I0760450

EVA CHASE

The Heart of a Monster: The Complete Series

First Digital Edition, 2024

Cover design: Covers by Christian

Ebook ISBN: 978-1-998752-85-0

Hardcover ISBN: 978-1-998752-86-7

CHOSEN BY VILLAINS

THE HEART OF A MONSTER #1

CHAPTER ONE

Torrent

I preferred Rollick's teeth pointy. The viciously sharp tips concealed beneath my boss's smooth veneers told the real story of what you were getting into. They showed that he was as much a monster as I was.

There weren't any veneers that could disguise *my* true nature these days.

But since he could blend in with the mortals we lived among, most of the time he did. When I answered his latest call, I found him standing in his penthouse office in human-like form.

"There you are," Rollick said before I'd even emerged from the shadows, with a flash of those shiny false teeth. "I always appreciate your promptness, Torrent."

And I always arrived as quickly as I could, no matter how far off I'd been soaking in the depths of the ocean just off Santa Monica Beach—farther than any of the mortal guests at his resort hotel dared to swim. I wasn't going to let even a minor delay undermine the respect I'd managed to earn with the formidable demon.

Traveling through the shadows had wicked the dampness from my skin, and I emerged into physical form totally dry. I extended two of my tentacles alongside my own human guise. My damaged legs wouldn't hold me up without those additional appendages supporting part of my weight.

Vibrations my ears couldn't pick up carried to my extra limbs through the floor: the pulsing bass from the nightclub on the hotel's lowest two floors, the mellow jazz from the rooftop bar and lounge. I kept the tentacles turned so the suckers didn't press too firmly against the thick carpet. It looked clean enough, but the suction cups were more sensitive than my eyes or nose as well.

I'd seen enough of what went on in Rollick's office to know I had no interest in tasting the trace evidence. As it was, I caught faint whiffs of blood and semen in the area by his broad ebony desk, both of them fresh, before I tuned out those streams of sensory input with practiced care. I dipped my head to him. "I'm at your service."

I'd never seen my boss actually sitting behind his desk in the leather executive chair. At my remark, he sauntered around one of the gray suede couches that framed the open stretch of floor by the office's entrance—the section that served as a sort of audience room.

Everything in the office was black, gray, or red like the deep maroon of the carpet, including his outfit: a sleek, charcoal-gray suit paired with a dove-gray dress shirt and a wine-red tie with gray stripes. It played down the physical heft of his human-like form while adding a different air of menace at the same time. Anyone with half a brain, mortal or shadowkind, could tell with one glance that this was a man you didn't want to mess with.

"I have a new job for you," he said in his low, languid voice, coming to a stop in the middle of the room but facing the door rather than me. "Unfortunately, right after I called for you another matter came up that I need to attend to swiftly. If you wouldn't mind waiting in the shadows a few minutes..."

He kept my presence on his staff private—it was useful to him to have lieutenants he could call on for work he didn't want his name associated with. That was fine by me. Holding my physical form on land was more of a strain than it was for most shadowkind, as he no doubt realized. I was just glad I'd never gotten the impression that he thought any less of me for my weakness, despite all the sneers and mockery I'd had thrown my way from beings with much less power than he wielded.

"Happy to oblige," I said, and released my solid body to meld into the patch of darkness beneath the desk. My awareness of the sights and sounds in the room around me hazed only slightly with the transition, but Rollick didn't mind me watching. I'd seen an awful lot of his business from this or similar vantage points before. If it'd been anything that required particular discretion, he'd have asked me to leave completely.

He reached to his mouth to pop out his veneers, a clear indication of exactly what kind of meeting this was going to be. At least these sorts of sessions were typically brief. A few minutes sounded about right.

A moment later, the door opened. Two of the trolls who worked as club bouncers and overall hotel security marched a smaller being into the room. From his lithe figure, luminous eyes, and the greenish bits woven into his hair, I suspected their captive was fae or similar.

Rollick smiled at the lithe man without baring his jagged shadowkind teeth. The trolls kept their hands clamped around the fae's wrists, exerting enough pressure to hold him in physical form in case he tried to vanish into the shadows around the room. Pain and apprehension were etched all across his pale face.

Rollick let his lips draw back slowly, the points of his fangs glinting. Then his entire body began to shift from its human guise into his full monstrous form.

His frame stretched until he stood seven and a half feet tall, muscles bulging across his limbs and chest as his suit vanished. A ruddy hue swept across his previously peachy skin. His short, fawn-brown hair lengthened and darkened to black, falling in rumpled strands to his broad shoulders.

Two narrow, curved horns jutted upward from the sides of his skull, adding another two feet to his height. His tail, slim with a tuft of black hair at the end, lashed back and forth. Cloven hooves replaced his feet.

The fae man let out a sound that was almost a bleat and squirmed in the trolls' grasp. Rollick loomed over him, grinning even broader. His voice rolled out of his mouth, deeper than before with a rough edge that made the air itself shiver. No one with even a fragment of a brain could have mistaken his aura of power now.

"I hear you've been glamouring unwilling human patrons of my club so you can fuck them in the bathroom," he said in a cool growl.

"I—I—I thought that's what they're here for," the fae man stammered. "Isn't that why you run this place? So the shadowkind have easy hunting grounds?"

"The Sunshine Sin Hotel exists so that those who play by the rules can get their needs met. But the most primary need is *mine*: that the human patrons keep coming. They won't if word gets out that customers are regularly getting 'roofied' and defiled, you sniveling nitwit. And the very first rule is that all shadowkind who want to make use of the facilities pass my approval before they indulge."

"I'm sorry, I—I didn't realize. I'd only heard stories about this place. I—"

"You thought I'd be too busy with other concerns to notice." Rollick's smirk managed to stretch even wider. "But I notice everything. And I'm going to make sure you remember never to cross me or anyone like me again."

He moved incredibly fast for his massive size. One second he was standing there, the next he was springing forward, his hand swiping out with the short but razor-sharp claws that'd protruded from his fingertips. With one slash and a twist of his wrist, they carved four jagged lines in the fae man's face from his temple all the way across his nose and mouth to the opposite side of his jaw.

The fae man cried out. Plumes of his smoky blood gushed up from his wounds. The flesh would seal soon enough, but cuts that deep would leave scars he'd never lose.

Rollick stepped back with a dispassionate air. "Try to glamour those away, and they'll hurt as much as they do right now. And if you set foot anywhere near the entire city of Los Angeles again, I'll carve the rest of you up until you're hellhound kibble." He tipped his head to the trolls. "Get this trash out of my sight."

The security guards hauled the whimpering fae man out again. As the door thumped shut, Rollick swiveled toward me, contracting into his human guise and reforming his suit as he did. I stepped out of the shadows, recognizing my summons.

He brushed his hands together and smiled at me with a reddish gleam in his dark blue eyes. "Now, about that job."

"Whatever you need," I said without hesitation. I'd repaid him for giving me a chance despite my limitations by rising to every challenge he'd thrown at me, and I didn't intend to break that streak of success.

He was hard on those who pissed him off, but he rewarded those who deserved it well.

My boss ambled over to his desk and drummed his fingers on the polished surface. "This particular mission requires a high degree of discretion, which is why I'm giving it to you. There's no one else I'm sure I can count on to handle it properly. You haven't seen any reason for concern in your squad-mates?"

I shook my head. "They're completely loyal and committed." Lance, well—he wasn't exactly the most stable being I'd ever met, but he'd never faltered when it mattered. Crag was as solid as the rock he was made out of. And I knew both of them appreciated the opportunities Rollick had given them as much as I did.

"Excellent." Rollick propped himself against the desk. "There's a mortal woman who's caught my interest. I'd like you to keep a close eye on her for the next six months. Watch for any unusual behavior or phenomena in her vicinity, as well as any signs that other shadowkind have taken an interest in her."

This was unexpected. In the half a century I'd been working for him, Rollick had never shown much interest in any specific mortal before.

I was careful not to let my surprise show on my face. "And if we do observe anything along those lines?"

"Report back to me immediately. Otherwise, return and make your report when the six months is up. And if any of our fellow shadowkind take their interest to the point of attempting to capture or harm her, fend them off and take her somewhere safe until you can get in contact with me. I'll give you the locations of a few properties that would serve well for that purpose in the area."

The way he said "the area" told me this was not only an unusual job, but one taking us much farther abroad than our usual work. I was already familiar with Rollick's key holdings in California and the adjacent states.

"It is especially important that no other beings discover my interest or involvement in this situation," Rollick went on, and produced a sleek cellphone from his pocket. He handed it to me. "This has a phone number programmed into it. Use only this device and only that number to leave a message for me should you need to."

"Understood." I shoved the phone into my own pocket and studied my boss's face. I didn't normally press for more information about my missions, but in this specific case, I felt uncomfortably uncertain about what I might be up against or what we should prepare for. "What's significant about this woman?"

Rollick hummed to himself. "Your mission will help me determine that. It's come to my attention that other shadowkind may see some advantage to be gained by devouring her." He shot one of his wide grins at me, his pointed teeth flashing. "If that turns out to be true, I'd like to have the chance to devour her first."

CHAPTER TWO

Quinn

There was nothing quite like seeing the city in the first few minutes after the sun dipped below the horizon. Enough of a glow still hazed the sky to catch on the details of the downtown buildings, but in the thickening darkness, the gleam of their lights outlined their walls with streaks of neon blue and yellow like some kind of cyberpunk landscape.

And there was nothing like seeing the view from the edge of a roof forty floors up.

I sat a couple of feet back from the narrow concrete lip, my legs braced in front of me, my sketchpad resting on my knees. This high up, the breeze held a bit of a chill despite the heat of the summer day that was just ending. I drank in the fresh air, totally free of the urban smells of downtown Jacksonville below me, and smiled at the sensation of goosebumps tickling over my arms. I'd brought a thin hoodie along, but I didn't think I'd bother putting it on over my tank top.

This was my third time breaching the upper floors of the new office complex next to the river: sneaking up the emergency stairs, climbing the maintenance ladder, and shoving open the hatch that led out onto the roof.

The thrill hadn't worn off yet. The light was always a little different depending on the weather; the glowing patterns in the windows around me shifted evening by evening.

I liked to think that seeing the city and its buildings this way gave me a perspective that'd lend something special to my work—to the designs I was sketching of structures I hoped to see built from my own blueprints someday not too far away. I'd spent my first hour up here working on a project for one of the online summer courses I was taking to speed along my architecture degree, and the rest of the time I'd given to my dream designs.

I traced my fingers over the lines of the spiraling high rise I'd drawn last. I didn't know how much time I had left in this world, but I was damn well going to leave some kind of mark on it if I possibly could. Something that people would look at and get the same sweeping sense of exhilaration I felt gazing out over downtown right now.

If I could manage that… well, maybe it wouldn't matter that I'd get a whole lot less time than the average person did.

The sketchpad was just for initial concepts. When I got back to my computer, I'd need to figure out all the logistics of scale and exact proportions. But there'd be nothing to construct in that digital landscape without doing some dreaming first.

Biting into the apple I'd brought, I watched the sky dim from hazy blue to the near-black shade of dusk. The sweet juice trickling down my throat made my stomach gurgle with a pang of deeper hunger. I'd told my parents I'd be home late and not to hold up dinner on my behalf, but Mom would have set aside a plate in the fridge for me to warm up when I got in.

I stuffed my sketchpad into the messenger bag I kept slung crossbody so there was no chance of losing it and stood up. Walking the few steps back to the open hatch with the breeze buffeting me set all my nerves jangling giddily. Death might be lurking in the near future, waiting for a second chance to sink its claws into me, but I defied it on a weekly basis.

No one would be able to say I hadn't *lived* in the time I'd gotten.

I eased down the ladder, tugged the hatch into place above me, and padded down the maintenance stairs at a brisk but careful pace, my hand following the railing in the dark. I'd taken the elevator up—I wasn't a glutton for punishment—but now the offices were closed for the night.

Going down took a lot less energy than going up, and it kept me out of the security guards' notice.

At least, it normally did. I was turning the corner on a landing when my foot skidded on a slick spot where someone must have spilled a drink. I caught my balance against the wall, and my shoulder thumped on the door.

A distant voice filtered through from the other side. "Hey! Is someone there?"

Shit. Just my luck that a guard would have happened to be patrolling on this floor right when I slipped.

My pulse hiccupped, and I dashed for the next flight of stairs. I ran as hard as I could, whipping around one landing and then another, until the squeak of hinges reached my ears from above. Then I tensed and slowed, still moving but setting my sneakers as softly as possible on the steps.

The darkness wavered as the guard must have swept the beam of a flashlight over the stairs a couple of flights above me. My heart hammered at my ribs. I'd managed not to get caught in my urban exploring since a couple of careless moments when I'd started up the hobby in high school. Somehow I figured the authorities would be a little harsher on a twenty-one year old than a reckless teen.

I kept slinking onward as the guard's feet thudded across two landings to the next floor, which I'd already passed. The glow of the flashlight beamed brighter with his approach. But he stopped there, let out a sigh, and pushed past the door back into the hall.

A grin stretched across my face. Another challenge conquered.

I left the building via the back entrance and trotted around to the street, rubbing sanitizer from my ever-present bottle over my hands in a gesture that was automatic after all these years. Cars rumbled by beneath the streetlamps. The familiar humid air filled my lungs. After a rooftop trek, the sights on the ground felt painfully mundane.

If I'd had the money, I'd have gotten an apartment downtown so my favorite haunts would have been close at hand. Thankfully, Mom and Dad's house was less than a half hour's walk from the river at my usual swift pace. And having me home for the summer eased their minds and cut down on the worried comments about whether I was pushing myself too hard in my studies.

They were pretty good about giving me space. After some frank discussions in family therapy about not going too heavy on the coddling or protectiveness, we'd found a good balance. They allowed me plenty of independence, I didn't feel like I was leaning too much on them, and we got in our little bonding moments like our Sunday board game nights.

And if every now and then I wanted to throw myself into Mom's embrace and bawl like I was a little kid again, I stuffed down that urge and put on the same impervious front I'd been perfecting for the past nine years. They'd already been through enough because of me.

It was easier for them if they didn't think *I* worried all that much. And easier for me too, shoving aside those worries instead of giving in to them. Freaking out about the inevitable would only slow me down and get in the way of my actually enjoying however many years I had left.

As the park came into view up ahead, my phone vibrated in my pocket with its silent alarm, programmed to go off twice a day. My hands moved automatically, unzipping the side pocket on my bag, flicking open the right flap on the pill organizer I'd recently filled for the week, dropping the three evening tablets into my palm, and popping them into my throat. I chased them with a gulp from my water bottle, ingesting them in three quick swallows. Then it was done, like it'd been nothing at all.

Totally normal, nothing to see here. Just a gal making sure her body didn't wake up and realize the transplanted heart stitched into her chest didn't really belong to her.

When I'd been dependent on what was technically an alien creature inhabiting my body since I was twelve, the darkness cloaking the park wasn't all that scary. The shortcut along the paths, quiet and still in the deepening night, cut several minutes off my journey. What had all those self-defense classes been for if I let my life be dictated by vague fears? I'd walked through here dozens of times and never been accosted.

If anything, striding along the paved strip that cut through the grass with the tree branches rustling overhead gave me a pleasant jolt of adrenaline. Any time I got away with thumbing my nose at my fears, I won a little victory.

Of course, I didn't throw caution totally to the wind. I let one hand rest on my hip, on the lump in my pocket—my ever-present multitool, which included a knife *I* wouldn't want jabbed into me.

My gaze skimmed over my surroundings, dim in the intermittent glow of the security lights that stood far apart along the path. One of the benches farther off by the dog park had a crooked slat on the back. I squinted at it, my fingers itching with the desire to see if I could screw it back into place—my multitool had plenty of other uses, after all—but I'd be better off waiting until I had better light to examine it by anyway.

Besides, it might need a whole new screw. I couldn't tell for sure in the dark. But a #10 or #12 would usually do the trick for something like that. I could bring a few possibilities when I passed through here next.

Fixing things someone else had designed wasn't anywhere near as satisfying as seeing a design all my own brought to life, but I had the basic engineering knowledge, and using it in tiny ways here and there was a chance to make a small impact right now. It reminded me that I was leaving my mark already, even if no one really noticed.

I was halfway through the park, just passing the pond, when a strange wobbly sensation passed through my chest. It was faint but unignorable, as if the blood coursing through my heart had rippled with a puff of breath like the surface of the pond in the breeze.

My strides faltered. A flicker of panic shot through me.

I'd never felt anything like that before. What if it was a sign—the muscles of the organ starting to fail—?

Normally, I'd have shaken off the twinge of anxiety and walked on. When you had to monitor your bodily reactions as closely as I did, you got to realize that there were all kinds of random sensations that'd pop up that meant nothing at all.

This time, I didn't get the chance.

All at once, the shadows draping the landscape... thickened. Here and there across the grassy terrain around me, several patches of darkness condensed into solid forms. Forms with what looked like legs and tails and flashes of red and yellow eyes.

Some were as small as a cat and others nearly as tall as me. I'd swear... that one had spikes jutting all over its body. Another opened a gaping maw hung with fangs longer than my hand.

What the *hell*? A cold sweat broke over my skin. Plenty of weirdness went on here in Florida, but nightmare beasts were a completely different level even for us.

I blinked hard, making sure the sight before me wasn't just a trick of my mind. As my fingers closed around the handle of my multitool, the nearest path light shattered. In the dim wash of moonlight that remained, the shadowy creatures charged at me.

A shriek burst from my throat. I flicked out the knife and jerked backward toward the pond, which was the only place I hadn't seen any of the impossible things emerge.

I hadn't been trained in fending off nightmarish fiends, but my self-defense practice kicked in all the same. I punted one of the little creatures away with a swipe of my foot, trying not to think about the fact that I'd swear sparks burst from its mouth as I did.

A lumbering furry thing with an absurd alligator-like snout sprang at me, and I lashed out with the knife. The blade sank into flesh, but the beast bowled me over without flinching. Its claws raked across my forearm with a flare of pain that lanced all the way to my shoulder.

My chest—I had to protect my chest above all else. A blow to the tissue that guarded my replacement heart could be a death sentence right there. I shoved at the thing as hard as I could, terrified adrenaline spiking through my veins.

The creature's head reared back, its paws still pinning me down. Snaps and hisses careened from what seemed like all around me as the other beasts closed in. Oh, God, if even more of them pounced on me—

Another figure leapt out of the night, barreling straight into the alligator-thing and knocking it off me. The forms rolled over the path with gnashes of teeth and guttural snarls.

Pulse thundering and arm throbbing, I scrambled to my feet. More of the shadowy creatures raced toward me, little more than denser streaks in the darkness and flashes of eyes. They seemed to weave through the night from all across the park—how many of them were there now? How could there *be* so many?

How could these creatures exist at all?

I had nowhere to go except the pond. Normally I wouldn't consider stepping into stagnant water with an open wound that was just begging for an infection, but if these vicious things devoured me tonight, my suppressed immune system would be a moot point. Even if a normal gator had stopped by, I'd take my chances with it over the shadowy fiends.

I clutched my knife, more pain lancing through my forearm. I was just about to step backward into the shallow water in the hopes that the beasts wouldn't follow me there when two more figures wavered into being between me and the oncoming horde.

One of the newcomers stood only a little taller than me. The other was a shape so hulking and bulky it made my breath stop in my lungs.

The first raised his hands toward the charging horde—hands that looked at least somewhat human to my straining eyes.

"You don't want to do that," he announced to the streaks of darkness in a curt, hollow-sounding voice. "Back off. She's ours."

CHAPTER THREE

Quinn

The words echoed in my head, somehow more chilling than the horrifying creatures that'd been attacking me: *She's ours*.

Who with the what now? Since fucking when did I belong to anyone? Or any*thing*, as the case might more accurately be.

A shiver crawled up my spine, but I didn't have much of a chance to process what I'd heard. If some of the creatures descending on me backed off, enough of them barreled onward that I couldn't tell the difference in the night.

The figure that'd tackled the furry alligator spun toward the charging creatures. I couldn't see what'd become of the beast that'd clawed me, but it was obvious the thing that'd saved me wasn't any less grotesque, even with the little I could make out in the near-total darkness. It moved on all fours with swift jerks and a clacking of its own talons, slashing this way and that.

The figure who'd spoken, the one who'd said I was *theirs*, seemed to surge forward with more limbs than I'd initially registered. Or were those weapons? Something long and sinewy whipped out at both sides of the body I'd initially seen as humanoid, with sounds of impact as the lithe projectiles smacked into my attackers.

The hulking form that'd stayed silent so far lunged this way and that with more forceful blows, moving nearly as fast as its companion. It slammed itself down on a creature that let out a piercing screech, and the ground shuddered under my feet. The pain in my arm jolted with a sharper ache.

What the hell was going on? What were these things? How could this be happening?

I shook my head as if clearing it would somehow wipe away the unreal chaos around me. I'd just taken my pills—could vivid hallucinations kick in as a new side effect after years on the same maintenance dose?

As implausible as that sounded, it made more sense than the idea that I was literally being swarmed by… by what could only be described as *monsters.*

A splash from behind me was my only, brief warning that at least one of those monsters had decided to brave the pond in an effort to get past my defenders. As I whirled around with a lurch of my pulse, a cold, slimy form rammed into me and pinned me to the ground.

Something rough as sandpaper scraped across my already bleeding wounds. The fresh spike of pain shocked a choked gasp from my throat.

I flailed at the thing, and one of those thick, whip-like objects bashed into its side, sending it flying halfway across the pond. But more wet noises were carrying through the night.

"Get her out of here!" ordered the hollow-sounding voice from before. "Up and out. We'll regroup on the island."

The island? I opened my mouth, not sure whether I was going to protest or clarify—or whether the sounds that fell off my tongue would even be coherent—but it didn't matter. The next thing I knew, the hulking figure was catching me up in arms thicker than my thighs and launching itself off the ground toward the sky.

Something flapped past the edge of my vision with a warble of rushing air. I was crushed against a solid… chest? The surfaces pressing against the bare skin of my arms had the solid, grainy texture of stone, but the body was as warm as you'd expect a body to be, muscles flexing and shifting as the thing adjusted its grip on me so I wasn't quite as squished.

I started to squirm, gritting my teeth against the pain in my forearm, and then froze when the thing heaved upward with another swish of its wings. A glimpse of the roads below showed the streetlamps and headlights gleaming distantly against the dark like upside down stars. We'd already left them far behind.

Did I really want to escape this creature's grasp when the only avenue for escape was a plummet to my death?

I dragged in a shaky breath, willing my body to unclench—other than the fingers still wrapped around the handle of my multitool. I might have squeezed it so tight by now that it was embedded in my palm for all time. Another urge rose up to thrash and stab at the monstrous thing clutching me, but my sense of self-preservation overrode the impulse.

I had to wait until it put me down. When my feet were on solid ground again, I'd have a real chance to fight for my survival.

My pulse rattled through my veins. The wind whooshed past us, flinging my hair across my face. And a voice—deep and gravelly in a way that seemed to fit the stony body that restrained me—rumbled by my ear.

"Am I hurting you?"

The question came out gruff, as if the speaker was irritated that I wasn't expressing gratitude for the ride. My own voice snagged in my throat. It took me a moment to force it out.

"No. Not—not really. I'd like to go back down, though."

The creature grunted. "Almost there."

It—he? The voice had definitely sounded male—tilted forward, and the whole of Jacksonville stretched out beneath us, dappled with golden lights and here and there streaks of vibrant blue. I'd never seen the city from quite this high up before. For just an instant, I forgot the craziness I'd stumbled into beneath a swell of awe.

Then my mind jerked back to reality. I'd been stormed by a mass of monsters in the middle of the park and now I was soaring through the sky in the arms of a creature that felt as if it were made of stone. This was insane.

I was going to wake up soon, right? Jolt back into awareness and find myself tangled in my bedsheets? How could this actually be *true*?

But I didn't wake up. The lacerations on my arm continued to ache, the wind kept on tangling through my hair, and the rock-like arms held me securely and firmly.

We tipped into a dive. With a gentleness that startled me, not that our flight before had seemed particularly rough, the beast glided downward against the buffeting of the humid air. The lights fell away behind the edges of my sight; darkness clotted beneath us.

We dropped down into a small clearing surrounded by trees. The only light came from the half moon and the few stars that showed in the circle of sky above the ring of leaves. The creature set me down in a sitting position, but I shoved myself onto my feet immediately, whirling around, taking stock.

My messenger bag still hung against my back, the strap digging into my chest. I gripped the handle of my multitool, knife ready. I should dig my first aid kit out of the bag and do what I could to clean and then bandage the wounds on my arm, but I wasn't sure yet that I didn't need to defend myself from more immediate threats.

As the hum of insect life wavered up from between the trees, a mossy scent filled my nose. I had no idea where we were. The river wove around several islands within the city alone, and there had to be dozens more in the ecological preserve along its northeast bank. I didn't see any signs of human habitation around me, but then, I couldn't see much of anything at all.

I tucked my injured arm against my chest and glanced at my protector-slash-kidnapper. He looked... oddly not quite as hulking as before. What I could make out of his form in the darkness was still at least twelve inches taller than my five-foot-five, broad and brawny with muscle, but I could have sworn he'd been at least a foot taller than *that* when he'd sprung into being in the park.

Of course, there'd been a lot of bizarre things happening right at that moment. It was possible I'd imagined him as more immense in my confusion.

But I hadn't imagined the wings. We couldn't have flown here without them, right? Now I couldn't see them at all. Had he managed to tuck them completely out of sight behind his back?

All of him looked more human than I'd expected—limbs and facial features in all the right places—other than the harsh, blocky angles of his square jaw.

"Where are we?" I asked. "Why did you bring me here?" I flicked my gaze to the forest around us, but if this was an island, chances were I didn't have much chance of escape here either.

And what else might be lurking in those denser shadows between the trees?

"Getting you away from those menaces," my rescuer rumbled. "This is the spot we agreed on."

I hadn't agreed on it, but before I could point that out, something moved at the edge of the clearing.

I tensed, raising my knife, but the figure that stepped into the moonlight was a man, not a monster. Or at least, that's what he looked like at first.

He sauntered forward on two legs with a swaying gait, tall but within a more typical range as human beings went, muscular but not hulk-like. I made out a tumble of dark curls above similarly dark eyes that held a faint glint of what seemed to be amusement. His narrow jaw canted to the right as his mouth stretched in a broad grin.

As bewildered and terrified as I was, his face was so striking even in the darkness that my pulse hitched with a jolt of giddy adrenaline. He was savagely handsome, with a wild grace that showed in every movement of his body.

Then he raised his hand in a flippant gesture of greeting, and I noticed the claws.

They were dark too, so dark they'd blended into the night before he'd moved his hand in front of him. Talons tapering to needle-sharp points protruded from his lithe fingers, nearly as long as the fingers themselves. Not a man at all.

My pulse stuttered all over again, and my arm jerked up, brandishing the knife. The clawed man cocked his ferally gorgeous head in a motion that felt more animalistic than human. He let out a chuckle.

"We help her keep her hide, and she wants to take off ours?" he said to the giant beside me in a lightly bemused tone.

"She's scared," the other man said in the same gruff tone he'd used when asking if he was hurting me. "Like mortals are. You traveled quickly."

"We hitched a ride on a few cars. So convenient." The clawed man's attention shifted back to me, and his angular jaw twitched. "You're bleeding. One of the interlopers took a gouge out of you. We can't have that."

"I—" I started, not really sure what I was going to say, but he crossed the ground between us so quickly that any further words cut off in a startled squeak. He grasped my elbow, tucking his fingers around the joint so his claws didn't graze my skin, and lifted my arm.

I jerked backward automatically. "What are you doing? Let me go!"

I jabbed the knife at him, but he batted it away with a flick of his other hand —not hard enough to hurt, but with enough power that I could tell he *could* hurt me easily enough if he'd wanted to, and without even using those claws.

"Careful," he said in the same almost teasing tone. "You don't want to lose more blood than you already have."

"But I—"

"He can cauterize the wound with his fire," the giant announced, and in the same moment, the clawed man breathed over the throbbing gashes on my upper arm.

It sounded like a breath, anyway—a slow, emphatic exhalation. But a quavering glow washed over my skin at the same time, and a burning sensation seared all the way down into the muscles as if that breath really had contained fire.

I yelped, but the heat wasn't like the kind of fire I was used to. It was already condensing into a more soothing warmth—and my flesh was melding into a solid mass again. I gaped, staring down at the rippled patch that now looked more like a scar than a wound.

Could he really have burned away any chance of infection? What the hell *was* this guy?

Before I'd realized what he was doing, the clawed man leaned even closer and swiped out his tongue. It stretched only a little longer than a regular human tongue might have, but it licked over the healed skin with an oddly rippled texture that was totally alien.

A quiver of mingled alarm, revulsion, and inexplicable fascination raced through me. I yanked at my arm again. "What the fuck— What are you—"

After one more swift flick of his tongue, the clawed man released me and stepped back. "The saliva settles the burn," he said conversationally.

When I stared at my arm again, I realized the skin did look smoother than it had at first. The patch where the gashes had been was darker than the rest, but otherwise looked no different.

I retreated a little myself, sliding my heel along the uneven ground the way I'd learned to in my urban explorations, and tested my arm. The clawed guy had soldered the outer flesh back together somehow, but he hadn't erased every trace of the injury. My bicep still ached faintly with the movement. I couldn't be sure it was totally safe.

It was a good thing I had that extra prescription of antibiotics. After a scrape during one of my exploring expeditions had left me nervous, I'd convinced my main doctor to write me a "just in case" prescription.

It'd never occurred to me I'd be using it to kill whatever bacteria might lurk on a monster's claws or tongue.

I flexed my arm again. The pain was much milder now, but it grounded me. A lot of impossible things had happened tonight, but getting slashed up still hurt. Some stunning weirdo's breath and tongue couldn't magically make *everything* better.

"We should go to the safehouse," the clawed man said to the giant. "The city's crawling with more of the same beings looking to chow down. You can handle the flight carrying her?"

The larger man flexed his shoulders. "Of course." He reached toward me.

I scrambled farther back, swinging my knife with one hand and clutching the strap of my messenger bag with the other. "Oh, no. You're not hauling me off someplace else. Who are you? *What* are you? What the hell is going on?"

By the last question, my voice had taken on a scratchy, hysterical quality I didn't like at all, even if I couldn't suppress it. It wasn't as if I could *stop* the massive guy from carting me off again if he decided to force the issue. I suspected the little blade on my multitool would rebound right off his skin like it would a slab of stone. A punch would probably hurt my knuckles more than it did him.

The clawed man gestured with his thumb in what I guessed was the direction we'd come from, as blasé as ever. "A bunch of beasties tried to carve you open. We made sure it didn't happen. Did you want to go back to them? It didn't look like you were having fun."

"Why did they attack me? What do you mean 'beasties'? I've never seen anything like those... And why did you jump in?" Another thought struck me with a fresh chill. "And where's the other one? There were three of you who were fighting them off."

I couldn't have forgotten the figure who'd looked like a man all along, who'd defended me with his strange, whip-like weapons. The one who'd said I was theirs. What'd happened to him?

The clawed guy had said "we" when he'd talked about hitching rides.

Was the third man here too, lurking in the shadows with who knew what nefarious purposes in mind?

For the first time, a flash of uncertainty crossed the clawed man's handsome face. He glanced at the giant as if for guidance.

"You don't need to talk to Torrent right now," the stony man announced. "We need to leave."

"No," I said with as much defiance as I could put forward, as hopeless as it might be. "I want to see all of you. I want to know who I'm dealing with. And I want someone to explain why the hell any of this is happening to me!"

The clawed man clucked his tongue. "She is a moody one after all, isn't she?"

My lungs constricted even more. He sounded like he was referring to my full name: Quinn Moody. But how could he know *any* of my name?

"We don't—" the giant started, but then a figure wavered into being beside them in the clearing.

It wasn't like the clawed guy. With him, I could have believed he'd walked up from the shore of the island... however exactly he'd gotten across the river when he didn't appear to have wings. This man clearly materialized out of the air in front of me as if the darkness itself had solidified into a human form.

Humanesque, at least. His height and lean frame matched the man I'd seen next to the giant in the park, but from behind I hadn't noticed the strangeness of his face. One side curved inward instead of out, as if that cheekbone had been caved in. And at his sides...

I swallowed another squeak before it could burst from my mouth. The guy was dressed in fairly normal clothes, relaxed jeans and a casual button-up, but two long, sinuous *things* jutted from his waist beneath his shirt to arc downward, where they curved against the ground as if to help support his stance.

Tentacles, a distant part of my mind recognized. He had tentacles sprouting from his sides like extra-long bonus arms. *Those* were the weapons I'd watched him flinging at my attackers.

My feet darted backward of their own accord, with less care than I'd used before. My heel caught on a rough edge of rock, and I stumbled, only barely recovering my balance. My heart was pounding faster than I remembered ever feeling it before. And that weird wobble ran through it, just like the moment before the creatures had descended on me in the park.

"Is this better?" the tentacled man—Torrent?—asked in his curtly hollow voice. "Here I am. I thought you might feel better *not* seeing me, but since you insisted..."

He might have had a point. I couldn't say that the sight of his monstrous body particularly reassured me.

But he *had* listened. He'd presented himself like I'd asked him to when his friends could have just dragged me off if they hadn't cared at all about my feelings on the matter.

Possibly that was the only thing that stopped me from running screaming into the night. Well, that and the fact that I was on landmass surrounded by water, and unknown beasts that'd already ripped into me were still prowling around somewhere out there.

"What are you?" I said again, my voice shaking. I didn't see any point in bothering with the *who* this time.

Torrent's eyes, paler than his companions', gleamed in the thin moonlight. His voice stayed brisk. "We call ourselves shadowkind. Humans tend to call us 'monsters.' Some of us travel to the mortal realm to enjoy what it has to offer in peace. Others have more vicious interests in mind. You met a lot of the latter tonight."

I let out a huff of breath. "Yeah. Why were they coming at *me*?"

"There's something special about you," the tentacled man said, as coolly as before. "Something all those creatures wanted to snack on, as far as we can tell. But we'll ensure that doesn't happen. We'll keep you safe from them."

"Why?" I had to ask. He didn't sound all that happy about the offer.

He shrugged. "What's special should be preserved. Mortals would generally agree, wouldn't they?"

I guessed so. But— "What is it—what makes me special?"

"I'm not totally sure," he said. "But maybe you've felt a little of it. Back there in the park, right before the creatures came at you...?"

The first time I'd felt that weird wobble in my chest. He couldn't mean *that*, could he? What could that have to do with... with anything?

"I don't know," I hedged.

"Well, the situation is very simple either way," Torrent said. "Those creatures will keep coming after you. We have a place we can take you where they should have trouble finding you—where we can ensure your protection."

My body balked. "Can't—can't I just go home?"

The words came out with a wobble of their own. Embarrassment flushed my cheeks.

The tentacled man's grim expression didn't so much as flicker at my show of emotion. "They'd follow you there," he said. "And we can't easily fight them off, not when there'll be more all the time. Coming with us won't just be for your safety, you know. They won't care who they hurt on their way to you. They'll tear through your family without a second thought."

My stomach sank. In the back of my mind, I saw a horde of shadowy monsters bursting through the windows of the house, sinking fangs and claws into Mom and Dad. Phantom screams echoed inside my skull.

No. My parents had been through so much already because of me. I couldn't lead this impossible danger right to their doorstep.

But what choices did that leave me? Trust these equally implausible figures in front of me?

I swallowed hard. "I can't just hide *forever.*" However short my specific forever might be.

"Not forever," Torrent agreed. "Not even all that long. We only need time to regroup and come up with a plan that'll see you more permanently secure. The place we have set up is only a short distance from here. Crag can fly you there. You won't be hurt."

Crag—that was an appropriate name for a guy who seemed to be at least partly made out of rock. I swiped my free hand across my mouth. Then, slowly, I lowered my knife and flicked it back into the handle before shoving the multitool into my pocket.

I didn't like this. I didn't want to go. But my head was spinning so fast I couldn't even focus on what other questions I could ask.

I couldn't lead those things from the park to my parents. If the three monstrous men around me had wanted to slaughter me themselves, they'd had plenty of opportunities. By all appearances, they really did want to help me, however reluctant their sense of duty might have been.

How long did we have before the horde came after me even here?

I wet my lips and then nodded. "All right. Just to regroup. And I'm going to have a lot more questions in the morning."

Torrent smiled faintly. “Of course you are. We’ll do our best to answer them.”

At a crackling amid the trees, his head snapped around. My pulse jumped. His face turned even grimmer.

“It’s time to go.”

CHAPTER FOUR

Lance

The interior walls of the cabin were covered with this smooth wood paneling that gave off a smell more like plastic than trees. I wrinkled my nose at them and then applied my claws. With a few twists and flicks of my fingers, I carved a swirling design into the surface, cutting through the outer coating to the paler grain underneath.

The imagery didn't mean anything, but it pleased me simply to have bent the place a little to my will. To make it a little less mortal-seeming. It was ours—or our boss's, anyway—and the place should look like it.

Drawn by a whim, I moved farther along the living room wall. I trailed my claws in ragged lines and then scraped them up and down, enjoying the sound and the vibration through my hand more than the picture I was creating now.

Crag lumbered over from the short hall that held the two bedrooms and the bathroom and eyed me with typical impassiveness. It was hard to tell whether any of my habits annoyed the gargoyle or simply didn't matter to him at all. You'd have thought his human form was made of stone too.

"She's still sleeping," he announced, keeping his deep baritone low as if he were afraid of making that statement untrue.

He wasn't talking to me. We both knew the man who gave our direct orders was in the room. A second later, Torrent emerged from the shadows by one of the armchairs that stood in a cluster around a rattan coffee table. He sank into the chair immediately but left his usual supporting tentacles out, squeezed against the padded arms. Our commander liked to be ready for any eventuality.

"It isn't surprising," he said to Crag. "She was up late and stressed out, and we know she has some issues with her health. She'll be up soon enough."

He sounded awfully sure about that. I poked my claws right into the wall, stopping just sort of piercing it all the way through to the damp swampy air outside, and then yanked them out with a push off the wall to flip upside down. Curling my fingers, I avoided stabbing the floorboards. With a swift contortion of my body, I whirled around and over, landing on my feet again just shy of the dining table, grinning with the burst of exhilaration.

No one could ever predict exactly how they'd need to be ready for *me*.

"Did you talk to the boss?" I asked, without much concern either way. I wouldn't mind spending a little longer in this place. With no mortals around for miles, I could leap and tumble around the swamp lands in either of my forms without worrying about who might see me. And I hadn't found myself in a place quite like this before, where the heat was more damp than dry and the air pungent with the scents of vegetation both living and rotting.

The mortal world was bewildering at times, but you could never call it boring.

Torrent frowned and took one of those mortal phones out of his pocket. "I tried. I think one of the creatures we fought off last night must have damaged it. At least a couple of them had some kind of electrical affinity, and Highest only know about the others. All I'm getting is a clicking sound. I sent my message anyway, in case that's what Rollick intended, and I sent a text as well... If I haven't gotten a response soon, there are backup methods I can turn to."

"He wanted us to be very careful about bringing her in," Crag said, as if we'd have forgotten that heavily emphasized point. Torrent was the one who'd told *us* that. I rolled my eyes and picked at a bit of fish that'd gotten stuck in my teeth after my early morning hunting.

I could have simply melded into the shadows and reemerged to lose anything I didn't want to keep on my physical body, but working with my claws was more fun. It'd taken me a while before I could maneuver them nimbly enough to manage something like this without scratching my gums open.

"We have permission to report back in three months anyway," I said.

Crag's ample muscles tensed. "We can't wait *that* long."

"Why not? It's safe enough here." I waved my hand toward the swamp beyond the windows near the cluster of chairs. "I could feel the silver and iron barrier around the property when I was out earlier. All prickly and shivery. No one's feeling her out through that."

Torrent nodded. "The defensive posts should deflect all shadowkind senses. At least, in her current state." His narrow brow furrowed. "The impression she gives off got a little stronger last night. That's what drew the attack. I hadn't even realized how many lesser beings were gathering in the city. They must have picked up the general sense but not exactly where it was coming from—until that moment."

"Why do they all want to kill her, though?" I asked. "Whatever specialness she's got, it doesn't make *us* want to dice her up. Or not me, anyway." I considered my colleagues.

Crag grunted. "I don't feel any urge to harm her."

"No," Torrent said. "But we did notice that the vibe around her had a vague threatening quality. It heightened with the spike of the energy last night. It's obvious to us that she doesn't pose any danger, but lesser beings aren't exactly known for their wits. They acted on instinct—destroy the threat before it could get strong enough to destroy them."

"Running into a fight. Silly beasties. And then they die." I clicked my claws together.

Crag frowned. "It bothered them enough that they didn't back off even when we were defending her. Usually they have more sense of self-preservation."

Torrent shrugged. "Maybe her vibe affects lesser beings differently than it does us. We couldn't even pick up on the energy enough to be sure it *was* anything that unusual until last night. Rollick wasn't very clear on her specific qualities of interest. It doesn't matter anyway. He knows his own plans, and we know our orders."

His statement was punctuated by a shrill beeping that emanated from the room where we'd left the mortal woman sleeping. Ah, *that* was how

Torrent had known she'd wake up shortly. We'd heard the alarm go off over and over while we'd been keeping an eye on her.

I hadn't bothered noting the time or whether it was always the same time. The commander was better with details like that.

My keen ears picked up a rustle of fabric and a hitch of breath. The alarm shut off. Then there was a momentary silence. The woman inhaled shakily, followed by some more rustling.

Torrent held up his hand in a gesture for us to stay still and silent. We were all out of view of the end of the hall.

The bedroom door squeaked open, the woman's feet padded tentatively across to the bathroom, and water warbled through the pipes. Some more rustling. Then she edged toward the living room, coming to a stop on the threshold, still in the same black tank top and flexible jeans as yesterday. One of her pale hands clutched the silly knife she'd wielded yesterday; the other a familiar container of pills.

She peered at us for a long moment as if checking to see whether we'd changed our minds about the whole protecting her thing overnight and might launch ourselves at her with fangs bared. Her long blond hair was rumpled from sleep but tumbled over her toned shoulders to picturesque effect. I had the urge to twine my fingers through it and find out how it'd feel to the touch.

"Is the water here safe to drink?" she asked after she appeared to decide that speaking wouldn't provoke us into a murderous rage. "My bottle is empty, and I need—I need to take my pills."

Torrent motioned toward the kitchen area at the far end of the main living space. "It's all up to mortal standards."

She strode over to the sink with the swift, powerful stride I'd observed in her before. She couldn't use her body as deftly as I did mine, but then, few shadowkind even could.

From what I'd seen of humans, she was impressively nimble. We'd followed her up and through all sorts of buildings in the last three months. She seemed to take particular interest in any place that other mortals avoided out of caution. An interesting approach—one I completely approved of.

As she filled a glass with water and gulped down her pills, I stalked closer. She turned when I was just a few feet away with a swish of her hair and an abrupt widening of her bright blue eyes. Her pupils dilated, and she wet her lips with a little flick of her tongue that brought a grin to my face. A faint pinkish tone colored her cheeks.

She was scared… but she also liked what she saw. I'd observed this kind of reaction to me before. Something in my human form was particularly appealing to a large number of mortals. It'd come to my advantage once—at a time I'd rather not think about.

Her, I didn't need to worry about. She hadn't even been able to fend off the little beasties on her own.

"What are those for?" I asked her, tipping my head toward the pill container. She swallowed down an awful lot of them day by day. We hadn't observed any other signs of sickness in her.

Her hand tightened around the container. She grasped the high neckline of her tank top with the fingers still gripping her knife and tugged it low enough to reveal a thin line that was a darker pink than the rest of her skin, slicing from just below the level of her collarbone in a straight line down the middle of her chest. It disappeared into the shadows of her cleavage.

She let the thin fabric spring back into place. "When I was a kid, I got sick with a virus that ended up wrecking my heart. The only way I made it through was a transplant. If I don't take the pills at the right times every day, my body could reject the transplanted heart. Or do a heck of a lot of other bad things."

I blinked. She'd gotten a whole new heart? What kind of magic was that?

"Why—" I started, and Torrent cleared his throat.

"Lance, don't badger her with questions."

I smirked at him. "I'm curious."

"You're always curious," he retorted. "That's not her problem." He turned to the woman. "Shadowkind don't get sick, so we don't have the same concept of these things. Even if there was a germ in this realm that could affect us, it'd vanish the second we slipped back into the shadows."

"Oh. That's… handy." She appeared to rally herself, drawing her chin higher. "Actually, I've got some questions I'd like to ask all of you. You said you'd try to answer them."

Torrent's mouth formed a thin smile of his own. "I did." The end of one of his tentacles swung in a slow arch where it dangled over the arm of the chair.

"Last night," she said. "How did you know to be there? It seemed like you were ready when the other... shadowkind attacked."

"The same aspect of your presence that caught their notice alerted us as well," Torrent said smoothly. "When we saw what was happening, it became clear you needed protection from our... less considerate kin."

A wider smirk stretched across my face. He wasn't even lying. He was just leaving out the fact that we'd been watching for the beasties to catch notice for months beforehand. He'd mentioned to me earlier that she wouldn't take well to the idea that we'd been spying on her.

The woman arched an eyebrow. "You just happened to be in the park?"

"It has the most shadows," Crag put in with standard gruffness.

"But what were you doing in Jacksonville at all? Is it some kind of major monster tourist hotspot?"

Torrent gazed back at her evenly. "We 'monsters' have abilities of perception beyond what mortals are used to. We had the sense that something important was going to happen."

I managed to hold in a snicker, knowing Torrent wouldn't like me sounding as if I were mocking his answer. In this case, our special "ability of perception" had been named Rollick.

His answers seemed to diffuse the worst of the woman's anxieties. Her shoulders came down, her stance relaxing a little. She studied each of us again, her eyes lingering just a little longer on my face than the others. Oh, yes, there was a spark of interest there, a heat fascinatingly different from the fire I could draw up my throat.

"You look different," she said, and then, to Torrent, "Well, not you. I don't think. But... Crag? He had wings. He flew me here! And I think he was bigger too. And... Lance?" She said my name as if testing the flavor. "When I first saw you—or what I think was you—you didn't seem human at all."

"Shadowkind have two physical forms," Torrent said. "Our more natural one that'd get us called monsters, and one that's mostly human-like, other than we all have one or another aspect that we can't help carrying over."

"We assumed you'd prefer the human-like guises," I said, prowling close enough that I could have touched her if I'd reached out. "We could switch to the beasts if you'd like." I grinned with a flash of my square teeth which could shift into fangs in a matter of seconds.

Her pupils dilated all over again, her breath quickening in a way that stirred my own blood. "No, that's all right," she said hastily. "I think this way is better. Easier."

I did reach out then, grazing the back of my fingers down her bare arm and enjoying the deeper flush that spread across her face. It hadn't felt like a reward to get this kind of response while I'd been bound to someone else's whims. But every time I'd seen similar reactions from mortals since, I had to wonder what it might be like to let them act on it. To meet them halfway and see what those sparks could erupt into when fanned.

"I make a pretty monster too," I teased with another grin.

The woman's blush spread down her neck. She backed up a step. "I, um—" Her forehead creased as if she was thinking of more questions to ask us.

Torrent interrupted before she could form any of them. "I think our mortal had better get some breakfast into her. We don't want her starving to death after we've gone to the trouble of saving her life."

"Of course we don't," I said with a chuckle, and snatched an orange out of the fruit bowl we'd stocked overnight, along with the fridge and the cupboards. With a whisk of my claws, I'd severed it into eight perfectly even slices. She normally had an orange with the breakfasts we'd observed, if not quite so expertly cut. "If you want some fruit?"

Quinn gaped at the orange, my claws, and then me with a flare of something in her eyes that made me sure I was going to like having her around very much indeed.

CHAPTER FIVE

Quinn

I stared at Dad's reply to my hasty text from last night for several minutes before I could pull together the words to write back. I'd told him I'd run into a friend from school while I'd been out and ended up crashing at her place. My shock-and-exhaustion-addled mind hadn't come up with an excuse to keep me away for longer than that.

If it'd been a normal day, a normal excursion, I'd probably have called him so he'd be more reassured hearing my voice. But I was afraid that whatever he'd hear in my voice right now would have the opposite effect.

Trish found out about this architecture convention happening in Atlanta this weekend, I typed, picking the name of a random classmate I hadn't actually exchanged more than brief greetings with in class last semester. *It sounds really amazing—we're going to make a trip of it. I'll probably miss you and Mom when I stop by to grab my things. See you soon!*

The lies gnawed at me. There were a lot of things I hid from my parents for their own benefit, but they were only secrets that affected me, that wouldn't have done anything except make them worry more. And they were just passing lies, like, "I'm doing good," or, "I stopped by the mall" when actually I'd hung out on a skyscraper's rooftop.

The fact that ravenous monsters were prowling Jacksonville's streets felt like a totally different ballgame, as did a multi-day disappearance. But if I told them the truth, they couldn't have done anything to fix that either. From what Torrent had said, the creatures were after me, for whatever reason. They wouldn't bother anyone else if I wasn't there.

I had no idea what story I'd come up with if I ended up stuck in this swamp for more than a few days, though. Of course, I'd need a lot more than a story by then. I had enough pills to last me nearly a week, but then...

"Regrouping" shouldn't take *that* long, right?

I worried at my lower lip for a moment and then plugged my phone into its charger. Thank God this place at least had electricity. That device was my only way of keeping track of the time.

A faint ache ran through my forearm beneath the flesh Lance had mostly healed last night, but that was the only unusual bodily sensation I noticed. Like I had a few times since I'd woken up in the oddly cozy cabin this morning, I closed my eyes, exhaled slowly, and felt around inside me for any hint of some special quality. Anything that would explain why monsters were converging on me by the dozen.

Nothing inside me felt particularly different. I didn't even detect another of those little wobbles that'd run through my chest yesterday.

Maybe the whatever-it-was would turn out to be a temporary condition that was wearing off? That'd make my life a hell of a lot easier.

So I really shouldn't have gotten even a tiny quiver of disappointment at the thought that this all might be an accident and I was totally ordinary after all.

I shook myself and went back out into the living area of the cabin. A series of tall windows gave a view over a wooden deck and the sprawl of the surrounding swamp, all murky water, clumps of vegetation, and mossy trees rising up toward the sky. I couldn't see signs of any other habitation out there.

A cluster of armchairs stood in one corner of the room, an oak dining table in the middle, and the kitchen along the far wall, really just a short span of counter-topped cupboards next to an oven and a fridge.

A faint cedar smell drifted through the space. The wood-paneled walls were bare other than the scrapes and squiggles I'd seen Lance carving into them with those razor claws of his.

If they could do that to wood, how easily could they cut through a body? I shivered at the thought. The men had fought off the other creatures that'd come at me, but they still didn't feel exactly friendly toward me either. I couldn't quite tell whether I was a hassle or a welcome divergence from their regular lives.

The room had looked empty when I'd walked out into it, but I'd already caught on enough to realize that appearances were deceiving. These monstrous men who called themselves "shadowkind" could meld right into the shadows, after all. I never really had any idea which of them might be around or where they were unless they bothered to show themselves.

Before that thought could creep me out too much, a figure condensed into physical form—Torrent, sitting in the same armchair as before.

He didn't look totally comfortable here, the two tentacles I'd never seen him without squashed between his waist and the chair's arms. He slung them over the sides of the chair and folded his hands in front of him, the pale eyes I now knew were sea-green studying me from beneath his scruffy dark red hair.

"Did you need anything?" he asked evenly but with his usual cool, hollow tone.

Was it his collapsed cheek that gave that odd quality to his voice? By daylight, I could see I'd been right that the bone appeared caved in, giving him a physical hollow in the side of his face beneath his left eye, but the skin over it was smooth, only a smudge of a scar that barely showed against his already pale skin. The scar suggested the odd facial shape was the result of an injury, not his original form.

"I—I guess I was just wondering if you've come up with any plan other than us just staying here," I said. If the three of them had been discussing it, they hadn't brought me into the conversation, but who knew what they might be chatting about while they lurked in the gloom? "My parents will start to get concerned soon—there are only so many stories I can give them that they'll believe. And I've got two summer classes I'm supposed to be keeping up with. I can't do much without my laptop."

Torrent let out a huff as if dismissing the idea that my classes mattered at all, and my jaw clenched. He couldn't have any idea what it was like racing against the clock to get my certification so I could actually do any of the things I hoped to accomplish before my replacement heart gave out.

Maybe I'd get a new one when this one failed. Maybe there'd be a viable heart donated at the right time, and I'd be chosen to receive it. But there were no guarantees. I'd been lucky just getting the first one.

"It shouldn't take very long to come up with our next steps," Torrent said. "But I do need to wait and see what happens now that we've removed you from the immediate danger—whether the other shadowkind keep hunting for you or disperse will affect our approach."

"Of course," I said, hugging myself despite the warm air. How long was I going to be stuck in this same outfit? I guessed I could exchange my tank top for the hoodie in my bag, but I'd be sweating up a storm in that at this temperature.

Torrent seemed to guess my thoughts. "When we scout out nearby activity, we can also pick up some supplies for you, whatever essentials you'd need for the next couple of days."

Should I make them a shopping list? "I mean, some changes of clothes would be nice. And a toothbrush." There'd already been soap and toothpaste in the washroom, but I'd made do with scrubbing my teeth with my finger. "Oh, and some sunscreen, the highest SPF they have." I carried a small bottle in my messenger bag, but if we ended up traveling by daylight, it'd be good to have more. "I think that should cover it as long as it's only a couple of days."

"We can handle that," Torrent said. "For the clothes, we'll need to know your correct size, of course."

Of course. I looked down at myself, embarrassment prickling through me at the thought of the most vital pieces of clothing I'd want to change. "I, um, medium should be fine. For everything." Either they'd skip a bra or pick up a sports one in those kind of sizes.

"Duly noted. You may as well be comfortable while you're here."

He made it sound like my comfort was more of a secondary concern, but I guessed keeping me alive *was* the higher priority. It would have been a little much to expect them to have had the cabin prepared for my arrival ahead of time. They hadn't been expecting to suddenly sense my "specialness" any more than I'd anticipated the monster attack.

Although... certain parts of their story still didn't add up to me.

I glanced around the cabin. "So, this place belongs to the three of you? What do you need a house for if you can just live in the shadows?"

Torrent's lips curved with one of the thin smiles that were the closest thing to friendliness I'd ever seen him offer. "We might be able to spend all our time in the dark, but we do enjoy physical comforts and luxuries as well. We wouldn't bother coming to the mortal realm otherwise."

I couldn't shake the sense that he was avoiding answering my question clearly. "You just happened to have an isolated building set up in case you needed to run off to safety?"

"There are plenty of squabbles between the shadowkind. It can be useful to have a home base to retreat to as need be." He made a dismissive gesture with his hand, adjusting his position in the chair.

The movement reminded me that I didn't think *he* found the physical world all that comfortable, no matter what he said about it. It wasn't just the fact that the furniture in the cabin wasn't built for his peculiar body. Something in the way he held himself, especially the couple of times I'd seen him get to his feet since we'd arrived here, sent a twinge of recognition through me.

I'd spent more time in support groups for sick kids than I liked looking back on. I knew how a person moved when they were in pain, when they were picking every position with care to avoid provoking the tender spots.

Torrent handled it well, only a little stiffness showing here and there. I didn't think the soreness was from some injury he'd taken in last night's battle. It was something he'd been dealing with long enough that it'd either faded or he'd gotten very good at coping, or a little of both.

My current line of questioning didn't seem to be getting me anywhere, so I switched tactics. "Have you ever found another human being who attracted the kind of attention I'm getting?"

He shook his head. "I've been around for several centuries, and I've never seen a situation like this before. That's why we're not entirely sure how to handle it."

That was fair enough. I was still having trouble wrapping my head around the part of the situation that was knowing nightmarish beings were slipping from their home dimension into my world on a regular basis. Beings that could live for multiple hundreds of years?

At least it seemed to be true that they didn't usually stir up much trouble. They wouldn't be able to keep their presence a secret for long otherwise. But my brain was still insisting the whole idea was crazy, even with a dude sporting tentacles right in front of me.

"There are so many of you, and you own houses and all this stuff... How is it nobody knows about you?" I couldn't help asking.

"Oh, a few do. There are humans who hunt shadowkind. Sorcerers who've taught themselves how to affect us, to some extent. Collectors who set up little bestiaries, living or dead. And the rare ones who don't like the others and get in their way. But they don't want to spread the news any more than we do. Too many humans in the know would spoil their stew."

I could only imagine the chaos if everyone suddenly found out that monsters were real. My gaze slid back toward the window. I didn't know what else to ask him that would help me in any way—and I felt kind of guilty knowing he was only holding his physical form with whatever pains it presented so that he could talk to me right now.

A restless urge tugged at me. I needed to stretch my legs, breathe in the fresh air, and figure out what my options were in case I wanted to make plans that didn't include my supposed saviors. Until we knew exactly what was going on, I couldn't assume they'd continue protecting me—or that I'd agree with their version of protection.

"Is it a problem if I go outside?" I asked.

Torrent seemed to consider the matter for a moment. "There isn't very far to go without a boat or wings, unless you want to swim in the swamp. You wouldn't want to roam much beyond the deck anyway. The farther you get from the cabin, the more chance some other shadowkind out there will sense your presence. But as long as you stay close, it should be fine."

It was very convenient that his explanation was full of reasons that I should stay here of my own free will. He wasn't *forcing* me to stay... only making it clear that I could be committing suicide if I tried to make a run for it.

Of course, that didn't mean he was wrong.

"I won't do any swimming, and I don't think it's likely I'll sprout wings," I said. "I'll just take a look around."

He nodded. The moment I headed for the door, he vanished into the shadows.

I pushed past the door into the thicker humidity outside. Insects buzzed all around me, and something scampered through the trees nearby. I patrolled around the cabin, taking stock.

The deck surrounded three sides of the building. The back of the cabin sat against a stretch of ground that looked like a tangle of tree roots with mud filling in the gaps between. I could see the shimmer of water maybe twenty feet through the clump of forest. No easy escape route that way.

No boats were moored here. The deck held nothing at all except an outdoor shower stall by one back corner with a pipe that jutted out from the cabin. Useful if you needed to rinse off the muck after a dip in the swamp?

One of the trees stood close to the deck's side railing, its lowest branch just a couple of feet higher. I studied it before hefting myself onto the railing and managed to step over onto the branch. Then I scrambled higher up, setting my hands on the least mossy spots, working my way from branch to branch.

Within a minute, I was sweating even in my tank top. I pulled myself onto the next tree limb and then peered out over the landscape around me.

I'd clambered several feet higher than the roof of the cabin now. There were a few more branches above me that should support my weight no problem. This was one of the tallest trees nearby—I'd get a great view of my surroundings from up there.

I hauled and scrambled until I reached the highest point that wasn't outright insane, wrapped my arms around the narrowed trunk, and scanned the landscape again.

Torrent hadn't been kidding about the lack of access to this place. I must have been able to survey at least a mile in all directions from my current spot, and I couldn't make out any patches of land that were more than small, swampy islands, let alone other human-made structures. The dingy water gleamed beneath the sun in every direction.

I *could* swim, though, if I really felt I needed to. If risking whatever infectious crap might be stewing in the swamp water seemed a better bet than sticking around.

I'd have to watch out for the wildlife too. No doubt there were gators cruising nearby—it looked like their kind of digs.

Sighing, I leaned against the tree and let my forehead rest on the ridged bark. I could use a break before I swung myself back down to earth. I still wasn't sure what the right thing to do was, but at least I had a better idea of what lay around me.

I pictured myself slogging through the swamp, my chin high with determination. I could do it if I had no choice. I'd spent the last nine years learning how to take care of myself and avoid relying on anyone else in every area I could. I was already dosing myself with a course of antibiotics after yesterday's injury. Why should I be a burden even to monsters... especially when those monsters had motivations I didn't totally understand for helping me?

It would be an adventure—a wetter, stickier version of my usual urban exploring. No big deal. I pulled that thought around me and let it strengthen my resolve.

I'd been chilling out there for a while when I caught a ripple of dark movement from the corner of my eye. My head snapped around automatically, my pulse hiccupping. But I didn't see anything around me but the other tall trees, their leaves swaying slightly in the languid breeze.

It'd probably been a bird or a large bug. Who could blame me for being jumpy?

All the same, I sat up straighter, about to plan my descent. Before I could make my first foray downward, a winged form with jutting tusks and scruffy burgundy fur sprang at me out of the shadows dappling the tree next to mine.

A cry escaped my throat. I lurched sideways instinctively—but there wasn't much of anywhere to go.

My legs slid against the branch. I groped at the trunk, and the thing crashed into my body, throwing me off and snatching at me in the same motion.

The creature's knobby arms closed around my torso—and a roar reverberated through the swamp. A larger form, gray as slate, barreled into the creature holding me.

The thing let go—and I fell.

I snatched at the branches I tumbled past, bumping my elbow, scraping my ankle. A shriek broke from my throat. Just before my head whacked against the next branch, a blur of scaly deep green burst through the foliage and yanked me out of the way.

We fell the rest of the way together, the skin on the limbs that'd closed around me turning pliant instead of rigid with scales. When my rescuer's feet thumped onto the boards of the deck, his arms cradling me so I only felt a brief jolt of impact, Lance was totally human-looking again, from his dark curls to his golden tan. Well, other than the claws he'd curved carefully away from me.

The jolt had knocked the breath out of me, and having his ferally gorgeous face that close to mine, my body pressed up against his well-muscled chest, made it hard to get my air back. My heart thumped as I stared up at him, and he grinned back at me, somehow getting even more scarily stunning with that expression.

"No more flying sessions for you," he said.

"I didn't mean to—" I jerked my gaze away, my mind screaming that I *really* shouldn't be feeling this rush of heat over a guy with three-inch claws protruding from his fingers, and a crash amid the trees had me squirming out of his hold. "There was another monster. Something attacked me."

Lance put me down, but his knuckles grazed my back in a gesture that felt both purposeful and way more enticing than seemed reasonable. "Our living hunk of stone is taking care of the beastie," he said. "It shouldn't take long. There's not much that can take on Crag and come out better for it."

I peered through the brush, making out only twitches of the vegetation along with the grunts and thumps. "He's going to kill it?"

Lance chuckled. "Can't have it going off telling tales about where it found you, can we? Stupid thing should have known better if it wanted to live."

As if to punctuate that sentence, a shriek of pure pain wrenched through the air. There was a gristly sound of flesh being torn, vivid enough to make my stomach twist. Then the noises quieted.

For a moment, there was nothing. Just as I realized that Torrent had materialized on the deck near the cabin door, Crag emerged from the shadows beneath the deck's railing. Traveling through the gloom must have been easier than moving physically through the swamp when he didn't need to carry me.

He didn't look like a hunk of stone now—well, other than the blocky jaw that was the same slate-gray all of him had looked like in my brief glimpse when he'd collided with my attacker. In his human-like form, most of his skin—from the scalp that showed through his thin sheen of black hair to his muscle-bound calves where they protruded from his shorts—was a burnished bronze-brown.

"It's taken care of?" Torrent asked.

"Done," the huge man rumbled. I didn't see any blood on him, but I could imagine those large hands ripping into the creature far too easily. His dark brown eyes focused on me. "You shouldn't go up there again."

His brusque tone made me want to cringe. I folded my arms over my chest. "Obviously. I didn't know going *up* would be a problem."

"The beasties come from all directions," Lance said with a tsk of his tongue.

"It seems that way." Torrent frowned at the swamp around us. "You must have gotten high enough that the protections didn't totally disguise whatever vibes you're giving off. Definitely no more climbing."

A lump filled my throat with the impression of my world shrinking even smaller than it'd already gotten in the past several hours. The attack last night hadn't been a fluke. Whatever the monsters wanted in me, it was still there, maybe even more potent than before.

"They're going to keep coming," I said.

Torrent turned to me. "For the time being. We'll figure something out."

The three of them, he meant. Because what the hell could I do against these creatures full of stabby appendages that could spring out of a patch of darkness without warning?

I didn't like feeling this helpless, this dependent on men who were not only strangers but also monsters themselves. There had to be *something* more I could do for myself other than standing—or falling—around while they did all the work.

I squared my shoulders and gave the bunch of them a firm look. "If I'm in this much danger, I need to be prepared for the worst. Even if it'd only help a little bit, I want you to teach me every possible way that I could fight them myself."

CHAPTER SIX

Crag

The woman had pushed the armchairs and coffee table off to the side to clear more space. Now she was sitting on the hardwood floor with her legs stretched out in a V, leaning to one side and then the other as she warmed up her muscles.

The clothes I'd bought her hung a little loosely on her slim frame, even though I thought I'd found the size she specified. But then, mortals seemed to have relatively few options with such a range of bodies. It was probably impossible for anything to fit the same way the clothes we shadowkind conjured onto our human-like forms did.

The slight billowing of the T-shirt couldn't disguise the toned muscles flexing in her arms, or the strength and flexibility that showed through all her movements. From our time observing her, we knew that along with her hobby of clambering around and up various buildings, she was part of a rock-climbing club at her school.

She might never have been able to match any of us for speed or strength, but she was more capable than most humans I'd encountered. I wasn't sure if that was a good thing or a bad thing as far as our purposes were concerned.

I shifted my attention to Torrent where he was watching from the shadows nearby. I was meant to go out there and begin the combat training the woman had requested. That *Quinn* had requested—I should get in the habit of using her name. We needed her to stay at ease and compliant.

But doubts niggled at me. "Are you sure this is a good idea?" I asked our leader. "Rollick isn't going to want a mortal who can fight *him*."

Torrent snorted. "She'd have to transform into a completely different being to present any threat to him. And if any deadly demon-killing moves occur to you, don't teach her those. Doing some training sessions will keep her busy while I work on getting in contact with him. It wouldn't be a horrible thing if she could pitch in during any future attacks too."

I guessed that was a reasonable point—and Torrent knew best. I didn't kid myself about having any head for strategy. My strength was in getting the job I was given done quickly and with all necessary impact. Lance's mind was sharp, yes, but it was also scattered, more like a bag of pins than a blade.

The dragon shifter would probably have weighed in with one of his random, not always totally sensible remarks anyway, but he was off patrolling. We wanted to be sure no other shadowkind had caught wind of the recent beast's discovery.

I pushed myself out of the shadows into physical form, sticking to my human guise. I didn't imagine Quinn found me all that easy on the eyes even like this, with the rocky jaw that had prevented me from ever blending in with mortal society the way Rollick and many others did—the way Torrent used to, from what he'd said. I was a hell of a lot more imposing in my gargoyle body, though. Mortals who saw *that* up close tended to scream or flee, generally both.

If they were lucky. Occasionally my appearance had an even more profound effect. I was a beast, and they saw it. No point in risking those ill effects again. I knew what I was, and it allowed me to get my jobs done.

Mortals were far too fragile.

Quinn got to her feet, finished with her stretching. She set her hands on her hips. "So, where do we start?"

She was fragile too compared to me, in spite of her athleticism. I stepped closer and hesitated. Normally if fighting needed to be done, I leapt straight to doing it, no discussing the possibilities. And I had a very different physique to work with than she did. How was I supposed to play teacher?

Torrent had asked me to because I did know how to fight. I needed to figure it out. I knit my brow, studying her. "What would your instincts tell you to do against a mortal opponent?" We could build from there. I hoped.

Quinn tipped her head to one side as she considered the question. "Well, go for the sensitive spots like the eyes, the throat, the groin—I took a bunch of self-defense classes in my teens, and that's what they taught us." She demonstrated the motions she might use against a human attacker with brisk efficiency that eased my apprehension. At least my student wasn't as green at the subject as I was at teaching.

"Hurt them enough that they'll let you go and be too distracted to catch you, and then run away," she went on. "That's the basic strategy. I'm guessing it won't be so useful against monsters, though."

I grunted dismissively. "The same idea should apply. Hit them where it'll hurt."

"Oh." She looked momentarily chagrinned, and I wondered if I'd spoken too gruffly. I'd never gotten much practice at conversing with mortals, but even my fellow shadowkind sometimes seemed taken aback. I was never sure how much it was my words that intimidated them and how much the being they saw those words coming out of. Sometimes I suspected it didn't matter what I said, the reaction would be the same.

Often, that served my purposes just fine. But I wasn't meant to be terrorizing this human. When she tensed up after I spoke, I had the impression that I'd failed somehow. I didn't like the sensation.

"It would still take some adapting," I added, forcing myself to speak more slowly. "Different body shapes."

"And different sensitive spots?" Quinn said. "I mean... you're basically made out of stone, right? When you're in your 'shadowkind' form. Would hitting *you* in the throat do anything?"

"No," I admitted. "Not to me." She might break the bones in her hand if she hit me too hard. "But most shadowkind don't have the same natural armor I do. And even I have sensitive spots." I paused, wondering if it was really ideal to admit anything like this... but did I really think she'd ever stand a chance against me even with a little inside knowledge? She was tough for a human, but still terribly soft next to me.

There wasn't a lesser shadowkind out there who could match my strength, and few higher shadowkind could either. A mortal managing it was out of the question.

"Eyes are a good target across the board," I said. "Including for me. My ears are also sensitive if struck a particular way. And the inside of my mouth, if anyone got that far without me snapping off whatever they'd stuck inside."

Quinn let out a nervous laugh. "I think I'll skip testing that out. Eyes it is, then. Anything else that's fairly common for all shadowkind?"

I pictured a fight in my head, trying to get my instincts to kick in mentally so I could figure out where I'd normally strike. The acts came so naturally I rarely thought about them at all.

"Anything nose- or snout-like, most of the time," I said after a moment. "A good blow there can deflect an attack and possibly stun the creature for a moment."

"That's what you'd aim for?"

"I'd snap off their heads or tear their innards apart," I said automatically. "That's the only way to *kill* shadowkind. You won't be doing that."

She made a quick face. "Right. Got it."

What else could I offer her that she *could* do? I frowned. "You can also go for hands or feet—especially fingers and toes. Small and easily broken."

"Unless they're made out of stone."

"Of course," I grumbled.

Her face fell just for an instant, and I realized she'd probably been attempting to make a joke. Humor was definitely not among my strengths. My gut twisted with that sense of failure, but she appeared to have already bounced back, tossing her hair over her shoulder with a smile.

Whatever Rollick had planned for her, I'd rather not make the time leading up to it more unpleasant for her than it needed to be. She didn't seem to be a *bad* sort of human. It wasn't her fault she'd attracted attention, whatever that strange, subtle energy she gave off was.

I didn't know what to do except continue. "Positioning will be more of a concern. Some of the higher shadowkind will have human-like stances on two legs, but many of them drop to all fours—or more limbs, depending on the being—and nearly all of the lesser shadowkind have more animalistic bodies. And there's a major range in size."

"Higher and lesser shadowkind?" Quinn broke in with a quizzical tone.

Had no one explained that much to her yet? I wasn't sure I was the best for it, but I was the only one available.

I motioned to myself. "Beings like me and Torrent and Lance are considered higher shadowkind. We think about more than our basic urges, talk, make plans. That sort of thing. Lesser shadowkind are... like mortal animals. Eat, sleep, fight."

Quinn arched an eyebrow. "And fuck?"

I was pretty sure she was teasing me again, but there was an obvious answer. "No. Only higher shadowkind—who decide they want to—do that. The lesser beings don't have any reason to. We don't reproduce the same way mortals do."

Both eyebrows shot up. "Really? So, how do you then? Do you lay eggs or something?"

I glowered at her. "We don't have children at all. We just... arrive in the shadow realm, as we are."

"Hmm. Very mysterious."

I let out a rumble and drew myself even taller, looming over her. "Do you want to practice your defending or not?"

The amusement on Quinn's face vanished. "Yes, of course. Sorry."

Another twinge of guilt ran through my stomach, but she had gotten off topic. I was just getting the work done.

I crouched down so that my hands could brush the floor, an approximation of a beast on all fours. I was still far larger than most of the shadowkind that'd come at her so far, but it captured the gist of the idea.

"Give it a try," I said. "Go for my weak spots, or the spots that would be weak on another being. Dodge when I strike at you. I won't really hit you. We can take it slowly."

She raised her fists but didn't move beyond that. "Are you going to turn all stony? You don't have your special protection like this."

"It's better I don't shift," I said, not bothering to say why. "If you land a blow hard enough to disturb me, it'll be my own fault. But I don't think that's likely. You're much softer than me even like this."

"So cocky," she said, and then sobered, looking down at her limbs. "But I guess you've got good reason to be. Okay. Let's see. Well, if you were one of the shadowkind that's been attacking me, you'd be leaping at me, not just sitting there."

If she wanted me in action, I could give her action. I started forward with only half the speed I'd have given to an actual charge.

Quinn swiped at my face, aiming for my eyes. She misjudged the blow in her haste and at the unfamiliar angle, and would have clocked my forehead if I hadn't swiveled out of the way. I bumped my shoulder against her thigh, making her wobble on her feet. The faint vibrations of energy that her body gave off, the whisper of a threat, tickled over me. Ridiculous. The lesser shadowkind should have been able to see that even without three months of observation.

Maybe they did. Maybe seeing the clang of threat coming from such an easy target incited them even more.

"You'd have fallen," I said.

"Right onto my ass," she agreed, and let out a rough breath. "And then the beast would pounce on me, and I'd be screwed. Again."

I came at her a second time, and she shuffled sideways on her feet as she took her jabs, staying in motion so I couldn't as easily trip her up. I still *could* have if I'd really tried, but I had to admire her speed and determination—and her quick thinking at coming up with that strategy unprompted. If she'd been a shadowkind, she could have become a formidable opponent.

She saw the benefits of switching up her tactics too. She darted to one side and then the other, and aimed for my nose and ears as well as my eyes. At one point she leapt in and stomped her heel at my braced fingers, swift enough that my own defensive inclinations kicked in. Without thinking, I jerked my hand back and smacked my other arm across the backs of her knees hard enough to topple her.

A jolt of consternation hit me an instant later. I leapt forward, swinging my forearm beneath her shoulders and catching her head inches before it hit the floor.

Quinn's breath hitched out of her at the impact, grazing my chest with its warmth. She stared up at me looming over her, and I was abruptly aware of all the warmth contained in that softness. *She* wasn't made of anything like stone beneath that tender skin.

I had the strange, ridiculous urge to trace my fingers over its delicate smoothness like I'd seen Lance do a few times. To twine my fingers into the equally soft strands of her hair where it was spilling across my hand.

Her eyes started to widen, and I shoved myself upright. She wouldn't want my brutish hands all over her. She'd probably been worrying that I might pummel her into the ground after all.

"You'll have to be more careful than that, Softie," I said. Her weakness wasn't something to admire.

Quinn winced and scrambled to her feet before I could offer to help her. She paused, studying me.

"Thank you," she said abruptly. "I didn't say that before, and I should have."

I blinked at her, puzzled. "For what?"

"For fending off that thing that jumped on me in the tree. If you hadn't gotten there so quickly…" She gave a little shudder and then met my eyes again. "Saving someone's life seems like the kind of thing that deserves at least a thank you."

I hadn't noticed its absence. "It's what I'm here for," I said with a waft of uncertainty that left me off balance. But that was the truest thing I could have said in return. I shook off the uneasiness and flexed my muscles. "Should we continue?"

Quinn swept back her hair. "Sure, even if the training isn't going so well. Hopefully I'll do better against the smaller monsters." Her hand dropped to her side, and she pulled out the tool she'd held earlier, flicking open the blade that was just one of the metal instruments it held. "Will weapons do any good against shadowkind?"

"It's difficult to injure one of us enough to *kill* us, but a deep enough cut can slow us down. Let me see."

I held out my hand, and she passed the tool over. As I grasped the handle, a prickling sensation ran through my palm. I flipped over the tool and noted the small logo embedded in the bright red material. Silver.

It was small and thin, only enough to cause a tiny discomfort, though if I'd left it pressed against my skin for a minute or two, the pain would have increased. The blade itself was steel, the iron mingled with other metals in processes that eradicated their effects on us. But it did stir an idea.

I held that thought inside as I offered the tool back to her. "If you think you have a chance of stabbing something in the eyes with that, it would be useful. Otherwise, you'll move faster and more accurately with just your hands. A solid punch will do more than a light scratch."

"Fair enough." Quinn moved into a fighting stance, but before we could return to our practice session, a peal of electronic music carried down the hallway. She stiffened. "My phone. I'd better see who it is."

I watched her hurry down the hall to the bedroom and then stepped back into the shadows where I could sense Torrent's watchful gaze.

"She won't manage much against any but the weakest shadowkind," I said. "Not on her own. She could do more damage if we found her a proper weapon. A blade made from silver or iron or both, maybe?"

Torrent hummed to himself, but I recognized the skepticism in the sound before he spoke. "Let's not take this too far. We wouldn't want her stabbing a lovely item like that into one of us."

"Yes," I said. "Of course."

Because for all Quinn thought we were here to protect her… there would come a point when stabbing us might actually make her safer.

CHAPTER SEVEN

Quinn

Torrent didn't join us for dinner. Not that the frozen pizza made for a particularly inspiring meal, but he'd vanished into the shadows every time the rest of us had sat down to eat. I'd gathered that none of the shadowkind *needed* food to sustain themselves, but Crag and Lance seemed to enjoy it as some sort of indulgence.

The empty chair at the head of the table across from me gave me an uncomfortable feeling. Maybe it was too uncomfortable for *him* to keep his physical form simply to eat and join a companionable conversation around the table. We weren't talking about anything all that vital, but it still seemed awkward to exclude him.

Or maybe I was just projecting my own general dissatisfaction onto him. It'd been a whole day, and we didn't seem to be any closer to getting me back home where I belonged.

I watched Lance carve a slice in half with his claws, severing crust, cheese, and pepperoni with equal ease. He gulped the piece down in one go, managing to look just as gorgeous as ever while he did.

Crag ate more politely, holding the rather limp slices gingerly in his huge hands. It was hard to tell how much experience either of them had with this particular delicacy.

More curiosity itched at me. Torrent had indicated that shadowkind moved around my world—the "mortal realm," as the shadowkind called it—pretty extensively, but for beings like Crag and Lance, their ability to participate in what I'd consider regular life must have been limited. Even in their mostly human forms, they couldn't have walked into a restaurant or wandered through the streets with that jaw or those claws.

"What do shadowkind like you normally do here?" I asked them. "In the mortal realm. When you're not saving random humans from other shadowkind, I guess. You just hang out and enjoy the atmosphere?"

"We keep busy," Lance said breezily. "Always lots going on around here. Much more interesting than the shadow realm."

Crag shot him a baleful look and attempted to answer my question more directly. "Some shadowkind mingle with humans. That's harder for us." He rubbed his rocky jaw. "But it's still good exploring different terrain. Watching from afar."

"Or in your case, from above," I suggested, thinking of his wings.

He grunted, his voice coming out with a growl. "I can't let mortals see me flying around."

My nerves jumped at the brusqueness of his voice, but only for an instant. A second later, his jaw twitched with a hint of a grimace. I was starting to get the impression that he didn't *mean* to be as gruff as he sometimes came across. It was just his default state, nothing specifically to do with anything I did or said.

For all his grumbling while he'd been walking me through shadowkind fighting techniques, he'd actually been very patient. And helpful, even if I couldn't pull off many of the moves he'd suggested all that effectively against an attacking monster. And that moment when all that brawn had loomed over me on the floor, his arm wrapped around me to protect me from the fall...

Okay, I really shouldn't be remembering all the possibilities that closeness had stirred up in my head. It hadn't been that long since I'd last gotten laid.

But when had I ever gotten laid by a guy so physically impressive? It wasn't weird for me to be curious about *that*, right? At this point, I probably knew him better than most of the random dudes who'd caught my eye and been up for a quick roll in the sack, even if that wasn't very much. There'd never seemed like much point in aiming for anything more, when I couldn't exactly offer much in terms of commitment given my short expiration date.

None of them had made me wish for a longer commitment. The guys I ran into all seemed to be too cautious to embrace the thrills I liked to chase or too aimless in their recklessness to understand what it meant to have a sense of purpose too. They hadn't cared about me, only about getting off. Which didn't really matter as long as I got off too.

They had at least been *human*, though.

I jerked my mind back to the present, tuning out the heat that had unfurled in my abdomen as well as I could. "Okay, so you can't do a ton of urban sightseeing from the air. It still must be pretty amazing flying at all." The memories of my flights in his arms were exhilarating even when tempered by my worries.

Crag paused and then inclined his head. "I do enjoy it when I can. It is... freeing. I can be weightless even at my size."

I wondered if it felt similar to the rush I got when I climbed to the top of a high rise, defying gravity in my own way.

"Also makes for easier hunting," Lance piped up. "The gargoyle likes to pounce. Makes Torrent sad for the animals, though, so we mostly stick to human-made." He dropped another piece of pizza into his mouth.

"Getting to try different types of provisions is another benefit of the mortal realm," Crag said. He studied his second slice as if he wasn't totally sure he approved of this type.

"There's much better pizza out there," I assured him. "You've got to get it from a restaurant instead of a grocery store." I paused. "I guess that'd be difficult."

Lance chuckled. "Slink through the shadows, nab one off the counter, chow down someplace else. No problem. Too far to bring one like that here, though. It'd be ruined."

"So you steal on a regular basis?" I said. Should that surprise me? They were monsters. Maybe it was ridiculous to expect them to have any consideration for human laws.

I was anticipating a typically playful remark from Lance, but it was Crag who answered. "Humans steal all the time from each other."

Well, I couldn't argue against that. "*I* don't steal," I felt the need to say.

"Lucky you that you can get yourself a lovely pizza pie without having to," Lance said, tilting back his chair just a smidge shy of toppling over onto his back. Although he was so agile he'd probably have managed to land on his feet even if it had toppled. "We don't spend all day doing that. That'd be boring too. There's roaming and playing and our duties when we have them and—"

My mind homed in on that one word. "Duties? What kind of duties?" I hadn't gotten the impression before that these guys answered to anyone other than themselves—that any shadowkind did.

Before either of the men could answer, Torrent wavered into being at the far end of the table. He must have been hanging out in the shadows while we'd talked—under the chair? Getting a great view of our feet while he had to follow the conversation mutely? There weren't any ideal shadowy vantage points in the room that I could see, not where he'd be near us.

He stayed standing, his tentacles braced at either side of his body, and nodded to my plate. "Are you just about done? Now that you've had a break, maybe you should get in some more combat practice. Especially if we're hoping to leave the cabin soon."

The thought of leaving gave me a jolt of energy. I looked down at the half-eaten slice still on my plate, both greasy and overly chewy, and nudged the plate aside. "Sure. But I still—Lance mentioned duties. Do you all have *jobs* or something?"

Torrent frowned as if annoyed that I hadn't dropped the subject. Was that why he'd popped up all of a sudden—as a way of distracting me?

But Lance just shrugged, still rocking his chair precariously on its back legs. "I only meant our duties to ourselves, to enjoy the best possible life." He flashed a grin at me.

His comment hadn't sounded like that, but he obviously didn't want to tell me whatever he had meant.

I exhaled in a huff, giving up for the moment, and glanced at Crag, expecting him to direct my second sparring session. But it was Lance who leapt up. He flipped both himself and the chair, whirling in mid-air to land on his feet as I'd imagined. With a flick of his hand, he caught the chair and set it down easily next to him.

"I wouldn't mind stretching my combat skills," he said. "And you should mix it up. Too much time with Crag, and you'll start lumbering too."

The stony giant let out a brief sound of consternation but pushed away from the table without complaint. "I should patrol again."

When I glanced back at Torrent in case he objected, the tentacled man had already vanished. It was just me and the ferally handsome, fearsomely clawed shadowkind who already had my pulse thrumming faster with that grin of his. He waggled his talons, and a shiver crawled up my spine that really should have been all fear... but a significant part of it was excitement.

I wanted to squeeze every thrill I could out of my probably short life, hadn't I? How many people could say they'd faced off against a gorgeous monster?

I just wouldn't think about all the other things parts of me were contemplating doing with that monster. Between him and Crag, I might need a cold shower—or several.

"Where should I try to hit you when you're in shadowkind form?" I asked him. I'd only seen him as a blur of scales and limbs before. I was even less sure what he looked like as a monster than I was with Crag.

Lance's grin widened. "Telling you would be cheating, wouldn't it? With any other beasties, you'd have to figure it out for yourself. But I'll shift so you know what you're dealing with. It'll be more fun that way."

He'd only just finished speaking when his body started to morph. One second, he was standing there all human-like with his dark, curly hair, golden-brown skin, and crooked smile. The next, he was stretching out on all fours.

His head elongated alongside his torso, his clothes rippling away into emerald-green scales. Along his gleaming lips, his teeth curved into fangs. Spikes jutted from the back of his neck all down his back to the tip of his tapered tail, which was nearly as long as the rest of his body.

I gaped. He was... a dragon. That was the only word that fit. A sleek, sinewy, wingless dragon, about the size of a tiger, all vibrant gemstone colors.

The only concrete aspects that fit his human-like form were the ever-present claws and the violet eyes, now set beneath scaled ridges on his reptilian forehead. But the creature in front of me still *felt* like Lance in other intangible ways: the sinewy grace to its movements as it prowled around me in the living room, the feral air that reminded me a creature could be both pretty and incredibly dangerous.

I reeled in my slackened jaw and shook the shock from my limbs. I needed to concentrate. If a beast like this came at me wanting to hurt me, what spots was it most likely to be vulnerable?

Like Crag had said before, the eyes were an obvious target on just about any creature, and Lance was no exception there. I wasn't sure his snout would be all that sensitive, especially with the many sharp teeth it contained. More jewel-like plates covered his throat and belly, which didn't look like a good bet for a punch.

Maybe his feet would still be vulnerable? As long as I could stomp on them without skewering my own feet on his claws.

Lance apparently decided that I'd had enough time to contemplate my strategy. He sprang at me without warning, leaping through the air as if he could fly even without wings.

I threw myself to the floor and rolled out of the way. He swiveled as he landed, his tongue flicking over his fangs in an expression that looked like a dragon version of his usual smirk. In an instant, he was bounding off the walls, whirling around me, with the same nimble speed I'd seen from him in his human-like form.

I ducked and spun and jabbed, my breath already turning ragged. He didn't actually attack me, didn't touch me other than the slightest graze of his smooth scales against my arm here, my back there, but he was showing me how easily he could have. Each time I swung my arm or slammed out my foot, he was someplace else before my strike could land.

At least I could be glad this particular monster was on my side?

"You know, Crag let me ease into the fight," I said between gulps of air, doing my best to keep pivoting to face him. "I'm not some kind of shadowkind-fighting powerhouse already."

Lance snorted as if the thought of cutting me any slack was absurd—or maybe he figured he was already cutting me enough slack by not eviscerating me a hundred times over. I'd swear I saw a glimmer of flame flare from his mouth along with the sound, but it vanished a second later.

Well, dragon, fire-breathing—it went with the territory, didn't it? That was how he'd sealed up the wound on my arm.

"You have to at least be careful of my chest," I insisted. "You don't want to bash it and send my heart onto the fritz, or it won't be those 'beasties' that kill me."

I couldn't tell whether Lance understood how serious I was. He twined closer, and I heaved my shoulder into his scaled side, managing to dodge around him at the last second. His tail smacked my ankles. I wobbled and leapt over it, and rammed my elbow toward one of his flared nostrils in case his nose was sensitive after all.

My arm glanced off the side of his cheek instead. He whipped around and pushed me against the wall. His scales and fangs fell away, and suddenly it was Lance the man looming over me, his hands pinning my wrists to the wood paneling, amusement dancing like fire in his violet eyes.

"Too slow," he said in a singsong voice.

I was panting for breath, my entire body tingling with the exertion of the fight—as much as it'd even been a fight rather than me simply flailing. The awareness of the dragon shifter's body so close to mine sent a flood of heat through me that only amplified the tingles.

I licked my lips instinctively, and Lance tracked the movement. He leaned closer, his head dipping as if to inhale the scent of my skin.

My heart skipped a beat. All at once, I *wanted*—wanted something I couldn't put into words, with a sharp, heated craving that pulsed low in my belly. Like the flings with the guys who'd stirred up the exhilaration I was longing for once or twice until I'd realized they weren't enough. They weren't what I needed.

I'd never found what I really needed. I wasn't sure it even existed. But right now, a whole lot of me wanted to find out if it could be the monstrous man in front of me.

"Like what you see, baby girl?" Lance said in a languid voice that held a hint of mockery. The teasing note jerked me back to reality.

Scratching an itch, getting a quick jolt of physical satisfaction was one thing. Being curious about my unusual protectors, fine. But to seriously be considering making out with a literal *monster*? Even a stunning one? That... That couldn't be a good idea, right?

I told myself it wasn't, but somehow the craving didn't subside. What was wrong with me? A chill washed through me, the intensity of my desire scaring me enough to dull the heat. I jerked to the side, away from Lance, and he let me go.

"I think—I think that's enough sparring for today," I said, wiping at my sweat-damp forehead as I tried to gather my scattered thoughts.

Lance considered me with his head cocked as if he was trying to figure out what was going on inside my mind. Since I wasn't even sure of that, he probably didn't get far. He shot me another smile. "Whatever you want." Then he was flickering away into the shadows, leaving me alone.

Adrenaline was still racing through my veins. I dragged in one breath and then another, but the jitteriness didn't subside.

This was all just… too much. Too crazy. And I had no idea what to do with any of it. How to react to my supposed saviors. How to make it safe for me to leave. What to say to my parents or the professors who'd be wondering about my absence soon.

Fuck.

I rubbed my forehead, swallowing the lump that'd risen in my throat. A different sort of longing hit me—for Torrent to appear in his usual chair and talk to me, distract me from the chaos inside me.

I wasn't sure he actually liked me all that much, but his measured responses made for easier conversation than Crag's gruff answers or Lance's unpredictable teasing.

Why would he want to show up just to chat, though? My gaze fell on his usual armchair—identical to the other three, identically wrong for his monstrous body. It wasn't really fair of me to expect him to put himself in pain just so *I'd* feel better. Too many people had already sacrificed too much so that I could be here at all.

A twinge of an earlier impulse rippled through me. My fingers curled toward my palms as if to hold it off. I hesitated.

Oh, why the hell not? It'd give me something to do, and it'd make life a little better for Torrent, at least. I'd be giving back a tiny bit in exchange for not getting slaughtered. If he didn't like it, he had three other chairs to squeeze his tentacles into.

I strode over to the chair and patted my hands along the arms. As I'd expected, the hard bits were around the edges—the middle section held only padding beneath the fabric. That was simple enough to adapt.

I didn't think my pocketknife would do the best job, so I went to the kitchen and found the sharpest blade there, a carving knife about the length of my hand. Then I knelt by the armchair and dug it into the fabric.

It took some sawing, angling carefully so I didn't go too badly against the grain of the cloth, but after several minutes I'd cut out a chunk about a foot wide and half as high. I trimmed down the foam padding to smooth it out and then sliced through the layer of fabric on the inside of the arm.

The chair looked a little weird with that gaping hole in the side, but if I could find some glue or a needle and thread—heck, even a stapler—I could attach the spare fabric over the edges of the padding to make it more cohesive again.

For starters, I'd balance it out. I moved to the other side of the chair and wielded the knife again.

I was carving the third side of the rectangular opening when Torrent appeared behind the chair. He peered down at me, his brow furrowed beneath the fall of his rumpled red hair. "What are you *doing*?"

I paused and glanced up at him, a little concerned that it wasn't obvious. "I noticed the chairs don't... fit you very well. This seemed like an easy adjustment to make. And it's not like I've got anything else all that useful to do."

He stared at me for a moment before he spoke again, his expression and his tone coolly impassive. "Is this something you do a lot? Fixing random things for people?"

A blush crept over my cheeks. "Well, kind of. I've spent a lot of time studying how things are constructed—mostly buildings, but engineering knowledge is useful for figuring out how smaller-scale objects are designed as well—and if I see where I could make a quick improvement... Is it okay? Were you particularly attached to the chair the way it was?" It wasn't super modern but not old enough to pass for an antique. And why would a monster care about human historical value anyway?

"No," he said quickly. "It's all right. Very considerate of you. Thank you. I'll let you finish."

He didn't sound all that grateful, but then, I hadn't done it for a pat on the back. Still, he vanished back into the shadows so swiftly I couldn't help wondering if I'd made some horrible faux pas after all.

CHAPTER EIGHT

Torrent

The swamp's water was far from an ideal environment. It lacked the bracing tang of ocean salt and the rippling currents of deeper lakes. Most of it was too shallow or narrow for my full natural body to move through. Even in the deeper, more open stretches, I kept my shadowkind form partly contracted. But sinking into the sluggish, murky liquid still gave me a brief escape from the stresses beyond.

I drifted along the maze-like channels around the clumps of vegetation for several minutes, tasting and scenting the water at the same time for any sign of intruders. The only living beings I encountered were of the mortal variety: fish, turtles, frogs, snakes, and an alligator that sensed me from a distance and paddled in the opposite direction, some innate sense telling it I was one of the few creatures it might ever encounter that could mark it as prey rather than predator.

Not that I had any interest in harming mortal animals. They were no threat to me. There was a simplicity to them, an innocence shadowkind beasts with their extra abilities couldn't possess, that had always appealed to me. So perfectly straightforward and predictable. I'd had a dog once—well, a stray that'd liked to hang around me—before...

There was no point in thinking about that.

Far beyond the boundaries of the protective posts, I came across a freshly fallen log with shattered branches drifting around it. A sense of possibility sparked in my mind. Stretching my tentacles, I allowed myself the small indulgence of assembling the branches into a sort of picture. Fit together in the right way, they created the impression of a spindly creature lounging on the log.

It wasn't likely that any human would wander out this way and see my efforts, not before the weather wrecked the hasty sculpture, but I got a little satisfaction from it all the same. I might not be able to walk among mortals like one of them the way I used to, but I could still make a small mark on their world.

Any pleasure I'd gotten out of that act dwindled over the short trip back to the cabin. I slunk inside through the shadows in time to join my companions for breakfast—as much as you could say I was actually joining them.

I considered my options and settled into a patch of shadow cast across the kitchen counter by the fridge—an awkward angle but one that at least allowed me to see each of the beings' faces. I needed to keep an eye both on the mortal woman and the members of my squad.

The vibe between the three of them as they sat down around the table felt amicable in a way that unsettled me. It was only our second morning here, but Quinn had gotten out the cereal she'd somehow already determined was Crag's favorite. She simply laughed at Lance when he announced he was having rocky road ice cream for his breakfast.

And when he leaned over and skewered one of her grapes with a claw to pop it into her own mouth, she didn't flinch at the demonstration of his monstrous features. Her eyes lingered instead on his mouth. An odd, heated prickling sensation coursed through me as if I'd swallowed some of the swamp water and it was stirring up a fever.

She was too at ease with us. Too accepting. How could she really look at Lance's talons or Crag's hardened face and smile like they were her *friends*? Was it some kind of trick?

She was making the best of a bad situation. She didn't really want to be here, but we'd made it clear she had no choice. So she was sucking up to us in the hopes that we'd...

I didn't really know what she'd want at this point. We were already keeping her alive, fighting off beasts on her behalf. She couldn't know what else might be coming that we'd be offering her up to. She knew it was the threat of our fellow shadowkind forcing her to stay away from her home, not our own preferences.

Why couldn't she have stayed cringing in her room like most mortals would? Then I wouldn't have needed to speculate.

Mortals lived and died like flies compared to us. She was likely going to die soon anyway. Whatever there was about her that gave off the provoking vibe that'd incited the lesser beings, Rollick either needed it or needed to destroy it. He didn't make decisions like that lightly. Every move he made was perfectly calculated.

I shouldn't even have to be telling myself that.

I definitely shouldn't have felt my hackles rise when Lance reached over to brush his knuckles against Quinn's forearm—or when a hint of pink touched her cheeks in response. He made one of his teasing remarks under his breath, too low for me to hear from my vantage point, and she guffawed, her eyes locked on his face.

I supposed it was easier to ignore the claws when he came with a human guise so otherwise appealing by typical mortal standards.

Women had once responded to me more like that. I'd never had quite the magnetism the dragon shifter did, but I'd never had trouble scoring a hook-up when I wanted to either.

Every now and then, Quinn's gaze left my comrades to skim across the room. That was interesting. What was she looking for? Was she plotting something?

I thought she knew there was no point in striking off on her own, that she'd be throwing her life away if she left our protection, but we'd seen how agile she was in her explorations of the city. No doubt she could have found a way out of the swamp without a boat or wings if she'd tried to.

If some roaming shadowkind wouldn't have cut her down first.

Lance tossed back the rest of his ice cream straight from the bowl to his mouth and got up. He stroked the backs of his fingers across Quinn's shoulder blades as he came around the table, and the flush returned to her cheeks. When he reached the sink to set his dishes down, I extended the tip of my tentacle from the shadow just enough to give him a light tug.

Lance answered my summons immediately, slipping into the shadows next to me. His presence there didn't exactly have eyes, but his attention rested on me with a faint weight. "Ready for your orders, sir!" he said in a jaunty tone.

"You're going to take the first patrol," I told him. "But I wanted to talk to you first. You seem to be getting very wrapped up in the mortal."

He shrugged without any sign of concern. "She likes me playing with her. It doesn't hurt anything, does it? She has no power over us. I've been curious what it might be like, to try out the physical connection they enjoy so much."

"You've had plenty of opportunities at the club," I grumbled, tamping down another flare of inexplicable irritation.

"It's not the same," Lance said. "You never really know what you're dealing with. They're always coming and going."

"Too much chaos even for you?"

He chuckled. "I have limits, as obscure as they may be."

I hadn't encountered many of them. What *had* held him back from experimenting if he'd been as curious as he said? It wasn't as if the typical club-goers had any power over us either...

But maybe his caution made sense, after the whatever wounds he'd been dealt in the mortal world before. From the havoc he'd been wreaking through the shadow realm when I'd stumbled on him, those wounds had obviously run deep.

"Well, don't get attached," I said. "Playing is fine as long as that's all it is, but appreciating her for anything more than that will only complicate the situation. She isn't ours. She's for Rollick."

"Of course," Lance said. "But we might as well have as much fun as we can in the meantime. He's taking his time coming to collect."

"I'm sure now that the first phone message didn't go through. I'll get another device and reach out that way." A different, new phone with no connections to anyone seemed like my best bet for the discretion our boss had asked for. I just had to hope *that* message would go through and not be blocked because it was a number he wasn't expecting.

If I didn't get a response to that either, I'd have to reach out through other channels that got more precarious. Somehow I didn't think he'd want us flying the woman right to his doorstep where anyone could notice.

"Go on," I added, nudging Lance toward the door. One of his tumbling, whirling romps around the swamp might burn off some of his extra energy too.

When Quinn went off to the bathroom to wash up, I sent Crag on a trip of his own to the nearest town to pick up that phone and additional supplies. We'd only brought enough food for a few days, and the woman would definitely get restless if we couldn't keep her fed. Then I sank into deep thought, contemplating what I knew of Rollick's business ties and threads of influence, what I might best tug on if I wanted to send a message without anyone else realizing the significance.

I only vaguely noted Quinn's return to the room until she drove one of the screwdrivers on her multitool into the wall near the dining table with a thump. The sound jolted through the shadows. I pushed myself into physical form just as she smacked the tool into the wall about a foot from the first spot, leaving a second small hole that went through both the paneling and the drywall behind it. Both holes stood at about the height of her shoulders.

"What are you doing now?" I demanded, bracing myself against my tentacles. I'd been in this body a lot more than usual lately, and both of my legs started to ache the moment any of my weight pressed on them—which didn't exactly improve my mood.

The woman blinked those sky-blue eyes at me as if I shouldn't be surprised that she was jabbing holes, however minor, in the walls of our current home. "I just thought… Let me show you. It'll make more sense that way."

"Usually guests *ask* before they start knocking down walls," I pointed out, folding my arms over my chest.

"I'm not knocking it down," she said with a laugh as she bent to pick something off the floor. "And it's hard to ask you much of anything when you're off being a shadow most of the time."

"I can still hear you when you talk."

"Well, I never know for sure you're even around. Also, there's this saying about asking for forgiveness rather than permission…"

She wielded a stick about a half an inch in diameter and as long as her forearm. She'd obviously trimmed it. It was smooth other than two smaller but solid twigs that protruded from its length: one that curved up from the base by a couple of inches to form what looked like a hook and another that jutted out at a shallower angle by the narrower tip.

Quinn wiggled the hook-like twig into one of the holes until she could pop the base of the stick right in. She wiggled it around until she seemed to judge it stable, leaving it with the smaller twig angled upward. Then she did the same with another stick that was almost identical. She must have gathered those this morning while I'd been out and whittled them down with her little knife.

The two sticks now protruded several inches out of the wall. Quinn picked up a broad but thin chunk of bark and balanced it on the two sticks. It fit just about perfectly, the twigs ensuring it wouldn't slide off even if jostled.

She stepped back and motioned to her creation. "There. Now you can join us properly even if you don't want to come out of the dark."

It took me a second to register that she was gesturing more to the shadow that now slanted across the wall *beneath* the thing she'd built rather than to the thing itself.

With the position of the overhead light, the patch of darkness fell along the wall directly across from the end of the table that the others had been leaving empty. Where I would have joined them physically if I hadn't been conserving my bodily endurance for possible threats to come.

Quinn glanced at me, abruptly cautious. "I realized there wasn't any good shadowy spot for you to... hang out with us, or whatever, when we're sitting there. This way you can almost be at the table with us, even if you don't want to come out. But of course you can always sit in the chair if you want to be completely there."

"Of course," I said. My other words seemed to have fled me. I opened my mouth and closed it again, my throat abruptly tight.

She wasn't just *accepting* our strangeness. She'd observed my habits and found a way to cater to them as if she understood.

How much else had she picked up on? She hadn't mentioned why she assumed I might be avoiding lingering in physical form for very long, but she hadn't questioned me about it either. Maybe she'd noticed my discomfort and was simply being polite not bringing it up.

When had anyone ever catered to my infirmities this way? Rollick overlooked them, and that had been a gift in itself. Those who respected me ignored them; those who didn't sneered at them. What reason could this mortal have for trying to make things *easier* for me? Was this pity?

The remark that finally spilled from my mouth was harsher than I'd intended. "Are you sure it's not going to fall right back out of the wall in a few hours?"

"I don't think so." She cocked her head. "It's my swamp version of those wall hooks—well, maybe you don't know about them. But the twig on the inside of the wall should keep it all balanced."

Something about her easy confidence in her abilities rankled me. "You really do love going around playing Ms. Fix-It, don't you?"

She flinched at little at my tone in a way she hadn't even at Lance's claws, and my throat constricted more. Then she raised her chin. "I don't know how long I'm going to be in this world, so I'd like to at least leave it better than I found it. If you don't like the new shadow, you don't have to use it."

My gaze slid past her to the chair she'd already doctored—that I'd lowered myself into last night long after she'd gone to sleep and confirmed it was far more relaxing when my tentacles could sprawl out through the sides.

There'd been a time when I hadn't needed any accommodations like that. Fucking ridiculous that something as basic as a chair caused me problems now.

But I did already know that was how Quinn operated. In the three months we'd watched her from the shadows, we'd seen her tinker with one fixture or furnishing or another several times. I'd just assumed it was for her own benefit. Making a new patch of darkness on the wall didn't help her at all. It made it *easier* for me to avoid her.

And the soft tremor that'd run through her voice with her declaration resonated with the same impulse in me that'd driven me to construct my silly sculpture in the swamp. Leave a mark. Show we'd been here. Make a difference. That didn't come out of pity. It was a declaration of purpose. Of passion.

And she'd dedicated this one to me.

I didn't like the churning sensation that'd filled my chest like a gathering storm. I swallowed thickly and willed both it and my irritation down.

It wasn't her I was frustrated with, after all.

"I do like it," I said. "And the chair. I just wasn't expecting it. I suppose now you'll have a better idea where to find me if you need to ask about something else."

Then I stepped back into the shadows before I found myself saying anything else. Before I had to look too closely at the warmth that had flickered up inside me at the thought of her turning to me for anything at all. Trusting me to be there for her as she'd tried to be here for me.

She was just a mortal. She didn't *really* understand anything. After all my centuries in the realms, I knew better.

If her gesture looked like kindness, it was only because she appreciated that in some way I might be as weak as she was.

CHAPTER NINE

Quinn

I sat on the front section of the deck where there wasn't any railing, dipping my bare feet into the water and letting the cool sensation spread up my legs. I figured that little bit of contact with the dingy liquid was safe enough. Even with the sky overcast today, the humidity stuck to my skin both inside and outside the cabin. I hadn't realized how much I depended on air conditioning until I had to go without it.

My sketchbook lay on the weather-worn boards beside me. I'd tried to distract myself by working on my projects—both the latest one for class and my own assortment—but there wasn't much else I could do with them with just pencil and paper. And the knowledge of that I couldn't take them further without my computer prompted niggling worries I couldn't ignore.

Both the sense of the hours creeping by as another day slipped past me and thoughts of the new excuses I was going to have to make soon tugged at my mind. Not to mention the uncertainties about what exactly was happening to me.

A flutter passed through my chest—the same eerie sensation as the earlier ripple, only expanded all the way to my ribs. My pulse kept beating on in the same steady rhythm, so I didn't panic about the feeling meaning my borrowed heart was on the fritz. But I didn't know what it *did* mean. Where that feeling had come from. Why it was bringing literal monsters to my doorstep.

I still didn't think I'd gotten the full story even out of the monsters who'd saved me. It wasn't like I could force them to spill their guts to me, though.

I tapped the soles of my feet against the murky water, leaning back on my hands. A flash of emerald green was my only warning of an impending attack.

A sinewy, scaled body whipped past mine with just enough force to send me toppling over on the deck. I nearly crashed right into the water—would have if I hadn't managed to hook my fingers into a narrow gap between the boards. My legs splashed in up to my knees.

I rolled onto my stomach and heaved myself all the way out. When I looked up, I found Lance back in human form, perched on the deck a few feet away. He smirked at me. "Gotta work on those reflexes."

"You don't play fair," I informed him. He didn't even offer me a hand as I pushed myself upright. Jerk.

A stunningly gorgeous jerk, but still.

"Where's the fun in *fair*?" he asked. "You want to be prepared to fight monsters, you've got to expect monstrousness." He winked at me and flipped over in one of his acrobatic moves to land on all fours, his dragon form re-expanding his body at the same time.

I guessed I couldn't argue with that point. And maybe I shouldn't have called him a jerk, even in the privacy of my head, because he wasn't really. He was exactly what he'd said, what I'd already known he was—a monster.

But I was starting to figure out that "monster" didn't necessarily mean maliciously evil, only inhuman. He wasn't operating under the same set of rules I took for granted.

None of them were. That was part of the reason I worried, wasn't it? They might not be evil, but brutal violence did seem to be their go-to solution. They didn't have families, so how could they understand my responsibilities to my own? I had no idea how their minds worked at all... or what they might have been keeping to themselves in those minds that I'd actually have wanted to know.

Water puddled around my feet. At least I was a little more cooled off now.

Lance's sleek dragon head weaved back and forth through the air as if taunting me, his violet eyes glinting with mischief. I shoved the sweat-damp waves of my hair back from my face and raised my hands in a defensive posture.

"We'll see who ends up in the swamp next," I said. The taunt gave me a little burst of invigoration, even though I didn't have much doubt that I'd be the one receiving most—if not all—of the soakings here if I gave him the chance.

I started to warn him not to try but clamped my jaw against the words. I wanted to go back out into the world where ferocious shadowy creatures were waiting to attack me. These three men might not always be around to protect me—and even if they were, they couldn't take on an entire horde alone. How could I be strong enough to defend myself if I was too busy worrying about swamp microbes?

Lance's lithe tongue darted over his fangs. Looking at his reptilian face, I couldn't help reflecting on how weird it was to be sparring—both verbally and physically—with a being I wouldn't have believed even *existed* two days ago. My breath still caught a little when I took in his otherworldly form, but it was as much with awe as anything like fear.

Dragons were *real*. And they could be gorgeous in their own mythical way too.

Of course, I didn't have much time to reflect or admire anyway, because a second later the dragon was lunging at me.

He leapt forward but twisted at the last second, snapping to the side. I'd gotten used to Lance's hasty changes of direction, though. I leapt right over his body, managing not to scrape my feet on the spikes that lined his back, and landed with only a slight bump of my knees on the deck's boards. As he whipped around toward me, I jabbed out backward and managed to clock him in the muzzle with my heel.

Lance let out a snort that sounded like a chuckle, his head swinging to the side and the rest of him rushing onward as if he hadn't taken a blow at all. He bounded sideways and flicked his tail into my calves just as I was scrambling up. I fell forward, barely catching myself on the edge of the deck, one hand splashing into the water.

He aimed another whack at my ass that would have propelled the rest of me into the swamp, but I threw myself to the side in a roll that brought me closer to the cabin. My heart was pounding, but the adrenaline racing through me felt *good*. I was hardly winning this skirmish, but I was at least holding my own. He wasn't dropping me in an instant.

Of course, he might be going easy on me. I did complain last time that he didn't give me enough of a chance.

Lance ricocheted off the wall and lunged at me, and I kicked him in the jaw. He snorted again and slammed the rest of his body down on me.

I didn't have anywhere to go other than back into the swamp—but I wouldn't always be able to run away anyway. Instead of trying to dodge, I jerked around to meet his pounce head-on, smacking the side of my hand into one of his eyes.

Honestly, I expected him to snap out of the way at the last second. I put more force into the blow than I would have if I'd actually believed it was going to land. But my kick must have thrown the dragon shifter off just a bit, and all he managed to do was blink before my hand rammed against his eyelid.

The grunt he made then had an obvious twinge of pain to it. I froze with him looming over me and winced on his behalf. "I'm sorry. I didn't mean to hit you that hard. Are you okay?"

Lance the dragon reared back, transforming into Lance the not-quite human as he did. He touched his right eye, the lid there a little ruddy from the impact but otherwise undamaged, and raised a quizzical eyebrow at me where I was sprawled on the deck by his feet. "The whole point was hitting me hard, wasn't it?"

"Well, I mean..." I groped for the words to explain what I'd thought would be self-explanatory. "Not really. I want to practice the right moves for hitting the bad guys hard if they come at me, but I don't want to hurt *you*. You're helping me."

His slight frown looked as puzzled as the arched eyebrow. "It bothers you."

Was it so hard for him to understand that? The men who'd rescued me had seemed to agree that it'd be bad if *I* got hurt.

"Yeah," I said. "I wouldn't want to hurt anyone unless I had to so they wouldn't hurt me. And you and I are... friends, or something like that, so I especially wouldn't want to hurt you."

Did shadowkind have a concept of friendship? It'd seemed as if the three of them were pretty companionable, but I hadn't actually seen a whole lot of them interacting. I had no idea whether they hung out or ignored each other when they slipped into the shadows, or why they'd come together in the first place.

Before I could ask about that, Lance gave a swift nod. "Other humans don't care—about hurting when they don't have to. I like your philosophy."

A sudden lump filled my throat. Other humans—had someone harmed him in the past? Was that why he'd been surprised that I'd mind? It was hard to imagine any mortal creature doing much damage to this guy, but his reaction said more than any words could have.

Whatever Lance had experienced didn't seem to have affected him all that deeply, though, because an instant later he was grinning again. "I barely felt it—your hit. It's good that you landed it. You're getting quicker and smarter, just like you should be."

His gaze traveled over me where I was still sitting on the deck before him, and my body tingled with awareness of how my tee and shorts clung to my curves with the perspiration I'd worked up. Heat washed over my skin in the wake of his attention.

"Then the training is working," I said, yanking my mind back to more important matters.

Lance clucked his tongue. "It is. But if you want to stop because it's getting too intense for you, we shouldn't strain your mortal sensibilities."

I glowered at him. "I'm just fine. Sorry for worrying about you. I'm not going to surrender just to spare you a few minor smacks."

His grin turned into a smirk. "Glad to hear it." Then he was springing into dragon form without a moment's warning.

A yelp jolted from my throat, but my limbs reacted on instinct. I heaved myself to the side and hurtled to my feet in one motion, dodging his leap.

I managed to land one glancing blow against his scaly side before he whirled around on me. It was impossible to get a good stomp on his feet when they whipped across the ground so fast I could barely see them. I'd only managed to hit his eye by embracing his pounce, which didn't seem like an ideal strategy in anything except desperate circumstances.

Where else might a monster like him be vulnerable?

I darted around the side of the cabin to where the deck railing would give me more options for maneuvering. With a playful gnash of his teeth,

Lance had me vaulting off the boards and over him. His tail slapped at my ankles. I spun around, eyeing its glinting length.

Maybe that part of him would be sensitive too? If I could find a way to stomp on his tail without jabbing my feet on any of the spikes that jutted across it too.

I tried to test out my suspicion while swerving and ducking to escape the swipes of Lance's snout and feet—always carefully angled, I noticed, so that his fangs and claws didn't split me open. He'd avoided aiming any blows at my chest, too, like I'd asked him before. I'd have been in a lot more trouble if he'd *really* been fighting me.

Every time I leapt at his tail, it lashed away from me again... or toward me, forcing me to scramble to avoid those spikes. Hopefully most other shadowkind that came at me wouldn't be quite this quick or canny.

Lance bounded off the railing and bumped his shoulder against mine, forcing me backward. I dashed farther back when he spun around into a full-out charge—and realized at the last second that was exactly what he'd wanted. He swiveled around me so quickly it dizzied me and then bumped my legs to send me careening into the outdoor shower stall.

He dove after me just as my elbow bumped the control, sending warmed tap water spurting down over both of us. Lance's smooth body pushed me up against the back of the stall, and then he was in his human form again, pinning my wrists to the damp boards and smiling his crooked smile.

"Do you surrender now?"

His violet eyes gazed into mine from just inches away, glinting slyly. His ferally gorgeous face filled my entire frame of sight. His muscular chest had come to rest against mine, warmer than sticky humidity of the day or the water that'd sprayed us. A sharper heat sparked between my legs.

I couldn't have shoved him off me if I'd wanted to... but I wasn't sure I *did* want to.

Why the hell was I resisting these impulses? Wasn't my main philosophy that I should run at everything that called to me? No delaying, nothing left untried or untasted—no regrets. He'd made his own interest clear. Since when did I back down from the unknown simply because it was unknown?

With a surge of giddy resolve, I leaned in and pressed my mouth against Lance's.

For a second, I thought I'd made a horrible mistake. He'd been so flirty in his teasing I'd assumed he'd leap at my blatant invitation, but who knew what was flirting to a shadowkind anyway? His breath stuttered over his lips against mine in what felt like shock, his body going still.

Then he kissed me back. The flicker of my relief turned into a renewed rush of heat with the melding of his mouth against mine.

He kissed me as if he were putting his whole body into it, as if every part of his being was concentrated on the meeting of our lips. As if he was absorbing every tremor of *my* breath, the little gasp that escaped me, the minute movements of my mouth.

I'd kissed a fair number of guys over the years, but I'd never been kissed like this. Every inch of me caught fire. I couldn't think of anything except kissing him more.

Lance released one of my wrists to wrap his arm around my waist, tugging me tighter against him. My free hand shot to his hair of its own accord, my fingers tangling in the glossy curls. When his mouth left mine, a moan of protest tumbled out of me that would've been embarrassing if the heat of the moment hadn't burned away all my capacity for shame.

He trailed his lips along my jaw and down the side of my neck, tasting my skin with flicks of his tongue that enflamed me even more than before. Then he murmured against the crook of my shoulder, "This is good." He drew back enough to catch my gaze again, his eyes outright smoldering now. "Very good. Why not have fun while we can?"

My body was screaming out in agreement, but something about his phrasing made my gut twist.

While we can.

As if there was some endpoint to this entire situation that he already had in his sights, something that would mean we definitely *couldn't* anymore.

The hint of finality jarred against my impression that none of the men protecting me knew how long this would go on or how much protection I'd continue to need. I'd just opened my mouth, torn between crushing it against his again and asking what he'd meant, when footsteps thumped onto the deck from around the side of the house.

"Dinner!" Crag announced in his typically gruff way.

Lance's tongue darted over his lips. He sprang toward the door with his breathtaking nimbleness.

"More fun later," he promised, beaming at me. But all at once I couldn't help wondering what else that promise included that he might not be telling me.

CHAPTER TEN

Quinn

After taking my pills and washing up for the morning, I came back to my bedroom to the ringing of my phone. My pulse hiccupped. I snatched it up, my heart thumping harder when I saw the call was from Mom.

I'd managed to avoid talking to her and Dad outside of texts for the past three days, but I probably needed to take this. If they didn't hear my voice, they were going to start wondering if I'd been kidnapped and some villain was making excuses in my place. It wasn't like I'd ever vanished for this long without warning before.

Drawing my spine up straight as if I could conjure confidence with my stance, I brought the phone to my ear. "Hi, Mom."

"Sweetheart! I'm so glad I caught you at a good moment. Can you talk for a bit?"

"Sure," I said, ignoring the churning of my stomach at the thought of all the lying I was about to do. "I'm sorry for the sudden trip. It just seemed like too good an opportunity to pass up."

"Of course! The conference sounds amazing from what you've said, and it's great that you're getting to spend more time with a friend."

I swallowed thickly. My friendships—or lack thereof—had been a constant if low-level point of tension between my parents and me. My sudden childhood illness and the stress around my heart transplant had been too much for a lot of the kids I'd hung out with in elementary school. Most of them had faded out of my life... except for my best friend Brandy, who'd run herself ragged trying to be there for me every way she could.

The symptoms of my impending heart failure had been awful, and recovering from the transplant hadn't been any picnic either. But it'd almost been worse seeing the toll my condition had taken on the people I cared about.

Mom and Dad—well, it was impossible to tell your parents you shouldn't matter so much to them. Even when their worries were draining them. Even when the treatments were draining their savings and all the dreams that money had been meant for. But I did everything I could to make the rest of my existence as un-stressful as possible for them.

I hadn't had any choice about relying on them, but I'd been able to spare Brandy. After seeing the dark circles growing under her eyes for weeks on end and catching murmurs about how her faltering grades had meant she'd missed out on getting into the private high school she'd had her hopes pinned on, it'd become obvious that being friends with me was taking a hell of a lot more from her than it was giving. I'd started avoiding her at school, refusing invitations, failing to return calls—pulling out of her life as much as I could.

Eventually she'd stopped reaching out, just as I'd intended. I hated thinking of the hurt in her voice the last time she'd talked to me, but it'd been better for her in the long run. She'd made new friends who wouldn't end up at death's door again by their twenties.

I hadn't been able to hide from Mom and Dad that I wasn't exactly a social butterfly in my high school years. I'd made up stories about parties and other get-togethers to cover for my burgeoning urban exploring habit, but they'd known I never brought anyone over to hang out at home. They hadn't missed the silence of my phone. Thankfully, once I'd headed an hour and a half away to the university in Gainesville, I'd been able to deflect more of their concerns since they couldn't see how quiet my social life was firsthand.

"Yeah, it's so lucky I ran into her," I said to Mom, keeping my voice as chipper as possible. "And I feel like I've learned a ton here." That wasn't totally untrue, even if she was in the dark about where exactly "here" was.

"That's wonderful. We never want to get in the way of you getting out there and living your life, you know. I just can't help wanting to check in."

"Of course."

There was a rustle as Mom shifted her position. "Will you be heading home now? I assume the conference only lasted to the end of the weekend. And you have your summer classes still going, don't you?"

The excuse I'd come up with still sounded flimsy to me, but I hadn't been able to think of anything better. I was gambling on my parents not poking around much in my room and realizing that I hadn't actually come back to collect my things. I was pretty sure I'd left my laptop in the drawer built into my bedframe, so it wouldn't be immediately obvious at a glance that it was still there.

"Actually... Trish asked me if I wanted to crash at her place for a while so we can work through some class stuff together. She's taking one of the same summer courses as me. We might even ask to do a joint project for it. I think we'll go to campus a few times to get stuff from the library and chat with the professor, and her apartment is already in Gainesville. I'll still be back for a bunch of the summer, of course. I'd miss you otherwise."

I added that last bit in the hopes it'd ease the sting of my unexpected absence. I *did* miss them—and everything that was normal at home. She had no idea how much. I might have been getting used to the strangeness of my shadowkind protectors, but it wasn't as if I wanted to be hunted by monstrous fiends for the rest of my life.

If I was here for a couple more days, I'd *need* to at least grab my supply of medication. But if we weren't ready to leave the cabin by then, one of the men would probably insist on going alone. I wouldn't want to drop by while my parents were home anyway, not with the danger that'd be nipping at my heels.

"Oh, that's totally all right," Mom said. There was something bittersweet about her tone, as if she was both sad to be losing the time with me and overjoyed that I was getting along so well with one of my classmates. "Do you need to pick up anything else from the house?"

"I can wash the clothes I brought at her place, and I have everything else I need. Thank you for understanding!"

"There's nothing to understand, sweetheart. I'd rather you got out and spent some of your summer with friends even if some of that's schoolwork too."

"You know what a workaholic I am," I said with a laugh that was only a little stiff. "But I can fit in some fun around it."

Saying "fun" made me think of Lance's comment yesterday afternoon. My heart gave a giddy skip at the memory of his mouth against mine, even though an uneasy twinge still lingered in my gut from his comment afterward.

I was probably reading too much into it. It wasn't like I expected a marriage proposal or something from him.

"That's what I like to hear," Mom said. "Go enjoy yourself, and don't work too hard in the meantime. We'll have plenty of game nights and family dinners when you get back."

She was being so chill about my absence that the guilt twined through my chest amplified. It took me a second before I could say my goodbyes without sounding choked. "I'll see you soon!"

I hung up and sank onto the edge of my bed, dropping my hand onto my lap. A sudden gloom rolled over me like a thundercloud, punctuated by another of those weird flutters—or was it a tremor now?—around my heart.

I'd done my best to keep busy here and convince myself that I was making progress toward... something. Being able to protect myself? Showing my gratitude to the men who'd protected me when I couldn't? Keeping up with the work I'd meant to be doing?

But who was I kidding? Whether I could leave this place without becoming monster chow wasn't really up to me, and I wasn't sure how much it was even up to my defenders.

From what they'd said, there were a lot of shadowkind in the world. It seemed like nearly all of them other than the three who'd appointed themselves my guardians wanted a piece out of me. How could they fight all the rest off forever?

How could I go back to a remotely normal life while I was a magnet for murderous monsters, drawing them toward not just myself but everyone around me?

I smeared on the sunscreen that was an automatic part of my daily routine, not that skin cancer was at the top of my list of current fears. Then I went out into the living room, where I found Crag just heading out the door.

"Where are you going?" I blurted out.

He glanced back at me with a frown. "I have to check the area farther around the swamp for shadowkind activity."

I faltered at his tone and his stern expression. "Oh. Okay."

He considered me, all stony solemness. "Was there something you needed?"

"No." Nothing that he could give me. At least not nothing more important than making sure a new horde of monsters wasn't descending on us. "Maybe when you get back, we could do a little more sparring? I've been improving with Lance, but it's probably better if I get different kinds of practice."

Crag hesitated, and my gut twisted. He'd been patient with me before, yeah, and I didn't think he wanted to be cruel, but that didn't mean he enjoyed catering to my whims either. "You don't have to, obviously," I added quickly. "Just a suggestion."

His expression turned a bit gentler even though his tone stayed gruff. "You're very dedicated. That's a good thing. I only worry about hurting you accidentally, Softie."

Even though the nickname highlighted my deficiencies, the fact that he used one at all eased a little of my uncertainty. I didn't think he meant it as an insult, just a statement of fact.

I managed a smile. "What was it you said to me? If I get hurt, it'll be my own fault."

He grunted, but I thought I caught an upward twitch of his lips before he turned away. "If there's time, then. This will take a while. Lance will be patrolling closer by to ensure nothing reaches the cabin."

He strode out. The whoosh of his wings as he shifted and took flight carried through the wall.

And now I was alone. Or at least, I appeared to be. Crag had indicated that Lance was out roaming the swamp, but he hadn't said anything about Torrent.

I wandered from one end of the room to the other, peering through the window. I could have gone outside and called for Lance, but keeping an eye out for murderous intruders was obviously more important than alleviating my boredom.

My restlessness crawled over my skin. I couldn't go *anywhere* except in this cabin and around the deck. I couldn't even climb the freaking trees without becoming a target.

Less than a week ago, I'd been climbing up skyscrapers, and now my world had shrunk to the size of a goldfish bowl.

Did my shadowkind protectors even understand how much it mattered to me to get out of this place? Keeping me here was easy for them. *They* could come and go whenever they wanted.

My gaze settled on the patch of shadow under the makeshift shelf I'd fixed to the wall by the head of the dining table. I couldn't tell whether Torrent was there—or in any of the other shadows around the room. But he didn't seem to venture out of the cabin as often as the others did.

I debated asking him to show himself and balked. He stayed in the shadows most of the time for a reason, didn't he? I didn't want to put him in pain just to ease my loneliness.

He could still hear me in the shadows anyway, like he'd said. Maybe... maybe I should make sure he knew why I wanted to get home so badly. I'd gotten the impression I'd earned a bit of good will from him with the chair and the wall fixture. If he could see how much I was losing with every day I had to spend here, he might work toward a solution a little harder, right?

It couldn't hurt anything to tell him.

I sank sideways into the chair at the head of the table, which put my face level with the patch of shadow. Staring straight at the wall felt strange, so I leaned my shoulder against the back of the chair and gazed vaguely toward the kitchen.

"I want you to know that I appreciate everything the three of you have done for me," I said, tuning out the awkwardness of talking to empty air and my doubts about whether anyone was even here to listen to me. "I mean, you saved my life. I would have died without your help. I'd be dead right now if you all decided it wasn't worth the hassle of looking after me anymore and took off. So I don't... It's not that I'm ungrateful."

No response. No indication at all that anyone had heard me. Oh, well. I soldiered on determinedly.

"The only reason I'm impatient to get home, or back to my old life however I can—well, okay, there are a lot of reasons—but the biggest one is that I really don't know how much life I have left at all. I told you about my heart transplant..."

My hand rose to trace the line of the scar where it ran down my sternum. "I guess you wouldn't realize because shadowkind don't do things like organ transplants. You only have to worry about dying if some bigger creature attacks you. But there's a time limit on these things when it's not your own organ, a lot shorter than even a regular human life. The average transplanted heart lasts twelve years. I got mine nine years ago. Since I was so young, the doctors say there's a good chance I'll get a little more time... but I could also get less. You never know for sure. It could start to fail on me any day."

I dragged in a breath and kept going despite the silence around me.

"I've accepted that fact. I don't know if you can grasp what it's like to not just know you're going to die, but that there's a significant chance you could die really soon, but... it sucks. It sucks, but I dealt with it. I might get another donated heart, if there's one that's a match at the right time—or I might not. And even if I'm lucky and do, that'll just add another 'average twelve' years to my life. It gets me to my thirties. Still not even half a full life for a human.

"So I've been busting my ass trying to cram everything I can into the life I've got. Experiencing things, accomplishing things..." I glanced toward my bedroom, thinking I should have brought my sketchbook but hesitant to interrupt whatever momentum I'd built up. "I want to design buildings—for people to live or work in. I might be able to see at least a couple constructed if I can finish college soon enough, if I make connections with the right people."

The room around me stayed perfectly still. I swiped my hand across my face, emotion starting to clog my throat. I willed it down like I had so many times over the past several years.

"Anyway, that's the thing. There are monsters waiting out there to kill me. But this heart could kill me without my ever leaving this cabin. And I'm not sure whether I'm more scared of the 'beasties' or the possibility that I might lose my chance to do and feel and have at least a little more of what this world can offer. So if there's anything at all we could try or that I could help with that has even a tiny chance of letting me leave here, I'd want to give it a shot. I thought you should know that."

In the continuing silence that followed, a heavy weight sank through my abdomen. I rested my arm on the top of the chair back and tipped my head against it, closing my eyes.

This was stupid. I'd probably been talking to no one but myself the whole time.

Then a gentle pressure grazed my temple. As I opened my eyes, it stroked tentatively along the side of my face, warm and velvety soft.

I raised my head slowly. The thing that'd touched me retreated, but I could still make out the tip of a tentacle, a few inches of burgundy skin dappled with a couple of pale suckers, protruding from the patch of shadow as if part of that swath of darkness had condensed into solid form.

When I didn't recoil, the narrow tip lifted toward me again and brushed over my cheek. It wasn't a suggestion or a solution, but it felt like an answer. A confirmation that I wasn't anywhere near as alone as it'd seemed a moment ago. He didn't have answers yet, but he'd heard me. And he wanted me to know that.

"Thank you," I said quietly. An ache spread through my chest that was as bittersweet as Mom's voice on the phone.

I might not get to leave this place alive. This dull existence might be how I spent the last of my days. But I wasn't on my own. That counted for something.

CHAPTER ELEVEN

Lance

I could hear Quinn not-sleeping through the walls of the cabin. Her breaths hadn't evened out into the slow, subdued pace of human slumber. Every few minutes, the sheets rustled as she rolled one way or the other.

She'd gone to bed an hour ago, but something was keeping her awake. And my awareness of her was distracting me. I could have gone out into the swamp to get some distance, but my thoughts kept drawing me back to the mortal woman in the next room.

The vibe she gave off was getting stronger, sending little pulses of warning through my senses. As if I could have believed she was any sort of threat after what I'd seen of her. She'd gotten distressed over the possibility that she'd accidentally caused me the tiniest of injuries. Not even Torrent or Crag would have given a second thought to a minor accidental smack.

No, she wasn't any kind of danger to me, no matter what the strange energy she gave off implied. And I didn't want to stay away from her. There were so many delicious possibilities hovering between us.

She'd kissed *me* yesterday. She wanted to do more than look. And so did I. It'd been good—better than I'd even hoped. Like devouring the most thrilling flavor of ice cream, except warm instead of cold, and having the sweet heat of it flood my entire body.

That thought sent me out of the shadows to the kitchen. I considered the cartons in the freezer—despite my requests, Crag had only brought back three flavors, which was hardly enough variety—and settled on caramel ripple. I scooped out a dollop with my claws, plopped it into a bowl, paused, and then grabbed another bowl to fill. The frozen treat was my favorite food because of the particularly enjoyable contrast between the cool creaminess and the echo of fire that lingered in my throat even in human form, but mortals loved this stuff too, didn't they?

I found two spoons and carried the bowls over to Quinn's bedroom. The door was closed, so I simply carried the ice cream into the shadows around it and emerged on the other side with everything still in order.

Moonlight streamed over her from the curtainless window. She was lying with her face toward the wall and her eyes resolutely closed, as if she could convince herself to sleep by strength of will. Her determination about all things really was delightful. I moved one of the bowls over so I held both with the splayed claws of one hand and sat down on the edge of the bed next to her.

As I'd expected from past observations of human behavior, she startled. Her mouth opened with a yelp of surprise, and I clamped my hand against her lips to muffle the sound so the others wouldn't come running to her rescue. "It's just me," I whispered.

Quinn huffed against my palm and rolled onto her back as I removed it. She glowered at me. "Just you, sneaking into my bedroom and smothering me like a maniac."

"Is there something wrong with being a maniac?" I asked. "Anyway, I brought you ice cream."

She grumbled something inarticulate to herself but sat up to accept the bowl. "Were you planning on waking me up for this midnight snack, or could you tell I wasn't asleep?"

"You're a very noisy not-sleeper. By shadowkind standards."

"Well, when shadowkind don't sleep at all, I guess I won't worry too much about that." She eyed the ice cream and took a tentative spoonful.

The way her face softened at the taste of it, a faint smile curling her lips, sent that heat I'd felt while we'd kissed unfurling down through my abdomen again.

I wanted to lick the traces of the cream off her mouth, but then my own portion would go to waste. There was plenty of time for all wonderful things. I popped a heaping spoonful into my mouth, gulped it before it could melt, and beamed at the sensation of the sugary chill sliding down my throat.

"You are deeply weird," Quinn informed me, as if she wasn't polishing off her ice cream as quickly as I was.

I turned so that I could rest my elbow on her raised knees, only the thin sheet separating our skin, and shot her a grin. "And you like it a lot."

Her mouth flattened, but the flush that spread across her pale face told me why she didn't argue. There wasn't anything to argue about. I was right.

Of course, I was coming to like her a lot too. I hadn't spent this much time around any one human before, at least not one who'd given me a choice in the matter. Mortal reactions and quirks really were entertaining. And now that I'd had a taste of this one, I couldn't help being increasingly curious about what other reactions I could provoke beyond the color in her cheeks and the dilation of her pupils. What effects those reactions would have on *me*.

A whole new area to explore that I'd never indulged in before.

I let my gaze travel over her as I finished the last of my ice cream. The sheet had fallen to her waist. She was wearing a tank top and nothing underneath it, the small nubs at the peaks of her lightly curved chest poking against the fabric.

I'd seen men and women—both human and shadowkind—embracing in Rollick's club or out on the beach plenty of times, and it seemed the women particularly liked having those nubs and the slopes around them caressed. That and farther down. What did she have on under the sheet?

Quinn set her bowl on the bedside table and licked her lips, the motion yanking my attention back to her mouth. I tossed my bowl onto the floor with a thunk and slid closer.

Her eyes widened with the tiny catch of her breath I was starting to savor. "What are you doing?"

"You like this too. Why shouldn't I do it?" I curled my fingers to angle my claws away from her flesh and traced one knuckle lightly across her lips.

Quinn pulled back, but only a couple of inches, her flush deepening. "Just because someone *likes* something doesn't mean they necessarily want to go ahead with it."

I cocked my head. "Why wouldn't they? If you know you would enjoy something, then why avoid it?"

"I was trying to sleep."

I snorted and reached a little farther to graze her cheek. My finger skimmed down over her jaw to the side of her neck, where her pulse jumped against my hand. "You weren't doing a very good job of it. This is more interesting than lying there not-sleeping, isn't it?"

"Why do *you* want to do it?" she asked abruptly, folding her arms over her chest and hiding those enticing curves.

"It's enjoyable for me too. It's something different from all this waiting around here, isn't it?"

"So, you're bored."

"I'm curious." I extended my claws and teased just the very tips along her jaw, easing them back when she shivered. "I won't hurt you. My reflexes have gotten very good. I don't slice and dice anything unless I intend to."

"Well, that's a relief," she muttered, but her breath had quickened. I wanted to drink it in. All those little signs of desire pulled at me like a magnet.

Maybe she needed the reminder of just how much fun the collision of our bodies could be.

I tucked my hand behind her shoulders and pulled her to me, bowing my head to claim her lips the way she'd captured mine yesterday in the water. A soft sound escaped her, and then I was reveling in the pliant heat of her mouth, turned even sweeter by the lingering traces of caramel.

Yes, this—this was what I'd been craving. This and more. My tongue flicked out to sweep between her lips, and her tongue rose to meet it. A stutter ran through her breath. She clutched the front of my shirt, her mouth pressing even more emphatically against mine.

No wonder humans got so worked up when they saw another being they wanted to mesh with like this. Nothing else I'd ever encountered matched this feeling.

I kissed her again, my hand starting to stroke down her bare arm, and Quinn pulled back. Her cheeks were ruddy and her eyes starkly bright with hunger, but she placed the heel of her hand firmly against my chest as if she thought she needed to hold me back, that words wouldn't be enough.

Or maybe she was holding herself back from me.

"What did you mean yesterday?" she said. "About—about having fun 'while we can'? What are you expecting to happen that'll mean we can't?"

I couldn't tell her what I knew, what Torrent had reminded me of so pedantically. When Rollick knew we had her and came to collect, we were handing her over to him, whatever his intentions were.

I found it hard to believe that our boss was literally going to devour this woman, but it was hard to tell with the demon. Sometimes beings that powerful did inexplicable things. Possibly he'd meant a more metaphorical devouring like the one I'd like to engage in right now.

Picturing him looming over her on a bed like this brought a flare of emotion I couldn't explain into my chest. A growl formed at the base of my throat. *Mine.*

She wasn't, though. Since when did I collect humans—or anything else, for that matter? She was his.

But for now, until he got his head out of his ass and realized we were waiting for him, she could be mine temporarily. I'd make it the most pleasant possible wait for her.

"You don't want to be here forever," I said, keeping my answer simple. "You'd like to be going back to your regular life as soon as we can arrange it, wouldn't you? It's not as if I should be staking a permanent claim."

Something flickered in her eyes that I couldn't read, but her shoulders relaxed. "Well, true. I wasn't expecting you to."

I let my lips pull into another grin. "Then what's the problem? Let's continue having our temporary fun."

She hesitated for only a second longer, and then she pushed forward to kiss me like she had yesterday.

Somehow it was even more delicious when she took that first step. But as her mouth moved against mine and her hands trailed down my chest, a shiver that wasn't entirely pleasant tingled through me.

The wonder and desire tangled through me were knotting into something that felt closer to *need*. Like she was entangling me, like I might find myself unable to break free.

No. It wasn't like that. *She* wasn't like that. I'd watched her for long enough to know. I wouldn't be doing this otherwise, after restraining my curiosity for so long before.

I knew there wasn't any real danger, but I slid my hands down her arms to her wrists instinctively. Without releasing her mouth, I tipped her over on the bed and straddled her hips. Then I stretched her arms over her head and pinned them to the pillow just above the rumpled waves of her hair.

Her body shivered under mine with a fresh waft of heat. She didn't object. She might even like my assertion of control.

She'd believed me when I'd said I wouldn't hurt her.

I smiled against her lips, my twinge of anxiety fading as quickly as it'd risen up. Now I could take my time exploring every plane and crevice of the delicacy that was her mouth.

When her tongue twined past mine to dart into my own mouth, a sharper clang of lust jolted to my groin. My blood was collecting there, turning me hard and sensitive with the inescapable urge to thrust myself against her.

Into her.

Not yet. There was so much else to discover in the friction between us. I left her mouth to nibble the crook of her jaw, the underside of her chin, the column of her throat, marking every spot that provoked a headier gasp from her. The sounds she made offered sparks of elation I'd never encountered before.

There was so much joy to be unearthed in this kind of melding. Why had I never tried it before?

I knew the answer to that, but I'd rather not look at it. Not while I was having such a good time.

I wanted to see what I could conjure in this woman with more than just my mouth. Tugging her arms closer together, I encompassed both of her slim wrists with one hand, my long fingers holding them both in place. Then I teased my other hand down her side.

She arched into my touch, those graceful mounds brushing my chest. I swiveled my palm over one, watching and feeling how the nub hardened at the contact. A little whimper spilled from Quinn's lips.

Yes. Perfect. I repeated the motion, seeing how far I could raise the peak. Then, with a glimmer of inspiration, I stroked the tips of my claws over the nub.

"Fuck," Quinn murmured, her eyelids fluttering.

I couldn't restrain a smirk. "Good?"

"Good. No complaints here."

I chuckled, but I was finding myself irritated with the layer of cloth that separated her flesh from mine. I could provoke even more intense sensations without that barrier, couldn't I?

Without questioning the impulse, I raked my claws down the center of her shirt, just forcefully enough to slice through the thin fabric while only skimming across her skin. A noise that was half yelp, half gasp burst from Quinn, turning into a ragged moan as I brushed the severed pieces aside with a graze of my claws across her naked breast.

"You're wrecking my clothes," she grumbled, her voice too breathy to give any punch to the protest. "I don't have that much here, you know."

I grunted dismissively. "Crag can go get you more if you need them. It was in my way. Now I can do this."

I bent over and lapped the tip of her breast right into my hungry mouth. For now, she *was* mine, and I intended to explore all of her in every possible way.

CHAPTER TWELVE

Quinn

This was crazy, right? Making out with a monster? I felt kind of crazy, writhing beneath Lance's sculpted body, gasping as he tested his teeth against my nipple. But not at all in a way that made me think I should stop this.

We'd barely gotten started, and he was already drawing more pleasure through my body than I'd felt in ages. Maybe ever. What other hookup had been this exhilarating?

What other man could have sliced open my shirt with his bare hands?

He swept his tongue over my breast again, and this time it felt a little different, new flexible ridges hugging the sensitive tip. A choked sound jolted out of me with the rush of unexpected pleasure. My arms jerked against the firm hand that pinned them above my head, and Lance eased back to grin at me.

"Enjoying yourself, baby girl?" he said, giving the nickname the same teasing lilt he had when he'd used it before. "I can bring out my dragon tongue for you as much as you want. If you ask for it."

"Yes, please," I mumbled, but a deeper impulse gripped me. That wasn't what I wanted most. I wet my lips. "Would you... would you use your claws again?"

Something sparked in Lance's violet eyes, turning him even more feral and gorgeous than usual. He flexed the fingers on his free hand and trailed the pointed ends of his claws over my skin, skimming the curve of my other breast, one of them flicking right over the nipple.

The movement was so precise my nerves jittered at the cutting edges, but he didn't damage a particle of my skin. Just a tender caress that could have killed me if he'd jabbed downward for an instant. My pulse leapt at the sensation, my panties soaking even more than they'd already been.

"Like that?" he asked, studying my reaction with interest so avid it lit me up just as much as his touch.

"Just like that," I said. "It feels amazing."

He gave a pleased hum, his grin slanting into a smirk. "Lie still, then."

He traced patterns all over my torso, giving special attention to my breasts, like he meant to carve my skin like he did the cabin walls. Every inch of me was tingling with the awareness that he *could*, but he never broke the surface. The giddy pleasure sparked everywhere his claws grazed—and I never knew where they'd dart next. I held myself as motionless as I could, ragged noises tumbling from my throat with each new caress.

I wasn't going to say there was anything okay about hordes of monsters wanting to shred me to pieces, but I'd never have gotten to experience *this* thrill if I hadn't needed saving. Maybe there was a tiny bit of a trade-off.

Lance started swiveling his claws around the nipple he'd been licking while swiping his ridged tongue over my other breast. My whimpers turned even needier. I couldn't stop my hips from swaying upward, seeking out a fuller satisfaction.

The dragon shifter shifted his weight over me, a taut length beneath his slacks suggesting he wasn't remotely unaffected either. He gave my breast a light nip and glanced down my body toward my sex. "You want to be touched down there."

Just the thought of him dragging his claws all the way to my pussy nearly made me explode. "I—yes. Please. If *you* want to."

"Hmm, I'm definitely not done with you yet. So much more terrain to uncover."

He reached for the sheet that'd pooled around my waist and then paused, glancing up at his other hand. He couldn't move any farther down my body while keeping my wrists clamped down. An odd uncertainty crossed his face.

"Would you rather if I didn't touch you?" I asked tentatively. "I mean, I'd like to, but if it'd bother you for some reason—you just need to tell me. You don't have to hold me down." At this point, I'd agree to just about anything to find out what other miracles he could conjure with those claws and that tongue.

Lance gazed down at me with an unusually pensive air and then abruptly offered a beaming smile. "You can touch. You wouldn't hurt me any more than I've hurt you."

"Of course not," I said, with the twist that'd come into my gut before when he'd hinted at how other humans had treated him. Then he released my wrists to peel back the sheet and reveal the panties that were all I'd worn to bed on my lower half, and I lost my breath at the glide of his claws down my thighs.

"So wet," he said, sounding a little breathless himself as he lowered his face toward my sex. "And your scent..." A soft snarl escaped him. "I know you have extras of these. Crag brought back a whole pack."

Before I could process where he was going with that statement, he jerked his hands past my hips and severed the sides of my panties in one swift movement. My chest had only just hitched in eager surprise when he nuzzled the swath of fabric away and buried his face between my legs.

His tongue stroked right through my slickness, over my clit and down across my folds, and pleasure erupted in its wake. I bucked into his mouth, my hands flying down to curl into his messy hair. I hesitated for a second, afraid I might have gone too far despite his claim that he didn't mind being touched, but he showed no indication of even noticing the contact. I gripped the silky strands and gave myself over to his fervent worship.

He lapped at me like I was an ice cream cone, with all the enthusiasm I could imagine him bringing to that task as well as this one. His tongue flicked and swirled, his lips suckling more bliss from my clit. The knot of need in my belly expanded, swelling to fill my entire abdomen with ecstatic fire. I couldn't restrain a moan.

Did the other two men know what we were getting up to? Hell, for all I knew, they could be in the room, watching from the shadows. The possibility should have made me cringe, but somehow it sent my desire sparking even hotter.

I might not be a monster, but I'd let them see me lose myself in savage abandon. I could be as wild as they were. I wasn't going to shy away from one bit of this delirious adventure I'd embarked on.

Lance raised his head just slightly to focus his attentions on my clit. As the ridges of his tongue gripped the sensitive nub with swipe after swipe that radiated pleasure through my core, he tucked one of his hands between my thighs. He couldn't extend a finger into me, of course—that was one place I didn't want any claws to travel—but he rocked a knuckle between my folds, filling me with just enough pressure to inflame me.

"So good," I muttered. "Don't stop."

He didn't let up, not even for a second. Shudders traveled through my body. The heady mix of desire and exhilaration surged through me.

Lance caressed my hip with the claws of his other hand while nipping my clit, and I unraveled with a cry. My release flooded my whole body, leaving me shaking and then limp. My head tipped back into the pillow.

As my hands fell from his hair, Lance peered up at me. "I brought you there," he said, not quite a question. "To the place you wanted to go."

A laugh spilled out of me. "Hell, yes, you did."

He gave my thigh a playful nuzzle and loomed up over me again, his eyes glinting. "Does that mean you're done? Or can you get there again?"

I stared at him, my mind spinning. Those words clicked into place with little pieces I hadn't quite understood before, starting with his initial hesitation when I'd first kissed him. The possibility stunned me enough that it took me a moment to regain control over my mouth.

"Is this… the first time you've done something like this?"

Lance flashed a grin, showing no sign of self-consciousness about his inexperience. "It's exciting new territory I'm delving into. I'm doing well so far, it seems?"

Holy fuck. I was having the best sexual encounter of my life with not just a monster, but a virginal monster who was figuring this shit out as he went. I blinked, having trouble arranging my thoughts back into coherent order.

Lance raised his eyebrows. "You *are* enjoying it, aren't you?"

A blush burned my cheeks. "Yes. A lot. I—I was just surprised. Because you're so good at it."

His smile turned wicked. "I'm paying attention to what gets those tasty little sounds out of you. There seem to be plenty of things that do the trick."

My mind tripped back to the questions that had started us on this subject. He'd wanted to know if I could keep going—presumably because he wanted to.

I slid my hand to the back of his head and tugged him up to fully rejoin me. "You're doing a very good job. And I'm definitely not done." I hadn't gotten the chance to hear what sounds I could get *him* to make for me, after all.

The revelation gave me a rush of confidence I hadn't felt before. *I* was the closest thing to an expert between the two of us. He wasn't comparing me to hundreds of women across however many centuries he'd been in existence. I'd never had sex with a shadowkind before, and he'd never had sex before, period, so the playing field was definitely a lot more level than I'd assumed.

When his mouth crashed down on mine, I kissed him back hard, my tongue darting between his lips to encourage his own out to play. He'd let the dragon ridges subside, but they formed again as our tongues twined together. A giddy shiver passed through me just from that small but startling sensation.

I hadn't gotten to touch very much of him so far. He teased his claws down my side to blissful effect, and I ran my hand down his chest to the fly of his slacks. His erection strained against it, electrifyingly hard against my fingers. When I gripped it through his pants, Lance made a rough sound.

"Ah, yes," he murmured. "I approve of your explorations too."

I couldn't help giggling, not that he appeared to mind. But my body was still on fire after my first orgasm, the craving to be filled even more deeply forming an ache in my core. There was way too much fabric still between us... and none of it was on me.

"We need to get you out of all this clothing," I grumbled, tugging at his shirt. "And I don't have any claws to tear it off you."

Mischief twinkled in Lance's eyes. "That's easy to take care of." Without so much as a farewell, he blinked out of existence.

I'd barely sucked in a breath, my lungs tight with a jab of bewildered loss, when he sprang back into being braced over me in almost the exact same position. He'd ducked into the shadows, I realized. And come back completely naked.

The rest of him looked as gorgeous and as human as his face did. For a few moments, I could only brush my fingers over the planes of muscle that filled out his chest, flicking my thumbs over his small, dark nipples that stood out against his golden-brown skin, making myself every bit as much an explorer.

Lance gave me free rein, his eyelids dipping low as if he were basking in the caresses. Then he seemed to decide it was time for him to take lead in our joint expedition. He rocked his hips, and the rigid cock I'd only glimpsed jutting down below rubbed over my clit.

I gasped, pleasure spiking through me from my core. My hips arched toward him of their own accord in a plea for more.

Lance dipped his mouth to my shoulder. A nick of the gentlest possible pain tickled though my flesh, and I realized he'd brought out his dragonish fangs as well as the tongue. When he tested his sharper teeth more firmly against the muscle there, I quivered with inexplicable excitement.

Why did it feel so good to know he could tear me apart and yet wouldn't? It just did. What could be more enlivening than the knowledge that I was not just defying my possible death but fucking it?

"There's one place I haven't explored yet," he remarked with his lips brushing my skin, angling his hips so the head of his cock slipped down to my drenched slit. "Not fully."

My knees rose beside his hips automatically. Every particle in my body screamed to urge him onward. From what Torrent had said about shadowkind never getting sick, I wouldn't have had to worry about STDs even if Lance had been more experienced, so the extra condoms I kept in my bag were a moot point. But a tiny part of me that still retained some practicality had the wherewithal to confirm one essential fact. "Crag said shadowkind don't have babies?"

I had an IUD, just in case one of my flings went wrong, but I was pretty sure no one had checked those for effectiveness against monstrous cum.

Lance chuckled. "No babies, so no need to worry, baby girl."

"Then what are you waiting—"

He didn't let me finish the question, thrusting inside me as swiftly as he did so much else. I was so wet and relaxed after coming that the stretch of his erection was only a heady pleasure, not a hint of pain despite the abrupt penetration.

I whimpered and lifted my hips to meet him, but the dragon shifter just held there for several seconds, a low rumble reverberating through his chest.

I traced my hands down his sides to grab his ass, and something flared in his gaze.

"Mine," he muttered with a puff of heated breath, snatching one wrist and then the other and pinning them over my head again. He kissed me, his mouth scorching against mine, and nipped the side of my neck with his fangs. A ripple of fire on his breath and a flick of his tongue sealed whatever marks he'd drawn there.

"Mine," he announced again, more forcefully, holding my arms with one hand as the other kept him braced above me. I might have protested the claiming or the restraining, but then he started to move, and the swelling roar of pleasure drowned any argument out.

I'd happily be his as long as he was making me feel this good.

Somehow he slid deeper with every thrust, stretching me more with that incredible, blissful burn. I swayed to meet him, a keening moan like I'd never made before slipping from my lips. I did feel wild then, like an animal driven only by my basest needs, like the kind of being that would fuck with claws and fangs.

The ravenous growl Lance let out only made me wilder. I pushed myself faster to meet his speeding thrusts, and his growl turned into a groan.

He pounded into me, a more potent wave of heat emanating from his body, setting every part of me it touched alight. I hardly ever came without any stimulation on my clit, but I was close. So close to shattering all over again—

He bit my shoulder with those tiny splinters of perfect pain, and I cried out with nothing but pleasure. Ecstasy raced through my veins. I clenched around Lance's cock, and his breath stuttered. His hips jerked, more heat flooding me on the inside.

He let out a low, languid groan and eased to a stop, his eyes closing completely. His grip on my wrists loosened. I eased one hand free and reached up to touch his cheek.

"A good experiment?" I felt the need to ask.

His eyes opened into slits, gazing down at me. "One of the best. We'll do that again."

It was a statement rather than a question, but I wasn't inclined to debate his decision, so I let the assumption slide.

Lance stretched his frame before pulling out of me. His brow knit as he considered my shoulder, and he healed the small marks left by his fangs with a spurt of breath. Then he shot me one last grin. "Maybe exploring will have tired you out enough that you can finally sleep."

He vanished into the shadows before I could respond.

I lay there, slack and sated, for a few minutes before I started to take stock. Both my tank top and my panties were ruined—but what the hell did that matter right now anyway. I pulled the sheet up over my nakedness, already feeling the weight of exhaustion creeping over me.

I'd almost drifted off when the strange sensation in my chest burst into being again, this time feeling not so much like a flutter as an entire sparrow beating its wings against my ribs.

CHAPTER THIRTEEN

Quinn

When I woke up the next morning, at first I just stared at the paneled ceiling, my muscles tensing in anticipation. The fluttery-flapping sensation in my chest had jolted me out of sleep twice during the night. I wasn't sure it wouldn't hit me again.

After a minute or two, something wavered between my ribs, but it wasn't as emphatic as the most recent feelings. Like the bird that'd somehow gotten trapped in there was settling down and simply giving its wings a gentle stretch. I swallowed thickly, counting the beats of my heart until my breaths evened out.

My phone alarm went off, and I grabbed my refilled water bottle and my pill container. The rows of mostly empty segments unnerved me. I'd need to talk to the men about that.

I needed to talk to them about a lot of things. The growing urgency of the sensation in my chest made it all the more obvious that this "special" quality I was harboring wasn't going to just fade away.

Maybe we'd been coming at this problem from the wrong angle. Maybe we shouldn't be trying to figure out how to guard me against the monsters coming at me but how to squelch the thing inside me that was calling them in the first place.

The sense that *something* needed to change soon had me shoving my phone and charger into my bag. The battery was full, and I got a tiny bit of comfort from knowing all of my essentials were together.

I pushed aside my sheet and the fragments of cloth that were left from my interlude with Lance last night, a flush tingling through me at the memory. He hadn't left any lingering marks, carefully healing the few places where he'd briefly broken the skin, but the memory of his touch echoed across my body.

We'll do that again. Not only did I have no intention of debating that point, a pretty large part of me couldn't wait to jump back in. If that was how much skill he'd been able to bring to his first attempt at sex, imagine what the second would be like. The tenth. The—

Another soft but insistent flutter around my heart brought me back to earth. I had bigger concerns than getting laid.

I got dressed, pulling on a shirt and shorts that were a little stiff from being hand-washed in the sink and then hung over a chair to dry. Even if they weren't the most comfortable, I had a little modesty when I crossed the hall to take my shower. When I emerged feeling more refreshed and ready to face the conversations ahead, I headed straight to the living room.

The first thing my gaze caught on was the new carving Lance must have etched into the wall sometime after I'd gone to bed. The whirling gouges he'd drawn with his claws were as abstract as usual, but something about the shape of them, the hint of one form curving over another, sent me back to our encounter, his head bowed as he worked his tongue over my clit. A sharper flush heated my face.

Was the impression intentional, or had I just turned into a monster-sex-crazed maniac overnight?

Knowing Lance... possibly both.

At that moment, Crag emerged from the shadows by the door, probably returning from one of his patrols. At his arrival, Lance blinked into being too—poised in a headstand on one of the undoctored armchairs. He flipped off with his usual agility and rolled his shoulders, his eyes sparkling with enthusiasm.

"Any peril out there today?" he asked Crag.

The larger man grunted, rubbing his hand over the sheen of black hair on his bronze scalp. "Very quiet."

"You say that like it's a bad thing. I can go find some beasties for you to beat up if you're getting bored."

Crag's expression turned even more stern. "Don't bring trouble."

Lance held up his hands. "Fine, fine, no unexpected guests. Better that we keep our moody mortal all to ourselves anyway." He aimed his grin at me and reached out to tease his claws down my bare arm.

A pleased shiver passed through me even as I stepped away. I might have gotten turned on by the idea of Crag and Torrent watching our hook-up from the shadows, but the idea of a PDA while I could actually *see* either of them watching gave me a little jolt of embarrassment.

"I'm not that moody," I retorted lightly, and then frowned, pretty much contradicting my point.

He'd called me "moody" before, when the three of them had first rescued me. It'd stuck me as odd at the time, but there'd been so much else going on that was even more insane that I'd forgotten the brief oddity.

But if he was actually referring to my last name, if he'd known it already on the first night, that would only be possible if they'd known about *me* before I was attacked. If that was the case, one of them would have mentioned it by now, right?

It was probably just a coincidence. To Lance with his carefree vibe, anyone who ever got worried about anything probably seemed moody.

I told myself that, but my gut had constricted more than it'd already been at the thought of the conversation I wanted to have.

Food. We should all get some food into us, and then I could demand more answers. Or at least demand that we figure out how to find some more.

I walked over to the kitchen area and automatically pulled three bowls from the cabinet. "You want the usual, Crag? And should I pour you some cereal, Lance, or are you on an all-ice cream diet now?"

Lance laughed and licked his lips. "I think there are a few other things I'll continue to enjoy eating."

"We can get the food ourselves," Crag rumbled, striding over.

A few days ago, the brusque remark would have made me flinch and worry that I'd offended him. But I felt reasonably sure by now that he didn't actually have any problem with me.

So I just paused and glanced up at him when he loomed next to me, a question in my gaze. His jaw shifted from side to side, and he put his hand over one of the bowls. His voice came out still gravelly but more measured this time. "You don't need to do anything for us."

There, that was all he'd meant. The boost in confidence melted any lingering apprehension I might have felt standing next to his formidable bulk. I tapped my elbow playfully against his arm as I retrieved the Mini-Wheats he always seemed to go for from the cupboard. "You guys are handling all the defensive maneuvers and gathering of supplies. The least I can contribute is tossing some cereal into a bowl."

"You're hiding here out of fear for your life," he insisted somberly. "You're dealing with enough." But he wasn't petty enough to jerk his bowl away when I went to pour the cereal. He did glower at me before getting out the milk for himself, but I simply smiled back at him, knowing he was more annoyed with himself for not managing to stop me from helping him than with me for wanting to.

He could call me "soft" all he wanted—I'd figured out he had a secret sweet side underneath the rocky exterior.

Lance had laid out some strips of bacon on a plate, ignoring the bowl I'd taken out for him. With a gush of his breath, they sizzled and turned crispy. That must have been a different fire setting from the one he'd used to heal up my arm.

My eyebrows shot up. "Um, could I get some speed-fried bacon too?"

The dragon shifter popped one piece into his mouth and smirked at me as he chewed. "Lay 'em out, and I'll torch them."

A couple of minutes later, I was sitting at the dining table with several perfectly cooked strips of bacon and a piece of toast. Not what my doctors would generally have recommended as a dietary choice, but I could make up for it with a bunch of fruits and veggies at lunch time. I was pretty sure avoiding getting killed by monsters was a more urgent concern than a few days off my strict nutritional regimen.

As I savored the salty, greasy goodness, my gaze settled on the shadow on the wall across the table from me. Had Torrent joined us like I'd meant for him to? He seemed to make the final calls about who did what around here. I needed him present for the conversation if I was going to make any headway.

I needed to see him, to gauge his reactions, even if that meant I had to put him in a little physical discomfort.

I washed the bacon down with a glass of orange juice and leaned my elbows on the table. Lance had just polished off his bacon and an apple he'd sliced up, and Crag was pushing aside his now-empty bowl. They both paused, taking in my stance as if sensing that I needed their attention.

I almost balked, but then another flutter passed through my chest. I couldn't just ignore it.

"I need to talk to you," I said, and looked pointedly at the shadow. "All of you. Torrent?"

The lean man materialized in the chair at his end of the table. His tentacles unfurled on either side of his seat, and his pale eyes contemplated me with even more gravity than the other two shadowkind had shown.

"What's the matter, Ms. Fix-It?" he asked, brisk but not as curt as he'd sometimes been in the past.

One of my hands moved to my sternum of its own accord. One thing I couldn't fix, at least not on my own.

I dragged in a breath. "You've all probably noticed, because you could sense the same thing that was drawing the other shadowkind to me—whatever's happening to me or in me, it's getting stronger. I can feel it more, but I still can't make any sense of it or what it has to do with any of you."

Even Lance's expression briefly sobered at my words, but only for an instant. "So, what you're saying is you just keep getting more special," he teased.

I narrowed my eyes at him. "I'd rather not be if the only thing it does is make monstrous creatures want to murder me." I glanced around at the others again. "I—I know how it feels inside me, but it's just a physical sensation, so whatever you all must notice has to be different. Do you have *any* idea what the 'special-ness' is now that it's stronger? What does it even feel like to you?"

"It's a sort of energy," Torrent said evenly. "One that sparks a sense of interest. I'm not sure exactly why that interest is hostile in so many."

His voice sounded especially bland with that remark. Was it really the whole truth?

I let out my breath in a huff. "Well, can you sense any way to get that energy *out* of me? We wouldn't have to worry about anything else if I just... wasn't 'special' anymore."

Lance tipped his head to one side. "You want *us* to carve you open and see what we can toss away?"

Crag squared his shoulders. "We can't damage her."

Something about his phrasing brought back my prickle of suspicion. He sounded like he meant it not as in it was impossible but that they weren't *allowed*. But who would even know about it if they tore me to pieces right now?

There were too many niggling bits of this situation that didn't quite add up.

My head jerked toward Lance. "Why were you calling me 'moody'?"

He blinked, looking both puzzled and amused by the change of subject. "Sometimes it seems fitting, especially because—"

"Because Lance thinks everyone is moody if they don't cater to his every whim," Torrent interrupted in a firm tone.

Lance, uncharacteristically, shut his mouth. The prickle of my apprehension deepened.

I crossed my arms in front of me. "You were going to say 'because it's part of your name.'"

He smiled at me, all toothy innocence. "Is it? I thought your name was Quinn. Which is a very good name on its own. No need to add to it."

Suddenly, frustrations I hadn't even known I was holding in boiled over. I found myself pushing to my feet, my hands slamming down on the edge of the table.

"There's something more going on here," I said, my voice coming out at a higher pitch than I liked. "There's something you haven't been telling me. I need to know what it is—I need to know *everything* so I can figure out how I'm getting out of this mess."

Crag went rigid in his seat, but I couldn't tell whether his reaction indicated guilt or simply defensiveness in the face of my aggression. Lance slung one arm carelessly over the back of his chair, all simmering amusement.

Torrent frowned at me from the other end of the table. "We've told you everything we can. There's nothing else we know that would help you figure out what's happening to you or how to keep the other shadowkind creatures away."

His wording sounded way too careful, as if he was doing his best to avoid telling the truth without outright lying.

I stared him down across the table. "But there are more things you know about me, or about why you're here, or something. I want to know exactly what's going on—what's been going on. It's my life. I *deserve* to know, don't I?"

He sighed, as if I was being an exasperating child instead of asking for information potentially vital to my survival. "Quinn—"

It still didn't sound like I was going to get anything useful out of him, but I never got to find out how he'd dodge the subject this time anyway. Before he could continue his sentence, a force like a demolition ball rammed into the cabin door.

The door burst open, the frame shattering at the same time, chips of wood flying everywhere. A huge creature landed on the threshold, filling the entire battered space.

He stood on two feet like a man, but his humanoid form was obviously monstrous, his skin deep blue, tusks jutting from his jowls, and his bared teeth revealing heavy fangs. His gaze swept over us with a gleam of intelligence I hadn't seen in any of my previous attackers' eyes.

This one wasn't just some rampaging shadowkind creature. This was a higher shadowkind being like the men who'd protected me.

Terror rattled my pulse. I scrambled around my chair instinctively, gripping it like a shield. My men all leapt up, Torrent's tentacles lashing, Lance slicing his claws through the air in a threatening gesture.

The intruder let out a bark of a laugh that was almost as much a snarl. "You don't want to make this a fight. Give me the mortal girl, or you can all die."

CHAPTER FOURTEEN

Crag

Rage blurred my vision as I stared at the gargantuan troll that'd barged into our cabin. I didn't know how he'd realized Quinn was here or what he wanted with her, but I didn't care. I just wanted him destroyed for daring to threaten us.

I barreled toward him, shifting into my gargoyle form as I went. He wasn't anticipating my speed—or perhaps my increased size either. I slammed into him with the full force of my hurtling body and sent both of us careening out of the cabin and across the deck.

The troll shoved out of the way just before I could propel him all the way into the swamp. He slammed his massive fist at my head, and I swung to the side, finding myself thinking of how I'd identified my ears to Quinn as a weak spot. One of those balled hands clocking me in the right spot wouldn't stop me, but it would send my brains spinning around in my head, as much as I had of them.

"You can't win this battle," the troll snarled, lunging at me in an attempt to heave me away from the doorway. I whipped upward with a vast flap of my wings and raked my clawed feet across his face.

He couldn't quite manage to jerk out of range. His head snapped to the side, smoky blood trickling from the rivulets I'd carved in his face.

A sinewy green body flashed past me. I didn't need Lance's backup in this fight—I was handling it just fine on my own. But before I could tell him to stay out of the way, my gaze followed his path and realized it wasn't the troll he was heading toward.

More shadowkind creatures were charging out of the shadows amid the swamp's nearby vegetation—more even than there'd been in the park the night we'd first saved Quinn. Most of them were clearly lesser shadowkind, springing toward the cabin with animalistic savagery, but I spotted a few other higher beings in their midst, approaching just as swiftly but with more wary alertness.

No, the three of us couldn't hope to win a battle against an entire horde of beasts at once.

Why were they so intent on having her?

I leapt back toward the cabin doorway, knowing our best chance of survival was escape. My distraction made me an easier target. Before I could reach the threshold, the troll landed a blow to my chest that sent me sprawling on the deck.

I rebounded right into his legs with a smack of my shoulder. Grunting, he stumbled backward and flashed his fangs.

I could understand how the strange energy Quinn gave off had incited the lesser shadowkind, but it hadn't affected me or my colleagues the same way. Why was this brute giving in to the ridiculous urge?

"She isn't any danger to us," I growled at him. "Are you like a dumb beastie who can't think past its impulses? There's no reason to slaughter her."

The troll let out a rumbling chuckle. "Oh, I'm not looking to slaughter her. The ones who sent me have much better uses for the girl."

The ones who sent him? I hurtled myself at him again, determined to get the upper hand. "Who sent you? Why does *anyone* want her?"

Why did Rollick, even? He'd known something like this would happen before the other shadowkind had even homed in on Quinn. What did all these beings know that we hadn't figured out in three months of observation?

How could I figure out how to win this fight when I wasn't even sure what we were really fighting over?

The troll didn't answer, pummeling me with his fists as he tried to fend me off. I rammed him into the cabin wall hard enough to dent the siding and then headbutted him so far down the deck that he crashed into the railing. The boards splintered under his weight, and this time he did crash into the water.

Feral shrieks and gnashes of teeth carried from all across the swamp. Lance was leaping across the clumps of vegetation, skewering every slavering beast he could. The slap of a tentacle into one of the higher shadowkind who'd nearly reached the deck told me Torrent had jumped into the fray as well.

Quinn was still in the cabin—Quinn was on her own. And all these creatures meant to... to tear her apart one way or another.

I moved to barge into the wider battle, but the troll was heaving to his feet. He launched himself at me with even more power than before.

All thought seared from my mind other than the knowledge that I had to stop him. Had to end any chance of him carrying out whatever foul purpose he'd come here with. He'd led all these creatures here. Let them see him fall.

I sprang to meet him, hurling my stone fists with all the strength contained in my hardened body. My wings swept around to batter him with their horned tips. His limbs battered my body, but I tuned out the momentary bursts of dull pain, not letting up my assault for an instant.

My fingers managed to clamp around his jaw. I threw him back, landing on top of him, and smashed his head against the boards of the deck hard enough to crack both them and his skull. Again and again, slamming it down harder each time, until the smoke of his blood was gushing up toward the sky in a plume and there was nothing but fleshy pulp and shards of bone beneath my hand.

Only then did a flicker of doubt penetrate my combat fury—he'd known things, things about Quinn's attackers that might have helped us.

There was no time for regrets. If I'd toyed with him longer to avoid killing him, the other beasts would have gotten an opening to attack her.

I hurtled off him toward the mass of creatures descending on us.

Most of them were much easier to deal with than the troll had been. I crushed one small beast's skull with a single blow and snapped another in two with a stomp of my heel. A rabid fox-like being with spines poking up along its spine lunged at me, and I flung it into a tree trunk before ripping its chest right open, eviscerating its heart.

The smoke of shadowkind essence was flooding the air all around me, and still there were more darting, snapping bodies racing toward the cabin. Lance was nothing but a greenish blur. Torrent's tentacles lashed out in all directions, slapping aside creatures in physical form, wrenching others right out of the darkness they'd tried to remain cloaked in.

From inside the cabin, Quinn screamed.

Adrenaline surged through my body. I tore across the swamp toward the small building and landed on a skeletal creature that'd just reached the open doorway.

The bones visible through the thing's taut, translucent skin fractured under my weight. More essence billowed up, obscuring my view. I sprang through the cloud into the cabin.

A taller, gaunt being with fingers that were little more than razors jutting from its palms was stalking toward Quinn. She'd ducked right beneath the table, pulling the chairs in closer as a flimsy barrier between her and the monstrous predator.

In the split-second before I charged, I could already see how she was bracing herself to throw a kick the second the thing got close enough. As I flung myself across the cabin at her attacker, an unexpected flare of pride lit in my chest.

She might be mortal, but she'd have done her best to defend herself against these creatures no matter how much they frightened her. That soft body contained more boldness and bravery than most beings could imagine. How could they want to savage something so... so astoundingly rare?

I heaved the gaunt creature into the wall. Its claws raked across my stony skin, only managing to scratch the surface.

The pinpricks of pain gave me an extra jolt of rage with which to propel it into the floor, one fist following the other. With a final roar, I tore its head right off its spindly neck and crushed its chest in for good measure.

A few more, smaller beings had managed to make it to the doorway despite my colleagues' efforts. I raced toward them and crashed into their midst, pummeling and slashing until they were barely shreds of beasts.

A choked sound carried from beneath the table. Had something got past even me?

I leapt across the floorboards and thumped to a halt just a few feet shy of the table, fangs bared and breaths rough. Quinn was alone, unharmed other than a bruise blooming on her forearm.

She stared at me with wide eyes, and a chill rippled through my body. This was the first time she'd seen me clearly in my monstrous form. Her face had paled, her lips parted. I braced myself for her scream.

Instead, she blinked, and the fear faded from her expression. A *smile* curved her mouth, bright as a beam of sunlight.

"Crag," she said, as if there was no one she'd have welcomed more happily.

A sensation unfurled deep inside me like a vast swath of fabric blanketing me with warmth from the inside out. She recognized me. She wasn't frightened of *me*, as terrifying as I knew my gargoyle form was to humans, as many mortals as I'd sent fleeing before me in the past.

She was something even rarer than I'd realized earlier.

I couldn't let one creature out there lay so much as a finger on her. The thought of even Rollick drawing her in with his pointed teeth gleaming in his smile...

I'd come here to protect her, and in that moment I'd have defended her from *anything* that threatened her, no matter what it required of me.

"Come out," I said, wincing inwardly at the harsh rasp of my voice in this form. "I have to get you away from here."

She scrambled forward without hesitation, courage and trust twined together in a combination that amplified the warmth in my chest even more. As she pushed past the nearest chair, her gaze darted to the hallway. Anguish tightened her pretty face.

"My bag," she said. "It's got my medicine, and..."

I didn't force her to finish. Her medicine kept her safe even more than I could at times. Whatever else mattered to her that she was afraid of losing, I'd protect too.

"We'll grab it," I said, holding out my arm. She looked at me in surprise as she scooted the last few steps to me, but she didn't release more than a brief gasp that was more relief than shock when I swept her off her feet.

I held her close against my shoulder as I took off down the hall. As I barged into Quinn's bedroom, a scaled beast that looked like a distant, shrunken cousin of Lance's shadowkind form leapt out of the shadows. I shouldered it aside, whipped my free arm through the strap on Quinn's canvas bag, and spun toward the window.

The glass pane was nowhere near big enough to admit me. I burst through it and the wall around it back-first, sheltering Quinn from the flying shards and splinters. She tucked herself closer against me, one arm looping around my neck to keep her more secure. I bounded off the deck outside and cast off into the air.

A few flying beasties blinked out of the shadows in the swamp to careen after me, but none of them could match the flaps of my much larger wings. Below, a roar rose up that I recognized as Lance's, tinged with triumph.

My colleagues could retreat now. We'd regroup. We'd shore up our defenses.

I slid my other arm around Quinn's slim form, and she relaxed even more into my protective embrace. A slight tremor ran through her body. I held her firmly, soaring steadily through the air. We'd picked a spot far from any human habitation. When I was sure I'd left the battle far behind, I dropped lower to skim the treetops where no more distant mortals would be able to see me.

With Quinn's soft form nestled against my stony skin, the tangy-sweet scent of her filled my nose. A different kind of warmth flickered through me. It came with images of stroking my hands over her softness the way I'd seen Lance tease her. Of drinking in that scent not just with my nose but my lips and tongue as well.

I'd never been with a human woman that way. I'd never been able to show myself around mortals at all in any capacity other than to terrorize and kill. But there'd been shadowkind women who'd valued me as a partner for my size. If she wasn't afraid of me—if I could impress her, satisfy her the way I had during those occasional encounters of the past—

Her wavering voice broke through the rush of longing that'd flooded me.

"They found me," Quinn murmured. "Even with everything you were doing to hide me, they figured out where I was."

Her comments washed away every trace of heat other than a faint burn of shame at my lust. How could I be imagining that when I'd nearly failed her? Just because she wasn't terrified of me didn't mean she'd *desire* me.

And she was right. The creatures had found her—multitudes of them. The knowledge made my teeth clench in frustration.

But feeling the fragility in her body where it pressed against mine, where my mind went next wasn't to the question of how her attackers had found us. Instead, I found myself remembering the fierceness she'd shown less than an hour ago, staring down Torrent across the dining table as she'd demanded answers.

No matter what other feelings she harbored for me—or didn't—she was counting on me. She *needed* me in a way no one else I'd fought for in the past ever had.

We couldn't leave her in the dark anymore. She deserved the full truth, as much of it as we knew. I'd dare anyone to tell me she hadn't proved herself worthy of it.

And if I couldn't convince Torrent of that… I didn't know what I'd do. I'd never questioned his leadership before.

But I wasn't letting this woman down, whatever the consequences.

CHAPTER FIFTEEN

Quinn

My nerves kept jangling for a long time after Crag had whisked me away from the terror of the shadowkind onslaught. I leaned against his chest, the rhythmic flap of his wings and the odd warmth that seeped through his rocky flesh gradually soothing the worst of my panic.

My messenger bag swayed where he'd slung it over one of his arms. Guilt jabbed my gut when I remembered how I'd insisted we grab it instead of immediately taking flight, but the thought of leaving behind not just my pills—which could be replaced, if with a little difficulty—but my sketchbook as well had wrenched at me even more.

I didn't have just drawings in there. Those were my *dreams*... even if right now it was hard to imagine I was ever going to get a chance to fulfill them. How the hell could I imagine anything close to a normal life when shadowkind monsters were hunting me down no matter how carefully my protectors hid me away?

The question sent a deeper ache through my stomach with a twinge of queasiness. But I couldn't look that far into the future right now. I had to focus on simply making it through today.

"Where are we going?" I asked Crag, tipping my head in the hopes that it'd help my voice reach him through the buffeting of the wind. The whistling currents of air blew my pale hair across my face and then down over my shoulders.

He grunted. "Torrent always has backup plans. We picked a regrouping spot. He and Lance should meet us there."

"And it'll be safe from the other shadowkind?"

The gargoyle paused. I peered up at his face, as well as I could see it in my current position cradled against his massive chest.

He wasn't the most emotive guy at the best of times, but it was particularly difficult to read his expressions in his monstrous form. I'd barely recognized him when he'd first barged into my view while I'd been crouched beneath the dining table.

His hard features had turned even more ridged: a heavy brow protruding over deep set eyes that held a ruddy glow, sharp-edged cheeks and a hooked nose like shards of granite, and the constant blocky jaw. All of it—all of him—was the same slate-gray hue now.

Two small, curved horns jutted from his totally bald scalp, just above his large, bat-like ears. Twin fangs curled from his jaw, jutting over his upper lip. When he'd spoken, I'd caught glimpses of more vicious teeth inside his mouth.

He was still the gruff but brutally protective Crag he'd been in his mostly human form, though. He'd torn apart the creatures that'd been closing in on me without pausing for breath—who knew how many he'd destroyed outside the cabin too. He'd gone for my bag simply because I'd asked him to, because he must have been able to tell it mattered to me.

Even with all the things I'd been angry at my defenders about, I didn't think I could blame him for their lack of transparency. He'd never presented himself as anything other than what he was—and he was a hell of a lot. I had the urge to reach up and touch his face, to demonstrate the affection spreading through my chest, but I was afraid of jostling his hold on me. I'd rather not make this rescue any harder for him than it'd already been.

A familiar pang of guilt resonated through my gut. How much might he have given for me already that I hadn't realized? Why should he be putting his own life on hold for me?

He'd been around for centuries, I reminded myself. Probably he had centuries more. If he wanted to spend a few days on what might be simply an adventure, or a chance to feel good about performing some kind of duty that had very little to do with who I was personally, then that was his decision. I couldn't be taking *that* much from him.

I had to believe that, because I didn't think I stood much of a chance of talking him out of whatever he'd decided his current mission should be.

I couldn't see the ground from his embrace, even when I craned my neck. I had no idea where we were heading until Crag dove down toward the ground.

He landed on a low hill with a large, paved parking lot. A chain hung across the entrance to the lot, marking it as temporarily closed. It appeared to be some kind of lookout spot—for taking scenic pictures or something like that. I glimpsed the ocean in the distance, across a stretch of landscape that alternated between forest and fields. It *was* kind of pretty.

Crag loosened his hold enough to allow my feet to lower to the asphalt. I had the embarrassing urge to lean closer into his embrace, to burrow my face into his solid shoulder and keep his protective warmth wrapped around me. He rested a hand on my back, and a tingle raced over my skin at the span of it, nearly broad enough to reach across both my shoulder blades.

But I had to stay strong. I had to be able to hold my own as much as possible. If I gave up on myself, then I'd only be letting down him and the other two shadowkind who'd come to my aid. They'd have thrown themselves into the fray for nothing.

Dragging in a breath, I squeezed his arm and then stepped away. There was no sign of Torrent or Lance, but then from what I'd seen, they didn't typically travel as quickly as Crag's wings could carry him.

Worry condensed into an ache in my chest. "Are you sure the others are okay? They were out there in the fight too, weren't they?" Both Lance and Torrent had vanished into the shadows less than a second after Crag had shoved the blue-skinned monster out the door. I assumed they'd gone to join the battle outside. It'd sounded as if a whole army had been descending on us.

Crag nodded. "It was mostly lesser creatures coming at us. The two of them should have been able to find an opening to escape without much trouble." He handed me my bag and glanced around the lot, his jaw flexing. His tone turned oddly uncertain. "I don't like to leave you alone, but I should check our surroundings for any sign of potential attackers. No shadowkind should be able to get at you easily here—not without warning."

I took in the stretch of pavement again, and understanding clicked in my head. It was smooth, barely any dimples or cracks—not much in the way of shadows for a creature to slink through, invisible to my human eyes. Crag had brought us down right in the middle of the space.

I nodded. "I'll be okay."

He let out another grunt. "If you see anything worrisome, shout."

The corner of my mouth twitched with bittersweet humor. "I can definitely manage that."

Crag launched himself across the lot. The second he reached the vegetation at the edge, he flickered out of view. I peered around me again, resisting the urge to hug myself.

In the direction where there weren't many trees, I could make out a road winding along not far beyond the base of the hill. A car cruised by, a perfect picture of human normalcy. The sight brought a lump into my throat.

In the same moment, an impulse quivered through my senses. The road wasn't that far away. Another vehicle sped by as I watched. I could make a break for it: dash along the lane beyond the chained entrance, flag down someone to drive me to civilization... Figure out some solution other than me staying under guard for the rest of my life.

Maybe I didn't know how to fight the shadowkind, but the creatures weren't impervious. And when I was in the city, they'd come at me in a secluded spot at night. They might not dare attack me in broad daylight with all kinds of mortal witnesses around. How could I know that my protectors had been telling the truth that hiding me away was the safest option?

There were definitely things Torrent had been hiding *from* me. Maybe Lance too. And I couldn't say any of my protectors made progress toward a solution of their own in the days we'd spent in the cabin.

A sharper ache hit me, full of homesickness and desperation. I'd spent the past several years chasing danger, sure, but this was a lot more peril than I was comfortable with. I wanted so badly to step back into the existence where everything had made sense. Where *I* got to choose how closely I toed the line of risking my life.

And then these three men who'd been strangers less than a week ago wouldn't need to risk anything else for me either. It would be perfectly fair. That was how I liked to live my life—without dragging anyone else down with me.

I took one step forward, and another. Then I stopped, clutching my bag to my chest, a wave of uncertainty washing over me.

I thought of Crag, holding me so firmly and yet carefully just minutes ago. Of Lance, grinning with delight after he'd made me come. Of Torrent reaching out of the shadows with his tentacle to offer me a small fragment of reassurance.

Even if there were things they weren't telling me, did I really think they meant me any *harm*? I couldn't summon any conviction behind that thought.

And who was I kidding if I thought I could fend for myself if the monsters came after me again? I wasn't sure an entire police force could deal with those creatures that bled smoke instead of blood and kept going until they were utterly smashed or torn apart. What good did safety by daylight do me when night fell every twenty-four hours? Who else would die when darkness fell and the fiends swarmed after me again?

I might not like relying on the three men who'd already saved my life more than once, but they were definitely better equipped to handle this problem than anyone else I could turn to. And even they had needed to whisk me away both times the horde had attacked rather than facing all the creatures down.

How could I expect my parents or even random bystanders to act as my protectors instead? And going it completely alone, away from human civilization, would basically be suicide. I'd probably be dead before the day was over.

There were a lot of things I wasn't sure of, but I knew I wanted to live.

So I stayed where I was, my feet planted on the pavement and my arms tight around my bag, drinking in the fresh air that wasn't as cloyingly humid as the swamp's. The sun beamed down over me as it rose toward its peak in the sky, keeping the shadows at bay. I felt almost calm by the time not one but three figures shimmered into being at the edge of the lot.

Crag had switched back into human-like form. He headed toward me with Lance striding along next to him. The dragon shifter walked with a spring in his step as if he'd come from a dance party and not a brawl.

Torrent followed the other two with stiffer steps. Watching him, it occurred to me that I hadn't seen him really move around before. He usually just appeared in whatever pose, sitting or standing, suited him at the time. I'd assumed he'd brought his tentacles with him because he had no choice in the matter, like Crag with his jaw and Lance with his claws.

But from the way he was leveraging them at his sides now, I could tell he needed them to support his weight. He was using the extra appendages like dual walking sticks, leaning on them to steady each step. Could his human-like legs even hold him up on their own?

Maybe his tentacles *didn't* inherently come with his human form. They were a lot larger than the monstrous features that stuck with Crag and Lance. Torrent might be bringing them out only to use them, like Lance had transformed his tongue and teeth last night, rather than because he couldn't disguise them.

I'd never paid much attention to his footwear before, but it occurred to me now that the ankle-high hiking boots were an odd choice for the summer heat. Lance wore thin sneakers like mine, and Crag always seemed to go barefoot. It could be that Torrent needed the extra support the boots provided too.

What had happened to his legs to leave him like that? Was it the same incident that'd caved in his cheek?

The men didn't appear to talk to each other, but from the glances exchanged before they reached me, I had the sense that I'd missed a private conversation they'd had before appearing in my view, one they were still processing. Crag stopped a few feet from me in a pose like a sentinel and looked expectantly at Torrent.

Lance rolled his shoulders as if shaking off spare energy and looped a strand of my hair around one of his claws with a flick of his finger. "You got through okay, baby girl," he said in the teasing tone he always gave the nickname.

My cheeks heated anyway, but my thoughts darted back to what I'd gotten through. "How did all those shadowkind find us all of a sudden?" I asked, focusing my attention on Torrent. "I thought there was some kind of barrier that stopped them from sensing me."

Torrent sighed. "The vibe you give off has been getting stronger. It must have reached the point where the protections weren't enough to disguise it."

Of course. The ripple had turned into a flutter and then that outright flapping sensation. I'd been right to worry about it, even if I hadn't known why.

"There were so many of them already in the swamp right by the cabin," I said. "They attacked suddenly, all together—it wasn't just one here or there like the thing that jumped at me when I climbed the tree."

He nodded with an air of resignation. "This assault looked more... organized than before. There were a few higher shadowkind in the bunch who appeared to be directing or at least moderating the others." He paused. "From their behavior, I also think that it's possible they didn't want to kill you, at least not this time. They were trying to take you away alive."

A chill swept through me. "Take me where? *Why?*"

"They won't," Crag insisted.

A grimace twisted Torrent's mouth. "I don't know," he said in answer to my question. "I wish I did. But the fact that they mostly emerged around the cabin rather than inside it, when they were clearly capable of coming up with a coherent strategy... They were hoping to draw us away from you. If their intention was simply to kill you, they could have appeared much closer and done it in an instant, like the being that caught you in the tree tried to. Possibly they were aiming to kill *us* before they took you at all, to be sure no one would be left who knew about it."

I swallowed hard. I believed him when he said he didn't know why. The weary frustration in his voice sounded totally genuine.

His observation made the situation ten times more complicated. It wasn't just rabid beasts wanting to tear into me. Some of the other shadowkind had a *purpose* for me, or someone else they were answering to...

I shook my head, but I couldn't dispel the bewilderment gripping me. "Why would anyone want me?" I demanded. "What is it about this 'specialness' that would be useful to any shadowkind? You've got to at least tell me that much."

"We want to," Crag said gruffly. "We would." He shot another look at Torrent.

Lance clucked his tongue, his grin turning crooked with the slant of his jaw. "You're a tricksy mortal, keeping too many secrets."

"I'm not keeping them on purpose!" I burst out. "I have no idea what's going on here."

Torrent cleared his throat. His voice took its more usual brisk tone, but it still wasn't quite as terse as usual. "We understand that. I can tell you...

the impression your energy gives off to us is that you're some kind of threat."

My eyebrows rose. "What?"

A faint smile crossed his face. "It seems strange to us too. Nothing else about you appears to pose any danger to us. I assumed the lesser shadowkind were driven by base instincts, noticing only the energy and not paying attention to any other factors that would make them realize it was a mistake. But for higher beings to be involved as well, to be orchestrating some kind of capture..." His narrow forehead furrowed. "I'm confused too."

"Which means we need to find out the reason," Crag said in a prompting tone.

Torrent dipped his head. "Yes. We've already seen that the best protections we could arrange aren't enough to keep us safe while we're staying in one place. And if we have to keep moving around, we've agreed that we should use some of that time to try to figure out what exactly is 'special' about you. If you're up for that."

I opened my mouth and closed it again, letting his offer sink in. We'd go investigate the mystery of this strange energy inside me, somehow or other—they'd help me figure that out?

"Won't we keep being attacked?" I asked.

Lance flashed his claws through the air. "We're faster. If one or two stumble into us, we'll shred 'em. Never stay anyplace vulnerable for long enough that a bunch of them could join forces, and they're shit out of luck."

"And I have some ideas about how we could safely rest for a decent stretch in between traveling," Torrent said. "I have a friend in the area who should be able to help with that."

He studied me in his penetrating way, his sea-green eyes as fathomless as the ocean to my left. "We'll need your help, of course. We can't work out what's happening to you without your participation. We don't know what we'll find out or how unnerving it might be. Are you sure you want to go down that road?"

A shiver passed through me, but I raised my chin. He didn't know me very well if he had to ask that.

"What are my other options? Just wait around for the horde to finally catch up and slaughter me? I *need* to know why this is happening—that's the only way I'll have any chance of fixing it."

He gave a curt nod. "Then we'll start right away, before the creatures after you have a chance to catch up again."

"Wait." I shifted my bag in my hands. "I'm almost out of my medication. I only keep a week's supply right on me. I have a bunch more pills at home. But if I go back there—if the creatures follow me— Mom and Dad..."

Something shifted in Torrent's expression that I couldn't identify. "I'll go," he said abruptly. "We'll pass through the city again within the next day or so, and I'll get them for you. It won't do our investigation any good if your heart gives out before we get any answers, will it?"

"No," I said with a rush of relief—and a twinge of something softer. "No, it won't."

They'd told me more than they had before, and they were willing to work with me to find the answers I'd been desperate for. Torrent wasn't keeping only me safe but my parents as well. I still wasn't sure I had the entire story, but I had enough to soothe my doubts.

I slung my messenger bag across my back. "Let's get started then."

CHAPTER SIXTEEN

Quinn

When Torrent had said his friend was a leprechaun, I guessed I hadn't totally believed him. That was, until I found myself in front of a spritely shadowkind man who couldn't have been more than four feet tall, with a twinkle in his eye, a dimple in his rosy cheeks, and heaps of reddish-gold curls. He even had a gold pin in the shape of a four-leaf clover clipped to the lapel of his trim forest-green suit.

It must have been because of the suit that he kept the air conditioning in here so cool my skin had broken out in goosebumps. I resisted the urge to rub my arms for heat.

"Goldie," Torrent said in greeting in his usual even tone. I couldn't tell whether the nickname came from the hair or the golden teeth the leprechaun flashed in his smile, which I assumed were his unalterable "monstrous" feature and not a fashion choice, although he must have passed them off as the latter. Torrent had said he didn't even know the guy's real name, that everyone had called the leprechaun "Goldie" for centuries.

It was weird thinking that the petite man who could have passed for a preteen in the right light had centuries under his belt. But it was even *more* weird when he leaned against the shelving unit in the back of his pawn shop, where we'd met him, and his eyes sharpened with a sudden maturity that made those centuries abruptly plausible despite the youthfulness of his face.

"It's been a while, Torrent," he said. "Where did you slosh off to?" His gaze lingered on Torrent's marred cheek as if he wasn't used to seeing it, but he didn't comment on the damage.

"I took up other habits," Torrent said, folding his arms over his chest. He'd propped himself against the door frame the second he'd appeared from the shadows—without his tentacles. I could see subtle signs of strain in his stance already, but he obviously didn't want his friend realizing the extent of his injuries. "It looks like you've kept up your typical line of business. Whatever anyone needs, you can get it for them, and fast—is that how it still goes?"

The normally-tentacled man glanced around the back room with its shelves packed with a wild assortment of antiques and modern-day collectables. A stack of Elvis records sat next to an ornately carved mantle clock, a boxed action figure I vaguely recognized beside that. I didn't see anything in here that could solve our problems, though.

Crag shifted his weight where he flanked me. It was a tight squeeze in here with the four of us—Lance was prowling through the shadows outside, keeping an eye on the area. Apparently Miami was a hotbed of shadowkind activity, to the point that Torrent had figured I was safer meeting his long-time associate than hanging around anywhere else near the city.

He'd asked Crag to stay visible and with me at all times as a sort of disguise for me. He'd pointed out that if his friend picked up on my "special" threatening vibe, the leprechaun should naturally attribute it to the man who actually looked like a threat.

I couldn't deny the cleverness of the strategy. Too bad it wouldn't work on the beings who were already hunting a mortal girl.

Goldie rubbed his slim hands together. "Of course I can get you whatever you're after. It's my particular gift. And I'm always happy to help out a friend, especially one I owe at least a few favors to still. What is it you're looking for?"

"A boat and a car," Torrent said. "With key specifications." He motioned to Crag, who stepped forward just far enough to hand the leprechaun a piece of paper, and I realized that maybe the gargoyle was also here as part of the show of Torrent's competence. Crag could move around when Torrent couldn't easily, and they made it look as if he was merely a lackey doing his boss's bidding.

Why was it so important to him to hide his injuries from his friend?

As I puzzled over that question, Goldie scanned the list of features and clucked his tongue. "This is doable. Definitely doable. The boat isn't difficult at all—I'm sure I can set you up with something appropriate right now. The car will take a little longer, but I should have it ready by midnight. You want it waiting in Daytona Beach?"

I tamped down my surprise as Torrent nodded. It made sense that he didn't want anyone knowing our actual destination, right? It wouldn't be a long drive from there back to Jacksonville.

"No trouble at all." Goldie tucked the paper into his breast pocket and peered up at the taller man speculatively. "What's all this for? You got bored of swimming?"

Torrent chuckled as if our mission was of no great importance. "I've been branching out into all kinds of new activities. An opportunity popped up that I hadn't anticipated but wanted to take advantage of. Glad I happened to be in the neighborhood. I knew I could count on you to supply the goods."

"Well, if you want to become more of a regular customer, I'm good for whatever you want. And open to all kinds of payment." The twinkle in the leprechaun's eye turned a little more pointed as his gaze swept over me. "A piece this pretty would be worth a few cars."

He'd barely finished speaking when Crag lunged forward, his massive arm sweeping in front of me protectively, the rest of him looming over Goldie, who looked miniscule beneath him. "She isn't for sale," he barked.

I gripped his forearm, startled by his vehemence—and abruptly twice as conscious of the firm muscles flexing all across his frame. Having him tuck me against his chest had warmed me this morning; now that warmth blazed into a spike of pure heat like when he'd loomed over me on the cabin floor.

Torrent motioned for Crag to back down. "Goldie can't resist looking for a bargain. He didn't mean anything by it."

"Not at all," the leprechaun agreed with a playful tug of his suit jacket. "More complicated dealing with mortals than it's generally worth anyway. She's all yours, big guy. Although I'm sure you're getting your share too." He winked at Torrent.

Crag let out a disgruntled huff as if he didn't quite believe the man's intentions were innocent, and I had to hold myself back from clarifying that I *wasn't* Crag's, not like that—or Torrent's for that matter. But maybe it was better if Goldie thought I was.

The memory came back to me of Torrent rising up in front of the shadowkind horde in the park and declaring me *theirs*. Somehow the idea wasn't so chilling now.

The leprechaun stepped to the side to make a quick call and then gave Torrent directions for where to find the boat at the Miami Beach Marina. I memorized them silently, knowing I was going to have to make the trek there without much other guidance. None of my shadowkind men could stroll around downtown Miami without drawing way too much concerned attention from my fellow humans.

We left quickly, me walking through the shop and the men vanishing into the shadows. I hailed an Uber to take me to the marina, knowing they'd slip into the patches of darkness inside the vehicle to join me.

The boat turned out to be a small motor yacht: one large cabin room with a tiny deck on the bow and larger shaded one on the roof. As I stepped on board, grabbing the railing to steady myself against the bobbing in the water, my three companions materialized beyond the glossy windows. I stepped into the cabin to meet them.

It was a fairly tight space with a long, curved leather sofa along one wall behind the navigation area and a narrow set of cupboards built into the other. Down a few steps lay a double bed that took up most of the cramped bedroom. The ceiling was low enough that Crag had to hunch his shoulders to avoid bonking his head.

I set my messenger bag down on the bed and checked my phone to see if I should start charging it. Torrent moved to the captain's seat and started poking at the controls, his tentacles sprawling over the sides of the padded chair.

"Do you even know how to drive this thing?" I asked him, coming back up the steps. He looked awfully sure of himself.

"When you've been around for several centuries, you pick up a wide variety of skills," he said matter-of-factly. The engine started with a rumble. "We'll travel out beyond view of the land and then head toward Daytona Beach. By the time we get there, it'll be starting to get dark anyway. As the sun goes down, we need to stay on the move."

"In the car you asked Goldie for?"

He nodded. "It'll go a lot faster than the boat—and most of our investigations will need to be conducted on land anyway."

I hadn't really seen him in his element before, I realized. He could fight when he needed to, sure, but he was a planner. A commander. And now he could actually direct some action instead of sitting around trying to figure out a solution in the cabin's shadows. Maybe he'd never really wanted to hole up there in the first place—it'd only been for my benefit, while he'd thought the protections around the building would shield me.

There was a deeper assurance to his stance while he rested his hands on the controls, an air of unshakeable power. Suddenly it wasn't all that hard to imagine why Goldie might have assumed his friend could easily get other kinds of action too.

I yanked my gaze away, tamping down the unexpected jolt of attraction, and glanced around. "And we don't have to worry about attacks from other shadowkind out here during the day?"

"Too much sunshine, not enough shadow!" Lance said. "No beasties are getting close to us unless they put on a show for the mortals—and they know how to swim."

"There were higher shadowkind in the last attack," I had to point out. "Couldn't they take a boat out just like we are?"

Torrent shrugged. "They could if they think they can find us. We won't stay in one place for long even in the boat, and they won't be able to bring a whole army of back-up. If they try, we'll deal with them."

He spoke with so much authority that I believed him. He should know his own kind better than I did, shouldn't he?

I collapsed onto the sofa, the stress of the day washing over me. But when the speedy boat had left land far behind, Lance and Crag headed out to climb to the rooftop deck, and my curiosity propelled me after them.

The rush of the salty ocean air reinvigorated my spirits. I turned my face to the wind, warmed by the late afternoon sunlight radiating over me, and then sprawled out on one of the deck chairs. The padding embraced my body. I could get used to this kind of life, at least for a little while.

After a few minutes, Torrent materialized to lean against the railing, one tentacle looped around a bar. He must have gotten the boat on the right course and left it on autopilot.

My stomach chose that moment to grumble. Loudly. I hadn't eaten since breakfast, and now that the panic of getting to safety was wearing off, it occurred to me that I'd somehow missed lunch quite a while ago.

Lance cocked an amused eyebrow at me from where he was perched on one of the other lounge chairs. "I think your insides are demanding food."

I swallowed thickly. It wasn't good for my continuing health to skip meals, but one small slip shouldn't be too big a deal. "It's not like there are any grocery stores or restaurants we can pop into out here. I'll survive until we get to Daytona Beach."

Crag stared out over the open water and grunted. "I can catch you something." He spared a brief glance at Torrent and then sprang into the air, transforming into his winged gargoyle body in mid-leap.

Lance whooped and jumped onto the railing, balancing on his nimble feet and then showing off with a slow cartwheel. Torrent's mouth flattened. He turned to face the other direction.

I didn't totally follow what was going on until there was a distant splash and Crag returned with two foot-long fish speared on his gargoyle claws. They were still twitching a little.

Lance had mentioned that Crag liked to hunt—and that Torrent wasn't super keen on seeing random animals killed. Funny from a guy who'd ripped apart who knew how many creatures of his own kind to protect me.

I caught his gaze. "It really bothers you, seeing mortal animals killed?"

The tentacled man gave a shrug as if trying to brush off the subject. "You need to eat. It isn't a problem. I prefer not to see creatures in pain that haven't done anything to deserve it, though, yes."

Ah. So it'd been the fact that those other beasties had been trying to kill me—or him—first that'd made the difference. Maybe it'd been unfair of me to assume his approach would lack that kind of nuance. All three of my monstrous defenders had turned out to be more complex than the average brute.

Crag brandished the fish in my direction. "Mackerel." Then he held out his rocky hands toward the dragon shifter. "A little fire?"

Lance grinned and hopped down from the railing. "Happy to supply." He breathed over the fish, the air in front of his mouth wavering with more heat than he'd applied to my wounds, and the creatures' scaled skin crackled and crisped like our breakfast bacon.

Crag set the fish on the deck table next to my lounge chair. "Wait," he ordered me in his gruff way. "They should be cool enough in a few minutes."

I basked in the sun's rays until the savory smell of roasted mackerel had my mouth watering too much to ignore. I picked up one of the fish gingerly and found that the crispy skin peeled off without much trouble. The cooked flesh underneath flaked from the bones at my nibbling, the mildly fishy flavor both salty and sweet with a smoky undertone from Lance's cooking efforts.

"You two should open a restaurant," I said, digging in more eagerly.

Lance snorted. "What would they make of a chef with claws? Maybe I should find out sometime." He twisted his torso in a stretch that brought me straight back to our interlude last night, feeling those taut planes of muscle pressed against me.

I licked my lips and yanked my attention back to the fish in my hands.

Torrent had vanished during the cooking. I wasn't sure if he was even still on the boat until I'd finished off the second fish, my stomach much happier with me than before. As Lance whisked the remains up to dump them into the water, the leader of our motley crew reappeared right in front of me.

"You've gotten the nourishment you needed," Torrent said. "Now it's time to start our investigations."

I blinked up at him, the somberness of his gaze making me uncertain. "How are we going to do that out here in the middle of the ocean?"

"This is hardly the *middle* of the ocean," he said dryly. "But we don't need anything other than what's on this boat. You were right before that we need to understand not just our opponents but also what's drawing them in. And I'm thinking we should start by analyzing the energy right at its source: *you*."

CHAPTER SEVENTEEN

Quinn

An uneasy quiver ran through my nerves at Torrent's announcement. "What do you mean? How are you going to analyze *me*?"

Torrent sat down on the lounge chair Lance had recently vacated. He held up one of his tentacles, the tip curled inward like a question mark. "The energy that's affecting all the shadowkind is being generated by your body somehow. If we can narrow down exactly where and how, that should help us in figuring out what and why. My suction cups can pick up more sensory input than most eyes, ears, or noses."

My arms rose to cross over my chest instinctively. I held my voice steady, arching an eyebrow at him. "So you're going to give me an exam, Dr. Squid?"

A short laugh tumbled out of Torrent that appeared to surprise even him. His lips quirked into the closest thing to a real smile I'd ever seen from him, though it still wasn't entirely relaxed. I wasn't sure the guy ever really let loose, at least not in physical form.

"Essentially," he said, his voice still brisk but lighter. "I won't even need to touch you, just bring my tentacle close. We can do this out here or in the cabin if you'd feel more comfortable there. Unless you're not interested in what I might find out, Ms. Fix-It?"

Was there a dare hidden in his even tone?

I forced my arms to lower to my sides, bracing against the padding of the deck chair with the gentle bobbing of the boat, and exhaled slowly to release the tension that'd wound through me. "I want to know. Go ahead. I think I'd rather stay out here." I liked having the sun's warmth beaming over me. The soft warble of the ocean wind mixing with the thrum of the yacht's engine would make it easier to tune out the weirdness of the situation.

Torrent raised one of his tentacles to the level of my head. I closed my eyes, figuring it'd also be easier if I couldn't see him not-quite groping me with the thing.

But I could *feel* him even if I couldn't see what he was doing. He didn't touch me, just like he'd promised, but the air shifted slightly against my skin as his tentacle swiveled around my hair. It displaced a few flyaway strands, which I couldn't really blame him for. The sunlight against my closed eyelids dimmed as the suckered appendage glided past my face.

He moved down to my shoulders, curling loosely around each of my arms and skimming down my back. Here and there, he grazed the fabric of my shirt just slightly. Just enough to set all my nerves tingling.

Maybe it was actually worse not seeing. It gave my imagination too much free rein.

I opened my eyes just as Torrent lowered his tentacle down along my chest, arcing over my breasts, and the tingling only deepened. Suddenly I was wondering what it would feel like to have those soft suckers actually stroking me, skin to skin. If Lance's claws and fangs could spark such a thrill...

I squeezed my eyes shut again as if I would dismiss the lustful thoughts that way. It wasn't weird for my mind to be wandering in those directions, right? Hooking up with Lance *had* been one of the most intense thrills of my life. Why wouldn't I be curious about the other possibilities monsters could offer?

But they weren't sex toys for me to experiment with—they were... people, or close enough, with their own thoughts and feelings. Thoughts and feelings that sometimes seemed pretty alien to me, but valid as anyone else's.

And it wasn't as if Torrent had any interest in exploring *me* the way Lance had.

When he spoke, his voice confirmed as much. For all the heat that had started to flow through my veins, his tone remained calm as ever. "I'll need you to stand up."

"Right." I pushed myself to my feet, hoping he hadn't noticed the blush coloring my cheeks, and looked down at him as he continued his inspection.

His expression remained impassive too, his gaze trained on whatever part of me his tentacle was moving over with penetrating focus. I found myself studying the broken angles of his face below his rumpled red hair.

Even with the caved-in cheek, he wasn't a bad-looking guy. Those intense eyes, the contrast between his dark hair and pale skin, the elegant lines of his features that remained intact. He might have been nearly as striking as Lance was before the injury.

When he hadn't needed his tentacles out to help him move around, he must have been able to pass for human, unlike his two companions. How different had he been then from the coolly curt man he was now? Goldie had obviously known him as something of a ladies' man.

Had Crag and Lance known him back then? They'd never made any remarks about his past habits.

I lifted my eyes. Crag was staked out by the side of the bow, his watchful gaze scanning the sea in all directions. Lance was watching Torrent's progress, his head cocked with obvious curiosity. When he noticed my gaze, he shot one of his smirks at me as if my heated reaction hadn't escaped *him* and strolled across the deck again.

Hooking his legs around the railing, he draped himself over the side of the boat without a hint of fear of falling. The rasp of his claws against the hull told me he was scratching his random designs like the ones he'd left all over the cabin.

Torrent's tentacle had reached my feet. I sat back down and lifted them up so he could flick it under my sneakers, since he seemed to be aiming for total thoroughness. He withdrew the extra limb and leaned back on his lounger, his expression pensive.

"Could you tell anything from that?" I asked when he didn't give an immediate report.

He exhaled slowly. "I can pick up the impressions of a threat you give off all through your body. It's most concentrated around your chest, but then, all of your energies are most concentrated there, like they are for any mortal." He frowned. "The only thing that tells me for sure is that it's something quite woven into your being, not an external force that's been attached to you somehow."

"Great," I said. "So, I just naturally incite shadowy beasts to want to slaughter me."

Torrent glowered at me. "It was worth checking. And we do know more than we did before. If it *had* been an external force acting on you, we'd have needed to figure that out to deal with it."

It'd probably have been easier if it'd been something like a magic spell that'd been cast on me and not an inherent part of who I was. I swallowed thickly. My thoughts jumbled for a moment, and I couldn't really have said why this question popped out now out of all the things I'd been wondering and worrying about.

"You don't have to keep your tentacles out. You didn't with Goldie. What's your shadowkind feature that you can't transform?"

Torrent blinked at me, looking surprised but thankfully not offended. Then, without a word, he tugged one of the elbow-length sleeves of his linen button-up higher on his arm. He turned so I could see the two rows of nickel-sized suction cups that ran down the back of his arm from close to the pit to a few inches above his elbow. I assumed he had a matching set on the other arm.

"I'm lucky they don't go all the way down to my wrists," he said briskly. "They'd be a lot harder to hide. Not that it makes much difference these days." His mouth flattened after that remark as if he wasn't totally happy he'd made it, and he jerked his sleeve back down before nodding to the cabin. "You should get some sleep while you can. Once we reach Daytona Beach, we'll be on the move for the rest of the night."

His dismissal was clear. The sun was still out, if close to the horizon now, but he did have a point.

"I'll try," I said.

I didn't think I had much hope of dozing off, but when I sprawled out on the bed inside, the exhaustion of the day's chaotic events rolled over me. I closed my eyes, tucking my arms close to my head, and that was the last thing I was aware of until I was jolting awake with the hitch of the boat.

In that first moment, it was totally dark in the cabin, only a faint gleam of distant lights penetrating the night beyond the far windows. My arm brushed my pill case lying on the bed next to me—I must have taken last night's doses on autopilot when my alarm went off and then gone right back to sleep without fully waking up. It'd happened before. Having the same routine for nine years will do that to a person.

Then the cabin lights flared on, and a body hurtled onto the bed next to me.

"Rise and shine!" Lance crowed, bouncing up and down on the mattress and then springing over in one of his acrobatic flips. He spun around and grinned down at me. "Although there's not much shining going on out there right now."

"Lots of gloom for the shadowkind creatures to lurk in," I said, my stomach knotting as I scrambled off the bed. I didn't know exactly what this trip had in store for us. I snatched up the pill case, grimacing at the faint rattle. There was only one dose left, for tomorrow morning.

But Torrent had said we could get my full supply from home tonight.

"Let the beasties come at us." Lance swiped his claws through the air so fast the air hissed around them. "I'll carve them up real nicely."

Torrent's voice carried from the captain's seat. "We'll be fully docked in a few minutes. Take care of whatever you need to now, because we'll want to move out the second we can."

Right. So those "beasties" didn't have time to home in on my new location.

I ducked into the tiny bathroom to do my business. An ache that wasn't just anxiety had gripped my chest by the time I emerged, punctuated by a fresh fluttering of the weird energy inside me. I grabbed my messenger bag, gripping the strap tightly as if it could keep me grounded.

Crag was just landing on the deck. When I stepped out into the open, salty air, which even near land was mildly warm rather than sweltering in the wee hours of the night, he'd already shifted back into man-like form.

He handed me a couple of chocolate bars. "I flew to land when we got close. I didn't know what at the store you'd like most. But you won't be hungry."

A different sort of hunting. I smiled up at him, accepting the snack. The night around me didn't feel quite so intimidating when I had a being as intimidating as *him* on my side.

"Thank you," I said. "These are great."

He gave one of his gruff grunts, but I thought he looked a little pleased.

Lance leapt onto the dock we'd moored at, his agile feet barely thumping on the boards, and lashed the yacht in place. Crag moved to help him.

Torrent came up behind me. "The car should be waiting in the lot here. A black sedan with tinted windows."

I frowned. "How are we going to get the keys?"

"They'll be in the glove compartment. Thankfully some of us can slip inside without needing the doors unlocked. But we're going to stay out of sight while you walk over."

"I haven't seen any shadowkind prowling nearby yet," Crag reported.

The three of them vanished in the darkness, and I hurried along the dock, my nerves jumping at every faint creak of the boards. There weren't many lights on in the marina, just a few security lamps that cast the surroundings in an orange haze.

No one else was here for a late-night boating expedition. The parking lot stood vacant other than the one car, so it was easy to find the right vehicle. I walked over to the black sedan, and suddenly Torrent was sitting in the driver's seat. The locks whirred on the doors, and he reached over to open the glove compartment.

I got into the back, setting my bag on my lap, and to my surprise Crag appeared next to me. It must have been more cramped for his bulk than the front seat would have been. He glanced around the parking lot with a wary air that suggested he felt the need to be as close as possible to protect me from lurking dangers.

Lance sprawled out in the front passenger seat. Neither he nor Crag bothered with their seatbelt, but I guessed if we got into a crash, they could just blink into the shadows before any damage was done.

Such a handy talent.

"Are you sure you're comfortable to drive?" I asked Torrent, eyeing the way he'd propped a tentacle over the side of the seat against the gear shift. We were heading back to Jacksonville, which would take at least an hour even with the speed limits he was breaking while the roads were this empty. I'd never seen him hold physical form continuously for that long.

"I'm the only one who can," he said.

"*I* can."

"I think it's better if I stay in control of the several tons of steel careening at high speeds when we don't know for sure what might cross our paths." He started the engine. "I'll be fine. I'm not an invalid."

His tone had gotten a bit sharp. I winced inwardly. "I know, I just—" I didn't know how to finish that sentence.

"Maybe I'll learn to drive sometime," Lance said conversationally as the car rumbled toward the highway. "Zoom all over. It's too bad you're supposed to stay on the roads, though. So many other places to go."

"Remind me never to get in a vehicle when you're behind the wheel," I teased, kicking the back of his seat lightly.

Despite the dragon shifter's chatter, the atmosphere in the car was somber. I glanced out the window at the darkness beyond the streetlamps, apprehension creeping over me again.

So many horrible things could be lying in wait just beyond my view. Torrent thought this strategy of keeping on the move would stop too many creatures from catching up with us at once, but he'd also thought the cabin would be safe. The horde had almost gotten the better of us there.

Maybe it was silly, but my hand crept across the seat of its own accord and grasped Crag's. My fingers curled around his much larger ones tentatively, half expecting him to pull away. The gargoyle sat still for a moment in stony silence and then eased a little closer to me on the seat, clasping my hand more firmly. Even with my seatbelt on, I could now lean against his massive bicep. The fear that'd risen up inside me eased back just a little at the warmth of his arm against the side of my face.

The car swayed as Torrent pulled onto an on-ramp, and Crag's knuckles brushed my thigh. All of a sudden, I was thinking more about what thrills those immense hands might be able to provoke in me than how well they could defend me.

I was glad that the night hid my blush. When had I become such a horn dog? These men had woken something up in me that I didn't know how to send back to sleep… or if I even should.

Those kinds of thoughts definitely weren't helpful at this particular moment. I focused on the protective posture of the man looming over me rather than any other wonderful assets he might have and talked to fill the silence. "What exactly are we going to do once we get to Jacksonville?"

"I want you to give us a tour," Torrent said. "All the places where you've spent significant amounts of time over the course of your life. I'd like to see if we can pick up on anything about or around them that might have affected you."

"Okay." I knit my brow, starting to compose a mental list. "But why would any of those places have affected only me and not everyone else there?"

"I don't know, but it's somewhere to start. We have to make use of whatever leads we've got."

"Of course," I said, chagrinned. I was as much a mystery to him and the other men around me as I was to myself.

By the time we reached the Jacksonville city limits, I'd come up with several locations we should check and even sorted them into a vague loop starting in the south. First, the hospital where I'd gotten most of my treatments, including the transplant operation. Then my high school, my elementary school, the daycare center I'd attended for several years, and the mall where I'd done most of my larger shopping trips, either with Mom or on my own.

At each of them, Torrent had me stay in the car while he and the others prowled around and through the sites. Each time, he returned without much to say and prompted me for the next location. After the mall, my heart had started to sink.

"I can't think of anywhere else I'd have been to *that* regularly except for my house. Maybe the little park that's near it? I played there a lot as a kid. Oh, and just in the past few years, the university in Gainesville. I guess we could drive all the way out there and check it out too."

Torrent shook his head. "Whatever's in you, I think it's been developing longer than that. Where's this park?"

I directed them to it and watched from the windshield as they stalked through the small grassy field and around the playground equipment. Lance poked at one of the swings and chuckled when it swayed.

The times I'd spent running around that place felt like multiple lifetimes ago. Before I'd found out that monsters existed and wanted to have me for breakfast. Before doctors had carved my old heart out of my chest and stitched in a new one. It was hard to wrap my head around the fact that I'd ever been a carefree little girl clambering over the monkey bars.

I'd survived, but in a way the girl I'd been before the virus had rampaged through my body *had* died. The Quinn who'd taken her place wasn't really the same person. But it was hard to mourn her loss. I had no concept of who I would have been if I'd never gotten sick, of what I'd have had that I didn't now.

I just wished she hadn't taken so much from everyone else around her as she'd slipped away.

"Nothing?" I said when the men returned to the car.

Torrent didn't even bother answering the question. "Let's go to your house. We needed to collect your extra pills anyway. Where are they?"

I dragged in a breath, my chest clenching up at the thought of being that close to home but not even being able to go in and soak up the familiar surroundings, to say hi to Mom and Dad and show them I was still okay. Turning up in the middle of the night would only make them more worried, not less. And the last thing I wanted was even one vicious creature noticing me inside the building and taking an interest in the other inhabitants.

"In my bedroom," I said. "It's the one next to the second-floor bathroom that looks over the backyard. Get all the pill bottles out of the drawer in the bedside table. Thank you."

A pang ran through me at the thought of all the other things I'd have liked to take, but we had to stay mobile. Focus on the essentials. It wasn't as if I could really concentrate on my studies or anything else until we got my monster-stalker problem sorted out.

Torrent bobbed his head in acknowledgment and vanished along with Lance. Crag remained in the back seat with me instead of joining them like usual.

"We've lingered in this neighborhood for a while," he said. "One of us should stay."

I wasn't sure whether to be more grateful for his attentiveness or nervous about the possibility of an imminent attack.

No hordes of murderous creatures descended on us *this* night, though. Maybe ten minutes had passed when Torrent and Lance materialized in the front of the car. Torrent immediately turned and held out not a handful of pill bottles but my entire school backpack, bulging full.

"I put the bottles in the outer pocket," he said brusquely. "And I grabbed a few more changes of clothes and your computer as well. I thought you might want those."

My spirits leapt. My laptop—I could catch up on my classes after all. Well, as long as I wasn't too busy fleeing shadowkind beasts.

As I took the backpack and hugged it to my chest, a lump rose in my throat. It hadn't occurred to me that Torrent would consider any of my wants or needs beyond the most obvious. At least now I could avoid falling totally behind.

Before I could say anything, Lance piped up. "Quite the collection of medicine. You could start a pharmacy."

Torrent's voice got even terser. "She needs it. It isn't that much considering she had her entire heart replaced."

The heart in question skipped a beat at the way he'd leapt to my defense, not that I'd really needed protection from the dragon shifter's joke. I hugged the backpack to me.

"I really appreciate it," I told him. "It might not seem like much, but it means a lot to me."

Torrent glanced back at me, his pale eyes unreadable in the dimness. "I listen," he said. "And you should make as much as you can of the time you still have."

A chill shivered through me at the unspoken words I didn't think he'd meant for me to pick up on. *However little that is.*

CHAPTER EIGHTEEN

Torrent

When we returned to the marina in Daytona Beach, the sun was just starting to peek over the horizon, sending golden glimmers across the expanse of water. How pretty.

A century ago I'd have wanted to pop a hallucinogenic mushroom or smoke a joint while appreciating the view. That'd been the old me. Not a care in the world until my carelessness had sent me up shit creek.

The thought made me glare at the ocean as I slipped through the shrinking patches of gloom to the yacht's helm. Lance and Crag made quick work of the moorings without being asked. As I started the engine, they vanished again, wary of watching mortal eyes while we were this close to civilization. Our one acceptable mortal, Quinn, hunkered down in the small lounge area on the bow and immediately pulled out her laptop.

Amazing that she could still be thinking about her schoolwork despite everything else that was going on around her. I didn't think I'd ever met another mortal so dogged in her goals. I checked the controls and ensured the wifi was on, for however long we'd have service as we headed out to sea.

I raised my voice to call through the window. "Don't tell anyone where you are."

Quinn waved her hand in a gesture that seemed to say, "I'm not stupid, don't worry about it." Which I could picture her saying with her mouth just as easily.

It wasn't her wisdom I was worried about. As I guided the yacht out of the marina and left the city behind for open water, an unfamiliar sense of uncertainty itched at me more insistently than the dull ache in my legs. The pain had expanded during the drive, even though I'd used my good foot to manipulate the pedals, but I was used to it. My lack of clear direction was much less familiar.

I'd sent another message to Rollick shortly before the attack on the cabin—a longstanding method I hadn't needed to turn to often, placing a classified ad in a newspaper he checked every morning. In it, I'd indicated that we had the "prize," but at the time I hadn't known that we'd be making a hasty break for it and leaving any property where he'd think of looking for us behind.

He'd be aware that I was trying to reach out to him now and that the original method had failed. I could leave another phone message giving him the details of our current whereabouts. But something in me had balked ever since we'd left the cabin.

Crag had insisted that we should find out exactly what our mortal companion's significance was. Crag, who barely ever spoke up about anything, least of all to go against established orders. If he felt that strongly about Quinn, maybe I should give the matter more consideration.

And investigating her power benefitted Rollick as well. We didn't really understand the situation, and he hadn't seemed to be sure of what was special about this woman either. What if she *was* dangerous to our boss in some way? What if there was some factor he hadn't realized that would affect his next steps?

I was merely doing my due diligence as his loyal lieutenant.

With the land slipping out of view behind us, my shadowkind companions blinked into view around Quinn, Lance dangling a bag of breakfast food he'd grabbed on our way back. Quinn set aside her computer to dig in with the two of them. She smiled at Crag and laughed at some antic of Lance's, and her blue eyes glittered almost as bright as the sunlight in her pale hair.

She raised her arms over her head to stretch them, and her breasts lifted beneath the thin fabric of her tank top. My cock twitched for an instant before I jerked my gaze away.

I focused on the navigational console in front of me. Yes, this woman was resilient and clever and bold, and someone more inclined to poetry might claim she was as pretty as the sunrise dancing on the sea. She was also human, and therefore as ephemeral as that light. Mortals bent to *our* whims—when we could act on them—not us to theirs. One rare example who was offered something unexpected didn't change the way our worlds worked.

None of us should be spending more than the bare minimum of time admiring her assets. Any of them.

We needed to make more progress in our search. The past day had turned up nothing productive except the stiffening of my groin while I'd examined Quinn's lithe body with my tentacle yesterday. The sooner we knew the full picture, the sooner I'd be ready to hand her over to the boss.

Then it wouldn't matter how smart or considerate or pretty she was. The increasingly loud internal voice that wanted to debate my decisions could shut up, and everything could go back to how I knew it actually was.

Quinn and the others headed up to the rooftop deck. As their muffled voices faded away completely, I pulled out my phone and dialed Goldie's number.

"Twice in as many days," my old friend teased when he picked up. "Lucky me. I trust both vehicles met your specifications."

"They're perfect," I said. "Thank you. I knew I could count on you. There's one more thing I need, but it'll only take a little of your time, nothing else. I can always add to your stash of gold if you want me to."

Goldie scoffed. "I'm not going to nickel and dime someone I go so far back with, Torrent. Repay me by not being so much of a stranger from now on. What is it?"

"I'd like to know if you've noticed or heard about any unusual surges in shadowkind activity in Florida. Or any unusual incidents in the area involving shadowkind."

The leprechaun hummed to himself. I didn't figure he'd have heard anything from Jacksonville, considering there wouldn't have been much in the way of witnesses to any of the attacks there or in the area, but who knew what else Quinn's predators had been getting up to.

"There has been a sort of uneasy vibe in the local community lately," he said. "I couldn't point to any specific source, just a feeling that I get of beings on edge or stirred up. And come to think of it, I've noticed more activity than usual at the local rifts—not a *lot* more, but definitely a higher influx than I'd typically see around here."

"More beings arriving from the shadow realm?" I clarified.

"Yeah. Not sure what that's about, though, so sorry I can't help more. As for incidents, I don't think— Hmm. How far back do you mean by recently?"

"What's the most recent incident you can think of?" I said dryly.

Goldie drew in a breath with a slight hiss through his teeth. "Well, it was a few months ago... Four or five. There was a bit of a commotion in the community about a major sorcerer family that got murdered by shadowkind just outside of Miami. No one was totally sure who did it, only that it'd been some very badass mofos. Before it happened, I hadn't even known the sorcerers were *there*, so I couldn't tell you more than that."

"Good riddance," I muttered automatically, but the information didn't help me all that much. Sorcerers enslaved shadowkind and bent them to their will—as much as the limited human magic they were able to tap into allowed—so I was never going to be sad to hear any of them had left this world. But I didn't see how that attack could relate to the ones on Quinn.

She obviously had no associations with sorcery or others who practiced it. She hadn't even known shadowkind existed until the other night. We'd seen no signs of anything remotely resembling magical practice while we'd watched her for the three months before we'd had to reveal ourselves.

At most, there could be a tenuous connection in that shadowkind might have started roaming the state more freely once that family was out of the picture, meaning more potential attackers had been around when they'd noticed Quinn's odd aura.

"That's it?" I asked.

"That's all I can think of," Goldie replied. "But you know me. I mostly deal in concrete goods, not information. If I can't test my teeth on it, it's not worth much to me." He guffawed.

"I appreciate it all the same," I said. "And I'm sorry for the long silence. I got wrapped up in some things that took me pretty far from my usual habits."

Goldie snorted. "Tell me about it. And really, *tell* me about it. What in the realms have you been up to all this time, man? It's been, what, seven decades? Eight?"

Seventy-three years, to be exact, but I didn't want him to know how closely I kept track. "Something like that. It's complicated and boring—believe me, nothing you could sink your teeth into."

"Oh, come on. I know you've got to have a few stories in you. I can't believe Mr. Party Hard lost his wild side completely."

No, I hadn't lost it. You could more say it'd been torn from me against my will.

Goldie went on before I could answer. "Remember that party out in Boston at the turn of the century? You were so high you went through five girls without breaking a sweat. *I* was so high I dropped all the trinkets I'd lifted from the mortal crowd off the fucking pier. But then I managed to convince a mermaid to take me for a very enjoyable swim, so it all worked out. Man, I haven't had a time like that in a while."

I did remember that party, vaguely and with an uncomfortable prickling over my skin at how blurred the memory was... like so many of my memories from the first several centuries of my life. "It was quite a night."

"Aw, come on, Torrent. That's the best you can say about it?" The leprechaun clucked his tongue. "I'm starting to think someone gave you a personality transplant. Who'm I really talking to here, and what have you done with my real friend?"

"Hey," I said. "It's been a long time. I found new pastimes to enjoy. But if you hear about another party like that one, drop me a line and we'll recreate a little history."

I didn't actually mean that—I just wanted to stop his line of conversation. But as his words sank in, the wheels in my head started spinning.

Goldie laughed and said he'd be in touch, and I barely paid attention to my parting remarks. I set down the phone, checked that there weren't any obstacles in sight, and engaged the autopilot. Then I headed up to the rooftop deck.

It would have been easier to climb the stairs if I'd traveled through the shadows, but something about Goldie's remarks had woken up a renewed stubbornness inside me. I gritted my teeth, gripped the railing beside the steps, and forced my damaged legs to carry me up as my tentacles braced my weight. The ache throbbed deeper, but I endured it.

Lance had opened the awning that shaded most of the deck and was leaping back and forth between it and the railings, showing off his much more impressive balance. Because of course he was. Crag hadn't allowed himself the luxury of the padded lounge chairs, instead sitting poised on one of the storage compartments, scanning the horizon for trouble as always. He gave me a quick nod when I reached the deck and went back to his surveying.

Quinn was typing something on her laptop, sprawled on one of the loungers. As I sat down on the chair next to her, the pain easing again with my weight off my legs, she clicked a button that created the whooshing sound of a sent email and glanced over at me.

"What's next?" she asked before I even had to bring up the subject. "I know the idea is that we rest during the day out here on the water where it's safer, but what are we going to do tonight?"

She wanted answers just as much as we did—maybe even more. I couldn't suppress the flicker of admiration that passed through my chest as I looked back into her bright but determined gaze.

She was mortal, but I could admit I hadn't met any quite like her before. Had Rollick meant he literally wanted to devour her? It seemed like a waste.

But why should I pity some random mortal woman I hadn't known just a few months ago? I'd survived this long despite my infirmities because I looked out for myself first, the small number of other beings I trusted a distant second, and everyone else not at all. I was done with chasing fleeting highs and bodily indulgences that could distract you into your doom.

Most of the time, I didn't even miss them. At least not enough that I allowed myself to notice.

"I had a new idea about that," I said, adjusting my tentacles around my frame. "There's one major factor we haven't investigated yet—the origins of your borrowed heart."

I motioned to her chest, and her eyebrows rose. That factor should have occurred to me earlier, but the idea of transplanting a significant piece of one body into another was so foreign to shadowkind practices that the full nuances of the scenario, the fact that a key part of her had once belonged to an entirely separate human being, hadn't really sunk in until Goldie had made his wheedling remarks.

"You think my new heart has something to do with it?" Quinn said. "You didn't mention sensing anything about it in particular yesterday."

"I didn't, but it would fit with the impressions I did get—the energy concentrated in your chest but spread through your body, which could be via your blood. There's no reason to assume it's definitely related to your 'specialness,' though, other than the fact that none of the other possibilities we've checked out have gotten us anywhere."

She smiled at me with a warm familiarity that sent an unwanted hitch through my pulse. "And you believe in considering every possibility."

My lips started to curl in a responding smile before I caught them. I dropped my gaze and then forced it to meet hers again—but it was already too late. Her face had fallen slightly with a shadow of concern. She'd picked up on my discomfort even if I didn't think she could possibly guess at its source.

Although, she had figured out an awful lot about me that I hadn't anticipated already, hadn't she?

That was what made part of me shout so loudly to stand between her and anyone who came at her, regardless of my loyalties. She wasn't just a superficial indulgence, a morsel that would evaporate the moment I partook. With every conversation we had, I couldn't shake the growing sense that she *saw* me. Saw things about me I'd kept tightly under wraps. Things no other being around me had been able to recognize.

It unnerved me, but at the same time, the urge gripped me to let more spill out. To solidify the connection. To revel in the poignant ache that suggested I wasn't cut off from the life I'd have wanted after all.

That maybe I didn't have to be alone in every way that really mattered.

I clenched my jaw, shoving the errant longing down as far as I could. Who was I kidding? I knew my place in this world and how I'd gotten here, and imagining anything else was pointless.

My voice came out curter than I'd intended. "Do you know anything about the other human your heart came from?"

Quinn didn't react to my tone. She sat up straighter, tucking her legs in front of her on the lounger. Her expression turned pensive.

"I do, actually. It was a girl around the same age as me—she had some kind of fatal accident. I wrote a letter to the family a little while after the transplant, thanking them for letting her heart be donated. You want us to go visit them?"

"We can at least take a look around and see if there's anything unusual about their situation. If you mailed a letter to them, I assume you know where they live?"

"They're in Florida," she said. "I'm not sure how close to Jacksonville. I sent it through the hospital—privacy reasons and stuff. But the hospital will have the family's name and the address somewhere in their records, I'm sure."

I allowed a smile then, somehow feeling my heart lift with relief even as my stomach sank with a vague sense of dread, both at the knowledge that we might be reaching the end of our journey. "All right. Then tonight I'll sneak back into the hospital and find out where we're off to next."

CHAPTER NINETEEN

Quinn

I'd never realized how difficult it could be to sleep while the sun was still up, especially blazing away in all its midday glory. Even with the blinds pulled down over the narrow windows in the bedroom area of the boat, an emphatic glow seeped around the edges. And plenty more spilled down the steps from the higher area with the sofa and captain's seat.

I sprawled on my stomach, my side, my back, and then my stomach again with my face buried in the pillow. I counted sheep and ran through the relaxing meditations I'd learned to help keep my stress levels down—fat chance of that right now!—and still felt not the least bit on the verge of sleep. Finally, I flopped onto my back once more with a thump of my arms against the mattress and a frustrated huff, my eyes popping open to glare at the ceiling.

In an instant, all three of the shadowkind men flickered out of the patches of darkness around the room to peer at me. "Are you all right?" Crag demanded, his gaze roving over the entire space with fearsome intensity, as if he thought some beast might have snuck in here and assaulted me without leaving any visible evidence.

"Maybe we need to chase away nightmares," Lance said with a chuckle.

I sat up, embarrassed and annoyed that I was embarrassed. "No nightmares. I can't get to sleep, that's all. But I don't want to be exhausted for tonight's road trip."

Torrent's eyebrows arched slightly. "I don't think bullying sleep into arriving has ever worked out well for anyone."

I resisted the urge to stick my tongue out at him. "No kidding. I don't know what else to do." I rubbed my eyes. I wasn't exactly brimming with energy either. I just couldn't completely unwind so that I'd drift off.

Lance sprang onto the mattress and crouched next to me. He teased his claws over my calf, gently enough that he didn't break the threads of the sheet draped over my legs. "Maybe you need a little physical exertion to tire you out, baby girl. We could manage that without you even leaving the bed."

He lifted his hand to hook his claws around the edge of the sheet and tug it off, and my pulse skipped with a rush of giddy heat. But the flush that raced across my cheeks wasn't only because of the suggestiveness of the dragon shifter's remark.

"Er, we're not alone here," I said, in case Lance had forgotten. Which with his periodic single-mindedness did seem possible.

"The more the merrier," he declared, leaning in to nuzzle my neck. "I bet you'd enjoy them too."

"Um," I said ever so articulately, my face blazing even hotter. It wasn't as if I hadn't had those sorts of thoughts about both of the other men in the past couple of days. But did I really want to put all my imaginings into reality in one go?

It didn't just depend on what *I* wanted, of course.

Before I could even catch his eyes, Torrent swiveled away from us, his posture even more rigid than usual. His voice came out equally stiff. "I'll leave you to it." He vanished an instant later.

Crag had tensed too, his eyes widening—but he hadn't taken off in apparent disgust. He studied me with an unreadable expression and then backed up a step. "I wouldn't want to presume..."

A brief but fiery light flashed in his eyes, and my throat went dry. Had that been desire?

The thought of him turning away too, of believing I wasn't at least as interested as he was, made my chest constrict. My heart thumped so hard it took me a second before I could focus on finding the right words. They tumbled out of my mouth.

"You could stay. If you—if you'd like to."

He paused, his gaze searching but the ruddy gleam reappearing. "*You* would like me to?"

I wet my lips, struggling to sort out my tangled feelings. Remembering the moments I'd been pressed against his brawny form, when I'd imagined how his powerful hands would feel moving over my body in more intimate ways.

Was this crazy? I'd never hooked up with two men at the same time before, let alone two monsters. But there wasn't any reason *not* to, was there? It was another experience, another chance to squeeze every pleasure I could out of this life.

And really, I trusted Crag even more than I did Lance. A lot of the time I couldn't tell what was really going on with the dragon shifter behind all his jokes and antics. The gargoyle seemed to be exactly who he presented himself as. He was the first to leap to my defense in an attack. As far as I could tell, right now he was most concerned about overstepping *my* boundaries, not his own feelings.

"I think Lance is right," I said, earning an approving chuckle from the dragon shifter as he nicked his emerged fangs against my shoulder. I sucked in a gasp and did my best to stay focused on Crag. "I think I might enjoy it a lot. If you would too. I don't know—I realize shadowkind don't necessarily indulge in this kind of thing..." Lance had been a virgin. Had Crag ever had sex?

Crag appeared to pick up on my unspoken question. He shifted his substantial weight from one foot to the other. "Many of us do," he said gruffly. "I haven't with— Because of my size and my looks—" He motioned to his rocky jaw. "I've only had occasional encounters with shadowkind women. I'm not very practiced."

Lance snorted, propelling a wash of heat over my neck. "I had no practice at all. Our mortal is good at showing what she likes."

Crag hesitated again, and my resolve solidified. I held out my hand to him. "Come here."

He moved the second I beckoned him, making it even clearer that his concern for me had been the only thing holding him back. The mattress dipped with a faint squeak at his weight. He sank down at my other side, his gaze fixed on my face.

I lifted my hand and cupped his jaw. As my fingers explored the only currently monstrous part of his body, he held perfectly still.

The stone surface of his jaw was as warm as skin—like all of him was in his gargoyle form. It felt less pliant to the touch than regular flesh but still had a little give that stopped it from feeling totally inorganic.

I traced the line where it merged with his bronze-brown skin below his cheekbone and then skimmed a fingertip across his lower lip, which was smooth but firm like polished marble. A sudden, searing desire unfurled low in my belly.

"Can I kiss you?" I murmured.

Crag let out a rough sound, and then *he* was kissing me, his thick fingers tangling in my hair as he gripped the side of my face. The contrast of the harder lip below with the softer one above, both of them growing hotter by the second, set off a quiver of delight right between my legs. The bulk of him looming over me overwhelmed me, shocking the breath from my lungs, but I couldn't say I found it unpleasant.

Lance laughed and grazed the tips of his claws up and down my bared legs from my ankles all the way to the hem of my shorts. I had to resist the urge to squirm at the tingling pleasure his dangerous touch provoked. If he stabbed me, it'd be *my* fault, not his lack of care.

Crag rumbled more emphatically and tucked his other arm right around me, enveloping me with his brawn and solid warmth from the waist up. His mouth pressed harder against mine, not as artful as Lance's kisses had quickly become but with a passionate intensity that electrified me. I flicked my tongue between his lips experimentally, and he parted them to allow me entrance.

"She likes the shadowkind bits coming out to play," Lance advised. "I've seen your gargoyle tongue—it could be a lot of fun."

He reached for my shorts at the same moment, and I eased away from Crag long enough to halt the dragon shifter before his claws severed the fabric. "These are my clothes from home," I chided him. "I don't want them in shreds too. As much fun as *that* is."

Lance's violet eyes glittered with mischief. "Fine, fine. We'll get extras for plenty of shredding next time."

The way he said that sentence really shouldn't have sounded so sexy. I tugged off my shorts, knowing my panties were now damp—and they became absolutely drenched when Crag helped me slide the shorts over my feet.

He slid his palm up my leg, over my knee, and down my thigh like Lance had with his claws, watching my expression intently the entire time. His massive hand engulfed my leg, putting my muscles honed by urban exploring and rock-climbing at the university outdoor recreation center to shame. When he reached my hip, he paused.

"If I use too much pressure or if anything hurts, tell me," he said.

"Of course. It's all felt very good so far," I assured him. Then, with a spark of boldness, I set my hand over his and guided it over to the spot where I was aching most.

When Crag's fingers prodded my sex, I couldn't hold back a gasp. A growl escaped him as he stroked my panties, feeling how wet the two of them had already made me.

I arched into the gargoyle's touch, and Lance captured me in a kiss. The dragon shifter dipped his ridged tongue between my lips to twine with mine, caressing my other leg with his claws. I moaned into his mouth.

"So soft and tender but so much strength," Crag rumbled. He bent his head toward my shoulder. He must have taken Lance's advice, because a tongue that felt twice as long as any I'd encountered before slicked along the crook of my neck, provoking a tremor of bliss. His solid fingers continued to massage my clit and the folds beneath like he was going to mold them into the perfect orgasm.

I was totally okay with that.

Lance had additional ambitions. "I think this shirt needs to come off too, baby girl," he murmured by my ear, giving me a chance to handle it before he brought his claws to bear. I tugged the tee off, and Lance unsnapped my bra with a deft twist of his finger. He nudged me down on my back and grinned at Crag. "Dig in."

Lance swiveled his claws over the peak of one breast while the gargoyle's eyes shimmered starker red. Crag leaned down and swiped his tongue, which had turned several inches long and gray but not at all stony, over my other nipple. His firm hand kept up its massage between my legs. Pleasure rippled through my chest and flared across my nerves. As a whimper spilled out of me, I bucked with the movements of his fingers.

Crag bent to twine his tongue all the way around my nipple, and Lance teased the other with tiny pinpricks of pain that had me gasping all over again. I'd thought hooking up with just the dragon shifter was amazing—I hadn't known sex could get even *that* amazing—but this was some completely new level of heaven right here.

I was starting to pant, heat surging in faster and more urgent pulses from my pussy with each stroke of Crag's hand. I could feel myself rushing toward the edge, but suddenly this wasn't how I wanted to go. I needed one of these men right inside me.

Maybe both of them.

That thought came with an even headier thrill. I tugged at my panties, and Crag gave me room to strip them off. Before he could continue his passionate attentions, I glanced at him and Lance. "I shouldn't be the only one naked here."

If I was going to have a threesome with a couple of monstrous men, I wanted all the goods on display, thank you very much.

Lance performed the same trick as before, blinking out of and back into view while leaving his clothing behind in the shadows, however that worked. Crag watched the dragon shifter's example and then copied it, lingering a few seconds longer in the darkness before he returned.

The sculpted muscles bulging across the gargoyle's limbs and chest stood out even more impressively without their coverings, but I couldn't stop my gaze from shooting to the spot between his legs. He was already erect—and oh, boy, was there a lot of him. Both thick and long, jutting from between his immense thighs. Lance was at least approximately regular human-sized. Imagine what Crag would sport in his even larger gargoyle form.

The image would have melted my panties again if I'd still had them on, but Crag stayed standing beside the bed almost warily. Was he worried I'd be intimidated—that he'd be too much for me?

An impulse gripped me, and I followed it. I crawled across the bed and closed my mouth around the head of his stunning cock. What better way to show that I was completely on board, after all?

I could barely fit my mouth around the head, getting nowhere near the rest of his length, but Crag gave a stuttered groan and grasped my hair. "Quinn," he muttered, and then something inarticulate that conveyed his appreciation better than any words might have.

I wrapped my fingers around his shaft and gave myself over to the act, swiveling my tongue around the head, tilting to slick it along the underside of his cock, pumping him firmly but slowly. His grip on my hair tightened, provoking just the tiniest jolts of pain in my scalp that I welcomed wholeheartedly.

As I worked Crag over, Lance knelt behind me. At the brush of a claw over my clit, my breath stuttered over Crag's erection. Lance chuckled and repeated the gesture, caressing my hip with his other hand.

"I think I should get you warmed up for this giant hunk of rock," he said playfully. "You like my dragon claws and fangs and tongue—how about the dragon cock?"

Before I could ask what he meant—and anyway, my mouth was full—a rigid length pressed against my slit. As Lance sank into my slick opening, I understood what he'd meant. The head of his transformed cock bulged noticeably wider than before, stretching me until I gasped. As he started to pump in and out, the expanded head stroked against my channel with the most amazing sensation, as if he were curling multiple fingers into the most sensitive part inside me over and over again.

Oh, hell. I whimpered and panted over Crag's cock, squeezing it and lapping at the head with the limited concentration I had left. The most ecstatic burn I'd ever experienced expanded through my body.

Lance pounded into me without restraint, his own breath turning joyfully ragged. He clutched my thighs, his claws only just nicking the skin, and propelled himself even faster. Even more pleasure blazed through my nerves, and I unraveled.

I cried out, glad that we were out at sea dozens of miles from any fellow humans who could have heard me. My body clenched and shook, and Lance roared his own release. The bliss surged through me in a tidal wave and left me with my head pressed against Crag's taut abdomen, still quivering.

The gargoyle caressed my hair, his breath coming roughly. Before I could pull myself together enough to finish what I'd started, Lance was flipping me around.

I found myself sprawled on my back again, with my legs dangling over the side of the bed in front of Crag. The dragon shifter nuzzled my temple and flicked his claws over my breasts.

"Kneel down, and you'll be just the right height to fill her," he said to his friend, and swiped his ridged tongue across my earlobe. "If you're ready to explore even more, baby girl."

God, how could I say no? I managed to nod, scooting even closer to Crag. His eyes outright smoldered as he got to his knees as Lance suggested, which did bring his cock almost perfectly aligned with my sex.

He eased my legs apart and moved between them, but then he simply bent over me to recapture my lips. He kissed me long and hard, with a growl reverberating through his chest. I slid my fingers over the sheen of his hair and down his corded neck.

"*My* Softness," he rumbled against my lips, the new nickname sounding far more fervent than the old one ever had. Drawing up a little, he rubbed his cock over my pussy.

We both groaned at the sensation, mine extending into a longer moan when Lance nibbled on my shoulder. I spread my legs even wider.

Crag eased into me one inch at a time. Even after Lance's expanded cock had stretched me, the gargoyle's girth brought a fresh burn. But it was a giddy heat, one that sent shivers of pleasure all through my body from my hips. I'd swear everything from the tips of my toes to the crest of my scalp tingled with it.

Crag palmed my breasts as he sank deeper, rotating the heels of his hands against my nipples. The sparks of delight relaxed me even more into the pressure building inside me. I gasped and started to rock into him, urging him on. With a breathless grunt, he pushed forward the last few inches.

I'd never felt so full, and it was the most searingly heady sensation I could imagine. I made a choked sound, bucking up to meet him. "Yes. Just like that. It's *really* good. Don't stop."

From the ragged snarl that escaped Crag next, I wasn't sure how easily he could have if I had wanted him to. He thrust into me with increasing power, his breath quickening. My body quaked, rising with each pulse of his cock inside me. I was splitting apart and melting together in a puddle of ecstasy all at once.

Lance was still there with us, punctuating the maelstrom of bliss with nicks of his claws and grazes of his fangs. "Oh, what a pretty picture you make," he murmured.

I moaned and bucked and clutched at Crag's forearms where he'd now braced them on either side of me. He pounded into me harder, deeper, claiming every empty place inside me, and I kept flying, higher, higher—

Lance reached down to swivel his knuckle over my clit, and I exploded, a keening I barely recognized as my own voice echoing through the yacht's bedroom. Crag drove into me again, and bowed over me as he followed me into release. Heat flooded my sex.

For several seconds, I couldn't move one fragment of my body. My bones had dissolved; I was nothing but putty in these monstrous men's hands.

Crag pulled out of me and lifted me farther onto the bed with surprising gentleness. "You are—all right?" he asked haltingly, looking abruptly apprehensive.

A giggle spilled out of me. I grasped his arm again and beamed up at him. "Very, very all right. We can do that again any time you want. Well, not right now. I'm not sure I'd survive a third orgasm like that in a row."

I squeezed Lance's thigh and grinned giddily at him too so he wouldn't feel left out of the compliment. I couldn't seem to do much more than that. My eyelids were drifting shut. That whole physical exertion thing seemed to have done the trick just as Lance had suggested.

The two men tucked the sheet over me. Lance might have left again, but Crag's weight remained on the bed beside me until I slipped completely into sleep.

CHAPTER TWENTY

Quinn

When the sign showing it was just 25 more miles until Miami flashed in the headlights of the sedan, I let out a whoop of approval. "Finally! We should have just stayed here in the first place."

I could feel Torrent's glower from his tone even if he couldn't look at me from behind the wheel. "We didn't know we'd be coming back to Miami then. And we did need to pick up your things from your house."

I let out a huff, but I couldn't really complain. He'd been doing all the driving as well as all the preliminary running around. After explaining to Crag in painstaking detail how to drive the boat, he'd slipped away and... I guessed swum? Over to shore a couple of hours ahead of us so he could zip over to Jacksonville and get his hands on those transplant records. He'd re-emerged on the yacht just a few minutes after Crag had brought us to a stop within view of the marina.

It turned out that my donor had lived off the beaten track beyond the outskirts of Miami. A few minutes after we'd spotted the sign, Torrent pulled off onto a smaller highway that would lead us west of the cities that sprawled along the Atlantic coast rather than right into them. He motioned for Crag, who'd taken the front seat this time, to show him the directions he'd written down.

The lights of civilization fell away, leaving us cruising through darkness broken only by occasional lamp posts along the road. The sole sound was a periodic crunching noise as Crag munched on a hunk of quartz he'd grabbed along with our more typical dinner. He'd explained that the minerals helped keep his strength up in physical form.

I couldn't say listening to a gargoyle literally eating rocks was the most comforting sound. It did give me something else to focus on when one of those flutters whirled between my ribs. I'd had a few stronger ones, the beating-bird-wings type, since I'd woken up.

Beyond the windows, fields gave way to looming trees. In the night, they looked as monstrous as some of the deadly creatures I'd encountered. I restrained a shudder.

"You shouldn't be scared of the dark after how much fun you've had with shadows," Lance teased from beside me, grazing a claw up my arm.

I made a face at him. "A little fun and a lot of running for my life. I do appreciate the former, but I'm still not super happy about the latter."

He shrugged. "It's all an adventure. Skewer a beastie. Romp in bed. Chow down on some breakfast. As long as you don't die, what's there to worry about?"

"The fact that I've come awfully close to dying at least once," I said dryly, and gave him a light kick in the shin. "Don't worry. I don't mean any criticism of your extensive abilities at adventuring."

He smirked at me. "I know. That's your favorite part."

I couldn't even argue with him. With another huff, I leaned against the window, hugging the messenger bag I'd brought along on my lap and peering at the silhouetted shapes streaming past the window.

At least the most predictable threat to my life was under control now. I'd restocked my weekly pill case before we disembarked, and there were plenty more in the prescription bottles I'd left behind on the yacht.

With each turn we took, the roads got narrower and bumpier. The trees pulled closer. The chirping of insect life started to penetrate the windows, almost as loud as the racket they'd made in the swamp.

There probably was a swamp around here somewhere. You didn't get much wilderness in Florida without bog water in the mix.

Torrent pulled over briefly to study his notes and a map on his phone in more detail, and then drove on even slower than before. There was no way we were making it back to the yacht before sunrise, but I guessed it didn't matter as long as we were on the move one way or another.

Finally, he turned onto a lane so narrow the vegetation hissed over the side of the car in places. I jostled in my seat as we thumped over a pothole. Just a minute or so down it, he parked where the shoulder got wider for a short stretch. Not that blocking the road was likely to have been much of a problem when it didn't look like people drove down here often... or maybe even ever.

"I'll take a look on my own from the shadows," he said. "You two stay with Quinn for now."

He wavered away before any of us could answer. Lance stretched out his lean legs between the seats and raised his hand to carve a few intersecting lines into the ceiling. I really hoped Goldie wasn't hoping on getting back the vehicles he'd handed over—or at least not in the same condition they'd been in to start with.

"Why do you do that?" I asked Lance with a sudden itch of curiosity.

He shrugged, adding more details to his abstract design. "Who needs reasons? I like how it looks. It feels good on my claws. Also good practice for the other uses I might put them to—knowing how much pressure gives what results." He flashed another smile at me.

I tapped him with my foot again. "I hope you're not planning on carving me up."

"Only as much as *you* like it," he teased.

Crag made a rumbling sound and opened his mouth to speak, but just then Torrent blinked into being in the driver's seat. He hadn't usually conducted his investigations that quickly.

As I knit my brow, about to ask what was up, he motioned to the other men. "Come with me. There are no beings around. She'll be fine for a few minutes."

His voice was even but terse, what I could see of his expression tense. I leaned forward, going on the alert. "What did you find?"

His gaze flicked toward me for no more than an instant. "Don't worry about it. Stay here." Then he and the other two vanished.

"Of course I'm going to worry about it," I snapped at the shadows they'd disappeared into. "Come back and tell me what's wrong. We're supposed to be working on this together."

No one re-emerged. I didn't know if they'd even heard me. They'd probably already slunk off to make their own investigations while leaving me in the dark, literally this time.

Apparently I was good enough for hooking up with but not for being let in on our mission to find out why I'd become a monster beacon, even though *I* was the only one here actually affected by it.

Torrent had said there weren't any other shadowkind nearby. I hesitated for just a second and then pushed the door open, digging my phone out of my bag and switching on its flashlight. If they weren't going to explain, then I'd just have to go with them whether they liked it or not.

I marched along the overgrown drive for several minutes. The thin beam of artificial light turned the shadows of the trees into deformed giants. My heart beat faster with each step. Every rustle in the trees made my nerves jump.

When Torrent appeared out of nowhere right in front of me, his tentacles braced beside him, I had to clap my hand over my mouth to stop myself from shrieking.

"What are you doing?" he demanded in a low, curt voice.

"This is my problem," I shot back in a firm whisper, casting the phone's beam toward the ground. It lit him with a hazy yellowish glow. "We're here *because* of me. You said there's nothing dangerous. I want to know what you saw that bothered you, that you needed Lance and Crag to check out."

He scowled at me. "We can check it out a lot faster without you tramping around."

Something in my chest plummeted at those words. Torrent had rarely been outright *friendly* with me, but I'd thought we'd at least reached a state of some kind of mutual respect. He'd understood my frustrations enough to bring me my laptop unprompted. He'd been awfully considerate about his examination of me.

But when it came down to the most important thing, the question of what was happening inside my own body that was threatening my life more than my health problems ever had, he didn't think I had a right to be a part of it.

I sucked in a breath, annoyed by the burn of tears that prickled at the back of my eyes, and kept my voice as steady as I could. "I know I'm not as strong or fast or whatever else as the three of you. I know I'm just some fragile mortal to you. But I'm doing my best. I don't think I've done that badly considering I had no idea beings like you even existed until a week ago."

"Quinn," Torrent interrupted with a clench of his jaw, his expression fragmented by shadows.

I didn't let him stop me. "Look, when you need me out of the way for my own protection, that's fine. I get it. I just don't want to be treated like I'm not a part of this situation. The main part. It's *my* life, my... specialness. I'm the one those things are trying to kill or kidnap or whatever. I need to know what's going on—all of it. And if insisting on that is what gets me killed, then oh well. It'll be my fault."

I heard Torrent swallow. "I'm sorry," he said abruptly, the apology startling me. "I know you can handle a lot. You might as well come—just be quick about it. It's about a quarter mile farther. I'll meet you at the house."

"Do I have to worry about anyone seeing me?" I asked before he could vanish in the darkness.

He shook his head, his mouth twisting. "There's no one there."

What?

He melded with the shadows before I could ask him anything else. I set off at a faster pace, raising my feet high the way I'd learned to when hustling through abandoned buildings and tunnels where I couldn't be sure what might be strewn across the ground. There wasn't much on the dirt lane other than twigs and tufts of weeds anyway.

Maybe five minutes later, the trees fell back ahead of me. I emerged into a clearing that held a sprawling bungalow, its walls a mix of wood and stucco. Tall windows glinted with the reflected glow of my light next to the front door; a few tiny ones ran along the side.

Across from the house, there was... a heap of rubble?

It took a few seconds for my mind to process what I was seeing in the eerie darkness. The jumble of wooden chunks, broken shingles, and mangled metal had probably been a garage. A garage that'd been battered nearly beyond recognition, along with one or more vehicles inside. A grimy strip of yellow caution tape lay on the well-trodden earth in front of it, torn from wherever it'd been attached before.

That was one construction failure the multitool in my pocket wasn't going to fix. Holy shit.

All three of the men materialized around me. "Someone had a big temper tantrum," Lance remarked, but his lilting tone didn't sound quite as playful as it usually did.

"What happened?" I spun toward Torrent. "You said no one's here?"

He motioned for me to follow him.

As we reached the door to the house, I spotted another ragged piece of caution tape that'd stuck to the base of the wall. From its position, I guessed it'd used to be stretched across the door. Whatever had happened here, it looked like the police had investigated it quite a while ago.

Crag pushed the door open and hesitated on the threshold, blocking me. "You might not like this," he said gruffly.

"I already don't like it," I muttered. "But I think I'd better see it all anyway."

As I stepped inside, I immediately found something else not to like: the smell. A sour, rotten stench hung in the air. Torrent left the door open after we'd all stepped inside, but the sluggish current of the breeze did little to displace the stink.

There was a living room immediately in front of us: sofa and chairs, a shattered coffee table, a framed picture that'd fallen off the wall. Deep gouges marked one of the armchairs, the stuffing spilling out. A chill rippled over my skin.

We walked on through a dining room and kitchen, around a corner into a hall—and there, I stalled in my tracks. My flashlight beam caught on dark splotches on the hardwood floor. From the thickened sour smell, it was hard to imagine they were anything other than blood stains.

Bile rose in the back of my throat. I wrapped my free arm around my chest, hugging myself. "What *happened* here?"

Torrent and Crag exchanged a glance. Lance was swaying from side to side on his feet, clicking his claws together, looking like he was gearing up to shred the whole place to pieces.

"I talked to Goldie today," Torrent said. "He told me that earlier in the year, some shadowkind slaughtered a family of powerful sorcerers who were living near Miami." He tipped his head toward pale markings on the floor near one of the bloodstains. "That's the start of a chalk circle. And in here..."

He led us to a large room down the hall that held a broad wooden desk and shelves full of books and other paraphernalia. My light caught on candlesticks, carved daggers and broaches, sealed jars, and wooden boxes etched with unfamiliar occult-looking symbols. The chill inside me deepened despite the mugginess of the air.

"Sorcerers," I repeated. "You mentioned those before—that's humans who've learned how to use some kind of magic on shadowkind, right?"

Torrent nodded. "Sorcerers can capture beings already in the mortal realm—or, with enough power, draw them straight from the shadow realm—and force them to do their bidding. So you can understand why we wouldn't be all that keen on them. Most likely a few beings they enslaved broke free and turned on their attempted masters. I've heard of that happening before. There's a poetic justice to it."

I walked over to the shelves, giving the items there a closer inspection. "What's all this for? How does it even work?"

"I don't know," Torrent said, his voice sharpening. "They don't exactly hold public forums on their practices."

I made a face at him and picked up one of the daggers, wiping away the thin layer of dust. Metal bands inlaid its wooden handle. When I eased it out of the leather sheath, the blade gleamed with a vicious edge. It'd be a step up from my multitool's knife.

I hesitated, glancing back toward the men, who'd stayed by the doorway. Whoever had owned this was long dead, but no inheritors had come to collect it. These people might have been enemies to the shadowkind, but a whole lot of shadowkind had made themselves *my* enemies. Torrent's attempt at keeping me away earlier only proved that I needed to be more resourceful in defending myself. He needed to believe I could stand on my own.

"Is there any reason I shouldn't take this?" I asked. "It doesn't have any, like, spells on it or something, does it?"

Lance twitched. "Just don't stick it into any of us," he said in that same teasing but strangely tight tone.

"Of course not."

Crag cleared his throat. "It'd do us more damage than a regular blade. It's silver and iron. They're both toxic to shadowkind."

"Oh!" I stared down at the blade. Then I looked at the three men again. "You didn't tell me that before. I could have gotten something made out of silver and iron to fend off the creatures that attacked me back at the cabin."

"Forgive us for not wanting to arm you with a weapon equally deadly against us," Torrent said tersely. "Go ahead. Take it. It might be useful to you in another attack." He turned toward the hall.

I shoved the knife into my shorts, thankful that I'd picked all my clothes to have deep pockets for collecting anything of interest during my urban explorations. Only a bit of the hilt protruded by my hip.

Then a wave of bewilderment washed over me. The carnage in the home had distracted me from our original purpose for coming here.

"*This* was the address listed for my organ donor?" I said. "Was there a mistake? Or these sorcerer people moved in later?" It had been nine years.

"I don't think so." Torrent moved across the hall, the other men flanking him, and I hurried after them. I found myself in a small room that held nothing but a mahogany side table with what appeared to be memorabilia placed all across its surface. There was a beaded bracelet, a bronzed baby shoe, a scruffy teddy bear... a framed photo of a girl with long blond hair who looked maybe ten or eleven.

My lungs constricted. It looked like a shrine. Like a memorial to someone who'd passed away. Like a family might make for a child who'd—

I shied away from finishing that thought, but the implications sank in anyway. I pressed my hand to my chest.

My heart—my borrowed heart—pounded away against my palm.

I swallowed thickly. "My new heart... It came from the sorcerers' daughter? Is *that* why the monsters are after me? They don't want any piece of them left?"

"That seems like a reasonable theory," Torrent said stiffly.

"But—I'm not—*I'm* not a sorcerer. I have no idea—" I cut myself off, thinking of the ripples of energy that kept forming in my chest. I had no idea how to wield any supernatural power, but had my new heart come with a magic of its own?

Something that alerted the shadowkind nearby. Something that gave them the impression I was a threat to them. Oh, God.

Crag drew in a rough breath, but before he could say anything, a noise made us all freeze: the thrum of an engine and the rasp of tires over the ground outside.

CHAPTER TWENTY-ONE

Quinn

The squeak of a brake filtered through the walls of the sorcerers' house. My gaze darted around the sort-of shrine room, but it had only a small square window set high in the wall—all I could see through the glass was darkness.

Should we make a run for it? Which way would we go? It didn't seem likely that shadowkind attackers would have approached in a human vehicle, but then, *my* shadowkind men clearly didn't have any trouble using mortal technology when it suited them. Maybe our enemies were upping their game.

"What should we do?" I murmured as quietly as I could manage.

Torrent jerked his hand toward the doorway, and he and Lance immediately vanished. Crag stayed with me, clamping his hand on my shoulder.

"We should move to where we could escape if necessary," he said brusquely, guiding me toward the hall. He had to duck to avoid braining his forehead on the doorframe. "It might only be mortal business, but they could get upset if they find you here."

"Whoever came would have seen our car when they squeezed past it on the lane," I pointed out. "They'll know *someone* is here."

My stomach knotted. What fresh hell were we facing now?

There was an abrupt thump and then a roar from outside. My pulse skittered. I lurched forward instinctively with the vague sense that I should be defending the men who'd gone ahead to defend *us*.

An oddly cheery female voice rang out, halting me as much as Crag's hand did. "I think we can resolve this peacefully. Just back off each other, and no one has to get charbroiled. Because if anyone's getting barbequed here, it'll definitely be you."

Crag growled low in his throat. He hesitated for a second, all his muscles tensed, looking torn between springing to his companions' aid and keeping me as far from the conflict as possible.

I pushed forward, helping him make the decision. As he barged after me, we came into view of one of the living room's broad windows.

An RV was parked outside the garage. A pretty unusual RV, with streamers dangling from its walls and a propeller spinning idly at its rear. Its headlights were still on, casting a hazy illumination over the figures gathered in the yard between it and the house.

Torrent had brought out two more tentacles—I hadn't realized he had a collection he was keeping in reserve. Two were bracing him as usual and the other two were waving back and forth like the hands of a kung fu master waiting to strike. He was staring down a man just as massive as Crag, with glowing red eyes and darkly feathered wings that proved he was a shadowkind too.

Lance had shifted into full dragon form, crouched on the ground with tension coiled through his body, ready to spring. His fangs were bared, his talons raking against the earth. Across from him loomed a dark dog-like shape, if dogs loomed as tall as the average human and had rivulets of searing orange winding through their fur.

In the middle of it all stood a woman with bright red hair pulled back in a ponytail, her athletic frame clothed in a black tee and sweats. As far as I could tell at a glance, she looked totally human, but she spoke to the shadowkind as if she saw them more as difficult children than monsters.

"That's it," she said in the same upbeat tone, holding out her hands in a peacemaking gesture. "Take a few steps back, put your human-y faces on, and let's see who we're dealing with, all right? We don't *want* to pulverize you."

She sounded awfully confident that they could pulverize my men if they changed their minds about wanting to. Her friends hadn't managed to overpower my protectors in the initial skirmish, though.

Seeing that the others weren't in immediate danger, Crag stopped where he was, grasping my shoulder again to hold me in place too. But a voice carried from somewhere beyond the view of my window, this one male but nearly as perky as the woman's.

"The other two from the car are inside, Sorsha—the one that tasted like stone and the human."

Tasted like stone? When had he *tasted* Crag? And how could he have known how many of us had been in the car?

The woman—Sorsha?—clapped her hands together and then made a beckoning gesture. "Come on out, whoever's hiding inside. We know there are four of you. We just want to find out what you're doing here."

"I don't see how that's any of your business," Torrent said flatly. "What are *you* doing here?"

Sorsha cast him a baleful glance. "Put away your tentacles, and we'll talk about it."

"And we're supposed to believe that after what happened to the people who lived in there?"

She wrinkled her nose in an expression of such disgust that I believed her next words without hesitation. "What? We didn't have anything to do with the sorcerers who got slaughtered. It's good to know that *you* didn't either. We're a little concerned about whoever did. That's why we've had this place monitored."

It didn't sound like they were here for me then, or because they'd been planning to ambush us specifically. But I wasn't sure if my men would stand down of their own accord. They did seem to lean toward violent solutions.

I set my hand over Crag's to give it a reassuring squeeze and tugged him toward the door. "Come on. I don't think they're the enemy. Which means they might be able to help us."

He made a discontented noise but stalked ahead of me, stepping into the doorway first as a shield. I peeked out through the small gap beside his arm.

"Hi," I said, figuring it was better if I spoke up rather than him. "I'm all for talking rather than having these guys tear into each other. We were just looking around—we didn't know what had happened here until we arrived. We thought the people living here had... something we needed." I didn't know how else to explain it.

Before anyone could answer, a tremor of the strange energy reverberated through my chest. I clutched Crag's arm instinctively as three pairs of eyes shot to me—not just the dog-like beast's and the scary angel's, but the woman's as well.

If she'd felt it, then she *wasn't* human, was she?

Another figure sprang into existence just a couple of feet from the doorway. The man, tall and slim, peered past Crag at me with wide green eyes beneath a tumble of golden curls. His human-like face was all youthful beauty until his tongue flicked across his lips and I saw it was forked.

"What was that?" he asked with what sounded more like curiosity than apprehension. "You're human, but there's something else about you."

"Um, yeah. That's kind of why we're here."

Sorsha knit her brow. "Interesting. I think you'd better tell us the whole story."

Crag cleared his throat. "We can't stay here for long. Other creatures are attracted to her energy. They've been tracking her. If they catch up with us, we'll have a bigger fight."

"Got it. Well, as long as you promise not to do any maiming, we could take a ride in the Everymobile while we chat." She jabbed her thumb over her shoulder at the RV.

"And why should we trust *you* enough to get into enclosed quarters with you?" Torrent asked.

Sorsha rolled her eyes at him. "You're pretty pathetic shadowkind if you can't hop out into the shadows whenever you feel like it."

"Quinn can't," Crag growled.

The redhead paused. She swiped her hand across her mouth and then offered us a crooked smile. "I don't suppose any of you heard about a big to-do about six years ago? A phoenix burning down a whole mass of shadowkind enemies before they could let loose something that would have destroyed both our realms? A whole bunch of other shadowkind rallying in support of her to stop the Highest from imposing sanctions?"

I had no idea what she was talking about, but Crag frowned. Torrent folded his arms over his chest, his tentacles still raised for battle. "What about it?"

Sorsha blinked. There was a whoosh of flame, and two fiery wings flared from her back. A wavering light danced in her eyes. "I didn't save all shadow and mortal kind just to go around incinerating random beings for poking around in strange places. If I wanted your woman dead, she'd be ashes already. So let's get on with the talking?"

The wings contracted as quickly as she'd extended them, and she looked like a perfectly normal woman again. My breath caught in my throat. Crag had gone totally rigid in front of me, and Torrent...

He lowered his tentacles, staring at Sorsha. "*You're* Ruby?"

She let out a huff. "I generally go by Sorsha. Are you coming or what?"

Torrent paused only a moment longer. Then he waved to the rest of us. "I think they're okay. Let's hear what they can tell us."

Sorsha clucked her tongue as she led us over to the RV. "I'm thinking that the bunch of you should probably start this story."

Several minutes later, I was perched on the end of a curved, padded bench inside the RV, which somehow looked way more spacious on the inside than my architect brain suspected it logically should.

Crag had insisted on squeezing in between me and our hosts. Next to him was the slim pretty boy with the golden curls and the forked tongue, and directly across from me was Sorsha. Torrent was leaning against the kitchen counter beside the dining area, all but his usual two tentacles tucked away. Lance had vanished into the shadows, but I assumed he was listening from there, like Sorsha's massive winged friend.

The enormous glowing dog had transformed into a grouchy tawny-haired guy who'd scowled at us before taking the RV's wheel. A fourth man, one with little horns protruding from his dark brown hair and a perpetual smirk, had propped himself in the little hall between the kitchen/dining area and the driver's seat, watching the proceedings with apparent amusement.

Sorsha braced her elbows on the table, cocking her head as she took in the explanation we'd stitched together between me, Torrent, and Crag. "So the extra shadowkind activity we've been seeing in Florida—that's been centered on *you*?" she said, eyeing me. "Because of this odd energy that seems to be coming from inside you."

I nodded. "We don't know what that energy is or why it's happening, though. It doesn't seem to actually *do* anything. We thought maybe it was because of my heart transplant"—I motioned to the top of my scar peeking from the neckline of my shirt—"and the records showed that the girl who donated it used to live at that house."

Sorsha sucked in a breath. "Did you write them a letter? The family of the girl—thanking them?"

My pulse stuttered. "Yeah. How did you know that?"

She sank back against the bench, and the forked-tongue guy, whose name I'd determined was Snap, slipped his arm around her with a concerned look. I didn't know what kind of monster he was, but I could tell he'd be leaping to defend her the second he felt he needed to.

"We came out to the house back when the murders first happened," Sorsha said. "It's kind of our thing—we go around checking out clashes between shadowkind and mortals, intervening in whatever way means the fewest beings get hurt... The sorcerers had an adopted daughter who escaped the attack. She told us that her older sister had saved someone when she died and about the thank you letter. I didn't realize exactly what she meant by 'saving' before."

My heart really had come from someone in that family of sorcerers, then.

My fingers curled toward my palms beneath the table, and I forced my hands to unclench against my lap. "That shouldn't matter, though, should it? I mean, *I'm* not a sorcerer. I have no idea how to work any kind of magic. I didn't even know magic was real until a week ago! And my donor was just a kid. Would they have put spells on her that'd have affected her heart—that could still be affecting me?"

"It's probably not quite like that," said the guy in the hall, who Sorsha had called Ruse, with a languid air. "It seems like sorcery affects the practisers right down to the genetic code."

Sorsha nodded. "When you get families who keep practicing the magic and marry with other sorcerers, the power gets stronger across generations. And that family was particularly established. The girl would have had a talent for sorcery etched into her DNA—which is in her heart. I don't know how much it would have passed on to you in any way you could practice it, but it's obviously expressing itself somehow."

My hand rose to my chest again. "What can I do about that? It's not like I can go back to the hospital and return this heart, asking for a new one."

Torrent spoke up again after his stretch of silence. "Can you think of any reason why shadowkind would be interested in Quinn other than wanting to destroy what feels like a threat? It seemed as if some of the recent bunch were looking to capture her rather than kill her on the spot."

I managed not to wince at his casual reference to my near-death.

Snap stirred, flicking his tongue with a faint hiss. "Heart," he said. "The organs."

Sorsha rubbed her forehead. "Yes, I was just thinking of that."

"What?" I demanded, urgency overcoming my sense of caution with these relative strangers. "What about the organs?"

The guy in the driver's seat let out an inarticulate snarl as if the very mention of the subject pissed him off. Ruse shot him a bemused look and turned back to us.

"There's a rumor that's gone around for ages that shadowkind can gain extra power by eating the vital organs of sorcerers," he said dryly. "A lovely delicacy."

Sorsha glowered at him before returning her attention to me. "What the incubus is inconsiderately trying to say is that when we found the bodies of the family, they'd been cut open. Their major organs were missing. We don't know whether their killers were just mutilating their bodies or testing that rumor, and if they were testing the rumor, there's been no evidence that anything came of it. But if they *were* trying to level up their powers, and they found out there was a heart from a member of that family they hadn't gotten to yet..."

Crag rumbled threateningly at her implication.

My stomach listed with a surge of nausea. "They don't just want to kill me—they want to eat my heart."

Sorsha grimaced sympathetically. "And it was higher shadowkind who carried out the killings. They may have convinced other beings to work for them, to track you down and bring you to them."

I gestured vaguely in the air. "How would they even have figured out there was another sorcerer heart out there in someone else's body?"

"Maybe you saw that little shrine in the house? Your letter was on it. But when we got there, the frame had been shattered and the letter was gone. That's why Ashley told us about it. It had at least your first name on it, right? And presumably you mentioned the transplant." Sorsha sighed. "I'd guess that they've been trying to track you down ever since then. You said you only started getting the sensations recently. That was what helped them locate you."

Snap tilted his head to the side, studying me. "What would have set off the heart *now*?"

"I don't know," I said. "Nothing different had happened to me right beforehand."

Sorsha tapped the tabletop. "It could be a whole bunch of factors converging. These higher shadowkind came to kill the sorcerer. Then they started scouring the area for the heart recipient. They might have called on a bunch of creatures from elsewhere to help them look, and then others started gathering here out of curiosity. The surge in activity is why *we* drove down here to take a look at the situation. Having more shadowkind around could have triggered your heart, responding to their presence. Which put a bull's eye on you."

"Great." My shoulders sagged against the bench, a wave of hopelessness washing over me. I glanced at Torrent, hoping he'd have some useful insight, but his face tightened and turned a sallower shade than usual, as if what we'd just heard had nauseated him too.

I looked back at Sorsha. "Do you have any idea what I can do about it?"

"We'll destroy the beings that want her," Crag growled before she could answer.

Sorsha arched her eyebrows at him. "That's the general idea—if we can't convince them to back down, which is generally my preference. But I'll admit it doesn't always work, and these ones have already shown they're murderously inclined. The trouble might be finding the masterminds behind the attacks. We haven't been able to determine which shadowkind were responsible for the initial sorcerer killings—not even what kind of beings they were."

"Whichever one renovated the garage was very large," Ruse put in, not particularly helpfully.

I remembered the ruined building and shuddered. Would that have been a shadowkind even bigger and stronger than Crag? *Could* my protectors "destroy" these fiends, no matter how much they wanted to?

It didn't matter. We had to try, right?

I pulled myself together as well as I could. "Then our first step is that we need to figure out who's calling the shots."

"Exactly." Sorsha snapped her fingers. "Unfortunately, we haven't made much progress at that. But we were already planning on being in Florida for at least a couple of days longer. Give us your number, and we'll give you a heads up if we find out anything useful. And if *you* find them, shout for us and we'll jump in to help any way we can. I'd offer to stick with you in the meantime, but it sounds like you've got a pretty solid strategy worked out for avoiding the beasties, and we'll be more likely to find answers if we're pursuing different leads."

Torrent stepped forward with a heave of one tentacle, pulling out his phone. "I'll take your contact info and give you mine. And then we'll need you to cycle back around to the sorcerers' house. There's someone local I know who might be able to lend some insight. He crosses paths with a lot of the higher shadowkind who come through this area."

"Sounds good." Sorsha exchanged phones with him and tapped her number into his contacts. After she handed it back, she stood up. "Now that we understand each other better, I'd like to have a little chat with Quinn one-on-one." She met my eyes. "If you're okay with that."

I had no idea what the phoenix would want to say to me in private, but I didn't have any fears about *her* hurting me now. "Sure," I said.

Crag shifted as if he wanted to protest, but he obviously couldn't think of a good reason. Sorsha led me to the back of the RV and into a bedroom with an impressively sparkly purple duvet.

"The guest bedroom," she said with a laugh, sitting on the edge of the bed, and patted the space next to her. I sank down at the opposite end, still not sure what this was about. She eyed me for a long stretch before saying, "Are you okay?"

That was so not what I'd been expecting from her that it took me a moment to find my words. "I mean, no, not really. I haven't been okay since the attack in the park. I can't go home, I can't do any of the things I've wanted to do. And now it turns out a whole bunch of shadowkind don't just want to kill me, they want to tear me open and eat me? And I've got some superpowered heart that's not powerful in any way I can actually use."

Sorsha let out a light chuckle. "Yeah. It's a lot."

I looked down at my hands. "I'll keep going, like I have been. I'm not the kind of person who gives up. I'm just being honest."

"I appreciate that." Sorsha was quiet for another moment, her gaze going distant. "I have some idea what it's like—realizing there's more to you that you never suspected. Having powers inside you that you can't control and that are making your life more difficult rather than easier. It's not a ball."

I blinked in surprise. I'd assumed all shadowkind knew what they were and what they could do when they came into existence. It seemed rude to ask her why she hadn't.

"How did you handle it?" I asked instead.

"Depends on who you ask. Omen would say disastrously." Her lips quirked up as if at a joke. "It was a lot easier after I stopped trying to deny it and started seeing how it could work for me. Not that you'd want to use any kind of sorcerer power. Their entire thing is turning shadowkind into slaves. But if you could tap into the energies inside you a little more, maybe you'd be able to turn down the volume or something. Or turn the vibe off completely."

The thought sent a wash of relief through me. "That would be amazing. Do you really think it's possible?"

"It can't hurt to try." She gave me a hopeful smile. "While we're on the road, why don't I take you through a few of the exercises that helped me focus and improve my control? Maybe they'll work for you too."

"Sure," I said, because really, what did I have to lose?

If I couldn't get this sorcerer energy inside me to chill the fuck out, sooner or later one of the shadowkind beasts was going to come carve it right out of me.

CHAPTER TWENTY-TWO

Lance

The entire clearing stank of sorcery. It itched in my nose no matter what form I took—even in the shadows where I barely *had* a nose—closing around me like a vise.

I stalked around the yard outside the house as if I could outpace the sensation. Torrent had said we wouldn't stay here very long. Crag and I had already shredded a few stray beasties that'd ventured out this way. Thankfully it seemed like they were still wary of the location where the sorcerers had done their dirty work, not totally convinced they were gone for good, but their hesitation would only last so long.

Were the sorcerers actually gone? One of their hearts was still beating in Quinn's chest. I glanced at her, my fangs prickling as they emerged instinctively.

She still looked like the same lively, lovely woman she'd been before, but now I knew what that odd energy seeping out of her was. It hadn't been strong enough for me to pick up the exact taint before. It was *their* kind of power—that sickening, twisting, suffocating power that shouldn't even *exist*.

Torrent had been popping in and out of the shadows all around the exterior of the house, always positioning himself so he had a nearby tree to casually rest a hand or a shoulder on without his tentacles out. He'd just finished a circuit of the property with the leprechaun, who as far as I could tell was only doing a lot of hemming and hawing without offering any useful insights.

"If you see anything at all that could help us identify who was behind the attack, from what you've observed of the powerful shadowkind who've come through Miami recently or anything you've overheard, I want to know about it," Torrent said by the doorway. He'd had to come up with a fake story to avoid putting even more of a spotlight on Quinn, something about suspecting the same beings had stolen an item he needed for a business enterprise.

"I try to steer clear of the murderous type of shadowkind," Goldie said with a chuckle as he headed inside. "So far all I'm seeing is that I definitely wouldn't want to mess with these monsters."

Useless. But Torrent had thought having him look around was worth trying, because what else did we have that we could try? The beasts who'd descended on this place had come in the middle of the night without leaving any witnesses. If some minor creatures in the woods had noticed the attack, it wasn't as if they could tell us anything. They were useless too.

Even if we found out, then what? I should congratulate the murderers for a job well done. Who knew how many shadowkind those villains had bent to their will over the generations?

At the thought, my fangs grew larger. I threw myself into dragon form and lunged into the forest.

Bounding off the tree trunks, I whipped through the underbrush until my fire-tinged breath grew ragged in my throat. I transformed into human-like form and gouged the bark with my claws, leaping and tumbling. Then I sprang back into the dragon to race all the way to the top of one tree before flinging myself to another and another.

I was free. Nothing chained me. Nothing constrained me. Nothing ever would again. I was proving it with every pang of my muscles, every hiss of air over my scales or skin.

I skidded down a trunk and leapt over a mossy log. Fallen branches crunched beneath my feet. I flipped onto my back and writhed, digging the spines along my back into the earth and reveling at the friction.

But even that couldn't wipe away the memories that'd risen up, clinging to the corners of my mind no matter what I did.

I'd left those images behind before. They should be *gone*. I could always slip away from them, escape into some other sensation.

When would Torrent be finished? I wanted to get away from here.

Footsteps rustled through the nearby vegetation. I spun onto my feet and around, hoping it was him calling me back but knowing he'd most likely have already spoken up if it was.

My gaze caught on a head of pale blond hair. Those soft tresses I'd nuzzled and stroked. I could smell her on the breeze, a scent like windblown wildflowers, like mortal spring. But I could feel her too, the faint vibration of energy that emanated from her between the larger pulses. My claws dug into the dirt.

Quinn paused, gazing steadily at me. Even with apprehension quivering through my nerves, there was something intoxicating about having a mortal look at me in my most vicious form without showing the slightest sign of fear.

I bared my fangs with an experimental growl, and all she did was knit her brow, looking both confused and concerned. But not for herself. "Lance?" she said tentatively, taking a step closer.

Torrent had asked her to stay out of sight while he and the leprechaun inspected the house, so she'd been lurking in the shadows of the forest almost like one of us. Crag was probably watching over her from someplace nearby.

"Are you all right?" she went on. "You seem more... worked up than usual."

I shook my body, willing the clashing emotions away as well as I could, and shifted into human-like form. My fangs stayed out. I dragged my claws idly over a nearby tree trunk to remind myself how much destructive capacity I held even in this shape.

"We've stuck around a long time," I said in a purposefully careless tone. "Aren't you bored? Dreary, stinking sorcerer house and dreary, sticky forest." Even as acclimatized as I was to heat, the summer weather brought sweat onto my skin within moments of transforming. The beams of morning sunlight that pierced the canopy shimmered like captured flames.

Quinn tipped her head to the side, eyeing me. "I agree it's not where I'd want to take a vacation, but it's hard to be *bored* when I've just found out something so huge. And we're still trying to figure out who these shadowkind are that seem to be after me."

What did it matter? Rollick wanted her too. It was them or him. Then she would be gone, and our job would be over, and that unsettling energy would be gone from my life too.

Along with the laughs and the smiles and the gasps...

"*I* am bored," I insisted, and carved a chunk of wood right out of the tree. My claws skittered over it as I held it between my hands, slicing it to slivers in a matter of seconds. The chips pattered to the ground at my feet.

"Are you sure that's all it is?" Quinn said. "I'm pretty sure I've seen you bored before. It's not like life in that swamp cabin was a laugh riot. This seems... different."

"If I say I'm bored, then I'm bored." I jabbed my claws all the way into a different tree, snarled at it, and wrenched them free. Then I turned away from her. "Also bored of this conversation."

But she wouldn't give up. Of course not. This human didn't give up. That was why she was still here at all.

She walked after me as I sauntered away, still doing my best to look nonchalant. "Are you worried about the shadowkind who attacked this place?" she asked. "I'm sure between the three of you and Sorsha's crew if we call them in—"

I couldn't restrain a stuttered laugh. "Worried about the sorcerer-murderers? No." I took a couple of swipes at the air. "They removed a little poison from this world. Set some beasties free. The ones that bled got what they deserved."

Quinn halted. At first I thought she was disturbed by my remarks, that she wasn't sure she even wanted to talk to me anymore, and somehow that both relieved me and irked me at the same time.

Then her voice came out quieter and gentler than before. "You've mentioned humans who didn't treat you well. Have you been caught by sorcerers?"

I growled, but I couldn't intimidate the truth out of existing. I didn't have to say much about it, though.

I jerked my hand toward the house. "Not *those* ones. But I'm not going to be sorry for them."

Quinn advanced again. I held my ground, a little uncertain about what I'd do if I let myself move. One of those sharper shocks of energy rippled out of her, and I flinched as her expression twitched with it. She halted.

"I'm sorry. I—my heart—" She pressed her hand to her chest. Her normally bright eyes dimmed. "I remind you of them. Of what they did to you."

Images from the past flashed through me—pain and bindings, groans and shrieks, flesh flayed apart.

My voice turned rough. "The worst wasn't me. The worst was the others. It's done now. It doesn't matter." I waved my arm toward the forest around me, letting the momentum spin me. "I'm here. Lovely trees. Things to explore."

"But it still bothers you." Quinn was silent for a moment. Then she added, "If *I* bother you—if it's uncomfortable for you to be near me, now that you know—I'll leave you alone. I was just worried about you. I don't want to make it worse."

There was so much anguish in her voice that the part of me that wanted to wrap her up in my limbs—to devour her in all kinds of ways that would make her gasp only in pleasure, not agony—overwhelmed the uneasiness in my nerves. I found myself moving toward her, reaching for her and then drawing back my claws. Claws that had torn—claws that had savaged—

"You don't make it worse," I said. "You've been a very good adventure." And more than that, really. Somehow even with the treacherous heart thumping behind her ribs, the tenderness in her voice and her expression was driving back the memories more than anything I'd done on my own had.

She crossed the last distance between us and raised her hand to my cheek. "I'm so sorry," she said. "I didn't realize— I don't know what all they did to you, but no one should be bound up and forced to do things against their will. That's bad enough. Of course you're angry."

"I'm not—" I started, and cut myself off as a spurt of the very emotion I was denying flared in my chest.

I didn't like to feel it. Didn't like to notice it. It was easier to be careless and following the whims of the present as if the past had never happened.

Before, when I'd first gotten free, I'd had only anger to fight back the pain. None of it had felt good. But Torrent had found me and showed me how to be more than that, and I'd left it behind.

Only I hadn't really, because it was still here.

Suddenly I didn't know what to do with my body other than pull Quinn into my arms. I tucked my head next to hers and inhaled her scent from her hair like it was some kind of drug. The soft warmth of her body washed over me.

She hugged me back, a little catch coming into her voice as if she were trying not to cry. For *me*.

"If there's anything I can do to make it easier, you let me know, okay?" she said, her words muffled against my shoulder.

I didn't know what to do with that offer either, but it pealed through my heart. My throat constricted, and I closed my eyes, squeezing her tighter. The tortured sounds of the distant past kept echoing up from the back of my mind, fading but still audible.

I hadn't saved any of them. I'd tried and I'd failed and they'd all given their essence back to the shadows.

But maybe I could save her.

That would be a good thing, wouldn't it? It wasn't her fault where her heart had come from. She hadn't asked for it.

Resolve dug its own claws into my chest. This lively, lovely woman was a victim of the sorcerers' twisted magic as much as any of us had been, and I would not let them destroy her too.

CHAPTER TWENTY-THREE

Quinn

We spent most of the drive back to Daytona Beach in silence. Torrent tuned the radio to some weird new wave rock station and let it blare through the car. With the brightening sunlight, I slathered on some sunscreen and then tried to doze, since it was well into the morning already. Unfortunately, none of the car's surfaces made the most comfortable pillow.

I didn't feel right leaning on Crag, who'd taken the back seat with me again. I was harboring a power that wanted to enslave beings like him. And he'd already done so much for me.

Why should these three shadowkind men protect me at all? I wouldn't have blamed them if they'd abandoned me to the creatures stalking me. It wasn't as if any of us had any clue what might happen next.

When I couldn't drift off, I ran through the mental exercises Sorsha had walked me through. I breathed deep and slow and tried to tap into my sense of the tremoring energy in my chest that it now seemed almost certain was emanating from my transplanted heart.

I couldn't feel much of anything right now, though. It seemed that shadowkind beings could pick up on a low-level vibe no matter what, but

I'd only been aware of the energy when the stronger surges had rushed through me. I couldn't see any pattern to when that had happened, other than Sorsha's suggestion that the reaction had been heightened once more shadowkind had been prowling nearby.

I'd been very near at least three shadowkind for several days, which might have been why the surges had been feeling increasingly unnerving. But those shadowkind men were the only reason I hadn't been torn apart or gobbled up or whatever else by the other creatures out there. I couldn't call it a bad trade-off. The murderous creatures had been on my trail regardless.

In the front seat, Lance was swaying with the latest song on the radio, clicking his claws against the dashboard at a slightly off-kilter rhythm that somehow complemented the tune. I studied what I could see of his profile, my stomach clenching.

He'd seemed okay since we'd left the sorcerer's house behind. The hyper, almost desperate energy that'd gripped him there had simmered down to what at least looked like his usual odd but easy-going self.

I couldn't shake the memory of his voice when he'd talked about his past even in vague terms, though. The anguish that'd rippled through the words and tensed his stance...

He'd backed away from me. Yes, after we'd talked, he'd seemed to take some kind of comfort in my embrace, but I had trouble believing it was enough. I was going to be a constant reminder of the people who'd enslaved him and hurt him in who knew how many other ways. And there was nothing I could do about that.

The sorcerer family must have felt they were doing a good deed by allowing their daughter's heart to be used as a donor organ. Maybe they hadn't realized that certain effects would be passed on with it. Or maybe they'd hoped her powers would live on elsewhere.

Had she donated other organs? Were there other people out there with a lung or a liver that was giving off the same vibes?

Although, if there was, I'd have thought at least one of the shadowkind we'd talked to would have heard about it. Maybe her heart had been the only organ still viable after her death. I didn't know how she'd died. Or maybe other organs didn't carry quite the same concentration of residual magic.

What could I have done about it even if there were other recipients out there? I was barely managing to keep myself alive with the help of these three men. We knew *I* was carrying my donor's genetic legacy of magic, and that was plenty for me to worry about on its own at the moment.

Would these guys want to keep sticking their necks out to protect me now that they knew why all this was happening? I hadn't expected their help to begin with, and now it seemed like the stakes had only gotten higher. They were up against formidable foes we knew nothing about and who were determined to get what they wanted by any means necessary.

I stewed in those thoughts as the sun rose higher in the sky beyond the windows. Daytona Beach finally came into view up ahead.

When we reached the marina, the men disappeared into the shadows as soon as we'd parked. I knew they'd travel through the marina and to the boat faster than I could walk, confirming that no scary beasties were lying in wait for me, but a terrible sense of loneliness settled over me as I walked along the docks between the other boats to our yacht at the end closest to the ocean access point.

No one leapt out with any warnings, so presumably the boat hadn't been made a target yet. I stepped on board, and Torrent wavered into view in the captain's seat. I crossed the deck and ducked into the cabin.

"Crag is doing a broader circuit checking for beings in the area," Torrent said without looking up from the controls. "And Lance has gone to collect edible supplies, although it's hard to say what in the realms you'll end up eating with his tastes dictating the selection."

"I'm sure it'll be fine." I hesitated, and then sat down on the edge of the storage container next to the navigation area, just a couple of feet from his chair. The strap of my messenger bag chafed at my shoulder, and I slid it off. All the questions and worries that'd been whirling inside me bubbled up to the surface.

Torrent was obviously the de facto leader over the other guys. They looked to him for orders. I had the sense he was older than them, however much seniority mattered to shadowkind. There was a definite air of authority around him, anyway, and a sense of weary experience.

It was up to him more than the others whether they kept protecting me. And he might have a deeper sense of the consequences of that choice, of this entire situation, than any of the rest of us did. But he never seemed exactly eager to chat. I didn't know where to start.

He'd draped his usual tentacles over the sides of the chair, which at least didn't have arms to get in the way. My gaze slid down their sloping path, taking in the slightly awkward angle at which he'd set his legs as if bracing them straight against the floor would have been painful. He'd held his physical form for an awful lot of the past twenty-four hours.

A comment that had nothing to do with any of *my* problems tumbled out. "It's too bad you can't steer from the shadows."

Torrent shot me a sharp look. "I manage just fine. I've been managing for decades longer than you've been alive, so you don't have to worry about coming up with any more helpful solutions, Ms. Fix-It. You have enough other things to worry about anyway."

"Yeah." I sagged in my seat. "Well."

All my other words clogged in my throat as he finished preparing whatever he'd been doing with the controls in advance of our departure. When he dropped his hands from the console, a jolt of panic rushed through me that he might vanish into the darkness like I'd just suggested, leaving me essentially alone again. The fear propelled another question from my throat.

"What are we going to do now? I mean, I can't really expect the three of you to keep spending all your time and energy keeping me safe."

"We haven't minded so far," Torrent said evenly. "Remember that this is a much smaller blip in our extended lives than it'll seem to a human."

"So comforting," I muttered. "I just—it's not only protecting *me*. You're protecting a piece of someone who'd have been your enemy. Powers that could activate more, in ways we can't predict. I could tell what we found out bothered all of you. Lance was really upset."

Torrent turned toward me, his voice outright flat now. "I'm sure both of your boy toys will get over any hesitations they have about you quickly enough, if they haven't already."

I winced at his phrasing, my cheeks flaring. Was *that* what he thought I was bothered about—losing my sexual partners? Neither of the encounters I'd gone along with had even been my idea.

"That was the last thing on my mind," I said shortly. "And I don't see them as toys. I don't see any of you as toys."

Torrent shrugged as if he didn't totally believe me. "Whatever the case, I'm sure any tension over this discovery will evaporate. We'll continue resting during the day and making inquiries about the shadowkind who've targeted you by night, and hopefully we'll come across more information sooner rather than later."

He sounded tense. It occurred to me that I hadn't really talked to him, not one-on-one, since yesterday when I'd had my interlude with Lance and Crag.

I'd assumed Torrent had removed himself immediately because he hated the idea... but maybe he felt excluded somehow? Or like he'd been put in an uncomfortable position? By Lance, technically, but I could see him blaming me.

"You know," I said tentatively, "what happened yesterday—I had no idea Lance was going to suggest any of that. It must have been kind of awkward for you when we're all stuck here on this boat. I probably should have shut him down."

"It's perfectly fine," Torrent said in a terse tone that suggested otherwise, returning his attention to the navigation console. "Why shouldn't you all enjoy yourselves? I don't have any illusions about being appealing in that department these days, so I wouldn't have expected an invitation."

His last remark jostled free a spark of understanding. Did he think the invitation hadn't included him? Or rather, he'd left because he'd assumed I would reject him, not because *he* had no interest.

Maybe he hadn't been interested anyway, but then why wouldn't he just say that?

How long had it been since the days when Goldie had known Torrent as a ladies' man? Decades before I was born, Torrent had just suggested. Had he simply closed himself off from desire for all that time?

I guessed if he'd normally pursued human women in the past, he couldn't easily do that now, what with the necessary tentacles and all. But I wasn't put off by his monstrousness, and the damage on his face didn't repulse me the way he obviously assumed it would.

I pushed myself to my feet before I'd thought through what I was going to do, driven only by my sense of *his* loneliness hidden under all his cool curtness. My hand rose to his caved-in cheek, resting lightly on the rough skin of the scar, moving with the jerk of Torrent's head as his gaze snapped back to me.

"I'd have been happy for you to stay," I said, holding his startled gaze.

"It seemed like you were offended by the suggestion, or I'd have made that clearer."

Maybe I needed to make it even clearer still. I dipped my head and brushed my lips to his scarred cheek.

Torrent drew in a rasp of breath. When I pulled back, his gaze had hardened. "Are you just looking to collect a full set of notches in your belt?"

I couldn't hold back a full flinch at the barb in the question. Anger rushed in to burn away the sting. I folded my arms over my chest, taking another step back.

"Of course not. Yeah, I go chasing excitement sometimes, but I wouldn't be hooking up with anyone in a situation like this if I didn't like you."

"*Like* us," Torrent repeated in a scornful tone that only made me more annoyed.

"I do," I retorted. "Lance makes me laugh and is weirdly sweet even when he's acting like a psychopath, and Crag is so brave and unshakeable, and you—even if you're being a real jerk right now, you stepped in to protect me and I can tell you look out for the other guys too. You're smart and dedicated, and you don't let your physical limitations stop you, which it shouldn't surprise you is a quality I can appreciate."

Torrent opened his mouth, but I barrelled on over anything he might have said. I needed to finish.

"If you don't want to go there with me because you're not attracted to me or whatever, that's fine. No insult taken. But if it's only because you're assuming *I* couldn't possibly admire you or I've got some other unsavory intentions, then... then I don't know why, even after all the time we've spent together, you'd think the worst of me."

I spun around, planning on soothing my wounded spirits by flinging myself onto the bed where really I should be trying to sleep anyway. But before I made it more than two steps, one of Torrent's tentacles caught me, snagging around my waist.

I halted and turned at his tug. He'd swiveled all the way around on the seat, his mouth tight and his gaze searching. His grasp loosened, but he nudged me closer toward him, and I came.

When I was close enough that his knees grazed my thighs from his perch on the raised seat, he touched my cheek with his hand like I had his. His fingertips skimmed across my skin. Warmth unfurled in their wake. I suddenly found it difficult to breathe, held in place by the strange mix of anguish and hope in his sea-green eyes.

He swallowed audibly. "It looks like I've been giving you the wrong impression there too," he said, his voice gone hoarse. "The problem is that I *can't* think the worst of you."

Before I could even try to make sense of that statement, he pulled me to him.

Torrent's mouth crashed into mine with so much passion I gasped against his lips. Neither Lance nor Crag had been particularly skillful in their kisses. The tentacled man might not have had much recent practice, but there was no missing the assurance with which he claimed my mouth now that he knew I'd welcome the gesture.

He coaxed my lips apart to deepen the kiss with the perfect amount of pressure. His fingers stroked down my neck, setting off a trail of giddy shivers. I kissed him back hard, clutching the front of his shirt, not wanting to give him any chance to doubt whether I really did want this.

Torrent's other hand dropped to my waist. It almost brushed the handle of the silver-and-iron dagger I'd taken from the sorcerers' house and then jerked a little higher to avoid it. I was about to pull back to see if I should set it aside completely, but he grasped me so tightly I had no doubt that he was perfectly okay with me as is.

I had the urge to sink onto his lap but wasn't sure if that would hurt his legs. Instead, I clambered onto the captain's seat with only the slightest break in the kiss, bracing my knees on either side of his thighs without putting any weight on his limbs.

An approving sound thrummed through Torrent's chest. "Fuck," he muttered against my lips, and then, in a very different tone, "Fuck it." He yanked me to him again, devouring my mouth so thoroughly my entire body quivered.

While one hand teased into my hair, the other slid up to cup my breast. He thumbed my nipple, deftly drawing it to a point, and I whimpered. My fingers curled against his neck, fingernails digging in just a little, and he chuckled. "Bringing out your claws?"

I smiled, stealing another peck. "They may not be as impressive as Lance's—"

He let out a guttural sound that was almost a growl and gripped my hair harder. "Don't even say his name. Right now, you're only mine."

His mouth collided with mine again. In the depths of my mind, his voice from all those nights ago echoed up, ringing through the darkness as it pronounced me *theirs*. His.

Why wouldn't I want to be? I'd never met any human being who'd have stood by me through everything these three men had. Who'd have let me find the sweet parts of this horrifying adventure. Who'd have made me feel so terrifyingly yet electrifyingly *alive*.

Torrent pinched my nipple through my bra, making my breath stutter. But even with the bliss already coursing through my veins, I couldn't help noticing that he'd left his less typical limbs motionless around us.

I tipped back a few inches to catch his eyes. "I like all of you. I want all of you. This"—I stroked his cheek again—"and these." I lowered my hand to trail my fingers over one tentacle. "*They're* not a problem."

A strained noise worked from Torrent's throat. He recaptured my mouth, but at the same time, one tentacle slipped around me.

Its warm, flexible tip dipped under the hem of my shirt and traced up my spine as his fingers continued to work over my breast. One sucker and then another came to rest against my bare skin, provoking a gentle tingling that felt like a promise of so much more to come.

I ran my fingers down his chest encouragingly, tilting my head so our mouths slid together with an even headier sensation. Torrent's tentacle wrapped right around me, teasing along the base of my bra. My breath caught, I arched toward him—

And Crag burst out of the shadows on the deck.

"Torrent!" he said in an urgent voice. "Rollick's here."

CHAPTER TWENTY-FOUR

Quinn

Torrent's body went so rigid against mine that I scrambled right off him. I had no idea what Crag's announcement meant, but everything about the men's demeanor and the atmosphere that'd abruptly descended over the boat made my nerves clang in alarm.

My hand automatically shot to snatch up my messenger bag from where I'd set it on the storage bin. I slung it across my body in case they were going to need me to make a run for it by land or air rather than by sea.

"Who's Rollick?" I asked. "Or what?"

Torrent pushed himself to his feet with a heave of his tentacles, his gaze flicking from the gargoyle toward the docks and back again. He barely seemed to have heard me.

"Where is he?" he said tightly, all the warmth I'd found in him seconds ago vanished.

"I noticed him near the marina buildings," Crag said. "I didn't speak to him—I thought I should tell you first. But he wouldn't be here if he didn't know that we are, would he? Did you call him in?"

Torrent's face had darkened. "No. Not—not recently enough to have given him this location. But I'm sure he has ways..." He glanced at the navigation console, his fingers twitching as if he were thinking of starting the engine right now.

None of this made much sense to me. Why were they agitated about someone they knew, who Crag thought Torrent might even have summoned here on purpose? My pulse skittered with my growing panic.

I smacked my hand against the wall to try to get their attention. "*Who* is Rollick? What's the big deal? Why are you upset?"

"I'm not upset," Torrent snapped at me, the ice in his voice turning that statement into an instant lie. He shook his head, rubbing his temple. "Sorry. We can't just— We have to talk to him."

Crag frowned. "But he—"

Torrent shot him a pointed look. "He didn't know any details. He hardly knew anything. And I'm not even sure what his intentions were."

"He said—"

Torrent cut him off again, even more firmly. "Do you really think we could simply run away, if I was willing to do that?"

My heart was thumping faster with every exchange. I didn't think I wanted to meet this Rollick guy, but I had to do something to stop them from ignoring me.

I marched over to the cabin entrance. "Well, if you're not going to tell me who this guy is, I guess I'll go find out for myself."

Crag leapt in front of me with a spurt of a roar that made my nerves jump, even though the swing of his head suggested he was aiming it at potential threats rather than me.

"Quinn," Torrent started, and then Lance blinked into being at the edge of the deck, carrying two bulging plastic shopping bags.

His head wove from one side to the other, his eyes sparking more wildly than usual, which was saying a lot. "Rollick's coming up the dock. You told him?"

He kept his usual blasé tone, but there was an edge underneath it not that different from how he'd sounded when he'd been bouncing off the trees in blatant distress by the sorcerers' house. My skin started to creep with deeper uneasiness.

"I didn't," Torrent said sharply. "But he's here, so let's see what exactly he wants. We owe him at least that much." He glanced at me. "There's a lot to explain, and not much time. He's a very powerful shadowkind, a demon, and we've worked for him. Just... come with us, but stay back and keep quiet. We'll sort this out."

He and the others had worked for this guy? They didn't seem to like him very much.

I followed them across the yacht's deck to the dock. "What if he's in league with the shadowkind who've been hunting me down?"

Torrent shook his head. "I'm sure *that's* not the case."

"How can you know?"

"I just do," he said tersely.

He stepped onto the dock and then hesitated, tucking his supporting tentacles behind his legs. There weren't any other marina-goers nearby, but I could see a woman in a floppy sunhat a few rows over, and an older couple farther off than that. Maybe from that distance Crag's stone jaw would look like a very thick five-o'clock shadow, and Lance could keep his claws curled mostly out of view, but there wasn't any way for Torrent to easily disguise his bodily crutches.

It turned out he didn't need to. He started to move forward after all, but before he'd gotten more than a couple of steps, another figure shimmered out of the shadows around the neighboring boats, less than ten feet away. The three men froze, so I did too, even though the man sauntering closer to us didn't strike me as particularly intimidating.

He *was* good-looking. Even in my anxious state, I couldn't avoid noticing it. Not in Lance's ferally gorgeous way—more like a clean-cut, all-American celebrity, polished to perfection. The kind of guy you'd expect to see flashing his teeth at you from film posters and magazine covers.

The kind of guy you wouldn't expect to look that polished and perfect in real life without the help of photo-editing magic, only this dude could have stepped straight out of a movie trailer, bringing all the special effects into reality with him.

He was tall and well-built by human standards, though no match for Crag's height and bulk. His tawny hair was cropped close to his smoothly handsome face, artfully ruffled. He was wearing a dress shirt, slacks, and tie that seemed overly dressy for a stroll along the waterfront, but his grin was all casual warmth, bringing out smile lines at the corners of his lips that were obviously well-worn.

If I'd encountered a guy with those movie-star looks at another time, my heart might have skipped a beat. But I was too wound up to appreciate the view. I scanned him for any evidence of his shadowkind status and came up with nothing, but then, Torrent's original monstrous features weren't obvious, only the additional ones he brought out on purpose. I hadn't been able to spot anything that marked Sorsha or her canine shifter friend as shadowkind at a glance either.

There was a confidence to the guy's posture and grin that sent another rush of apprehension through me. Whatever he was, he held himself like a man who thought he was in charge. Who *knew* he was in charge, and that he could step over anyone who got in his way.

When he came to a stop near the stern of the yacht away, Torrent confirmed my suspicions with a nod. "Rollick. You were able to figure out our location."

Rollick cocked his head and raised his eyebrows. "It did take some doing. What happened to the phone?"

Torrent grimaced. "Broken in an early skirmish, or I'd have used it. I turned to the most discreet alternatives available to me."

"You kept it quiet enough. I suppose it's a bit much for any plan to go perfectly smoothly. Especially in a situation that's become this frenzied." Rollick's gaze slid to me where I was peering at him from between Crag and Torrent, half-hidden by Crag's massive arm. "So this is the girl. She doesn't look like much for there to be such a commotion around her. But I suppose it's not really about her, only what's beating in her chest, isn't it?"

He knew about my heart—about the other shadowkind wanting it. And I didn't like the way he spoke about me, as if I was a painting he was considering buying and not a person who could hear him perfectly well. My mouth got away from me.

"You don't look like much either," I retorted, which was true by shadowkind standards. "Who the hell *are* you?"

Since none of the guys seemed to want to tell me, maybe the man himself could give me a clue.

Rollick simply chuckled, with a coolness to his amusement that sent a shiver up my spine. "She does have some spirit, clearly," he went on, still as if I wasn't there. "Well, let's get out of here. Florida is *not* the type of mortal atmosphere I prefer to absorb."

"I'm not—" I began, but Torrent held up his hand, still tense enough that I obeyed the gesture.

"What do you want with her?" he said, low but steady. "What are you going to do?"

Rollick shook his head chidingly, as if Torrent should have known better than to ask. "Once you hand her over, it's my business from there. No need to concern yourself with it."

"Well, this once I am concerned. I'd appreciate you enlightening me."

Crag shifted on his feet as if to add his substantial weight to that request. Lance's claws clicked together in a vaguely threatening sound.

"I don't think this is the time or place for that," Rollick said, obviously dodging the question. I couldn't think of any *good* reason for him to do that.

Neither could Torrent, clearly. He squared his shoulders. "You don't *need* her or her heart. If you knew—if we could talk about it first—"

"I know everything I need to about her and her value to *me.*" Rollick took the three of them in and tsked his tongue. "Are you staging a mutiny? Over some mortal woman? Come on now, the bunch of you—this had better be a joke. Let's finish the job and go."

Though he didn't sound particularly worried, a dark edge had crept into his tone. But it was the words themselves that made my stomach lurch. "What *job*? What are you talking about?"

Torrent had said they'd worked with Rollick in the past, but not— This guy couldn't mean—

"Quinn," Torrent said, like a warning or maybe a protest, but anything he might have added was lost in Rollick's rolling laugh.

"You didn't think this bunch came to your rescue out of the goodness of their hearts, did you?" Mr. Movie Star's grin widened as he focused on me. "They came out to this hellhole to protect what I meant to be mine. And now I'm going to claim it. I'm afraid you don't have any choice in the matter, but it'll be less painful for you if you hop along and don't make a hassle of it."

"You're not taking her," Crag growled. "Not if you're going to hurt her."

His words washed over me, barely catching hold. He hadn't denied what Rollick had said. None of them had.

What did it matter if the gargoyle was making a little show of protectiveness now if all the rest was true? All this time they'd sworn they wanted to defend me because it was the right thing to do, because they thought I deserved to live… and really they'd only been waiting to serve me up to their demon master.

Icy fingers wrapped around my gut. I stepped back from the men I'd thought were shielding me toward the edge of the dock, closer to the boat. One hand closed around the strap of my messenger bag over my chest; the other dropped to the hilt of the knife in my pocket.

All the things I'd wondered. All the little pieces that hadn't quite added up. I'd dismissed my minor uncertainties when it'd seemed like my protectors were working with me, but I'd never gotten a full explanation, had I? Why they'd so conveniently been there to leap to my defense. How Lance had seemed to know my full name. Their lack of concern about finding a long-term solution until I'd pushed for it.

Because this bodyguard job had never meant to be long term. They'd only been waiting for this guy—their boss?—to show up and take me off their hands.

I'd thought they'd had some kind of honor. I'd thought they *cared* about me.

Oh, God, I'd been so fucking stupid.

My jaw clenched. They were monsters. They'd told me that from the start, and I'd let myself think it didn't count when it came to them, not enough to scare me away. They'd dragged me into a trap pretending it was safety, and even now, Torrent was simply discussing the details like it was a business negotiation.

Rollick's next words rang through the frantic thump of blood past my ears. "If she complies, it can be perfectly painless. I only torture beings who've wronged me. You know me better than this. Bring her over, or I'll—"

I wasn't interested in what he meant to do. I just needed to get out of here.

My gaze flicked along the dock, and my instincts honed by years of urban exploring hurtled me into action.

I leapt onto the edge of the yacht, the lip that protruded just a few inches out from the railing, and darted along the narrow strip. I meant to dash right past Rollick and sprint on down the dock. But as I shot past him, he grabbed at me with a flash of his bared teeth that looked more monster than movie star in that moment.

His fingers closed around my wrist. Shouts had risen up behind me, but I couldn't focus on anything but my shrinking window of escape.

I whipped the dagger out of its sheath and rammed the blade toward Rollick with all my strength.

In my panic, I didn't aim all that carefully. Everything Crag had told me about weak spots went out the window. But Rollick was in human-ish form, and most of the human rules applied. I did have the wherewithal to aim lower than his ribs, and the dagger plunged right through his shirt and into his gut like a knife into softened butter.

That smoky shadowkind blood stuff gushed up between us. His hand on my arm spasmed as a strangled sound of agony burst from his lips.

I wrenched my wrist free, and the demon snatched at me again, faster than any human would have been able to. I dodged, losing my grip on the dagger—but better I kept my life than it.

Hurling myself away from Rollick and the monstrous men who'd claimed me for him, I pelted down the dock toward civilization as fast as my legs could carry me.

CHAPTER TWENTY-FIVE

Crag

"Quinn!" I bellowed as she hurtled away down the dock. I leapt after her, but Rollick flung the dagger she'd stabbed him with into the sea with a hiss and slammed his arms around me.

He'd unleashed his demonic claws from his fingertips. They sank into my flesh with spikes of pain. I spun around, lashing out with one of my thick arms. A prickle of transformation rushed over me, the urge to shift into gargoyle form for this fight, but I yanked myself back with a jolt of fear.

It was broad daylight. There were other mortals around. What were they already thinking of however much of this skirmish they'd witnessed from a distance?

Rollick wouldn't want to reveal himself either. In a way, it was luckier that we were fighting this way, because while his demonic form could have posed a real challenge, in human shape he was no physical match for me.

I heaved him away from me and tried to run after Quinn again, but he caught my foot and wrenched hard enough that I felt a bone snap. More pain jolted up my leg. I stumbled and flung myself around onto my ass to try to kick him in the face.

Rollick whipped out of the way of my blow, smaller and less powerful but even faster than I was. In that instant, as I stared into the face of the being who'd taken me on decades ago, who'd given me everything I'd ever asked for—as modest as my wants were—in exchange for services I'd found it easy to provide, my stomach sank.

He'd given me a purpose. He'd ensured my happiness. And now I was pummeling him like a brute.

But he'd been going to destroy Quinn's happiness, purpose, and everything else about her. It'd been obvious from the way he'd spoken. And in the past week, she'd somehow managed to give me something he'd never come close to. Something even I hadn't fully realized I needed.

It didn't matter where one piece or another of her had come from or what sort of power it might contain. *Quinn* wasn't like the sorcerers. She was the farthest thing from those cruel slavers that I'd ever encountered, soft and kind alongside her strength. Her heart had opened to all of us.

I would not let the demon take her.

As my resolve hardened every inch of muscle on me, Lance leapt in to slash at Rollick's face with his claws.

"She's ours," he snarled, his face contorted, his violet eyes blazing. "*Ours*. Find yourself your own human."

Rollick swayed, his shadowy essence streaming from those smaller wounds and billowing from the gouge the sorcerers' dagger had dealt. In his injured state, even his keen reflexes had difficulty fending off two separate attackers. His own eyes flared, and he swung a fist at Lance that crackled with supernatural power—

And a tentacle slashed through the air, smacking Rollick in the gut and sending him toppling right off the dock in the gap between two of the boats.

"Come on," Torrent said in a rasp. "Through the shadows, after her. It won't take him long to recover."

Rollick was already groping at the side of the dock, sputtering curses at us. "When I get my claws into you turncoats—"

I didn't wait to hear the rest of his threat. All three of us sprang into the patches of darkness along the dock and raced from one to the next in the direction Quinn had fled.

Unfortunately, I'd lost track of her in the skirmish. She must have passed the end of the dock and crossed the open area near the marina buildings. I caught no sign of her on the terrain ahead.

My body ached to launch myself into the sky, but there were no shadows in the open air. I couldn't fly around all gargoyle-like with so many humans around. A few around the marina were already staring in the direction of our dock.

Lance and Torrent rushed along beside me, vaguely urgent presences in the fragments of gloom. I wasn't surprised that Lance had joined me, but Torrent...

He'd worked with Rollick even longer than I had. He'd been one of Rollick's most trusted lieutenants, if not *the* most trusted. And he hadn't seemed to warm up to Quinn all that much. I wasn't even sure I could believe what I thought I'd seen happening between them right before I'd warned him of Rollick's approach.

Was he really on her side, or did he have some other game plan here? There wasn't any reason for her to matter more to him than the average mortal did. Maybe he'd just realized that Lance and I could overpower Rollick under the circumstances, and he intended to grab Quinn and present her to the boss on his own, later.

On the other hand, he had been questioning Rollick rather than offering her up right away. He'd *sounded* like it mattered to him what happened to her.

And his motivations didn't matter at all if we couldn't find her.

We reached the street beyond the marina, the cars roaring past us. Quinn was nowhere to be seen.

Where had she gone? I swiveled, thinking of our car, but Torrent spoke before I could start back to check it.

"I have the keys. She'd have no way of opening it. But that doesn't mean she couldn't have gotten into some other vehicle."

Lance drew up beside me. "I can sense her. The sorcerer energy she gives off. It's gotten even stronger." A growl crept into his voice. "That means any other shadowkind around here will be able to pick up on where she is more easily too."

"That's probably partly how Rollick managed to find us," Torrent muttered. "He knew what he'd ordered us to do and what tactics I was likely to turn to. The other shadowkind will have been chasing us around as we moved with her, but he figured out where to lie in wait." He seemed to shake himself. "So we find her before any other being does. We know *her*."

"Do you?" Lance shot back, twisting around me toward Torrent. "It seemed like you were happy to hand her over if he said the right thing. Rollick *can't* have her."

"She doesn't belong to us," Torrent said tersely. "We protected her *for* him. I needed to know why. She'd have been safer with all his resources guarding her rather than just the three of us if he'd actually been willing to guard her."

"She doesn't belong to *him*," Lance hissed back. "I say she's mine. And she's not safe with him if he's planning on eating her like those other beasties are. He told you he wanted to devour her."

"I didn't know if he meant that... like that."

"How else could he mean it? You just wanted to finish the job and have him pat you on the back."

"No," Torrent snapped. He paused to gather himself, his voice coming out more evenly again. "Do you remember how lost you were before our paths crossed? You were roaming all over the shadow realm, pissing off every being in existence. *I* helped you center yourself. *I* showed you that you could still have an actual life, no matter what you'd been through."

"I don't owe you *her* in gratitude," Lance said.

"That's not my point. The only reason I could help you is because Rollick did the same thing for me. He treated me like more than a fucking cripple. He's brutal when he needs to be, but I've never seen him hurt anyone just for the sake of it. I had to be sure before I went against him. That's all."

"Are you sure now?" I had to ask, bracing myself for how I might need to respond to his answer.

Torrent's frustration resonated through the darkness. "Yes. He dodged the questions. He has a motive to kill her for her heart—he does like amassing power. Maybe I should have been sure sooner..." He trailed off with a harsh sigh. "She's just a mortal. She might only have a few more years left anyway. But... she's more than that too, isn't she."

It wasn't a question, but I answered regardless. "Much more. She's *Quinn*. She needs us."

"She was meant for us," Lance said definitively. "Not to be monster food. She's got so much more in her than whatever came with that heart, and we're going to tear apart anyone who tries to say otherwise."

"All right," Torrent said. "Then let's go do that."

If he'd sounded totally confident, I might not have trusted him. But I could hear how hard it was for him to set aside his loyalty to Rollick. If he'd wanted to trick us, he'd have pretended to be caught up in unwavering devotion, not admitted his doubts.

He hated turning his back on our boss, but he was doing it anyway. For her. That was enough for me.

"This way," Lance said, and darted onward through the shadows. I could catch a faint quiver of Quinn's energy in the air, but the dragon shifter appeared to have a sharper awareness of it. Maybe because of past exposure to that kind of magic. If we got close enough, I'd be able to identify the unique vibrations of her movements, but for now I'd trust his sense of direction.

"We don't just need to find her," I reminded him and Torrent as we hurried along the streets together. "We need a way to set her free. She can't keep living with all these beings chasing after her. Even if there's nothing permanent that can be done, we have to come up with something that'll at least give her a break from the danger."

"Yes," Torrent agreed. "It doesn't do any good saving her if she's still trapped by being on the run. But it's not just the unknown monsters we're dealing with now—it's Rollick too. He knows us; he knows most of our resources."

Lance let out a jagged chuckle. "Then we make him think it isn't worth messing with her."

I frowned. Rollick was the most powerful being I'd ever spent much time around. How in the realms were we supposed to do that?

CHAPTER TWENTY-SIX

Quinn

As I tore along the dock and across the marina grounds beyond it, I didn't dare shoot so much as a glance over my shoulder. The thumps and grunts suggested some kind of scuffle was taking place, but I had no idea who was on which side and whether it'd turn out in my favor. Or whether *any* of them winning could be in my favor after what I'd just learned.

My messenger bag thumped against my back, and my feet pounded over the boards and then the pavement. "Hey!" a marina-goer called to me, but I didn't stop to find out what help they might try to offer.

They couldn't help me, not when my enemies were shadowkind. Beings they wouldn't even believe existed. Beings with powers no human could match. Even the sorcerers had failed to defend themselves.

As long as any of those shadowkind knew where I was, I was in danger. That one fact had been drilled into me well over the past several days. Once I was out of their sight, I wasn't *safe*, but I was a hell of a lot saf*er*.

I raced around the marina building and spotted a bus just pulling up at a stop a little ways down the nearby street. Hell, yes! The men had talked about hitching rides in the shadows of cars—human vehicles could move faster than shadowkind could travel on their own. Even if one or more of them gave chase and saw where I went, they wouldn't be able to catch up.

I pushed my legs faster, summoning an extra burst of speed. Just as the last person waiting at the stop stepped on board, I scrambled after her, breathing hard. I fumbled in my bag for my wallet and shoved a five into the fare box, pretty sure I was overpaying but not really caring. It wasn't like I had time to stop and make change.

It was early afternoon now, well before rush hour, and the bus was only half full. I flopped into a seat partway down, my pulse slowly settling back into a more normal rhythm as the bus pulled away from the curb and sped up heading down the street. I had no idea where it was going, but I didn't care about that either. I just wanted to be *away*.

I hugged my messenger bag to my chest and closed my eyes for a moment, my throat tightening. What the hell was I going to do now? Even the men I'd thought had my back had turned out to be villains. All kinds of shadowkind were still hunting me. How was I going to keep ahead of them on my own?

I couldn't keep moving forever. The jolt of panicked adrenaline during the confrontation with Rollick had driven away my creeping of fatigue, but it would come back. I hadn't slept since a brief doze in the car early last night.

My hand slid to the pocket that contained my phone. Sorsha had given her number to me as well as Torrent.

But... she was shadowkind. Her men were shadowkind. How could I be sure *they* had really meant well either? My judgment was obviously off. Torrent had trusted them, and he'd turned out to be the most untrustworthy of all.

I barely knew them. It wasn't worth the risk of finding myself in an even worse trap than I already had.

The bus rumbled along for a half hour or so before I realized it'd turned in a loop and now was heading back the way we'd come. Back toward the marina. Definitely not where I wanted to be.

I got off at the next stop and took stock. I'd ended up in a pretty ordinary-looking strip of shops and casual restaurants, a little shabby but not horribly rundown. Pedestrians were ambling along, chattering with each other or lost in their own little worlds like mine wasn't on the verge of ending.

My legs itched with the urge to keep moving. I strode down the street, stopping only long enough to grab a chicken wrap from a café, which I dug into as I kept hustling along. I headed north without much reason other than the map on my phone showed that direction would take me farther from the marina rather than closer.

I left the commercial strip behind for rows of modest houses. What next? Where could I hole up for the night? How long would it take before the shadowkind caught up with me? I couldn't sleep on a bus the whole night.

Inspiration sparked in my head. Maybe I could—if I could find a cross-country bus. Or a train. Was there a train station in Daytona Beach? There was probably one at least close. That would run up my credit card bill, but hopefully it'd keep me ahead of any creatures wanting to sink claws or fangs into me for a day or two.

I looked up directions, wincing at the sight of how low my phone battery was getting. I hadn't had a chance to charge it since yesterday, and the flashlight app drained it fast. I memorized the directions and then brought up the Uber app.

Before I could confirm my location, my last few percent vanished. "Shit!" I snapped.

It was okay. I'd just keep walking. Quickly. I knew where I needed to go. If I saw a taxi passing by, I'd flag it down. Once I got on a train, they had outlets, and I could charge it up again.

No big deal. I could handle this.

The shadows were starting to stretch a little longer across the sidewalk. A few cars were pulling up into driveways as people arrived home from early shifts at work. Kids out of school for the summer played in the yards. An uneasy prickle ran down my spine.

What if the shadowkind beasts decided to attack me here even with all these people around? They had to be getting more desperate. Who knew how much sense of caution the lesser beings had to begin with?

I veered through the streets, trying to work my way back to somewhere a little less family-oriented. After several blocks, I found myself passing a big outlet store that looked like it'd been closed for months if not years from the grime on the windows.

No one much was hanging around in that parking lot—or anywhere else nearby. I picked up my pace, my nerves prickling with apprehension that was totally self-preservation now.

I'd made it halfway past the parking lot when the first creature eased out of the shadows.

It was about the size of an alley cat, but hunched and furless, its shoulders jutting high from its wrinkled back. It hissed at me, eyes flashing amber, and I stalled in my tracks.

I'd had to leave the damned dagger behind in Rollick, or I might have been able to tackle this beast. Of course, it wasn't that big anyway. Maybe I could hit it hard enough to get it to back off even without special weaponry.

I raised my hands in a fighting stance as if it were going to come at me like a boxer. The thing lunged at my legs.

My reflexes had obviously benefitted at least a little from my sparring with Crag and Lance. My foot shot out at just the right angle to punt the creature over the low steel fence around the parking lot. It skidded to a stop on the other side, claws skittering against the asphalt.

A momentary spurt of relieved pride washed through me, and then the wrinkled cat-thing was leaping over the fence again. Two more creatures, these ones closer to the size of Dobermans, slunk out of the patches of darkness to surround me.

Okay, clearly walking hadn't been moving quickly enough.

I swallowed, finding my mouth dry, and tried a little bravado. There was some kind of wild animal you were supposed to yell at to intimidate it into leaving you alone, right?

"Get out of here!" I shouted, looming as menacingly as I could in one direction and then another. "Beat it! Nothing for you here. I'll make sure you regret it."

As the words tumbled inanely from my throat, the bald cat-like creature and another of the things launched themselves at me from opposite sites.

I yelped, dodging and blocking as well as I could. My knuckles smacked into the cat-thing's head with a solid-sounding smack, but the other creature clamped its jaws into my thigh.

Pain splintered through my leg. I gasped, teetering as I hurled my fists at the thing, and the third creature leapt up to chomp on my elbow.

Panic blared through my mind even louder than when I'd faced Rollick. I flailed around, a desperate scream for help bubbling in my throat even though I didn't want to subject any other human being to this madness—

—and a tentacle whipped through the air, smacking one creature's jaws right off me. A flicker of claws sliced straight through the neck of the thing on my elbow so its body thumped to the ground just seconds before I shook off its detached head.

Smoky blood plumed up toward the sky, and I whirled around in its midst, my heart hammering even harder than before.

Torrent, Lance, and Crag stood around me. Crag looked stern, Lance was grinning as he flexed his claws, and Torrent—the tentacled man's broken face was as unreadable as ever.

"We have to go," Crag said gruffly, nodding to the car parked down the street. In my terror, I hadn't even noticed it pulling over. "There'll be more coming."

I hugged myself, conflicting emotions tangling in my chest. "What, so you can drag me back to Rollick?"

"No," Torrent said, his voice crisp but firm. "So we can keep you away from him and all the other beings that are after you."

"And why exactly should I believe that? He did send you to collect me for him, didn't he? Wasn't that your job?"

Torrent's expression tightened. At the sound of an approaching car, he sank down to sit on the parking lot's fence so he could tuck his tentacles out of sight. "Yes. He sent us to keep an eye on you and see if anything unusual happened, to step in if you were in danger. That's why we were there in the park the night you were attacked."

Keep an eye on you. "How long were you watching before that happened?" I demanded.

"Three months," he admitted.

Three *months*? All that time, everything I'd been doing, they'd been spying on me—

Then understanding struck me so hard my eyes widened.

I jabbed my finger at him. "It's *your* fault. You were hanging around near me for months—you set off whatever this stupid power is in my heart. Maybe I wouldn't have been attacked at all otherwise."

"It would have happened, moody one," Lance said, his gaze sliding away from me across the lot. "There was already a vibe to you when we showed up. Only a little one, but it was there."

He leapt abruptly and landed on a creature in the shadows that he forced into physical being with his pounce. The iguana-like thing let out a brief squeal before the dragon shifter's claws severed its life from its body.

"We might have sped things along," Torrent acknowledged. "But it's better that it happened when we were here. Otherwise you wouldn't have survived at all."

"I also wouldn't have had you stalking me, scheming about how to offer me up to your boss for dinner," I shot back.

"He's not having you for anything," Crag growled.

"Why not? What changed? Why should I believe you?"

Torrent shifted on his awkward perch. His voice came out low with a bit of a rasp. "Because you made *us* believe. We believe that you should get all the life you've been making the most of, as much as that heart will allow you. I've never—"

He cut himself off for a second, glancing away with a grimace, and then yanked his gaze back to me. "Mortals were playthings to me once, and since then they've become obstacles or beings of no consequence. But you aren't like any other I've met. You've woken something up in me, something that can't bear to see you gone, and I don't know how to turn it off. So you can come with us or you can run away, but either way I'm going to be right there with you fighting to keep you in this world."

My throat choked up abruptly at his declaration. He wasn't saying that he's suddenly realized the value of all human life or anything like that. He *was* still a monster, still a being that'd watched millions of us come and go in our relatively brief lives, seeing us the way the average human probably looked at ants swarming on the sidewalk.

But somehow I'd earned that kind of devotion from him anyway. He was willing to be monstrous on *my* behalf rather than Rollick's—rather than a fellow shadowkind he'd apparently served for a long time.

Even so... "You lied to me all this time."

"I know," he said. "I thought I had to. I thought it didn't matter."

"He was wrong," Lance piped up.

Torrent glowered at the other man but didn't correct him. "I see things differently now. Rollick... Rollick doesn't know you. He didn't give us a chance to make a case. I thought he'd be better than that, but obviously I was wrong about him too."

He exhaled sharply. "These two have been shifting their allegiances since well before I have. You shouldn't doubt *their* commitment to the cause of keeping you alive. What else do you need from me? Ask whatever questions you want."

"Maybe in the car away from the creeping beasties?" Lance suggested. His expression clouded when he considered the wounds on my thigh and arm, where blood was seeping alongside the stinging in my flesh. "I don't want them ripping you up any more, baby girl. I can close up those cuts for you."

I didn't know how to deny the affection in his voice, or the protective ferocity that emanated off Crag in the instant before he smashed another creature out of the shadows to its smoky death. How many more beasts were dashing toward us even now?

Even if trusting these men again was the wrong decision... making any other choice was still basically suicide, wasn't it? I'd *tried* to make it on my own, and within a few hours, I'd nearly become monster chow.

Bringing my gaze back to Torrent, I still had to ask, "Where do we go from here? How do we stop them all—the beings who killed my donor's family, Rollick, all the lesser creatures...?"

A faint smile touched his lips, and somehow that was what convinced me. That he could smile at me at all while still looking pained, as if it mattered more to him to try to offer me a tiny bit of comfort than to focus on his own discomforts.

"We don't have a full solution yet," he said. "But we've been hashing out a lot of ideas while we searched for you, and I think we've come up with one strategy that will buy you some time. I suspect we'll need your design expertise to take it all the way to reality. If you'll come with us, we can get started."

He didn't stand, just sat there waiting for my response, braced for more questions or accusations.

I reached out and found Crag's hand with mine. He squeezed my fingers immediately with the rock-solid gasp that could become so gentle when he touched me.

"Okay," I said. "Let's hear how you're really going to save me this time."

CHAPTER TWENTY-SEVEN

Quinn

A half hour later, I slumped against the tinted backseat window and gave the drawing in my sketchpad a final once-over. Lance scooted to sit closer to me like he had when he'd cauterized my wounds with his fiery breath, tucking his chin over his shoulder. "Can I see?"

"It doesn't look like much," I said, tilting the pad so he had a better view.

Clothing was far from my expertise, but I'd fixed torn seams and lost buttons over the years. I had a basic understanding of how the pieces needed to fit together and what sorts of construction made sense. I'd just have to count on an expert to figure out the precise logistics.

The sort-of vest I'd sketched out looked like a broad-coverage sports bra, the neckline curving along my sketched model's collarbone to two narrow straps, the base set a couple of inches below the breasts. I'd drawn a closeup of the materials I wanted stitched together for the entire piece other than the straps: flat beads woven in an interlocking pattern so that they could shift with my movements but left only the slightest gaps in between them.

"I think it should work," I said. "I mean, as much as anything should, if this works at all. I figured we'd ask for alternating silver and iron beads so that both metals have an evenly distributed effect." I sucked my lower lip under my teeth. "Do you really think this will suppress the sorcerer vibe I give off? I thought it was in my blood too. I can't go around in a full hazmat suit of this stuff."

My question was directed mainly at Torrent, who'd suggested the metal vest solution. He'd been behind the wheel for the entire time I'd been drawing, cruising north along the highway. He figured we had the best chance of finding someone who could build what we needed in Jacksonville, since it was the biggest city anywhere nearby. I hadn't wanted to stick around Daytona Beach with Rollick searching for us there anyway.

"The effects of the metals worked for a while when we were at the cabin," he said. "There were posts of silver and iron under the water around the property to discourage other shadowkind from coming near, and it took a few days before your energy got strong enough for it to seep through."

"But if it *keeps* getting stronger—"

He shot me a brief glance over his shoulder. "That should be less of an issue once the other shadowkind aren't stalking you as closely—and we'll be keeping more of a distance rather than being in close quarters with you 24-7. This shield will also create a much more concentrated effect directly around the most potent source of the energy. I can't guarantee it'll work, but it's our best chance."

I couldn't really ask for more than that, could I? I slumped back in my seat. "All right. Now how are we going to find someone to put this together—and fast?" The afternoon had only gotten later, the sun dropping ever closer to the horizon, and it wasn't exactly a normal project at the best of times. "We'll have to pay them a lot too, especially for a rush job."

I started mentally calculating how much I could take out of my bank account in one go from an ATM. Would any branches of my usual bank be open by the time we got to Jacksonville so I could ask for more in person? It was coming up on the end of the afternoon. Random independent seamstresses weren't likely to take a credit card.

"I can take care of that," Torrent said before I got very far in my assessment. "Money isn't a problem. Crag, give her my phone."

As the gargoyle handed the device over with a worried frown, Torrent went on. "Find someone in Jacksonville who's got the resources, can work quickly, and can start right away. Offer them a hundred thousand dollars if you need to."

My jaw dropped even as my gut twisted. "I'm sure *someone* would do it for that, but are you kidding me? I can't ask you to give me that kind of money." It was at least twenty times more than all I had to my name.

Torrent let out a scoffing sound. "I've had centuries for my accounts to accumulate interest. Believe me, that's a drop in the bucket. You'll find most shadowkind who've spent much time mortal-side have no cash-flow problems."

"Oh." That made sense. But a knot remained in my stomach as I started searching the internet for local clothes makers and designers.

A whisper of a memory rose up in the back of my head of overhearing Mom and Dad murmur to each other about how much the insurance would cover, how they'd leverage their retirement funds and other investments to cover my treatments. All the trips and minor luxuries they'd once talked about us enjoying someday had vanished with my hospital stays.

They'd also used to talk about me someday having a little brother or sister, but that idea had evaporated too once my health problems had drained their accounts.

I'd done everything I could not to be a burden since then. I knew it wasn't my fault and that my parents would rather have had me still alive than have kept the money. But still…

I stared down at the phone, blinking away the sudden blur of tears, and set my jaw. This was different. Torrent had made it clear he could easily spare the money. It mattered more to *him* that I survived the next few days than to hold on to his cash.

And if the fact that I might really matter to him a hell of a lot more than I'd believed a couple of hours ago sent an uneasy wobble through my chest, this wasn't the time to examine that feeling too closely. Before, I'd managed to tell myself that my shadowkind men were only protecting me out of some sort of general sense of honor or justice, since after all they hadn't really known me.

But that had changed. They'd somehow become dedicated to my survival to the point that they'd defied a very powerful demon they'd once answered to.

How much more would they lose trying to keep me alive?

I closed my eyes for a second and shook off those thoughts. They didn't want to lose *me* either, so I'd better get on with making sure they didn't, right?

I tapped out hasty messages to the freelancers I'd looked up, giving a few details about what I needed and the preferred timeline. A couple of people responded as if thinking it was a joke. One said they'd need a week. Then the fourth messaged me back saying she was a night owl and would appreciate the challenge. Would I call to discuss the details?

I dialed her number, my pulse thumping harder. "Hey," she said when she answered. "That was fast."

"Yeah," I said with a nervous little laugh. "Like I said in my message, this is pretty urgent. Do you really think you can make it happen tonight?"

"I'm hoping so. The structure should be pretty simple, and my roommates can help with the beading. I've got to check with a friend who does metal work, but he's been putting together a bunch of types of beads and other fixtures in different metals. I'm sure he has silver and probably iron too. They might not be the exact shape you were picturing, though, since it sounds like there isn't time to customize..."

"That's fine," I said. "I wasn't sure what would work best anyway. As long as they're relatively light-weight and small enough to allow a good amount of movement, that's what's most important."

"Okay. Send me a pic of your sketch so I can get started working out the logistics. Exactly how high is your budget for this? I've got to put off another project I had on the go."

"Whatever you'd usually charge for a rush order with this much customization, triple it," I said.

I could almost hear her eyebrows rising over the phone. "That'd put us at about fifteen K since I'll need to give my roommates a slice. You're really okay with that?"

I held back a laugh, thinking of what Torrent had offered. "No problem at all. More than worth it for the short notice."

"All right then. It is kind of crazy, but for that kind of money—and hey, I always like stretching my skills. I'll send you my address so you can come by and I'll measure you. We can work out the deposit details then, once you see I'm a real person too."

For the first time in ages, the weight of worry I'd been carrying since the attack in the park lifted. "Great. I'll see you soon."

My seamstress turned out to be a woman who looked only a few years older than me, with wild curls and sparkling eyes that matched her enthusiasm for the unusual work. When I stopped at her apartment for the second time, after she'd texted me that the vest was done, she flung open the door with an exuberance that felt like a bit much for the late hour. I'd managed to get some sleep nestled in the back seat of the car while Torrent drove around and we waited for my new protective clothing to be finished, but I wasn't exactly at full alertness.

"It came together so well," she said in an excited whisper, and motioned toward the apartment behind her in explanation for her volume. "My roommates have all crashed. But it wasn't even as hard as I was worried it'd be. Come in. You've got to try it on."

I stepped inside, set down my messenger bag, and held out my arms so she could ease the vest over my head. She'd made the fabric in the straps flexible so it pulled on easily despite the shallow neckline.

The beads, a mix of dime-shaped silver and slightly thicker iron squares, tinkled faintly against each other. But once the vest was lying flat on me over the thin cotton of my regular tank top, they were spaced enough apart that they barely clinked unless I twisted around abruptly.

"It'll be even quieter if you wear something over it to weigh them down," the woman said, cocking her head. "Not that you'd want to layer up in this heat. And I assume you're hoping to show it off. I did make sure it's nice and sturdy like you asked—shouldn't have to worry about threads snagging and breaking. What's it for, anyway? Some kind of theater production? Special fashion statement?"

"Something like that," I said, wishing I could sate her curiosity after how well she'd come through for me. "Thank you so much. You got it together incredibly fast."

She giggled. "With what you're paying me, I'd have finished it even sooner if my hands could work faster. I hope it's worth it."

So did I. Torrent had picked up money somehow or other while I'd slept so that I could pay the rest of what I owed her in cash. I got the envelope out of my bag, stood there awkwardly while she counted it with widened eyes, and then hurried downstairs to find out whether our plan had been a success. *I* couldn't tell whether the vest had changed anything.

I slipped out of the apartment building and rushed around back to where the sedan was waiting, knowing at least one of the men would be tracking me through the shadows for extra protection. When I opened the back door, Crag materialized at the opposite side, Torrent and Lance already up front. All three of them gave a little flinch as I dropped into my seat.

I glanced down at the vest. "Crap. I didn't think about—it's uncomfortable for you being near me while I'm in this thing, isn't it?"

"We're fine," Crag said gruffly. "We could handle being in the cabin surrounded by the posts; we can handle this."

"We're just trusting you not to give us any bear hugs while you're in that thing," Lance said around the side of his seat, shooting me a wink.

He'd said it flippantly, but the words struck me hard anyway.

It was true. The trust went both ways in this situation. It wasn't just me counting on them not to turn on me, either directly or by betraying me to their boss. They'd arranged the means for me to hurt them if I wanted to.

The sense of resistance to accepting their commitment coiled through my gut again, but it didn't squeeze quite as tightly as before. Maybe it was okay that they were staking so much on me. I'd taken a risk voluntarily, and so had they. We were in this together.

"Is it working?" I asked, focusing on the most important question.

Lance tipped farther between the front seats. Torrent watched as the dragon shifter examined me. Lance's lips stretched with a smile, and he rubbed his hands together. "I can't pick up a quiver even when I'm this close. None of the beasties will have a clue."

Relief rushed through me so abruptly that I found my eyes welling up for the second time since the three men had caught up with me this afternoon. "Good. No, that's fucking fantastic. Does that mean—is this enough? As long as I can figure out how to keep this thing on me, I'd be able to go home and head back to college in the fall and all that?"

Torrent's mouth slanted at an apologetic angle. "Not quite. This is a big step, and it buys us time. It should get the other shadowkind off your back, since as far as we can tell, they didn't know anything about you other than whatever was in that letter you wrote. They're clearly not as adept at tracking via human methods as Rollick is. They were relying on picking up the energy to hunt you down, but he found out your full name and where you lived before you even started giving off enough of a vibe to draw notice."

My exhilaration dampened. "I can't go anywhere I'd usually go then, can I? He'll be keeping an eye on my house and maybe other places too."

"That would be the most logical approach once he realizes he can't locate you any other way." Torrent hesitated, as if he didn't like what he had to say next. "He might even chat up your parents or other people from your regular life to try to gather more information. I don't think he'd *hurt* any of them, at least not unless he saw a reason to believe you'd find out and he could use it as leverage..."

Any good feeling in me swept away under a wave of nausea. "Oh, no. So then, what? I'm supposed to basically go into witness protection and cut all ties with everyone and everything that mattered to me?" What was the point in even staying alive for another few years if I did that? Everything I'd been working toward would still be thrown in the garbage. My parents would suffer for ages wondering what'd happened to me—worse than if I'd simply died.

"We have to find a way to get him to back off," Crag rumbled, his expression hardening as he took in the anguish that must have been written on my face.

"A way, a way, to make him go away," Lance chanted, sliding down in his seat and sticking his feet on the dashboard. "He's a wily one."

"We haven't come up with a definite plan for that yet," Torrent said. "But we haven't had a lot of time to either. We can lay low for a few days and think it through."

But that didn't guarantee we'd come up with a solid plan. And in those few days, who knew what Rollick might do to Mom and Dad?

As Torrent started the engine, I knit my brow. "Could we ask Sorsha for help? Even if he's too powerful for the three of you to stop on your own, she and her guys seemed pretty fierce."

Lance hummed to himself. "The flaming bird."

Torrent shook his head. "We don't really know them. I've worked for Rollick for decades and I still didn't know *him* as well as I thought I did. We can't trust strangers to solve our problems for us. For all we know, they'll decide it's better to destroy Quinn's heart so no one gets their hands on it than to try to protect her."

Crag let out a growl at that idea. Okay, yeah, I didn't really want to take that risk either.

I bit my lip, my thoughts spinning. "Your boss just wants me, right? He wants my heart like this other bunch of shadowkind do too?"

"As far as I can figure from what he's said," Torrent said. "Rollick wasn't specific when he gave our orders. I'm not sure *he* knew back then whether there'd be any reason to pursue you at all. He wanted us to observe you and to protect you if any other shadowkind came after you so that… so that you'd be saved for him. But he also said that if we didn't see anything unusual after several months, that we should just leave. When he came to the marina, though, he was obviously more aware."

My mind latched on to one part of what Torrent had said with a glimmer of inspiration. "He was worried that if I turned out to be something he wanted, someone else might get to me first. And then he couldn't have me at all."

"That sums it up pretty well."

"Then… is there some way we can make him believe that another shadowkind *has* gotten to me? That I'm not around at all, so he might as well just go back to wherever he came from and stop looking?"

All three of the men were silent for a long moment. Lance clicked his claws together. "Clever. I like it. But also tricky."

Crag frowned. "I don't think he'll give up based on rumors. He'd need to be totally convinced."

"I agree." Torrent drew in a slow, thoughtful breath. His silence stretched as the car's engine rumbled. Then he nodded. "There may be a way we can arrange some 'evidence.' We might even be able to pull it off tonight, if luck is on our side."

I sat straighter, peering at him in the shadowy space lit only by the passing streetlamps. "What are you thinking? Whatever it is, let's do it."

He let out a humorless chuckle. "Maybe you should wait until you've heard the idea. You might not like it. You're going to need to get up close and personal with human mortality—and we'll need you to bleed."

Crag let out a grunt of protest, and Lance hissed through his teeth, but I lifted my chin even as a chill washed over me.

I'd thumbed my nose at death plenty of times. No big deal. And as for blood—if it was spill a little or spill a lot, I knew which option I preferred.

These three men had sacrificed their security and their jobs and risked their own lives to save mine. How could I say no to *anything* they asked of me to accomplish the same goal?

"I'll face whatever you need me to if it means I can get out of this mess," I said. "What's a little more blood in the grand scheme of things anyway?"

CHAPTER TWENTY-EIGHT

Quinn

Getting into the restricted areas of the hospital was surprisingly easy. At three in the morning, it was only a skeleton crew anyway, the few nurses and doctors on duty busy with essential tasks. The men slipped inside through the shadows, one of them unlocked a staff side door to allow me in, and we slunk down to the basement without encountering anyone other than in distant voices filtering through the walls.

Crag stayed in physical form beside me, his solid fingers curled around my elbow to guide me in the dark as we left the active levels of the hospital behind. His eyes glowed with a ruddy gleam in the dimness. I held my arm away from my side so there was no chance of his skin brushing the silver-and-iron vest, but he didn't reveal any outward sign of discomfort.

Torrent and Lance had gone ahead through the gloom to scope out our destination. When we reached the door, Lance pushed it open. "Lots to choose from!" he said with hushed cheerfulness.

As I stepped through the doorway, my stomach clenched up. The smells of the space closed in around me, both the standard hospital smell of antiseptic cleaners and a more pungent waft of the chemicals employed in this specific section. The chilly air raised goosebumps on my arms.

Torrent had switched on a desk lamp at the far end of the room to cast a thin glow over the space without risking too bright a light in case someone else ventured down in the basement halls. I peered around me at the shiny exam tables, the tool cabinets, and wall of stainless steel cubbies. Images flashed through my mind of what lay behind those doors, and I closed my eyes.

I'd risked death every time I'd gone out on one of my urban exploring adventures, sure. I'd been at its door every time the shadowkind beasts had launched an attack. But I'd never looked it in the face quite as vividly as I was right now.

The morgue didn't hold any adventure or excitement, any sense of making the most out of life. It was wrenchingly banal in its finality.

If my transplant operation had gone wrong nine years ago, or if there hadn't been a viable heart available in time, I'd have ended up down here. Just a husk of a body, already starting to decompose. Any day, any hour, any minute, my new heart could fail, and I'd be behind one of those doors by the next day.

I shivered, my lungs constricting. I didn't know if I believed in an afterlife. I *wanted* to, but the older I'd gotten, the more it seemed like wishful thinking. And even if it did exist, there was so much I still wanted to do in *this* world. Even with all the thrills and experiences I'd chased, I wasn't close to finished.

Lance roved over to the cubbies and started opening the doors, peeking inside. Torrent had emerged into physical form near one of the empty exam tables. He considered me, his mouth tight.

"Are you all right?" he asked.

I squared my shoulders, willing down the icy tendrils of nausea. I could do this. I *had* to do this if I wanted to live. Even if it felt like shit to know that I was stealing from someone else to survive just like the first time.

Don't think of it that way, the counsellor had told me after the operation. *The girl who gave you her heart was already lost. She'd be* happy *knowing that she saved someone else, that she managed to do one more good thing.*

Hopefully whoever we picked down here would feel the same way.

"I'll manage," I said, and touched the hem of my vest. "Do you need me to take this off?" He'd said I should come with them to the morgue if we wanted to improve the chances of this plan working. The men could compare the overall human vibe my body gave off to the ones in here to make sure they found someone who was as close a match as possible. If we picked someone too different in physical composition, Rollick might sense something was wrong.

Torrent shook his head. "It only disguises the energies coming from that area of your body. We can pick up on your general essence from any other part."

Crag's hand slid to mine, and he lifted it to his nose as if to breathe in that essence. I held still and then extended my fingers to graze his cheek.

He gave my hand a little squeeze. "The strength beneath your softness is always impressive."

"My strength, my softness. *My* baby girl," Lance declared lightly, without sounding particularly put out by the other man's attentions. He teased his claws over my hair and leaned in to give the back of my head a quick peck.

Torrent curled a tentacle around my other wrist. I remembered him saying that his suckers could pick up on things his other senses couldn't.

I caught his eyes, feeling abruptly uncertain. My relationship with him had yoyoed all over the place in the past day.

He stepped a little closer and raised my hand so he could brush a quick kiss to the knuckles. It was a brief flutter of sensation, but it made my heart skip a beat.

"It will be worth it," he said, with total conviction, and added, "You don't have to get any closer to the bodies. We should handle the choosing anyway."

"Okay," I said. But I still saw the white-shrouded corpses as the men slid one and then another partway out, undoing zippers for closer inspections. My stance went rigid, holding me in place even though part of me longed to bolt for the door.

This wasn't my fate. Not yet. I had at least a little while longer.

The men came back to me one at a time to refamiliarize themselves with the details of my essence and then continue their search. There did appear to be quite a large selection on this particular evening, although this was the biggest hospital in Jacksonville, so maybe that wasn't surprising. Accidents and illnesses either sudden or finally terminal, probably at least one murder...

"I think this one," Lance said, tapping his claws against the tray in a cubby he'd doubled back to. "Not the same but the closest. And her hair looks similar too, in color anyway."

The other men joined him to study the corpse. "She's older but not so much older that I think Rollick will notice once we've set everything up," Torrent said after a moment. "Heavier, but that won't really matter. I agree. This one."

I swallowed thickly, wondering who this woman was that we were going to use in our scheme in ways she definitely didn't deserve. "What now?"

Torrent glanced at me. "Crag can carry the body through the shadows. Lance will help you navigate back to the door. I'll go ahead to the car so we can drive off quickly. It won't be dark for more than a couple hours longer."

Guilt clamped around my gut as I left the room behind. Lance tsked as he ushered me through the dark halls. "Why worry about her? She's gone, wherever the part of her that matters would go, if it goes anywhere."

"It's still not something anyone would want to happen to their body, if they did know," I murmured. "And she probably has family or friends, people who could find out and who'll be upset..."

"*We* would be very upset if we couldn't stop Rollick from taking you," Lance informed me, his grip on my arm tightening.

I didn't know how to tell him that knowing how invested they were in my survival unnerved me as much as it reassured me.

What if this didn't work, and I was going to end up taken and eviscerated no matter what they did? What if I'd ruined their lives for nothing?

Maybe it would have been better if I'd never tried to get to know them, never shown any concern for them, kept my distance the way I had with every normal person in my life. *I* took the risks for me. I'd never expected anyone else to.

But these men weren't normal, and the situation wasn't either, and now here we were. What could we do other than keep going forward?

We drove through familiar streets to the park where the shadowkind men had first leapt to my rescue. It seemed fitting. They figured Rollick would have headed this way both following my energies before I'd put the vest on and then investigating my usual haunts when that beacon had vanished. We needed him to find the body first or at least quickly.

Maybe my safety would be secured in almost the exact same place I'd lost it.

Crag carried the body through the darkness again, and Lance followed his impressions of the other men. He led me through the shadowy park to an isolated spot far from any of the paths, sheltered by trees and shrubs. The gargoyle laid the corpse on the grass there.

I stared down at the woman's bluish face, and Lance raised a hand, extending his claws, to begin the work.

"Wait!" I whispered urgently, and bent down by the dead woman. "I'm sorry. I hope you're at peace, wherever you are. I wouldn't do this if I didn't think it'd save more people than just me."

The men waited until I straightened up again, not commenting on my little speech, and then they descended on the body without any sign that the act bothered *them* at all. I supposed it didn't.

Lance and Crag tore into the torso with their claws. Torrent slammed the thicker part of one tentacle into her face hard enough to crush the skull and batter the woman beyond recognition. In between, the dragon shifter warmed the ravaged pieces to a more lifelike temperature with shallow huffs of breath, so Rollick wouldn't think "I" had cooled too quickly.

The sounds of ripped and pummeled flesh made my stomach heave. I had to turn away and put my hands over my ears. I'd wanted to bear witness, but I was afraid I'd puke and ruin the scene we'd meant to construct. My gut kept lurching, bile creeping up my throat.

It only took a minute. I didn't see what they did with the heart they removed from the flayed flesh. Torrent touched my shoulder with his hand.

"We need your blood now," he said. "And then you'll have to take off your vest so he can track your energy here."

I nodded. My legs wobbled as I turned around. Lance blinked in and out of the shadows, the gore vanishing from his claws with the trip. For these guys, darkness was the ultimate disinfectant, erasing everything except the essentials of their physical presence when they reformed. Torrent had said not even germs could travel with them. I couldn't have asked for a cleaner blade.

The dragon shifter took my hand with a gentleness I'd never seen him extend to anyone or anything other than me. "We won't let you lose too much. I'll seal it up quickly."

"I know," I said, but my voice came out choked. I forced myself to step over to the ravaged remains that barely looked human anymore.

A meaty smell hung in the air. I clamped my mouth shut, breathing as shallowly as I could, and held out my arm.

Lance severed one of my veins so neatly it was only a brief flicker of sharper pain and then a radiating but duller ache. Blood spurted down over the wrecked corpse. I moved quickly around the mess, guiding the traces of scarlet liquid all around the scene so that a little of my essence would cling to every part.

I had to give enough blood to make this trick work. If Rollick realized we'd tried to pull one over on him… I didn't know if I or my men would make it through the night.

I kept holding out my arm and letting my blood fall until one of Torrent's tentacles caught me carefully around my waist. "That's enough," he said in a low voice.

I was starting to feel a bit light-headed, although I didn't know how much that was the blood loss compared to my jittering nerves and the roiling nausea that kept bubbling up inside me.

Lance raised my wrist to his mouth, blew his fiery breath over it to cauterize it, and then soothed the momentary burn with a slick of his dragon tongue.

"So handy," I said with a wobbly laugh.

He grinned at me. "It is. I'll always patch you up."

If I didn't end up torn up beyond repair like the corpse we were standing over.

I squashed down that thought and stepped back, tugging off my vest. Crag had already vanished into the night to watch for Rollick's approach—and to dispatch any unwanted shadowkind who crept this way before their boss reached the site. Torrent sent Lance after the gargoyle with a brisk gesture. Then he motioned for me to follow him.

"You stay crouched here," he said, ushering me to a cluster of bushes about ten feet from the body, which were dense enough that I'd be invisible to anyone near it. They formed a semi-circle that would shield me on both sides as well.

"As soon as any of us alerts you, put the vest on," Torrent said. "At that point, I think it'll be safer if you stay in this spot rather than try to go back to the car or anywhere else. We'll be here helping manipulate the situation."

I glanced behind me, in the one direction where I'd be exposed. "What if Rollick comes from that way?"

"We should know before he gets close enough to spot you in the dark, and we'll move you. I've already scouted out a couple of other hiding spots." Torrent paused and then touched my cheek with his hand. His cool gaze held mine. "This is a good plan. It's *your* plan. The ultimate fix-it."

The old guilt wound through me again. "I know. You don't have to—none of you have to—" I sucked in a breath and gathered my words. "It'd be safer for the three of you too if you stayed in hiding and didn't show him you're here, wouldn't it?"

"But not safer for you," Torrent said calmly. "We'll be helping sell the story. And if he doesn't see us then, he'll probably track us down just in case we were responsible. This will help settle things between him and us too."

I raised my eyebrows. Rollick hadn't struck me as the type to simply let a transgression go. "Is he ever going to forgive you either way?"

Torrent shrugged. "Forgive, no. Recognize that he's got better things to do than make us suffer when no one knew we were running this mission for him anyway? Absolutely. He cares more about maintaining his reputation on a broad scale than retribution. The longer he lingers around here, the more chance another party will find out he was mixed up in this mess, and he definitely didn't want that."

"So it might be easier for you if you did just disappear."

Torrent was silent for a moment, studying my expression. I wished it was easier for me to read his face.

One of his tentacles eased toward me, simply coming to rest against my ankle. "Do you *want* us to go? Would you rather be rid of us once we've dealt with Rollick? You will be reasonably safe with just the vest."

I folded my arms over my chest. "Would you—or Crag and Lance, anyway—leave even if I told you to? You don't seem to be very good at that."

He gazed back at me steadily. "I'd make them. If that's really what would make you happiest. I know a whole lot of chaos has come into your life along with us, and we lied to you for a long time—it'd be understandable if you didn't want to be reminded of that. But we—*I*—would only be leaving for your benefit. I..."

He glanced away for a moment and then jerked his eyes back to me.

"I've never felt anything close to the way I feel when you're with me. It's not something I want to lose. I don't want to lose *you*. That's why I'm here, in case I didn't make that clear enough earlier. It isn't just them, even if they've been better at showing how you've affected them. All right?"

A strange sensation bloomed in my chest—not the flutter of inexplicable energy, but a heady warmth that grounded me in the night. Because the three of them had done the same for me, hadn't they? They'd brought a lot of chaos with them, but they'd also opened up my life to all kinds of things I'd never even known were possible.

Imagine what it could be like if we pulled this off and I had the freedom to have both normalcy and a little chaos on the side.

They were here for me... and I was giving them something in return. It wasn't just take take take, me draining them in my quest for survival, the way it'd always seemed with my parents and my former friends.

I could have lied. I could have told him I never wanted to see any of their faces or sense them lurking in the nearby shadows again. But it *would* be a lie... and it sounded like leaving might actually hurt them more than staying would, even if this ended in catastrophe sooner rather than later.

"I just don't like putting you in more danger," I said quietly.

Something shifted in Torrent's face, bringing a gleam of longing into his gaze that I couldn't deny. His voice came out raw. "*You* aren't the danger. You're what makes things right. Our indomitable Ms. Fix-It."

There was nothing but affection in the once-sardonic nickname. It drew me in. I stepped forward and answered Torrent the best way I could, with no words at all. Bobbing up on my toes, I pressed my lips to his.

He returned the kiss without hesitation, his tentacle rising to rest against the small of my back, to hold me in place. When I eased back, I added, in case it was necessary, "I don't want to lose you either."

A smile softer than I'd ever seen from him before touched Torrent's lips. And then Crag leapt out of the shadows beside us, his stance tensed. My pulse hiccupped, and I moved to tug on my vest.

"No," he said before I got very far, and turned to Torrent. "I haven't sensed Rollick yet. Neither has Lance. And more lesser creatures have been intruding on the park. I don't know how much longer we can wait."

CHAPTER TWENTY-NINE

Quinn

My throat closed up at Crag's words. "We can't *give up*," I forced out. "You were sure Rollick would have come up to Jacksonville by now."

Torrent nodded, looking grim. "You were here for hours before we got the vest and could cloak the energy you give off. There's no reason for him *not* to have followed the trail. Unless something even more important diverted him..."

No. *No.* If we couldn't see this plan through now, when would we ever get another chance to ensure everyone I cared about was safe from the demon?

I dragged in a breath and let it out slowly. An idea took shape in my mind. It wasn't an idea I liked all that much, but that could be said for an awful lot of the schemes I'd entered into over the past few days.

I'd be sticking my neck out, putting myself right in front of the threat, but that was what I excelled at, wasn't it? Stand on the edge of a skyscraper, dangle myself in a villainous demon's face—it was all good.

"You and Lance have only been patrolling near the park, right?" I said to Crag.

"We couldn't keep a close enough watch if we went much farther," he said. "We wouldn't want him getting past us and catching you unaware."

"All right, but what if he couldn't get past you to me... because I was with you?"

Torrent cocked his head. "What solution are you designing now, Ms. Fix-It?"

I motioned to Crag. "If Crag's okay with it, he could carry me and go farther out into the city. There are barely any people out at this hour, and it's dark enough that he should be able to avoid anyone noticing him. He could see if he can figure out where Rollick is and get him to realize that I might be nearby. Give him a more urgent trail to follow back here." I caught Crag's gaze. "I'm counting on you being able to fly faster than he can run."

"I can," Crag said sternly, as if worried his abilities had been doubted. "But we don't know who else is working with him. He could have other tricks up his sleeve. It'd be dangerous."

"I know," I said firmly. "I'm okay with that. It's better taking that risk than risking our plans getting ruined."

Torrent rubbed his mouth. "It isn't likely that Rollick has much of anyone, if anyone at all, helping him in his search. He sent us because of how discreet he wanted to keep his involvement. This approach would put you closer to harm's way, but I think the trade-off is worth it. It might be the only way we can salvage tonight."

Crag paused and then grunted with determination. "I'll keep you safe," he said with a hint of a protective growl, and hunched down, expanding into his gargoyle form at the same time. His voice carried from his transformed throat with a deeper rumble. "It'll be easiest if I carry you on my back."

I left the metal vest in the semi-circle of bushes where I'd need it as soon as we returned. Even with Crag crouched close to the ground, it was a scramble heaving myself onto his stone body, using his knee as a foothold. I scooted as high up as I could between his thick wings and wrapped my arms around his neck. "Is this okay?"

"No problem at all, Softie," he said, and rose into the air with a flap of his wings.

I was putting my absolute trust in him—and he was putting his in me, that I wouldn't react in some way that would draw attention and screw him over. The sense of mutual reliance soothed some of the lingering guilt still prickling in my gut.

Crag soared between the trees, avoiding the paths with their intermittent lamps. Only a few cars cruised by on the roads beyond the park. In a gap between them, he launched himself higher. He landed on the roof of a store-top apartment and then glided along with shallow flaps, staying close to the buildings so he couldn't be spotted from the streets.

"I'll go south first," he said, "since that's the direction he'd have been coming from."

"That makes sense." I hugged him a little tighter, his stony skin reassuringly unyielding against my arms as the air licked over me. "Thank you. I—I hope you don't feel too awful, going against the guy who was your boss."

Crag let out a short huff. "He gave me things to do... and I thought they were the *only* things I could do. I thought I could only scare people. But I don't scare you."

The blooming warmth Torrent's words had provoked unfurled further through my chest at Crag's. "No, you don't. I think you're... incredible."

He hummed low in his chest, the reverberation tingling through my skin. "So I'd rather be with you, where I can be more."

He said the simple statement with so much certainty that I couldn't argue with him. I just leaned the side of my face against the back of his neck and soaked in the warmth he offered so freely.

Crag flew in silence for several more minutes. Then he froze on the edge of a rooftop, his breath catching. "I think—" He shuffled to the side with a sharp inhalation. "He *is* here. His body gives off specific vibrations I can sense when he moves through this world—they're close to us now."

My heart leapt. "Is he coming this way?"

"Let me see. I'll make an easy path to follow."

He stalked back the way we'd come over the tops of a few buildings and then paused again. After a moment, he nodded. His voice dropped even lower. "He's on our trail. Now we hurry."

I held on tight, and Crag sprang through the air. We bounded across the buildings and over streets, sometimes flying, sometimes simply running on all fours. A couple more times, Crag stopped to confirm Rollick hadn't fallen too far behind, but only for a matter of seconds. The demon was nearly keeping pace with us.

As we neared the park, Crag clarified why. "He's got a car. I feel its resonance too. He can't follow us on a straight path, but he's coming fast."

"Well, he'll have to get out once we're at the park," I said. Hopefully that'd be enough time for us to get everything ready.

Crag swooped into the cover of the trees and soared the rest of the way to the site of the savaged corpse with swift flaps. The second he landed by the bushes, I dashed into their shelter and picked up the vest. As I raised it, I noticed a few beasties already prowling through the shadows toward the clearing.

How many more were converging on this spot? More than my men could dispatch all at once?

Shit. We needed Rollick here *now*.

So I did what seemed like the easiest thing to bring him running. I sucked in a breath and screamed like I really was being torn apart.

The sound reverberated up my throat and split through the air. I wrenched the vest over my head and down across my torso to cut off the energy seeping out of me. Then I ducked between the bushes.

Crag and Torrent vanished. My pulse thudded on and on and—

There. Footsteps hurried across the terrain nearby. They slowed as they drew nearer. A curse in a voice I recognized from our brief confrontation tumbled from Rollick's lips.

When I tipped my head, I could make out a sliver of the scene between the bush's spindly branches. Rollick's form moved into view, somewhat less confident than on my first encounter with him. I couldn't make out his expression through the shadows.

He knelt down by the mangled body. He was checking it, confirming it was me, like my men had expected.

My heart raced on, and I pressed my lips tight together. Would he hear the thumping in my chest? Make out my nervous breaths? What if he realized—

A soft thump of footfalls told me that my men had leapt from the shadows around him. Rollick jerked around just as Crag's voice boomed out with apparent agony. "We didn't get here fast enough. What have you *done* to her?"

He sounded so furiously horrified that *I* almost believed he thought Rollick had killed the woman, even though I'd been there for the mutilation.

Rollick's posture drew authoritatively straight. "This wouldn't have happened if you hadn't gone looney over the girl. *I* didn't kill her. Some prick got to her first."

"Sure," Torrent's voice said coolly. "And you just happened to be hanging out with her dismembered body. That checks out. For fuck's sake, Rollick. I didn't think you were this crazed over her."

"I didn't do this," Rollick snapped. I suspected he was glowering. "Maybe I can figure out which creature did, though. The power in her—for it to be fucking *lost* to some random beast—although that might be better..."

He trailed off, bending over the body again. Had my men counted on him examining it for an extended period of time? I'd gotten the impression they'd thought he'd leave fairly quickly once they confronted him.

"You ripped her apart and now you're rubbing your nose in the mess," Lance chimed in with a singsong tone obviously designed to needle the demon. "Like a wild dog. Why did I listen to your orders so long anyway? Much better things to do."

"You should be glad I'm not making sure you'll never do anything at all again," Rollick growled, but his attention stayed focused on the body. He paused over a particular strip of flesh.

My stomach lurched. Could he tell something was off? How long would it take him to realize that wasn't me?

We needed him to leave. What could possibly scare him off?

The distant thrum of a car engine made me stiffen. If more people came, mortal witnesses, he wouldn't stick around acting like some kind of psycho, would he? He'd taken care not to be seen at the marina, only emerging from the shadows when he'd been close to us.

I didn't have time to weigh the risks. If he realized we'd tried to trick him, this was all over anyway. I had to do my best... and count on the men who'd supported me this far to cover me if I needed it.

Staying low, I backed out of the bushes as quietly as I could manage. Then I slunk away across the park with as much speed as I dared.

A stomp shook the ground from behind me, followed by a threatening snarl, and I realized through my jolt of panic that Crag must have distracted Rollick just as I'd hoped.

I needed people... a lot of people, too many for Rollick to decide that dispatching one more mortal wasn't a big deal. God, this had better work.

When there were enough trees between me and the site of the corpse, I ran faster. A car zoomed past with a lone driver—not good enough. I made out a woman silhouetted against the light in an apartment window, but I couldn't tell if she was on her own, and I couldn't shout out to her without risking being heard from the park.

Then a gaggle of college-age guys meandered around a corner down the street, laughing and clinking beers like they'd been roaming the streets since getting kicked out of a late-night bar. There were six of them—that had to be enough.

I dashed over to them, not needing to fake my panic. "There's a body!" I said. "In the park. All torn up. I don't know what to do. It's awful!"

I might not have played it up that way with a different set of people, but a morbidly curious light lit in the guys' eyes like I'd suspected it would.

"What the fuck?" one said, heading straight toward the park. "Where?"

I pointed wildly. "Where the trees are thicker, not too far from the fountain. Someone needs to call the cops!"

A couple of the guys were already fishing out their phones. "Can you imagine if we're the first to post about this?" one mumbled to another. I heard a third making a report to what I hoped was a 9-1-1 operator as they vanished into the darkness.

What did I do now? Crap, what if Rollick left and headed this way? I spun around, looking for a place to take shelter.

All the businesses were closed this late at night—or early in the morning, depending on how you counted it. I darted farther down the street toward an alley where I could watch the park from out of view.

Sirens started to wail in the distance. Relief trickled through me. Even if Rollick had continued lurking while the college guys surveyed the scene, surely he wouldn't stick around once the police arrived. And they wouldn't leave until the mess was all cleaned up, no more chance for him to inspect it.

I'd just reached the alley when a form materialized right behind me—and clapped a hand over my mouth that would have made me squeak against it if I hadn't recognized the gesture and the faint prickle of claws.

"Tricksy girl," Lance murmured with a chuckle. "Changing up the plans."

"It seemed like I needed to," I whispered when he released my mouth. "Is Rollick gone?"

"Gone from the park, at least." He nipped the shell of my ear and then nuzzled my hair. "We did it, baby girl. Time to get you home."

CHAPTER THIRTY

Quinn

Getting home wasn't quite that easy, of course. After Lance hustled me back to the car, I spent the last hour of the night and a bunch more of the day snoozing in the back seat while my shadowkind men found a sheltered spot to conceal the car and then took turns monitoring the streets for any sign that Rollick hadn't been convinced after all. They watched my house and the roads around it, and Torrent even returned to the boat in Daytona Beach.

When I woke up, a little groggy from the awkward position and my messed-up sleep schedule, he'd set the backpack that held my laptop on the floor of the car next to me. I'd left it behind in the boat.

"We haven't seen any sign that Rollick has stuck around," he told me. "I think we should wait until tomorrow morning just to be careful, but chances are he's already headed back to California."

"Very pissed off," Lance put in, and the corners of Torrent's mouth twitched.

"Yes."

I listened as he called up Goldie and made it sound as if he'd heard about the corpse in the park second-hand: "Some crazy shadowkind attack—they tore up the woman, her heart was missing and everything. Any idea what that could have been about?" He figured the leprechaun would start the rumor mill churning so that any higher shadowkind in the area who'd been keeping a lookout for me would ease off on their search.

Now that they couldn't sense my weird sorcerer energy, it shouldn't be hard to convince them there was nothing left to find.

We drove around a little more, locating a restaurant with a bathroom where I could quickly relieve myself and grabbing some food for good measure. After we ate in the car, I found I was exhausted enough after the very long night previous that right after I'd popped my nightly pills, I zonked out with my head on Lance's knee.

When I woke up, it was still dark out. All three of the men seemed to have vanished, but I assumed at least one of them had remained in the shadows of the car. I sat up and checked my watch. There were still a few more hours to go before dawn.

Both Torrent and Lance reappeared a moment later. Torrent twisted in the driver's seat to look at me. "I was able to confirm that Rollick has returned home. He was in a photo from his club posted on the internet last night." He shook his head as if in bemusement at human social media habits, as much as they worked in our favor.

I sagged in relief and winced at the pinching of the vest against my skin. After sleeping with the thing over my tank top for two nights, the beads were starting to dig little dents into my chest and back, thin as they were. I tugged at it.

"I'm going to have to figure out some strategies for wearing this constantly without ending up covered in welts," I said. "And without my parents noticing anything weird." But that was a small price to pay for actually being able to see my parents again. A smile sprang to my face despite the minor discomfort.

Torrent nodded. "We'll drive over to your house once it gets light out. You can have breakfast with them."

Imagining how happy—and relieved—Mom and Dad would be to see me made my smile stretch wider. But as I looked from Torrent to Lance, I hesitated.

"How are things going to work between us now?" I asked tentatively. "I mean, you can't exactly drop by the house like normal guests, but I can obviously meet up with you outside it. Assuming you want to keep spending time with me and not just lurk around warding off beasties."

Lance snorted. "Oh, we're not done with you! There are so many more things we haven't explored."

My cheeks heated. I rustled my vest again. "*That's* going to be kind of difficult while I've got to wear this thing all the time."

The dragon shifter smirked at me and scooped up my foot to start massaging my calf. His claws grazed my skin with tingling strokes between each press of his fingers. "I'm sure we can find ways to work around that. The *most* important parts of you—for exploring purposes—aren't covered."

Torrent coughed, and my cheeks flared hotter. "I'm sure there are other ways we'd enjoy your company that don't require quite so much physical contact too," he put in, shooting Lance a pointed look.

Lance opened his mouth, probably to make some remark that would scorch my cheeks right off, and Crag blinked into being in the front passenger seat with a creak of the car's frame at his haste.

"We have to go!" he said. "There's—"

Torrent was already jerking around to twist the key in the ignition, but the warning had come too late. A massive form crashed down on the hood of the car, the engine crunching and sputtering. The image of the collapsed garage at the sorcerers' house flashed through my mind.

I cringed against Lance, who snarled at the intruder. The thing on the hood peered through the windshield with eerie yellow eyes, but it wasn't the only sudden arrival. Shadowy figures with spines or talons, wings or extra limbs, stood all around us in the otherwise empty parking lot. And in their midst—

"Goldie?" Torrent sputtered, his gaze latching onto the leprechaun at the same moment mine did.

The small man gave an apologetic grimace and winced as the figure behind him, a monster nearly twice his size, squeezed his shoulder with a barbed hand.

"I had a debt to pay," he said thinly. "And you've been gone a long time." He glanced at the creatures around him. "Here they are, just like I promised. That's the woman you wanted, isn't it? She's all yours."

COURTED BY BEASTS

THE HEART OF A MONSTER #2

CHAPTER ONE

Quinn

Monsters surrounded me. In the faint glow cast by the distant streetlamps along the edge of the mostly vacant parking lot, their claws, spines, and searing eyes glinted eerily. The massive beast crouched on the hood of our sedan leered at us through the windshield as if the tint in the glass didn't obscure his vision at all.

After being swarmed by hordes of shadowy creatures multiple times in the past, maybe I should have been getting used to this scenario. No such luck. My heart hammered in my chest, my fingers curling against my palms tightly enough to dig my fingernails into my skin. I jerked my arm through the strap of my messenger bag automatically—it held my medication and other essentials—but my whirling mind couldn't see any way of escaping this time.

Dozens of the creatures prowled around the car on all sides. The leprechaun who'd apparently led them here, the man one of my protectors had considered a friend, was still staring at Torrent with a tight, pained smile.

Our luck had run out. Our one sort-of ally had turned on us. The vest of silver and iron beads I'd commissioned to stop the shadowkind creatures from tracking me down didn't do me any good when they already knew exactly where I was.

Where the hell did we go from here?

Torrent turned his head toward Crag. Whatever communication passed between the tentacled man and the gargoyle was totally silent. Beside me, Lance hopped up nimbly into a crouch on the seat, flexing his vicious dragon-shifter claws.

The huge fiend on the hood raised a fist to smash right through the windshield, and the men around me sprang into motion in an instant.

Torrent hit the button to activate the car alarm. The sudden blare echoed through the vacant lot, startling the beast on the hood in mid-punch. Creatures all through the horde surrounding us flinched, heads jerking toward the nearest buildings in an instinctive fear of discovery.

At the same moment, Crag dove into the shadows of the car and re-materialized practically on top of me in full gargoyle form. His bulging arms yanked me against his immense chest. He grunted as my vest smacked against his stony skin, and I realized that coming into close contact with the metals toxic to shadowkind must be hurting him, but he didn't hesitate. Without missing a beat, he threw himself into the door shoulder first.

The car door burst right off its hinges. We hurtled out into the night, the flap of Crag's wings sweeping us up over the heads of most of the throng. I shifted in his embrace, hugging my messenger bag and adjusting my position so as little of my vest was outright touching him as possible. I had to make myself as easy a burden as I could.

But our enemies had come prepared this time. They'd seen how the gargoyle had carried me to safety before. Several winged bodies launched themselves after us, most of them smaller, but a couple were nearly human-sized and one was almost as large as Crag's gigantic form. My pulse stuttered.

The wind warbled past us as Crag soared higher. My pale hair whipped around my face. Hisses and shrieks rose up from below, where the car alarm had cut off. Torrent and Lance would be fighting for their lives—they couldn't just leap into the air and take off. Would they be able to escape all those attackers?

My chest ached at the thought of abandoning them, but our own escape was looking more precarious by the second. The effects of the silver and iron in my vest must have been tiring Crag, because the other flying beasts were catching up. A rasp had crept into his breath. I wanted to fling the vest right off me, but I didn't have the room to maneuver without risking his hold on me.

A creature that looked like a barracuda melded with a bat shot toward us. Crag clutched me firmly with one arm and swung his other fist at the thing. With a crunch of fracturing bone, it tumbled down through the air, the smoky substance shadowkind had for blood pluming up in its wake.

Three more of the smaller shadowkind lunged at us from different sides. Crag's wings whooshed as he spun and flipped, dizzying me. His heel shattered one thing's skull, his thick fingers snapping another's spine. The third flitted past him, aiming its curved talons straight at me.

I didn't have time to think, only to react—but I knew what the most powerful weapon I had on me was. I managed to fling out my arm, snatching the creature's wing and yanking it even faster so that it slammed right into my vest.

The thing's skin outright sizzled with the contact with the noxious metals. It screeched and shoved away, and Crag bashed its head into a pulpy mess.

He was still breathing hard—and the larger creatures had almost caught up. He pushed his wings faster, careening over the tops of the Jacksonville buildings with the city lights glinting through the darkness from below us, but the monstrous forms tore after us just as quickly. One of them made a low, guttural sound it took me a second to recognize as a chuckle.

"Stay still," Crag muttered, the only warning I got before he plunged into a dive. He shot between two high rises and swerved around a condo building. If anyone was up at this way-too-early hour of the morning and looking out their window, they'd have gotten quite a view.

I craned my neck and spotted two of the monstrous figures still on our tail. My throat constricted.

"You could land and put me down," I said over the rush of the wind. "You'd be able to fight better if—"

"No," Crag said gruffly. "That would give them the chance to snatch you. They're not getting you, Softness."

His emphatic insistence and the affectionate nickname sent a bittersweet pang through my chest. The three shadowkind men who'd rescued me from more murderous examples of their kind a week ago had already been through the wringer to protect me. They'd fought battles, gone on the run, even defied the boss they'd all spent decades working for.

They'd dedicated themselves that much to me... but what if the decision ruined them?

Yes, they were monsters too, but in the past week I'd discovered that they were so much more than that. The thought of Crag with his brutal protectiveness—or Lance and his playful wildness, or Torrent and his curt determination—being cut down on my behalf wrenched at me.

The slightly smaller of our two foes, a beast that looked like a winged, scaly jaguar, hurled itself the last short distance toward Crag. Its claws raked across Crag's shoulder as the gargoyle swiveled. Smoky blood streamed from the gashes.

Crag lashed out with his own clawed hand. He shredded the edge of the creature's wing, but the thing only bobbed before regaining its balance. The other flying fiend had almost reached us.

Crag pushed away with a heave of his wings and kicked out with both of his powerful legs. He caught the scaly beast in the face with one foot, cracking open its snout. It still managed to snarl through the gush of smoke, but the pain turned it wilder—and more reckless. It sped at Crag, who whacked it to the side and crushed its neck between his heels.

By then, the largest creature was on us. It sprang too quickly for Crag to reorient himself in time, and the sound of ripping flesh made me flinch. The gargoyle listed to the side with a snarl resonating through his clenched teeth. My stomach lurched.

This creature was way too big for me to help in the battle, though. I couldn't hope that contact with my vest would do more than briefly irritate it, and trying to strike out at it myself would only put my limbs in Crag's way. As he whipped around in the air, I held myself as still and small as I could, my pulse thundering through my head.

Our last opponent didn't let up for a second. It swung a fist here and swept out a taloned leg there, its sinewy body contorting this way and that to evade Crag's blows. He dipped lower, still favoring one side, and a deeper terror gripped me.

The beast had injured his wing. He was having trouble just keeping us in the air. Maybe he'd *have* to come down to earth.

I wasn't totally sure that was a bad thing, but Crag seemed determined to hold us aloft as long as he could. He struck out at the creature with his legs and the arm that wasn't holding me tight against him, even battering the thing across its oddly pointed head with his good wing.

The fiend just gave another of those low, unnerving chuckles as if this was all a game to it. As if it wasn't the slightest bit worried about the outcome of the battle.

A chill coursed through my veins. Crag spun, and the creature leapt in the opposite direction. With another tearing sound, Crag grunted and dropped even farther. Smoky blood hissed from his wounds.

He beat the creature off as well as he could, but it wasn't a fair fight while he was clutching me, dealing with the pain of my vest and his failing wing. The beast landed a strike to his head, scraping its claws right through one of the pointed gargoyle ears Crag had told me were a vulnerable spot and slamming its spiked tail against his side. More smoke streamed up, and almost all of it was Crag's.

Tension wound through my torso alongside a prickling sensation that spread out across the rest of my body. *No*. I couldn't let this happen. I had to do *something* to save the man who'd given so much to protect me.

If I didn't, we were both going to die.

A now-familiar fluttery wobble of energy ran through my chest. It seemed to cast a bubble into the base of my throat. My heart thumped, propelling a quiver through my blood that I could almost taste, like something electric crackling all through my flesh.

The thing lunged at us again, and my mouth popped open. I expected to scream or cry out.

Instead, a shout burst from my lips: a string of syllables that meant nothing to me but that rang from my mouth with a sense of urgency and purpose I couldn't explain. The electric energy surged out of me with that sound.

The fiend jerked backward as if I'd slapped it. It shook its head, its muscles tensing, but its wings were already whirling it around. It took off in the opposite direction like a shot.

As Crag plummeted into an alley even darker than the quiet street beyond, I stared after our attacker. The gargoyle didn't say anything about the weirdness of what had just happened, but he didn't have to. Nausea coiled around my gut.

Did I really need to wonder what had happened? The heart now beating fast but more steadily in my chest, the one that'd been transplanted into me nine years ago after a childhood virus had ruined the one I'd been born with, had come from a sorcerer's daughter. We'd already suspected that some of the magic those rare mortals could use to control the shadowkind had carried over to me with it.

And I'd just drawn on that power without even understanding what I was doing. In whatever language had come to me instinctively, I'd ordered the fiend to leave... and it had.

Maybe I should have felt triumphant, but I couldn't summon excitement from beneath the sick feeling in my gut. That power might have saved us just now, but technically it made me an enemy not just to the monsters that wanted to capture me but to the men who'd protected me as well.

Crag's feet hit the ground in a landing much less graceful than usual. He was still streaming smoke from multiple wounds. The second his grip on me loosened, I dropped to the pavement and swiveled toward him, groping at my bag. Was there anything in my first aid kit that could help a being made of stone and shadow?

"I'll heal," the gargoyle said in his gruff way, but he couldn't hide the thread of pain in his voice. In the thin light that seeped from the street, I made out the imprint the beads on my vest had burned into his muscular chest, turning the gray flesh nearly black. A fresh wave of nausea swept through me.

Then the little bit of illumination we had dimmed even further. A sedan had pulled up to the curb just outside the alley—but not ours. The black one we'd used for the past few days was ruined now anyway. This one was silver.

As I braced myself to run and Crag grasped my shoulder, a figure wavered into being next to the car, having skipped the need to open the door. Crag's former boss, Rollick—the one hostile shadowkind I'd thought we no longer needed to worry about—rolled his shoulders and aimed a knowing grin our way.

CHAPTER TWO

Quinn

As Rollick strode into the thicker shadows of the alley, Crag wrapped a protective arm right around me, his wings fanning out on either side of him. The other man stopped in his tracks and raised his hands in a gesture of peace.

"Don't strain your wounds more than you already have, Crag," he said in a smoothly assured voice. "I'm not here to threaten her. You need to listen to me."

Everything about the guy radiated assurance. When I'd first seen him on the dock a couple of days ago, I'd thought he looked like a movie star who'd stepped right out of the screen in full cinematic glory, and that impression hadn't diminished. And that was true even though I had even more reason to distrust him now than I'd had before—partly because it'd become clear that he wanted to grab my heart for himself just like our other enemies did... and partly because I doubted he trusted *me* after I'd stabbed him while making a run for it.

I still had no idea what monstrous attribute he brought with him into his mortal guise. Other than the aura of power that tingled off of him over my skin and woke up another quaver of energy in my heart, he looked completely if stunningly human. He smiled again with a flash of those white teeth and ran his fingers back through his tawny hair, leaving it perfectly ruffled. I saw no hint of the injury I'd given him. The cut from the silver-and-iron dagger must have healed already.

"You can't have her," Crag rumbled, hugging me close. "You're not setting one finger on her while I'm here." But the fact that he hadn't taken off into the air didn't bode well for his ability to do so. How long would it take *him* to heal?

How well could the gargoyle fight off Rollick in his current state if he couldn't flee? Torrent had said that their former boss was a very powerful demon.

"Well, I suppose that depends on how you look at it." Rollick stayed where he was and tipped his head toward the street. "Would you really rather *that* mob got their hands on her? They're already heading this way—they saw what direction you flew in. You'll have trouble outrunning all of them in your current state."

The monstrous horde was on the move—which meant they weren't fighting my other shadowkind men anymore. My pulse stuttered.

"Are Torrent and Lance all right?" I blurted out.

Rollick blinked and focused on me rather than Crag for the first time. One eyebrow arched. "If you think they're going to save the day, you've greatly overestimated what they're capable of."

My jaw tightened. "That's not what I was thinking about. I just want to know that those creatures didn't... didn't kill them."

I couldn't stop my voice from wobbling. For a second, the demon in man form looked outright puzzled. Then he shrugged. "I'm not sure about the welfare of my mutinous employees. They are very adept at getting out of jams. I've only seen your other pursuers from a distance. I wasn't looking to get up close and personal."

We didn't just have to worry about the horde tracking us down on their own, it occurred to me. I hadn't enslaved the being I'd used my sorcerer magic on, only given him a single command. How long would that stick? He knew exactly where we'd been—he could lead the others right to us the second he snapped out of the spell. Which he might already have, for all I knew.

I eyed the man in front of me, tucking my hand around Crag's arm so

I'd be ready to help him carry me as much as possible if he determined we needed to take off. Could I use that power on Rollick to give us a chance to escape?

I had no idea how I'd summoned enough energy to begin with. It wasn't crackling through my body the way it'd been in that moment. Maybe if he came at us and provoked enough desperation, that would trigger the same reaction. But I didn't know how to generate it on my own.

And who knew if it'd even work on a being as powerful as my men had suggested he was? They hadn't believed they could defeat him in a fight even three against one.

"How are you even here?" I asked, for the sake of drawing out the conversation—and giving Crag more time to recover from his wounds. "Torrent saw a photo of you back in L.A."

"Oh, I did go home," Rollick replied. "Quite the trick the bunch of you pulled with that body in the park. It actually convinced me. But I have eyes all over the place. I got word that shadowkind had amassed in Miami and then headed north, and I knew that meant there was still a prize to be had here. So I flew straight back, and I've been cruising around keeping watch for you for the past couple of hours."

My skin prickled uneasily at his words. "I'm not a *prize*."

He gazed at me steadily. "To a whole lot of my monstrous brethren, you most certainly are."

"And to you?" I shot back.

"I recognize your value." His gaze lifted to meet Crag's eyes again. "That doesn't mean I'm going to hurt her."

"You wanted her heart," the gargoyle growled. His wings extended and contracted at the edges of my vision, and I could tell the damaged one was still barely mobile. More smoke was coursing off the ragged tears in its leather surface. Shit.

"Yes, well, I happen to think that heart is much more useful while still in the body currently harboring it." Rollick aimed a wink at me, as if we were all having a grand time here and not in a life-or-death standoff.

"What do you want, then?" I demanded.

He paused as if considering his answer and slung his hands in the pockets of his fitted slacks. "You're a piece on a very large playing board, one you don't even know the half of. I prefer to hold as many pieces as possible. But I meant what I said. I don't intend to harm you, certainly not to kill you like some of those lesser shadowkind might if given free rein. I can help you figure out what to do with all that unexpected energy inside you."

My pulse hitched again, but this time it wasn't with fear. He might know how to deal with the sorcerer magic lodged in my heart? How I could control it or even get rid of it? The memory of the strange word that'd reverberated up my throat and the way the creature I'd aimed it at had fled came back to me again with a chill.

I might not know how to turn it on at will, but the power was getting stronger, more active. I hadn't used it on purpose. What if I accidentally turned it on one of my men next? If all three of those men had even survived the latest horror show I'd dragged them into.

But Torrent hadn't believed that Rollick would protect me. He'd defied his boss specifically to protect me from *him*. The demon in front of me could be lying through his teeth, and I'd have no clue.

I wet my lips. "Why shouldn't we just walk away? What are you going to do if I don't agree to go with you?"

Crag shifted his stance behind me, drawing himself up even taller as if in an attempt to look as threatening as possible.

Rollick considered both of us calmly. He folded his arms over his well-muscled chest. "You can't fly right now," he said to Crag. "We both know it, or you'd already have jetted off. I don't *want* to fight you, if only because I'd rather not traumatize the girl by having her see what I'd have to do to you, but I will if I need to. There's no one watching here that I need to hide from. You'd be taking on the demon."

I kind of wondered why he hadn't launched into battle already. He had to be pissed off at Crag for disobeying him and then tricking him. Was he really that worried about my emotional well-being? It seemed unlikely. But then, I got the impression Rollick played a long game on that board he'd talked about. Who knew what his full motivations were?

We could still run for it. I curled my fingers tighter around Crag's thick forearm, prepared to let him heft me up so he could charge off down the alley. At the same time, my back pressed more firmly against his chest, and I felt the faint flinch he couldn't suppress at the feel of my vest.

Could he even run fast enough to outpace Rollick the way he was now? What would Rollick do to him if we forced him to give chase?

The gargoyle's head twitched, his attention seeming to shift to something beyond the alley. A low growl escaped him. He didn't say anything in front of Rollick, but a chilly certainty washed through me.

Crag had told me that he could sense the presence of other shadowkind when they were close enough. The ones hunting us must be nearby—maybe no more than a few blocks away now.

"What guarantee do I have?" I asked abruptly.

"Quinn," Crag protested, his arm tensing around me. "You don't have to—"

"Guarantee?" Rollick interrupted, cocking his head.

"That you won't hurt me," I said. "You could say whatever you want, and then as soon as I don't have Crag guarding me, you'll be ripping my heart out."

Rollick's mouth twisted slightly in what looked like genuine distaste at the thought, but it could have been an act. He contemplated the question for a moment. Then he raised one hand and flicked his fingers. A spread of black claws shot from the tips where his fingernails had been an instant before. They were only half as long as Lance's talons but equally vicious-looking.

He poised the claws over his other arm where bare tanned skin showed beneath the rolled-up sleeve of his dress shirt. "I'll give you my demonic oath. You come with me and do as I say, and I'll defend you from bodily harm to the best of my ability."

Crag went rigid behind me. I glanced up into his monstrous face, searching for affirmation of Rollick's claim in his angular gargoyle features.

"It would be binding," Crag confirmed. "That kind of oath—he wouldn't be able to break it unless you failed your end."

I dragged in a breath. Maybe it would be okay, in that case. I couldn't really expect the demon to offer that kind of promise without getting something in return. And if I disagreed with his demands, hopefully by then we'd be in a better position to flee.

All of us. As the idea took hold, I raised my chin. "I can agree to that as long as you swear the same for Torrent, Lance, and Crag." Assuming the first two were still in one piece.

Rollick stared at me for a second, appearing taken aback for the second time since this conversation had started. He recovered quickly. "Also dependent on your cooperation," he said.

"Of course."

Crag bowed his head close to my ear. "This isn't necessary. I'll fight if I have to. The others will catch up."

Even as he spoke, a roar rang out what sounded like no more than a block away. The hairs on the back of my neck stood on end.

He might be right, but we didn't know when Torrent and Lance would reach us. We didn't know how close all of our other pursuers were. Torrent had at least used to trust this demon, enough that he hadn't run away when Rollick had first shown up. That was more than I could say for any of the other fiends who'd attacked me.

I could go with him, see what he could tell me about my powers, and ensure our safety at least temporarily, or send Crag into a battle I doubted he could come out of alive and end up in Rollick's clutches anyway, with no agreement in my favor at all.

"We'll find Torrent and Lance before we leave," I added. "They're coming with us—if they want to." I didn't know how they'd feel about the deal I was making, but I couldn't exactly ask them ahead of time. "All right?"

The dawn light that was spreading through the streets glinted in Rollick's dark blue eyes. "You drive a tough bargain, mortal. But I'll accept in the interests of getting us out of here."

He dug two of his claws into his flesh, carving a swift sigil that released tendrils of smoky blood. "I will defend the human Quinn Moody and the shadowkind Torrent, Lance, and Crag from bodily harm to the best of my ability, after first seeking out Torrent and Lance, so long as Quinn complies with any requests I make of her. This oath will remain binding until either of us violates the terms or for ten days, at which point we may revisit it."

I hadn't expected that last part and wasn't sure whether it benefitted me or not. But there was a bit of relief in knowing it wasn't an eternal contract no matter what either of us did. I didn't love how open-ended the phrasing about Rollick's requests was, but another snarl carried from down the street even as I absorbed his words.

We didn't have time to debate whether he should include an addendum. If I didn't like what he requested of me, I could simply not do it, and our deal would be broken.

Rollick stepped back toward the car and opened the back door like a chauffeur, his confident demeanor erasing any impression of servility. Chest tight, I squeezed Crag's arm and tugged him with me toward whatever our future held now.

Please, oh please, let me not regret this gamble.

CHAPTER THREE

Quinn

It was clear from the moment Rollick's private jet arrived in L.A. that the demon *really* didn't want anyone knowing that he'd brought me back to the city with him. First, he made me wait on the plane while he checked out the car he'd had brought to the tarmac and the surrounding area. Apparently he didn't trust any of his underlings all that much. Or maybe he was being extra cautious now that three of them had recently turned on him.

As soon as he'd vanished near the doorway, I turned to the three men *I* trusted. My heart leapt with relief all over again taking in Torrent and Lance, looking not particularly worse for wear. We'd managed to find them fairly quickly on the streets of Jacksonville with Crag helping with the search, and they'd escaped the onslaught of enemy shadowkind with no major injuries.

I hadn't been able to express my relief all that thoroughly yet, because Rollick had kept us apart and in view during the flight. He'd insisted that I sit at one end of the cushy leather seating area and his three former employees stayed at the other while he lounged in the middle of the space, periodically glowering at them.

All three of the shadowkind men moved to join me where I was waiting near the door, and I immediately motioned them even closer. Lance hooked one hand around my elbow, careful as usual not to let his ever-present claws do more than graze my skin. Normally his touch sent tingles through my body, but right now my insides were too knotted up to feel anything except anxious.

"Tricksy, tricksy," the dragon shifter muttered, his violet eyes even wilder than usual beneath the fall of his erratic dark brown curls. He cocked his head, and I couldn't stop my gaze from shooting to the new scar that marred the smooth, golden-brown skin at the crook of his neck. A scar he'd gotten during the battle earlier this morning—he hadn't made it out completely unharmed. "We could make a run for it while he's distracted."

He glanced over at Crag, who'd come up behind him and set a hand on my shoulder. The gargoyle was back in human-like form, nothing hinting at his true nature other than the rocky jut of his jaw, but his otherwise bronze-toned face had taken on a grayish cast to match it. I didn't think he'd fully healed from his own wounds, although it was hard to tell how badly his wings were doing with them invisibly tucked away.

The gargoyle ran his other hand over the sheen of black hair on his skull and ducked his head. "I'm not sure of how far or well I could fly yet."

We all looked toward Torrent, the de facto leader of the trio, who'd come up at my other side. Seeing how drawn his pale face was beneath his scruffy dark red hair, I swallowed hard and reached out cautiously to slide my arm around his torso, just above the spot where his two supporting tentacles emerged from his waist. I'd have hugged him more tightly if I hadn't wanted to give him enough distance that the silver-and-iron vest I was still wearing wouldn't touch even his clothes.

My growing understanding with Torrent had been a lot more tumultuous than my connection with Lance and Crag. I wasn't sure how he'd react to the choices I'd made.

"I think we should wait this out and see how it goes," I said before he could speak. "We're safe under the deal I made for ten days at least. If we go against it, who knows what he'll do to any of us. Crag needs time to recover, and it could be a good thing to find out what Rollick knows about my heart. It seems like he realized there might be something important about it before any other shadowkind did, considering he sent the three of you to watch over me way before I got attacked."

Torrent gazed down at me with his pensive sea-green eyes. "I agree," he said. "There's too much we don't understand about this situation. It'll be easier to determine how to tackle our enemies while we have fewer of them —and access to Rollick's resources. He can't break the deal he made. When the ten days are up, we'll be much more prepared for whatever we need to do."

He raised his hand to my shoulder and leaned over to brush a kiss to the top of my head that brought a larger lump to my throat even as it reassured me that he wasn't pissed off with me. All the same, I felt the need to say, "I'm sorry. It seemed like the best out of a bunch of bad options. I didn't even know if you were still alive… or if you would be for very much longer if I didn't make a deal with him, now that he knows you all tricked him."

"It makes sense," the tentacled man said. "I wasn't there, but I don't think I'd have wanted you to choose differently." He frowned in the direction of the door. "He's been good to me in the past. He's more generous and fair-minded than the majority of shadowkind I've met, even if that isn't saying a lot by your human standards. The fact that he offered the deal at all… Maybe we did simply misunderstand his intentions."

He didn't sound as if he totally believed that was true, but I was glad he thought it was possible.

"If he asks anything of you that you feel is unreasonable, do what you can to get out of it and get to us before he can turn on you," he added firmly.

Before I could say anything else, Rollick blinked into being in front of the door. He waved his hand in my direction. "Quinn, come with me. The three of you, assuming you're sticking around, make your way through the shadows and don't show yourselves until we reach my private rooms in the hotel."

Lance let out a little growl, but when both Rollick and Torrent shot him a warning glance, he pecked my cheek and grudgingly faded into the shadows. The other two men did the same. Clutching the strap of my messenger bag where it was slung across my chest, I tramped down the plane's boarding stairs.

The silver sedan waiting outside looked a lot like the one Rollick had driven in Jacksonville. He motioned for me to get into the back. I found an oversized suede purse sitting in the middle of the seat.

"Put everything in there on," the demon told me as he started the engine. "Mortals are always snapping photos and plastering them all over the internet. The last thing we need is one of the beings who's got his sights on you spotting you in an image from the hotel."

When I unzipped the purse, I understood what he meant. Inside was a knee-length, high-collared silk dress with a billowy cut that I could tell would fit over the vest to disguise it, a wig of long black hair, a make-up bag, and a pair of sunglasses with large, round panes that would hide half of my face.

"Am I going to have to be going incognito the whole time I'm at this hotel of yours?" I asked as I quickly tugged the dress over my vest, the tank top I had on underneath, and my jean shorts.

"You'll be staying in my private suite," Rollick said. "Once you're settled in, there won't be anyone around to see you who shouldn't. You'll even be able to take off your very creative anti-shadowkind armor without any beings sensing your presence. I had the building constructed with a layer of silver and iron a few floors below the penthouse to discourage uninvited visitors and ensure no one could exert unwelcome influence on my living space or my guests."

"You thought of everything," I muttered.

He chuckled lightly. "I haven't stayed alive and well for as long as I have by leaving my fate to chance."

I studied the back of his head, the short fawn-brown hair framing his ears with just the slightest trace of a curl. "How long *have* you been alive?" I knew from past conversations that Torrent had been in existence for several hundred years, and I'd gathered that Crag and Lance both had at least a couple of centuries under their belts. There wasn't much that killed shadowkind other than being pulverized by another monster.

"Long enough to have watched nearly every civilization your kind has created rise and fall," Rollick said, as languidly as ever. "Get yourself together now. It's your life we're protecting here."

Right. I peered at myself in the little mirror that came with the make-up palette and dabbed on red lipstick when we were stopped at a streetlight. Then I smudged on some bronzer to give my skin more of an olive tone. There didn't seem to be much point in bothering with my eyes when they'd be concealed behind the sunglasses anyway. It wasn't my typical style for my occasional nights out, but I wasn't looking to find a quick hook-up today.

I managed to get the unfamiliar wig cap over my long hair and tugged the wig over that. When I looked at the mirror again, I barely recognized myself. That seemed like a good sign.

As I put the supplies away, I turned my gaze to the world beyond the window. For a few minutes, all I could do was stare.

We'd driven into the city proper. In some ways, Los Angeles wasn't that different from Jacksonville. Palm trees stood here and there along the streets; the roads were clogged with cars rumbling and periodically honking at each other.

On the other hand, everything was so much *bigger*. The skyscrapers loomed taller, and there seemed to be a gazillion of them. The streets were wider. I felt abruptly very small.

But even as the intimidated part of me shrank back a little, the architect-in-training took the sights in with an expanding sense of awe. Imagine designing a soaring high-rise to stand among *these* giants. Would I be able to come up with something that would strike the same awe I felt in people who were used to living someplace like this?

My fingers itched for my sketchpad. I almost pulled it out of my messenger bag to see what I could come up with on the fly, but taking full stock of my surroundings seemed more important. I wouldn't be able to become any kind of architect if I ended up a prisoner of shadowkind—or a worse sort of victim—for however much longer my borrowed heart would keep beating.

I thought I spotted a sign for a nearby train station. There was a police station... not that cops were likely to be much help against shadowkind attackers.

The buildings were starting to look increasingly posh. I saw more and more people on the sidewalks snapping pictures with their phones and consulting the street signs—tourists. I'd have been following our route on my own phone's map if Rollick hadn't demanded I hand it over the second I'd accepted his deal. I guessed it made sense that he didn't want there to be any chance that I'd give away my location, but its loss left me even more uneasy.

It wasn't much longer before Rollick pulled the sedan into a driveway outside a tall, white-washed hotel with vivid purple trim. He drove past the curved section out front and over to a secluded side door that looked like it'd be mostly used for deliveries, where he parked to the side of the lane.

"The door will be unlocked," he said. "Go in and follow the hall until you can first take a right. You'll find an elevator there. Get on, and once you're inside, I'll enter the code to get us to the right floor. I'll be with you the whole time in the shadows."

I wasn't sure if that information was supposed to reassure me or threaten me, but I wasn't inclined to argue anyway. I was in this situation now, wherever it led me.

Clutching my messenger bag, I eased out of the car into the sweltering summer heat and hurried over to the door. It didn't look like there was much of anyone around here to notice me anyway, but Rollick was clearly being extra careful. I slipped inside and couldn't help sighing as a blast of air conditioning washed away the heat.

Forward and then to the right, he'd said. I hurried onward over a hall runner that was thick and velvety even in the maintenance part of the hotel. Muffled voices carried from up ahead. I passed what must have been a kitchen area where dishes were clinking and savory cooking smells wafting from beneath the door.

My mouth started to water. I'd had a snack in my bag to pass for breakfast, but it hadn't been all that substantial, and it was almost lunchtime.

When I reached the next hall, where a solid door stood between me and the front section of the hotel, I turned right as instructed. The elevator was just a few steps farther. It opened immediately when I pressed the button. I stepped on, jabbed the Door Closed button, and flinched when Rollick popped into being next to me.

"So jumpy," he said in a lightly teasing voice, and leaned past me to flick his fingers over the display next to the door. He angled his body so I couldn't see the code he'd entered. Was it a general code or only required to go up *to* his special rooms, not to return to the public floors? If I managed to get back to the elevator, maybe I'd be able to get out of the building if I needed to.

When the demon pulled back, his arm brushed mine, but he stepped to the side to give me a little space. "No need to worry. I think you'll find your new accommodations very adequate."

The elevator rushed upward, and my stomach dropped. It pinged and opened to a small vestibule.

"My office," Rollick said, indicating the door across from us. "You won't bother with anything in there." He led me over to a small staircase, the door to it opening at a press of his thumb against a digital pane. I wasn't opening *that* on my own without cutting off the digit to bring along.

The private staircase only descended one floor. We emerged through the next door into a suite as grand and luxurious as I'd expected from the demon.

The deep maroon carpet hugged my feet. Black leather sofas and armchairs stood in a cluster by a gas fireplace. A vast flatscreen TV stood in a tall entertainment unit near the corner. Built-in ebony bookshelves filled the opposite wall, packed with a diverse assortment of volumes from aged linen spines to garish modern paperbacks. A scent that was both sweet and faintly smoky laced the air.

At the far end of the living room, floor-to-ceiling windows looked out onto a broad terrace with a view of the ocean beyond. There were doors in the walls on either side of the stretch of windows, both of them open. Peeking past one, I found a bathroom as big as my bedroom at home, with a huge jacuzzi tub as well as a glass shower stall and double sinks, everything mottled black-and-gray marble.

Across from the bathroom lay a bedroom with an immense bed I had to think was some size larger than a king surrounded by an ebony wardrobe, vanity, and small matching desk.

I halted in the doorway between the living area and the bedroom, my skin prickling. "This is where *you* live. Where am I supposed to sleep and everything?"

Rollick propped himself casually against the back of one of the armchairs and aimed one of his warm grins at me, as if we were friends having a companionable discussion. "You have free run of these rooms, including the terrace—it's totally private. I don't *need* to use any of the facilities here."

Right, because shadowkind didn't require sleep any more than they did food.

"If I feel the need to indulge other urges of mine, I can do so elsewhere," he added, his grin widening. "If you're not interested in enjoying those benefits of my attention too, that is."

Did he mean—*oh*. My face flared, and I hugged myself instinctively. "Um, no, I think I'll pass, thanks." Sure, he was possibly the hottest guy I'd ever seen, but he was also a potentially murderous demon who'd been threatening to bash one of my actual monstrous lovers into oblivion earlier today. I did have standards.

I'd only just finished speaking when all three of my lovers wavered into being near the door. However they'd traveled here, it hadn't taken them much longer than Rollick's driving. Lance started toward me at once, his gaze intent on me and a smile flashing across his ferally gorgeous face, but Rollick held up his hand.

"Hold on," he said. "We need to discuss what I'm going to do with the three of you."

My spine stiffened. "You swore not to hurt them."

The demon shot me a baleful glance. "I do remember that." He patted his arm where the small sigil still showed faintly, pink against his tanned skin, and turned to the three shadowkind men. "Let's be clear: I'm not happy with any of you over your little rebellion. But I suppose the worst you did was follow my orders *too* well when it came to protecting her. That and your long history of service are the only reasons I haven't yet decided to eviscerate you."

Torrent's mouth tightened, and Crag appeared to suppress a wince, but the gargoyle spoke up anyway. "We'd like to continue protecting Quinn, if—"

Rollick waved whatever else Crag would have said away. "Yes, yes, I'm sure you would. But I think you're enraptured enough as it is. A little distance to clear your heads would do you some good."

"We're not just letting you take her—" Lance started to hiss.

Rollick snapped his fingers. "That's *not* what I'm saying. You want to be useful to the mortal? Wonderful. Then our ends are aligned. I want to know everything you can find out about who the beings after her are and how we can foil their plans. And finding that out requires you be out *there*, not hanging all over her in here."

Lance shifted on his feet, but he couldn't seem to come up with a firm argument against the request. Rollick had played his cards well, I had to admit. I suspected that knowing they were working toward my long-term safety was the *only* thing that would have kept the three men from insisting on staying near me.

"It's okay," I said, even though my lungs constricted around the words. "I'll be all right. I want to know how we can defeat those monsters too.

That matters more than... just about anything." As much as I was aching for the comfort of their arms around me.

My gaze slid to Rollick. "What about me? *You* wanted me for some reason. What am I supposed to be doing while I'm here?"

Rollick met my gaze with an unconcerned expression. "I haven't made a definite decision yet. I don't believe in committing to action without seeing what I'm working with." His dark blue eyes skimmed down over my body, making me feel abruptly naked despite the three layers of clothing I had on.

I hugged myself tighter. "Can I get my phone back? And my computer —I need to give my parents some kind of story, and if I could keep up with my classwork—" Torrent had thought to take my school backpack with him from the car when he and Lance had dodged the attacking beasts, not wanting them to find any clues about my full identity, though Rollick had confiscated that item too.

The demon gave his head a slow shake. "I'll bring up your other bag, but I'm holding on to your devices. No contact with the outside world. These rooms *are* your entire world for the time being."

"I need the alarm on my phone to make sure I'm taking my pills on time."

Rollick studied me for a moment and then reached into his pocket. He pulled out the phone and flicked open the small compartment at the base. "Fine. Then I'll take out the SIM card so it's basically just an alarm clock. You can forget about getting the WIFI password."

Oh, come on. An automatic protest tumbled from my mouth. "But—"

He lifted his eyebrows. "Do you really want to see what'll happen to your family or your schoolmates if the fiends after you catch on to those connections?"

My voice died in my throat. No, I didn't. We didn't know how much the other shadowkind had figured out about who I was beyond the energy my heart gave off, but Rollick had managed to determine my full name and address. The more I interacted with anyone outside of the four men in front of me, the more likely I'd put everyone I cared about in danger.

I closed my eyes and girded myself, tamping down the niggling anxiety. I'd already given my parents a story that'd cover my absence for a week or two. If I fell a couple of weeks behind in my classes, I could make that up when I got back. The important thing was making sure I *could* go back eventually.

"Okay," I said. "For now. Open to further negotiation later."

Rollick chuckled softly, the sound sending a quiver over my skin that wasn't entirely unpleasant. "Negotiation is one of my favorite pastimes. I look forward to your counter-offer." He handed over the partly disabled phone and nodded to the room around us. "Make yourself at home. I have to inform my disgraced employees of their first missions."

Then the four of them vanished, leaving me alone and adrift.

CHAPTER FOUR

Quinn

It took me a long time to decide what to do with myself in Rollick's suite. I knew he'd said he'd gone off to talk with the other men, but I couldn't shake the feeling that he might be watching me from the shadows, observing me for whatever purposes he hadn't wanted to share yet.

I wandered around the living room restlessly for several minutes and then remembered he'd said I could take off my protective vest.

The seamstress who'd created the unusual piece of clothing for me had done a fantastic job considering that she'd only had a matter of hours to pull it together. The thin silver and iron beads, a mix of round and rectangular, weighed a lot less than I'd imagine full chainmail would but deflected the shadowkind's ability to sense my heart's sorcerous energies. It still weighed on me quite a bit more than my typical cotton tanks and tees did, though.

I pulled off the billowy dress and then the vest. A shudder of relief ran through my body as the weight lifted. I draped the thing over my messenger bag, not sure where else to put it at the moment, and rubbed my arms.

I felt... grubby. I hadn't had a proper shower in a regular bathroom in days, and it'd been a few since I'd even had the benefit of the cramped stall on the small yacht we'd sailed around on. I glanced around the room again and raised my chin.

Fuck it. If Rollick wanted to perv out, let him. I wasn't going to sit around stinking the place up out of probably imaginary fears for my modesty. For all I knew, those intense blue eyes could see right through my clothes even when I was wearing them.

I headed into the bathroom and found a stack of luxuriously thick towels on a shelving unit in the corner, along with a basket that contained everything from shampoo to bath oils. Why would a being who could erase all the grime from himself simply by slipping in and out of the shadows need all that?

Ah. Presumably it was for the female guests he'd hinted that he regularly hosted in his bedroom.

The thought of those guests and the proposition he'd made to me left me feeling twice as grubby as before. I hustled over to the shower stall and turned on the water.

It heated up quickly, filling the room and my lungs with a pleasant steam. I grabbed the shampoo, conditioner, and body wash and stepped under the hot deluge.

At first, I just stood there and let the liquid heat stream over me. Wouldn't it be nice if this shower alone could sweep away everything that was wrong with my life right now? But the sense of escape only lasted a few minutes. Then all my worries started creeping back in.

I lathered myself thoroughly from head to toe, breathing in the sweet lilac scent of the bath products, and rinsed myself until I was sure every particle of dirt and grease had to have gone down the drain. I'd just turned off the water and stepped out onto the plush mat to grab the towel when Rollick's languid voice carried through the door.

"I'm just letting you know that I've dropped off your backpack, sans computer. In case you wanted anything else in there."

My pulse skittered, and I tugged the towel around my body, but he didn't make any move that I could hear toward coming into the bathroom. It *would* be nice to change into a fresh set of clothes from the backpack.

"Thank you," I called tentatively.

The demon didn't respond. Maybe he'd already left while I'd hesitated.

Oh, well. Considering everything, showing him gratitude wasn't at the top of my priority list.

I peeked out into the living area and found it empty at least to my human eyes. Rollick had left the backpack just outside the bathroom door. He'd probably gone through it looking for anything else he wouldn't want me having while I was here, but I couldn't see anything missing other than my computer.

I retreated into the bathroom to pull on a clean tank top and shorts and then brought the backpack, my messenger bag, and the vest over to the bedroom. Even if it gave me the creeps thinking about what Rollick usually got up to in this bed, the covers smelled freshly laundered. It wasn't all that different from sleeping in any regular hotel room—actually, I wouldn't be surprised if the demon kept his own abode to a higher standard of cleanliness.

It'd beat sleeping on the sofa, anyway. Besides, who knew what he'd gotten up to *there*? It wasn't like he'd have changed the leather cushions every time.

Okay, now I was never sitting on the sofa ever.

I pulled the granola bar that was my last snack on hand out of my bag and gulped it down. What was I supposed to do for food after that? Rollick would remember that I needed to eat even if he didn't, right?

He'd sworn not to cause me bodily harm. That should include starvation.

I flopped down on top of the comforter and stared up at the ceiling. Fatigue rolled over me. My sleep schedule had gotten awfully messed up over the past week of monster escapes, and I'd been too keyed up to nap on the plane. I'd just close my eyes for a minute or two...

The next thing I knew, I was waking up to sunlight slanting at a much lower angle through the window. I sat up, rubbing my eyes, and checked my phone. It was almost evening.

My stomach grumbled louder than before, but I ignored it to walk to the sliding door that led onto the same terrace I'd seen from the living room.

As I stepped outside, a crisp ocean breeze swept over me. It was still hot, but not quite the same as I was used to in Florida. Even here by the ocean, the heat had a drier feel to it, not quite so sweltering with humidity.

I walked across the clay-tiled floor past the lounge chairs to the railing and peered over the edge. Jazz music was traveling faintly from somewhere nearby, but I couldn't see the source. Like Rollick had said, the terrace was totally private. I couldn't make out anything but a stretch of white wall on either side of the space, and it was high enough and close enough to the beach I had to assume was below that I couldn't make out the sand, only the expanse of turquoise water.

No one would have been able to see me except by swimming far out or sailing by in a boat, and at that distance I doubted they'd even be able to tell whether I was male or female, let alone recognize exactly who I was.

There were no boats in sight now. I gazed out over the rolling water, a sense of awe rising inside me. I typically preferred views with more architecture to admire, but I'd always had a healthy respect for oceans. So big and powerful, almost eternal.

Another pinching of my stomach sent me back inside. I looked around for an intercom or hotel phone or anything that might have let me contact my host, and just then a whirring sound emanated from the wall to the right of the fireplace.

There was a fixture there that I hadn't paid much attention to before: a square cut into the wall at about waist height, about a foot and a half wide and tall, with a notch that I realized might be a handle. I walked over to it and tugged it open like a door, just as a large tray carrying two covered plates rose into place in the compartment on the other side.

At the same moment, Rollick emerged from the shadows next to the suite's door. "I see you discovered the dumbwaiter."

Oh. I'd heard about those but never stayed anywhere that actually had one before. I peered at the two plates with their steel dome covers, silverware and glasses set around them. "This is dinner?" A sweetly savory smell that had my stomach gurgling again reached my nose.

"Yes. I thought we could eat together." His eyebrows arched slightly. "Unless you have some objection."

"Um." I hesitated, and then decided it was better to save any arguments for subjects that mattered more. I didn't really *want* to spend more time with him than I had to, but I was going to have to find out what he wanted with me at some point. Maybe he'd enlighten me over the meal. "Well, all right."

"Such enthusiasm. I promise I'm an excellent dinner companion." He strode over, and I stepped back so he could lift the tray, seemingly effortlessly despite how much it held.

He carried it to the terrace and opened the door to the terrace with a motion of his foot that must have given off a pulse of supernatural energy. Goosebumps prickled up my arms at the overt show of power. He didn't emphasize it, though, just stepped out, set the platters on the small patio table off to the side of the terrace, and brandished a bottle of sparkling water he'd had tucked under one arm.

"I'd have brought some excellent wine, but I understand alcohol doesn't always interact well with your medications," he said as I eased out after him.

I blinked, startled that he'd even considered that factor. "Yeah. Thank you."

"It wouldn't do me much good to take you into my protection and then send you into heart failure, now would it?" His grin turned a little crooked on one side, and okay, it was kind of charming. When I wasn't reminding myself about that whole thing where he'd maybe wanted to *eat* my heart just a few days ago.

He motioned me toward the table, and I came, abruptly curious about what might lie beneath the domed covers.

"You do have everything you need in that department, don't you?" Rollick asked. He poured the sparkling water into both glasses and then pulled out my chair for me. "Torrent said he picked up your full supply of medication from your house."

I nodded, thinking of the pill bottles I'd stashed in my messenger bag. "I usually get ninety days at a time with my prescriptions, and I stocked up not long ago. So I'm good unless I'm here for more than two months or so."

I studied the demon's expression, wondering how likely he thought that was, but he didn't give away any hint of concern. "I'm glad to hear it," he said smoothly. "Of course I could easily have arranged an additional supply if you had needed it—I have sources for just about anything anyone could need." He flashed those bright teeth at me again and lifted the lids off the platters before settling into his own chair.

The rich smell filled my nose twice as strong as before, with a hint of lemon. The plate held a glazed salmon fillet and a large assortment of roasted vegetables, and I could already tell from the scent that they were going to be delicious.

It was also the perfect meal to fit within the sort of diet my doctors preferred I kept to—the one I normally *had* kept to except for on special occasions until the shadowkind had barged into my life. I hadn't been able to be as picky about my eating habits while we were on the run.

My gaze darted up to meet Rollick's. The demon lifted his fork. "I'm very pleased with the hotel's main chef. This seemed like an ideal option that you'll enjoy without any guilt." He winked.

My throat closed up for a second. I didn't know how to handle this much thoughtfulness from a man I'd expected to hate. I forced myself to pick up my own fork and take a bite of the salmon.

It was perfectly tender, melting in my mouth with the savory, citrusy flavor, a balance so delicious I nearly swooned. "It is good," I had to say, and then I couldn't stop myself from shoveling several more bites into my achingly empty stomach.

To my relief, Rollick didn't study my reaction to the meal too closely. He dug into his own dinner with a pleased expression that suggested he really did enjoy the food too. But then, the other shadowkind men had told me mortal food was one of the pleasures that brought them to the mortal realm in the first place, so I supposed that wasn't surprising.

Curiosity bubbled up despite my initial desire to get this encounter over as quickly as possible.

"How do you know so much about... human health concerns?" I asked. "The other guys barely seemed to understand that it was possible to have a heart transplant."

Rollick waved his fork in a casual gesture. "I've been around a lot longer than any of them. And I make a point of educating myself as thoroughly as possible on any matter that's of interest to me. Like you are." The corners of his dark blue eyes crinkled with well-worn smile lines. Somehow the slight marring of his otherwise smooth face made him even more striking to look at.

His explanation prompted a whole different line of questioning. I knit my brow. "You knew there was something special about me—or about the heart transplant—or something. You sent the three of them to keep an eye on me and see whether anything happened. You knew where they'd find me—the other shadowkind looking for me were only following the energy my heart gives off." And they hadn't tracked me down until months after his three underlings had already been observing me.

The demon hummed in agreement. "I find that a large number of my brethren don't make very good use of the resources available to us mortal-side. They can't be bothered to learn new technologies or human social customs unless it's something they can pick up quickly out of necessity. Whoever exactly it is who's set their sights on you, it appears *they* didn't really understand what it meant that the sorcerers' daughter had given you her heart, let alone how to trace the journey that heart had taken."

"But you did," I filled in. "You dug into the hospital records… How did you know to look for me at all?" A chill washed over me. "Were *you* part of the attack on that house in—"

He cut me off with a brisk shake of his head and a grimace. "If the idiot sorcerers don't bother me and mine, I don't bother them. You learn pretty quick that there's no point in seeking out trouble. But I understand the beings that did orchestrate the attack found some evidence that pointed them in your general direction. Word went out through various back channels that important figures were looking for a girl in Florida named Quinn who was in possession of a sorcerer's heart."

I swallowed thickly. "So they figured I had the heart in a jar or something?"

Rollick let out a bark of delighted laughter that left his eyes sparkling. "That sounds about right. I put the pieces together and did a little digging into the family that was killed and the destination of the daughter's heart, and that led me to you." He cocked his head. "You're *lucky* most shadowkind aren't so medically or technologically aware."

"I guess I am." I looked down at my dinner plate, my appetite having vanished. But I needed the fuel. I poked my fork into a chunk of sweet potato. As I chewed, I couldn't help wondering how much this dinner was actually kindness and how much Rollick was simply trying to butter me up for… for whatever he wanted with me.

It wasn't as if he'd admit to manipulating me. But since he'd mentioned tracing medical records, I could ask about another worry that'd been on my mind.

"If you looked up the daughter who died—do you know if there were any other organs donated?"

"A very good question," the demon said with an approving tone that shouldn't have warmed me the way it did. "You're unique. The other essential organs were too damaged in the accident to be of use."

Well, at least I didn't need to fear for the lives of any other human beings who otherwise might have been facing the same danger I was. I let out a breath and considered Rollick more closely, doing my best not to let his movie-star aura distract me.

"Are you going to tell me yet what it is you expect me to do here?" I asked after a moment.

He gazed back at me with a similarly contemplative air. Then he said the last thing I'd have expected.

"I want you to tap into your sorcerer powers."

For a second, I could only stare. Then I regained control over my tongue. "You want me to try... compelling shadowkind?"

"We might as well determine what the limits of those powers are and how they can be used. I hear you compelled one of the fiends that came after Crag this morning—that both of you might have died if you hadn't."

So Crag had noticed what I'd done—well, how could he not have? I wet my lips, my gut knotting even more than before. "I didn't even mean to. It just happened."

"Survival instincts are a wonderful thing," Rollick said conversationally. "But you'd rather know what you're doing, wouldn't you?"

I frowned at him. "Would *you* really want me to know what I'm doing? What if I started compelling you around?"

He gave another laugh, lighter than before. "I don't think you're going to reach that level of power in an instant, if you do at all."

But what would he do to me if he decided I could get there? Would he kill me after all, as soon as he could without violating his oath? Any warmth I'd gotten from his presence fled with the salt-tinged breeze.

"I—I don't know if that's a good idea," I said.

Rollick considered me. "Why wouldn't it be? Wouldn't you like a little more say over your fate?"

When he put it that way—hell, yes, I would. But the situation was more complicated than that.

"The more power that stirs up inside me, the easier it's been for the other shadowkind to track me," I pointed out.

Rollick flicked his fingers dismissively. "I assure you I have more than enough protections here."

And there was also... I hesitated and then allowed myself to admit my biggest fear—the one that should have been his biggest fear too. "What if I wake up more power, but I still don't know how to control it? I don't want to hurt anyone."

The demon gazed back at me steadily, his forehead furrowing just for a split-second. "I think that's very unlikely," he said. "I'll see that you're properly guided."

"*How?*"

"Leave that to me."

When I didn't answer right away, still tangled up but not sure how to express my resistance any more convincingly, Rollick stood up, his plate cleaned. "This isn't a request. It's a condition of our deal. You cooperate, I keep you and my three mutinists safe. I'll have everything in place for you to start practicing soon, so you should get used to the idea."

He vanished into the shadows without giving me a chance to protest.

CHAPTER FIVE

Torrent

I watched Rollick slide into the back seat of the chauffeured sedan, aiming a wave at the patrons lined up outside the hotel night club as he did. The car drove off into the L.A. night. I waited in the shadows in front of the hotel for several minutes longer to be absolutely sure he wouldn't double back for one reason or another.

Not that he typically did. But I no longer trusted my instincts when it came to my former-and-possibly-still-current boss. I wasn't even sure whether I'd misjudged him only a little or horribly to begin with.

There was definitely plenty he *wasn't* telling me, my men, or Quinn, and as long as I didn't have the full story, everything about him was suspect.

I was reasonably sure that he wouldn't be back for at least a few hours. His evening business meetings tended to involve a lot of drinking and schmoozing, something he'd playfully complained to me about more than once. He wouldn't want to show any sign to the outside world that something had changed about his habits, even around mortals. You could never be totally certain who else might be watching.

Anyway, he hadn't forbidden us from having any contact with Quinn at all. If he caught me schmoozing with *her*, he might be pissed off, but he couldn't claim I'd gone against explicit orders.

I slipped through the shadows up through the hotel. On the high level where silver and iron slats lay interlaced within the floor, there was no way for the average shadowkind to continue upward other than via Rollick's secure elevator… or through a secret entrance he'd keyed to just a few select employees' energies with his demonic magic. Thankfully his shaken trust in me had been outweighed by his desire to have as many invested parties as possible keeping his "prize" safe, or no doubt I'd have been locked out of that.

I had to be careful in his own rooms, of course. I wouldn't put it past Rollick to have surveillance in his private space, video or audio or both. If I could avoid him finding out about this visit, I'd prefer to.

The terrace outside his suite looked clear enough. I scanned the eaves and the walls and saw nowhere a camera could be hiding. It was just a matter of getting Quinn out here.

She was in the lounge room, tucked into one of the armchairs with a book open on her lap. There mustn't be much for her to do stuck in that suite. It'd be killing her being so cut off from her family and school.

My mouth twisted at the thought. I wasn't sure my visit would make things much better, but at least I could offer a little company and information about what was going on outside these rooms.

I emerged into physical form on the darkened terrace, just close enough to the sliding door that I could touch the handle with the tip of one tentacle. I gave it a slight jostle, small enough that it could pass for a gust of wind but loud enough to make Quinn glance up.

As her gaze caught on my face, I held my finger to my lips. She'd startled a bit at the noise, and thankfully that covered any additional shock from her first sight of me. Being the astute woman I'd discovered her to be, she composed her features into an expression of calm and turned back to her book as if she hadn't seen anything at all.

Satisfied, I drifted through the shadows to the side of the terrace to wait. Impatience gnawed at me, but I wouldn't want her to come too quickly and give the game away.

Moonlight rippled over the ocean. I watched it and listened to the distant chatter and music from the rooftop lounge overhead until the door from the bedroom whispered open. As I dragged myself back out of the gloom, Quinn eased outside to meet me. She walked over to the railing next to me and then raised her eyebrows in question, not even sure whether she should speak.

She'd learned a lot of caution in the past several days—or maybe she'd developed that instinct years ago thanks to the restrictions of her health.

"I think it's fine for us to talk here," I said quietly. "But I checked earlier—the hotel room around the corner of the building is empty. If you trust me to help you over, we could talk even more freely there."

Quinn nodded without hesitation, sending a pang through my chest. She'd only known me for a matter of days, and in that span she'd uncovered at least one major betrayal, but she believed in me enough to put her life in my hands. I guessed I had saved it far more times than I'd put it in danger, but her trust felt like a gift all the same.

"Stay here," I murmured, and leapt into the shadows along the building. It was a long span of wall to reach the corner, and then a few feet around the side to the railing of the other room's balcony. There, I re-emerged and unleashed two more of my tentacles than usual, leaving me with eight limbs: four from my shadowkind state and four humanesque.

My natural appendages were far stronger than my human-like ones. I hooked one tentacle firmly around the railing and then drew myself back around the building by gripping the wall with my suckers. Quinn didn't show any sign of alarm at my increased monstrousness. She waited while I got a solid grip on her railing. Fully extended, I could hold on to both, but I wouldn't want to risk stretching myself across a much farther distance.

I held out a third tentacle to her. "I'll hold on to you and carry you across," I said.

"Okay." She clambered onto the upper part of the railing with the skills I'd seen watching her tramp around abandoned buildings and high-rise rooftops back in her regular life, and I looped my tentacle around her waist. It was a little strain drawing her to my torso, but she wasn't all that heavy.

She smiled at me when we were face to face. As I passed her to my fourth tentacle, her gaze slid down the building, taking in the lights and other terraces below. Then I was hefting her around the corner to where she could scramble onto the other balcony.

I followed quickly, heaving myself over the railing after her and ducking into the shadows to unlock the balcony door from the inside. The moment I opened it, Quinn darted inside—and flung her arms around me.

"I'm so glad you're here," she murmured against the fabric of my button-up, her warmth spreading all across my body. "I'm so glad you're still *okay*. Lance and Crag—"

"Are just fine too, last time I saw them, which was this morning," I reassured her, and allowed myself the simple but nearly overwhelming pleasure of hugging her tighter to me with my arms while my tentacles braced my damaged legs.

The gargoyle liked to call her "soft," but what I felt more than anything was the strength in her. The resilience that had kept her going through so much chaos and so many setbacks.

As much as I wanted to gather her up completely for myself, I forced myself to add, "They'd be here too if they were able to. Rollick sent them on missions farther afield, and they haven't gotten back yet. He's gone out too—we should have at least a couple of hours before there's any chance he'll notice I've kidnapped you."

"Is that what you're doing?" she asked, tucking her head against my neck. "Kidnapping me? I thought we agreed that it was better to wait out the deal and see what we could find out with Rollick's input."

"That is still the plan," I admitted. "This is only a temporary kidnapping. I figured you'd want to be filled in on what we know so far—and to have the chance to talk to someone other than him, as enthralling a conversationalist as I know he is."

Quinn snorted, which told me Rollick had at least tried working his charms on her. The thought made my arms tighten around her, even though she obviously wasn't particularly impressed by him.

What Rollick wanted, he tended to get, one way or another. Which was all the more reason we had to figure out how to free her from him for good before that happened in a more permanent fashion.

An ache was starting to creep up my calves from standing like this. I adjusted my weight minutely, not wanting to disturb Quinn, but she reacted immediately. She'd always been particularly alert to my difficulties, which both irritated me and tugged at my heart.

"You should sit down," she said, glancing around the room. The only places *to* sit were a narrow armchair that I could already tell would squish my tentacles—it wasn't as if Quinn could carve that into a more monster-friendly version in the short time we had—and the bed. A pang that was both uncertainty and anticipation wavered through my chest, but Quinn drew me toward the bed without a second's hesitation.

I sat down on the edge near the foot and swept my gaze around the room in another precautionary glance. It seemed unlikely that Rollick would risk putting cameras in the guestrooms where there'd be a scandal if one were discovered, and I saw no sign of one. I relaxed just slightly, setting my hands on the covers.

Quinn switched on one of the small bedside lamps so we could see each other better and hopped up next to me, turning toward me and sitting cross-legged. She obviously wanted to have a real part in this conversation, not just to lean on me for comfort. That was part of why I'd fallen for her too.

"What have you found out so far?" she asked. "Do you have any idea who these shadowkind are that keep sending their horde of allies after me?"

Right down to business. My lips twitched with a fond smile. "We know more than we did before. From combining what Rollick's been able to tell us about what happened after the sorcerer family was attacked in Miami with our own observations over the past several days, we're completely sure that whoever's searching for you—and putting pressure on Goldie and whatever else—was also behind that attack. We also know that this is part of a longer pattern. Rollick's dug up information on a dozen or so prominent sorcerers across the continents who've been slaughtered in similar ways."

Quinn winced. "With their vital organs removed?"

"Yes," I said, because it wouldn't do her any good to shy away from the full truth. "It's starting to seem increasingly likely that the one or few higher shadowkind responsible *have* gained some sorcerer power of their own and are using it to compel some of the lesser beings to their bidding, along with more typical methods of coercion. Although I'm sure some of them are simply along for the ride to win favor or for the thrill of it."

Her shudder reflected how unnerved I felt by that revelation. A shadowkind compelling other shadowkind... It was bad enough when humans enslaved us and manipulated us to their will. To turn that perverse power against your own... There were some lines that shouldn't be crossed, no matter how much of a monster you were.

"Who *are* they?" Quinn asked. "Do you know anything about the powers they had before they started murdering sorcerers? Or about what they want to do with all the new powers they're getting?" She paused, her head drooping slightly. "Or why they seem to want to capture me now rather than tear me apart on the spot? Although maybe that's just so the underlings can bring me to their boss, and that's when I'll get torn up."

"That is possible," I admitted, as much as I hated to. "We've talked about it, and even Rollick agrees that at this point it seems unlikely. They've put a lot of energy into tracking you down, and with the number of sorcerers they've already devoured, one heart doesn't seem like it should be so important to them."

"But what else could they possibly want from me?"

I dragged in a breath. "We've determined that they have at least one higher being with persuasive abilities working with them—she can't compel shadowkind, but her powers work on mortals, and she's used that to help during their search for you. It could be that they want to have you in their grasp so they can compel *you* into compelling other shadowkind."

Quinn knit her brow. "And that would be better than eating my heart?"

I smiled thinly. "Power direct from its natural source is a lot more potent than power diluted by mixing it with other factors. Quite possibly once you get a handle on your abilities, you'd be able to command more shadowkind alone than our enemies could with a dozen sets of organs in their guts."

A shiver ran through her slim frame, and she hugged herself. Wisps of her pale hair fell across her cheeks as she glanced down at her lap. Then she squared her shoulders and met my eyes again with those stunning sky-blue eyes. "Well, we're obviously not letting that happen. What about my other questions?"

I thought back to what else she'd asked. "The mastermind—or minds—behind this whole situation have kept themselves very much in the background, letting their lackeys do all the grunt work. We're not sure what kind of beings they are or their natural powers. We do seem to have benefitted from their not being all that familiar with this country. Most of the other killings were in Europe and Asia, and they've only been 'recruiting' assistance here on the ground pretty actively in the past several months—they don't seem to have had much of a presence on this side of the ocean until recently."

Possibly that was the only reason we'd been able to stay a few steps ahead of them.

"We're still working on that," I went on. "It's only been a couple of days. Rollick sent Crag off to talk to a being who tangled with the group and might have clashed with the leader directly to see what we can find out there. Lance is following another trail. I'll try to update you again soon—maybe all of us will be able to come together. Rollick has meetings and other events pretty frequently."

Quinn gazed past me toward the balcony, her expression pensive. Then she met my eyes again. "*He* wants me to tap into my sorcerer powers. Rollick. He told me that yesterday."

I frowned. Was that all the demon wanted—a pet sorcerer he could use to compel shadowkind to his bidding? The idea made even less sense to me than the thought that he'd wanted to devour her heart and take on that power for himself. I could maybe see him enjoying adding to his own capabilities, but he exerted plenty of authority over any shadowkind he encountered already. Getting a human to order them around in his place didn't sound like him at all.

Quinn was studying my reaction. "That's not what you'd have expected."

"No. I have no idea why he'd want to bring out your magic—but I doubt he'd tell me if I asked."

"He wouldn't tell *me*. And you're not even supposed to know, since we aren't supposed to have talked about it." She sighed. "Before this whole thing, you respected him, didn't you? You didn't think he was some horrible villain."

"I didn't think that," I agreed. "He... I mean, we're all shadowkind, not human. There's a reason we get called monsters, and it's not just because of how we look. I won't claim he follows the same moral compass someone you'd consider a "good person" would, but neither do I. I can say that in the decades I've worked for him, he's only seemed harsh when prompted, not out of pure sadistic enjoyment. And while he plays with the mortals who come to this place, it's never been in a way that leaves them scarred. He doesn't let the shadowkind patrons outright harm them either."

"So he's got *some* sense of morality," Quinn muttered. "Or at least of maintaining a balance for whatever selfish reasons."

"I don't think it's all selfish." I flexed my tentacles on either side of me. "He didn't need to take me on as a lackey and then a lieutenant. When I presented myself to him and asked for whatever work he could give me, I expected him to laugh in my face. I haven't gotten much more than sneers and ridicule from other shadowkind over my infirmities... and I can't deny that they make me less capable. But he saw something in me and decided it was worth taking the gamble. He's the only one who gave me a chance like that."

Quinn was quiet for a moment. She scooted closer to me, and I shifted my nearer tentacle so it slipped around her, letting her get close enough that she could rest her hand on my thigh.

"What did happen to you—to injure your legs and...?" Her hand rose to my bashed-in cheek. "If you don't mind telling me."

I didn't like talking about the past with anyone. Shame burned through my body at just the briefest memory of those times. The words rose in my throat to put her off—but she'd told me about the most traumatic parts of her own life. She'd bartered her freedom to save me from Rollick's anger.

She deserved to know exactly what kind of man—and monster—I was, didn't she?

I forced myself to speak. "For most of my existence, I wasn't anyone you'd have admired or probably even liked. I got a thrill out of all the indulgences of the mortal realm, and that was what I focused all my time and energy on. I grifted to make money and connections; I roamed from party to party; I delved into every recreational drug there is; I went through multiple sexual partners in a night."

Quinn hadn't tensed or shown any sign of distress yet, just waiting patiently for me to go on. I swallowed hard and continued.

"I don't even remember exactly what happened, I was so high at the time. All I know for sure is that I got it in my head to hassle some other beings in some way, a prank or something like that, and it turned out they were more powerful than I must have realized in my messed-up state or I wouldn't have targeted them. They were pissed off, and I didn't have the wherewithal to really defend myself. They battered me good... I wouldn't be surprised if they'd have killed me if we hadn't been on a beach and I managed to propel myself into the water where I was more at my element and could flee."

I paused, and then reached to untie the laces on my boots. Let her see the full extent of my deformity. This was who I was now. This was who she could decide to stand by or push away from.

As I slid the boots off, a little pained sound worked from Quinn's throat. On one side, the foot was merely broken, the ball and toes missing just as the very tip was on the matching tentacle when I was in full shadowkind form. My ankle canted inward at an odd angle too.

The other side was worse. My attackers had crushed everything from below the anklebone so completely that my left foot had simply fallen away. There was nothing but a stump. The boots I conjured out of shadow held the necessary fixtures to keep me upright when I needed them to.

Quinn's fingers curled around my arm. I found myself unable to look at her.

"That's the story," I said, my voice roughening. "That's who I was. The beating worked as a wake-up call. I *couldn't* indulge the same way I had before, since I couldn't move among mortals on just my two feet, and I didn't want to lose even more by keeping up the same carelessness anyway. But I still love a lot about this realm. The job for Rollick gave me access to a few minor pleasures. And the rest I can at least enjoy vicariously here and there."

Now she'd seen it all. She knew just how much of a ruin I was. My muscles clenched, bracing for—I didn't even know what, but some act to extricate herself from me.

Instead, she bobbed up to press a kiss to my fractured cheek like she had in the yacht a few days ago. My heart wrenched.

Quinn stayed there with her head tipped close to mine, her breath tickling over my skin. After a moment, she spoke softly by my ear. "Thank you for telling me. It doesn't change who I know you are now. Or how I feel about you."

I finally dared to turn my gaze toward her. "And how's that?" I murmured.

She touched my jaw and brought her lips to mine.

As our mouths melded together, something hummed through my chest, as if she were pouring pure light straight into me. I wanted to soak it all in, to revel in the passion she still meant to offer me.

Here we were on this bed with no one to disturb us. I had her all to myself. And if she wanted me, then I was going to make sure she got every possible pleasure I could offer *her*.

CHAPTER SIX

Quinn

Torrent's answering kiss was only hesitant for the first split-second when our lips met. Then he leaned into it, his mouth aligning perfectly with mine, claiming me as if there was nothing in the universe he'd rather be doing. With every passing moment as his hand rose to cup my cheek and the tentacle he'd slung around my hips teased up my back, more confidence radiated off him.

Good. I hadn't liked the sense of shame I'd gotten from him while he'd given his confession about his past. If he really thought I'd judge him for the injuries he'd taken or how he'd acted ages before I'd even been born, this was the best way I could show him how wrong he was.

If anything, now I was more impressed by the calm leadership with which he'd directed our little crew, knowing how hard-won that self-control and assurance was. Knowing that he'd spent decades remaking himself into a man he *wasn't* ashamed of, even when most of his kind had seen him as a lost cause because of his disability.

And he was still remaking himself when he saw the need to. He'd recognized that I was more than a pawn to be used in a game between his boss and whoever else wanted me, and he'd abandoned his former loyalty to fully protect me because he'd felt that was the right thing to do. There weren't many humans who were willing to adjust their sense of morality that easily.

Of course, morality wasn't exactly the first thing on my mind right now. Torrent hadn't touched me anywhere all that sensitive yet, but he'd encased me in his warm embrace, and every inch of my skin was tingling for more. I kissed him again and again, wondering if this was what it felt like to be drunk.

Only one tiny practical part of me stayed alert enough to pull me just a couple of inches back from him, my breath gone ragged. "We don't have to worry— You're sure Rollick won't be back for a while?"

Torrent's eyes gleamed, no doubt understanding why I was asking. "I'd expect him to be out for at least a couple more hours, if not longer," he said. His tentacle trailed down my spine, and the tip hooked under my shirt. "And if he returns early and realizes what we've gotten up to, then let him. He can't hurt us."

A thrill quivered through my chest, unexpected and yet familiar. I'd always liked taking risks, thumbing my nose at danger when I felt I could get away with it. We both knew Rollick wouldn't be *happy* about us taking this interlude together, but he hadn't ordered us *not* to do it. Defying him added an extra spark to the giddiness already bubbling through my veins.

"Then there's no reason not to enjoy the moment to its fullest," I said with a grin, and dove in for another kiss.

I hadn't gone farther than this with Torrent before. The one time we'd gotten into a heated make-out session, Rollick's arrival had interrupted us before we'd done much of anything. I *really* hoped the demon didn't show up soon enough to stop us before I got to experience everything he had to offer.

Torrent's tentacle grazed up and down my spine beneath my shirt, the suckers pressing into my skin with a subtle pressure that felt like he was kissing me all across my back too. His hand tucked between us to fondle my breast through my bra. When he flicked his thumb right under the cup, a gasp jolted out of me.

"There's so much I want to do with you," he murmured, dropping his head to kiss the side of my neck. "So much I *can* do for you that no other mortal woman could have handled. Do you want all of it?" His second tentacle reached over to glide across my thigh.

An ache of need was already forming between my legs. Lately I'd been discovering just how stimulating monstrous features could be in bed, from Lance's dragon claws to Crag's gargoyle tongue. I'd just let this man carry me over a fatal height with his tentacles—trusting them with my body in less death-defying ways was a no-brainer.

"Yes, please," I said, my voice breaking with a whimper when he swept the curve of his tentacle right over the seam of my shorts. Just like that, my panties were drenched.

Torrent captured my mouth again with an approving hum that reverberated through me and set off all kinds of other tingles. The tentacle at my back deftly unhooked my bra, giving him access to caress my breasts without that barrier in the way. I gripped the front of his shirt, at first simply holding on through the waves of heady sensation and then fumbling with the buttons.

My other monstrous men had removed their clothes simply by stepping into the shadows and leaving everything that wasn't their innate physical form behind. Torrent let me peel his button-up off him, tracing my fingers over the leanly sculpted muscles of his shoulders and arms as I did. A sound carried from his throat that was closer to a growl than a hum.

My hands encountered the ripples of other scars, low ridges that marred his equally sculpted torso. Superficial but still unshakeable remainders of the long-ago assault. At first brush, I jerked my fingers back instinctively, afraid of pressing a tender spot. But when Torrent's muscles tensed at my hesitation, I stroked them carefully and then more confidently, hearing the hitch of his breath that was nothing but eager.

"You don't have to worry about hurting me," he said, nipping the lobe of my ear. "It's only my lower legs where there's any residual pain, and it comes from putting my weight on them, not simply being touched."

"Okay," I whispered. "Good." I ran my hands down his chest again, all the way to the waist of his slacks.

When I skimmed the bulge behind his fly, Torrent groaned. He shifted his weight, tugging me with him to tumble over on the bed, and yanked off my tee with hands and tentacle as we sank down. He caught my jaw in his fingers and kissed me again as two tentacles tucked around the hem of my shorts and pulled them off as well.

He'd brought out more of them, I realized through the haze of pleasure. Along with his hands and mouth, there were four sinewy, suckered limbs teasing over me now. Two of them coiled over my breasts, setting a sucker over each nipple and squeezing as if plucking them.

The rush of bliss was so intense I jerked into his hold, kissing him even harder. He delved his tongue between my lips like a smaller echo of those lithe appendages. As it tangled with mine, he squeezed my nipples again and again. The pleasure shot me higher each time until I was writhing against him, desperate for more.

Torrent didn't leave me hanging. His tongue kept exploring my mouth and his tentacles continued working over my nipples, but another eased under my panties to curve across my sex.

He let out another rough sound at the wetness he found there. The tip of his tentacle glided back and forth over my opening while a lower sucker settled against my clit. When it squeezed on the little nub like the others were plucking my nipples, I nearly arched right off the bed.

The giddying bolt of sensation left me quivering. When he did it again, I couldn't help crying out against his mouth. Torrent swallowed that sound even as he coaxed more out of me, sliding his tentacle farther so it could curl right up inside me.

I'd been fingered before, but this—this was something totally different. Something totally heaven. No human fingers could have filled me like his lithe extra limb did, or reached so easily to the sensitive spot inside that produced the most pleasure. No fingers could have pulsed into it so perfectly while flexing against the walls of my pussy and massaging my clit at the same time.

I clung to Torrent and bucked with the sinuous thrusts, all kinds of gasps and whimpers spilling from my mouth now. Between his grip on my pussy and his continued suckered caresses to my breasts, bliss flooded every thought from my mind. All I could do was soar higher and higher on it, until so much was swelling through my body that I thought I might literally explode.

"That's right," Torrent murmured. "You take to it so well. I always wondered what I could do if—" He hesitated and kissed the crook of my jaw. "I'm glad I got to find out with you. It'll only be you from now on."

I couldn't find my voice to answer him despite the pang of affection his words sent through me. Somehow the wave of sensation was propelling me even higher still. My fingernails dug into Torrent's shoulders. He plucked at my clit a little more firmly than before in perfect synchronicity with the pulsing against my G-spot, and I careened right over the edge like I'd leapt off a cliff.

The blaze of ecstasy was like the whipping of the wind, hurling me higher instead of letting me fall. My throat choked up. I all but sobbed, my head jerking back against the pillow, sparks dancing behind my eyes.

Torrent wasn't done with me even then. He eased on the pressure while I floated hazily down and then ramped it up again, stroke by stroke. I'd have thought I'd be wrung out after that epic orgasm, but somehow more pleasure was building in me already, propelling me toward another peak.

As I rocked with his strokes, that final tentacle slipped around my hip to draw my panties right down to my knees. It rose again and traced the line between the cheeks of my ass. The contact woke up an even headier shiver.

"Have you taken anyone here before?" Torrent asked in an unusually husky voice, swiveling the tip of his tentacle around my back opening. In combination with the bliss he was summoning all through the rest of my body, his touch there made me buck even more wildly.

"No," I mumbled, struggling to speak at all. "I—I've been curious, but —it's risky, for infection and things—"

I wasn't sure how coherent that answer was, but Torrent seemed to understand. His lips moved against my cheek with his reply. "We'll wait until I can prepare you better for the full experience, then. I'm looking forward to filling you in every possible way."

If it somehow felt even better than the way he was simply rimming me now, I was looking forward to it just as much. I writhed between his tentacles, moaning as he sped up his thrusts in my pussy and his plucks of my clit and nipples. I probably looked crazed, but every particle of my body was singing with the pleasure he'd brought me. It seared hotter and brighter, fresh jolts crackling through me and stealing my breath.

"Oh, God," I mumbled. "Oh, Torrent. Fuck." And then I shattered all over again, even more epically than before. For a few seconds, I couldn't even feel my body, only a roar of bliss that swept me away.

I sagged bonelessly into the bed, and Torrent kissed me on the mouth, his lips curved with a smile. Then his tentacles started to work me over yet again.

I gasped, shivering with delight, but I'd come back to earth enough to know that this wasn't all I wanted out of our encounter. I slid my hand back down to the fly of his slacks again and cupped his erection through the fabric.

"Your tentacles feel fucking *fantastic*," I said, feeling the need to make that clear after his earlier uncertainty, "but I want you to come with me this time."

Torrent's eyelids dipped, lust darkening his eyes as I rubbed his cock. Without a word, he helped me peel off his slacks and drew his probing tentacle out of my sex. As he poised himself over me, he paused and gazed down into my face as if searching for something there.

I raised my hand to caress his caved-in cheek while curling my other fingers around his rigid erection. "It isn't hard on your legs, holding yourself like this? We could—"

"I'll be fine," he said in a strained voice. "I want you under me. I just—it's been a very long time. I might have had plenty of practice in the distant past, but I don't know how long I'll last after all this time. And when it's you."

The adoration of those last words brought a poignant ache into my chest. I beamed up at him. "You've already made me come—*twice*—so hard it'll be a wonder if I can walk for the next day. Believe me, I couldn't be more satisfied. I just want to feel you totally with me now."

Something shifted in his expression, tender and almost peaceful. He dipped his head down to kiss me, softly and then more passionately. As his mouth moved against mine, he plunged inside me.

It wasn't the same sensation of having my centers of pleasure perfectly stimulated, but it felt so good all the same. I rocked with his thrusts, absorbing the tremors of delight that ran through his body, reveling in the way our bodies aligned in harmony, seeking our release together.

Sweat had started to form on his skin. I stroked my fingers over his chest and then along his sides, following the base of his tentacles where they protruded near the base of his rib cage and then lower down his waist. He groaned and wrapped one across my chest again to suck at my nipples while he used his arms to brace himself over me.

I was so wrung out from the first two orgasms that I wasn't sure I could have gotten there again anyway. But when Torrent's breath started to stutter and his hips jerked faster as he neared his own climax, the sense of him giving himself over to this moment with me renewed the spark inside me. I arched into him, and he tucked another tentacle between us to flick just the tip against my clit.

I gasped and clenched around him, coming more like a gentle wave than a tsunami this time but enjoying it no less.

Torrent swore under his breath. He bucked even faster and tucked his head next to mine as he came inside me.

He sank down onto his side and immediately pulled me into his arms, his tentacles wrapping around me for good measure. I rested my head against his sweat-damp shoulder.

"Anyone who can't handle the tentacles has no idea what they're missing," I muttered.

Torrent let out a startled guffaw and kissed my temple. "They're all for you, so everyone else will have to keep missing them."

I glanced up at him, the joy of the moment dampening at the thought of how brief our interlude was likely to be. How long it might take before we could spend any time together even talking again.

"Do you really think we can find a way out of this?" I found myself asking.

I didn't need to explain what I meant. Torrent's arms tightened around me.

"I don't know," he said a little hoarsely. "But I'm going to do everything in my power to see that we do."

CHAPTER SEVEN

Rollick

"The nymph said the one she was around briefly never showed his shadowkind form, but he had a sort of earthy vibe to him," Crag reported, standing stiffly by the door to my office. "And a strong vibe in general, very large and powerful. The ground shook with his steps. She never saw any other being that was clearly in charge, but the earthy one referred to 'we' a few times in a way that made her think he wasn't making his plans alone."

I strolled through the room, turning over everything he'd told me in my mind. "Earthy and very powerful... Could be a particularly established giant or troll, or an earthen elemental... Dwarf seems unlikely given the size. I can't think of any specific being I've crossed paths with who'd be a definite candidate. But then, I haven't traveled much overseas in recent decades."

I'd been focused on the hotel and establishing my business ties here in L.A. Putting down roots as well as one ever could in the mortal realm. I didn't expect *this* location to stand the test of time across centuries, but if I continued solidifying my network as I'd always done, it'd take no time at all to rebuild wherever I liked. I'd been through that cycle more times than I could count as human society shifted, rolling with the punches and coming out back on top.

But these new fiends... they were a problem I'd never encountered before.

"At least we have more information?" Crag said, giving me a hopeful look.

I'd have appreciated the gargoyle's dedication to this quest more if I hadn't known it was mostly for the mortal woman's benefit and not my own. I stopped by my desk and leaned against it, folding my arms over my chest and holding his gaze. There were other plans I needed to set in motion. I could never have kept my spot at the top of my game if I wasn't juggling a dozen balls at once.

"It's a start," I said. "Too early to tell how much of one when we don't know how long a trail we'll need to follow. You're impatient to tackle these fiends."

I definitely didn't like the firmness with which Crag gazed back at me, totally at ease with the admission he was about to make. "I want to know they won't get near Quinn ever again. They've hurt her enough as it is."

I raised my eyebrows. "And do you think that playing her protector is going to stop her from getting bored with you? You expect that her gratitude will make her feel obliged to continue that dalliance even after the initial thrill has cooled off?"

Crag's mouth twitched into a frown. "That wasn't something I'd worried about to begin with."

"Oh, my poor fellow. You've never associated with mortal lovers before, have you?"

His hand rose to rub his rocky jaw. "I haven't had the opportunity. But Quinn doesn't mind—she accepts the—"

I waved off his protest before he could even finish it. "Of course she doesn't *mind*. You've found one of the curiosity-seekers. Rare but predictable. She gets off on how unusual you are, but they're just like the shadowkind tourists in reverse, you know. Dabbling with the fun of the other side but never committing to anything. It's just a way to get her kicks until she's tired of that and on to something new."

I expected the gargoyle to look concerned or embarrassed, but instead he only drew up his ample frame straighter with an air of undeniable and irritating defiance. "You don't really know her. She didn't seek us out as lovers. Lance was the one who pushed for that sort of intimacy. She trusts us—she cares for us. And I *will* be worthy of that trust."

"I'm only trying to look out for you in your inexperience, friend," I said with a tsk of my tongue. "How long have *you* known her, really interacting with her rather than watching from the shadows—a little more than a week? Humans don't typically form long-lasting bonds even with each other in that short a time. How could you fit into her regular life if you can win it back for her?"

"We would figure it out," Crag said gruffly but without hesitation.

I didn't want to harp on the subject and risk building more animosity toward *me*. The best thing was to have planted the seed so it'd have time to sprout and grow. Not that the soil appeared at all fertile. I supposed it wasn't surprising that the gargoyle could be stubborn as stone.

Well, that too had been only a start. I made a dismissive motion, and he wavered into the shadows without another word.

Time to work on yet another angle of my plans. I gave my humanesque body a little shake to dispel any tension from the unsatisfying conversation, flashed my brightest smile just to warm up my expression, and headed downstairs to my private rooms.

I didn't bother knocking. It was a careful balance between showing consideration for the woman's preferences and keeping her just a little off-balance. She should never forget whose generosity she was relying on right now—who these rooms belonged to.

Quinn didn't notice my arrival at first anyway. I spotted her sitting in a patch of shade on the terrace, her sketchbook propped on her lap. Her head bowed with concentration as she moved a pencil over the page. She didn't react to my presence until I eased open the sliding door to step outside.

Her head jerked up, her pencil stilling. I ambled over to peer at the picture she'd sketched: a tower that curved like a narrowing helix up to a magnificent spire. I couldn't say I'd seen a mortal building quite like it before, but that might mean it wasn't especially practical. She did have a taste for grandeur.

"I expected you to relax and recover after your ordeal," I teased. "And yet it seems you can't help putting yourself to work."

Quinn shrugged and closed the sketchbook. "It isn't really work. I love imagining what I might be able to see built from my designs—it's *fun*. Anyway, it makes me feel a little better about the fact that I can't do my *actual* work since you've confiscated my laptop." She narrowed her eyes at me.

I had to grin. Her obstinacy did make my life a little harder, but her boldness was enough of a delight that I wasn't sure I minded. Most humans —most shadowkind, even—automatically cowered at least a little before me, sensing instinctively that in the universal hierarchy they were prey and I was predator.

This woman had definitely acclimatized to the idea of monsters very quickly during her time with my mutinous underlings. She was wary of me, absolutely. But she didn't see me as enough of a threat that she felt the need to kowtow—or at least, she didn't give enough of a shit about the consequences to rein in her snark.

It was very refreshing.

"Give you that laptop and I might as well throw you straight to the wolves," I said. "You wouldn't want that. Not only would it be very painful, you'd also lose out on more of my delectable company."

Quinn tried to control her reaction, but I caught the flicker of a smile before she schooled her expression into blandness. She did enjoy the banter whether she wanted to or not.

"You think very highly of yourself," she said dryly.

I grinned and leaned against the doorframe. "I'm simply drawing the most obvious conclusions from the available evidence. Are you deprived of anything—other than disastrous contact with the outside world? Let's see if I can't provide it."

Quinn raised an eyebrow. I had the sense that she was debating trying me—seeing what she might get away with. The thought invigorated me more than it probably should. I did love a challenge, and so little challenged me these days.

She looked as if she were about to say something, her lips parting in a way that sent a twinge to my groin, but then she shut her mouth again and shook her head. "Okay, I'll admit you've been catering to my needs very well."

I stepped closer, letting her absorb the heft of my presence without actually touching her. It'd be so much better if she crossed that final distance first if we were going to mesh that particular way. And if we didn't, well, I'd survived worse disappointments. There was no denying she'd be *fun*, though.

"What about your wants?" I said, letting my voice turn silky. "Your desires? There was something you almost asked for. Don't hold out on me now."

If I'd turned that voice on another woman—or man, as the mood took me—I'd have expected them to melt into a puddle of compliance in a matter of seconds. I thought I saw a little quiver run through Quinn's body, but then she simply shrugged. Fascinating. Maybe that sorcerer heart of hers gave her extra resilience against my innate demonic magnetism.

"I guess I'd just like to know when you're going to get on with this plan of yours that I factor into somehow," she said finally, studying me with the distrust I knew to expect.

I kept my stance casual and chuckled. "I was under the impression you needed time to get accustomed to the idea of taking on your natural role. But if you've had enough time, I have the necessary pieces ready to begin our experiments into human sorcery."

Her posture stiffened automatically at the word, a most unusual response. She should have been *glad* to have access to that kind of power—the opportunity to potentially work it against her enemies.

Instead she was mulishly worried about how it might affect my three traitors.

I didn't actually believe what I'd said to Crag. I'd watched many bouts of human affection come and go, and Quinn clearly cared about a lot more than what my mutinous men had in their pants. It wasn't the thrill of being with a monstrous being that made her so reluctant to experiment with a magic that might hurt them.

No, she was genuinely concerned about their well-being. I didn't know how it had happened or how long it would last, but the devotion was there on her side as well as theirs.

And it was highly inconvenient.

"I've been thinking about that," she said, drawing out the words.

"Yes? And what conclusions have you drawn?"

"I still think it's a bad idea."

I resisted the urge to roll my eyes and instead tilted my body forward, resting my hand on the back of the lounge chair just an inch from the cascade of her light blond hair. Tipped that close, I caught her scent: a tang of sunscreen mixed with something fresher, like spring wildflowers just coming into bloom.

"Maybe you've forgotten," I said. "Our deal—the whole part where I keep you and the men who defied my orders safe—is dependent on *your* cooperation with me. You wouldn't want to violate that over some vague fear of the unknown, now would you?"

Quinn gazed up at me, a hint of sharper warmth flowing from her skin just for an instant. She wet her lips, drawing my attention to that lovely mouth again. Her eyes darted away from me momentarily before returning to meet mine.

"I was thinking about that too," she said. "And I wondered… since you did swear not to cause us any harm, and *you* can't know for sure that my powers won't harm them—or me… if *I* honestly believe that the sorcery could harm us, then wouldn't it violate our deal for you to insist that I try anyway?"

I blinked at her, my mind abruptly whirling. She couldn't really have found a loophole—surely that logic couldn't hold—

But I was abruptly certain that it did. She'd found a weak spot in our agreement, one that gave her a free pass to ignore me without consequences over her own worries. Frustration prickled through me, my teeth itching to shed the veneers that hid the vicious points.

This was a little *more* of a challenge than I'd have preferred.

I kept my composure, because I hadn't lived millennia by losing my cool every time events didn't go exactly my way, and let my grin widen instead. "I suppose I'll just have to soothe those fears to the best of my ability, then."

"Not sure how you're going to do that," Quinn said steadily, but her pupils had dilated. Oh, I did have some effect on her. No being mortal or shadowkind was totally impervious to the impact of my presence.

"Hmm." I straightened up and took a couple of steps away, rubbing my chin as if debating my options. But I'd already known one move I wanted to make, and this gave me a reasonable opening.

I turned to face her, flexing my shoulders in the fitted suit that would have been sweltering in the summer heat if I hadn't been built for climates even hotter than this. "Maybe you need a little help wrapping your head around the idea that using those powers could *protect* whoever you want to save more than they're likely to hurt them. Because the beings we're up against could very well be even more imposing than me."

"I don't think you're—" Quinn started, and then her mouth snapped shut as I shifted into my shadowkind form.

I loomed even taller and broader, my shadow stretching across the terrace to her feet even under the midday sun. I swiped my hand past my mouth to remove the veneers, revealing the rows of razor-sharp teeth. My clothes vanished, leaving behind only a landscape of ruddy skin over bulging muscles. It was marred here and there by paler scars, including a slash of one just above the side of my waist where this particular mortal had stabbed me a few days ago, but those added character to the terrain. A reminder of how much I'd survived without faltering.

My horns shot up from just above my ears. Claws jutted from my fingertips. My tufted tail lashed beside my hip, and my feet condensed into cloven hooves most mortals associated with pure evil. I flexed my shoulders and grinned.

It was always a relief, letting my demonic self loose. Filling all the space I was meant to.

Quinn's eyes had widened. She couldn't disguise her reaction now—both the horror and the spark of interest that danced alongside her animalistic panic. Especially when her gaze dipped to particular endowments.

"You have two," she blurted out, and flushed flame-red, jerking her eyes upward again. "I mean—I've never seen—it's no big deal."

I smirked wider, letting my pointed teeth gleam in the sunlight. Oh, let her just imagine how big a deal two substantial cocks could possibly be. She liked her men monstrous—she might as well know what she was missing out on if she passed on the most monstrous of those on hand.

"My apologies," I said in the more resonant voice that came with my true form. "We monsters tend not to go around clothed while we're being monsters." I flicked my tongue over my teeth. "Lucky for you, I'm on your side. But imagine facing off against a being like me—or even more savage—and knowing you could have defended yourself and everyone with you... if only you'd figured out how to purposefully draw on your accidental powers."

Her throat bobbed as she swallowed. She tucked her legs closer to her chest, but her pupils were still huge. A little frightened? I should hope so. But also so very, very curious.

"That's a lot to think about," she said, keeping her voice steady and even a bit tart.

I had to suppress a startled guffaw. She'd pulled most of her composure together with incredible speed.

This one was going to be hard to crack. But I'd get there. I was more than familiar with playing a long game.

"I'll leave you to that thinking, then," I said in a low rumble, and gave her a wink before ducking to step back into the lounge.

As I reached the far door, I shifted back into my human-like body, conjuring my clothes around me again. The full demon presence would lose a little of its impact if I went around flashing it everywhere.

Besides, I kept my phone in my trousers, and I couldn't hear it ringing if I dismissed it to the shadows. It did start ringing now when I was halfway up the stairs to my office. I checked the number and raised it to my ear.

"Yes, Aspen?"

The lackey on the other end drew in a hasty breath. "I'm sorry to bother you, Rollick, but there've—there've been some new developments in Florida that I figured you'd want to hear about sooner rather than later."

CHAPTER EIGHT

Quinn

When dinner arrived, a single covered plate humming to the top of the dumbwaiter, I was still having trouble shaking the image of Rollick in his full demonic beastliness from my mind. I carried the plate over to the coffee table in the sitting area on autopilot, not able to summon much hunger.

My men had told me he was a demon—a powerful one. But I'd never seen him in anything other than his human guise, which was compelling and sometimes even electrifying but hardly monstrous. Now, there was no denying just how immense a foe he'd be if I defied him.

In physical heft, he wasn't that much larger or more beastly-looking than Crag's gargoyle body, which I actually kind of liked now that I was used to it. I wasn't used to Rollick's demonic form, though, and I sure as hell didn't trust him never to tear into me with those jagged teeth and claws or pummel me with those bulging limbs. And the aura of power that emanated off him even when he looked like a man, full of equal parts promise and menace, had amplified to the point that *my* whole body had shivered with it.

If he was right and the other foes I was up against were as formidable as him—or worse—I couldn't help thinking that I was totally screwed.

Annoyingly, I wasn't even totally unnerved by Rollick's display. I might not trust him, but I was now well aware of how... enjoyable certain monstrous features could be. A small part of my mind couldn't help speculating about what it'd be like to have a monstrous lover I *could* trust who came endowed with not just one but two cocks. That image kept swimming up from my memory too, the one jutting out over the other above a single set of balls, both sized to match the rest of his massive frame even when flaccid.

God, how big must they be when *erect*?

I slapped my hand to my forehead as if I could jostle those unwanted thoughts out of my brain and forced myself to focus on my dinner. I needed to eat and keep my strength up, because who knew if I'd need to go on the run again with no more access to hotel-quality food.

I'd say this for the demon—he had been very conscientious with my meals. Every spread that'd appeared in the dumbwaiter, three times a day, had offered up something mouth-watering but within the realm my doctors would have approved of. Yesterday a delicately flavorful mango sorbet had arrived at just the right timing for me to indulge right after I'd finished my dinner without it being at all melted.

So, the whole being held under captivity experience was ten out of ten for sustenance, which was about all I could recommend about it.

Tonight's spread included a chicken breast drizzled with nuts and a fruity sauce, with a fresh-baked whole-grain roll and a pear and spinach salad on the side. Plus another bottle of sparkling water, since Rollick seemed to feel I shouldn't be reduced to drinking from the tap with my meals even if I couldn't partake of his preferred beverages.

There was also, poised on the edge of the plate as if it didn't totally belong there, what it took me a moment to realize was an apple carved with deft precision into an ornately petaled rose.

My chest hitched with a pang of sudden affection. I recognized Lance's work immediately. He mustn't have had a chance to come right up to see me, but he'd stolen a moment to show he was thinking of me and to sneak this little present in with my meal.

I picked up the carved apple, cupping it between my hands. I wasn't sure I could bring myself to eat it—but then, I probably shouldn't leave it lying around, because I doubted Rollick would approve.

For a second, tears pricked at my eyes. God, how I missed the dragon shifter's sly warmth and playful energy. I could just imagine spending hours in here telling him about all my adventures around Florida and explaining the parts of human life he didn't totally understand, finding out more about his life before he'd crashed into mine, challenging him to an impromptu sparring session… and of course all the other fun we could have been having together, alone or with the other two men.

He didn't seem to take much very seriously—other than my protection. It'd have been so much easier not to let my worries consume me with him around.

I swallowed thickly and made myself bite into the apple. Mouthful by mouthful, I swallowed it down. Closing my eyes, I savored the sweetness and the texture of the carved petals and imagined telling him how much I'd appreciated the little gift when I did get to see him again.

However long that took.

When I set the core aside, I considered the rest of my dinner. My gaze caught on the knife at the right side of the plate. With past dishes, I'd only ever received a dinner knife. This one was a steak knife—for greater ease of cutting the chicken breast, I assumed. The serrated edges gleamed under the room's artificial lights.

I picked it up and cut into the chicken. The meat parted with only a light pressure, as if I were slicing through butter. Of course, the hotel restaurant wouldn't want to give its guests ineffectual cutlery.

How convenient that it could also be a weapon.

I ate the rest of the food mechanically, only paying enough attention to note that it was as delicious as always but not taking much enjoyment out of the fact. A different memory was replaying in my mind now—the moment when I'd first fled from Rollick after he'd come to collect me from the other men. When I'd stabbed him in the side with the silver-and-iron blade I'd grabbed from the sorcerers' house, buying me a chance to escape despite his strength and supernatural prowess. I'd seen the small mark of a scar I assumed was from that wound on his side today.

This knife would be stainless steel, of course. No way would a shadowkind keep literal silverware around. The men had said that the iron in steel didn't affect them the same way as the pure metal because of the different composition.

But shadowkind *could* still take regular physical injuries. It'd been the beast's claws, not any kind of magic, that'd torn up Crag's wing. A blade like this could make the difference between freedom and imprisonment, or even life and death if push came to shove.

The kitchen staff wouldn't bother the hotel owner about it if a knife didn't happen to return from his rooms, right? They'd assume it'd been misplaced and would be sent back when it was discovered. Not worth hassling the man in charge when they'd have plenty of other knives to work with.

The decision to hang on to it sent my mind spinning off in other related directions. After I'd finished eating, I got up, keeping the knife in my hand, and prowled around the room examining every object and fixture in it with fresh eyes.

I stopped by the empty fireplace, eyeing the ornate mantle clock perched there. The arched case looked like mahogany, and the numbers on the face were printed with aged ink, but the needle-like hands glinted with a silver sheen.

It looked old and fancy. The makers wouldn't have used steel for a display piece like that, would they? I could just see Rollick taking a perverse delight in having a tiny bit of the noxious metal in his rooms, like showing off to any other shadowkind he allowed to come up here that he was impervious to it.

And probably it didn't bother him at all with such small pieces tucked away behind the glass face. But if someone stabbed one of those pointy bits into, say, his eye or his throat, he wouldn't be laughing about that.

With a rush of resolve, I grabbed the clock and went to retrieve my multi-tool from the pocket it'd been relegated to in my messenger bag, since I hadn't had much use for it here. I stuffed the steak knife into the same pocket and got down to work.

Sitting cross-legged on the bed, I found the glass face popped open on a hinge. All I needed to do was unscrew the pin that held the hands in place and then tug the minute hand right off. Since it was longer, I figured it'd be a bit more useful.

Of course, Rollick might very well notice that his clock no longer had a minute hand. Then again, how much did a demon care about the time?

The clock was just a decoration, one he'd seen thousands of times. There was a decent chance that one small change wouldn't actually catch his attention, at least not for a little while.

And if he did realize it was missing, well, he hadn't ordered me not to take steps to protect myself. I could claim that I'd repurposed it as a weapon against powerful shadowkind other than him. I mean, I'd happily stab any of the other monsters that wanted to capture me too, so that wouldn't even be a lie.

This two-inch long sliver of silver wasn't going to do me much good on its own, though. I pondered my options and after some experimentation determined that I could actually fit the hand into the lead end of one of my mechanical pencils. I adjusted it so it was half in, half out, figuring that was the most stable position that still allowed for a fair bit of stabbing length.

I stood up and was contemplating how best to keep my makeshift weapon on me where I'd be able to grab it quickly and effectively when a sudden warmth wafted over my skin with the materializing of a body right behind me.

"What an impressive contraption," Rollick said, peering over my shoulder, his chin nearly grazing my hair. "Were you planning on jabbing it into me?"

He arrived so suddenly and with such horrible timing that I couldn't restrain a yelp. I practically jumped right out of my skin. My fingers twitched, and I had to fumble to avoid dropping the pencil-turned-dagger on the floor.

I whirled around, my heart hammering at my ribs, holding the weapon down by my thigh even though a significant part of me wanted to jab it into the demon right now. When I'd already lost the element of surprise, I wasn't going to get anything out of the attempt other than wrecking our deal surprise.

"How long have you been spying on me?" I demanded, my entire body rigid. Had he seen me tuck the steak knife away in my bag when I'd first come into the bedroom?

Rollick gave me an amused look. It was deeply disconcerting seeing his movie-star handsome face with my recollection of his demonic form overlaid on it. "I don't think it's 'spying' simply to walk into a room in my own suite. The door was even open."

Damn it. I'd assumed the fact that he hadn't joined me for dinner meant that he wasn't going to show up anytime soon. It sounded like he'd presented himself pretty much as soon as he'd arrived, though, which at least meant he shouldn't have realized about the knife. And I still had my excuse for the weapon he had noticed.

"I'm sorry about your clock," I said. "I didn't figure you needed it as much as I needed a weapon against potential shadowkind attackers." I allowed myself to raise the makeshift blade, eyeing it with a trickle of embarrassed anticipation. "It *is* silver, isn't it?"

Rollick chuckled. "Of course you would find the one bit of the stuff in the entire suite. Are you that uncertain of my protective abilities? I promise, none of the idiots searching for you will find you *here*—as long as you don't tell anyone where you are. Which I've made sure you can't."

He didn't sound as if he was particularly worried that I had intended to use the silver against him, which didn't relieve me as much as it should have. Maybe he simply knew it wouldn't have done much anyway.

"Torrent and the others thought we were safe lots of other times when it turned out we weren't," I said quickly, shoving the weapon into my shorts pocket. "It seems smarter to be prepared for the worst. I don't suppose you've found out anything more about the shadowkind that are after me?"

"That's not for you to worry about," Rollick said breezily. "If you can contribute to our investigative efforts in any way, I'll let you know. *You* need to focus on getting control of your sorcery."

I grimaced at him. "We already talked about that."

"And I was hoping you'd reconsidered." He sighed and pulled his phone out of his pocket. "But maybe you need additional motivation—thinking of *all* the people you might want to protect. I got word this morning about some activity in your home city that made me concerned your stalkers may be identifying your usual haunts."

I stiffened all over again. "In Jacksonville? You mean like my house?"

"I've averted potential catastrophe." The demon flicked at his screen and then held it toward me. "Your parents will be perfectly safe for the next several days under my roof."

It took me a few seconds to process what I was seeing. The photo Rollick was showing me was of my parents: Mom with her fancy camera hanging around her neck in full tourist mode, Dad with the dorky headgear he called his "safari hat." They were standing at a gleaming black reception counter, a logo showing on the wall behind them in vibrant red: *Sunshine Sin Hotel*.

"You brought them *here*?" I said, my insides recoiling from the idea.

"It was safer than leaving them in Jacksonville," Rollick said without the least sign that it'd occurred to him I might object. "I arranged for them to 'win' an all-expenses-paid trip here. They'll have a wonderful time."

He grinned at me, but the shiny white teeth only brought back the visual of the jagged tips I'd seen this morning. I swallowed thickly.

The demon was acting like he'd invited my parents here out of the goodness of his heart to keep them safe for my benefit. But I wasn't an idiot. The implicit threat was clear.

I hadn't made him promise to do no harm to my family. It hadn't occurred to me in the moment we'd made the deal that my parents would factor into the situation. Now they were under his roof, under his control...

If I continued resisting, even if I technically met the terms of our deal, there was nothing to stop him from exerting pressure to get what he wanted in other ways.

Like seeing that my parents met some unfortunate accidents.

"Thank you," I said roughly, since it seemed wiser to play along rather than to make the threat that much more concrete. "I'm glad they'll be okay. I guess I can't see them while they're here."

"Not in person. As far as they know, you're still in Florida."

"Right." I inhaled slowly and raised my chin. "Okay. Fine. Tell me how you want me to try out this sorcerer stuff, and we'll see how it goes."

CHAPTER NINE

Quinn

"We'll ease into it," Rollick had assured me last night, but it didn't feel like all that relaxed an approach when he turned up right after breakfast the next morning to make sure I was ready to get started. He waited until I'd put the empty dishes back in the dumbwaiter and washed up before pointing to one of the armchairs. "Sit down, gather your focus, and I'll be back in a few minutes."

It was the chair I'd normally been sitting in, I couldn't help noticing. Was that just a coincidence, or had he been paying that much attention to my behavior?

As I sank down onto the soft leather surface, the demon vanished, a stark reminder of just how easily he *could* pay attention to me without me having any clue. But he hadn't mentioned the steak knife yesterday. That one time he hadn't been peering at me from the shadows for very long before he'd announced his presence.

Other times... who knew?

Rollick had told me to gather my focus, but that was awfully difficult when my thoughts were being pulled in so many different directions. Would he really keep my parents safe here? What would he do to them if he wasn't happy with my progress? Was giving in to his demands that I try out my powers a mistake?

What if I *could* get strong enough to compel him a little, despite his confidence that I'd never get that strong? It was worth a little risk to give myself an advantage over both him and my other enemies, wasn't it?

I just wasn't sure whether it was only a little risk or a huge one. I felt like I was balancing on the edge of a rooftop with only clouded darkness below, no way of knowing whether I was walking next to a drop of five feet or five hundred.

And at least when I was navigating a rooftop, I knew what I needed to do to avoid a fall. I had no clue what was the safest way of testing the strange energies inside me and what might speed us toward disaster.

Selfishly, I wished the three men were here. My men. Torrent would have assessed the situation for me in his pensive way, giving me a more accurate sense of just how much shit I might be throwing myself into. Crag would have loomed menacingly as if he could intimidate my powers into behaving. Lance would have cracked jokes and flirted with me like nothing could possibly go all that wrong.

But it was better that they were far away when we conducted this experiment. Less chance that anything I woke up inside me would hurt them. Especially Lance. The thought of how unnervingly wild he'd gone after we'd visited the sorcerers' house where my donor had lived, almost frantic in his rampage through the forest, made my stomach twist up.

Other sorcerers had already hurt him—hurt him badly enough that it'd surprised him that I'd hate the thought of doing the same. I never wanted his joyful demeanor to shatter because of something I'd done.

My mind was just meandering in yet another direction, wondering what the three of them were up to now and whether Rollick's orders were putting them in other kinds of danger, when the door swung open. I straightened up in my seat, a little surprised that Rollick hadn't just slipped through the shadows, but then I saw the man he was ushering in ahead of him.

The guy was human—it seemed I'd spent enough time around the shadowkind that I could sense his mortal status at a glance. He didn't look much older than me, maybe his mid-twenties, skinny enough that his elbows stuck out in points where he had his arms folded over his narrow chest and his dark eyes seemed to protrude a bit from his sallow face. He glanced at Rollick nervously, and the demon prodded him forward.

"There she is. Go have a chat. Be cooperative, and you can go back to your awful but insignificant existence soon enough." Rollick lifted his gaze to meet my eyes. "I've brought in a minor sorcerer to talk you through the basics. It seemed like a good idea for you to get a grounding in the theory before you actually try to boss any more shadowkind around. In the magical way, at least."

He flashed one of his charming grins at me and then wavered away into the shadows again, though I had trouble believing he was actually *gone*. He wouldn't let me talk with a sorcerer without listening in on our conversation, would he?

The man crept forward with tentative steps and lowered himself into the chair opposite me. He looked at his hands, at the now-empty coffee table, and finally at me. "He—he said you want to learn sorcery," he mumbled.

Geez, how badly had Rollick traumatized the guy "bringing" him in?

"Want" was way too strong a word for my actual feelings on the subject, but I didn't think it'd help the situation to get into the complexities with my unexpected guest.

"Yeah," I said. "Sort of. I mean..." It occurred to me that I didn't even know where to start this conversation. There was so much about sorcery I didn't know and so little I did. "How did *you* start learning?"

He wet his lips. "It was my mother. My mother taught me. It's mostly in families, you know. We aren't a very strong one, though. There's no reason to kill us. We'd never even try to work our skills on a higher shadowkind." His gaze darted toward the rest of the room as if he was talking more to Rollick, wherever the demon was lurking, than to me.

My gut twisted. "*I* don't want to kill you. And I think he only wants you to teach me." Rollick had sounded like he meant it when he'd told me he didn't bother sorcerers as long as they didn't hassle him.

The man's shoulders twitched. "There've been—we heard—just in the past few days, a couple of other families were slaughtered. More powerful than us, but not *that* prominent."

Oh, shit. So the shadowkind after me were ramping up their efforts to devour all the sorcerer organs they could from other sources too. My stomach turned.

"That wasn't Rol—that wasn't the shadowkind who brought you here," I said, remembering at the last second that Rollick probably wouldn't want his name tossed around freely. "We're trying to stop the monsters that are killing people. If I can learn how to use sorcery, that might help."

At those words, the man seemed to calm down a little. He peered at me. "Are you from a family? I realize every now and then someone totally new gets brought in as an apprentice, but I don't know how to check whether they'll be capable, or how to awaken the right energies..."

As if on cue, an emphatic flutter of the energy that'd already awakened in me beat at my chest. I restrained a flinch. "Actually, I've already got some power. I—I had a connection to a sorcerer family that I didn't know about until recently, and they can't teach me now. I just need to figure out how to use it."

"Okay." The man let out a shaky laugh. "That's the most important part right there. Tapping into it. Once you're aware of it, you just need to use it, and with practice you get better at knowing how. It comes more and more easily."

I frowned. "But I don't know how to use it in the first place. There was —I compelled one shadowkind, but it was totally by accident. I just said some words I didn't even realize I knew, that I can't remember now, and it worked."

The sorcerer nodded eagerly. "That's how it is. The power and the language to wield it are written into our own beings. We just have to open ourselves up to it and let it emerge, and you'll simply *know* how to conduct it."

This all sounded way too woo-woo and not at all concrete enough. I thought back to what I'd seen at the sorcerers' home near Miami. "I thought you used drawings and symbols, like with chalk and things—summoning circles or—"

I cut myself off when the man shrugged. "Those are tools that can help ground your intentions. But you still need to open yourself up to work them right. The symbols and shapes come from inside you, and you use your energy to make them real and potent."

I tipped my head to the side, still having trouble wrapping my head around how ephemeral his explanation was. "You're really saying that it's all inside me—everything I need to become a sorcerer? To become a major one, even? There aren't any, like, guidebooks or special rituals or whatever that I'd need to learn? Where does the energy even *come* from? How can it work like that?"

He splayed his hands. "I don't know. Honestly, it's kind of a fantastic mystery. I used to ask my mother a lot of questions when I was first getting the hang of it, but after a while, you just accept that as the way things are."

Just accepting and letting things happen as they felt like it wasn't my usual approach. I believed in figuring out what I needed to do and then doing it step by step—that was how I'd approached my architecture studies and my urban exploring as well, delving into abandoned and off-limits buildings. But as far as I could tell, this guy really didn't know anything more than what he'd said.

"How do you open yourself up?" I asked finally. "Is there anything special you do to tap into the energy and let the understanding or whatever come to the surface?"

"I wouldn't call it special," he said. "It's like meditation. You focus on the energy and... sort of listen to it. It's almost like it whispers into your head if you pay enough attention to it. And you hear it more and more clearly the more often you welcome it. You can picture what you'd like to accomplish and it'll answer that. But once you get good at using however much power you've got, it'll become more automatic. You think what you want to do and it comes to you without having to pause and really concentrate."

More color had come into his face as he'd talked about sorcery, as if even thinking about using it invigorated him. I guessed there was something pretty exhilarating about being able to command monstrous creatures to do your bidding even if you only had enough power to do it with the animal-like ones. If you didn't think they deserved free will anyway.

I rubbed my mouth, straining my brain for anything else I should ask and coming up empty. "I think that covers everything then," I said. "Thank you."

Rollick appeared next to us an instant later, abruptly enough that the sorcerer startled in his chair. It appeared he didn't have any questions of his own, because he simply motioned the man to his feet. "You've served your purpose. Good man. Let's get you out of here."

I stood up too with a hitch of my pulse. The guy hadn't been especially helpful, and I had pretty iffy feelings about sorcerers in general, but he had tried to help. And it didn't sound as if he was personally doing anything all that horrendous.

"What's going to happen to him now?" I asked Rollick pointedly. I didn't think the demon would want a sorcerer running around able to say that a demon had brought him to this specific hotel so he could talk to a woman with my description.

Rollick chuckled. "No need to worry about this pipsqueak." He patted the slight man in the head with a patronizing air. "I have a succubus on staff who can compel him into not even thinking about, let alone speaking of, what went on here. As far as he'll know, he went on a little day trip to the next town over."

Okay, so the guy definitely wasn't getting murdered. He looked relieved even as he tensed up at the demon's words. "You're going to mess with my—"

Rollick shot him a firm look. "Would you rather I messed up the rest of you? How many shadowkind minds have you addled over the years, hmm?"

The man's mouth snapped shut. Apparently he couldn't come up with a very good counterargument to that point.

I shifted my weight, resisting the urge to hug myself. "What about the other sorcerers out there? He said they're being targeted—murdered. Wouldn't we want to stop that? I mean, I know you don't like them, but it does mean the murderers are getting more power."

Rollick waved off my concerns dismissively. "Not much, from what I've gathered. I'm not extending my resources guarding all of those pricks. They knew the risks they were taking when they decided to start enslaving our kind."

"It could be a chance to find out more about the beings we're up against," I pointed out.

Rollick gave me an amused look. "Why do I think that's hardly the real reason you're concerned? Such a bleeding heart, mortal. I can add keeping an eye on the more powerful sorcerer families I'm aware of to your favorite trio's duties, though only because it serves *my* purposes."

He nudged the sorcerer toward the door and called one last remark over his shoulder. "You've got the rest of the day to work on listening to those whispers, sweet sorcerer. We're going to begin target practice tomorrow."

CHAPTER TEN

Crag

"He might not be gone for very long," I felt the need to point out as the three of us raced up through the shadows toward the hotel's upper levels.

"We have enough time for a brief talk," Torrent said. "When Rollick breaks out one of those crystal bottles of cognac, he plans to savor it. We just won't let ourselves get sidetracked by unnecessary diversions."

I suspected that last comment was directed mainly at Lance. The dragon shifter was by far the most likely among us to get distracted, and the woman we were hurrying to see had become his favorite diversion. Every time we'd been able to talk amongst ourselves since arriving in L.A., there'd been an irritated edge to his jokes, along with some grumbling about certain demons restricting our access to "our mortal."

"Gotta take the time we have, or he'll steal even more from us," he said now in a jaunty but urgent tone, rushing ahead of the two of us.

"Hold on." Torrent's tone was firm enough that Lance slowed. Our squad leader took the lead as we moved through the small opening in the layer of silver and iron. "We need to handle this so that Rollick doesn't realize we snuck in. He probably has surveillance in his rooms, but I've checked over the terrace, and it seems clear. But we'll need Quinn to come to us."

"Yes, yes, invite her out to the party." Lance leapt forward again. "I can be careful."

He could, or he wouldn't have been part of the squad to begin with. We were the ones Rollick sent on the secret missions he didn't want anyone knowing he was invested in. No other shadowkind was even aware that we worked for him.

Which was a good thing now that half of the beings that'd been rampaging around Florida had seen one or all of us, or even this hotel wouldn't have been safe for Quinn.

When we reached the terrace outside Rollick's private suite, Torrent emerged by the railing overlooking the ocean. Lance and I followed suit. Our leader was the only one who'd managed to speak to Quinn since Rollick had sent us off a few days ago; he knew how to best handle the situation.

Or, I thought that, anyway. Lance started toward the glass sliding door, and Torrent caught his arm. The dragon shifter let out a soft growl of annoyance, but hung back next to Torrent as the other man extended one of his tentacles to lightly jostle the glass.

I hadn't spotted Quinn at first. But as I stepped forward to stand beside my companions, I noted a hint of her pale blond hair peeking over the top of the armchair that faced away from us. It didn't stir.

"You need to smack it harder," Lance said to Torrent.

Torrent gave the dragon shifter an amicable nudge to the shoulder. "She heard. She'll know. She's just being smart and waiting a few minutes so that it won't be obvious she thinks there was something significant about the noise. Come on, we should stay as far back from the windows as we can."

He darted through the darkness and reformed in the most shadowy corner of the terrace. Lance and I came after him on foot. It was getting late into the night, stars glinting in the vast sweep of the sky overhead, the ocean not much more than a vague expanse and a rhythmic hiss of waves. I couldn't make out the thumping bass of the nightclub on the lower floors anymore, but the less aggressive melodies from the rooftop patio filtered down. If it was still open, we weren't calling on Quinn at an unreasonable hour.

Lance stirred restlessly on his feet, and I tamped down similar impulses inside myself. It'd been too long since I'd been in our woman's presence. I'd sworn to myself and to her that I'd protect her, I'd done everything in my power… and it hadn't been enough. She'd had to make this deal to protect *me* as well as herself. My jaw clenched at the thought of the scars that still ached a bit when I extended my reformed wing, which would never quite be the same.

Quinn didn't leave us waiting too long. She came out through the bedroom door, closer to our current post. The smile that sprang to her lips at the sight of all three of us was so brilliant it nearly erased all my agony at being apart from her.

She dashed forward, and naturally Lance caught her first, snatching her into an embrace so swift and emphatic it was a miracle he didn't skewer her with those fatal claws. He spun her around and nuzzled the side of her face with a long inhalation as if drinking in the scent of her hair. "I've missed you, baby girl." Then he kissed her so deeply an approving sound hummed from Quinn's throat.

"I missed you too," she said in a choked-sounding voice. "Thank you for the apple."

Delight sparked in his eyes. "I'll toss more in whenever I get the chance."

I wasn't sure what they were talking about, but he didn't get to soak up *all* her affection. As soon as she'd eased back from him, I tugged her into an embrace of my own, reveling in the softness of her body against my solid frame—and the strength I could feel emanating from within that softness. "He's not the only one who missed you," I said gruffly.

Quinn squeezed me back tightly and bobbed up on her toes to press a kiss to my mouth that brought my more heated desires roaring to life. "And I missed you too. All of you." She glanced around at us, her gaze settling on Torrent, and smiled at him. Then she turned back to me with a flicker of concern in her eyes. "How's your wing? Has it healed up all right?"

I hadn't known I could feel fonder of this woman, but a renewed surge of affection rushed through me. I let my wings extend from my back without transforming all the way into my gargoyle body, letting her see the sealed tears with their mottling of scars in the thin flesh. "Almost good as new. If we need to fly, I'm ready."

"Hopefully that won't be necessary." She stepped closer, running her fingers tentatively over the marks, and a shiver of my own delight shot straight to my groin. The flesh there was sensitive both to damage and to a more tender touch. I swept the wing forward, tucking her into an embrace next to me, and she leaned against my arm with a sigh of contentment.

Her gaze slid back to Torrent. "Are we hopping over to the other room again?"

Something about the slight arch of her eyebrows and the unusual warmth to Torrent's answering smile made me wonder exactly what the two of them had gotten up to when he'd visited alone two nights ago. But then, it wasn't as if I should resent Torrent for getting to embrace Quinn as intimately as I already had. The three of us were in this together, watching over her together… Showing our adoration in every possible way together.

"I don't think there's any point," Torrent said. "Rollick's downstairs in the club—I wouldn't want to risk staying more than half an hour as it is. We can talk just as easily out here."

Quinn tensed against me. "Are you sure it's safe for you to have come at all?"

And that was exactly why I knew Rollick had been wrong when he'd suggested Quinn was only using us for a thrill. Her first thought wasn't to be upset that we couldn't stay longer and engage in the more thrilling pursuits we'd discovered together—it was to be worried about how our visit might have negative consequences for us. She might be rare among mortals, but there was no denying her commitment to us.

I would have fought to the bitter end to ensure her freedom, but she'd given it up so that I could keep my life. Rollick had no idea what he was talking about.

I *was* going to prove myself worthy of her devotion. She needed to believe that her imprisonment here was only temporary, that we were making progress toward destroying all her enemies and clearing the path back to her former existence. If I couldn't accomplish that for her, then she was the one who should have been scorning me, not the other way around.

"I'll sense if he's approaching," I said. The one useful feature of the demon's immense power from my perspective was that I could sense the vibrations of his presence through my rocky nature at a much farther distance than the average being. I wasn't aware of him right now through the layer of silver and iron, which was exactly why Rollick had added it to the building—though mainly so he couldn't be sensed when he was up here, not the other way around. But as soon as he traveled past it, I'd know.

Torrent nodded. "If he comes while we're still here, we can make ourselves scarce."

"I still say we slice and dice him," Lance announced, clicking his claws together. "Too tricksy—so annoying. Keeping us apart from you, giving us all the work."

Torrent made a dismissive noise. "It's more than just his 'tricksy'-ness that's the problem, as you know. If we don't have to fight him at all, we're a lot more likely to come out of this situation still standing. And the work we've been doing should eventually help us come up with a feasible plan."

Quinn hugged herself within the shelter of my wing. "It's going to be even harder going against him now. He brought my parents here to the hotel—he says it's for their protection, but our deal doesn't cover them. Even if I'm technically sticking to the terms, if he isn't happy with me, he could take it out on them."

My muscles flexed automatically, my fangs itching at my gums, eager to emerge. "We won't let him harm them either."

Torrent frowned. "That does complicate the situation... but really, we need to neutralize the threat of the other shadowkind after you, who don't seem inclined to make any deals at all, before we worry about Rollick anyway."

He was right, even if the difficulties with accomplishing that task loomed as large as a mountain in the back of my mind, more daunting than an actual mountain would have been. But we had to find a way. They couldn't have Quinn. That was all there was to it.

"Have you found out anything else about the beings who are searching for me?" Quinn asked.

Lance raked his claws through the air and then slung his arm around her waist to pull her away from me to nuzzle her again. "*They* like to slice and dice. No deals. No negotiations. Anything in their way, they pulverize it."

Like the crumpled garage at the sorcerers' home, an image that made me wince inwardly. I prided myself on my strength, but strength might not be enough against these brutes.

Torrent was nodding. "They seem to be pretty... old-school in their approach. All overt violence, turning to aggression to handle any problem

—earning the 'monster' label very thoroughly. The two or more beings in charge have stayed in the background letting their followers handle most of the work, so we're not sure of their exact powers yet, but they're clearly not afraid of other shadowkind noticing their activities."

"Like Rollick is," Quinn said. "I mean, he's been very careful to make sure no one finds out he's at all interested in me and my powers, right? He sent you out in secret. Does that mean these beings are even more powerful than he is?" Her mouth twisted.

"Not necessarily," Torrent said. "Rollick's mostly concerned with running his businesses and enjoying the fruits of his labors. He wouldn't get anything out of all-out war. So it suits him to avoid it, whereas these other shadowkind seem to welcome that kind of conflict. Maybe they're out to prove themselves the top dogs around. Maybe they've got a specific agenda." He let out a frustrated huff. "We're still not sure what their end goal is."

"They've been killing other sorcerers." Quinn motioned vaguely to the world beyond the hotel. "At least a couple of other families since we arrived here."

"Good riddance," I said automatically, and regretted the words at the tensing of Quinn's stance. I wasn't going to wish for the safety of the malicious humans who enslaved shadowkind, but I had to remember they were closer to her own kind than we were. And she didn't seem to like to see any sort of being suffer.

"Serves them right, but it's no good for shadowkind to grab those powers," Lance said with a snarl for emphasis. "They should be better than that."

"I might not be safe even *with* Rollick protecting me then," Quinn said. "If these monsters are close to as powerful as he is and more willing to fight..."

Torrent extended a tentacle to give her forearm a reassuring squeeze. "Oh, he'll fight if he needs to. He just prefers to choose his battles wisely. He obviously thinks defying these fiends is important, or he wouldn't have involved himself to begin with."

"What does *he* want with Quinn?" the dragon shifter murmured, pressing a kiss to the back of her head. "Other than her loveliness. That's enough for me, but I don't think so for him."

"No," Quinn agreed, her expression clouding.

I pictured what a battle like that might look like, shadowkind assaulting the hotel, Rollick hitting back with his demonic powers and the allies he could call on. The whole place might end up rubble by the time both sides had finished battering each other...

The thought brought a spark of inspiration into my mind, a sensation I wasn't all that familiar with. It took me a moment before I felt confident enough to voice it.

"What if... what if we let them deal with each other?"

Torrent cocked his head, studying me but with interest rather than the skepticism I'd been afraid of. "What do you mean?"

"If we made it so the other shadowkind found out that Rollick was keeping Quinn here," I said, "they'd attack, and he'd *have* to fight back. They'd take out a bunch of each other's forces, maybe even take *each other* out and leave no one in any shape to continue chasing after her. We'd have to make sure she was safely away before the fighting started, of course, but..." I glanced between the others' faces, hoping my explanation hadn't sounded completely absurd.

Quinn nodded slowly. "That makes sense. Let them exhaust themselves against each other... Even if neither side is totally destroyed, they should both end up a lot weaker than they are now."

Lance grinned. "Very tricksy. We can play that game too."

Torrent rubbed his chin. "There could be something to that. We'd need to set it up very carefully—if Rollick got wind that our enemies were coming much in advance, he'd take off with Quinn and leave them nothing to find. And even if they take him by surprise, if she turns out not to be here, that could diffuse the conflict and simply leave him *very* pissed off at us."

"We have time to think through the possibilities," Quinn pointed out. "The deal holds for at least another six days. The more we know about who we're up against and why they're doing this—on both sides—the better. At least now we have the start of an approach that could work." She aimed one of her bright smiles at me. "It's a really smart plan, Crag. Better than anything I've been able to think of."

I couldn't help beaming back, as strange as the expression felt on my face. She was impressed by an idea *I'd* come up with. And if we needed to, we'd see it through, whether Rollick liked it or not.

CHAPTER ELEVEN

Quinn

I had no clue what to expect from the "target practice" Rollick had mentioned. With every passing minute after I woke up, I dreaded it more. Not even the joy of seeing my three men last night could stand against my anxiety.

I forced down my breakfast of spinach omelet and fruit salad, took my morning pills, and finished the rest of my typical routine on autopilot. Then I paced around the living room, unable to sit down for more than a minute or two without a restless urge driving me to my feet again.

Somewhere on one of the floors beneath me—or out in the city, if they were getting in some sight-seeing—my parents were roaming around, unaware of the dangers circulating around them. Unaware that I was possibly just minutes away.

But how could I have told them even if I'd had a way to reach them? If I'd warned them about monstrous attackers now or when I'd had the chance before, they'd have thought I was crazy.

They probably *were* safer here than back in Jacksonville... as long as I didn't defy Rollick. As long as I kept him happy.

I'd tried to meditate with my apparent sorcerer powers like the guy yesterday had instructed. Before, following the suggestions of a shadowkind woman named Sorsha who'd been trying to help me suppress those energies, I'd only concentrated on suppressing and disguising them. But that hadn't worked so well.

When I focused on them and encouraged the wavering sensations in my chest, I did get a reaction. The wobbly flutters had been coming more frequently since my first attempts. I'd gotten to the point where I could provoke one if I tried to, not that I really wanted to. And with them came little murmurs of sensation, as if some innate instinct I didn't understand really was whispering in my ear, directing me in how to use it.

I'd had nothing to aim those instincts at, though. All I'd been left with was even more jitters inside me and a knot in my gut.

I didn't know whether to be relieved or upset that Rollick arrived fairly promptly, just a half hour after I'd started my pacing. How well did he know my morning routine? He entered without a knock, as usual, carrying a black box about the size of a cat carrier.

"Ready to go?" he asked me with a dimpled smile. He really shouldn't be allowed to look that gorgeous while acting as my jailor.

"What are we doing?" I asked, eyeing the box. "What's in there?"

He motioned for me to follow him out onto the terrace. There, he set the box on the patio table where we'd eaten dinner just a few days ago. "This is a contraption developed by the human 'hunters' who catch shadowkind beasts either because they want to exterminate them or to sell them to collectors," he said. "You mortals do come up with some interesting inventions. I don't care for the practice in general, but it worked for my purposes for today. I believe in making use of all the tools available to me."

It took me a few moments to piece together that rambling explanation enough to draw a clear conclusion. "There's a shadowkind creature in there?"

He nodded. "Just a weak little thing, not much more than a lost kitten. One shaped like a lizard with little spikes instead of scales, but given the chance, it'd wisp away rather than confront you. You have nothing to fear."

I swallowed thickly. Did *it* have anything to fear? "What do you want me to do with it?"

"I want to see if those sorcerer powers of yours have woken up enough that you can put them to some small use on demand. I'll open up the box, you compel the beastie to, oh, let's say hop on top of it and stay there. That's simple enough, but not what it'd do given the choice."

I raised an eyebrow at him. "And if I fail and it disappears into the shadows? Do you have a whole menagerie ready to stock these experiments?"

The demon shot me an amused glance. "As little faith as you apparently have in me, I can manage to wrangle one minor shadowkind. It can't get very far from this level of the building anyway. If it runs, I'll bring it back. We have all day. I'm sure you'll tap into your inner sorcerer eventually."

"Maybe you could tell me why *you* want me to tap into these powers so much," I suggested, partly procrastinating and partly because I really did want to know. "It'll help me to focus my attention properly."

Rollick guffawed. "Nice try." He offered a languid smirk. "How about you give it a shot, and we'll see how conversational I'm feeling if you pull off a little compulsion?"

I managed not to grit my teeth in frustration and yanked my gaze to the box rather than his face. Apparently satisfied that I was cooperating, Rollick slid out the two latches that secured the container's door and eased it open.

A light was beaming inside, brightly enough to highlight a patch of shadow that was quivering within the box, even though it barely appeared to have any physical presence. That was the creature he wanted me to compel. I opened my mouth and closed it again, an ache forming behind my sternum.

The shadowkind *hated* mortals who used this power. It was stealing their free will as much as Rollick had stolen mine—more even.

"I'm pretty sure nothing will come of simply staring at it, though you're welcome to prove me wrong," the demon put in.

I darted a hasty glower at him and focused on the little shadowy beast again. I wouldn't be like other sorcerers because I didn't *want* to be. The very fact that I was so uneasy about using this power meant I wouldn't use it badly, right?

Asking this little creature to sit on top of a box was hardly terrible. And what Rollick might do to my parents if I didn't make the attempt could very well be.

I inhaled deeply and let part of my mind detach from the outside world, concentrating on the rhythm of my pulse and the flow of energy around that most vital of organs inside me. Strange sensations rippled through me with each beat of my heart. When I acknowledged that energy, it seemed to twitch to attention in awareness of the shadowkind nearby—both the little thing in the box and the much more powerful presence standing next to it.

It recoiled from Rollick, obviously aware that I was in no position to compel *him* into doing anything just yet. But it seemed to reach through me toward the lesser being eagerly, with a tug on my nerves.

On top of the box. I wanted the creature to step out and hop up there, that was all.

Sweat broke out on the back of my neck, though I couldn't have said whether it was from effort expended or just my trepidation. I opened my mouth again, a quiver raced up my throat, and a few unfamiliar syllables fell off my tongue like when I'd sent the flying beast away.

The shadowy patch shuddered and then leapt forward. As it burst from the box, I caught a glint of the spikes Rollick had mentioned and a gleam of eerie green eyes. A conflicted jolt of triumph hit me in the second before the creature spun around—and dashed toward the edge of the terrace rather than taking the seat I'd intended.

Rollick leapt forward twice as quickly, faster than any human even with that muscular body could have moved. He snatched the moving shape of what was mostly still shadow—and it solidified into a hissing, writhing creature in his hands, his fingers clamped around its neck.

He tsked his tongue at it and brought it back to the table, where he set it next to the box and looked expectantly at me. "The world didn't end, did it? See if you can persuade this beastie a little better the second time."

"What, you weren't looking for a workout?" I said glibly, but the joke landed flat. My heart was beating too fast, and I was too aware of the fact that the power I had exerted was flowing from that organ. The organ that'd been stitched into my chest from another girl, that I only managed to keep in my body because my twice-daily meds convinced the rest of me that it was a welcome friend rather than a foreign invader.

Over the years, I'd come to think of the medications as reflecting a reality my body simply had trouble accepting. Right now, it was hard not to think that my body might have been right after all.

Rollick glowered at me, his lips still curled in amusement. "I know you can master this, Quinn. We just need to work on *you* knowing that."

His confident words sent a weird buzz of exhilaration through me—to have a millennia-old, immensely powerful demon praising *my* capabilities. Of course, it was probably just a pep talk to get me to do what he wanted.

Which I needed to do anyway. I dragged in a breath and scowled at the spiky creature.

It'd remained in physical form, maybe nervous of what Rollick would do to it if it tried to escape again. That made it easier for me to concentrate. I pictured it leaping on top of the box, the *need* for it to do that condensing within my ribcage.

I had to prove to Rollick that I was cooperating. That I didn't need any further motivation, especially not of the cruel kind.

It was just a short hop. No reason for the creature to not want to do it. Just give it a little nudge...

One of those unsettling wobbles ran through my chest, forceful enough to make my pulse stutter. Another burst of meaningless sound spilled from my mouth. I hurled it at the creature, my skin tingling with the energy my voice carried—and the beast stiffened for just an instant before springing on top of the box as if its life depended on it.

Rollick gave me a languid round of applause and a pleased smile. "There we go. Now let's see if you can compel it back into the box. It won't want to go in there, so you'll have to be firm about it."

Wonderful. But maybe once it was in the box, the demon would be satisfied for the day and we could stop this charade of me being a sorcerer.

That flimsy hope girded me. I tensed my arms at my sides and stared the lesser shadowkind down.

Into that glowing space. In between those walls. It *would* go there, because I demanded that it did.

A jolt of power surged up my throat. My heart hitched. I spat out the unfamiliar words rushing up from my chest. They didn't mean anything to me, and yet at the same time, I understood that I was saying, *Go inside there, NOW.*

This time, the creature didn't even pause. It darted right into the box. My shoulders sagged as a mix of relief and revulsion rolled over me.

I'd done it. I'd forced the little beast to go against its instincts, to do something it'd hated. Hurray for me.

My heart was thumping hard but not so quickly now. My chest felt tight. I had a very strong urge to lie down and close my eyes and hope I didn't wake up until this whole horrible situation was over. Except I didn't think it could be over if I tried to simply sleep through it.

"Very nice." Rollick strolled over to stand next to me, his body so close that the bare skin of my arm woke up with giddy awareness. "What should we have it do next? A tap dance? I wonder if you could convince it to leap right onto that silver spear you made."

My spine went rigid. "I'm not telling it to do that."

The demon continued in a nonchalant tone. "It would be a fantastic test of your powers. But if you don't like practicing on innocent beasties, we do have other trial subjects around. I could call the dragon shifter or the gargoyle in to see how well you can play with a higher shadowkind. I'm sure they'd be willing to offer themselves up just for your sake."

I tensed even more than I had already. My arms jerked up to fold over my chest defensively. "I'm not using any powers on them. It isn't *playing*. This isn't a game."

Rollick smiled down at me, the intensity of his presence making my pulse wobble in a totally different way. "Oh, but it is in all the ways that matter. Everything is a game, really, to the ones who make the decisions that affect the outcomes. You'll learn that soon enough, reluctant sorcerer."

"I don't think I'm getting to make any decisions here at all," I shot back. "You're the one calling the shots."

He arched his eyebrows. "I've given you plenty of leeway. But if you'd like me to act more the part of a dictator, I believe I can call Lance up here right—"

I couldn't have said what came over me. I knew it was useless; I knew I shouldn't provoke him. But the thought of inflicting my emerging power on Lance after the torments sorcerers had already put the dragon shifter through hit me with a smack of horror, and my body simply reacted.

"No!" I said, and shoved Rollick away from me.

I barely budged him. The guy had a foot on me and probably a hundred pounds more muscle, and, y'know, the whole immensely powerful demon thing on top of that. But he reacted the second my hand smacked into his arm.

One instant, I was standing next to him. The next, he'd slammed me down on the tiles of the terrace floor. He cushioned my head and back with one arm just enough that the impact rang through my nerves but wasn't more than a brief shock of pain, but his other hand pinned my shoulder to the ground. His claws had emerged. He lowered my head all the way to the tiles and jerked his first hand around to tease them along my throat, braced over me with less than a foot between our bodies.

I trembled. Most of it was fear, but a tiny flare of heat lit between my legs. Fucking hell.

And Rollick noticed it. He smiled at me, still bright but fierce, transforming his movie-star good looks into something hauntingly gorgeous.

"You don't want to get into a fist fight with me, mortal," he crooned. "But I'm not sure that's what you're really looking for, even now. I think I could take you right here on the tiles, and you'd be gasping for more."

My jaw clenched. If I denied the attraction coursing through me, he'd just laugh. "I'd hate you afterward," I said. "I can't help how my body reacts, but none of it means I trust or respect or even like you."

The demon laughed anyway, a low chuckle that reverberated into me and woke up even more heat even as I stiffened against it. He lowered his head so that his breath ghosted across my lips, not quite touching them with a kiss.

"I'm not going for 'like,' sweet sorcerer. But it's much more fun to win more than just the body. One day I will fuck you with both of my dicks, and it'll be because you've welcomed me. And you'll be ever so glad you did."

Before I could formulate a response, he leapt off me with typical languid grace. He picked up the box with the shadowkind creature and sauntered off the terrace before I'd even willed myself to sit up.

The trial was over—for now. Maybe that was some kind of victory? But my muscles were still trembling, and I was starkly aware of the dampening of my panties. Not even the floor beneath me felt stable enough to hold me steady.

He wasn't right. I wouldn't let him be. I would *never* welcome a fiend who'd treated me the way he had.

But I had no idea what happened now.

CHAPTER TWELVE

Lance

I knew Rollick had arrived from the shifting of the energies in the shadows. His tricksy presence always loomed large even when you couldn't see it.

"What is it that you had to call me all the way out here about?" he drawled, but I could tell he wasn't happy about the request despite his casual tone. I might not be the most sensitive being around, but even I could pick up on the tremor of tension that emanated off him.

"You didn't want us consulting with anyone else," I reminded him. "And you also didn't want us stirring up trouble with shadowkind who aren't any part of this. How could you decide whether I should pursue this without seeing what I'd found?"

The demon made a dismissive sound, but he came closer. "What exactly *did* you find that's made you so nervous, dragon?"

I motioned to the mountain range we were positioned at the base of in the shadow of a spiky-leafed tree. Rollick had sent me roaming out to the area mortals called Utah because a few sorcerers had been slaughtered and devoured here a few days ago. I'd only been meant to check the murder scene for clues that might identify the beings involved. I'd ended up stumbling on what felt like a much more momentous trail.

"There are a few human paths farther along," I said, "but they don't really come out this way. *Something's* been active around there, though. Lots of rocks looking bashed up with claw marks on them. Shuddery energy left behind. The whole place gives me the impression that I should want to be anywhere but here, which isn't because of anything *I've* actually seen. It's shadowkind power, isn't it?"

Rollick let out a more thoughtful hum and motioned for me to take him closer. I leapt from shadow to shadow where they formed at the base of rocks and shrubs and dips in the earth across the uneven terrain. Where the slope really started to angle upward, I pointed to a mess of chunks that looked like a shattered boulder.

The sense that I should be going someplace else hit me stronger here. It made me want to dig my claws into the rocks and snarl at whoever was trying to boss me around with their magic. But whoever that was probably had pretty big claws too. Or some other sharp appendages. There were broad scratch marks here and there on the broken chunks of stone.

Rollick examined them, prowling around through the shadows, and then peered up the side of the mountain. "You haven't followed the trail much farther?"

I shook my head, knowing he'd sense the movement through the gloom. "There's another smashed rock like this a little ways up. After that I stopped. I can spy on whatever might be up there without being noticed, I think. But I don't know for sure what other magic they might have. Or maybe you can tell what being it is and that we shouldn't get involved."

I kind of hoped the latter was true. I'd much rather head back to California—to the hotel, where I might get to drop in on Quinn again.

And I didn't like the idea of a fiend with this kind of power being after her.

"I don't recognize it," Rollick said, and moved closer to one of the chunks of stone. "These aren't claw marks, though. Those are horns, or curved spikes of some sort." His frown came through in his voice. "How did you get here from the murder site?"

"There was a beastie hanging around the spot," I said. "It ran off when it saw me. I was thinking maybe it was keeping watch to see who came around. I followed it quietly so it wouldn't realize I'd seen it, but when we were close to here, there wasn't as much cover. So I smashed it. But if it was going to report to someone about me, I figured they'd be around here, so I explored some more."

Rollick nodded. "Or it could simply be that it was randomly passing by."

I shrugged. "I didn't say that wasn't possible. You asked how I got here."

"I did." Rollick paused again, with a pensiveness I didn't totally like. I was used to this solemn consideration from Torrent—it felt right from him. Rollick was all easygoing confidence except when he was really mad. If something about this situation outright worried him, there couldn't be anything good about it at all.

"Go up the mountain," he said finally. "See what you can see—but don't let anything or anyone see *you*. That's the most important part. If you don't think you can stay hidden, retreat and report back whatever you were able to discover."

I would have saluted him the way I'd seen humans do sometimes to people giving commands, but there wasn't much point in the shadows. "I can do that. I'll be sneaky. Twice as careful as with the beastie."

"If anything urgent comes up that can't wait until you can make it back in person, you know how to reach me by phone," Rollick reminded me. "Although I'm sure you're in a huge hurry to be back to that mortal woman."

I bristled instinctively at his reference to Quinn. "I'm here to make sure no bigger beasties get their claws—or horns, or whatever—into her. I won't let her down."

Rollick clucked his tongue. "I suppose you'd better hope she doesn't let *you* down then, hadn't you? I know this is all new and exciting to you, Lance, but humans don't settle down with dragons. And the more fiends try to stick their claws into her, the less thrilling she's going to find yours."

I thought of Quinn's eager shivers when I traced the tips of my talons over her skin and had to smile. "I don't think that will be a problem."

"Well, you know better than most what horrors humans are capable of. Just because she's shown you her softer side doesn't mean there isn't a vicious edge to her too."

I couldn't help snorting, as disrespectful as that might be to the man who'd somehow become my boss again. "She can be vicious against the beasts that deserve it. I'll cheer her on." I didn't have the slightest doubt that she'd never lash out at *me*. He hadn't seen how worried she'd been over a light smack to my eye.

"Fine," Rollick said. "Don't listen to the demon who's seen more human relationships begin and end than breaths you've taken. Go find out what we're dealing with here."

It didn't matter how many other humans he'd known. He didn't really know Quinn.

I set off up the slope, slinking from shadow to shadow, stopping in each one to test the energies around me and ahead of me. The vibe warning me off got stronger, but I didn't pick up on any other supernatural forces. I simply ignored it. No one was bullying me into changing my course.

At least, that was what I intended. I reached a point in the rough path that wound up the increasingly steep mountainside where I simply couldn't push myself onward. I looked at the shadow I wanted to leap to, I braced myself to jump—and my body refused to go on. A blaring *No!* echoed through my essence.

That was cheating. More tricks to keep me from finding out their secrets. I'd just have to figure out another way.

I slipped along the edge of that boundary, the point where my nerves couldn't withstand the push away. The energy woke up some sort of prey alarm in my brain that felt totally foreign.

I was a dragon. Nothing preyed on me. I was the one who slashed and slaughtered. But somehow I couldn't convince myself of that when I challenged the supernatural barrier.

After a while, I roamed right around the side of the mountain. There was a sharp peak ahead of me, topped with a layer of snow even in the summer. The growing chill itched at me through the shadows, but this part of the mountain range didn't appear to be quite as protected. I darted up it, moving faster but still pausing now and then to check my surroundings.

Whoever was lurking up here would be trusting their warning vibe to keep spies away. They wouldn't need many other protections if they were strong enough to propel even a being like me in the opposite direction.

The chill might have affected me, but traveling through the patches of darkness without any physical form didn't tire me particularly. Especially once evening fell and the whole landscape was dark. I raced to the edge of the peak and peered down over the terrain I'd circumnavigated.

Enough of a pale glow shone down from the mostly full moon that my already sharp eyes could make out many details even with the dwindling sunlight. In the distance, between this peak and a couple of others, a large lake shimmered. There were a few buildings near the edge of the lake, rough huts that I suspected only held one room each. The rocky terrain showed a few gouges large enough for me to make out even from the distance, as if some huge creature had dug right into the mountain.

I watched the water and the land around it. For a while, nothing moved. Then I made out a creature here and another there, one slipping into one of the huts, another heading down the mountain by the way I hadn't been able to come up.

There were probably more in the shadows, too far away for me to make them out, let alone tell what sort of beings there were. There could be just a few or dozens, even hundreds. No way for me to know.

I gritted my teeth in frustration. But then I caught a sense of motion from much closer by. Another being, a higher shadowkind but not all that powerful, passing through the gloom no more than fifty feet away.

Because I'd been crouched motionless and she'd been in motion, she hadn't picked up on my presence as far as I could tell. Nothing about her passage betrayed any nervousness.

I couldn't think of any reason for a shadowkind to be up here who wasn't connected to the bunch hanging out around the lake. That meant she might be able to tell me more, even if I couldn't get down there myself.

I waited until she'd come a little closer, moving on a diagonal past me, and then I flung myself across the short distance to tackle her.

Her sinewy form jerked and flailed as it snapped into physical form beneath my emerged dragon body. I hauled the being—not a type I'd encountered before, but with a scent that reminded me of the dryads I'd once met—around the slope out of view of the apparent mountain den. Then I pinned her down firmly and let enough of me transform that I could speak.

"You've come from the lake," I said with a growl in my voice.

The being just stared at me, her thin face bluish-gray, although maybe it was naturally that color and not just turned it out of horror. Her lips wobbled.

I leaned closer, showing my fangs. "You will tell me about it. Who's there? What are you doing? Are you the ones who killed the sorcerers near here?"

When she stayed silent, I dug a claw into each of her wrists. She let out a little squeal. Then she said, "I can't—I can't talk about it. It isn't allowed. There's nothing I can say."

I recognized the desperation in her words with a cold smack of revulsion. She'd been compelled—compelled like sorcerers did. Except there weren't any mortals hiding out up here in the mountains.

This was an enclave of the beasts we were fighting against—the beasts who'd been gulping down sorcerers' innards to take on their powers for themselves. And they'd used those powers on this being along with so many others.

A swell of regret washed through me. She might not want to be helping them. It might not be her fault at all. Not any more than it'd been the fault of any of the other shadowkind enslaved alongside me all those years ago.

"Can you come with me?" I asked. "The power will fade given enough time away from the ones who cast it. Or I might know someone who can help shatter it." Surely a demon like Rollick could manage to clear her mind from that influence?

But the shadowkind woman shook her head with a miserable expression. "I have my tasks," she said, her voice a croak now. "I must stick to my duties."

It was sickening, hearing her. A snarl hissed through my fangs. Well, I just wouldn't give her a choice then.

I shifted back into my full dragon form and clamped her to my scaled chest with one leg. My other limbs scrabbled down the mountainside as fast as they could carry me. Who knew what she might be able to tell us if Rollick could break through the magic on her? She could be the key—

She twisted in my hold abruptly. I whirled around, ready to snatch a firmer hold of her if she tried to escape—but she hadn't been trying to flee after all. At least, not that way.

She whipped her hand with its own much finer claws to her neck and tore it open all the way through to the spine.

Her filmy blood gushed up in a cloud. Her body went limp in my grasp. I growled in frustration, laying her down on the slope, but there was nothing I could do for her. She'd practically gouged her head right off her shoulders.

Had her masters ordered her to do *that* too? I grimaced with another surge of disgust.

I took only a moment to mourn the loss of my possible victory. I couldn't afford to stick around here in physical form very long. There was only one thing left I could do.

I sucked in the cool mountain air and then breathed my dragon fire over the body, just hot enough to incinerate the rest of her in a final gust of smoke without charring the ground beneath her.

She blew away in a quickly fading haze. There was no trace of her left—no evidence that anyone had caught her, that she'd been forced to take that desperate step. I glanced back toward the higher reaches of the mountain again, but a tug in my chest brought me leaping into the darkness down toward the base again.

There were powers here I couldn't challenge. But we'd discovered one of our enemies' bases of operations. That was some kind of victory still, wasn't it?

I just hoped I'd scrounged it up quickly enough for it to help Quinn survive these villains and their horrible intentions.

CHAPTER THIRTEEN

Quinn

By the end of my third session of sorcery, I'd compelled the little spiky creature to walk all along the railing from one end of the terrace to the other, jump into Rollick's arms—which it definitely did *not* want to do—and in an impromptu moment of inspiration for the demon, pounce on a gull that very unwisely decided to land on one of the lounge chairs.

The last command made me balk the most. I'd dawdled, hoping the gull would realize its impending doom and get the hell away. But Rollick had arched his eyebrows at me, and I'd thought about my parents somewhere below me. That'd been enough motivation to propel the strange words from my throat.

The creature had slammed the bird right off the chair onto the tiles as it tore open its throat. I didn't think I'd ordered it to *kill* the gull, but maybe the sorcery words for "pounce" and "slaughter" were the same... or maybe the mini monster simply couldn't imagine doing the former without also doing the latter.

Blood smeared across the tiles, and my stomach lurched. I jerked around, nausea continuing to roil in my gut.

Rollick seemed to realize he'd pushed me to my limit. He snatched up the beast by the scruff of its neck like it was an errant kitten, stuffed it back in the box, and did something with his supernatural powers that I couldn't follow but that resulted in both the bird and most of the blood vanishing within a matter of seconds. All that remained was a faintly pinkish smudge on the pale gray tiles. He cocked his head at it. "The next rain should take care of that."

The demon turned to me then, his dark blue eyes glinting slyly despite his haste to end the session. "You're doing very well, sorcerer. Maybe I'll bring a bigger beastie next time and see how well you can exert your will on it."

Maybe we should see what happens if I exert my will on you, I thought, but I kept the snarky words to myself this time. I hadn't forgotten how he'd threatened to make me practice on Lance. And over the past few days, I'd become increasingly conscious of the time ticking away before our deal was dissolved.

It'd been almost exactly seven days since the moment we'd made that deal. Rollick had snuck me into his suite a week ago. What was going to happen after three more days had passed? Was I impressing him enough, or would he decide my heart was more useful to him as dinner?

If I had impressed him... what was he going to want me to do next?

After he'd left, I roamed around the terrace and the living room, even more restless than usual. At least I might be able to negotiate safety for my parents if we set new terms. But on the other hand, I'd lost a lot of my bargaining power. Before, Crag could have fought for me on turf that wasn't any more familiar to Rollick than it was to the gargoyle. We could have made a run for it. Now, Rollick controlled almost everything about my situation.

What leverage did I really have?

Out on the terrace again, I squinted against the bright sun, peering at the terrace above mine. The one that jutted from Rollick's office, ending at the edge of his personal apartment's roof.

I'd made a lot of tricky scrambles over the past several years. Climbing up maintenance ladders, scaling fences designed to keep out the curious, hefting myself to a higher floor of an abandoned building through nothing but a hole in the floor. I should be able to manage that climb if I planned it carefully.

There was more on the uppermost levels of the hotel than just Rollick's office. I doubted the office itself was significantly bigger than his entire personal apartment, and the sub-penthouse floor had other regular hotel rooms like the one Torrent and I had made use of. I'd heard distant music and laughter from above before—one of the men had said something about a rooftop bar.

It still wouldn't be wise for me to let anyone else *see* me, but I'd like to know what I was working with here. Get a better sense of the layout of the hotel. Figure out what my potential escape routes might be if I felt I needed to make a run for it later.

Anything that might add one small advantage to my side.

I studied the patio chairs and dragged the sturdiest one over to the inner corner of the terrace. If I started to lose my balance, I could hop down on its padding, and it wouldn't be too bad a landing. I clambered from it onto the railing—first the stucco edge, then the steel bar that ran half a foot above the more solid wall.

From there, I could just reach the base of the office terrace. Rollick had opted for maximum visibility rather than privacy there, which served my purposes just fine. The whole barrier along the edge was made of steel posts with decent gaps in between them.

I grasped them and swung my legs up. I'd been keeping up my regular exercise routine during the long hours of boredom in the hotel room, and I hefted my weight without much trouble. In a moment, I was hooking my feet around two of the bars. With my legs holding the rest of me more stable, I pulled myself upright hand over hand until I could unhook one foot and then the other and swing right over the railing onto the terrace proper.

When my sneakers hit the tiles, which matched those on my own terrace below, I froze. For all I knew, the demon had come up to his office after he'd left me.

There wasn't much of anywhere to hide on this smaller outdoor space, which appeared to be intended mainly for schmoozing with potential business prospects rather than private relaxation. There were no chairs or loungers at all, only a couple of small, bar-height tables that looked designed to hold drinks while the people around them stood.

I waited for the space of several heartbeats, but no one emerged from behind the glass door that led into Rollick's office. Straightening up, I slunk over to it. Who knew what leverage I might be able to find in there?

I wasn't really surprised to discover that the door was locked, though. I peered through the glass into the shadowy interior, but I couldn't make out much beyond the thin wash of light that spilled through the windows, which revealed a thick carpet like the one downstairs and the shape of a desk with a bulky leather chair. Nothing particularly useful.

Better not to hang around on Rollick's immediate turf too long anyway. I went back to the railing, walking the length of it to get the full view from this slightly higher vantage point. I couldn't make out much more than the sprawl of ocean water I could see from my own terrace.

Jazzy notes were already lilting through the air from somewhere less distant now. I moved to the inner corner of the terrace and studied the wall.

The building protruded on either side of the terrace to hug its sides with solid, windowless stucco all the way up, no railing to clamber onto. But there was a rectangular bulge just above my reach, some kind of maintenance fixture, and a decorative slat above it that I thought would be wide enough to get my fingers around.

I eyeballed them for a minute, picturing the movements I'd need to make, and then dragged over one of the little tables. It wasn't as steady as the chair I'd used before, but when I braced it in the corner, I could heave myself onto it and balance with only a little wobbling.

From that height, I could hook my elbow over the rectangular box. I leapt up, bracing my feet against the wall, and caught hold of the slat by the fingertips of my other hand.

For one dizzy moment, I thought I was going to skid back down to fall on my ass. Then I managed to shove my legs farther up and push off the box. Once I had one foot planted on it, hauling myself upright wasn't too much trouble.

I could see onto the roof over Rollick's office now—and it was just roof. The music and faint chatter I could now hear from the bar seemed to be coming from beyond a tall white wall that ran along the roof about twenty feet away, making sure no patrons wandered too close to Rollick's private domain. The area I could see was a plain, smooth white surface, dappled with rain-streaked grit here and there.

It obviously wasn't meant for visitors. There was no railing at all other than a simple bar that stood less than a foot high along the lip. But I was familiar with rooftops. I yanked myself up and over, crawled a few feet from the edge for safety's sake, and then walked the rest of the way over to the wall.

I didn't want anyone on the other side to get a glimpse of me, but I had to figure out whether the patio bar was accessible to me at all. If the hotel patrons used it, there must be a way to get down through the hotel from there. A potential escape route for desperate times.

But I'd only just reached the slanted shadow that fell along the looming wall when an unfamiliar lithe figure leapt into being a few feet away from me.

He jumped into my frame of view at an angle as if he'd hopped over the wall. If I hadn't known shadowkind existed, I'd probably have believed that was what he'd done. But I knew he hadn't been there a moment ago—he'd flickered into being right out of the shadow above.

I backed up a step, tensing as he grinned at me. The stranger didn't look particularly monstrous at the moment, pale eyes gleaming amid peachy skin under a fall of rumpled chestnut hair, but I had no idea who he was either. And Rollick had been *very* clear that he didn't want any shadowkind at all finding out I was here.

Shit. Just how much had I potentially fucked up the security of my hideout by exploring like this?

And what the hell did I do now?

As my heart pounded, the shadowkind man cocked his head in a casual motion, looking me up and down. "You must be one of the owner's toys," he said in an amused tone. "Decided to do a little wandering? Has he kept you all caged up?"

"No," I blurted out. "I—I'm fine. I just wanted to get the best possible view." I motioned vaguely toward the seascape beyond the roof.

I had my silver pen-dagger in my pocket, but suddenly it felt woefully inadequate. I had trouble imagining where I could stab it that I could manage to land and that would slow this guy down even slightly. Attacking him might make the situation ten times worse. My hand dropped to my pocket just in case.

He stepped closer, and I automatically retreated, starkly aware of how much roof I had left before I couldn't back up at all. But the shadowkind man didn't pursue me any farther.

A slow smile stretched across his lips. When he spoke next, there was a strange melodic quality to his voice that shivered through my thoughts and into my bones.

"You'd like to play with me now. It's awfully hot up here, though. Better take that shirt off."

I wanted to sputter a laugh in his face. No way was I getting undressed because some random dude asked me to. But before my mouth could even open, my arms were rising, my hands grasping the hem of my tank top.

My pulse hitched. What the fuck? I tried to stiffen my muscles against the movement, but I couldn't stop them. It was like my common sense had been locked away by whatever magic he'd cast on me, and I couldn't regain control no matter how I wrenched at myself inside. Some deep part of my mind thought there was nothing odd at all about lifting the fabric up over my bra and—

With the cloth pulled up partly over my face, I only saw a blur of motion. There was a thump and a hiss and the start of a shout, cut off with a gurgle. The vice-like grip on my free will shattered. I whipped my hands and my shirt down, my skin damp with a chilly sweat.

In full demon form, Rollick had the other man, whatever kind of monster he was, pinned to the rooftop. He'd already slashed right through the guy's throat with his claws, sending smoky blood billowing up. He snarled down at the intruder, his demonic face twisted with vicious fury.

"This is what you get when you mess with me and mine," he spat out, and snuffed out whatever life had been left in the man by crushing the remains of his neck.

I hugged myself, my pulse still racing, as Rollick straightened up. Gripping the body, he dove into the shadows and returned an instant later empty-handed. Only a small smudge of smoke remained, wisping away into the air as I watched.

The demon turned toward me, wiping his hands together as he contracted into his less monstrous form. His normally cheerful face was darkened by a savage frown.

"Was that—was that one of the shadowkind that've been killing the sorcerers?" I asked. "He compelled me—he made me—"

Rollick was already shaking his head. His frown relaxed a little. "There are many shadowkind who can manipulate *mortals* to their will," he said. "We just generally can't control each other by that sort of means." He glowered at the spot where he'd caught the other man. "Too many cajoling merfolk around when you're near the ocean. Never trust a siren."

"Oh." My gaze slid to the water, mythic tales swimming up through my mind.

Was that how it felt for the shadowkind when sorcerers compelled them? I'd gotten one brief taste of supernatural persuasion, and even that had been horrifying.

I looked back at Rollick. "How did you know I was here?"

His expression turned to pure amusement. "I don't imagine you can blame me for being curious when I see the mortal who's *supposed* to be staying in her very nice rooms clambering around the hotel. But as you can see, I wasn't going to let you get into any actual danger. You're welcome, by the way."

"Thank you," I said automatically, but then a prickle of anger rose up inside me. The way he'd tackled the siren hadn't been so different from how he'd pinned *me* down just a couple of days ago, making promises that'd only been a shade distant from threats. I raised my chin. "Let's not pretend you're such a hero, though. You only protected me because you don't want anyone messing with your plans or inconveniencing *you*."

If he'd had the sort of persuasive power that other shadowkind had, maybe he'd have simply brainwashed my compliance just as quickly without a twinge of conscience. The only reason he hadn't let his succubus do it was because he didn't want her knowing I was here.

Rollick let out a huff that sounded more teasing than actually offended. "Whatever you think of my motivations, you're much better off now than you were five minutes ago. Did you discover all you hoped to, little adventurer?"

I gritted my teeth. "I just wanted a better sense of where I actually *am*. I wasn't going to let anyone see me—I didn't think anyone would be able to get over to this part of the roof."

"You came too close to the wall," Rollick informed me. "He wouldn't have been able to approach or affect you if you'd been over by the edge. But it's done now." He motioned to me. "Come on, let's get you back where you belong and see if we can't keep you in one piece for at least a few days longer."

CHAPTER FOURTEEN

Quinn

Any lingering anger I'd felt faded away into apprehension over the rest of the day. Rollick's growled words to the siren echoed through my head: *This is what you get when you mess with me and mine.*

He thought I belonged to him, even though I'd made it clear in every way I possibly could that I wasn't happy about being in his grasp. That I was only cooperating with him to protect myself and the people I cared about.

I was grateful for the deal he'd extended to me and the protection he'd offered, but the debt I sensed myself racking up was starting to weigh on me. Just how much was he going to end up asking for in return beyond what he'd already demanded?

I didn't know how to answer that question, and my attempts at getting more control over my situation had only made me more indebted to him. I checked my makeshift silver dagger in my pocket, not that it'd done me much good with the shadowkind stranger, and ran through my workout routine again, but no amount of exertion could burn off the uneasiness gripping me.

So, when a now-familiar soft tap sounded on the sliding door, relief rushed through my body. Maybe they couldn't fix everything that was wrong, but there was nothing I'd have welcomed more than the chance to spend more time with any of the three men I didn't mind calling me *theirs*.

I forced myself to hold off on going over to the terrace for a few minutes, puttering around sticking my dinner dishes in the dumbwaiter and finishing the current chapter of the book I'd been reading, even though the words barely sank in. Then I ambled over to my bedroom. There, I stretched my arms leisurely and drifted to the terrace door as if the mood had just happened to strike me to take in the fresh air.

My spirits lifted even higher when I saw that not just one but all three of my monstrous men had joined me again. I hadn't seen any of them in three days, and that past meet-up had been wrenchingly brief.

"It's so good to see you," I said as I hurried over to them. "How long can you stay this time?"

Torrent gave me the quiet but warm smile that he rarely brought out and that never failed to send a pleased shiver over my skin. "A few hours should be safe." He nudged the gargoyle's shoulder. "Rollick actually specifically asked Crag to keep watch down below while he had to zip out of town for the night. I don't think he expected Lance and I to make it back as quickly as we did."

"He didn't specifically say I *couldn't* watch over you from right beside you," Crag rumbled with an uncharacteristic hint of slyness in his dark eyes. I decided I liked it.

"I can't think of a better vantage point," I said with a laugh.

I grabbed them each in a hug—and naturally Lance swept me into a kiss as well, tracing his claws lightly down my spine until I was quivering against him as he claimed my mouth. Torrent cleared his throat, and the dragon shifter lifted his head with a grin. "We've left her alone too long. Need to make up for it."

"I'm sure there'll be plenty of time for that," Torrent said in a tone that managed to be both dry and laced with heat. He tipped his head toward the side of the hotel. "And since we've got the time, we can have a more relaxed conversation if we hop over to that other room. It's empty again."

Crag shifted without any further prompting, unfurling his leathery gray wings from his stony gargoyle form. My gaze lingered on the scars that gripped through the taut skin there, but he didn't show any sign of discomfort.

The first couple of times he'd flown me anywhere, I hadn't known whether I could trust him, whether he might be whisking me off to my doom. Now I stepped into his arms without hesitation. I couldn't imagine anywhere I'd feel safer.

The other two men vanished into the night to travel through the darkness to the balcony around the corner of the building. Crag leapt over the railing and crossed the distance with a few brisk flaps, staying close to the wall where it was darkest. It was only a little past dinner time, the sun completely set but lights still beaming in many windows and along the perimeter of the property I could now see below me.

The second he'd landed on the balcony, Crag transformed back into his still impressive but not quite so gigantic human appearance. He'd always seemed a bit reluctant to let me take a good look at him in his monstrous form, even though I didn't find anything about him horrifying.

Lance wavered into being next to us at the same moment as Torrent blinked into being on the other side of the balcony door. The tentacled man unlocked it and slid it open to admit us.

Torrent had told me last time that he would arrange fresh linens for the bed after he'd brought me back to Rollick's rooms. We didn't want any of the staff realizing someone had been using the suite without permission. I couldn't tell if it'd had any guests since then. The air smelled crisp and clean but a little stale. I left the sliding door open so the fresh ocean breeze could wash through the room and sat on the edge of the bed.

"How have your investigations been going?" I asked. "Have you figured anything more out about the shadowkind who're hunting for me?"

"We're hunting them right back," Lance announced, slicing his claws through the air, and shot me a brilliant grin that turned his always ferally gorgeous face even more stunning. "I found their den. Or one of their dens, anyway. We know one place they like to hang out with the poor beasties they've turned into slaves."

The triumph in his tone darkened with those last few words. He bared his teeth, his dragon fangs out in his otherwise human face. A pang of sympathy filled my chest, sharper with my guilt over the way *I'd* been bending one beast to my will over the past few days. I hadn't liked doing it, but I'd bowed to Rollick's will anyway.

I tried to push those thoughts aside. "Is it nearby? Do they seem to suspect that I'm in L.A.?"

Lance shook his head and dropped onto the bed beside me, tucking his arm around my waist. "Not even in the same state. I still don't know *what* exactly they are. They like mountains, and they play with rocks."

"One of them, anyway," Crag rumbled. "I did talk to a being that'd been around them briefly who said one of the apparent leaders gave an earthy impression."

"It's probably not their only base of operations," Torrent said. "Most likely they've got at least a few camps spread around in this country and others abroad, just like Rollick has all his properties—as much as he likes focusing on this one for the moment." He paused. "It is useful information, though, for making our own plans. We know where to find them."

If we wanted to pass on a message about my current location, he meant. "Well, that's something." I tried to sound optimistic, but I suspected I'd failed.

"We'll put all the pieces together and then shred *them* to pieces," Lance said with typical vicious confidence. I wished I could be that optimistic.

Crag gazed down at me, his broad brow furrowing. "Are you all right, Quinn? You seem more… dispirited than before."

It was true that my initial joy at seeing them had faded with the realization of how far we still were from a solution. I hadn't meant to disturb him with my worries, even if it brought a pang of affection into my chest to know he'd noticed despite my efforts.

I wasn't going to lie to him now that he had picked up on my feelings. I rubbed my hand over my face. "It's just—there are only three more days in the deal. I don't know how Rollick will want to change it then, or whether he'll even agree to making another one."

"If he won't guarantee your safety, we'll figure out something else," Torrent said. "You know we can get to you and take you away from here if we absolutely have to."

"But there's still so much we don't know about who we're up against or what they want."

"We have three more days to figure that out," Lance declared. "We've made a lot of progress already. Have faith, baby girl." He nuzzled the side of my face playfully and then trailed his claws along my arm, his voice dipping lower. "Maybe what you need is a distraction from all the worries wiggling through that pretty head."

I swallowed thickly, but a flare of heat had washed over my body at his skillful touch. "What kind of distraction did you have in mind?"

He snorted in amusement and leaned in to nip the crook of my jaw. "I think you know. I haven't gotten to enjoy my lovely explorer in a *week*. We can do all the things you like, and maybe discover new things you do too."

The vibe in the room had shifted, the air seeming to warm despite the cool current from the air conditioning system, all three of my men's focus narrowing down to me with an intense alertness. Another quiver ran through me, but it seemed to provoke a jolt of energy through my heart—a jolt of that sorcerer power that made my pulse shudder. I sucked in a breath.

"I've been compelling a shadowkind creature," I said abruptly. "A little lesser beast that Rollick's keeping caged. He's getting me to tap into the magic more and more."

I expected Lance to recoil at my statement, even braced myself for it, but the dragon shifter's lips kept nibbling down the side of my neck. "When we get you away from him, you won't need to do that either."

Something in me unwound just a little. If even Lance, who'd been tormented by sorcerers for I had no idea how long, didn't blame me for going along with the demon's demands, then maybe I shouldn't blame myself either. Maybe I shouldn't hold myself back from what I wanted out of some sense that I didn't deserve it.

I did want this—I wanted the shadowkind men who'd stood with me through all the chaos so far. Not just to stoke the heat kindling low in my belly, but to reconfirm with kisses and caresses as we already had with words that nothing could tear us apart from each other. Rollick hadn't been able to stop us from having this interlude, and we wouldn't let him stop us from winning our freedom either.

For a moment, it seemed that simple. I raised one hand to stroke my fingers into Lance's silky curls and over his scalp. He let out an encouraging hum and grazed his fangs across my shoulder. At a much more enjoyable skip of my pulse, I glanced up at my other two men.

Crag had shared me with the dragon shifter before in an encounter on the yacht, the memory of which made the heat inside me flare twice as hot. But Torrent... that time, Lance had invited both of them to join in, and the tentacled man had turned his back on us before I'd even been able to agree.

But that was before we'd understood each other better. Before I'd been able to show him that I saw him as more than a curiosity, and he'd shown me that he'd defy his own boss to protect me. We were in a very different place now, and not just geographically.

As if he sensed my uncertainty and wanted to reassure me, Torrent met my gaze and sank down onto the bed at my other side. He let one tentacle trail across my shoulder in a tender caress. "I look forward to seeing how much you can enjoy yourself with all three of us on the task."

So did I, especially when that hungry note crept into his voice. I reached toward Crag to make sure he knew he was fully included, and the gargoyle gave me a smile that was almost shy as he knelt at my feet. "We'll take very good care of you, Softness."

He slipped off one of my sneakers and then the other, the undressing oddly seductive even though it was only my feet. Lance tugged at my shirt. "You don't want me slicing this up."

It could be thrilling having him undress me in his... uniquely savage way, but— "I think Rollick might notice if one of my few outfits ends up in shreds. And my current wardrobe is small enough as it is."

"I'm sure we can manage to take care of your clothes too," Torrent said wryly, tucking his tentacle under the hem of the top. With a deft tug and the lift of my arms, he pulled it right off me.

Lance had watched that motion with an avidness I didn't totally understand until he caught my arms before I lowered them again. He glanced across at Torrent with a sly grin. "Hold her wrists." Before I could worry that he was still nervous of me after all, he licked his tongue along my jaw and murmured, "It shows her how much she's ours."

Well, if that was the only reason he wanted me restrained, I wouldn't argue about it. Especially because a giddy shiver ran through me as Torrent carefully coiled his tentacle around both my wrists, pinning them together above my head. The suction cups seemed to mouth my skin like a dozen simultaneous kisses, and the slight stretch made my breasts rise within my bra.

Lance managed to flick open the clasp with his nimble claws without severing the fabric. He tugged the bra aside with his teeth and flicked his now-ridged dragon tongue over the peak.

I gasped at the shock of headier pleasure, and there was something erotic about the way my hands caught in Torrent's grasp. Holding me on display, baring me for my men's attentions—making this moment all about what they could do for me without any expectation or even possibility of me returning the favor.

I did want to return the bliss as much as I could before the interlude was over, but for now, this was a different sort of fun for all of us.

As Lance worked over my breast and Crag stroked his large hands along my legs, Torrent leaned in to capture my mouth. His kiss had the passion of a stormy sea, the yearning in it leaving me breathless. When he released my lips, he eased behind me on the bed to leave more room for the other men, never loosening his grasp on my wrists.

He slipped another tentacle around my torso to pluck at my other nipple with the suckers until I leaned back into his lean frame with a whimper. The need building between my legs made me squirm. Torrent let out a heated chuckle and tucked the tentacle under my breast as if to offer it up to the man in front of me.

Crag didn't hesitate to accept the invitation. He pushed up on his knees and leaned in to taste my breast, his tongue stretching from regular human shape to its extended, sinuous gargoyle anatomy before my eyes. He wrapped the tip right around my nipple and tugged, and I jerked with a desperate mewling sound.

Lance was still conjuring all kinds of sparks in my other breast with his own special tongue. He wasn't diverted from finding even more ways to bring me pleasure, though. He delved his hand between us to deftly undo the fly of my jean shorts. Crag rumbled and tugged the shorts off me without pausing his administrations.

The dragon shifter stroked his claws lightly over my sex, and I spread my legs wider with an eager trembling at the delight his wicked touch provoked. Then a tentacle was slipping down my belly to pluck my clit the way it had my nipple. A full-out moan reverberated from my lungs, and Lance raised his head in time to catch the end of it with his mouth against mine.

I swayed and writhed between the three men, bliss rushing through me from so many directions that the room around me blurred. But I heard Crag's deep thrum of a voice clear as anything when he said, "I haven't tasted her yet."

"Mmm," Lance murmured. "You shouldn't miss out on that. Better than any food I've ever eaten." He laughed and began charting a new scorching path along my neck.

Crag gazed up at me as he tugged my panties down. Without the use of my arms, I couldn't reach out and pull him to me to show him how much I wanted this experience too, but I shifted my hips toward him. "If you want to…"

"Oh, very much," he said with an odd formality that somehow made the moment even hotter. Torrent raised his tentacle to tease across my breasts again, clearing the way for the gargoyle to lower his head between my legs.

His tongue slid over my clit, encompassing it so thoroughly another moan burst from my lips. "Even softer here," he said with a sound like a sigh, and then he was pressing his whole mouth against my pussy.

His upper lip massaged my clit while his extended tongue delved right inside me. It had the same wonderful flexibility as Torrent's tentacles, but the combination of his hot breath and the rocky texture of his jaw against my thighs made it a totally different sensation. A fucking amazing sensation.

I rocked against his mouth, unable to do more than that and whimper as Torrent tweaked my nipples and Lance trailed his claws over my belly and down my back. God, when had I ever felt as *alive* as right now, with these three fearsome men focusing all their attention on bringing me to the greatest heights of pleasure they could supply?

Whatever happened in the future, I was definitely never going back to mortal guys. None of them had ever really understood me anyway. With these three men, as inhuman as they were, I felt strangely understood. Seen in ways I'd never felt comfortable letting any person get a glimpse of.

Crag growled and lapped his tongue deeper inside me. I was shuddering with the unfurling bliss now, rushing higher and faster with every movement of his mouth and the other men's touches. "Oh, fuck," I mumbled as he clamped his lips even more firmly on my pussy, and arched to meet him. Then my release crashed over me, leaving me shaking and slack between the three men.

Lance nuzzled my hair. "And she does enjoy the meal so much," he said with fond amusement.

Crag pressed one last kiss to my folds and beamed up at me, his normally hardened face radiant with his satisfaction. "Then that makes two of us."

The dragon shifter vanished and reappeared in the blink of an eye, leaving his clothes behind in the shadows. He swiveled me toward him, his violet eyes gleaming. "My turn. It's been too long since I got to feel her all around me. My favorite place to be."

He grinned at me, and an urge came over me to make this my own claiming as well as theirs. If I belonged to them, then they belonged to me just as much.

I yanked at my wrists, and Torrent must have sensed there was a different quality to the motion than my earlier instinctive resistance. His tentacle uncoiled, and I swiveled around to land right on Lance's lap, straddling him.

Surprise flickered across the dragon shifter's face, but it came with a flare of hunger. "Our mortal wants to take charge," he teased. "What are you going to do with me now, baby girl?"

I rocked my slick cunt against his already rigid erection, making him hiss as his eyelids drooped with pleasure. His total trust that whatever I had in mind would be just as enjoyable for him too set off a surge of twined affection and exhilaration inside me. "I'm going to let you feel me all around you," I said with a smirk, echoing his earlier words, and sank right down onto him.

His cock filled me so well, even more so when I felt the head swell larger inside me into its dragon shape. My breath caught, and Lance smirked right back at me, knowing the effect his monstrous features had on me. He glided his claws up and down my thighs as he gazed at me.

There were other benefits to sitting up instead of being pinned under him, I realized. As I found the best position over Lance's lap, swaying up and down over his cock experimentally, the other two men drew closer on either side of me. They'd only meant to keep up their assault of pleasure, Torrent trailing his tentacle over my body, Crag capturing my mouth, but it occurred to me that in this position, I could bring them all with me and Lance on this ecstatic journey.

"Both of you, clothes off too," I mumbled around a groan as Lance pushed his hips up to meet me, filling me deeper than before. They performed the same trick the dragon shifter had, shedding their clothes in an instant and revealing their own sculpted bodies to my eager gaze.

I kissed Crag again, stroking my hand over his bulging arm, and then turned to where Torrent was kneeling beside me. With my other hand, I traced the rows of suckers that protruded from the back of his upper arm—

the one shadowkind feature he couldn't leave behind completely, although his tentacles were almost essential now to support his legs. He brushed one of those beneath my chin to giddying effect, and it occurred to me that I hadn't tasted *him* yet. His cock was standing at rigid attention within my sights.

I twisted at the waist and lowered myself carefully, stretching my arm to trace my hand down Crag's body at the same time as I dipped toward Torrent. Catching my intent, Lance leaned back on his hands and both of the other men shifted even closer. Torrent's chest hitched as I flicked my tongue over the head of his erection.

"Quinn," he muttered, nothing but longing in the way he said my name. It made me twice as eager to take him.

I wrapped my mouth around his cock and my fingers around Crag's thick shaft at the same time. Lance had held still, watching my progress with apparent delight. As I found a rhythm with the other two men, he started to roll his hips against me again.

"That's right, baby girl," he said, his voice becoming strained with need. "You were meant for all of us. Look at you."

His last words cut off with a growl. He thrust into me more forcefully, and I gasped around Torrent's cock. Rocking with the dragon shifter, I slicked my tongue around Torrent's length to lap up the salty flavor that tasted so much like the ocean and gripped Crag's shaft tighter with the pump of my hand.

The gargoyle groaned and pressed kisses over my back. Torrent looped a tentacle all the way around my waist, the tip dropping to stroke my clit just above where Lance and I were joined. I moaned and sucked him down as deep as I could without choking. His hips jerked toward me with a growl of his own.

It was a maelstrom of desire and bliss, and it wrapped around me so thoroughly that everything faded away except the joint motion of our bodies and the pleasure blazing through me. Crag's fingers dug into my hair with a grasp that was just shy of painful. I squeezed him harder, and he came with a grunt and clamp of his mouth against my shoulder blade.

Lance hummed encouragingly and rocked with me faster. Torrent's tentacle tightened around my waist, the tip strumming my clit into a chorus of ecstasy, and I swayed with them both, driving us all toward release.

Despite my intention of getting the men there before me, I broke first. Lance surged up inside me at just the right moment with the flick of Torrent's tentacle, and pleasure exploded through my body.

My pussy clenched around Lance, and he came with me in a spurt of heat. My mouth closed more firmly around Torrent too, and he grasped the back of my head. "I'm going to—"

Good. I sucked him down, and he emptied himself into my mouth with a ragged cry that nearly tipped me over the edge all over again. *I'd* brought him that much pleasure.

I'd taken all of them, my monstrous lovers, and shown I could handle it. Shown just how good we were together in every possible way. They understood me, and I understood them. Maybe we'd all become something more by finding each other.

Lance yanked me down next to him on the bed, and the other men tucked themselves close. Surrounded by their heat, I let myself doze for just a moment, adrift on the satisfaction of knowing this one thing Rollick couldn't steal from us.

CHAPTER FIFTEEN

Quinn

I woke up in Rollick's bedroom to the beeping of my alarm. As I sat up and grabbed my pill case, the memory of last night's encounter with the three shadowkind men—whose bedrooms I'd rather have been staying in—rushed through my body with a pleasant achiness of muscles well-worked. Then I thought of the hour we'd spent afterward, dozing companionably and then talking about all the things we'd want to do together when I wasn't being pursued by any kind of villains, and the heat turned into an ache of affection.

Maybe I really could someday swim in the ocean with Torrent, and fly over Crag's favorite landscapes with him, and sample every flavor of ice cream in the supermarket with Lance. People had overcome worse obstacles than this, hadn't they? I'd like to think so, anyway.

I missed them already, but something about the sensation gave me a fresh burst of confidence. I still had cards to play. I wasn't a total victim. By the time Rollick showed up after I'd showered and eaten, I was ready for him, bolstered by my growing resolve.

He stepped into the room carrying a black carrier that looked a little larger than before. I remembered his suggestion that he'd bring a creature that was more of a challenge this time. My chest clenched up momentarily, but I stood firm, bracing my feet against the floor and squaring my shoulders.

Rollick took in my stance and paused rather than walking straight across to the terrace. He raised his eyebrows. "You look like a woman with a mission," he said with a smile as if he enjoyed seeing it. "Still plenty of energy to spare, I see."

I wasn't sure what he meant by that comment when it was first thing in the morning. What would I have been expending my energy on before now? But the demon could shove his charm up his ass regardless.

"Before we do any more training, I want to see my parents," I said.

Rollick's eyebrows arched a tad higher. "I thought we'd already covered *very* thoroughly why any interaction with people from your regular life is a bad—"

"I'm not asking to talk to them," I interrupted. "I know I can't do that without making a big mess. But they've been right here in this hotel for days. You're a super powerful demon. There's got to be some way you can let me get a look at them in person, even if they can't see me. I just want to confirm with my own eyes that they're totally okay."

And it was an excuse to take a look at more of the hotel itself as well. What surreptitious ways would Rollick bring me through the building that I might be able to make use of on my own later?

Rollick set the carrier down on the sofa and leaned against the arm in a casual stance. "Unfortunately, that's impossible."

I resisted the urge to roll my eyes at him. "Impossible, or you just don't want to?"

"Your parents aren't here anymore," he said. "I arranged for their trip home yesterday, which to the best of my knowledge went perfectly smoothly. The activity happening back in Florida that concerned me petered out, and there was no sign that they'd be in any further danger there. Frankly, if the idiots after you aren't looking for you over there any longer, your parents are safer outside your current orbit."

"Oh." I didn't know what to say to that. I didn't know what to even think about it. He'd given up a major point of leverage over me... Probably because he'd decided I was cooperating enough that he didn't need the immediate threat to propel me along. It wasn't as if we didn't both know that if he wanted to hurt my parents, he could have them in his clutches again in a matter of minutes.

But the information had taken the wind out of my sails. I couldn't stand firm and make demands when fulfilling those demands actually *was* pretty much impossible. I sucked my lower lip under my teeth but caught myself before I'd worried at it more than a few seconds. Then I narrowed my eyes at Rollick. "How can I be sure that you really did send them home and you're not just saying that so I won't insist on seeing them?"

"I don't know," he said, sounding not at all bothered by the possibility that I might consider him a liar. "It's very difficult to prove the *non*-existence of something—in this case, the non-existing of your parents within this city. I could take you on a tour of the entire hotel and no doubt you'd accuse me of tucking them away someplace else. We have more important matters to focus on." He tapped the top of the box he'd brought.

My hackles rose. "Important to *you*. I didn't want to be throwing my sorcerer powers around in the first place."

"But look at how much progress you've made already! It really is impressive. If you have another horde come at you like I'm told has happened a few times already, you'll at least be able to deflect a few of the lesser creatures without any trouble. Maybe even send them after their own allies." He motioned toward the terrace. "Let's get on with it. I'd rather not conduct this experiment inside. I like my furniture enough not to want to see it clawed up."

My frustration at yet another failed strategy boiled over. My back went rigid. "No. I don't want to participate in any more 'experiments' until you tell me what it is you're hoping to gain out of all this. I know you're not just looking to help me protect myself. You wanted me. You think I'm going to be useful to you in some way. I think it's about time you properly explained."

Rollick cocked his head, still smiling. My hands clenched against the urge to smack the grin right off his face. I could practically hear him thinking how ridiculous it was that I thought I could demand anything from *him*.

I wasn't sure what I would do if he refused. At what point would he claim I was reneging on our deal and bring out more concrete threats to my own safety? But I was so tired of him assuming he could call all the shots here.

To my surprise, he didn't threaten or argue. He pushed off the sofa and strolled closer to me, his grin turning sly.

I backed up a step, but I was already just a couple of feet from the bookcase. I stopped before my shoulders hit it, my pulse thumping faster. And, damn it, when he loomed over me close enough for the warmth of his body to touch me even though no part of him had actually brushed my skin, the adrenaline rushing through me wasn't only apprehension.

"Is my sorcerer so restless that she needs other kinds of stimulation?" the demon asked in a crooning voice. He traced his fingers through the air following the line of my arm but not quite grazing my flesh, and a shiver ran through my nerves. "Have I not been giving you enough attention after all? You only need to ask for what you're craving."

"I'm not craving *you*," I spat out. Some stupid part of my body was curious about what he could do for it, sure, but I had no problem ignoring that part when it came to how I actually acted.

"Maybe I just haven't found the right approach yet," Rollick suggested. "Would you like me better if I took the decision away from you? Tied your arms over your head so you had nothing to do but respond to me? Hmm, from the look that just came into your eyes, I think that might be just the thing."

"Don't you dare—" I started, and then froze with a rush of cold that washed away even the flickers of attraction I'd been suppressing. The image he'd presented sounded way too specific. Way too familiar.

He'd never said anything about restraining me before, and now, the morning after Torrent had "tied" my arms over my head on Lance's instructions, the demon was bringing it up out of the blue? And bringing it up so confidently too, as if he'd been sure I'd react well.

I jerked away from him, moving around him into the more open area of the room where I had space to maneuver. My heart was suddenly thumping twice as fast, but it was only horror reverberating through my veins now. "Were you *watching*?" The men had said that Rollick had left town for the night, but it could have been a set-up—had he suspected and wanted to catch us?

But he hadn't confronted us then or even now… What was he playing at?

"What was there to watch?" he asked, but I thought his gaze had gotten more intent as he studied my reaction. "Have you been naughty, my little mortal?"

My teeth set on edge. Every nerve in my body was screaming to run from here, but there was nowhere to run. No way of getting away from him. And what if I was just imagining the connection?

My mind tripped back through our entire conversation and stuck on that odd remark he'd made about how much energy I still had. As if he knew I'd been occupied in a rather intense physical encounter last night.

No, it couldn't be just a coincidence. Maybe *we'd* been idiots to think he wouldn't find out.

"So you're a pervert and a liar," I shot at him. "You can't even own up to... to..." To violating my privacy. To leering at us from the shadows. Just thinking about it made my skin crawl.

Something shifted in Rollick's expression. A hint of a fiercer light glinted in his eyes, a glimpse of the monster lurking behind them showing through. "I know everything that goes on in this building, no matter how clever the beings within it think they are. A prime sub-penthouse room doesn't stay empty just by happenstance. And I have every right to record what goes on within my property."

To record... Then he hadn't been there in person. He really had left last night, but he'd had some kind of cameras running. I didn't know if that made the situation better or worse.

It occurred to me in another icy splash of revulsion that the first time he'd been particularly provocative with me, when he'd shown off his demonic form not just as a threat but a sort of promise of sexual gratification, it'd been the morning after my first interlude with Torrent. My stomach churned.

"So you treated me like pornography and then decided to use what you saw to advance your own agenda, whatever the hell that is?" I snapped.

The demon blinked slowly, that fucking smile still in place if cooler now. "I've never hidden the fact that I believe in drawing on every advantage at my disposal. You're a difficult one. But if I understand you better, then it's to your benefit as well as my own."

Because he still thought I was going to let him put his hands on me. I suppressed a shudder, backing away one step and another. Rollick prowled after me with languid steps, his grin turning wry again. Like he figured he could charm away my horror.

I had my silver sort-of dagger in my pocket, but I couldn't imagine stabbing him with it doing any real good. I tried to picture jabbing it into his eye—but then what? Even if I pulled off that move without him stopping me, I'd have a furious demon on my hands and nowhere to go.

I wavered, definitely not at all predator now no matter how I'd taken charge with my men last night. In Rollick's presence, I felt all prey—and it wasn't a comfortable feeling.

The demon advanced again, and instinct took over. I darted into the bedroom and slammed the door. It was a useless gesture against a being who could slip right through the tiny gap beneath it—or smash the whole door down—if he wanted to, but the gesture gave me a fragment of a sense of control.

"Leave me alone," I shouted through the door. "I'm not doing *anything* for you or with you, so just—just go away."

And then I braced myself for the retribution to come.

CHAPTER SIXTEEN

Quinn

I stood in silence for one minute and then another. No sound carried from the living room. A gust of ocean wind warbled past the windows across from me. Then I thought I heard the click of the suite door closing.

Could Rollick really have *left*, just like that? I was still shaking, both keyed up and afraid, and the thought of opening the bedroom door to check made every muscle in my body lock up even though it was hardly a significant barrier to the demon anyway.

I gulped in breath after breath, struggling to settle my nerves. But my mind kept leaping from thought to thought, each jolting me with fresh spikes of panic.

Had my men and I said anything incriminating during our guestroom interludes? Did Rollick have audio recording in the room or only video? We'd been out on the terrace when we'd first discussed turning our enemies against each other, but was it possible Torrent had missed a recording device out there?

Would Rollick have focused on my sexual proclivities if he thought we were plotting against him? I had no idea. He obviously played a long game, by standards incomprehensible to my human morality. I had no idea what he'd consider acceptable, what he'd be willing to let slide for now so he could turn it against us later.

I stalked over to the sliding door and then back to the bed, my hands opening and closing at my sides. My thoughts slipped back to last night, to the tenderness and passion I'd enjoyed with my three men, and queasiness bubbled up inside me. I couldn't take any comfort in the memories now that I had to imagine Rollick watching the whole scene, taking in every gasp and moan I made, scheming about how he could manipulate me by knowing what turned me on.

He'd watched every single intimate moment I'd shared with my lovers since I'd gotten here. Ogled my naked body. Watched me writhe and shudder with abandon...

My stomach outright heaved. I shoved open the bedroom door and only just made it to the bathroom in time to puke my breakfast into the toilet.

I crouched there on the cool tiles for several minutes until I was sure I wasn't going to vomit again. The shakes gradually subsided, but I still felt off-balance, both in my head and my stomach. Gradually, it occurred to me that if Rollick *had* still been lurking in the suite, after that display he'd probably have come to make sure I was all right.

Gathering myself, I crept out into the living room. By all appearances, the demon was gone, as was the carrier he'd brought. I guessed he'd figured I needed some space to process what I'd learned. No doubt he'd be back again in a few hours, acting like nothing had changed, expecting us to go on with my training session after all.

My body went rigid at the idea. Resistance clanged through every part of me. To go along with his demands, to keep bowing to his whims, when he'd shown just how monstrous he could be... I'd rather throw myself off the damn terrace.

The second that thought passed through my mind, everything in me went still. I paused and then walked over to the sliding door.

The breeze was light today, wafting over me with a faint saltiness and tickling my hair across my shoulders as I stepped out onto the tiles. A grayish haze muted the summer sunlight, making the ocean look darker and deeper. I glanced at the spot where I'd met up with my three men last night, but of course they weren't there.

Rollick would have sent them off on some new mission, of course. Who knew if he'd even let them come see me again at all? He'd known they were sneaking in all along, so he probably had ways to keep them out if he really wanted to. Now he'd gotten all the information he needed, and he knew his tactics had been uncovered. He wasn't learning anything else from me in this hotel.

I couldn't wait for them. I couldn't count on them getting to me before the deal ended and Rollick could set new terms—or simply have me for lunch, if he decided that was the best option. I still had my phone. He'd taken the SIM card, but it had Torrent's phone number programmed into it. If I could get out of here now, while the demon thought I was too shell-shocked to do much of anything, I'd be able to find another phone and get in touch with them again.

I wavered over the decision for a few minutes, knowing how risky it was. But every time I considered sticking this situation out, waiting until Rollick came with more demands, my gut twisted tighter and my skin started crawling.

I *couldn't* stay. I couldn't stand to spend one more minute in that monster's presence. My parents were back home—and he couldn't threaten them if he couldn't talk to me about what he might do. I just had to get away, as far away from him as I could.

My pulse thrumming faster, I pushed into the bedroom and dug the silver-and-iron vest out of the bottom of my backpack where I'd stuffed it. Running away wouldn't get me very far if the demon and my other enemies could track me the second I moved past the protective barrier a few floors down.

I pulled the vest on over my tank top. Then I filled my water bottle to the brim, grabbed the remaining snacks from a basket that'd been sent up a few days earlier in between meals, and stuffed everything into my backpack, including my messenger bag. It'd be easier to carry one bag rather than both. I slung the straps over my shoulders, secured them tight, and headed back out onto the terrace.

I already knew I could handle the climb to the roof. I also knew that there were guestrooms with balconies around the corner of the building beyond Rollick's suite. I couldn't reach them directly from the terrace without the help of tentacles or wings, but I could go up and over. At least in theory.

There was no telling when Rollick might return. For all I knew, he was already watching me from the shadows. Another shiver of horror rippled over my skin, and I hurried over to the corner.

I went through the same motions as yesterday briskly and efficiently, knowing exactly what I needed to do now. The backpack threw off my weight a little, but by the time I'd clambered onto Rollick's office terrace above, I'd adjusted to it. I normally carried a bag with me during my urban explorations, so the sense of bulk on my back was more familiar than going without.

With another quick scramble, I made it onto the roof. I hurried over to the side where I knew the guestroom balconies were, staying within a few feet of the edge rather than venturing closer to the barrier wall where the siren had used his persuasive influence on me. Rollick had said there were protections here.

But none of them were strong enough to stop *him* from moving all over the hotel. How had I ever thought I could stand a chance going head-to-head with him?

My deal had bought myself and my men some time. Maybe that time had ended up exposing me to the demon in ways I'd never have wanted, but I wasn't going to let myself regret that choice. Now I just had to make some new ones.

At the northern side of the building, I peered down over the edge of the roof toward the balconies below. To my relief, I discovered that there were rooms on the same level as Rollick's office as well as the floor below. I didn't have to attempt a twenty-foot descent to find solid ground. All the way below was the side alley where Rollick had dropped me off. No one was walking around in there. The building across from the hotel had only a few windows on that wall. I should be able to go unnoticed.

Even a ten-foot descent was going to be a little unpleasant. Now I appreciated the tiny railing along the roof. I gripped it with both hands and eased my body over the edge, walking my feet down until the soles of my sneakers hit the edge of the room's window frame. My metal-beaded vest rustled against my torso. I pushed a little farther, my toes skidding against the glass and my body stretching, and then let myself drop the last few feet.

The impact jarred my legs, but I'd felt worse. I shook them out and peered through the balcony's sliding door into the guestroom above the one my men and I had occupied for a short while just yesterday.

No one stirred inside. I jiggled the door handle and confirmed it was locked. Too bad I wasn't a shadowkind who could just slip through the shadows—although then I'd have been trapped by the silver and iron Rollick had built into the hotel anyway.

It was easier to take a lay of the land by daylight. Glancing along this side of the building, I saw there were two more balconies, each spaced just a few feet apart. I should be able to manage that jump. At least one of them was occupied, a towel draped over the railing to dry and a book left on a table next to a lounge chair. That didn't mean the door would be unlocked, but if the inhabitants were around, I could hope they'd let me through their room. Or at least give me an opening to make a run for it through the space to the door.

If none of them opened... I supposed I could find a way to descend to the next level of balconies. I didn't want to think about that yet.

The nervous adrenaline coursing through my veins pushed me onward. I scrambled onto the bars of the far side of the balcony railing, wishing that these ones had the same stucco wall as Rollick's private terrace for a broader base, and studied the gap I had to cross.

No looking down. Looking down would only eat away at my courage.

I needed to be as light as possible for this leap. I took off my backpack and tossed it across ahead of me. The ease of the throw and the soft thump of it hitting the floor on the next balcony soothed my nerves a little.

With my hand against the hotel wall for balance, I braced my feet on the top bar, crouched with leg muscles coiled, and sprang.

I knew better than to try to hurl myself right onto the balcony. Instead, I only aimed to catch the opposite railing. I flung my arms over it as my chest smacked into it and simply clung there for a few seconds, catching my breath and recovering from the impact. That probably hadn't been great for my heart.

But Rollick was a hell of a lot worse for it.

Gritting my teeth, I hefted myself over the railing and checked the next room. No sign of the guests staying there; no response when I tapped on the glass. That door was locked too. Shit.

One more to try on this level before I had to worry about my journey getting even more complicated. If the next door was locked too, I could always smash the glass and get in that way, right? If I could manage to hit the pane hard enough—they'd be made of tough stuff. And that might set off an alarm...

I pushed those worries aside to focus on simply getting over to the last balcony. First, toss the backpack over. Then, clamber up on the railing. Prepare and leap—

It should have worked as easily as the first time. But I hadn't realized that whoever was staying in the last suite had gotten the railing wet, maybe with a hanging bathing suit they'd since taken inside. My arms slammed over the top of the railing—and slid on the layer of water before I could get a proper hold.

I groped out at the railing as I started to plummet. My fingers snagged around a vertical bar, but they were pulled down by the weight of my falling body, and an instant later they smacked into the base of the railing. The impact broke my hold.

My heart lurching to my throat, I clawed at the wall beside me—and grasped a decorative hook where maybe hanging flowerpots were sometimes displayed. I managed to scrape my feet against the wall enough to slow my fall, clinging on to the hook as tightly as I could. The thing was only as wide as my hand. My palm was already aching, the metal edges digging into my skin.

I slapped one hand on top of the other, leaning against the hotel wall as well as I could while dangling and fighting through my panic. I was maybe three feet below the balcony I'd been aiming for—there was no way I'd be able to reach my arm high enough to pull myself back up there.

Back to where I'd left my bag. My phone, my pills, all my things—

I squeezed my eyes shut, doing my best to tune out those frantic thoughts and the pain spreading through my arms and shoulders. None of that mattered if I ended up flat as a pancake on the ground below.

I cast my gaze downward for the first time, my gut flipping with dizziness at the sight of the several floors below. Then I realized something even more horrifying.

The suite I was dangling next to didn't have an outdoor area at all, only a row of tall glossy windows. The one at my other side had a small balcony, but it was farther off to my right, the top of it level with my knees right now. If I tried to swing in that direction, I was afraid the remaining strength in my hands might give out.

And even if I could land my feet on the railing, that wouldn't do me much good. I needed to hook a limb right over it to be sure of catching myself when I let go. I wasn't sure I was tall enough to manage that.

Tears started to burn behind my eyes, as much from fear as the pain creeping steadily deeper into my hands and arms. I swallowed thickly, scrambling for a solution.

And then the sound of screeching metal brought my head jerking up.

Rollick was crouched on the balcony I'd tried to jump to. He was in human form, but he'd exerted his demon strength to wrench the bars aside so he could lean down toward me. Somehow he was still fucking smiling.

"Looks like you got yourself into a bit of a jam, my stubborn sorcerer," he said, extending his arm. His hand reached to just a few inches above my own where they were locked around the hook. "It's a good thing I noticed you were missing and came looking. Grab hold, and I'll pull you up."

I stared up into his smiling movie-star-handsome face, and something in me recoiled. A chill washed through my whole body, sharper than my panic over the fall beneath me.

No. I couldn't put myself back under his power. Couldn't let him cage me up again with even less hope of escape now that he knew how far I'd go.

I might as well be dead if I let him control my life. I might be *worse* than dead.

Maybe it would be better to just let go. A few seconds of horror, and then it'd all be over, painful but immediate. No more monsters chasing me down or trying to use me. No more worrying about how the strange power in me might lead to the people I cared about being hurt—might even force *me* to hurt them.

I could leave it all behind me, just like that. How many years had I really had left anyway?

Rollick's smile faltered when I didn't immediately take his hand. His forehead furrowed, and he pushed himself closer. His fingertips brushed my knuckles.

I almost let go right then. My fingers started to loosen. But an answering surge of emotion, even more defiant than my initial revulsion, rushed through me.

I wanted to live. That was all I'd ever wanted—to squeeze all the time out of this world that it would give me. As long as I was alive, there was a chance to get out of this mess, no matter how small it was.

I couldn't quite convince myself to give up that hope completely, no matter how miniscule it was.

A sob caught in my throat. I glanced over at the balcony that was just a little too far away again, not that I could have escaped Rollick by that route now that he'd found me regardless. Then, with a tearing sensation searing through my abdomen, I thrust one hand upward to clasp Rollick's arm.

CHAPTER SEVENTEEN

Rollick

Quinn hadn't spoken since I'd brought her back to my suite. She'd barely *moved.* She'd sunk into what appeared to be her favorite armchair and had been simply sitting there for the past half an hour, her arms wrapped loosely around her knees, which she'd folded up to her chest. Her gaze stared aimlessly across the room.

I'd brought her a glass of water in case she needed hydration after the shock of her near-death, but she hadn't touched it. She'd taken no notice of the backpack I'd retrieved and set near the base of the chair.

I'd lounged on the sofa near her for a little while in case she decided to talk and then wandered around the suite, hoping her tongue might loosen if I gave her some space. I couldn't quite convince myself to leave. It'd been when I'd left last time that she'd set off on her desperate scramble around the hotel.

She *had* nearly died. If I'd tracked her down a minute later... I couldn't remember the last time I'd felt alarm like the icy jolt of fear that'd stabbed through me the moment her grasp on the railing had slipped—or the wave of relief that had flooded me when I'd determined I could get to her in time.

But it hadn't been enough. There'd been a moment when she'd seriously contemplated letting go rather than taking my helping hand. I'd seen it written in her expression, reverberating through her hesitation when I'd reached out to her. I wouldn't have been able to catch her then. For all my demonic powers, I had no ability to fly.

Some part of her, a large enough part to override all mortals' instinctive drive toward self-preservation, believed death might be a better option than returning with me.

It didn't make sense, and my uncertainty gnawed at me. I'd thought I'd known what we were playing at between us. She'd taken on the role of defiant but tempted captive, and I'd been the seductive jailor, and we'd been cruising along toward our inevitable collision.

We'd bantered. I'd seen desire light in her eyes. She hadn't *seemed* scared. I knew what scared looked like.

At least, I'd thought I did. There was something painfully broken in the slump of her shoulders now, something I'd had no idea she was hiding underneath that tartly rebellious exterior.

After another few minutes passed without her stirring, I returned to the sofa. Her gaze didn't move to me as I settled onto the cushions. I gave her a moment to begin the conversation and decided I'd better take the first step if I wanted any to happen at all.

"It's become clear to me that my understanding of the situation we've found ourselves in is flawed," I said, keeping my voice smooth but serious. I was reasonably sure that she wasn't in the mood to be cajoled with jokes or charm. "It wouldn't have occurred to me that you'd go to the lengths you just did to escape what I thought I'd made clear was a safe haven. Has your time in my home been that awful? What do you need that I'm not offering?"

Quinn's attention shifted to me slowly, but the disbelief etched on her features sent an uncomfortable twist through my gut. I wasn't used to feeling this off-balance with any other being, let alone a mortal, and I didn't enjoy it at all.

"Do you really think this is about whether the suite is properly luxurious or the meals tasty enough?" she said, her voice raw but steady. "You've made it clear that you've got some purpose in mind for me that you won't tell me about. The only things I know for sure are that you're determined to make me use a power that I hate even having, and there was a point when you wanted to murder me and eat my heart, if you're not *still* considering that. That's not even getting into..."

She trailed off with a shiver, but I was stuck on her initial point anyway. I knit my brow. "When have I ever indicated that I was interested in seeing you dead? Let alone snacking on your innards? I know the fiends after you have been devouring sorcerers, but—"

Quinn's eyes narrowed as she interrupted. "You told Torrent that *you* wanted to devour me, didn't you? He and the others—all three of them are sure that's what you originally meant to do. And you seemed awfully hesitant to explain what you *did* want with me when you first came to take me off their hands."

The twisting sensation inside me pulled tighter. Ah. I hadn't quite thought—but yes, I could see how I could have made a miscalculation there. Mainly in that I'd failed to consider how much information my associates would have shared with her. It was hard to think of their connection being more than carnal even after the evidence I'd seen, but I knew there was more going on there. I should have taken their closeness properly into account, as strange as it was.

I hesitated, debating my options. She might not believe me no matter what I said. But all my wry remarks and shows of power before hadn't swayed her, so a different tactic was in order. What did it matter if I was a little more honest with this mortal than I generally was with anyone? She could hardly ruin my reputation.

I leaned forward, clasping my hands in front of me. "Quinn, I never had any intention of killing you. I've always very specifically wanted you *alive*. I sent those three mutinists out to Florida specifically to make sure you stayed that way. What I said to Torrent— The less anyone knows about my exact plans before I've carried them out, the better. It was the simplest explanation, and not one I expected him to have any concerns about."

"You didn't have any problem even with pretending you were going to 'snack' on me?"

I grimaced. "I'm a brutal, incredibly powerful demon who rules over my empire with an iron fist. Haven't you heard? If I want to make sure that people fall in line with a minimum of additional brutality, which honestly is pretty tiresome most of the time, it's best if I play into that perception rather than away from it."

Quinn lowered her legs so she could fold her arms over her chest instead, but I could tell she was paying attention, evaluating what I'd said. "Why would a brutal, incredibly powerful demon with an iron fist care so much about keeping a random human alive?"

I shot her a baleful glance. "You know you're not just a random human. You're something more valuable even than the sorcerers who brought your donor into this world, and you're worth much more than whatever minor power could be transferred by consuming your heart. As I suspect our opponents have figured out as well."

Her forehead furrowed. "Torrent mentioned that an actual sorcerer would have more power than they get from consuming the organs. Is that what you mean?"

"It's not just that. You have access to a sorcerer's powers," I said, motioning toward her. "A sorcerer with a long heritage of that power, compounded across generations. But *you* weren't raised as a sorcerer. You weren't taught techniques for shutting out shadowkind influence. You haven't learned to despise us or to see us as nothing but tools. Which makes you the perfect combination of powerful and vulnerable. You could become a tool for shadowkind, if you could be convinced to use those powers on our behalf."

Quinn studied me for a long moment. "That's what *you* want me for too. So I can be your tool. So I can enslave shadowkind for you?"

"No." I laughed, even though she wasn't totally wrong about the tool part. "I have no interest in collecting slaves. I *do* have an interest in ensuring that no idiotic ancient shadowkind go off on some crusade that'll ultimately serve only to their benefit and screw over the rest of us. There's clearly something brewing. And you're the only being I know who might be able to stop them if it gets to that point. We're definitely screwed if they get their hands on you."

Her jaw tightened. "I wouldn't do anything for those beasts."

"You probably wouldn't have a choice," I said gently. "They'll have beings on their side like that siren who took all of two seconds to cajole you into taking off your shirt. They'd enslave you into being their slaver."

As I might have done, if I hadn't wanted to keep my interest in her secret. If I hadn't had faith in my own ability to win her over by other means. I'd thought I could simply flatter and seduce her until she wanted to appease me—yes, that task had been made harder by her entanglement with my associates, but in a way her affections had also made things easier, since I could use them as motivation too.

But it wasn't going to be enough. I could see that now. Maybe the suspicion had been creeping over me for days, and I hadn't wanted to accept it.

I wasn't going to delude her into going along with my goals. Wasn't going to cloud her mind with passion to the point that she'd do whatever I wanted as long as I took care of those needs. She didn't have an ingrained revulsion toward shadowkind, but she was sharp enough to stay wary no matter what desires stirred in her body. Stubborn enough to stand firm no matter what was at stake.

To see even losing her life as a viable option if it gave her the freedom she craved.

It was becoming increasingly clear to me how three of my most trusted and reliable men might have become so enraptured with her when they'd never strayed before. There was definitely something to her that most mortals didn't possess.

Quinn swiped at her eyes. She hesitated for a stretch before meeting my eyes again. "I don't want to be a tool—for them or for you. I don't want to be in this war, if that's what it's turning into, at all. I just want to go back to my life, however much of it I still have."

My mouth tightened with genuine sympathy. I could hear in her voice how exhausted she was from the unexpected trials she'd been put through, but I couldn't give her a more reassuring answer.

"I don't think you have a choice," I said. "And I'm not only saying that because I'm concerned about what will happen to me and my domain if you don't stand against these pricks. I suspect you won't like where they're going with their schemes either."

"How so?"

I shrugged. "Maybe they'll amass some more power and simply go back and mess around in the shadow realm… but I think that's unlikely. Whatever they have planned, it's probably going to affect the mortal realm too. Even if I could figure out a way for you to keep up your old life without them discovering you, which I can't see doing regardless, this is going to affect you whether you like it or not. It's better if we deal with them sooner rather than later."

Or we might not be able to deal with them at all, even if she was fully committed.

I straightened my stance and decided I could offer a smile now without it rubbing her the wrong way. "I can promise you this much: I'm not going to force you to use your magic against your will. And not out of the kindness of my heart, but because I doubt you'd be able to reach your full potential without your will being totally behind the cause anyway. I *will* keep reminding you of why it's important, and I'm not going to let you go running off to your doom. If that's irritating, well..." I spread my hands. "I'll attempt to be entertaining enough that you don't mind too much."

Quinn wrinkled her nose at me, but I thought her posture had relaxed a little. She seemed to believe me.

The fresh relief that spread through me at that thought was unnerving. As if it didn't only matter to me that she believed me for my own objectives but because having her distrust me *bothered* me in some ridiculous way.

Why should she trust me? I was a demon, a monster. I'd played the villain enough times.

I needed to get a handle on this game again. Put myself firmly in control, ensure she was devoted to me or at least dependent on me. That was the only way I could ensure I protected everything that really mattered.

"Truce?" I said, adding a seductive lilt to my voice.

Quinn exhaled slowly. Then she tipped her head in a hesitant nod that opened all the doors I needed.

"For now," she said.

Not a problem. I could take that and spin it into forever now that I'd gotten this potential disaster back on course.

CHAPTER EIGHTEEN

Quinn

My ninth morning at the Sunshine Sin Hotel, I choked down my breakfast with nerves on edge, braced for Rollick's arrival. He'd given me the rest of yesterday to recover from my escape attempt, but he'd taken precautions. When I'd tried to step onto the terrace just to get some fresh air in the afternoon, I'd found that both of the sliding doors were locked in some way I couldn't open.

I guessed I couldn't totally blame him for that when my last venture outside had nearly ended not only in my getting free of him but in my death as well.

I couldn't really rest easy in the suite, though. He'd said he had no interest in killing me, and he'd sounded like he meant it. But the expectations he did have for me weren't much better. I didn't want to be the key figure in some supernatural war. And no matter how he phrased it, he clearly did see me as a tool... or he'd have cared more about my feelings on the subject.

Whatever he'd said, I was a prisoner here. I was trapped both by what my unwelcome powers meant to the shadowkind and by Rollick's determination to use me to stand against them.

At least I had a better idea of the full situation and his intentions now. My escape attempt had gotten me that much, somehow or other.

When the demon finally did stroll into the suite—without knocking, like usual—I found his lack of concern for my privacy weirdly comforting. If he'd waited outside politely, I wasn't sure I'd have trusted that to be real concern anyway rather than a gambit to try to convince me that he was reformed from his previous habits. He still saw me and these rooms as totally his.

I didn't like it, but I knew where I stood.

He was carrying the same larger black box as yesterday, the one that presumably held a somewhat stronger shadowkind creature. I eyed it and then him as I got up from the chair where I'd been attempting to concentrate enough to work on a sketch. Rollick stopped on the other side of the sofa from me and arched an eyebrow as if inviting a comment.

Yeah, he was still the same arrogant jerk as he'd been before, even if he'd opened up a little more. Also still way too stunning to look at, but I could keep ignoring that. All I had to do was remember how he'd remarked on my supposedly private interlude with my men, and any heat that'd formed over my skin crawled away in disgust.

"Are you going to risk your upholstery or will I be allowed terrace access again?" I asked, keeping my voice dry even though my heart was thumping at an uneasy rhythm.

The corner of Rollick's mouth quirked up in a crooked smile. Maybe he was relieved that I had enough spirit left to hassle him about his security precautions.

"I thought, just for the one night, it was better to give you time to totally gather your thoughts," he said. "I don't want to restrict your movement any more than necessary to keep you safe, even if it's from yourself. But we do need to work together, which means a certain level of mutual trust is required. Are you willing to fully cooperate for the time being?"

"I won't run off like that again," I said, and meant it. I didn't for a second believe he was really going to give me the leeway to try. He'd probably set up additional security to prevent me from getting anywhere near that far across the building even once I could go out onto the terrace again.

It was better if he thought I trusted him, though. The more freedom he allowed me, the more space I had to figure out other plans.

"Then we have no problems," Rollick said with a wider smile. "Come on, I think you'll like this beastie. We won't do anything bloody today."

Not today, but maybe tomorrow, that remark implied. I sighed and followed him out.

Once I'd stepped into the bright sunlight, I couldn't help glancing around at the walls, checking for concealed devices. "Have you been recording me out here too? All over your suite?" In the bedroom? In the bathroom? I restrained a shudder.

Rollick paused, cocking his head as he studied me. "You're still very bothered about that one point, aren't you?"

I glowered at him. "You violated my privacy in a huge way. I didn't want to star in a porno for your enjoyment. And you were trying to use it against me, to manipulate me—of course that 'bothers' me."

The demon set down the carrier on the usual table and then walked over to lean back against the railing. The breeze ruffled his light brown hair. He looked unusually serious while he pondered his answer.

"I can see that," he said finally. "I thought we were playing a different game from what it turned out to be. And really, I shouldn't need to resort to deception to convince you of my charms. It was an ill-advised shortcut that I will not attempt again. I'm sorry."

My eyebrows rose with automatic skepticism. "Are you really?"

His smile came back, sly around the edges. "I'm not going to get down on my knees and beg for your forgiveness. That's not really my style. But yes, I'm sorry that I intruded where I wasn't welcome and upset you."

"Because now it's going to be harder to charm me."

He laughed and gave a brief shrug. "Sure, that's part of it. But I also don't like that it drove you to the point that you risked hurting yourself yesterday. And I'm not a sadist—I only enjoy tormenting beings that deserve it, which as far as I can tell you don't. I regret doing so inadvertently."

"For a millennia-old demon, you sure aren't well-versed on what things upset humans," I said with a grimace.

"Oh, you might be surprised by how many mortals get off on voyeurism. But like I said, I thought we were engaged in a different sort of game. Absolutely my fault." He glanced toward the suite. "As for the rooms here, there are plenty of things I don't want there to be any concrete record of *me* doing. And I have better things to do than spy on your every movement or peep at your body. If I want to see a naked woman, there are plenty who are happy to show off right in front of me downstairs."

"So reassuring," I muttered. I didn't know if he was telling the truth about all that, but he still hadn't shown any sign that he was aware of my scheming against him with the other men on the terrace, so maybe we were safe at least out here.

I paused and decided I might as well find out if I could push whatever leverage I'd gained yesterday a little farther.

"I want to see Torrent and Crag and Lance again," I said, fixing him with my steadiest stare. "Without them having to sneak up here or worry about how you'll react. If you want me cooperating, it'll help a lot if I can actually spend time on a regular basis with the shadowkind I *do* totally trust."

I thought Rollick's jaw tightened just slightly, though he didn't let his smile falter. "You won't have the opportunity to make use of the guestroom next door again."

"I don't care about that. I don't only enjoy their company for hooking up, you know. It'd give me someone to at least *talk* to now that you've cut me off from all the rest of society."

"My conversational skills are so lacking?"

I rolled my eyes. "Other than the fact that you're not even here for most of the day—not that I'm suggesting you should stop by more often—I'd *rather* talk to them. Sorry if your ego is so fragile that you're offended by that fact."

Rollick blinked at me and then tipped his head back with a laugh of pure amusement. "Well, when you put it that way, I really can't deny you, can I? They *are* quite busy with discovering all we can about your real enemies, a mission I'd imagine you wouldn't want to interrupt—they'd have been sneaking in more often if they'd had the chance, no doubt. But the next time they have a break, I'll let them know there'll be no punishment for coming up here for a visit." He tsked his tongue teasingly at me. "Just don't do anything I wouldn't do."

I couldn't help snorting. "Somehow I have a feeling that doesn't cover very much."

"You wouldn't be wrong." The demon was outright grinning now, so I guessed the request hadn't bothered him too much. He motioned to the carrier. "Can we begin, or do you have more demands to make, my stubborn sorcerer?"

Stop calling me yours, I thought, but I kept my mouth shut on that one. I could choose my battles for now, and somehow I suspected he'd laugh harder at that request. "Bring it out."

When he opened the door to the carrier, this creature emerged of its own accord, slinking from the brightly lit space and cringing at the sunlight outside. It was an oddly spindly thing, nearly skeletal in the vague shape of a wiener dog, with wings protruding from its back that were covered in flesh so gauzy it might have been made out of spun spider webs. It glanced at me and bared a mouth full of piranha-like teeth.

Okay, I definitely didn't want to get too close to that one.

"What do you want me to do with it?" I asked doubtfully.

Rollick tapped a finger against his lips. "Let's start with a sprint around the terrace. Give it a good warm-up."

I dragged in a breath and focused on the small beast the way I'd been learning to do. Part of my concentration roused the wavering energy in my chest. My pulse beat faster, one of those unnerving wobbles rippling through it.

I pictured the creature darting around the edge of the terrace, focusing on the idea of it staying clear of me while it did, which I definitely wanted. And in that way I still didn't understand, a surge of energy pushed a burst of sound from my lips.

The creature leapt forward. It jumped off the table and dashed past me toward the far end of the terrace. I spun to follow its course, and weirdly... *felt* as much as saw when my control started to slip.

As it reached the far wall, its muscles coiled to spring right over the railing into the shadows farther along the building. But I knew that less because of observing its odd anatomy and more because a hint of the impulse flickered through me: to flee, to get away.

Or maybe I was only imagining that from my observations because it matched my own urges so well. I opened my mouth, knowing I needed to rein it in and having no idea how—but my sorcerer instincts kicked in again of their own accord.

The magic crackled up from my chest and over my tongue. I barked a command, and the thing swiveled in mid-spring. It darted around the side of the terrace by the suite windows without missing another beat. Then it stopped and huddled under the table where it'd started. The edges of its body hazed, but when Rollick crouched next to it with what must have been an implicit threat, it flinched and resolidified.

He looked up at me from that vantage point, grinning. "That was a nice catch. You're adapting well on the spot."

Only I had no clue how or why… I didn't understand *any* of this still. Cool nausea clamped around my gut again. How was I supposed to be the deciding force in a battle when I couldn't really control my own powers or predict how they'd present themselves? I *would* be just a tool if all I did was follow Rollick's commands by rote.

Not to mention…

"It wouldn't have worked if I couldn't see it to know I needed to adapt," I said. "My magic wasn't controlling it completely. And it's just a little lesser creature, not the powerful higher shadowkind you think we're up against."

"Patience," Rollick said. "You've made major strides in just a few days. Usually with these sorts of things, once you've grasped the basics, the rest comes much more quickly."

He couldn't know that for sure, though. He'd just been telling me yesterday how rare I was.

I paused and met his gaze. "Why are you relying on *me*? You're a super powerful demon, as you like to remind everyone around you as often as possible. If you're so worried about these assholes, why don't you just crush them before they can carry out their plans?"

"We don't know who we're up against yet," Rollick reminded me. "It is possible they could prove a real challenge to me on my own, although I'm flattered by your faith in me." When I wrinkled my nose at the assumed compliment, he laughed and went on. "I think I might have mentioned before that I like to be thorough in my preparations. It's better if you're ready if we need you, don't you think?"

"Sure," I said, but I doubted that was the main reason. He'd also mentioned more than once that he didn't like to draw attention to himself by interfering with other shadowkind or even sorcerers. He probably just wanted to hang back in the shadows and not take any of the heat, even if tackling these villains directly would have been much simpler and easier for the rest of us.

As I turned my attention back to the creature under the table, anticipating the demon's next instructions, a renewed sense of resolve eased my earlier edginess. Rollick might not *want* to deal with the other shadowkind head on, but if I got my way, he wasn't going to have a choice. This was his fight, his game, and so he ought to be the one playing it.

CHAPTER NINETEEN

Torrent

I'd have been happier about Rollick's declaration that I could use my free time to drop in on Quinn if he hadn't made it with a slyly suggestive gleam in his eyes.

"She did seem *very* eager to have your company," he said as he ambled around his office, in a tone that somehow conjured all kinds of illicit imagery without him saying a single actually provocative word.

I didn't show any outward reaction to his teasing from where I was standing near the door. "I'm sure it puts her more at ease when she can spend time with us, since we're the only shadowkind who've completely had her back."

Rollick paused and arched his eyebrows at me. "Implying I don't. I've made my peace with her. In case you weren't clear on this either, I never had any intention of literally devouring her."

"I'm glad to hear that," I said dryly. He had his own motivations, though—motivations we both knew were to further his interests, not Quinn's. In the back of my head, I could still hear the way he'd talked about her when he'd come to retrieve her from us in Florida, like she was an inanimate trinket we'd stolen for him. The memory made me tense up inside along with a jab of guilt that I'd let *myself* think of her as nothing but a possession for so long.

Was I that much better than the demon in front of me? Well, I *had* adjusted my mindset eventually. I'd made up my failings to Quinn in every way I could since then. It seemed to be enough for her.

"You've always been so focused on the work," Rollick went on in a casual tone. "I'm surprised to see you getting so caught up in a bit of... leisure, should we call it? If you were craving more time to indulge with the mortals, you only needed to ask. I've got a hotel full of them."

My gut twisted for a second. I *had* craved it, and I'd stuffed down those cravings because I'd known as well as Rollick must that there'd been no way I could "indulge" in the same way I'd used to in my current physical state. I couldn't appear in the middle of the club with my impossibly collapsed cheek and tentacles showing and sweep some woman off her feet.

But what I'd found with Quinn wasn't like that at all. It didn't feel like an indulgence. It felt... like a calling, like a mission I'd been meant for far more than any of the jobs I'd carried out for Rollick, as much as I'd appreciated his faith in my abilities.

"I know," I said simply. "You've always provided whatever I needed. I'm sorry our goals ended up putting us at odds." And I meant that.

Rollick nodded. "I am too. I never doubted that I could count on you before, and I thought our partnership was important to you. I'm aware that you had troubles because of your recreational activities in the past... I hope you know what you're doing here. Even if I wasn't exactly pleased about the mutiny, I wouldn't like to see you going astray."

When he'd first took me on, I'd told Rollick an abbreviated version of the history I'd recently shared with Quinn. It'd been reasonable for him to ask, since if there were any continuing grudges against me, that would affect him too. He'd never held my past carelessness against me, and the concern he expressed now sent an uncomfortable prickle over my skin.

Maybe it made sense for him to be concerned. He was only outside looking in on our strange relationship, and for most shadowkind, this sort of association with a mortal would have been more about getting off than anything else. Had I let my growing affection for Quinn distract me in ways that could get me—or her, or my squad—into trouble?

I couldn't think of any, but the implications lingered even when I tried to shake off his words. "I appreciate that," I said. "As well as your leniency as far as the mutiny went."

Rollick shrugged, the corner of his lips quirking upward. "Good help is hard to find. You're still the best lieutenant I've got in many of the ways that count most."

One of which was the fact that no one knew I worked for him, so I could investigate these other powerful shadowkind without them targeting him. Somehow I doubted he'd have the same confidence in me if he knew the full extent of the discussions I'd been having with Quinn.

Discussions we were going to continue now.

I made myself look at my boss—really look at him, both the shiny human-like guise and the demon I could sense lurking within. He was striding forward as he always had, bolstering his power, protecting his empire. I couldn't blame him for that. Just as he shouldn't really blame me when I made whatever moves I needed to in order to defend what mattered to me.

A prickle of discomfort was spreading through my calves. I shifted my tentacles against the floor, looking forward to the reprieve of diving back into the shadows. "I do my best. Thank you for your trust." Even if I was going to betray it again.

It was a short trip down through the gloomy innards of the building to Rollick's personal suite one floor below. There was something to be said for being able to simply step out of the shadows right next to where Quinn was already lounging in the living room rather than needing to go through the song-and-dance of pretending to be the wind tapping on the windows.

Lance and Crag had already arrived. Lance had plopped himself down on one of the armchairs and collected Quinn on his lap, where she was laughing as he gave an account of his exploits that was ending with, "...and that was the last time they ever sold balloons at that zoo." The gargoyle, leaning against the entertainment unit a few feet away, gave a grunt that seemed to dismiss the story as frivolous. They all looked up as I emerged.

"The boss gave you a free pass too," Lance observed with a grin. "I'm starting to think our mortal is even more tricksy than he is."

Quinn snorted. "I'm working on it." She gave him a peck on his cheek —which he answered with a pleased growl and a nip of her neck—and then got up to wrap me in a hug. "It's good to see you."

Something about the press of her arms around me suggested that she needed this embrace more than her breezy words implied. I hugged her back, a mix of worry and anger rising in me as I wondered what had happened to her in the past couple of days to shake her up. There was a slight catch to her breath, a tiny tremor that ran through her limbs that I only picked up thanks to the sensitivity of my suction cups, that spoke of a vulnerability I hadn't sensed in her the last time we'd spoken.

"Are you all right?" I asked quietly, letting my lips brush her hair and inhaling the freshly sweet scent of her.

"Yeah. Pretty much. I mean, it's not the greatest situation still, right." She eased back and seemed to gather herself. "There are some things I'd like to talk about. Maybe we should go out on the terrace. Rollick said he doesn't have cameras in here, but the only place I'm pretty much sure of is outside. For more private matters."

I tipped my head toward the wall. "We can't make use of any of the nearby guestrooms today, unfortunately. Someone's checked in—"

"We couldn't anyway," Quinn broke in with a grimace. "He—he set us up. He recorded everything that happened in there."

Oh. *Oh.* Fury seared through me so abruptly and forcefully my vision briefly hazed red. My jaw clenched. Rollick had given no indication of it when we'd spoken... Well, why would he? I doubted he wanted to chat with me about what he'd witnessed if he'd decided to dismiss our flouting of his unstated rules.

It shouldn't have surprised me. I'd even thought to check for recording devices—I just hadn't done a thorough enough job of it, obviously. I hadn't managed to protect Quinn in that most basic way—he'd watched her, maybe even enjoyed seeing her pleasure when it hadn't been meant for him at all...

Quinn grasped my arm, bringing me back to the present. Lance had sprung off the chair with a snarl; Crag had marched forward to grip Quinn's shoulder, his gaze searching the room.

Our woman glanced around at all of us. "I'm okay. He and I... hashed it out, as well as it could be hashed out. I'm not happy about it, but it's already happened, and... and if everything works the way we hope it will, then soon it won't matter. So don't go rushing off to defend my honor or anything. I'd rather you were here with me."

"I should skewer him," Lance muttered, waving his claws through the air. "Turn him into a demon shish kabob."

"Easier said than done," I replied, understanding Quinn's request. We wouldn't gain anything by taking Rollick to task for it, not anything that would help her. We might very well end up shish kabobs ourselves. "Come on, let's go get some fresh air. And I'll make a particularly careful sweep of the terrace before we talk further."

It felt strange, stepping out into the warm mid-morning brightness outside. I didn't normally take on physical form outside in a setting like this by daylight. A burst of laughter carried up from the beach far below; faint strains of animated chatter filtered from the rooftop lounge. But no one could see me and my monstrousness in our current perch.

I made good on my promise, scanning every part of the terrace and its furnishings with both my eyes and my tentacles. When I was satisfied that even Rollick couldn't have concealed a device anywhere nearby, I sank down onto one of the loungers to rest my now-aching legs.

Lance paced around the terrace, leaping into a handspring with his usual agility but an energy that was more restless uneasiness than his usual buoyant spirits.

"What do we do now?" he said. "Less than two days before the deal ends and Rollick gets to make more demands. What is he going to want next?"

"Everything we find out about our enemies makes it clear how much of a menace they are," Crag rumbled. "I don't think we'll be able to destroy them quickly."

Quinn sat down on the chair next to mine and reached out her hand to rest it on one of my tentacles as easily as if she'd been taking my hand. I wasn't sure when I'd get used to her easy affection toward every part of me.

"Not if we're trying to do it using Rollick's subtle methods," she said. "I think we need to put the plan we talked about before into action. The morning when the ten days will be fully up—a little less than forty-eight hours from now. Let them deal with each other."

She spoke with a firmness she hadn't shown before. Her recent interactions with the demon had obviously solidified her resolve. I felt no desire to disagree with her after what she'd just revealed about him.

I pushed myself up straighter, letting my tentacle loop around her arm. "We still need to balance the factors carefully."

Quinn nodded. "I've been thinking about that. I have a couple of things I can 'hide' in the apartment that will show that I've been there, and

I think I know where to put them that Rollick won't notice them ahead of time. And once we've delivered the message, you can keep watch and recognize when the other shadowkind are acting on it. If you 'warn' him just a little before they get here, we'll have time for him to approve of a plan to get me to a different safe spot and gather his defenses, but not enough time for him to head them off completely."

"Then they smash each other!" Lance said, his eyes brightening as he smacked one fist into the other palm.

My chest constricted. "We can't cut it too close. If they catch one glimpse of you leaving—or if Rollick's no longer bound by the deal and decides it's safer to simply remove you more permanently—"

Quinn gave me a reassuring squeeze. "It'll be better if it's earlier in the morning anyway, before it's at all light out, when there aren't any people around. Crag can offer to fly me to wherever we'll be going—that'll be the obvious strategy anyway. And by the time Rollick is finished dealing with the rest of them, we'll have vanished."

She glanced at me. "Can you find someplace where we'll be able to get by at least until we take stock of how the clash turned out? I'll wear my vest the whole time, so we don't have to worry about anyone tracking me from my sorcerer energies."

She was putting so much trust in me—in all of us—to pull this plan off. For a second, my throat closed up.

There wasn't anything to be ashamed of in the devotion that'd kindled in me, more with every moment I spent with her. She'd earned it far more than Rollick ever had. Let him deal with the consequences of the conflict he'd gotten himself wrapped up in, not her. That was justice, not indulgence.

"I can manage that in the time we have," I said. "But—what you really wanted was to get back to your parents and your studies..."

Quinn's mouth tightened, but she held her chin steady. "I did, but if that needs to wait so that we're all safe and the people back home are too, then that's how it needs to be. I'll be one step closer to being really free. I can't complain about that."

Well, she could. She just wouldn't, not with that fierce stubbornness to survive that'd already kept her going so long.

I couldn't resist tugging her to me, slipping my arms around her again. Quinn tipped her head against my shoulder, melting into my embrace.

"He's going to be even more mad at the three of you," she murmured. "You were lucky he mostly forgave you the first time..."

I cut her off before she could follow that train of thought any farther. "Let him be angry, then. I'd rather deal with that than see him keep you on a leash."

Crag let out a thrumming sound of agreement, and Lance hissed through his vicious grin.

We were really going to do this. We were going to screw over one of the most powerful shadowkind in the realms in epic fashion...

And I didn't feel the slightest doubt about my decision, not while I held this strange and wonderful mortal woman in my arms.

CHAPTER TWENTY

Quinn

I was examining the frame of the bed when the rasp of footsteps in the living room reached my ears. I leapt to my feet, my pulse stuttering, abruptly overwhelmed with gratitude for my past self's wisdom in keeping the bedroom door shut so my visitor couldn't have seen me in that odd pose.

I opened the door to find Rollick on the other side, about to reach for the handle. He didn't look at all startled by my abrupt appearance, stepping forward to glance past me into the room with an upbeat but oddly intense air. "Do you still have the wig and the dress I had you wear for your arrival?"

My pulse hiccupped to even greater effect. "Of course," I said. "Why? Do I need to leave?" Had the plans we'd made been thrown off just a day before we'd meant to carry them out?

But Rollick took in my reaction and smiled in his annoyingly charming way. "Don't panic. You wanted to see more of the hotel. I might not be able to offer you a view of your parents anymore, but I'm giving you the chance to stretch your legs, so to speak. In a less precarious way than previously."

I blinked at him, taking a moment to process the words. "You're letting me go out into the rest of the hotel? But—"

He raised a hand dismissively. "I know what I said. I have a very good memory. That's why we're having you put on your fancy vest with the dress to hide it, and the wig to disguise your looks even more. And we'll stick to parts where you won't be available for close inspection, at least to begin with."

Why was he offering this gesture *now*? My heart thumped faster again, but this time it was more in anticipation than fear. I might get the chance to learn something that would strengthen our plans or help us stay ahead of the demon if he gave chase afterward. No way could I pass up the opportunity.

"All right," I said, managing to smile back. "Thank you." I grasped the door handle and looked at his position right on the threshold. "I'm going to close the door before I get changed. Just because you got a show without my knowing about it doesn't mean I want to do a repeat performance."

A bit of an edge crept into my voice with those words, but Rollick took it in stride with a chuckle. "Your maidenly honor is perfectly safe," he said, and turned on his heel.

As I pushed the door shut and turned to riffle through the wardrobe to figure out where I'd stuffed my previous disguise, Rollick started to hum a jaunty little tune to himself. At first, I thought he was trying to irritate me. Then a thought occurred to me that was startling enough that I froze in place.

He was making noise so I'd know for sure he was out there and not spying on me from the shadows in here. I hadn't really thought he would, but it'd been important enough to him to confirm it for me all the same.

I didn't know how to feel about that consideration.

Well, I'd known he *could* be considerate, or at least act like it, when he wanted something. He was still trying to win me over like he had been all along. He'd just learned more about what tactics I'd appreciate.

I couldn't trust a single thing the demon did, not really.

Finally I dug out the dress and wig from amid the heap of clothes Rollick kept in his bedroom for purposes I could only speculate on. There were women's and men's things, but I knew the shadowkind could conjure their clothes around their physical bodies as they took on concrete form. Mementos from past "guests"? Spare clothes in case those guests needed a change of outfit? Stale perfume clung to a few of the items, suggesting they'd been worn at some point.

I tugged on my silver-and-iron vest with a soft hiss of the beads and then layered the loose dress on top of it. Studying myself in the mirror, I adjusted it until I was sure it didn't reveal any odd bulges when I shifted my position. Then I pulled my hair into a quick braid so I could tuck it under the wig.

I'd left the makeup bag on the vanity, untouched since my arrival. I dabbed on some lipstick for good measure, deciding not to bother with the bronzer. It would probably look too obviously fake if I did end up passing close by anyone. I was no makeup genius.

When I emerged from the bedroom, Rollick stopped his ambling circuit of the room and his humming to look me over. I expected to cringe under his attention, but his gaze felt more assessing than leering. He gave a brisk nod of approval and motioned for me to join him.

"You should keep quiet unless I indicate that you should speak," he said as we headed out and up the stairs that led to his office level. "For your own safety. It's not likely we'll end up in a situation where we'll be chatted up anyway, but just in case."

"I get it." A nervous shiver rippled through me. As much as I wanted a better understanding of my luxurious cage, I couldn't help asking, "Are you sure this is a good idea?"

"I wouldn't be doing it if I wasn't," Rollick said smoothly. He shot me another smile. "You know, I didn't shut you away in my suite for any reason other than your own protection. I'd happily have given you free run of the hotel if I thought there wasn't a danger in it."

Yeah, I believed he would have. He'd have trusted that I wouldn't make a run for it because I'd have known how quickly he could track me down—and the consequences that I and the people I cared about might face for my defiance. My lungs tightened as I thought of my parents back in Florida—

No. If we escaped his clutches, if he had no idea where we were and was busy licking his wounds from a battle with my other enemies, threatening my parents wouldn't do him any good. And if I didn't get free before he arranged another deal, I might lose what little protection I'd already arranged, as well as my chance to escape.

We stepped onto the elevator, which whirred down to the second floor. It opened to a narrow hall where bass pounded through the walls. Rollick led me down the shadowy space to a door he unlocked with his thumbprint.

He slipped through the doorway first, paused, and gestured for me to follow. As I crossed the threshold, the music washed over me with a reverberation I could feel down to my bones.

We were in a room about the size of the bedroom upstairs, with a couple of small tables surrounded by sleek but cozy armchairs in the same wine-red as much of his other furniture. A window that filled the entire opposite wall let in multi-colored strobe lights and a view of the club beyond.

It wasn't that late, only around nine at night, but dancers already undulated throughout the space, both on the floor below us and on the second level of the club that stood across from Rollick's private, enclosed room. The strobe lights wavered over them, shifting to a green and blue that made their bobbing forms look as if they were rolling in the ocean surf. The boldest dancers—maybe they were trained professionals—gyrated on a low stage at the back of the room.

"Are all of these people staying at the hotel?" I asked, staring out at them.

Rollick came up beside me and shook his head. "Hotel guests get special benefits like a free drink, but the club area is open to the general public. It's quite popular. People line up for over an hour to get in. There've been catfights over the guest list."

I turned to face him. "Am I supposed to be impressed by that?"

"I suppose you wouldn't be." He swept his hand toward the hundreds of people enjoying the club. "It means something to all of them, though."

"So this is your grand achievement?" I asked, unable to restrain a note of skepticism. "You've spent millennia building up your power and influence so you could give people a place where they can party?"

The demon shot me a look that was both amused and baleful. Then he sank into an armchair that was just a couple of feet from the glass. He patted his knee. "They can see us too, if not in much detail. They should think you're 'entertaining' me if we want to keep up appearances. Come sit."

I balked. "Please tell me this isn't the real reason you wanted me to come down here. I'm going back to the suite—*alone*—if you're just looking to cop a feel."

Rollick laughed. "I promise I can keep my hands to myself. Just perch there; it won't kill you. I'd like to show you something—about the club, not anything perverse."

He sounded relaxed enough about the situation that I relaxed too. I didn't want anyone looking up and thinking Rollick had brought a woman around who was acting strangely. If suspicion somehow came down on him before we were ready, that could be disastrous.

Tentatively, I walked over and lowered myself onto his lap, trying not to look awkward about it while staying perched a few inches away from the rest of his well-built body. No way was I going to lean right into him like I was actually cuddling up with the demon.

Rollick let out a soft chuckle and set his hand on my waist to steady me. It stayed there, a mild warmth seeping through my clothing to match the warmth of his thigh beneath mine, and didn't venture anywhere more sensitive. Still, every nerve in my body was on edge.

"There," the demon said. "That isn't so horrible, is it? I can behave myself when I need to."

I ignored both him and the thrum of tension that had formed between my legs at the feel of him beneath me, focusing on the dancers beyond the window. My stance swayed a little with the rhythm of the music. "What is it you wanted to show me?"

"All work, no play." Rollick tsked teasingly at me, his thumb tracing a careful arc over my side. "Take a look at all those people out there. Notice anything unusual?"

I frowned and leaned forward, squinting through the uneven patches of light. At first, I had no idea what he was talking about. The dancers shimmied and swiveled in their club clothes—a little fancier than I typically saw at the club near the university that I occasionally popped into, but that was the only difference.

Then a few details here and there caught my eye. A guy near the platform adjusted the hat he'd left on, and I'd swear I caught a glimpse of a shape like a small horn above his ear. Another man deeper into the crowd twisted in a way that brought out the impression of small spikes down his spine pressing against his shirt just for an instant. And a woman near him spun with a flash of red in her eyes.

If I hadn't known the shadowkind existed, I might not have noticed those glimpses at all or would have assumed they were tricks of the light. But I did know now, and I also knew who this club belonged to.

"You have shadowkind patrons too," I said.

Rollick hummed in agreement. "It's hard for all of them to stay completely under the radar to someone alert. But if they can pass, they're welcome. Nearly half of the beings here tonight are shadowkind, like usual."

"*Half*?" I stared at the dancers again, picking out a few more figures who looked supernaturally attractive or graceful or whatever—though not so much that I'd have thought they were anything other than exceptional humans before. Others, I had no idea which might be mortal and which were simply pretending at it.

"Why do they all come here?" I asked. "I mean, I'm sure you're a great host and all, but they really care about dancing that much?"

"It's not just about the dancing." Rollick gazed past me out the window in a moment of unusually pensive contemplation. "You took a jab at me about what I've built over all this time. I've built places where the shadowkind who feel more at home in this realm than our own can enjoy everything it has to offer while knowing their interests will be protected, and I'll continue to build more every time the currents shift."

I cocked my head. "Do they really need protecting?"

"Does Torrent?" Rollick asked simply. "Or Lance, or Crag? You seem to think they do, and there are plenty of beings down there less capable than they are. I'm not going to deny that there's a tendency in us toward aggression and brutality. There's a reason mortals have labeled us monsters on the rare occasions they've stumbled on us. But plenty of us aren't interested in indulging in those urges unless forced to, and I keep those who'd want to hunt and exploit out so they can't bother anyone. I lay down rules so less experienced or... intelligent beings don't make any mistakes that'd come down on the rest of us."

He made it all sound so fair and even generous. The impression didn't sit totally right with me. "What about all the mortals down there? Who's protecting them?"

"Don't you worry about that," Rollick said with another stroke of his thumb. "I might not always have enormous respect for humankind, but I have nothing against them. Some of them are amusing or charming in their own ways." He tapped his fingers against my side as if to count me in that number. "They get to have a good time within the rules I've laid down too, no one harmed or disturbed. Unless they try to play predator themselves, in which case I think a little terror is good for them."

I couldn't say he was wrong. I glanced over my shoulder at him, my skin increasingly flushed from our closeness. "Why did you get started on this mission of yours?"

Something shuttered behind the demon's dark blue eyes. He gave me a lazy smile. "That's a long story and not particularly interesting. I just thought it might help you in arranging your priorities to know more about who you're working with. What I stand for. What I'm trying to preserve from idiots who think they can rearrange the structure of both the realms."

The mark he was leaving on society, whether most of us humans had any clue or not. The thought tugged at me in a way that hollowed out my stomach.

Maybe he *had* built something impressive, something admirable, whatever his reasons were for doing it. He'd gotten thousands of years to lay the groundwork, and he probably had thousands more to repeat his successes.

My own life felt as miniscule as a handful of sand, the grains currently slipping through my fingers too quickly for me to catch them.

A sudden melancholy swept over me, dulling the energetic beat of the music as completely as if someone had tossed a thick blanket over my head. My throat tightened. All at once I wanted to be anywhere but here. And definitely not with the company I currently had.

"All right," I said, with conscious effort to keep my voice even. "I've seen it. Can we go now? It's probably better if I'm not on display for very long anyway, right?"

If Rollick was bothered by my abrupt request, he didn't show it. He gave me a gentle nudge, and I stood, folding my arms over my chest and holding back from outright hugging myself. He set his hand on the small of my back to guide me out of the room, and I didn't argue. It was all for appearances anyway.

"There's one more thing I'd like you to see," he said as we walked down the hall to the elevator. "It won't put you on display at all."

"All right," I said, not wanting to make a big thing of my mood—not wanting to invite questions.

We got off at the top floor by his office, but instead of turning to the stairs that led to his private suite, Rollick ushered me in the other direction, to a different flight that went up. We stepped out into cooling night air onto a patio scattered with empty tables and a shadowed bar area beyond them.

"The rooftop lounge is closed for 'maintenance' tonight," Rollick said in a dry voice, and motioned me over to the wall at the opposite end of the bar. As I approached it, my heart somehow soared and plummeted at the same time.

The only view I'd gotten from the hotel before now was the vast stretch of the ocean. This was the city side.

Before me sprawled Los Angeles. Beneath the sprinkling of stars, the buildings glowed with vibrant colors: purples, blues, ambers, and here and there a gleam of hot pink. Cars wove between the buildings, casting the streams of their headlights in front of them. It was an immense urban jungle, but a gorgeous one.

My fingers curled around the railing at the top of the wall, clutching it tight. More pressure filled my throat and formed behind my eyes. I felt as if I were clinging on against nearly as stark a fall as I'd faced yesterday morning.

"I thought you'd appreciate seeing the city from up here," Rollick said, leaning against the railing a few feet away from me. "What with all your architectural interests. There aren't many vantage points as good as this."

He spoke casually with no hint that he saw the gesture as anything momentous, but his words broke a crack in the dam I'd been holding against my emotions. Before I could catch myself, a sob burst from my throat. I clapped my hand over my eyes as tears gushed out faster than I could blink them back.

Shit, shit, shit. I sucked in a shaky breath, swiping at my eyes, struggling to get control of myself. He must think I was pathetic. How could he possibly understand the fears I'd been grappling with most of my life, the sense of loss that was growing with every day that slipped through my fingers because of this stupid magic I'd never wanted inside me?

It would have been hard enough to make my own mark on the world before my time was up and my heart gave out even before the latent sorcerer powers had kicked in. Now... now I had no idea if I'd ever finish another project for class, let alone see one of the breathtaking skyscrapers I'd imagined brought to life.

Every time I tried to steady myself, another wave of anguish rocked me.

I gulped and sniffled, turning away so at least the demon wouldn't get to witness me falling apart—but then Rollick's hand was on my shoulder, light but solid, easing me back around toward him.

"Hey," he said, sounding a little bewildered but not at all mocking. "I didn't mean to upset you."

"It's not— You weren't—" I couldn't quite choke out the words to form any kind of explanation. "I'll be fine." Couldn't he just bring me back to the suite and be done with it?

Apparently not. He leaned closer and wiped a tear I'd missed from my cheek with his thumb, his expression almost inquisitive, as if I was displaying a rare phenomenon he'd never witnessed before. "You're not fine right now. What can I do for you?"

He could give me my life back. He could make everything go back to normal. Except he couldn't actually do either of those things. He couldn't do anything at all—he wouldn't even if he could—*he* was part of the problem.

I shook my head, still struggling to get a grip on myself. The flood of tears had slowed, but they were seeping out in a trickle, my breath hitching.

Rollick gave a thoughtful hum and glanced past me toward the view. "It's a very sad thing if you like *Jacksonville* so much that the City of Angels disappoints you."

The remark was so wry and ridiculous that a laugh tumbled through the gloom that'd been wrapped around me. I sputtered something not quite a giggle or a sob and found I could take my next breath without it catching in my throat. "As always, you think very highly of everything to do with you."

"Only because I have ample evidence that it's deserved," Rollick replied with total assurance, a subtle smile returning. "But I suppose we all have our own tastes, as wrong as some of those might be."

I managed to glower at him, and he shot a full grin back at me, and suddenly my balance felt steadier again. I didn't exactly feel *good*, but I wasn't on the verge of a total breakdown, so I'd call that a win.

"Agree to disagree," I muttered at him.

He chuckled. "Fair enough. May I escort you back to the suite, Quinn? I'm sure you've had enough of my company for tonight."

I'd had enough of his company for a lifetime, but it seemed rude to point that out when he was being so gracious about the whole situation, pretending I hadn't just fallen apart in front of him when he could have been heckling me about my mortal sensibilities or something.

I simply nodded and walked with him back to the suite. He saw me in with a promise that we'd "have more fun tomorrow" and a onceover that was only slightly more pensive than usual, and then he let me be.

And as the door shut behind him, I found myself weirdly glad that he'd been there when I'd had the meltdown. That I hadn't been on my own, drowning in the emotions with no one to snap me out of them.

A prick of guilt formed in my gut. I scowled and strode through the suite to toss myself onto the bed.

I wasn't going to have any regrets about doing whatever I had to do to escape this place and the demon who'd brought me here. Even when he was theoretically being kind, it was always for his own benefit.

Nothing was going to sway me from making whatever desperate grab I could at reclaiming the life I was supposed to have, short as it might be.

CHAPTER TWENTY-ONE

Quinn

On my tenth night in the Sunshine Sin Hotel, I had to pretend to sleep even though my nerves were jittering too hard for me to do more than doze for short spells. Maybe Rollick had been telling the truth when he'd said there were no cameras in the suite, or maybe he'd been trying to lull me into a false sense of security. I wasn't sure I could take anything he said at face value.

And the last thing I wanted was for him to suspect at all that I was anticipating what was going to happen in the wee hours of the morning.

After hours of lying there with a knot in my stomach, enough exhaustion finally closed in on my mind that I actually did drift off. I woke up with a start at the sound of my name.

"Quinn!"

The voice was so brusque I didn't recognize it as Rollick's until I'd jerked upright with a jolt of my heart. The room was still dark, only a thin wash of moonlight spilling through the tall windows. The demon was standing in the doorway, his handsome face gone taut with more tension than I'd ever seen on it.

I was groggy enough from my interrupted sleep that I responded exactly the way I should have, not yet remembering the full situation. "What's going on?"

"It seems the fiends who want you have somehow gotten wind that I might have taken an interest as well," he said, still terse, striding into the room. He opened the wardrobe and grabbed the wig and discarded dress from inside, then spun to scan the rest of the space. "We need to get you out of here, temporarily at least. And remove every trace that you ever were here."

I blinked at him and pushed myself off the bed. There was a real urgency to the moment even if I'd been ready for it. Things wouldn't go well for me if I wasn't gone in time.

"Can't you fight them off, Mr. Powerful Demon?" I asked, because it seemed like the sort of thing I would have said if I hadn't been counting on him not doing that until his hand was forced. I grabbed my backpack and started stuffing in the few belongings I'd left out so that it wasn't obvious I'd packed for this moment.

"That would only confirm to them that I have something to hide," Rollick muttered. "A being who has no idea what they're nattering about would graciously allow them to search the premises for you in case you snuck in without my noticing, as if that's possible. Put on that vest of yours —we don't want them catching wind of you once you've left the shielded section of the hotel."

I yanked the vest out and tugged it over my head. Then I pulled on an extra T-shirt for good measure, because I already knew what answer I hoped to get to my next question. "Where am I going?"

"Crag will fly you to another secure location until I let him know it's safe to return," Rollick said, to my relief. "It's dark enough that he should be able to avoid notice, and our unwelcome guests haven't gotten close yet. But they're coming on fast, so move quickly!"

Everything had worked out. Well, so far—I couldn't count my chickens until I was actually out of here. I yanked on my shoes and stuffed my phone into a pocket on my bag, purposefully steering my gaze clear of the places around me where I'd stuffed a couple of things I didn't want Rollick seeing. They were tucked away well enough that he shouldn't catch sight of them just looking around in a hurry, but we were counting on the shadowkind searching for me digging a little deeper.

Tucked between the mattress and the box spring but right near the edge was a folded sketch that I'd signed *Quinn* and an unreadable last name on. And I'd slid a hair elastic with a few blond strands clinging to it behind the TV. Not places Rollick would expect me to have accidentally left something behind, but telltale giveaways if the intruders stumbled on either or both. The message my men had passed on should encourage the other shadowkind to pry.

As I swung my pack over my shoulder, Rollick prowled around me, his eyes taking on an eerie glow in the darkness. I suspected he could see in it much better than I could, but he was brisk in his perusal. He crouched to look under the furniture but didn't jostle anything around.

"Good," he said, guiding me out of the room with a hand on my back. "I trust the gargoyle will put as much effort into keeping you safe as he has so far, and the rest of your devotees will meet up with you at the safehouse. Nothing to worry about; just a small kink in our plans. We can get on with your training soon."

"Wonderful," I murmured. It wasn't as if he didn't already know I was hardly the most enthusiastic student. Then we reached the terrace doors, and Crag wavered into being from the shadows there in full gargoyle form.

My heart leapt at the sight of him. I'd have flung myself into a tight embrace if Rollick hadn't been standing there. It seemed wisest not to do anything that might provoke the demon in the middle of our precarious plan. Instead, I walked over to the gargoyle and lifted my arms so he could easily scoop me up in his preferred carrying position with me tucked against his broad, stony chest.

"Do *not* be seen," Rollick said in one final warning, and Crag dipped his head with a grunt to the affirmative. Then he took off into the air.

The gargoyle soared so high so fast that I lost my breath, staring up at the distant stars. I guessed the point was for us to be swallowed up into the darkness of the sky so no one all the way on the ground could make us out while we were still near the city. I leaned my cheek against the planes of Crag's chest and then tensed a little.

"I put the extra shirt on so the vest isn't pressing against your skin directly. Is it helping?" I could remember far too clearly how he'd started to struggle with the toxic metals burning him when we'd fled my attackers ten days ago.

"It's still not an enjoyable sensation, but it's less intense with the barrier," the gargoyle said with another swish of his wings. His voice came out in a deeper, rougher rumble than usual in this form. He started flying out over the ocean instead of up into the sky and lowered his head to brush his lips against my hair. "Are you comfortable?"

"I'd rather be here with you like this than anywhere else I've been all week," I told him, and kissed his shoulder. The combination of the granite-like texture of his flesh with the living warmth that emanated from it was strangely thrilling. "How far are we going?"

"Rollick thinks we're heading to a property of his out in the desert," the gargoyle said. "Torrent was able to locate a small island where he's stashed some supplies—nothing there for Rollick to connect to us. No other shadowkind around. As long as you have your vest on, no one should be able to find you there."

I wouldn't let myself question what would happen after, not yet.

We flew on and on. Dawn light started to turn the horizon gold, but we were far out enough over the ocean now that I couldn't even see the mainland. Crag started to drop. I twisted my neck and made out a splotch of land amid the deep blue water, like a birthmark on the ocean's surface. As we glided toward it, I saw palm trees and a wooden shelter that wasn't much more than a rough shack, large, jagged rocks catching the spray from the waves along one side and seaweed-mottled sand along the other.

Crag set me down on the sandy ground outside the shack, which only had three walls but held a few bundles of the supplies Torrent must have brought. I stepped away from the gargoyle quickly so that he could get some distance from my vest and then glanced around. With the brightening sky and the warm breeze rustling through the palm trees, the island looked like some kind of paradise.

"It's our very own desert island," I said with a little laugh. "And I didn't have to go through a shipwreck to get here." Relief surged up through me, stretching my mouth into a broad smile.

I was free. For the first time in ten days, I was out of Rollick's clutches. For the first time in nearly three weeks, there was no immediate threat of attacking monsters. They had no way to find me.

I couldn't stay here forever, obviously, but for the time being, it was a paradise in every possible way.

I set down my backpack in the shelter of the shack and then walked down to the water. The waves lapped at my toes, refreshingly cool in contrast with the already-rising heat of the tropical sun.

Crag followed me. He'd stayed in gargoyle form, either because he wanted to be sure he wouldn't need to whisk me away again or it simply hadn't occurred to him to shift back when I didn't mind him like this. I had to assume *he* felt more comfortable in his actual shadowkind form than the human guise he squeezed himself into.

"Is this the kind of place you'd want to fly out to when you weren't busy with some job for Rollick?" I asked, trying to picture his life before it'd gotten tangled with mine. How often did *he* get to feel free when he had to hide his true self so much of the time? "No humans so you don't have to worry about spreading your wings. Plenty of fishing opportunities."

The gargoyle let out a low rumble of a chuckle. "Maybe because of my nature, I'm usually drawn more to rocky terrain. Rushing up and down the slopes is quite a sensation."

"I bet it is." The thrill-seeker in me leapt in eager anticipation just imagining it.

"And there can be good hunting on mountains too." He flexed his clawed fingers with a satisfied expression that brought more warmth into my chest. Then he paused, seeming to feel the need to clarify, "I only hunt what I can consume—or for others, like when I brought fish to you. I don't enjoy slaughtering every creature in my path. Unless those creatures are vicious beasts trying to attack you."

"I think in that particular situation, it's understandable." I tucked my hand around his elbow. "What's best for hunting in the mountains?"

Crag tipped his head in a thoughtful way. "It depends on where the mountains are. There's a kind of horned sheep I'm very fond of. We could bring Lance along—you liked how he cooked the fish with his fire. Roasted sheep would be even better."

He spoke so easily about us traveling together, experiencing more of the world together without having to worry about fiends giving chase, as if he wouldn't allow there to be a future when that wasn't possible. Right now, with my newfound freedom stretching out in front of me like the vast sprawl of the sea, I could believe it too.

Tears sprang to my eyes. Crag peered at my face as I brushed my fingers across my eyes. "Are you all right? If you're not happy here—"

"No, I'm good," I said quickly, swallowing the lump that had risen in my throat. "They're happy tears. It's just amazing not to have so many threats hanging right over me." I still had things to worry about, I had no idea how our plan would pan out in the long run, but we'd won this part of the game. We'd managed to beat Rollick this once.

The exhilaration of the knowledge sent me back toward Crag. I grabbed him in a hug, meaning to keep it short because of the vest I had to keep wearing, but he wrapped his bulging arms around me and squeezed me back.

"Thank you," I said. "I know you've basically screwed yourself over with him. You could have kept working for him—he'd forgiven you—"

"That doesn't matter to me," Crag said in his usual gruff way. "I'm yours. You're my Softness. I'm only glad I could be a part of getting you free."

My throat tightened with emotion again. I lifted my head and bobbed up on my feet to press my mouth to his.

We'd never kissed while he was in gargoyle form before. I'd felt the sensation of his stony lower lip before thanks to his jaw that never shed its rocky quality, but the texture of both together and the brush of the fangs that protruded at the corners of his mouth sent an eager quiver through me. Heat flared between my legs.

There were no cameras here, no unwanted figures watching us. I was free in that way too. I could welcome this monster I'd fallen for without any fears that our intimacy would be violated.

But a second later, the body I was hugging contracted a few inches, the fangs vanishing and part of the mouth mine was melding with taking on the more pliant feeling of human flesh.

I pulled back to find Crag nearly human-like again, his skin bronze-brown other than his jaw, his horns and wings vanished, his facial features smoothing out, and his body shrinking just a little more into its still large but not monstrously massive stature. I stared at him, confused, and then understood.

He thought I wouldn't want to be kissing the "monster." That I'd rather have him like this. But it was the monster who'd saved me—now and many times before. Didn't he know by now I didn't see anything horrific in his natural form?

I raised my hands to rest them on either side of his jaw. "I like you this way, but I like seeing you as you really are too. I like... *feeling* you as you really are. I've gotten to enjoy your gargoyle tongue. Will you share the rest of you with me?"

Surprise flickered through Crag's expression. "Are you sure? I—it's more likely I could hurt you by accident. And… it's not as if I'm the most attractive man even in human form, but at least—"

My heart wrenched. I pulled him into another kiss, which turned firm and hot enough to make my knees wobble when he kissed me back. Then I eased away just far enough to say, "I think you're amazing in every form. You've been the gargoyle with other shadowkind before, haven't you?" He'd admitted to me that while he'd never taken a human lover before me, he'd had flings with shadowkind women in the past.

Crag's grunt told me I was right. "That's different. You're different."

"Maybe, but I want everything they got." I peered up at him, giddy with the glow of the dawn and the wild terrain all around us. "Give me the gargoyle, please?"

CHAPTER TWENTY-TWO

Crag

How could I deny this woman, mortal or not, when she looked at me like that? When she *spoke* like that, with longing humming through her words?

And an answering desire thrummed through me as I gazed down at her—to possess her as fully myself, as no other being had ever taken her. To feel the softness of her mortal body against and encompassing the hardened planes of my true physical form.

But there was a brutality to that hunger, to the craving to claim and possess. I'd never experienced the urge this strongly with any of my shadowkind lovers, as little as I'd known or cared about them beyond the brief release of the encounter. That was exactly why I couldn't give the beastly part of my nature free rein.

She was mine, but I had to preserve her as well as claim her. I couldn't let her tenderness be damaged.

I was a monster, but I was *her* monster.

I bowed my head over her and let my gargoyle self rise to the surface. My skin tightened and toughened, my wings flared from my back, and my face sharpened. My ears lengthened alongside the horns that poked above them up into the warm air. My largest fangs jutted from the sides of my jaw.

I was a beast in every sense of the word now. I'd used this form to terrify more beings both mortal and shadowkind than I could count.

I was good at that. It was what I was made for. I had trouble imagining how Quinn could look at me and see something to appreciate.

But she did. She smiled up at me and trailed her hand down the side of my face, tracing the ridges of my brow and cheek. Then she hooked her fingers around my jaw and tugged my mouth back to hers.

Her lips felt even softer than usual against my stony ones. I kissed her back carefully, only giving myself over to my eagerness bit by bit, increasing the passion of the embrace. When my lips parted, my fangs sliding against her skin, she gave a quiver that would have worried me if she hadn't tugged me even closer an instant later, giving every appearance that she was reveling in the sensation.

I hugged her to my chest as I kissed her harder, but the impression of her vest through her shirt sent a prickling over my skin that was much less enjoyable than the rest of this experience. She couldn't risk taking it off, even out here.

So I'd just have to bring her as much pleasure as I could around it.

I laid her down on the sandy ground and braced myself over her so we weren't pressed quite so closely together. With that bit of distance, the effect of the silver and iron was only a faint niggling I could tune out. It faded away completely when I captured her mouth again.

Quinn hummed encouragingly, her mouth slipping open so her tongue could twine with mine. As I teased my sinuous gargoyle tongue past her lips, she reached up to curl her fingers around my horns. Her grip on them, gentle and yet determined, inflamed me in ways I hadn't expected.

I wanted every part of her. I wanted to show her I could bring her to the same heights she'd reached with my companions all on my own. I couldn't resent the enjoyment and devotion they'd offer her, but right now she was only mine.

I let out a soft growl and trailed my fangs along her jaw to the side of her neck. Quinn whimpered and tipped her head back to allow me greater access. I had the urge to nip her to the point of drawing blood, to mark her and let the spark of pain fuel more pleasure the way Lance did, but I didn't have the dragon shifter's fiery breath to seal the wound.

Quinn was strong, but she was also fragile in ways even most mortals weren't. The illnesses of this world could affect her so much more easily than most. I would ravage her, but never to the point of threatening her.

As I slicked my tongue over her throat, Quinn let out an impatient murmur and ran her hands down my chest. She couldn't quite reach the fitted canvas shorts I normally wore in gargoyle form, but the arch of her hips toward mine told me exactly what her goal was. Her thigh brushed the erection already straining at the fabric, and I groaned.

I wanted to feel her on me, around me, everything—but she wouldn't be ready for me all at once. We'd had to take it slowly even in my human form, and I was even larger now.

Besides, there were other parts I wanted another taste of now that I'd discovered just what a delicious delicacy my mortal woman was.

"I'm going to get you good and ready," I murmured against her skin, and eased down her body to grasp her own shorts. Quinn squirmed out of them and her panties with my tugging fingers for help, and for a moment I just gazed down at her most intimate parts, the pale downy hair and the glistening folds that I was honored to witness.

A flush crept across Quinn's pretty face. "I can handle you," she said. "I'm sure I can. It just might take some... warming up."

"I'm only admiring you," I told her, which made her blush deepen. "But you'll definitely be warmed up when I'm through."

I bent down to lap my tongue over her slit. Quinn gasped, her hips bucking upward so I could devour her even more thoroughly. I gripped her hips, careful not to let my short claws dig into her skin, and lapped my long tongue right into her the way she'd enjoyed so much a few nights ago.

An even needier sound burst out of her. I drank in her tangy sweetness, like nothing I'd experienced with the few shadowkind women I'd dallied with, and my cock stiffened to the point of aching.

I was going to make her come at least once before I attempted to push *that* inside her. Let the rush of bliss relax her, and then we could find more delight together that much easier.

Lance had said once that it was easy to tell what would satisfy our mortal from her cues, and he'd been right. Quinn urged on every flick of my tongue and graze of my lips that inflamed her with her cries and growls and the swaying of her hips. She reached for my horns again, not holding on to them now but simply stroking them in a way I hadn't realized could provoke such pleasure in myself.

I plunged my tongue deeper, pressed it against the spot that brought out the most sound in her, and rubbed my upper lip across the little nub nestled in her folds that gave her such pleasure. Quinn came with the most beautiful noise, a choked moan that reverberated through her whole body as it quaked around me.

My wings flexed over me in response, her bliss radiating through my own body. I was on the verge of exploding just like that, but I wasn't going to rush this.

As she sagged back against the sand, I eased away only far enough to caress her with my hand now. Her muscles were looser with the release, but not quite enough that I was sure I wouldn't hurt her.

"Fuck, that feels good," she panted as I slid two fingers inside her. "I want all of you."

"Soon," I said, the word coming out in a hungry growl. "I'm going to stretch you so it's good all the way through."

I spread my fingers to stroke them around her channel, encouraging it to accept more and more pressure. Quinn sputtered another curse and rocked her hips, her juices coating my hand. I had the feeling that if I swiveled my thumb over her nub, she might come again just like that. But the next time she found her release, I wanted to be inside her properly.

Her overlapping shirts had ridden up to expose her stomach. I bent my head to kiss the soft skin beside her belly button as I continued working her over.

The swell of her breasts was too tempting even with the noxious materials that covered them. I couldn't resist. I slipped my other hand under the fabric of her tank top beneath the vest, ignoring the sharper pang of discomfort, and reached up to cup one of the silky slopes.

Another moan tumbled out of Quinn's mouth. She outright writhed beneath me, caught between my hand above and my stretching finger below. I massaged her breast and skimmed a claw over the nipple the way I'd seen Lance do to impressive effect. The gasping reaction I got was the perfect reward.

Her channel was so slick against my other hand, the muscles lining it gone increasingly pliant with each rotation of my fingers. I forced myself to stroke her a few more times before bringing those fingers to my lips and licking her arousal off them.

Quinn shifted up on her elbows with a ragged breath. "Kiss me again."

I was more than happy to oblige. Our mouths melded together, our tongues tangling, and her hands skimmed over my chest. Then I drew back to yank off my shorts. Quinn's gaze followed the movement, her eyes widening with obvious eagerness as she took in my thick shaft.

She showed no hesitation at all, spreading her legs wider in invitation, but I couldn't help halting just to check. "Are you sure?"

This couldn't have been how she'd ever imagined her encounters with men would go. When I had only my rock-like jaw as a reminder of my true nature, I was nearly as human as any of them. But like this...

"Right now, there's nothing in the world I'm surer about than the fact that I want all of you inside me immediately," Quinn grumbled.

There was no denying how much she meant that statement. A relieved chuckle spilled out of me. I tucked a hand under her hips to lift her to meet me and lined myself up.

Her channel expanded again to encompass me. Every inch I penetrated her, more pleasure raced through my own body, until I felt as if I were on fire with a heat I'd have happily burned up in.

Quinn groaned, pushing herself toward me as her fingers dug into the sand. The joy that washed over her expression and reverberated through her panting breaths set off a fresh flare of need in me.

I thrust into her, slowly at first and then with increasing speed as she showed no sign of pain. The sounds breaking from her throat now were nothing but gleeful. Sweat beaded on her forehead and glistened on her collarbone. I bowed over her to lick it off with a swipe of my tongue, and she clutched at me, holding me with her.

I kissed her on the mouth and then her neck, bucking into her even faster. A wild keening reverberated from her chest. She bucked in time with my rhythm with increasing wildness, her fingernails scraping over my stony skin, her breath fragmenting more and more. Pressure built at the base of my cock, but I held myself focused on her reactions, her pleasure, holding off my own final bliss until—

Her sex clenched around my cock, and a shudder ran through her body. It was as if she were wringing my own release out of me. With a groan, I spilled myself into her softness.

Quinn shivered again with a giddy grin. She held my face, gazing up at me with affection shining in her sky-blue eyes, and beamed as if she were the sun itself. As I eased out of her and gathered her against me, a strange sensation wrapped around my heart.

I wasn't ashamed of what I was, not generally speaking. I'd put my monstrousness to use to serve all kinds of needs. When things had gone wrong... it hadn't been on purpose, and I'd made what amends I could. Every advantage had its downsides.

But I couldn't say I'd ever felt outright *proud* to be the monster I was before this moment, holding Quinn in all her combined strength and fragility, knowing how much she trusted me to look after her. I would serve her for as long as she'd have me, and I'd put all my bulk and brutality toward ensuring she got every bit of life she deserved.

CHAPTER TWENTY-THREE

Quinn

The second time I woke up that morning, it was on the floor of the island shack, sprawled on the sleeping bag Crag had unfurled for me. From the angle of the sun and the small shadows cast by the men standing over me, it was nearly noon.

I pushed myself upright, rubbing at my eyes, and took in the newer arrivals. Torrent and Lance showed no sign of recent injuries, so they must have gotten clear of the hotel without any problems.

Lance dropped down onto the floor of the shack next to me with his usual carefree grace, and I motioned for Torrent to sit at my other side, mindful of the strain standing put on his legs. Crag stayed on his feet, alternating between peering over the ocean and glancing at us, but when our eyes met, a tingle shot through me in the memory of how we'd celebrated my newfound freedom.

Lance tucked his clawed hand around my elbow, and Torrent rested one tentacle against my back. I was left with the sense of being perfectly contained between my three monstrous men. We fit together so easily. Maybe having them in my life would be harder if I ever got to go back to a regular one… but with the harmony I felt in their presence, I had to believe we could make it work.

"How long have you been here?" I asked Torrent.

"We just arrived," he said. "I had to pull a small craft along with me over the water to carry the dragon shifter." He shot a wryly baleful look at Lance.

Lance let out a playful huff. "If you'd gotten a boat big enough to hold an engine and not just a shadow, I could have driven it myself."

"But we didn't want any chance of the wrong person spotting us. It seems that we got away clear." Torrent took my hand and ran his thumb over my knuckles in a way that provoked another tingle. "I know this place isn't up to the standards of your previous accommodations—I didn't have much time to work on it—"

"Wait, you built this?" I stared at the building around us. Yes, it was roughly made, but I hadn't realized it was a recent construction. Because the wood that made up the small structure was weathered... but not by the actual weather, I realized. They were pieces of driftwood, some of the ends ragged—mostly flat boards, but ones that had ended up in the sea one way or another.

When I squinted closer, I couldn't make out any nails or screws. The boards had been wedged against each other in a careful configuration that kept them stable, some of them presumably braced against the boulder at the rear of the building. Some kind of thick tarp or treated fabric had been wrapped over the roof to cover any cracks.

"It's amazing that you put this together at all," I said, taking in the details with an architect's perspective. It might not be the kind of structure I'd dreamed of designing, but it was sturdy and functional in its simplicity. Staying up and doing what it was supposed to do were the most important qualities for our purposes.

Torrent's mouth curved into a small smile. "I've sometimes enjoyed making sculptures and other fixtures along the beach for people to find. It's a way of staying present in the mortal realm even if I can't really show myself. I've picked up a few tricks over the years."

"Well, it worked just fine for me to catch up on some sleep." I yawned and stretched my arms over my head, but curiosity was already gnawing at me. "Did you see what happened at the hotel? Was there a fight? Has Rollick reached out?"

"We stayed behind watching long enough for the big bad beasties to show up," Lance reported, drumming his other claws against the floorboards. "All human-like, so we're not sure what kind of beasts they are."

Torrent nodded. "And they found something they didn't like. The window to Rollick's suite was smashed just as we were taking off. It seemed like it'd get dangerous to stick around anywhere nearby at that point."

My pulse hiccupped. If my monstrous stalkers had been busting up Rollick's suite, then they must have found at least one piece of evidence I'd left that'd convinced them he was lying about not knowing where I was. But in my focus on getting *me* out of the hotel, I'd forgotten— "What about the other guests—the human ones? If the other shadowkind attack Rollick and his people, will the mortals around be okay?"

"These beings have still mostly been keeping up appearances in their other activities," Torrent said, squeezing my hand. "I doubt they'd want to show off their monstrous forms in front of downtown Santa Monica. Both sides will want to keep the conflict contained away from mortal eyes."

Lance tugged at his ear. "I think I heard a fire alarm going off as we were zipping away. That'd clear out the building nice and quick."

Relief rushed through me. "Okay. But we don't know yet how the fighting turned out? Whether either side took significant damage?" As monstrous as Rollick had proven himself to be, he was still more on my side than the creatures who were going around eating sorcerers and trying to kill my men so they could enslave me. I couldn't help hoping that he'd come out of the clash better off than his opponents.

Torrent shook his head. "Rollick said he'd contact me by phone when everything was settled. I haven't heard from him yet, and no missed calls or messages from when I wasn't available to answer. We couldn't risk getting caught up in the skirmish by staying."

"Of course not. I'm glad you're okay. Both of you." I gripped his hand tighter and leaned against Lance's shoulder. A sigh slipped out of me.

The dragon shifter peered at me with a mix of concern and eagerness before reaching toward one of the bags of supplies. "Have you eaten yet? We made sure to grab many things when we were setting up."

"I remembered the snacks you like best," Crag put in with a pointed rumble.

Lance waved him off carelessly. "Yes, yes. But she needs all the vita-whats and so on too." He plucked out an orange and started carving it into slices with his claws without waiting for my answer.

My stomach did gurgle then. I'd been so tense from our escape and then exhilarated that we'd succeeded that hunger hadn't crept up on me before I'd dozed off. All I'd had was the gulp of water with my morning pills. "Thank you," I said, reaching to accept the slices from the dragon shifter.

As the tartly sweet juice filled my mouth, Lance rummaged around in the bag, partly shredding the thin plastic with his claws, and pulled out a chocolate bar. "There, you can be helping keep her fed too," he said, wagging it teasingly at Crag before handing it over.

It was actually my favorite type of bar—I must have mentioned that to the gargoyle sometime in our travels. I beamed up at him. "Thank you too. You all made this place perfect."

But the world beyond this island was far from perfect. I took another bite, more pensive thoughts creeping up over me. "So, I guess now we just wait and see how things pan out, and then we'll figure out where we go from here?"

I expected Torrent to agree immediately, but instead he paused as if debating whether to say what he was thinking. I straightened up to catch his gaze. "What?"

He tipped his head to the side, his mouth twisting at a crooked angle. "I did have a thought—something we might want to investigate while the shadowkind who've been searching for you are distracted."

"Okay, and what's that?"

He motioned in what I assumed was the direction of the mainland. "When I was scouting out enemy activities for Rollick, I came across evidence that there's a sorcerer family in Arizona that our enemies were trying to track down. I've spent some time in that area on other missions for Rollick before, and I think I know exactly where the family is located. From what you've told me about the sorcerer Rollick brought to talk to you before, this bunch is more experienced and has more power."

"I think most would be," I said. "He seemed like his talents were pretty weak. But why would that matter right now?"

"You still need to sort out the problem of the magic in you—understanding how to work with it or even getting it out of you, if that's possible," Torrent said. "We could try to talk to them today. Heading to their little settlement here, we wouldn't need to go anywhere near L.A."

Hope trickled up through my chest. "Do you really think they'd talk to me?"

Torrent shrugged. "I don't see why not. I'd imagine they'd have at least a little sympathy for your situation. If not, then we just leave, no harm done."

Lance had tensed a little at my other side. I glanced over at him, my stomach clenching. "But we don't know how they'd treat the three of *you*."

The dragon shifter put on a grin that only looked a little stiff. "We've got you to vouch for us, baby girl. And we can always stick to the shadows farther out if we don't want to tempt their voodoo."

Torrent tapped him with a tentacle. "*You* should definitely stay well back—you can keep watch over the road leading to their settlement. It'd be hard for them to affect any of us—from what I've seen before, only one might be powerful enough to even attempt to coerce a higher shadowkind of our power—but after you've had your mind muddled with sorcery once, you're more susceptible."

Lance gave a snarl but didn't argue. Crag drew himself up even taller, still in his gargoyle form, and spread his wings. "Torrent and I can keep a closer watch over Quinn. We won't let her be harmed."

"It'll still be a little risky for *you*," Torrent said, searching my gaze with his sea-green eyes. "There's always the chance of shadowkind noticing you and passing on word. You're safest here."

I dragged in a breath. "But I need to figure out how to leave here eventually, and the longer we wait, the more chance there is that some other beings will go after those sorcerers and kill them. It's better that we go now while we know the ones hunting me and them are distracted, like you said. Just a quick conversation, see if there's anything they know that could help. If you're all in."

The men around me inclined their heads without hesitation. I pushed myself to my feet, ignoring the nervous twist of my gut. "All right. Let's find out what these sorcerers can tell me."

CHAPTER TWENTY-FOUR

Quinn

Just this once, Torrent let me drive. I couldn't really see that as an act of faith when he hadn't had a whole lot of choice in the situation, but having my hands on the steering wheel and my foot on the gas pedal reinvigorated my sense of freedom.

I was tracking down answers, maybe even a full solution to my problem. What the people I was going to see could tell me might give me *complete* freedom from the problems that'd been dogging me for the past few weeks... From the monsters that'd been attempting to claim me as their meal or their tool.

The desert landscape whizzed by on either side of the lonely road: plains of rippled orange-brown earth dotted with scruffy shrubs leading to ruddy cliffs that rose in the distance. There was no sound from outside other than the whistle of the wind over the jeep Torrent had acquired for us somehow or other. The air conditioning blasted a steady stream of cool air over us, but I could see how hot it was outside from the shimmer on the pavement ahead.

The sorcerers had their sort-of ranch in a secluded valley just beyond the nearest of the cliffs ahead of us. We'd already left Lance in the shadows about a mile back, watching the road well beyond the influence of any enslaving magic. Crag was scanning the landscape from the backseat while Torrent checked his phone next to me and nodded to the road ahead.

"The road will be pretty rough since no one but them comes out here, hardly a road at all, but the jeep should be able to handle it. I don't think whatever shadowkind guards they have posted around the settlement will stop you when you're alone in the car. You know what to do if the sorcerers turn out to be hostile."

I nodded, my chest constricting a little. I might enjoy the chance to take the wheel, but I didn't love the fact that none of my men could stay right by my side for this meeting. Sorcerers saw shadowkind as enemies at worst and slaves at best, not as friends or lovers. They'd be even more wary of my men if they'd heard about the recent killings like the guy I'd talked to before had. If I turned up with a couple of shadowkind companions, they'd *definitely* be unhappy.

"Shout really loud," I said. "I think I can handle that."

"And we'll keep watch from our vantage point," Crag put in. "We'll be able to tell if anything's really wrong."

"As long as I don't go inside." I thought I should be able to manage that. How likely were the sorcerers to want a stranger poking around in their homes?

"If you get a bad feeling, you can just leave," Torrent reminded me. "We don't know for sure this group will be able to help you at all. There's no point in taking any more of a risk than you already are just by coming out here."

"I know."

It was late in the afternoon now, the shadows stretching long, and he still hadn't gotten any word from Rollick. I didn't know if that was a good sign, meaning the demon and our other enemies were still totally occupied with their clash, or a bad sign, meaning the other shadowkind had managed to batter him beyond capability of communication.

Either way, no one would be expecting to find me out here. If we faced any danger, it'd come from the sorcerers and the shadowkind *they* commanded.

As the cliffs loomed closer, Crag stiffened in the back seat. I eased up on the gas before he'd even spoken.

"There's a being up ahead," he said. "I can only sense it faintly from here. It's staying still—I think it's a lesser shadowkind, but it feels large and strong."

Torrent made a face. "They have guards, as we expected. I was hoping not so far out, but I guess it's not surprising."

I pulled over onto the side of the road and stopped completely. "Will you still be able to get close enough to see what's happening?"

He studied the sheer hills that framed the shallow valley we couldn't yet peer into. "There's a lot of high terrain. I think we should be able to find a spot where we can look down into the valley from the shadows while avoiding any sentries. But it might take us a minute or two to get to you from there." He paused and glanced over at me, his eyes darkening. "We don't have to do this. We can go back to the island and make other plans."

I inhaled slowly and touched my pocket with my old multitool, the one that'd helped me fix so many problems much smaller than the one I was currently facing. I had that. I had the steak knife I'd stolen from one of my hotel dinners and my silver pen-dagger in the other pocket. I had the moves ingrained from my self-defense classes.

And I was wearing my silver-and-iron vest, concealed by a fresh tee, which would make it difficult for any lesser shadowkind and even most higher to hurt me. Torrent had said it should block any persuasive vibes if the sorcerers had managed to enslave a being like a succubus or the siren who'd manipulated me on the hotel roof.

I'd spent the past ten days hiding away in Rollick's luxurious hotel, accomplishing nothing except putting on an inadvertent porn show for my captor and tapping into skills I didn't really want. I *had* to do something, had to try to take control over my life again, or what was the point in having gotten free at all?

I couldn't expect my shadowkind men to take all the risks on my behalf. That wasn't remotely fair.

"This is our best chance," I said. "And we don't know how long the shadowkind after me will be distracted for. Anything we do after today will only be more dangerous."

Torrent didn't argue with any of my points. He simply waited for me to work through my thoughts, easing one of his tentacles over to hug my knee. I rested my hand on the sinuous limb.

"We could try to hide in the vehicle, make ourselves as inobtrusive as possible," Crag said abruptly.

I glanced over my shoulder, raising my eyebrows. "As much as I'd like to bring you with me, I don't think inobtrusive is a word that could ever describe you." I turned to face the cliffs again. "These sorcerers have managed to avoid getting attacked so far. They must have a pretty good security system. I'll go in alone. They can't do anything *worse* to me than the monsters chasing me want to do."

They had no reason to want to hurt me, after all. I was just a fellow human seeking help.

"Then we'll part ways here," Torrent said, but he reached for me first, his fingers sliding along my jaw and tugging me into a kiss. The press of his mouth against mine felt like a promise and a plea that I'd return to him safely. I kissed him back hard, a sudden swell of emotion nearly overwhelming me.

There was a lot wrong with my life right now. There were so many things I wanted to fix. But somehow in the middle of the chaos, I'd found these three brutal but incredible men who'd lit me up inside and followed me into every challenge we'd faced.

Crag grunted from behind me, where he couldn't easily mimic Torrent's farewell gesture, but he took my hand and kissed the knuckles briefly. Then they both vanished into the shadows. I knew they'd have leapt from the car immediately to dart as quickly as they could over the landscape, avoiding the sorcerers' enslaved shadowkind guards.

I pushed on the gas again with a growl of the engine. The increasingly imperceptible lane led straight ahead between the two jagged hills and then downward with a slight curve into the broad, shallow valley between them. The jeep's wheels jostled over potholes and bumps, but the vehicle managed all right. Torrent had picked it well.

As I came around the bend, four single-story adobe buildings came into view around a larger two-story structure, all of them blending into the orange-y earth around them.

I hadn't seen any sign of sentries myself, human or monstrous, but probably some shadowy presence had taken note of me, decided I wasn't a terrible threat, and simply informed the inhabitants of my approach. I was still at least a hundred yards away from the nearest building, dust spurting up from under the tires, when a few figures emerged from the homes and headed up the road toward me. One of them raised her hands for me to stop.

Easing my foot on the brake, I ground to a halt there on what was pretty much just bare dirt at this point and put the jeep into park for the time being. Then I got out, grabbing my messenger bag and slinging it over my shoulder automatically, staying close to the vehicle. Even with the sun having sunk behind the western hill, the air was hot enough to bring sweat beading across my skin.

It was an older woman, her coiled hair a mix of white and steel-gray, and a younger couple who'd come out to meet me. The older woman, who was the one who'd motioned to me, appeared to be the leader. She strode a little closer with the man and the other woman, who I figured were in their thirties, following just behind.

"What are you doing here?" the first woman asked in a dry but commanding voice, squinting at me.

My pulse thumped faster. This was the deciding moment—whether they believed my story would determine whether I got any help from them at all.

"I heard that there were people who lived out here who had certain... skills. Skills I'd like to learn about, because I didn't get a chance to from my own family before I lost them."

It was a simplified version of the truth, because the last thing I wanted was anyone talking about a visit from a girl with a transplanted heart. The full story was too complicated anyway.

The man folded his arms over his chest. "*Who* told you that?"

"It was... it was in some notes my parents left behind," I lied. I wasn't going to tell them a shadowkind had directed me here. "I know about the rifts, and the monsters that come through them, and that it's possible to control them. Sometimes I feel like I should be able to, but I didn't have anyone to teach me. I don't even know if I *want* to do that—I just need to understand this power I've got so I can figure out what to do about it."

The three figures shifted on their feet, obviously uneasy. But their sentries hadn't given them any reason to worry about me, and from what I'd heard from and about other sorcerers, my story was plausible. The only question was whether they'd want to bother spending the time talking with me.

Before they could answer, a little boy came running across the uneven terrain. He couldn't have been more than four. He grabbed the younger woman's leg and stared at me, then up at the others. "Mommy, Daddy, who's this lady?"

My gut twisted with guilt at the lie I was about to tell, but I grabbed the opening he'd given me. These were people who stole the free will of shadowkind beings and forced them to do their bidding. I shouldn't feel bad about manipulating them just slightly in turn.

"I was about his age when I lost my mom and dad," I said, letting my voice turn rough with all the losses I had actually faced.

I could tell the tactic landed as I'd intended. The young woman's face fell. She squeezed her son's shoulder. "Go back to the house, Jonah. Ask Grandpa to read you a book." As the little boy scampered off, she returned her attention to me. "Your parents were sorcerers."

I nodded. "But I haven't been able to piece together much... I only just found some of their writing that made a little more sense of things I heard and saw when I was a little kid. My memories are all kind of a blur, though, and the journals didn't give many details."

The three sorcerers exchanged a glance. The older woman took the lead again. "This isn't a good time for pursuing an interest in the magic of the shadows. There are monsters hunting people like us. You'd do better to forget about it."

I folded my arms over my chest. "I don't think I can. I have this strange... feeling inside me. It's been getting stronger. Maybe if I could just get rid of it—is that even possible?"

She frowned and rubbed her mouth. "There is... Overseas, out where there are times when the sun never rises for days... Norway, I think? I've heard there's an enclave for sorcerers there, a place where those without power go when they're hoping to spark it in themselves. I don't personally know anyone who's taken that route instead of having it through their family line, though, so maybe it doesn't work. But if it does, it's possible someone there would know how to snuff out a power that already exists too."

My heart leapt, although I wasn't sure how I was going to get all the way to Norway. Minor details. "Okay. I guess that's a start. I don't know how soon I'd be able to actually look into that, though. Since I'm already here... is there anything you'd be willing to tell me about how you work with and control your power?"

The older woman sighed. "Since you *are* already here, I suppose we could talk a little. I'm not sure how much we could tell you, but you could ask a few questions. Come over to the courtyard." She motioned to the man, who from the similar dark eyes and hooked shape of their noses I suspected was her son. "Ivan, bring some lemonade or something. It's hot enough to invite the devil out here."

I followed the three sorcerers into the circle of their houses on cautious feet, hoping my shadowkind protectors still had me in their sights.

CHAPTER TWENTY-FIVE

Lance

Quinn needed to be here. She needed to know about the foreboding energy that'd gotten all twisted up inside her heart. I reminded myself of that as I twined through the shadows along the road.

I needed to keep watch. I was the first line of defense if anything ominous came this way. But my whole being itched with the uncertainty of what might be happening to Quinn off where she'd gone, down into the place where the sorcerers lived. What might those sinister mortals with their warped minds decide to do to her?

Was the real danger away from here or in the direction she'd gone?

The buried memories rattled at the inner cage I'd stuffed them into. Slivers of groans and agonized winces trickled out despite my best efforts. I flexed my shadowy sense of my claws, longing to dig them into the firmly packed soil, to gouge my presence, my *survival*, into this landscape.

No. I could already imagine what Torrent would say. We didn't want anyone knowing we'd come here. We didn't want to lead the monsters who'd claim Quinn to these other sorcerers even after we'd gone.

Even if these particular mortals would deserve whatever fate they met from the fiends.

The sun had dipped below the hills. Its glow still spilled over the sky and lit the clifftops, but gloom swathed the ground. I leapt and darted from one side of the road to the other, spinning this way and that, working the restlessness out of my being as much as I could without any real muscles to stretch.

So strange that I felt more at home in the physical body I pulled together out of the materials of this foreign realm than I did in the darkness now. The concreteness of it, the certainty of it, appealed to me in a way I couldn't put into words.

I liked that I could put my *claws* into it—there was the thing. What was the point of having claws if you couldn't slice and dice with them? And fighting was much more satisfying with bodies colliding than when tangling with another being while you were both wisps of essence that barely had a presence at all.

The car had vanished into the valley some time ago. Ten minutes? An hour? I didn't have much of an internal clock at the best of times, and this was definitely not the best.

What would the sorcerers tell Quinn anyway? That she should order around all the beasties like Rollick had her doing? That she should try to command all of us?

Well, maybe I wouldn't mind if she threw some of that power at the monsters who wanted to sink their claws and fangs into *her*. It would serve them right. Fighting back wasn't the same as hunting down beings who'd never done a thing to you. Quinn would use the magic in her properly. Quinn understood how awful it was—the things the other sorcerers did.

But I couldn't say the thought that they might know how she could toss the power away completely didn't wake up a flicker of joy in my chest. She could be rid of it, not a sorcerer at all. Then none of that taint would remain, and none of the others would want to steal her away, and she could be only mine.

All right, Crag's and Torrent's too. They'd stood by her when she needed them like I had. I would just have to steal her away for my own self, only the two of us, as often as I had the chance. I shouldn't have to share *all* the time.

A creeping sensation wavered over my body. I spun again, my focus sharpening. Was something—or someone—coming? From which direction? Maybe it was simply Quinn returning. I could hope for that.

The impression faded as quickly as it'd risen up, but I didn't think it'd come from the sorcerers' valley. I studied the more distant bulge of reddish rock that jutted from the ground and the bristly plants that dotted the flatter soil near me. I couldn't see anything traveling in the gloom, but I wasn't as sensitive to movement as the gargoyle was.

It could be just a tiny beastie. Maybe even one of the sorcerers' dupes patrolling farther. If I stayed still, it wouldn't think I was of any concern all the way out here.

Or it could be nothing at all. Just my nerves jumping because of the memories churning inside me.

I bared my teeth as if I could scare that possibility into submission, and snapped them a few times for good measure, but in the shadows they didn't make the satisfying gnashing sound. No, physical form was much better. I couldn't wait until we could leave here and I could stretch my limbs out properly.

A pebble rattled. I whipped in the direction of the sound, my ears pricked, my eyes narrowing. The tufts of coarse grass waved in the breeze. Somewhere off on the other side of the road, a rabbit hopped behind a bush.

Just a mortal beastie. Even less of a threat than a shadowkind one. Humph. Rollick would have chuckled at me. Maybe even Torrent would have laughed. Not Crag—most of the time he didn't really get even actual jokes.

And not Quinn. Quinn would have told me it made sense that I was uneasy. She'd be hurrying out of the valley as quickly as she could. She knew those sorcerers were no—

The surge of energy walloped me, so suddenly and with so much force that I tumbled right out of the shadows. I sprawled on the dry earth with my scales scraping the scattered stones and my thoughts whirling in my head. Panic flashed through them, jumbling them even more. That'd felt— It was too familiar— No, no, I couldn't let—

I reached to leap back into the shadows instinctively, and another wallop smacked into my body. I could practically hear my brains jostling inside my skull. The energy crackled through my mind, digging in like dozens of tiny claws. I couldn't move, couldn't speak, could hardly piece together coherent thought. What— How—

Another presence loomed, still far but large enough that I felt it even across that distance now. So powerful. So determined. And others—other shadowkind rippling into my awareness as they charged ahead of it.

They'd come. The ones we thought were busy with Rollick—they'd found the sorcerers too. They'd come. And Quinn was still there. I had to—

I was moving, but not because I'd decided to. My body morphed back into its shadowy state and lunged forward across the desert plain alongside the other racing creatures. An urge gripped me way down in the center of my being, with words I couldn't remember hearing with my actual ears reverberating through me.

Find all the sorcerers. Slash their throats. Leave the rest to me.

No. I couldn't do that. Especially not while Quinn was there.

I tried to fight the compulsion, but its claws had stretched into threads that wound all through my essence, gripping every particle of me.

Just like before—just like when the ones who'd kept me in that cage had given their orders.

A cry burst from my throat, silent to the outside world as the gloom swallowed it up. I strained at my limbs, but they kept hurtling forward, toward the place where I knew the sorcerers lived. The ones who were strangers to me... and one other besides. One lovely woman I'd sworn to protect, who, yes, was a sorcerer too, whether she wanted to be or not.

Icy panic washed over me, but it didn't dislodge the hold the magic had on my will. It simply closed around my gut with a queasy lurch. I couldn't give in, couldn't let this fiend control me. I had to break the spell, somehow...

But I'd only broken it before by getting my captor to let down her guard. I didn't even know where the being who'd compelled me was now. Somewhere behind, lurking while we ran ahead to carry out the most dangerous work. Driving us forward in front of him like a herd of deer ahead of a wolf.

Except we weren't the real prey here. The mortals with their tender flesh were.

I wrenched and flailed at my body as it whipped toward the valley, but nothing I did made the slightest difference. The command laced all through my being urged me on and on with visions of human necks sliced open, blood splattered across the ground.

Some part of me *reveled* in the thought, and I couldn't even tell how much that was the magic and how much my own fury at the humans who imprisoned our kind this way.

For a few fleeting moments, my anger seared through all my resistance and my horror. I would tear into them and let their lives leak out into the earth. They would never twist another being's will to their own again. I—

The image flashed before my eyes of a very specific pale neck I'd become familiar with, pale blond hair falling around it beneath a delicate chin, and another smack of cold nausea broke through the stirred-up rage.

Not her. She didn't count. She wasn't like them. I had to defend her.

Find all the sorcerers. Slash their throats.

The other beings around me didn't know Quinn was in the valley. I was abruptly certain of that. The immense being who'd given the command would have instructed them to leave her alive if it'd realized.

But I knew. And the compulsion in me demanded that I end her life too, that I serve the master who'd caught me in his leash to the full extent of my ability.

I'd been able to fight the hold the sorcerers of the past put on me a little —to delay, to bend their instructions in tiny ways. I'd never felt an iron grip quite like this.

Because my enslaver now was shadowkind. The compulsion came with an understanding of my nature no human could have held, as if the being that'd given its orders saw me and knew me inside out. How had any human even come near that kind of recognition to command shadowkind to their will?

That brief question fled as I flung myself down into the valley and the buildings came into sight up ahead in the fading sunlight.

There was the jeep I knew Quinn had arrived in. Even realizing it was probably empty, my fangs jutted with the impulse to leap inside and shred whatever was within.

No, no, *no*.

My agonized protests made no difference to the movements of my body. I leapt over the jeep, a glance through the window confirming no one was inside and allowing me to race onward. Then I burst out of the shadows in full dragon form, snarling and flexing my claws.

Other creatures were leaping from the darkness all around me. A few had already stormed into one of the houses, a shriek and frantic yelling spilling past the bashed door. The horrible, unshakeable tug inside me drew me past the buildings, following a trace of scent I couldn't stop myself from recognizing, from knowing that the woman attached to it was technically one of the sorcerers I'd been commanded to destroy.

There she was. The first glimpse of her bright hair and frightened face just about tore me in two, wanting to run to her and shield her, knowing my claws and fangs would rip into her of their own accord despite my wishes.

I cried out again, attempting a warning that snagged in my throat. Every bit of determination in my body rallied in resistance, straining against the magic propelling me onward—but it wasn't enough.

Crag was sweeping her up in his arms. He was going to carry her away, and the orders driving me toward them refused to accept that, as much as the rest of me wanted to shout for joy at her potential escape. I couldn't stop myself, couldn't do more than growl in a mix of rage and anguish as I threw myself at the two of them.

"Lance!" Crag roared in protest, whipping himself around so that my claws sank into his stony flesh instead of gouging Quinn's. Small mercies. I recoiled inside at the smoky blood that gushed from my friend's wounds, but my limbs and teeth slashed on.

No, no, please, no...

The protest turned into a silent wail inside my head. It didn't help me. Nothing could drown out the commands ringing through me—to stop the gargoyle, to savage him until he fell and I could wrench the woman from his grasp to claim her for the being that'd made himself my master.

CHAPTER TWENTY-SIX

Quinn

The lemonade cut through the worst of the heat, the perfect mix of sweet and sour as it slid down my throat, but it left my mouth sticky. I swallowed, looking around at the three sorcerers who'd offered it to me.

Ivan had stuck close to his wife, who'd introduced herself as Jenny. The older woman—the apparent matriarch over this small community—was Victoria. A few other figures had emerged from the buildings to listen in on our conversation, but they hadn't bothered to introduce themselves.

I still didn't feel exactly *welcome* in their midst. I clutched the strap of my messenger bag with my free hand, fretting briefly that my vest was showing under my shirt and they'd wonder about my weird fashion choices, as if that was what really mattered.

"Is this normal?" I found myself saying, thinking of my donor's family with their house in the Florida wilderness. "All of you living off in the middle of nowhere together? Doesn't it get kind of lonely?"

Victoria shrugged. "We have other properties in other places, in cities and towns or at least closer to them. This spot was meant for when we're harnessing a new demon and making sure they're fully under control, or simply to gather the extended family together. But with recent events... We've felt it's better to stay here where we can be more sure of our safety for a while."

"Where are you from?" Jenny asked, watching me curiously. I wondered if she'd ever met a sorcerer who didn't understand their powers before me.

It seemed unwise to mention my actual home state in case these people had heard about all the chaos shadowkind had been creating over there. "California," I said instead, which was at least true of where I'd most immediately come from. "Near L.A."

Victoria hummed to herself. "I don't know of any major established families operating around that city, but there are a lot more small-time practitioners who don't mingle much with the community. Although I wouldn't have expected you to have trouble with an emerging power you hadn't meant to call on if your parents weren't particularly skilled." Her eyes narrowed.

"Is it about skill?" I asked quickly. "From the things they wrote, it sounded like it's something that just... wakes up in you and almost tells you how to use it. Which sounds really weird. And I still don't know what I'm doing."

"There are strategies for getting more in touch with the power," Ivan put in. "Meditation and that sort of thing. And also..." He paused.

I focused on him, hiding my eagerness. The other sorcerer had already mentioned meditation to me, but maybe this group knew something more. "Also?"

He glanced at his mother, and Victoria gave a short laugh as if amused that he was deferring to her. She gave me a thin smile. "You do understand exactly what it is that we do, don't you?"

"You... you get control over the monsters that can come out of the shadows," I said. "You can tell them what to do, and they have to do it. Make them use their supernatural powers for your benefit and things like that."

"That's the gist of it. Well, this won't matter until you're confident enough to fully harness one of those monsters. And many practitioners dismiss this aspect because they feel it's abasing ourselves when we should hold ourselves much higher than the creatures we command. But we've always found, and I know other families who feel similarly, that you can wield your power much more effectively the better you've familiarized yourself with the demon."

I held my eyebrows from rising. "Familiarize yourself how?"

She waved a hand carelessly as if it didn't matter much. "Oh, however makes you feel you're developing a better understanding of them. When I've taken on a new subject, I'll spend hours in our training room with it, giving it free rein other than making sure it doesn't harm me, watching its behavior. Ivan takes his on hunts and shares the meal with them. Jenny likes to draw and paint hers. There's a sort of closeness that can develop that seems to bring forth more of the power."

Huh. I hadn't tried communing with the creatures Rollick had brought around. But then, neither he nor I had known there'd be any point in trying. The first sorcerer hadn't mentioned that strategy. "So that just works for the one creature you're studying, right?"

"That's where you'll see the greatest effect," Ivan said, his tone getting more enthusiastic. "But we've found that making those sort of connections makes it easier to control others as well. Partly because you need less effort to keep the ones you've developed a deeper understanding of under your control so you have more energy to expend elsewhere, but I think also because you understand monstrousness in general better."

"I'm not so sure about the last part," Jenny said, giving him a teasing nudge of her elbow before meeting my eyes again. "It definitely helps just in freeing up energy, though."

Interesting, even if it wasn't advice I ever expected to put into practice. "Thank you," I said, riffling through my thoughts for the next question I'd want to ask. "Is there any—"

Victoria stiffened so abruptly that my mouth snapped shut around the words I'd been going to say. Her head jerked around, her gaze darting across the terrain beyond the settlement, around where I'd parked the jeep. I swiveled, following her gaze.

The landscape was draped in shadows cast by the tall cliff to the west. I couldn't make anything out, but Victoria had obviously sensed something.

"Into the houses," she shouted abruptly. "Everyone, *now*. Call whatever creatures you can to our protection."

With the last words, she was already racing toward one of the buildings,

Jenny and Ivan right behind her. The other sorcerers darted off toward their own homes. I hurried after the three I'd talked to, but as I reached the door, Victoria spun around, motioning her son and daughter-in-law past her.

"*You* brought them with you," she hissed. "They followed you here. How else could they have found us right now?"

"What? I—"

Then the first shadowkind beasts lunged out of the shadows at the edges of the courtyard. As the monsters charged toward us, Victoria slammed the door in my face. The other doors had already banged shut all around me.

My stomach flipped over. I couldn't tell her that the monsters who'd been killing sorcerers had already been close to finding her before I'd ever come here, or I'd have to explain how I knew that, and I didn't think knowing I was chummy with some *other* monsters would endear me to her either.

There was no point in running toward the jeep. I'd have to push through a horde of shadowkind to get there, and they didn't look at all friendly. My heart thudding, I shoved myself around the side of the house. The lemonade glass slipped from my hand and shattered on the ground, but I didn't have time to think about that.

A shovel was leaning against a shed around the back. I dashed to it and grabbed it, knowing it wouldn't give me much protection but that it might at least buy me a minute or two in fending the creatures off. The shed itself was locked, so I braced my back against it, brandishing the shovel with one hand and groping in my pocket. Would the larger steak knife or the smaller silver blade offer more protection? I had no idea.

Had my monstrous men seen the coming onslaught? Were they on their way to get me out of here, or was I completely on my own?

How the hell was I getting out of this if they couldn't make it to me?

I clenched my jaw even as my pulse thundered past my ears. I wasn't going to be a useless mortal. I'd fend for myself as long as I could. I dug the silver pen-dagger out of my pocket and held it and the shovel ready.

The monsters that'd surged into the courtyard hardly seemed to notice me back by the shed, though. Hinges squealed and doors groaned as they hurtled themselves at the entrances to the houses. I flinched at the resounding crashes as one and another door fell. Someone inside one of the homes screamed.

Shit. I didn't want to see another family murdered. But I wasn't even sure I could defend myself, let alone the sorcerers who'd left me to my own devices.

A few smaller creatures veered my way. One that was shaped like an armored greyhound sped toward me with teeth gnashing.

As it reached me, I swung the shovel at its head and sent it flying across the dusty ground. Another beast leapt at my elbow, I whipped around to bash it away—and brawny arms with the feel of sun-warmed granite wrapped around me from behind.

"I've got you," Crag said in the deeper, gravelly rumble of his gargoyle voice. It was the most welcome sound I'd ever heard in my life.

I leaned into him, dropping the shovel and letting him take my weight. He hefted me against his chest, pushed off the ground—

And a bright green blur of motion launched itself at us from around the side of the building.

Crag yanked himself around before I could fully comprehend what was happening. His body lurched, and the grunt that jolted out of him told me he'd been hurt by whatever had hit him. It'd almost looked like—

"Lance!" he roared, and I choked on my own spit. How could the dragon shifter be attacking him—us. He would never—

The gargoyle jerked and growled, striking out with one arm while the other held me close. The answering snarl was far too familiar. A chill rippled through me as I remembered Torrent's remark about how it'd be easier for the sorcerers to bring Lance under their control because he'd been affected by that kind of magic before.

Easier for them… and easier for the shadowkind beings now wielding sorcerous magic too?

"Lance!" I cried out in an echo of Crag's protest, as if my voice would be able to penetrate the spell.

Crag tried to lift off the ground again, only to stumble with a ragged breath. When I looked up, I saw his smoky blood streaming off him like when the beasts had attacked us in the sky before. More shrieks and ragged shouts were carrying from the buildings near us, but all I could focus on was my wounded gargoyle and my dragon shifter turned rabid.

A sob caught in my throat. This couldn't be happening. Was there anything I could do to stop it?

Crag staggered, nearly dropping me. As my feet hit the ground, I clutched his neck to make it easier for him to sweep me up again if he could. Then a sinewy appendage whipped past us with a fleshy smack.

Torrent had emerged from the shadows to fight alongside us. Crag pushed closer to the shed, turning around enough that I made out Lance in his dragon form snapping and raking his claws across the tentacles Torrent had flung at him. The other man had even transformed his arms so he could maneuver four tentacles at once while two continued holding his legs steady.

One lithe appendage smacked the dragon shifter into the ground, but Lance rolled and sprang back to his feet in an instant, nimble as ever. A burst of flame erupted from his lips, and Torrent flicked one tentacle to the side before it was totally charred. The burgundy skin bubbled with a fresh burn.

Crag took in our surroundings and set me down. "Stay here," he growled. "Call for me if any more come." Then he leapt in to help Torrent subdue Lance.

He wasn't quite fast enough. Just before he pounced, the dragon managed to clamp its jaws shut on the end of one of Torrent's tentacles. The sinuous flesh ripped with a meaty sound that made my gut churn.

"No!" The protest burst from my mouth, and I was darting forward before I could think better of it. Torrent wobbled backward with smoke gushing from his mangled tentacle, Crag pummeled Lance into the ground, and the dragon shifter let out a screech as if the gargoyle was crushing his chest.

But it was still him. It was still *Lance*. It wasn't his fault—they couldn't *kill* him.

"Lance!" I shouted, my hands waving through the air like some kind of maniac. "Lance, it's us. We've got you. Just—if you can just stop fighting—"

I was maybe five feet away when the dragon somehow managed to squirm out from under Crag's massive body. He threw himself straight at me, eyes searing and jaws snapping.

I teetered backward, and Crag hurtled between us with a roar. One thick, rock-like hand whipped toward me to shove me to the side and clocked me across the face.

I crashed to the ground, blood bursting from a split lip, pain radiating through my jaw and cheekbone. Crag pounded Lance with his other fist, ramming him in the opposite direction. He pinned the dragon shifter down, and Torrent rushed over as fast as his unsteady legs could carry him. He whipped one tentacle against the top of Lance's skull, and the dragon finally sagged, temporarily knocked unconscious.

"We have to get out of here," Torrent said roughly, twining another tentacle around my waist and yanking me to them. Crag flung Lance's limp body over his shoulder, snatched me from Torrent, and sprang into the air as the tentacled man vanished into the shadows again.

I could barely think as the ground fell away beneath my feet and the wind gusted over my bruised face. The screams behind me had stopped—when had they petered out? I couldn't hear anything now except faint snaps and snarls.

Crag dipped and bobbed in the air, obviously struggling, but before I'd gotten my thoughts totally straight, he was landing on a ledge partway up the nearest cliff. The yawning darkness of a narrow cave loomed beyond him. He set me down in a sitting position and then really looked at me for the first time since the fight had started.

Unmistakable horror flashed across his monstrous face. He shifted back into man-like form in a blink, kneeling beside me. "Quinn, I—I didn't mean to—"

"I know," I said, and winced at the brush of my split lip against the upper one. I pressed the side of my hand to the wound and swayed to my feet. "I'll be okay. You—he really went at you—"

"It'll heal," Crag muttered, still looking agonized by my minor injury even as more smoke wavered up off his own back. Then Torrent reappeared behind us in the thicker darkness of the cave.

"We need to make sure Lance is restrained in case the effect of the sorcery hasn't worn off when he comes to," he said, his voice taut with strain. "Quinn, watch for any shadowkind coming this way. I don't know if they noticed us leaving—they seemed... occupied."

I whirled toward the mouth of the valley, backing into the shadows at the mouth of the cave as I did to reduce the chance of being seen. My messenger bag still hung from my back, and I clung to its strap across my chest with both hands. I'd lost my silver pen-dagger somewhere in the chaos, but it hadn't helped much anyway.

The other shadowkind couldn't sense me here, not with my vest on. That might be the only reason I was still alive. Lance had known about the magic I possessed, and those few minor beasties who'd come at me must have gotten it into their heads to attack any human who might interfere, but all the others had been focused on the sorcerers they could detect.

Most of the shadowkind from the attack must have merged back into the shadows. I couldn't make out many moving bodies in the courtyard through the dimness of what was now approaching twilight. Light streaked over the darkened ground from a few windows on the houses, but no forms moved through that illumination either.

A sickly chill wrapped around me like a wet sheet. They were all dead. Victoria, Ivan, Jenny, their relatives whose names I'd never gotten. Even the little boy, Jonah. Slaughtered by those creatures.

I knew the men shuffling around in the cave behind me might not mourn them. They'd hardly been kind to me as soon as trouble had arrived, and they'd been a human sort of monsters to the shadowkind they'd enslaved. But I couldn't shake the horror creeping through me.

They'd never be as monstrous as the actual monsters because they could simply never wield as much or as many different types of power. And now our opponents had merged the one human supernatural skill with all their innate abilities, to the point that they'd managed to control even Lance. I swallowed thickly.

Then something prickled through my senses, making me go perfectly still without understanding why. I peered through the valley for several seconds before the feeling became solid enough for me to focus on its source.

Something was coming. Something I couldn't see but that made the energy embedded in my heart jump and stutter like never before. Instinctively, I pulled the vest tighter against my chest as if that could ensure nothing out there picked up on my reaction.

There was another shadowkind down there, one that had only just arrived. One powerful enough to set all my nerves jangling. It must have slipped into one of the houses, because all at once a huge silhouette formed by one of the windows, blotting out most of the light.

The massive shape bent down, and the fleshy tearing sound that followed was violent enough that my ears caught a trace of it even across that distance. Or maybe I only imagined I did, knowing what must be happening.

That was one of the ringleaders. One of the powerful shadowkind Rollick had warned me I might have to face was devouring the sorcerers' organs and absorbing their powers, like it must have many before. A shiver passed through me, and I cringed deeper into the cave.

I couldn't tell how quickly the being passed from building to building, but I never got the impression that it so much as looked our way. I hadn't left anything behind except for the jeep, and maybe it would assume that'd belonged to the sorcerers living there. I didn't think the shadowkind invaders had followed us, because then they'd have focused on capturing me, not killing everyone else. It'd just been horrible luck that they'd managed to track down the sorcerers' settlement so soon after the attack on the hotel.

Or maybe this group had never been involved in that attack to begin with. The men had figured that there were at least two beings in charge. One could have gone to confront Rollick while the other continued searching for more sorcerers to snack on.

Just when I thought I couldn't get queasier, a shrill weeping that I definitely wasn't imagining split through the evening. I leaned forward again, my heart in my throat, squinting at the settlement.

A mostly human-shaped being, though not the huge one I'd seen in the houses, was dragging a small, squirming form out of one of the buildings. I swallowed thickly, my stomach heaving.

It was Jonah. I didn't need to make out the details of his appearance to be able to tell from his size and his alternately sobbing and pleading voice. That was the house Jenny had sent him into.

The shadowkind attackers hadn't killed him. They were *taking* him—carrying him away now as they hurried at a brisk lope up the road. What the—

Rollick's words came back to me. These fiends had wanted me because I was a human with sorcerer powers they could hope to influence, one who hadn't already been taught to ward off the shadowkind. Were they planning on using that little boy the same way they'd hoped to use me?

Someone moved beside me. I startled in the instant before I realized it was Torrent. He stopped next to me and stared out over the valley.

"They're leaving," I said. The ominously large presence I'd sensed was fading away, and the few shadowkind still in physical form were scurrying back the way they'd come. "They took the little kid. I think—I think they're going to try to make him their pet sorcerer like they wanted to do with me."

Torrent's mouth twisted. He reached for me as if automatically and then caught himself. I glanced over at him, and my chest hitched.

His hand. His right hand—the smallest two fingers were torn right off. The other two and the thumb were a mangled mess, distorted above the mashed mess of his palm. Even his wrist looked battered.

"You—" I stared with a fresh rush of anguish.

Torrent jerked his hand out of view. "It can't be helped," he said sharply. "I've made other accommodations. I can deal with this."

Lance had done that. Lance had mutilated Torrent's human-like body even more than it already was when he'd torn into his tentacle. Oh, God.

These men had come out here for me. They'd come out here to help me get answers, and now Lance's mind had been stolen from him all over again, Crag had been forced to hurt both his friend and me to get us out of there, and Torrent had lost even more of his ability to interact with the mortal realm the way he'd used to.

And that poor little boy...

Tears welled up in my eyes. A wrenching but undeniable certainty filled me.

I'd thought I might be able to run away from this horrible situation. To let my problems rip each other apart, to ask some sorcerer expert to carve the power out of me. But every time I tried to escape, the people I cared about got hurt even more. I couldn't let anyone else suffer on my behalf.

It was my battle too now, as much as I hated that. Which meant I had to face my enemies and fight, or I'd lose even more than I already had.

As that horrible revelation sank in, the faint thrum of an engine wavered through the valley. Torrent frowned, looking toward the road as I did. A dark car had just driven into view from between the cliffs. Even though we were both hidden by the shadows at the cave entrance, we both drew back a little farther, watching warily.

No beings attacked the car, but then, I hadn't seen any hanging around for at least a few minutes now. It parked next to my jeep. The figure that got out was mostly lost in the thickening darkness, but something about it and its movements struck a chord of recognition in me.

I stared as that figure headed across the terrain, not toward the buildings but toward our mountain. He glanced at something in his hand. I couldn't quite believe what I was seeing until he halted about twenty feet from the foot of the cliff and peered up at us with a wry tip of his head.

"Quite the mess you've managed to get yourselves into this time, my mutinists," Rollick said.

CHAPTER TWENTY-SEVEN

Rollick

For the first several seconds, if I hadn't known exactly where Quinn and therefore the three men who'd dedicated themselves to her cause must be, I'd have thought I was talking to thin air. The cliff above me was a mass of shadow-swathed rock.

I kept my arms folded loosely over my chest, my stance casual. No outward sign of the emotions roiling inside me. No indication of the wounds now sealed but still faintly throbbing on my back and thigh. You didn't get very far in our world if you couldn't disguise your weaknesses.

Sometimes even from yourself. I'd thought I'd known approximately how this reunion of sorts would go, but I was unprepared for the jolt of relief that hit me when Quinn's pale form eased into partial sight overhead. She was standing on two feet, both arms appearing to be attached—whatever carnage the fiends who'd reached this spot before me had carried out, she'd escaped it.

She was whole and well, and it was hard to say which of my conflicting impulses was stronger. Definitely the two strongest were the one to yank her into my arms as if I could hold her together longer that way and the one to tear her apart myself for the havoc she'd created back at *my* primary home, as much as they clashed with each other.

"What are you doing here?" she demanded in a voice that only wavered a little, still mostly cloaked in darkness. "What do you want?"

"Strange questions from a woman who just this morning agreed that we'd be meeting up again as soon as I took care of the little problem at the hotel," I said. "Well, I'm not waiting for an engraved invitation."

"You—"

Before she could say anything else, I stepped into the shadows and rushed up through them to the outcropping where she was standing. Before I'd even emerged back into physical form there, I could sense the long stretch of gloom in the cave where they'd taken shelter and the impressions of my three unreliable employees, although Lance's presence felt unusually subdued. Had *he* been injured?

Then I pulled my human guise together and looked Quinn straight in the face from just a few feet away, and every thought and emotion burned away in a blaze of fury that I hadn't been any more prepared for than I had the relief.

This anger wasn't directed at her. Her upper lip was split on the left side, blood marking it and the skin above it, where a bruise was also blooming across her cheek. My claws poked from my fingertips unbidden. I caught myself an inch from spitting out my conjured veneers and snapping my true, fanged teeth.

My voice came out in a rough hiss. "What wretched being did that to your face? Because when I get my claws into him—"

Crag pushed into view, strangely halting with an arm's length of distance between him and the mortal he so exalted—or maybe not strangely given what he said next.

"It was me," he said in a raw rumble. "I—I was trying to keep her out of the way—"

Quinn whipped toward him. "It wasn't your fault. You were protecting me as well as you could with so much going on."

She took a step toward him, reaching out, and froze when he jerked himself farther away. The gargoyle closed his hands into fists and stared down at them before taking in her injuries again.

Even if I'd still wanted to flay the perpetrator alive after finding out the circumstances, I couldn't imagine any punishment I could have visited on Crag that'd hit him harder than the guilt he was already clearly flagellating himself with. My own hands clenched. Seeing her lovely face marred still made me want to hit *something*.

Why should it? I should be furious with *her*. It was her own fucking fault. Her fault my hotel had been stormed. Her fault the four of them weren't securely tucked away in my safe house.

I was furious about that too. My jaw clenched against the acidic words I wanted to toss at all of them. But damn it if there hadn't been a swell of awe mixed with that searing rage from the very first moment the invaders of my hotel had snatched a sketch from beneath the mattress in my suite's bedroom.

She'd played me. This mortal woman who was barely even an adult by human standards had played *me*, a being who'd roved this realm for thousands of years. It was ridiculous and awful and impressive all at once.

She was lucky that I had been around long enough to see plenty of businesses rise and fall and to know how easily I could rebuild from the rubble, or I'd have been a lot more pissed off about the fact that the Sunshine Sin Hotel might never re-open. I certainly couldn't go back there for as long as these assholes were continuing their rampage.

And she hadn't even done all that just to get away from me. She wasn't sticking her head in the sand and hoping she could play house with my traitorous employees while the rest of the world went to hell around her. The very same day she'd escaped me, she'd come here searching for answers.

It was just too bad our enemies had arrived with bloodier interests at the same time.

Of course, she hadn't been clever enough to *completely* foil me. I wasn't an idiot; I'd known she might fly the coop like she'd taken off on me once already. I'd also noticed how closely she guarded the messenger bag she kept her most essential possessions in. It hadn't been any trouble at all to sew a GPS tracker into the lining where she'd never notice it.

Not that I was going to tell her how I'd found her so easily. Let her believe it was my amazing powers of perception or some supernatural skill I'd worked that she could never avoid.

Another figure stirred deeper within the cave. Torrent. "He's waking up," he called to Crag, and I knew immediately he was talking about the dragon shifter. My once-loyal lieutenant glanced at me from where he was crouched, his tentacles oddly stretched across a limp form I realized was covered in green scales. It looked as if he were... holding Lance down.

A hint of my confusion must have made it onto my face, because Quinn spoke quietly in explanation. "One of the beings that's been taking in the sorcerer powers was leading the attack. He must have gotten Lance under his control. He made him attack us."

My body tensed, a jab of worry lancing through my gut. Our enemies had gotten awfully far with the hearts and livers and so on that they'd already devoured, then. To sway a shadowkind as sharp as Lance, even if he'd been prey to sorcerers before... And that'd been before this being had gulped down the innards of the dozen or so magically inclined humans living here. How much might the idiot be capable of now?

This was not good at all.

The scaled body shifted, and a thin whine seeped from its mouth. Then the serpentine figure seemed to crumple inward into the smaller, human-like form that would allow Lance to actually speak. He coughed. "Torrent? I—they—sorcerous shadowkind—"

The last words cut off with a snarl and a gnash of his teeth. Torrent eased back his tentacles. "They're gone. It looks like their influence has left you too. They didn't try to bring you totally under their control—small mercies."

"They came up on me so fast. I didn't even know they were there before that one caught me up..." Lance swayed into a sitting position, hanging his head. "I—I'm sorry. I would never—I tried so hard to stop it—"

"It's not *your* fault," Quinn said emphatically, hurrying over as if she had no further concerns about my arrival. "We know you didn't want to hurt us."

His gaze darted up, and his stance went rigid. "You're bleeding. I could have—" A low, ragged groan rippled out of him.

Quinn's face twisted as if she were just as agonized as he sounded. She dropped to her knees in front of him and gripped his arms. "I'm okay. You can—you can heal it up, and I'll be good as new."

The dragon shifter eyed her with an air of bewilderment as if he couldn't totally believe she meant it—that she'd trust him to take care of her. But when she turned her head to offer the cut on her lip to him, he leaned forward and exhaled a flicker of his fiery breath over that patch of flesh.

Watching him flick his tongue over the spot afterward, almost a kiss, made my hands clench all over again in a way that didn't make any particular sense. I'd already observed her with all three of these men getting far more intimate than that gesture, after all.

The second he'd treated her wound, Lance swiveled away. He tipped over, slumping and stretching at the same time into his dragon form, his head swerving away from the rest of us to press against the rocky wall.

Quinn hesitated and then set her hand on his scaly shoulder. When he didn't shake her off, she leaned in, wrapping her arms right around his sinewy frame and resting her cheek against his scaled neck. She'd been the one who'd nearly died, and there she was offering *him* all the comfort she could, even while he looked as far from human as he could get.

She really didn't mind, did she? It wasn't just getting off on an unusual situation or exotic anatomy. It wasn't imagining away the full extent of their monstrousness. She saw him as being as much of a person as anyone else she might have cared about regardless of how inhuman he appeared in that moment.

Suddenly I wanted to rip him apart, which wasn't a reasonable reaction either. I spun on my heel with a brisk gesture toward Torrent for him to join me.

As I stared out over the darkness now blanketing the valley, he came up beside me at the mouth of the cave. He'd retracted all but his usual two supporting tentacles now.

"So," I said, "should I even bother asking what you're doing out here rather than at the meeting spot we agreed on?"

I wasn't going to admit that I'd realized they'd betrayed me to a far worse extent than that. I still needed Quinn—needed her on my side more than ever, if what had happened here today was any indication—and for now that meant I needed these unreliable underlings too.

My lieutenant lowered his head. "You knew how to contact me," he said with typical terseness. "We thought we'd have the chance to find out something useful about her powers while the other fiends were distracted. You *want* her to get a better handle on her sorcery, don't you?"

Oh, he figured he could turn this around and make it sound as if it'd been a favor to me, did he?

I held in a snort. "I would have preferred it if that training didn't come with a heaping side of bloodshed, FYI."

"We got her out of the way as quickly as we could—and it doesn't look like the other shadowkind even realized she was here."

"Dumb luck." I exhaled sharply and turned to him, just as he adjusted his arm at his side, and the remark I'd meant to make next fled my mind. I stared at his mangled hand—if it could even be called a hand now. Different words tumbled out. "Some part of *you* didn't get out of the way fast enough."

If he hadn't made it clear his loyalties lay elsewhere, I'd have winced a little at the insensitivity of that spontaneous comment. I knew how tormented he was by the infirmities he'd already had when he came to me. But maybe he deserved having the results of this misadventure rubbed in a little—just how badly his choices had gone for him.

It seemed my mutinous followers had gotten punished quite thoroughly before I'd even arrived.

Torrent tucked the damaged hand under his uninjured arm, his voice dropping. "Lance. When I was trying to keep him off Quinn. You know how fierce a fighter he can be."

I did. I hadn't expected him to ever turn those talents against his own squad, though. Fucking sorcerer-scheming shadowkind and their new brainwashing abilities.

I couldn't ignore the opening, though. "It doesn't seem to be working out so well for you—this whole playing guardian angel to the mortal thing. How many losses are you willing to take before you decide it's time to cut out?"

Torrent answered without missing a beat. "I knew there were risks in this line of work, and I knew there were risks in taking her side. I have no regrets. Not like I would have if she'd ended up in those assholes' hands."

I'd thought he'd been that unshakably committed to *me*. If he was even more devoted to her…

I glanced back at where Quinn was still snuggled up to Lance and caught her watching us in the fading twilight, her gaze lingering on Torrent's back, her expression strained. Her eyes darted away at the turn of my head, but I recognized the horror I'd seen written there. And suddenly I understood where I'd gone wrong.

This wasn't the right direction. There were fault lines in the unusual relationship my trio had formed with the budding sorcerer, but if I wanted to crack their unified front, I needed to push from the other end.

And the catastrophe they'd brought on themselves had given me my perfect point of leverage.

CHAPTER TWENTY-EIGHT

Quinn

The light of the electric lantern wavered off the walls of the cave, which we'd ventured deep enough into that little of the glow should show in the valley. It felt weird to be sticking around the place where our greatest enemies had just carried out a massacre, but the fact was that they believed they'd gotten everything they could out of this place. They hadn't noticed me while I was here, and no one outside the valley knew I'd come. This was the last place they'd return to.

I couldn't imagine bedding down in one of the blood-splattered houses, though. I hadn't wanted to face the carnage at all. I'd stayed up here while Crag and Rollick had gathered the lantern and a bunch of blankets to act as a makeshift bed.

We'd spend the night here, and then... Then we'd have to figure something else out. I assumed Rollick had ideas about that, but he'd stayed focused on our immediate situation so far.

My own mind was still a blur of shock and guilt, but I knew I couldn't just go back to being his caged sorcerer.

I sat down against the cave wall, ignoring the gurgle of my stomach. Crag had flown back down to the houses to see what food he could scrounge up. He seemed intent on taking whatever tasks he could that would keep him away from me, which only made the guilt wound through my gut grip me harder.

I rested my hand on my messenger bag, the one certainty I'd clung on to since the first shadowkind attack. Although my phone couldn't place calls and I had no desire to sketch, so its contents were becoming increasingly useless.

The phone alarm went off, and I reached for my pills automatically, chasing them with a gulp of water from my bottle. My heart thumped on in a heavy but steady rhythm. A ripple of energy passed through it.

Somehow it was getting hard to believe that the transplanted organ was my weakness and not the strongest thing in me—strong enough to transform me into a person I'd never have wanted to be.

The other shadowkind had all faded into the shadows, but Torrent wavered into view as I put away the pill case. He sank down next to me, keeping his ruined hand close by his side where it wasn't as noticeable.

"Managing okay?" he asked, his eyes searching mine. As if *I* were the one who'd been permanently mutilated today.

My throat constricted. "I should be asking you that."

Torrent's eyes narrowed, but his even voice came out in the gentler tone I'd only heard him use with me. "I've never wanted your pity, and that hasn't changed." A wry note crept in. "I've still got five fully functional limbs, which is more than humans even start with."

The fact that he could joke about it comforted me only a little. "I guess you can't just swap out which is which." Or he'd already have done that with his legs.

He shook his head, lifting one of his usual tentacles to slip around my shoulders. "There's a certain synchronicity between our shadowkind and human-like forms. I couldn't make this tentacle into an arm or a leg any more than Crag could convince his wings to sprout from the top of his head."

He lifted his wounded arm, considering its mangled state with a contemplative air. The flesh had all melded back together with those special shadowkind healing powers, if into a form that no hand or wrist should look like. "I might chop it right off. Then I could conjure some kind of fixture to work in its place like I do with my foot." He flexed the thumb and the two remaining fingers at their awkward angles. "I'll have to see how well I can still work with this in its current state."

His voice stayed calm, but I knew him well enough by now to catch the jump of a muscle in his jaw, the slight flattening of his lips after he stopped speaking. It hurt, moving that hand, just like standing on his battered legs did. The arm might hurt for the rest of his life even if he amputated the worst of it.

He'd only met me a few weeks ago, and our association had already amplified the pain he'd been enduring for decades in a way that might never leave him.

Torrent glanced at me, forcing his mouth into a crooked smile. "At least now you have confirmation of just how effectively Lance can defend you when he's in his right mind."

"I think I already had plenty of confirmation of that," I muttered, and then Rollick blinked into being near the cave entrance.

"Unwilling sorcerer," he said, brandishing what looked like a balled-up dish towel. "I brought something for you."

I pushed myself to my feet, all my nerves immediately going on the alert. Rollick hadn't accused us of anything other than taking off on an unexpected side-mission, but I had trouble believing that he *hadn't* put the pieces together that I'd purposefully left evidence of my presence in his suite. He was smarter than that. But also smart enough not to bring it up if rubbing our faces in the betrayal didn't suit his current purposes.

"What's that?" I asked, eyeing his supposed gift with skepticism. "You want me to do some washing up?"

He chuckled and walked over until he was closer than I really preferred. Torrent got up too, standing to the side and watching the interaction warily. He'd intervene if he thought he needed to, but I wasn't sure how much he *could* do against Rollick directly.

The demon simply raised the dishtowel to the level of my face, smiling one of his charming movie-star smiles. "The dragon shifter couldn't do anything for the bruise. It occurred to me that a little ice is good for mortal injuries."

"It's okay," I said, pulling back, but Rollick grasped my arm carefully but firmly and brought the chilly fabric to my cheek. From the texture of the lumps, I could tell the thin towel was full of ice cubes.

"It's not okay," he said, with a dark note under the silky quality in his voice that I didn't think was aimed at me. "I'm meant to be seeing to your safety. And I don't imagine any of your devotees likes seeing you looking battered either."

He glanced at Torrent. "Speaking of safety, while Crag is being a perfectionist about what constitutes an appropriate meal, why don't you keep watch over the road into the valley? I'll send the gargoyle to relieve you when he's back."

Torrent's shoulders tensed, and he caught my eye as if seeking my permission. He wanted to know if I actually felt safe with the demon looming over me.

"Go ahead," I said. "I'm sure if Rollick was planning on carving me up, he'd have gotten on with it already."

The demon snorted, but he didn't argue. Torrent nodded and vanished into the shadows.

I turned my focus back to Rollick, wishing his considerate gesture didn't require him to be standing just inches away from me, his stunning face filling almost my entire vision. Wishing he wasn't being so gentle about it. If he'd been raging at me, it'd have been easier for me to keep seeing him as the enemy.

I reached toward the balled towel with its icy filling. "I can hold it myself."

Rollick tsked his tongue and ignored my hand. "For some strange reason, I feel the need to ensure this task is seen through to my specifications. You have a continuing habit of improvising."

I couldn't easily deny that. "You're not obligated to protect me anymore," I reminded him. "The deal was only for ten days."

He shrugged. "I thought I made it pretty clear that I'm not keeping you alive and well simply because of a few words we exchanged. If anything, today's events have only convinced me more how important it is that you stay out of the grasp of those fiends. They're wreaking enough havoc as it is."

I didn't really want to know, because it'd make the guilt inside me swell even larger, but I couldn't help asking, "What happened at the hotel?"

Rollick's expression barely flickered. He did know how to keep up a poker face. "I was visited by many higher shadowkind, though all minions, as far as I could tell. They were convinced I knew of your whereabouts, and they attempted to force me to cough that information up. I made them regret trying. Unfortunately, I had to evacuate the hotel in the process. As far as anyone knows, there was a gas leak that's being investigated. It may need to continue being investigated for quite a while, since I don't think I can safely reopen until this other problem is dealt with."

He shifted his weight on his feet, and I thought I caught the faintest hint of a wince. How many of those minions had he needed to fight off on his own?

"Are you okay?" I asked before I could think better of the question.

"I heal faster than you," he said, which wasn't really an answer. And then, "The scar you gave me is still the most impressive one of the bunch. None of them were wielding silver or iron."

I bit my lip, restraining a wince of my own, but he didn't sound accusing about it. Was it possible he really didn't know we'd set him up? Maybe the other shadowkind had been so convinced by the message Torrent had passed on that they hadn't even looked for evidence, just gone straight into shaking Rollick down.

"What do we do now?" I said. That was the more important question.

Rollick cocked his head. "Did you find out anything useful from that bunch down there before they became monster food?"

I thought back to my truncated conversation with the sorcerers. "Not really. There might be some kind of enclave of sorcerers in Norway that has a better understanding of how powers can develop at all. And I'd have an easier time controlling the ones we're up against if I knew them better, which seems pretty unlikely to happen when they make their followers do most of the actual work."

The demon hummed thoughtfully, but my mind had darted to my last memories of the battle. To the little boy that one minion had dragged off. Jonah.

My mouth went dry, but the vague conviction that'd been sitting like a lump in my stomach took on a clearer form.

"We need to get the kid back," I said.

Rollick blinked at me. "What?"

"The little kid they took. We told you about that. They probably think they can use him the way they wanted to use me. Or they'll realize he won't be powerful enough in time and eat him too. But they kept him alive. We can save him."

"We're having a hard enough time saving you," Rollick said dryly. "One sorcerer kid won't make that much difference—in the near future, anyway.

The only thing I agree with these pricks about is that the fewer sorcerers are in existence, the better. Present company excluded, of course."

His casual dismissal rankled me. I pushed aside his hand with the icy towel, my cheek already numb, and stepped farther away, folding my arms over my chest. "No. He's just a little kid. *He's* never done anything to shadowkind, and he doesn't have any family left to teach him to anyway. And he wouldn't—

My throat choked up abruptly. I was *not* going to cry in front of Rollick again. I dragged in a breath, willing down my emotions, while he studied me.

"He wouldn't what?" he asked.

"He wouldn't have been taken if they hadn't gotten the idea of having their own sorcerer because of me," I said quietly. "Or if they'd managed to catch me. They took him because they *haven't* been able to capture me." Whatever ways they were tormenting him already, it was in my place. I hadn't wanted to make that kind of trade.

The demon studied me. He lowered his voice to match mine. "And now you want to stage some kind of rescue attempt? Don't you think your devotees have gone through enough just looking after you?"

He said it almost sympathetically, but the words hit on the main source of my guilt so dead on that I felt as if he'd punched me in the gut. I squeezed my arms tighter around myself. "I didn't want any of that to happen."

"Of course you didn't," Rollick said. "It's only a natural consequence of your precarious situation. Which is why you really shouldn't go running off on unplanned missions like this one. They're clearly going to follow you to the ends of the earth as long as you'll still have them."

Was this his way of trying to talk me out of wanting to rescue the kid? No matter where we went, I didn't know how to protect the men who were so determined to protect *me*. Torrent maybe would have stepped back if I could have convinced him that I really didn't want him around, but I had the feeling Crag and Lance would stalk me from a distance as long as I was still breathing, determined to make up for the fact that they'd been partly responsible for dragging me into the danger to begin with.

I wouldn't let the demon distract me. "Lance found a place in this part of the country where these shadowkind seem to be operating from, didn't he?" I said. "In Utah, I think he said? That's probably where they'll have taken the kid, unless you think they've got a hideout in every state."

Rollick let out an amused huff. "I agree that would be the most likely place, but that doesn't mean we should pay a visit."

I frowned at him. "It could be for more than just rescuing him. We need to know more about what kind of shadowkind we're up against anyway if I'm going to stop them, and that seems like the best place to look for evidence. You're a super powerful demon. Are you telling me you can't pull this off?"

"I'm telling you I don't see the point, and that I doubt it'll go well."

"Only if you don't pull your weight," I shot back, my annoyance at his callous refusal overwhelming all my other emotions. I paused, remembering the sense of foreboding that'd risen up in me right after the slaughter in the valley below. "I know I have to tap into my powers now. I know I can't just stand by and let these fiends do whatever they're hoping to do. I'll train or work with you however you want—but you have to help me with this."

I needed to start standing up to the monsters right away, or what was the point in taking a stand at all? Jonah needed me *now*, even if I couldn't do much more than snatch him from their grasp. If I'd been more willing to join the battle and work toward stopping these fiends before instead of putting all my energy into running away, maybe the villains never would have made it to the settlement to begin with.

I could fix this one thing. I wasn't backing down until I did. How could I live with myself if I gave up a literal child to be enslaved by fiends in my place?

Rollick arched an eyebrow. "Or what?"

I gazed steadily back at him. "Or I'll go off on my own again and probably get myself killed, and we'll see how well your plans work without me."

I didn't know if I'd have actually taken that risk, not with so much at stake, but the demon clearly didn't know either. He eyed me warily and then let out a huff of breath. "You do drive a hard bargain. We will see what we can find out and whether the attempt has any chance of success—"

"Figure out how to give it a chance," I broke in, picturing little Jonah again. "I'm not doing anything with you, not making any deals or helping with any of your plans, if you're going to let a preschooler die just because of what his parents did."

CHAPTER TWENTY-NINE

Quinn

Before Rollick could respond to my declaration, Crag arrived near the mouth of the cave. It appeared he'd assembled some sort of sandwiches, a little awkwardly with dents in the bread from his broad fingers, which kind of made it more impressive that he'd managed at all. He'd brought a whole heaping plate of them as if I had enough room in my stomach to gulp down five. Or maybe he'd figured all of us would dig in.

"I wasn't sure what to do with the other food in the kitchens, so I went with this," he said gruffly, setting the plate down by the lantern. Not even handing it right to me, as if moving that close could somehow damage me.

"Thank you," I said quickly, shooting him a bright smile even if I couldn't make it totally authentic when he was so obviously struggling with what had happened earlier today. I sat down by the plate and motioned to him. "Are you going to have one? This is way more than enough for me."

Crag shook his head with a jerk. "They're all for you. I wasn't sure what you'd like most."

Maybe I could have come up with something to say to make him feel better, but Rollick snapped his fingers, capturing the gargoyle's attention. "I need you standing watch by the entrance to the valley. I can't imagine our main enemies would head back this way, but we don't want any wandering shadowkind or humans stirring up trouble while we're still here. Tell Torrent he can take a break." The demon cast a downward glance my way. "And I need to go see about a few things, since my would-be sorcerer is as stubborn as ever."

My spirits lifted a smidgeon despite the possessive "my." Did that mean he was seriously considering launching a rescue effort for the little boy?

He didn't clarify, only stepped into the shadows a second after Crag had, leaving me apparently alone. The demon hadn't even bothered to tell me not to go wandering off myself—but then, I couldn't really wander anywhere when I had no way of getting off the cliff without Crag carrying me in flight.

I examined the sandwiches and determined that the gargoyle really had put together a wide variety. One was ham and cheese, another what looked like turkey or chicken along with a few leaves of lettuce, another roast beef with mayo. There was even an egg salad one, from egg salad I had to assume had already been mixed up when he'd found it. I couldn't picture Crag boiling eggs and then carefully cracking and dicing them.

He must have gone through more than one kitchen to find all that. Working so hard to make me happy. How happy had being with me made *him* today?

I swallowed the lump in my throat and forced down the sandwich with lettuce after it, since I figured getting a little bit of vegetables in the mix was probably a good thing. My doctors really would not have been pleased with the majority of my recent diet... other than the hotel meals Rollick had provided.

The thought of the hotel brought my spirits low all over again. Our plan hadn't worked, not really. Rollick had destroyed some minions—great. He hadn't even gotten the chance to take on the real threat, and they hadn't slowed him down much. And he'd found us again so easily.

Maybe he'd spent enough time around me that he could track me just by my general vibe now, regardless of the vest. Or he knew how to trace one or more of the men. It would make sense for him to have some secret way of keeping tabs on his own minions.

My brief stint of freedom had only gotten me a little more information that I had no idea how to use, as well as put all three of my boyfriends through various sorts of trauma. Wonderful. I didn't know if we'd have been better off staying at the hotel, but it couldn't have been that much worse.

I was just finishing the sandwich when Torrent returned, emerging from the shadows with his usual stiff gait.

"Any sign of trouble?" I asked.

He shook his head. "Not a single vehicle within sight, and no shadowkind came anywhere near while I was out there. I think we'll be safe enough here for the night. Are you going to get some rest?"

"Soon," I said. I didn't think I'd be able to sleep just yet with all the anguish churning inside me. I looked down at the sandwiches and thought of Lance's enthusiasm for mortal food. "Where did Lance go? Maybe he'd like a little dinner too."

Torrent tipped his head toward the far end of the cave. "He slunk off through the shadows that way. You could take the lantern and go look for him. I don't need it. It might be good for him to have some company."

"Yeah." My throat tightened all over again. I got up, picking up the plate with one hand and the lantern with the other. "There's plenty to go around if you wanted to eat."

I wasn't surprised when he shook his head. Torrent had generally skipped our group mealtimes.

"I'll be here if you need me," he said. "Just call."

He'd already faded back into the nearest patch of darkness before I turned to venture deeper into the cave.

I crept onward cautiously in the glow of the lantern light. The rocky walls veered to the left and closed in until I could barely walk without brushing my shoulders on them. Then the cave widened again into a space about as big as the hotel suite's living room.

A blanket Lance must have grabbed from the heap near the entrance lay rumpled on the floor off to the side, but there was no sign of the dragon shifter himself.

"Lance?" I said tentatively, holding up the lantern and peering into the shadows. "Are you here?"

His human-like form wavered into being sitting cross-legged on the blanket. He gazed up at me with a somber expression that didn't look right on his normally eager face.

"Are we leaving?" he asked.

"No, not yet. Not for a while, I don't think." I sat down across from him, not sure how close he'd want me to get. He'd accepted the embrace I'd offered him after he'd first become conscious, careful as I'd had to be to avoid pressing my vest against him through my other clothes, but I hadn't been able to tell whether he'd taken much comfort from it. And then he'd slipped away to come over here, apart from all of us.

I set the plate on the uneven floor between us. "Crag made sandwiches. I've already had enough, so I wanted to see if you'd like anything."

Lance considered the clumsy sandwiches, and a small but sly gleam lit in his violet eyes that sent a surge of relief through me.

"The gargoyle is good for hunting," he said. "I don't think we should appoint him head sandwich-maker."

My lips twitched toward a smile. "Maybe not, but they taste perfectly fine. I'm sorry there wasn't any ice cream."

Lance hummed to himself and picked up the ham and cheese. He took a few careless bites, his gaze drifting across the cave as he chewed. Then he dropped the sandwich and shoved the plate away. "I don't really want this."

He fixed his attention on me instead. I saw the moment he started studying the bruise on my cheek in the tightening of his stance. "It still hurts?"

"A little," I admitted. "But I've gotten bruised before. I'm used to it. It'll heal up in a week or so."

Lance raked his hand through his black curls, which looked even wilder than usual. "Torrent won't heal."

I couldn't lie to him about that. He knew what shadowkind were and weren't capable of way better than I did.

"He isn't mad at you," I said instead. "And neither am I, in case I didn't make that clear enough earlier."

Lance let out a sound that was closer to a grunt, as if he didn't totally believe me. Watching him, I couldn't help thinking of bodily activities he'd enjoyed even more than eating. I hesitated and then scooted closer to him, touching his cheek with my hand. Maybe this was what he needed.

"I trust you," I said, stroking my fingers along his prominent cheekbone. "What happened today had nothing to do with *you*. I know when you want to put your dragon claws and fangs on me, I never have to worry."

Lance met my gaze again. For a few seconds, his expression looked torn between conflicting impulses while he held perfectly still. Then he reached out and teased the tips of his claws over the bare skin of my lower thigh below the hem of my shorts. "You still like the claws, huh, baby girl?"

A quiver of desire raced through me despite my concern for him—or maybe because of it, seeing how my admission had started to revitalize him.

"Always," I said, and leaned in to kiss him.

He might have been a little more tentative in the strokes of his claws than he'd normally been before, but he claimed my mouth with total enthusiasm. He grazed the sharp tips up and down my legs and then across my stomach below the base of the vest. I pressed closer to him with a giddy shiver and then eased back an inch both so the metals weren't so near his body—and so that I could run my hands up under his shirt to explore his smooth skin in turn.

Lance gave an approving growl and vanished for a split-second, which was all it took for him to shed his clothes. He captured my mouth an instant later, flicking his tongue between my lips and reaching for the waist of my shorts.

He might not have been interested in the food, but he was definitely hungry. The furor of his response was getting me all kinds of heated up too. It could be we both needed this, a hasty passionate collision to jolt ourselves out of the melancholy that'd fallen over us.

"My woman," he murmured, nipping a path along my jaw. "My Quinn. Always."

I squirmed out of my shorts and panties. Lance fingered the bottom of my shirt with a grumble, knowing as well as I did that we couldn't risk removing the vest.

To distract him from that minor setback, I clambered right onto his lap, nudging him down onto the blanket at the same time so I could take in his full naked glory sprawled beneath me.

At least, that was the idea. As I straddled him with my hands splayed against his chest, pushing him downward, Lance's whole body went rigid with a sudden flinch. His own hands shot to snap around my wrists as a hiss that sounded like a deadly warning rasped out of him.

It happened in a flash, and then his grip on my arms was already loosening, though he didn't quite let go. Anguish filled his expression again.

I scrambled off him to kneel beside him instead, and he released me then. "I'm sorry," he said roughly.

"You didn't hurt me." I showed him my unmarked wrists. An inkling crept into my mind of what the problem might be. He'd held my wrists before when we'd hooked up, though he'd been on top of me then. It'd turned out I liked the restraint, but at first he'd done it because of memories lingering in his head.

The only humans he'd really interacted with before me had been the ones who'd enslaved him.

"You felt trapped," I suggested. "I know you don't like that. I should have realized—"

"No," he interrupted, with a scowl I could tell was directed at himself rather than me. He shoved himself into a sitting position and pulled me tight against him, heedless of the vest. "I shouldn't be afraid with you. I know *you* wouldn't hurt me. You had nothing to do with those other ones. It just—my body reacted…" He trailed off mournfully.

I nestled my head next to his, pressing a kiss to his shoulder. We were even more entwined than we'd been a minute ago and almost totally naked, but the mood had shifted in a way I wasn't sure we could get back. But talking this through was more important.

"It makes sense," I said. "People like me were horrible to you. And you were just reminded of that time in the worst possible way today."

"They were *nothing* like you," Lance snarled, and hugged me even tighter.

I returned the embrace, wishing I knew how to heal the wounds inside him as easily as he could seal the ones I'd taken.

"Will you tell me about it?" I asked tentatively. "What happened back then? Maybe I'll be better at not stirring up those memories if I totally understand."

Lance let out a wordless mutter and tucked his face into the crook of my neck. It felt like a refusal, but then he turned me in his arms so my shoulder rested against his chest and his breath ruffled my hair.

"It isn't a very interesting story," he said.

"I'd still like to hear it, if you're okay with telling me. I want to know *you* as much as I can."

He made a noncommittal sound, but then he started talking. "I wandered through a rift into the mortal realm. I hadn't been here before, and it was overwhelming—and then this magic wrapped around me, like it was putting a cage around my thoughts and moving my body for me. The sorcerers must have lived near the rift, watching for beings they'd like to use."

He paused and then went on. "They kept us in cages. There were four of them and seven of us. All of us higher shadowkind. Those sorcerers were ambitious. But they didn't want us roaming around when we weren't following their orders, so, the cages. They would weaken us too. Jab us with silver and iron things. Make sure we were never at our full strength." He shuddered.

I slipped my hand around his arm and squeezed gently. "That's awful."

"It wasn't even the worst for me. I was the strongest because I was the newest. The others had been through much more. The sorcerers would send us out to take things or kill people... mortals who were always weaker no matter how we'd been weakened... I don't know what the sorcerers wanted, really."

"But you got away from them," I said.

The dragon shifter nodded, his chin brushing my temple. "I thought I would get us all out—all of us shadowkind they'd trapped. We all wanted to leave. The others were older—they had more that they missed—they would talk about it sometimes when they weren't feeling too badly... They would try to reassure me that I wouldn't be locked away there forever. They were right about that."

He stopped for a moment, and I gave him the space to find his next words. He kissed the top of my head.

"The sorcerer who'd put her magic around me—she liked how I looked. Maybe she wanted to know how my claws would feel too. I just knew... I had a little bit of power there. So I pretended that I wanted her too. To get her to open my cage. To let me touch her, when normally we couldn't. And when I did..." His lips drew back in a snarl, and he lifted one hand away from me to make a savage swiping motion through the air.

"She deserved it," I said without hesitation. After the description he'd given of his treatment, the knowledge that he'd murdered his captor didn't bring even a flicker of discomfort.

"Yes. But the others... I got their cages open, and the other sorcerers realized, and they had a strong hold still. Me and one other, we were bound by the woman I killed, and when she was gone we were free, but the rest—"

He stopped for a moment, his head drooping. "The sorcerers ordered them to attack each other. They weren't sure who was even under control then, they just wanted us all dead. I tried to kill those sorcerers too, but by the time I slashed the last throat… the other shadowkind with me, they'd torn each other apart."

Tears had welled up behind my eyes. From what I'd seen, I didn't think all sorcerers were quite that vicious, but it was easy to understand the shadowkind's immediate animosity toward them if any at all acted like that.

"I didn't save any of them," Lance said quietly. "They all died by their cages. I don't know—if I'd picked a different moment, or gone after the other sorcerers before letting them out, or—" A tremor ran through his body, and then his muscles stiffened. "Those mortals call us monsters, but they couldn't let us go even then. They'd rather see us die!"

I reached up to loop my arm around his neck, hugging him as well as I could in our current position. "And you can't blame anyone but them. You did everything you could—and you shouldn't have been in that position to begin with. And it was still… It was still helping the others a little. At least they knew someone cared enough to try to get them out. And they didn't have to go through any more of the torture."

"Maybe," Lance muttered, sounding unconvinced. "If I could tear those sorcerers apart all over again…" He growled in frustration.

My earlier guilt congealed in my stomach. "I'm sorry," I said, my voice faltering.

Lance pulled back far enough to see my face, his eyebrows rising. "You don't need to apologize. You didn't have anything to do with it."

"I know, but—I got you into the situation we're in now. It's because of me that you had to go through something like it again, having your self-control stolen from you. Bringing sorcery back into your life."

"No." In one swift movement, Lance flipped us. I found myself sprawled on the blanket under him, staring up into his flaring eyes. He braced his hands on either side of my shoulders and his knees by my thighs, gazing down at me. "Never apologize for that. I got you. I *have* you. I've never—you're the only being—I didn't know how much I was missing. I would go through all of the awfulness a hundred times over again if it meant keeping you safe and with me."

My pulse stuttered at the determination in his words. "Lance—"

"I love you, Quinn," he broke in. "That's what humans say when they feel like this, isn't it?"

I blinked at him, twice as startled as before. It'd never occurred to me to wonder whether the shadowkind could even feel love the way people thought about it. "I don't know."

He snorted and leaned in to nuzzle my face with a flick of his tongue along the tender underside of my jaw. "I want to be with you all the time. To hear you talking, to see what you'll do, to feel you next to me." He lowered his body so it rested against mine, his eyes peering into mine from just a couple of inches away now, his heat engulfing me. "I would go anywhere and do anything if it helped you. Isn't that what humans call love?"

I choked up for a completely different reason than before. I suspected that for an awful lot of people, love didn't extend even half that far. Who was I to tell him what he felt couldn't be called that?

And an ache had formed around my heart at the same time with the knowledge that I felt the same way. If he'd told me there was something all the way on the other side of the world, through deadly landscapes and past brutal enemies, that could protect him from the influence of sorcery or heal his guilt over the lives he'd failed to save, I would have jumped to get it for him without a second thought.

"I love you too," I said, almost as surprised by my words as I'd been by his. The emotion had been creeping up over me without my noticing, but the declaration felt so right.

Lance beamed at me, his previous somberness falling away. He lifted one hand to tease his claws along the side of my neck and bared his teeth with his dragon fangs glinting. "Do you? And not just my claws and fangs and—"

He rolled his hips, the erection I'd only been vaguely aware of before sliding against my sex. A whimper spilled out of me at the abrupt rush of pleasure, but I held on to my voice.

"All that stuff is very good," I murmured. "But I also love how adventurous you are, and how you can see the fun side of everything, and how you question things instead of just accepting them. You're brave, and you stand by the people you care about even when it's hard—not just me, but Crag and Torrent too."

A rumble vibrated through Lance's chest. "When they deserve it. You always do. My Quinn. All mine." He captured my mouth again then, stroking his cock over my clit until my hips canted upward in a plea. Then he plunged right into me, drinking in my gasp, sighing his own satisfaction with a tinge of fire.

As I lost myself in the rising wave of bliss our bodies kindled together, one clear thought penetrated the haze.

I loved all three of my shadowkind men, didn't I? I wanted to protect them as much as they'd protected me. But what had I really faced, what had I really risked on their behalf?

Lance had said he'd do anything for me, and I believed him. Shouldn't I be willing to go just as far to save him and the others?

CHAPTER THIRTY

Quinn

I woke up next to a warmly scaled body. Lance had stayed with me the whole night in the cave's deeper room, but sometime while I'd slept he'd morphed back into his dragon form.

I didn't mind. For a supposed reptile, he was awfully hot-blooded, and his scales were so smooth they felt almost silky against my skin. In his longer body, he'd been able to curl himself right around me, spooning me from behind with his tail tucked around my front so that I was completely engulfed in his affection.

I had about ten seconds to appreciate the peacefulness of the moment before Rollick's lilting voice echoed from the other end of the cave. "Any mortals around here who wanted to run a rescue mission should probably stop sleeping in."

Lance stirred as I sat up with a jolt. The demon was agreeing to go after Jonah? I didn't want to give him time to change his mind.

The dragon shifter stretched cat-like while I yanked my panties and shorts back on, and then sprang up into his human-like form. He grabbed me to press a quick kiss to the crook of my jaw with a much more upbeat energy than he'd shown yesterday. Maybe our talk... and all the other things we'd done... had helped him even more than I'd dared to hope.

"Who are we rescuing?" he asked as I tugged him with me toward the entrance to the cave.

He'd slunk off before the rest of us had discussed that part of the catastrophe. "The sorcerers had a little kid," I said. "The shadowkind that attacked yesterday took off with him, probably to try to make him work whatever magic he's got on other monsters. We can't let them do that."

Lance let out a humph that I couldn't decipher. He might not have been keen on doing anything that helped a sorcerer, child or not, but he wouldn't want our enemies using the boy either.

We found Rollick standing near the mouth of the cave, looking ridiculously dapper in his tailored suit in the middle of the rugged environment. I'd have thought he might have adjusted his fashion sense a little to fit the setting, but then, maybe it fit his personality to refuse to bow to his surroundings. My men seemed to wear pretty much the same thing all the time, so maybe shadowkind had particular clothes they found most easy to conjure, whether because of their nature or out of habit it was hard to say.

The demon motioned to a plate next to the heap of blankets that'd been supposed to serve as my bed, and I realized someone had gone down to the settlement again to make me breakfast. Scrambled eggs, a piece of toast, and an apple waited for me.

I didn't know whether Crag had gotten more ambitious with his culinary skills or if one of the others had taken a stab at feeding me. It was hard to picture Torrent working over a stove with his tentacles serving in place of his wrecked hand, but even harder to imagine Rollick lowering himself to playing cook for a mortal.

"What's the plan for the rescue?" I asked, sitting down on the blankets and wielding the fork.

Rollick propped himself against the rocky wall, alternating between watching me and peering down into the valley. "I've been able to confirm that the kid was taken to the camp of sorts that those idiots have set up in Utah—the one you found." He tipped his head to Lance. "I've set up a few distractions that I believe should draw the ringleaders away for long enough that we can crash their party without having to do battle with them directly."

Somehow that information both relieved and unnerved me. "Are you sure you can't tackle them head on? We could end this whole thing today if you took them down." Or was he still avoiding showing how invested he was, even now that they'd chased him out of his home?

Rollick's grimace suggested he wasn't happy about the situation either. "They're clearly powerful beings with a lot of powerful underlings, and they've already advanced their human-style sorcery beyond what I expected. I don't think I'd win against all of them on my own or even with just the four of you backing me up. Maybe if I summoned an entire army… but that would take days to organize, and they'd almost definitely catch wind of the activity, and then they'd stash the kid somewhere even harder to find. Which I don't think is what you want?"

"No." I swallowed a mouthful of eggs, finding my mouth had gone dry. "But is that what we'd do next—after we get him out? Raise a whole army?"

"I don't know," Rollick admitted. "I'm only going along with this whole rescue effort so I can get a better read on what we're up against. If we can simply pick them off using more cleverness than might, that's vastly preferable to staging a full-out war. To both me and you. There's no way there wouldn't be a lot of mortal casualties if it got to that point."

Lance's good spirits had dampened as we'd talked. He adjusted his weight from foot to foot restlessly. "Is it a good idea for me to go with you? If they work their new magic on me again…"

Rollick focused on him. "Do you have any reason to believe the being that imposed their power on you was a shadowkind on a similar level as yourself?"

Lance shook his head. "I didn't see him, but whoever it was, he felt very… large. And old. Heavy."

I remembered the sense I'd gotten of the being that'd arrived at the settlement after the other shadowkind had killed the sorcerers. "That's got to be the one that came to collect the organs."

Rollick nodded. "It seems doubtful that the ringleaders would be letting any of their underlings partake. They want as much of the ability as possible for themselves. So if we've diverted them from the camp, then you won't have anything to worry about." He splayed his hands, offering a crooked smile. "And if we don't manage to divert them, then we're most likely screwed anyway."

"Very comforting," I muttered.

"Take comfort in the fact that I know what I'm doing, and I've been pulling off whatever I want to for thousands of years," Rollick said, and turned back toward the valley. "Torrent and Crag are searching the sorcerers' houses in case there's anything in there we can use. I'd like to move out as quickly as possible, but since I'm not letting you out of my sight again, stubborn sorcerer, I'm hoping we can find a thing or two that might allow you to defend yourself a little better during this escapade."

I guessed the steak knife I'd still managed to hold on to wasn't likely to cut it. I sat up a little straighter, swallowing the last of my eggs and stuffing the apple into my messenger bag for the trip. "Definitely. If there's any way I can hold my own without the rest of you worrying about me, I'll take it. We can head down there now. I'll eat the rest of my breakfast during the drive."

Rollick shot me an amused glance with a brief flick of his gaze toward Lance. "Somehow I don't think there's anything you could do to prevent a whole lot of worrying from your devotees. But at least having you armed may mean they can focus *slightly* more on the task at hand rather than protecting that mortal body, as lovely as it is."

I hid my wince at the guilt his casual remark provoked. He was right, but I didn't know how to change that. I'd already tried running away, doing whatever I could to escape our enemies and this situation, and it hadn't kept them safe. Was there anything that could?

It seemed more and more certain that the only way I could really protect them was by stopping the fiends that were after me, whatever it took. And this rescue was the first step toward doing that.

As I got up, Crag appeared on the ledge outside the cave in gargoyle form, his wings already unfurled. "We've got something that might be useful," he told Rollick. "Can't handle it easily ourselves, though."

I stepped toward him. "Bring me down, and I'll take a look."

It killed me that he hesitated before reaching his arms out to me, as if he thought the simple embrace he'd used to save me from danger more than once might now injure me. I wrapped my own arms around his neck and tucked my head beneath his chin. "I'm okay. Let's go find whatever I can use to make sure I stay that way."

He grunted, but there was no denying the tenderness with which he held me against him as he lifted into the air. He didn't say anything as we glided down to the courtyard where I'd spoken with the sorcerers yesterday. When we landed, his hold on me tightened for an instant before he let go. "It isn't pretty. They left the bodies."

I got a preview of what he meant before I'd even moved away from him. By one of the bashed-down doors, a body was sprawled, the arm slumped across the threshold. Blood splattered the doorframe. A meaty scent already tinged with a hit of rot carried on the warming morning breeze. The sound of buzzing flies made me shudder.

Torrent materialized in a different, less bloody doorway nearby. He beckoned us over with his good hand. "One in here was using a weapon I think you should be able to handle. It worked decently well for her. She took down a few of the creatures before they overwhelmed her."

As I headed over, Rollick and Lance appeared alongside us after their slightly slower journey from the cave through the shadows. I braced myself before stepping into the house.

The smell got thicker, but at least it wasn't quite as putrid as the lingering stench in the sorcerers' house back in Florida. I averted my eyes from the stream of blood that'd trickled across the floor from the doorway to the kitchen and followed Torrent to what appeared to be a family room at the back of the house.

Another body was sprawled there, a woman whose face I vaguely recognized from the silent bystanders yesterday... and whose torso was gouged open from throat to pubic bone. Her chest was a mass of shredded tissue. I caught one glimpse of it and jerked my head to the side, my stomach flipping over.

Oh, God. And they must all look like that—Victoria and Ivan and Jenny, and all the others who'd never introduced themselves. Would the monsters decide to do the same to Jonah after all? They might have already...

With my hand clamped to my mouth, it took me the better part of a minute to get my nausea and horror under control. My gaze settled on a crumpled heap in another part of the room that was steaming dark smoke. Torrent stepped over to it.

"This is one of the shadowkind she shot," he said, and held up a contraption about as long as his forearm. It was made of metal and wood and looked like a combination between a crossbow and a gun. "The bolts are half iron, half silver. There are a few scattered around here and more in a room in the basement, but I can't handle them easily."

"Of course not." I girded myself and stepped into the room to pick up the bolts he indicated, each like a shiny metal pencil with an especially sharp tip. When I'd stuffed the handful into my bag, he led me down a set of stairs to the basement, which was thankfully free of corpses.

The storage room he'd mentioned was stacked with dusty boxes. One shelf held a plastic carton that appeared to be full of more of those bolts. I grabbed that and spotted a dagger similar to the one I'd found in the other sorcerers' house.

"I'll take this too," I said. The last one had come in handy.

As Rollick obviously remembered. "As long as you don't stab that one into any of us," he said dryly from where he'd followed us to the doorway.

"Don't be too much of a jerk, and it shouldn't be a problem," I retorted.

My gaze fell on a few faded but relatively modern-looking notebooks stacked on a higher shelf. I picked one up and flipped through it. It appeared to be a journal, written in a messy but readable scrawl, the dates in that one from a few years ago.

"Maybe they knew more than they wanted to tell me," I said, stuffing those into my bag as well. "I'll read through their notes when I have a chance."

Rollick motioned to me. "Come on, let's make sure you're prepared to use that thing."

I couldn't get out of the house fast enough. We tramped over to the cliffside, and Torrent handed me the crossbow. It was heavier than I expected—I needed two hands to steady it—but the mechanism looked simple enough. Without help, I figured out how to arm it with three bolts, which appeared to be as many as it could hold at one time. Then I puzzled over how exactly to ready one to fire.

Rollick stepped closer, examining the weapon quickly and then showing me a metal fixture I needed to pull into place. "You'll aim using the sights here," he said, tapping a notch.

I held the weapon at eye level with both hands, curled one finger around the trigger, and squeezed hard. The bolt smacked into the rock just an inch below the darker spot I'd been aiming at. Not bad for my first try.

Now that I knew what to do, it only took a second to ready the next bolt. I fired off the other two in quick succession, managing to hit my target dead on the third time. My arms were aching a bit from the strain of keeping the crossbow aloft and still, but that was a small price to pay for self-defense.

"It'll be harder with moving targets—and when you've got to worry about more than one," Rollick said. "You'll want to shoot at whatever's closest and keep your back to as much shelter as you can find."

"Right." I dragged in a breath and looked around at the other men. "Better than hitting them with a shovel, anyway."

Torrent cracked the smallest of smiles. Crag still looked intensely grave. Lance bounced over to point out where the bolts I'd fired had landed so I could quickly snatch them up. Their ends had blunted with the impact, but at that speed they'd probably still penetrate flesh. It seemed wiser to keep them just in case.

I didn't know how many battles I'd need this weapon for.

"Do you want to practice more?" Torrent asked, shooting a sideways glance at Rollick.

The demon had been hurrying me along, but I couldn't say he was wrong to. Every second we lingered here was another opportunity for the shadowkind marauders to decide the little boy was better eaten than enslaved. But I didn't want to falter in the middle of our raid either.

I reloaded the blunt bolts into the bow. "I'll do a few more rounds."

For several minutes, I went through the motions of readying and firing and reloading until the movements started to feel more comfortable and I could hit a head-sized target from several feet away while walking slowly. I doubted I was going to get much more competent than that in the limited time we had.

Rollick had apparently decided we were using his car. He'd already grabbed my backpack from the backseat of the jeep and tossed it in the trunk of his sedan. I guessed that made sense when the invaders had seen the jeep when they'd launched their attack, if they'd been paying much attention to it.

"Get in," he said after I'd lowered the crossbow, opening one of the back doors. "Crag, you stick close to her. We don't know what we might encounter on the way there."

I clambered onto the buttery leather seat, and Crag sank down on the other side, in human form now. He sat so stiffly that I was afraid to even reach over and take his hand.

I studied him as Rollick gave Torrent and Lance some instructions I couldn't hear. As the demon got in and started the engine, Crag's muscles tensed, and I was suddenly sure he was going to fade right into the shadows rather than stay where I could see him.

I caught his arm before I could second-guess the impulse and cringed inwardly at his immediate flinch.

"Don't," I said, unable to keep the pleading note from my voice. "I'm not scared of you, and you shouldn't be scared either. It was a lot better that I got a bit banged up than that Lance sank his claws into me."

Crag allowed himself to look at me as the sedan lurched forward over the uneven ground. Even with my voice quiet, Rollick must have been able to hear me, but he didn't offer any comment this once, thankfully.

The gargoyle's voice came out low but rough. "I don't like how easy it is to hurt you without even meaning to. I thought—I thought it wouldn't happen, but I still can. It could happen without me even touching you."

My chest clenched at his words, but I raised my eyebrows. "I don't think that's very likely."

He pulled his gaze away. "There was a woman once—she was stealing wallets at the hotel club. I went to frighten her into thinking better of doing it again. But she—when she saw my true form—it startled her so much that her heart failed. She died."

Oh, shit. Suddenly his reactions—all the way back to when we'd first been sparring, how careful he'd been of me, how long it'd taken before he'd let me get a clear look at his gargoyle body—made so much sense. And that moment yesterday had brought all his past anguish rushing to the surface just like it had for Lance.

"You know that won't happen with me," I pointed out. "I have no problems at all with seeing you as a gargoyle." But the reassurance sounded weak even to my own ears.

Maybe it wouldn't go quite like that, but I knew better than anyone how fragile my health could be. I couldn't promise him I'd live forever or that nothing we encountered together would push me past my breaking point.

Crag wrapped his fingers around my hand just for a second and then let me go. "I'll protect you in every way I can. But that also means it's safer for you if I keep a little distance."

I didn't know what to say to that at all. An ache clamped around my lungs like a vise.

These men cared about me so much, but it was getting harder to say that having me in their lives was all that good for *them*.

CHAPTER THIRTY-ONE

Quinn

We left the car near the base of the mountain, out of view in a stand of scrubby trees near the side of the road. After driving through the majority of the day with only a few brief pit stops, I had to stretch the stiffness out of my legs. Evening was setting in again, but having the cover of darkness for this raid would make it easier for us to sneak up on the camp.

I'd carried my messenger bag out of habit, slung over my back. Rollick eyed it. "You should leave that in the car. The less you have weighing you down, the better."

The thought of leaving behind my stash of medication—and my first aid supplies, and my water bottle, and all the other bits and pieces that went into keeping my health stable—made my pulse stutter. Although if we didn't make it back to the car, there was a good chance it was because I'd already kicked the bucket.

I tugged at the strap while holding on to the small crossbow with my other hand. "I've got the spare ammo in there."

"Stuff your pockets full," the demon said. "You've got a hoodie with your things somewhere, don't you? Put that on and fill those pockets too.

They'll be easier to grab for quick reloading that way." He turned away without waiting for my response. "You'll need to wait here for a little while anyway. I need to make sure the coast is clear and interrupt that repulsing magic Lance noticed here before."

How exactly was he going to do that? Rollick didn't stick around to explain, vanishing into the shadows the moment he'd finished speaking. I hesitated and then popped open the trunk so I could dig my hoodie out of my backpack.

He did have a point. The crossbow put me off-balance as it was. And at this elevation with the sunlight fading, the air was already turning cool. I might appreciate the extra layer once we were even higher up.

Crag stood stoically but not too closely by while I rearranged my belongings. After a moment, Torrent and Lance emerged from the shadows they'd kept to for most of the ride. Torrent leaned against the side of the car and flexed his tentacles. I assumed he'd make most of the trip in shadowy form, but it was reassuring to see him again before we set off.

Lance prowled around the trees, his head tilting to one side and then the other in a way that reminded me of his dragon form even though he was in his human body. "They work too much unnatural magic in this place," he muttered. "More than tricksy. Sick."

Seeing his uneasiness made my gut twist. "You don't have to come," I started. "You could hang back and guard the car—"

He whirled toward me with an emphatic shake of his head. "They got me when I stayed back before. Not again. We need to tackle the beasties together. I won't let them get in my head, and I won't let them get yours."

He flashed his claws meaningfully with that last statement, but his eyes still looked wilder than I liked. This mission was only dredging up more of that old trauma for him. He might have made some peace with it when we'd come together last night, but not enough to put it completely behind him.

"Rollick will make sure the beings with the sorcerer magic aren't around," I reminded him.

He hummed to himself. "I'd like to show them a thing or two." He scratched his claws across a tree trunk, starting to carve one of his abstract designs.

Torrent reached for him with his mangled hand, caught himself, and switched to snagging Lance's arm with a tentacle. He wasn't used to the new disability yet.

Of course he wasn't. How long had it taken him to adjust to his injured legs?

"We shouldn't leave obvious signs that we were here," he said to the dragon shifter.

Lance snorted. "They're going to know we came. There'll be pieces of their minions all over the place to show for it."

"They won't know it was definitely *us*. You made those carvings all over the cabin—some of their followers will have seen them. It's better to leave as little trace as possible."

Lance growled discontentedly, but he lowered his hand. He stalked over to me instead and wrapped his arms around me from behind, burrowing his face against the side of my neck. After the confession he'd made yesterday, his touch set off both a flare of heat between my legs and a softer glow of affection in my chest. I was abruptly doubly glad for the extra layer of the hoodie, protecting him from the worst effects of contact with my protective vest.

Torrent watched us for a moment and then stepped closer to loop one tentacle around my forearm, as if he felt the need to stake his own claim. I brushed my fingers over the row of suckers, and his gaze momentarily darkened with desire, but we both knew this wasn't the time or place for any more intensive indulgence.

Crag stayed poised a few feet away, his gaze flicking to us but his stance rigid. Would *he* ever touch me again, for more than a brief moment or a necessary flight?

I tried not to think about that possibility, soaking in the tenderness two of my men were offering.

It felt like no time at all when Rollick reappeared. "All right," he said. "The camp looks pretty sparsely inhabited at the moment. My distractions were effective. Let's get moving before they peter out and the head honchos return."

"What exactly were your distractions?" I had to ask.

"Let's just say I gave them reasons to think you might be a few different places where you definitely aren't and that aren't all that close to here." He jerked his head toward the mountainside. "Are we rescuing this kid or what?"

I raised my chin. "I'm ready."

Torrent squeezed my arm one last time and slipped into the shadows. Rollick followed him, but I knew even in the darkness that dappled the mountainside, he'd be leading the way for all of the shadowkind men to the spot where he thought we could best launch our attack.

Lance stepped away from me and shifted into dragon form. Crag shifted as well, his leathery wings sprouting from his stone back, and picked me up gingerly. As embarrassing as it was, I knew I was the slowpoke here. It didn't make any sense for me to insist on walking when the ascent would take us more than twice as long that way. Every minute counted.

I didn't want this expedition to turn into another disaster. We'd just grab Jonah, quickly observe whatever evidence there was to see about the nature of the fiends we were up against and their plans, and get out of there.

Crag took off into the air, staying close to the darkened rocky landscape as he flapped his wings. We soared up the slope at a more measured pace than I knew he was capable of, since he had to follow Rollick's course. I wanted to point out that I was perfectly safe here in his arms despite his worries, but after our conversation in the car, I wasn't sure if that comment would go over well.

It was probably better not to remind him of his fears right before we went into battle.

I hugged the crossbow to my chest so it didn't bump against him. "Are the bolts and my vest bothering you?"

"It's no problem for this short a flight," the gargoyle insisted in his gruff way.

Abruptly, he dropped to the ground by a scrawny sapling. He set me on my feet and glanced around, I assumed to check that at least one of the other men was in range to protect me. Then he lunged into the shadows.

I understood why several seconds later when he burst back into physical form farther up the slope, where I could only just make him out in the dwindling light. He had some kind of creature pinned to the ground for an instant before he ripped its foxlike head right off. Then he was diving back into the shadows with its smoking body, removing the evidence.

A sentry. We must be getting close. I peered beyond him to the jagged edge of rock between the two nearest mountain peaks. We seemed to be heading for that spot.

Crag returned to scoop me up again without another word. I heard a few more faint squeals and gurgles as we went, when one or another of the men on the ground must have dispatched other creatures they encountered.

Crag didn't come back to earth until we'd reached the ridge. I crouched down between two jutting spikes of rock and peered down toward the shadowkind camp.

The ring of mountains circled what looked like a massive crater with a rippling lake in its middle. A few rough buildings stood around it, maybe to hide supplies. Or maybe in preparation for housing me there. A sliver of ice ran down my spine.

A distant whimpering reached my ears a moment later. I stiffened, squinting at the buildings, but I couldn't make out any movement. Which one was Jonah inside? How many shadowkind were lurking in the gloom between us and him?

My companions emerged around me, studying the terrain equally intently. "I think there were more here before," Lance said approvingly. "We can handle this bunch. Slash and sever." He clicked his claws.

"Don't get too cocky," Rollick said, but his tone was languid, as if we were back in his hotel discussing dinner plans. Apparently he wasn't all that worried at this point either.

"Should we try to take any of them prisoner to question them?" Torrent asked.

The demon frowned. "I haven't seen any higher beings that'd be able to talk so far. It's mostly beasties they've left guarding the place. If you come across one and have a solid chance, go for it, but we don't want to leave ourselves vulnerable spending extra time scouring the place."

He motioned to the buildings. "We have a straight path to get to them but not much cover. Crag and Torrent will charge ahead and clear the way. Lance and I will hang back with Quinn. As soon as we reach the buildings, we check each one. Quinn cajoles the kid so he doesn't throw a complete fit, Crag picks up the two of them, and we get back to the car as fast as we can move. During all that, everyone keep an eye out for traces of the shadowkind who built this place that might be useful. Any questions?"

Torrent rolled his shoulders. "We go right now?"

"No time like the present." The demon glanced at me. "Assuming you're good to go."

It was hard to be offended by him singling me out when I was the least capable fighter among us by approximately ten miles. I brandished my loaded crossbow with all the bravado I could muster. "As good as I'll ever be."

Rollick flicked his hand, and Torrent and Crag leapt forward, Torrent vanishing into the darkness and Crag staying in his gargoyle form. As they barreled ahead of us, I heaved myself over the lip of the crater and dashed down the shallow rocky slope as quickly as I could while making sure I didn't trip on the uneven ground.

Lance's claws scrabbled against the stone surface behind me. I didn't look back, but I suspected Rollick had slipped into the shadows like Torrent had, though for different reasons.

Torrent could move much more easily that way. Rollick simply didn't want any witnesses that he'd been here.

How much would he intervene even if our lives were at stake?

I tightened my grip on the crossbow. I couldn't worry about that, only about doing whatever I could to ensure we didn't get to that point.

As the now-cool breeze whipped through my hair, the first wave of shadowkind creatures burst from the shadows to meet our charge. There were far fewer of them than we'd faced when they'd been the ones descending on us out of the blue, but my pulse still hiccupped at the sight of the unnerving shapes wavering into being as if from nothing.

One thing that looked like an elongated racoon popped into being right in front of me. My finger squeezed on the trigger once—twice. The second bolt caught the thing in the chest, tossing it backward with an agonized hiss and a spurt of smoky blood. As I ran on past its slumped body, Lance slashed through its neck to chop off its head for good measure.

Crag and Torrent caught most of the beasts before they got near me. Crag whipped in one direction and another, tearing through the shadowkind like they were made of tissue paper. Torrent didn't fully emerge, but his tentacles lashed out of the gloom to smash one creature's skull and hurl another all the way to the lake.

Feeling a little steadier after my initial victory, I fumbled in my pocket for more bolts and managed to fit one and then another into the crossbow while slowing my pace only a little.

A lizard-like being hurtled at me from the side, and I threw myself away from it, stumbling and landing on my butt. My shot went wild, but then a clawed, ruddy hand snatched out of the shadows and ripped its chest open.

Okay, so Rollick wasn't just hanging around watching the rest of us do all the work.

A bristly boar-like thing raced toward me, but I saw it quickly enough to aim properly despite my hitch of breath. I caught it square in the forehead. It tumbled over onto its back, and Lance finished that one off too with a triumphant snarl.

Shrieks and grunts were echoing all across the crater's sides now. Smoking bodies slumped everywhere I looked. I shoved myself to my feet and hurried on toward the semi-circle of buildings near the lake.

A sudden, sickening thought unfurled in my head, making my stomach clench. How many of these creatures even *wanted* to be fighting us? We had no idea how many were supporting our enemies because they believed in their cause or wanted to impress them, and how many had been forced into obedience with their overlords' new sorcerous powers.

It didn't really matter, did it? We had to get through them either way. If the shadowkind men around me felt any remorse about slaughtering beings who might be victims rather than villains, they weren't letting it stop them.

Torrent and Crag would have killed *Lance* to protect me yesterday if they'd had to. They wouldn't have wanted to, but they'd have done it.

For me.

That realization left me chilled from head to toe. I picked out my lovers' forms in the darkness: Crag rampaging across the landscape, Torrent flinging out his tentacles, Lance springing this way and that.

The gargoyle's face was set in a mask of grim determination. He was taking no pleasure or pride in this fight. Maybe he saw slaughtering as many of the attackers as he could as the only way he could start to make up for the minor injury he'd given me.

Torrent still hadn't completely emerged from the shadows. He was too wounded now to be able to fully fight, but he was still giving it his all because he refused to back down when my life was on the line.

And Lance leapt from place to place with his typical energy and grace, but I caught the nervous twitch of his head here and there as he cast quick glances around the crater. Afraid of who else might be lurking here and what they could do to him. How they might warp his mind so he barely belonged to himself.

My gut balled into a cold, queasy knot. Since I'd met these men, I'd lost a lot, but that was because of our enemies. The three of *them* had given me the chance to become something more than I'd been before. To discover new sides to myself, to recognize new skills and desires… Right now, I was standing up to these nightmarish creatures like I'd never have believed I could weeks ago.

But what had I given my men in return? Looking at them now, I couldn't help thinking that I'd taken more than I'd given. I'd left them with less of everything except the damage they'd been dealt.

What kind of love was that?

A larger creature loomed over Lance from behind, and my arms reacted automatically. I shot it in the head and the chest, and it stumbled enough to give the dragon shifter time to whirl around and finish the job.

I could protect the men a little… but not half as much as they did for me.

Something clicked together in my head, fragments of ideas colliding into a picture that filled me with a sense of horrified resignation. That emotion solidified into resolve as it sank in my chest like a stone.

They were willing to do all kinds of horrible things to defend me. I'd already pushed away my own parents and every friend I'd had or could have had to spare them the trouble and pain that came from being close to me, even when the only reason was my uncertain health. I'd gotten by on my own, keeping the burdens of my life to myself as much as I possibly could, for years. Why wouldn't I do the same for these men when they were facing so much worse?

If I really cared about them, if I really wanted to protect them properly, then I couldn't shy away from being as monstrous as they were.

My throat had constricted, but I didn't have time to wallow in the discomfort of the decision. I shoved more bolts into the crossbow, shot another small beast that scurried toward me, and then my sneakers were thundering onto the flatter terrain near the lake to reach the closest building.

Crag pushed ahead of me, jerking around me with an awkward motion to make sure he didn't come close to touching me. He slammed the door open. A shadowkind creature sprang at us from inside, but he wrenched its body in two without missing a beat.

The small room inside the hut was empty other than a few crates marked with grocery logos. Food for the shadowkind who enjoyed it or for the mortal prisoner they'd planned to keep?

We dashed onward, and a sob reached my ears from a hut around the curve of the lake. I pushed myself faster.

Torrent made it there first, one tentacle yanking the door off its hinges, the other whipping inside to snatch at the shadowkind guarding the boy.

"What's going on?" Jonah wailed.

I lowered the crossbow to my side as I hurtled through the doorway. The little boy was crouched by the far wall on a thin mattress, shaking, his eyes red-rimmed. For a second, he stared at me with as much terror as if I really had been one of the monsters. Then his face brightened slightly. "You're the lady. You were talking to Mommy and Daddy."

"I'm here to bring you someplace safe," I told him, bending down, and to my relief he raised his arms to welcome my embrace. An instant later, Crag caught us up from behind.

Jonah squealed and squirmed, and I squeezed him tight, struggling to keep my grip on my weapon at the same time. "It's all right," I murmured. "This one's a friend. We're getting you out of here."

The boy whimpered but clung to me without further resistance. Another creature flung itself at me, and I had no way of fending it off now. Its claws raked through my calf in the instant before Lance slashed through it. Then we were hurtling off into the air, my leg stinging, the little boy shivering in my arms, and this one small wrongness made right.

We'd shown our enemies that they couldn't call all the shots. That we wouldn't always be running away from them while they pushed us closer and closer to the edge of destruction. I was pushing back now, and I intended to drive them right out of this realm if it was the last thing I did.

But first I was going to have to do a little destroying of my own to fix the mess *I'd* made.

CHAPTER THIRTY-TWO

Quinn

The redhead set her hands on her hips as she looked down at the little boy in the thin dawn light. "You know, I never expected to be running a safe haven for sorcerer kids."

I rested my hand on Jonah's head where he was clinging to my leg. We'd met up with Sorsha, the shadowkind woman who'd given me and my men a hand when we'd been investigating the sorcerer killings in Florida a few weeks ago, on a desolate stretch of highway at the eastern edge of New Mexico. Apparently the RV parked behind her was able to travel a lot faster than Rollick's car thanks to some supernatural enhancements.

"I didn't know who else to ask," I said with an apologetic grimace. It'd taken some convincing just to get my shadowkind allies to agree that I should contact her, since we weren't totally sure of her or her companions' loyalties. But she hadn't betrayed us in any way so far, and she had offered her help if we needed it. And also... "You mentioned you'd taken in the daughter of the other sorcerers. He can't stay with us—he'd be in too much danger. I'm not sure how safe he'd be even if we dropped him off at Child Services someplace."

The sorcerer energy in me hadn't woken up until I was twenty years old, but who knew if it might be different for a kid who'd been surrounded by sorcerer family members from birth? Who was a sorcerer through and through rather than just having borrowed a heart from one?

I wouldn't have been surprised if Sorsha had washed her hands of the situation and told us to ship Jonah off someplace else anyway. But she cocked her head and then sank into a crouch so she was level with the little boy. She gave him a crooked smile that still managed to exude warmth.

"You must be having an awful time of it," she said. "I know how horrible some of those monsters can be. But if you come with me, you can make new friends. Including a little girl who's been through something a lot like what you've faced. She lost her family too, so we're building a new one. When you're ready, you might like being part of it with us."

Jonah pressed his face against my leg, and I stroked my hand over his short hair. It wrenched at me to send him away after we'd just rescued him from our enemies' clutches last night, but what I'd said was true. Those enemies would be searching for me even more vehemently now that I'd defied their attempt at replacing me. It was a fulltime job keeping ahead of them and working out ways to fight back without a little kid in the mix on top of that.

I wasn't that much less of a stranger to him than Sorsha was anyway. He'd seen me for all of a minute outside his house.

"She'll take good care of you," I told him. "Make sure you're safe. I know it's hard, but the monsters that came to your home have been coming after me too. You don't want to stick with me."

"I want Mommy and Daddy," he mumbled.

I swallowed hard. He knew they were dead, and I hadn't wanted to remind him of that fact any more than I needed to. I had no idea what else to say.

Sorsha glanced up at me. "Have you gotten a better idea what these fiends are after or what they even are?"

I paused, my gaze darting toward the shadows where I knew my men were lurking. They'd stayed mostly out of sight since we'd gotten back to Rollick's car and roared away from the mountain camp because Jonah panicked at any glimpse of their monstrous features. I'd told Sorsha that her more obviously shadowkind companions should stay in the RV for the same reason.

But Rollick, with his thorough disguise, had still driven us out here while I'd comforted Jonah as well as I could. He'd looked more pensive than usual. I had the feeling he'd seen something in the camp that'd gotten the wheels spinning in his head, but he hadn't shared his suspicions with the rest of us yet. He didn't appear to be inclined to with Sorsha either, since he didn't emerge.

Knowing his preferences for discretion, he probably didn't want her being able to identify him either.

"One of them has some kind of affinity to earth," I said. "I think that's the one that ordered the attack on Jonah's home. All I could tell about him is that he felt very big and powerful, which I know isn't super helpful. As far as what they're planning on using their new sorcery skills for, we haven't been able to figure that out either. But I'm guessing it's not anything good."

"Seems like a reasonable prediction," Sorsha said dryly, and sighed. "You'd think one psychotic megalomaniac shadowkind per decade would be enough. Are you sure *you* don't want to come back with us? There's plenty of room at the house, and we keep pretty tight security."

The offer tugged at my heart. Yes, I *wanted* to hole up somewhere safe and pretend none of this was happening. But the events of the past few days had made it amply clear that I couldn't run forever. And running to Sorsha and her companions would probably just bring my enemies down on them too.

I wasn't going to see anyone else hurt just so I didn't have to deal with this fate I'd never asked for but couldn't shake.

I shook my head. "I think I need to get ready to stand up to these monsters. We have a vague lead about a possible place in Norway where I could get a grip on my powers."

"I hope that works out for you. We'll keep our ears peeled as much as we can while we're settling this little guy in and let you know if we find anything else out on our end. And don't hesitate to call me if you need back-up." She gave me a firm look. "I mean that. I can be a lot more than a foster mom."

My cheeks flushed. "I'm sure you can. I just—we've had people we thought we could trust turn against us already—it was hard to know for sure who we could count on."

"Fair. I've seen that the shadowkind tend to be hesitant about joining forces in general." Sorsha scooted closer to Jonah and held out her hand to him. "You really should see the inside of the Everymobile. It's pretty amazing. And we picked up McDonalds drive-through on the way over. Do you like chicken nuggets?"

"It's okay," I told him, squeezing his shoulder. "See how nice she is?"

Cautiously, the boy detached his hands from my leg and took a step toward Sorsha. She scooped him up gently and pointed to the streamers waving along the side of the RV. "Check those out. Pretty cool, right? We've taken this thing through rifts a few times, and it always comes out a little more fun."

She tipped her head to me in farewell and carried Jonah into the RV, hugging him tighter when he started sniffling again. My hands clenched at my sides, but there wasn't anything more I could do.

I went back to Rollick's sedan to lean against the hood while the RV drove away. As it disappeared into the distance, there was a moment when it felt as if I were all alone amid the scruffy desert vegetation. There was no sound but a faint whisper of a breeze, nothing real but the hard-packed dirt beneath my feet.

Then the shadowkind men wavered back into view—all four of them, Rollick in front of me and the other three off to the side. Rollick folded his arms over his chest. "So you're wanting to jet over to Norway now?"

I opened my mouth and closed it again. The ache that'd formed in my chest as I forced Jonah to leave expanded, nearly smothering me.

I knew what I had to do. I'd known it since that moment during our raid on the mountain camp... maybe even before it, without admitting it to myself. The sorcerers had even given me all the information I needed to be sure I could do it.

But I didn't want to.

I closed my eyes. Was I going to be selfish, or was I going to show my love for the three men who'd offered theirs to me in every way they deserved, no matter how painful it was to *me*?

It wasn't even really a question. I knew the right answer. I hadn't been able to fix much in the past few weeks or to design anything worth admiring. Now that I had the chance to do something meaningful, something that showed what was important to me, I couldn't pass it up for my own comfort.

"I think looking for the sorcerer enclave in Norway is our best chance of figuring out how we can stand up to those fiends effectively," I said. "Unless you learned something in the camp that's given you some ideas?"

Rollick's mouth twitched with a hint of tension. "I have a few thoughts based on my observations, but nothing that comes with any obvious solutions beyond seeing you get a better handle on your powers. And it seems unlikely they'll be looking for us in Norway, which is a plus."

"Yeah." I sucked in a breath of the warm morning air. "But there's something I have to do first. It—it won't take long."

When I turned toward the other three men, Torrent gave me a quizzical look. Crag held himself with his usual stoic air, like he expected me to send him off on some new dangerous mission for my benefit. Lance beamed at me, equally ready to jump at my request. My resolve hardened.

I stepped closer to Torrent first, reaching up to caress the side of his neck with my hand. He wrapped his good arm around my waist, gazing down at me.

"I love you," I said. "I want to see all the other things you could make—I want you to get to make your mark on the world and enjoy every part of it that you can."

More confusion flickered through his expression, but it didn't diminish the fondness in his eyes. "Quinn..." He bowed his head next to mine, hugging me even closer despite my vest. "Love isn't a concept I've given much thought to. But I'd do anything for you—I can say that much."

I smiled through the pain radiating through my abdomen. "Then you'll understand."

Before he could ask *what* he was going to understand, I eased out of his embrace and moved to Crag. The gargoyle tensed as if worried that I was going to try to touch him too. I longed to give him one last hug, but I could tell he wasn't going to accept it.

"I love you too," I said, choking up. "You're so much more than a monster, and all the ways you've been here for me matter so much more than one little accident. I hope you can believe that."

Crag blinked, his forehead furrowing. "Softness," he said, his gruff voice unusually tender, but then didn't seem to know how to go on.

Lance's smile had faded as he watched, his mouth twisting with his own confusion. Maybe given what he'd been through he could sense where this was going even if he wasn't totally conscious of it.

"You know how I feel about you," he said when I moved to him.

"I do. And you know I love you too." *And I'm going to prove it,* I thought as I stepped in quickly to give him a tight hug. Oh, God, please let him understand.

I let him squeeze me back for just a few seconds before pulling away. I had to do this before my conviction faltered.

I gazed back at all of them, thinking of all the ways I knew them. Not just the way they moved or spoke, their everyday habits. I knew what they cared about, what made them smile and what made them hurt, how they reacted to a threat and how they celebrated a victory. I knew them in ways far beyond any connection the sorcerers I'd spoken to could have known the shadowkind they "harnessed."

So please, because I loved them, let this work.

I gathered all my agonized determination, all my fears, and all my love, and channeled it into my mouth alongside the energy that thrummed through my heart. The sorcerous magic sizzled through every inch of my body as a jolt of it shot into my voice, searing my tongue with its force.

"The three of you will go straight to the nearest rift and back to the shadow realm. You can go wherever you want from there, other than you'll stay far away from me, hundreds of miles, until the shadowkind who've been hunting me are no longer a threat. *Go.*"

The words wrenched out of me as if tearing me into pieces bit by bit. The last emphatic syllable nearly cracked me right down the middle. I swallowed a sob at the expressions that crossed the men's faces: Torrent all shocked recognition, Crag's horrified consternation, and Lance's frozen in panicked anguish. I only got that brief glimpse of them before they were all swiveling around, leaping simultaneously into the shadows away from me.

It was only when they were gone that the sob burst out. I clapped my hand to my mouth and squeezed my eyes shut. Every part of me ached from my throat down to my gut. My legs wobbled, and I stumbled backward to catch myself against the side of the car.

Rollick stayed silent as the impact of what I'd done sank in. Some desperate part of me pleaded for it not to have worked, for any of the three to leap back out and declare that they weren't going anywhere, but when I forced my eyes open again, the desert landscape remained still and quiet.

It was done. I'd made sure they wouldn't be hurt any more in any way while they tried to do the same for me.

Maybe they would hate me for it. Maybe it made me as monstrous as the sorcerers they hated. But I'd have been even more of a monster if I'd let them keep hurling themselves into harm's way on my behalf, when this was my battle.

The fiends only really wanted me. And when they got me, I'd be ready to take them on... or I didn't deserve to live at all.

I expected Rollick to toss out some dry remark, but when he finally spoke, he simply held up his phone, his expression opaque, his voice carefully even. "Should I book us a flight to Oslo, then?"

If he was at all offended that I'd cared more about his underlings' safety than his own, he didn't show it. We both knew I wasn't tackling the monsters who wanted me completely on my own. But Rollick never had any problem looking out for his interests over mine. He'd intended to use me as a tool, and now in some ways, I'd be using him right back.

I lifted my head and clamped down on the agony inside with all the determination I had left in me. "Yes, I think you'd better."

DEFENDED BY DEMONS

THE HEART OF A MONSTER #3

CHAPTER ONE

Quinn

If you'd told me a month ago that I'd soon find myself on a road trip through Norway with a powerful demon as my only companion, I'd have suggested you needed your head checked. But here I was, sitting next to said demon while he drove our rental car through a landscape of mossy-looking hills and sparkling lakes. We hadn't passed any human habitation in half an hour.

I frowned at the journal I had open on my lap, full of loopy handwriting that'd faded with age. "We don't know for sure that the mention of *Alta* means the town up here. It could have been someone's name or who knows what else."

The sorcerer of decades past who'd recorded some of his thoughts on the worn pages hadn't been all that specific. He'd just mentioned "associates from the vicinity of Alta" and a few pages later commented on how the "established families" like those associates were more reliable than greener practitioners. But it was the only reference to anything that *could* have had to do with Norway that I'd found so far.

Rollick—who might have been a powerful demon but at the moment looked like technicolor made flesh with his human guise's movie-star good looks—made a derisive sound. "It fits with everything else we know: what the sorcerers said to you about the enclave up here, the little tidbits I've been able to dig up from that starting point. There are certainly a lot of places in this area where a clan of sorcerers with their little training center could hide themselves away."

He swept his hand over his fawn-brown hair, his dark blue gaze skimming over the beautiful but remote landscape. He did have a point. With all the hills and the more distant mountains rising from the earth, we could rarely see more than half a mile away in any direction, often less than that. And sorcerers with strong enough magic to be able to provoke the same talent in people who'd never had it before probably had major shadowkind at their command. Those supernatural beings could possess all sorts of talents for avoiding discovery.

Even though it was coming up on the evening, bright sunlight still washed over the terrain. The sorcerers I'd talked to briefly—before they'd been slaughtered by the particularly monstrous shadowkind beings we were hoping to stop—had mentioned the extremes of daylight in this part of the world as being a key feature of the enclave. During the winter months, there'd be little sunlight at all, which I guessed made for more opportunities to catch and enslave shadowkind.

I hoped the enclave was still active during the summer. The sorcerers had to do *something* the rest of the year, right? Otherwise we'd have come all the way out here—and done everything else we'd had to in order to get here—for nothing.

A sudden gloom swept over me. I stared at the vibrant greens and blues beyond the window and thought of how much Lance would have loved leaping and tumbling across those slopes with his acrobatic grace. In his dragon form with his jewel-toned scales, he'd have fit in with the scenery perfectly.

Had Crag ever gotten to fly over this gorgeous terrain and admire it from above, soaring on his gargoyle wings? Would Torrent have enjoyed taking a dip in those lakes, or would he and his tentacles have been more at home in the ocean we'd left behind after following a stretch of highway along the coast?

It'd only been yesterday when I'd last seen the three shadowkind men I'd fallen hard for. I'd gone longer without their presence just in the past week. But this time… this time it might be permanent.

A pang shot through my chest alongside a wobble of energy in my heart. I pressed my hand to my sternum instinctively. I'd used the magic *I* held, the sorcerer powers I'd gained thanks to my childhood heart transplant, to send my three lovers away. In a way, I'd briefly enslaved them. I'd forced them to act against their will.

I didn't know how long my control over them would last before the energies faded with distance and time, but even when they did fade—if they did, which I couldn't know for sure—there was no guarantee that the men I'd fallen for would want anything to do with me again. I'd betrayed them in the most horrible way any human could.

I shouldn't *want* them to come back to me. I'd sent them away specifically because of how much it was hurting them trying to fight my battles for me. But my entire abdomen ached with the sense of loss. A fresh burn of tears formed behind my eyes.

I'd felt so many things with them that I hadn't known I could feel, discovered new confidence, realized how much I was capable of. But I didn't know how to protect them other than by forcing them out of my life. They'd protected me so much in the past month. I'd owed them the same in return, even if they wouldn't see it that way.

Rollick's gaze flicked toward me as he took a particularly tight turn around a jutting stand of dark gray rocks. "Don't be regretting your choices, reluctant sorcerer. We've got to stay focused on the problems ahead of us rather than behind."

"I know," I said tightly.

He flashed his shiny white teeth, which I knew were veneers hiding the savagely sharp tips underneath. "Maybe I should be insulted that you couldn't be bothered to protect me too. You did them a favor, keeping them out of this mess, but apparently I'm fair game."

I couldn't help rolling my eyes at him despite the pain tangled up inside me. "*You* haven't given me a whole lot of reason to care about your well-being." Until a couple of days ago, Rollick had been essentially holding me captive, forcing me to develop my sorcerer talents despite the reluctance he'd noted. "Anyway, this is your battle too. You wanted to take this sorcerer-devouring duo on. Torrent, Crag, and Lance only got involved for my sake."

"I can't argue with any of that," Rollick said in his typically smooth, charming way, not that I was particularly in the mood to be charmed.

I stifled a sigh and sank lower in my seat. "How much farther is it to the village you think is an ideal jumping off point?" He'd identified a community smaller than the town of Alta that he'd decided was our best choice for a base of operations while we searched for the enclave.

"About ten more minutes." He kept the same mildly teasing lilt. "Are you that tired of my company already?"

"You're a wonderful conversational partner," I said with an edge of sarcasm. "I'm tired, period." We'd taken a flight from Salt Lake City to Oslo with a brief stopover in Amsterdam, leaving and arriving in the middle of the day as if night didn't exist thanks to the time zone jump, and then immediately hopped on a local flight up to Alta. At this point, I wasn't sure how long it'd been since I last properly slept, only that it'd definitely been too long. It was only the periodic spurts of adrenaline I got when I remembered our mission that kept me going.

The thought of that mission—and the full reasons behind it—brought my gaze back to the landscape. It might still be sunny out, but the tall, craggy hills were dappled with patches of shadow. Stands of trees cast broader swaths of darkness at their bases. I scanned the murk, my nerves jangling at a flicker of movement that turned out to be a branch bobbing in a gust of wind.

"Can you sense many shadowkind around?" I asked. I wasn't sure how well the demon could pick up on their presence from inside the car while he was at least partly focused on keeping us on the road.

Rollick was perceptive enough to pick up on the worry underlying my question. "Just a few stray beings here and there, about what I'd expect in a place without much human presence. I don't see any sign at all that our enemies have marauded this far. Your heart is safe for the moment."

My mouth formed a tight grimace. Our main enemies were two very ancient shadowkind who were possibly even more powerful than Rollick—and who'd been killing sorcerers and eating their vital organs to take on some of the magic that would allow them to control their own kind in a way the monstrous beings usually couldn't. We didn't know what they were planning on using that power for now that they had it, but they'd also been very interested in getting their hands on me.

It'd appeared that the villainous duo was mostly active on the other side of the ocean right now, though. We were here in Norway to see if the sorcerers in the enclave—if we could find it; if it even existed—could teach me something that would allow me to get a greater handle on my own powers faster. Rollick thought it was possible that I might be the best chance of stopping these fiends now that they could brainwash their fellow shadowkind, since an actual sorcerer's powers would beat the bits and pieces of talent they'd absorbed from their violent meals.

Maybe I could also figure out how and why sorcery worked at all, and that would give us other ideas for bringing the fiends down.

I couldn't see the men I loved again until I'd eliminated the threat. That was the condition I'd put in my command to them. As long as it held.

Nestled at the base of a low hill up ahead, a cluster of buildings came into view, most of them houses. A few darker buildings were interspersed between the white-washed walls, the roofs deep blue or red, all of them with a quaintly picturesque vibe that made me feel like I didn't belong here at all.

Rollick drove straight to one of the two-story houses on the outskirts of the village, which had a hand-painted sign proclaiming it the Daffodil Inn. It didn't look like it was big enough to host more than a handful of guests, but then, how many tourists came out this way anyway?

As it turned out, it was really more of a bed and breakfast. The grandmotherly owner bustled out to meet us, eagerly taking my backpack and fussing warmly about what a long trip we must have made. It was obvious from my first step inside that she lived on the first floor. She led us up a narrow staircase, opened one of only two doors at the top, and ushered us into a decent-sized bedroom. It held a queen-sized bed in a simple Scandinavian-style beech frame, a matching dresser and chair, and a door through which I could make out a shower stall.

Only one bed.

"Make yourself at home and let me know if you'd like anything to eat before you turn in for the night," our host said with a pat of my arm, and vanished, closing the door behind her.

I folded my arms over my chest and eyed Rollick. "You only got us one room. With one bed."

The demon spread his hands, his lips curving into a slight smirk. "This town doesn't offer a whole lot of travel accommodations. I didn't figure it'd matter. It's not as if I *need* to sleep."

"I do," I muttered.

He tsked his tongue at me, still looking amused by my hesitation. "I won't even be here while you're doing that. You're very boring when you're asleep, you realize. I'll be off scouting around seeing if I can't determine exactly where this enclave is hidden away." He paused, and a sly gleam lit in his eyes. "Of course, we could share it if you'd really like to."

I made a face at him. "The only people I'd want to share it with can't be here."

I was trying to make a sharp retort, but my voice got rough with the last few words. I yanked my gaze away from him, not wanting to see him being amused by my sense of loss, but Rollick didn't push his provocative teasing any further than the little nudge he'd tested me with.

Maybe he realized just how much I wasn't in the mood for him to flex his seductive charms.

"What a shame that is. I'm sure you'd all have enjoyed that bed very much." He clapped his hands together. "Do you need anything to eat? Was the snack you picked up in Alta enough?"

He'd always been conscientious of my health, even when he was being a jerk about other things—I'd give him that. I rubbed my hand over my mouth, considering. I couldn't summon any interest at all in shoving more food into my knotted stomach. In an hour or so, it'd be time to take my second set of pills for the day to convince my body that my new heart belonged to me, and other than that, I didn't think I *needed* anything to survive until morning.

"I'm fine," I said. "I just need that sleep. Go do your scouting or whatever." I waved vaguely toward the door.

Rollick shot me another grin. "Pleasant dreams, my sweet sorcerer," he said, but he vanished into the shadows a moment later.

I sank down on the bed and nestled my head in the downy pillow without bothering to change my clothes. I barely wanted to move. And I couldn't fully change, not when the silver-and-iron beaded vest I wore under my shirt was the only thing ensuring that no other shadowkind, including our enemies, figured out where I'd gone.

Closing my eyes, I hugged myself. The squeeze of my own arms was a pale echo of the embrace any of my men would have offered.

How had my life ended up being so different from where I'd expected I'd be—where I'd wanted to be—just a month ago?

And what fresh hell was I going to find myself stumbling into next?

CHAPTER TWO

Torrent

It was always disorienting, being back in the shadow realm after a long time away. No color met my gaze, only a seemingly endless darkness, shifting between full blackness and dark grays with random currents. Nothing quite had a physical form—there was nothing exactly to touch or hold on to, although brushing too close to another being traveling through this space sent a prickle through my shadowy body. Only faint scents lingered in the wafting air, cool and almost mineral as if I were back in the cliffside cave I'd recently spent the night in.

How long had it been since I'd returned to what was technically my natural home? Years, definitely. Possibly more than a decade. Nearly all of my work for Rollick had required me to stay mortal side, and I had no interest in dropping in for a visit during my free time. Drifting through this dreary space and testing the quivers of energy that rippled through it was nowhere near as satisfying as a swim in the cool, vibrant depths of the ocean.

I'd have taken a swamp over this place.

As I prowled onward, I couldn't help thinking that as much as most mortal beings feared us when they met us, we shadowkind had to be meant for their realm. Why else were there so many rifts to give us access to the benefits of their vibrant world with all the variety of sensations it had to offer—portals only we could slip through, that the mortals had no awareness of at all? Why else did we all shift so easily into physical forms when we had the chance to?

We were born of this place, born out of the endless shifting gloom, but I couldn't believe it was all we were meant for. Whatever inexplicable powers called us into existence, they intended us to belong to the realm beyond the rifts as much as this one.

I just wished I'd understood how fully I could devote myself to that other world before I'd found myself forced back into this one. Maybe I could have convinced her—maybe I could have made her see...

I shook those thoughts aside and hurried onward, scuttling octopus-like with my now-ephemeral tentacles stroking through the darkness.

The others had to be around here somewhere. We'd all rushed toward the same rift, driven by the magic-laced command I could still feel humming through my body. But I hadn't been able to say or do anything other than give in to that command, and both of my companions could move faster than me through the shadows of the mortal world. I'd lost my sense of them before I'd even hurtled through the rift.

A faint tremor rippled through the miasma that gave me a vaguely familiar impression. Was that Lance's odd, erratic attitude rippling off of him? I propelled myself faster in the direction it seemed to have come from—and nearly collided with a hulking being nearly as big as I was and far sturdier.

I jerked to the side, and the other creature loomed, studying me with a menacing attention that weighed on me.

"Humph," she said in a voice that reverberated into me alongside the energies swirling through the shadows. "Cripple. Stay out of my way."

If I hadn't been so set on my goal, I might have felt more than the brief flash of shame that hit me before I shook it away. Why should I give a fuck what this monstrous stranger thought of me anyway? My limbs worked well enough to accomplish the most important things.

"My apologies," I said with just the slightest edge to my tone, and rushed on.

I passed a cluster of smaller beings scampering about in some kind of game of chase and a few higher shadowkind who were occupied with low rumbles of conversation. Then a hiss I recognized vibrated into my ears.

I dashed toward it, spotting a sinuous churning movement in the darkness up ahead in a shape that reminded me of the dragon shifter's physical form.

He was whipping between a couple of other shadowkind whose animosity was already thrumming off them. Then his energetic voice reached my ears, sounding more frenzied than buoyant at the moment.

"Don't you want to play a game? You think you're pretty tough, but can you dodge my claws? I won't go too hard on you."

"Get out of my way, nuisance," one of the shadowkind he was hassling growled, "or I'll—"

I sensed Lance moving to pounce and dove in with all the speed I could propel into my body. My tentacles swung out and lashed around the dragon shifter's body, shadowy essence colliding with shadowy essence. Where we touched, I could grip him well enough to yank him back toward me—just as he could have scratched up the beings he was antagonizing if I hadn't caught him.

Just as they could have pulverized him in retaliation.

We couldn't die here in the shadow realm. The atmosphere of the place sustained our life energy in a way the mortal world couldn't quite. But we could be battered to within an inch of death. Lance could have found himself pummeled to the point that he wouldn't have moved for months.

Of course, maybe that's what he'd been aiming for. He spun on me with another hiss and a swipe of a dragonish paw before he registered who I was. Then he froze, the guilt I'd sensed from him ever since our enemies had possessed his mind and forced him to fight us radiating off of him.

"I'll take care of him," I told the other beings, and dragged him farther away through the gloom.

"Torrent," Lance said in a mournful tone. "She sent us away. She put that magic into us and made us *go*." He squirmed out of my grasp with a violent twist, though still careful not to actually strike me with much force, and leapt wildly through the currents of shadow. "We can't go back. The sorcery has its claws in my head. I can't scratch it out. She wouldn't—I never thought she would—"

A sharp twinge ran through me, even more poignant than when I'd first found him picking fights and stirring up whatever trouble he could before

I'd brought him on board under Rollick's authority. Then, Lance had been distraught and unstable after his imprisonment by mortals he'd hated. Now one he'd cared about deeply had stolen his free will using the same sort of power. I couldn't even imagine what was going on in his head right now.

"Hey," I said, not trying to restrain him again but tucking one tentacle around him to try to settle down his restless prowling. "It was only one command. She didn't fully enslave us. It'll wear off. We just have to give it time."

"How much time? It feels—it feels different than when this happened before. Both of them, with the other sorcerers and with the beasts who ate them. The magic is holding on so hard, like she knew how to squeeze every part of me into the shape she wanted..."

He thrashed to the side again, and I let him work out the wild energy he couldn't seem to contain.

I hated to admit it, but I knew what he meant. I'd never had sorcery worked on me before, but Quinn's command was still echoing through me as if it'd penetrated every particle of my existence.

She knew us. She understood us. That was why I'd fallen for her in so many ways... and I suspected it was also why she'd bent our wills so easily.

"It *has* to wear off," I said, as much for my own reassurance as his. "Even shadowkind that are fully enslaved shake off the effects if the sorcerer leaves them to their own devices for too much time."

Lance made a strangled growl low in his throat. "And then what? She doesn't want us. She made us leave. She thinks I can't protect her enough, that I don't deserve to be with her."

I swallowed thickly. "I don't believe that's what she was thinking at all. She wanted to protect *us*. Because of how much we matter to her."

It was still difficult for me to wrap my head around that last part. Remembering the way she'd gazed at me as she'd told me she loved me brought a bittersweet ache into my chest that was laced with disbelief.

I'd known she'd cared about us a lot, that she felt a connection to us just as we did to her. Humans sometimes threw around those words far too lightly. But I'd been able to tell how much she meant them. How hard it'd been for her, knowing she was going to lose us, even if it was her own decision.

And she mustn't have fully understood how much *we* cared about her either. Otherwise I couldn't imagine she'd have banished us like this. I didn't care if the villains we were up against chopped off every limb on my body—I'd still rather be at her side, savoring every moment I could have with her.

This separation, the uncertainty about what danger she might be facing even now, hurt more than the mangling of my hand under Lance's fangs.

"We aren't the ones who need protecting," the dragon shifter was muttering, whipping his tail through the air with obvious agitation. "She's the soft one. The mortal one. Our Quinn." His next growl sounded mournful. "If those fiends get their maws on her…"

"She still has Rollick with her," I reminded him. "He might have wanted to use her, but he's been trying to use her *against* them. He's not going to hand her over to the enemy." I didn't trust our former employer all that much, but the demon stood a better chance of keeping Quinn away from harm than any other shadowkind I could think of other than the three of us.

Although we were only two right now.

I dragged in a breath and tugged at Lance with my tentacle again. He let out a huff, but he'd stopped thrashing around quite so much. The energy resonating off him had settled to a faintly frantic hum rather than a total cacophony of distress.

"We need to find Crag," I said. "He'll want to fix this as much as we do. Then we'll come up with a plan for how we can defeat those two brutes without being near Quinn, until we can get back to her. And for showing her that she doesn't need to worry about keeping us safe."

"Yes," Lance muttered. "The gargoyle. Where did the stony one go? He flies so fast."

"We'll find him," I said firmly. "We'll find him, and we'll set the rest of this situation right."

Or I didn't deserve the three words Quinn had offered me so emphatically.

CHAPTER THREE

Quinn

The road had just curved around the bank of a crystalline pond when Rollick said, "Stop the car there—right before that hill."

I coasted to a stop and jerked up the parking brake before glancing around. The hills loomed taller and pressed tighter together in this part of the Norwegian wilderness, another hour's drive down country lanes from the little village where we'd spent the past two days. Or, at least, I'd spent those two days there. Rollick had been gone for most of that time, sneaking around figuring out where the sorcerer enclave might be.

And he claimed to have succeeded. I lifted my chin toward the road ahead where it snaked around the nearest hill, shrouded in a pale mist. "It's over there?"

Rollick gave a casual shrug as if the answer wasn't all that important to him, but the unusual intensity in his expression betrayed his actual investment. "If it's not there, then I don't think it's in this country at all. That mist is being generated by a shadowkind creature who has no reason to do it or to produce so much of it here other than because it's under command. I've identified several other beings lurking around in a loose ring with a circumference of about three miles. They're clearly guarding something, not roaming around the way a free creature might. I assume the enclave is located approximately at the center of that circle."

I sucked my lower lip under my teeth, my chest tightening as I absorbed his certainty. I knew what the next step was—and that it required me to go in alone.

I'd confronted a small community of sorcerers on my own back in the US, but I'd still had a couple of my shadowkind companions watching over me. And it'd been a much smaller and less formal community than what I had to assume this enclave consisted of. If sorcerers were genuinely *created* here… I couldn't imagine what I was going to find beyond that mist.

"I assume you didn't let any of the lurking shadowkind notice you were poking around," I said.

"I'm glad you have at least that much faith in my abilities," Rollick said dryly, but his smile was a bit tight. I doubted the demon was worried about my well-being beyond whether I'd still be able to help him with his plans, though.

I peered at the mist. "Do you have any idea what I'm going to be dealing with as far as terrain from here on?"

He shook his head. "I couldn't get a clear view, which is obviously the intention. Just drive slowly and try to continue straight as much as you can. If you see any lanes smaller than this one, I'd give them a shot. Especially if you start to get the feeling that you definitely *shouldn't* go down them."

One of the shadowkind we'd dealt with before had cast some kind of supernatural vibe over a mountainside that'd discouraged intruders. "What if I can't get in at all?" I asked. Rollick had dispersed that repulsing energy last time, but he couldn't do the same here if he couldn't get close enough to find out it existed.

"Then we'll figure something else out," Rollick said breezily. "But they must allow *some* strangers to enter, or they'd have no one to train. Maybe your preexisting sorcerer powers will guarantee you admission. We'll just have to see."

"Right." I swallowed thickly. I didn't trust the demon beside me any farther than I could shove him, but a nervous wobble ran through my gut at the thought of continuing on without him. "You have to get out of the car now, I guess?"

He inclined his head and then fished around in his pocket before pulling out a simple gold pendant shaped like a dove in flight, dangling from a thin chain. I blinked at him as he held it out to me.

"It'd be a whole lot better for both of us if you get whatever information you can out of them and then leave without there being any trouble," he said. "Or if you can get yourself away from the enclave on your own even if there *is* trouble. But if the situation goes sideways and you're sure you're stuck, the pendant has a GPS signaler in it. Pull out the wing on your right, twist it ninety degrees, and fold it backwards. You shouldn't be able to activate it by accident, but it's a quick process if you need to do it."

I wrapped my fingers around the metal bird, simply holding it for a moment before moving to attach the chain around my neck. "And if I do activate it?"

"I'll get to you as quickly as I can." Rollick offered me a brighter grin. "I'm not letting you go in there completely defenseless, my sweet mortal. Not that I doubt your ability to hold your own if things don't get completely out of hand."

"Thanks," I muttered, but having the pendant nestled against my collarbone actually did reassure me a little.

"I realize it may take a while for you to fully infiltrate this 'enclave,'" the demon went on. "I'm not going to panic if you're busy with them for a few days. But if you can come up with an excuse to drive back into town and give me an update, I'll make a point of stopping by the bakery where we had breakfast this morning for an hour around noon every day."

I nodded. "What will you be doing the rest of the time?"

He made a flippant gesture with his hand. "A little of this and a little of that. Our enemies appear to have spent most of their time on this side of the Atlantic until recently. I intend to do some digging into their history while you investigate your fellow mortals. There's a rift not too far from here—I can use that to pop before this area and various other parts of the continent via the shadow realm."

"Sounds like a plan." I dragged in a breath and squared my shoulders, flexing my fingers against the steering wheel. "Well, you'd better get going. It's about time to find out where all this sorcery stuff comes from."

To my surprise, Rollick appeared to hesitate for a moment, as if he hadn't expected me to dismiss him so quickly. As if he was as reluctant to leave me to my own devices as I was to be left. Then he flashed another smile and vanished into the shadows as if he'd never been beside me at all.

I gave him a few seconds to be sure he'd left the car and then released the brake. As the car rumbled on down the road and around the hill, the mist closed in around me. In less than a minute, I couldn't make out more than hazy impressions of green and gray farther than ten feet around me.

Keeping my breaths steady, I focused on the road ahead, watching for any changes to it or any oncoming side lanes. The road itself wasn't on any maps—we'd checked. No doubt the vast majority of wanderers who ventured this far off the beaten path would have turned back when faced with such apparently inclement weather conditions. Only those who knew there was something specific to find by coming this way would continue on.

Maybe that was why I didn't encounter any repulsive force. Or maybe Rollick had guessed right that my sorcerer talents would somehow grant me access despite other protections in place. I crept along at five miles an hour for several minutes without encountering any obstacles. Then I spotted a wooden post to my right, appearing out of the mist moments before I passed it.

I slowed even more, and it was a good thing I did, because otherwise I might have missed the lane next to the post completely. The road I was driving on was already dirt, but it was at least relatively clear. The path that veered off to the right had a vague impression of tire marks amid patches of grass and jutting stones. I had to angle the car carefully to make sure the tires didn't bump into any particularly threatening-looking rocks.

It wasn't long after I took the side-road, if it could even really be called a road, when I felt more than saw the terrain slant upward. It swung to the left and then to the right again, giving me the sense that I was weaving my way up one of those hillsides. Or this could be a full-out mountain now for all I could tell.

Then, without warning, the mist started to fade. One moment I was cloaked in it; the next I hit the brake, finding myself staring at a broad building looming out of the trees that covered the steep slope ahead of me.

Several rooms seemed to jut from between the trees, walled with smooth dark wood that looked regularly buffed. They gleamed in the now-piercing sunlight. A couple of the rooms had tall windows that stretched across most of the front, shaded by blinds; others had only small rectangular panes or none at all. Decks of the same dark wood wrapped around and even under the rooms on multiple levels, scattered with wooden lounge chairs and in one spot a long table.

Staring at the structure with my architecture-fanatic's perspective, I had the sense that there was a lot more to the construction than what was immediately visible, hidden by the trees or even delving right into the mountainside.

It wasn't the kind of building I'd imagined designing myself—I wanted to create something soaring and awe-provoking—but the way this place seemed to be fused with the natural landscape around it set off a flicker of admiration in me alongside my apprehension. Whoever *had* designed it had put a lot of thought into their creation.

The building materials and style appeared quite modern, but as I got out of the car, I noticed signs that this spot had been in use for many decades if not centuries. A path of square stone tiles led to the deck on the lowest floor, where only flat walls met my gaze other than a gap between two windowless rooms that was shrouded in shadow. The edges of the stone squares had become rounded with age, their centers dipping after being worn down by innumerable feet. And there was a large shed off to the side built out of logs rather than smooth boards, deeply weathered with patches of moss on its angled roof.

This far north and at this altitude, a chill wrapped around me even though the mist didn't creep after me. The breeze brought a pungent pine scent with it. While I had obvious evidence of civilization in front of me, the flavor of the place was distinctly feral.

A shiver passed over my skin, and I tucked my hands into the sleeves of my thin windbreaker, wishing I'd brought a warmer hoodie to wear under it. Avoiding a chill hadn't occurred to me when we'd left the August heat of the southwestern US.

I slung my backpack over my shoulders and headed up the path from where I'd parked, but before I'd made it more than a few steps, a man who looked around the same age as my dad emerged from the shadowy area on the deck.

He had slate-gray hair still flecked with some hints of auburn and an arched Roman nose that dominated his face. His close-set eyes peered at me down that nose. I stopped in my tracks.

He said something in words I didn't know but that were presumably Norwegian, given where we were.

"I'm sorry, I only speak English," I said quickly.

He let out a soft huff and repeated himself, not exactly aggressive but definitely firm, with only a light accent. "Who are you, and what do you want here?"

"My—my name's Quinn," I said. When discussing our strategy, Rollick and I had decided that it was better for me to go with my real name so there was less chance that I'd slip up and reveal my deception in however long I had to stay among these people to learn their secrets. "Is this—I heard there was an enclave of sorcerers in this area. I came out here hoping to find you."

The man's lips pursed, but his shoulders relaxed at the same time. I got the immediate sense that I'd been recognized as one of his kind.

"You're looking to kindle the power in yourself?" he said.

A spark of excitement darted through my chest. Could they really do that, then? In that case, they had to know more about how this strange magic worked than any of the other sorcerers I'd talked to had.

"Not exactly," I admitted, clutching the straps of my backpack. "I have a little already. But I didn't have family to train me—they passed on before I was old enough to learn. I didn't even know I *had* any power until I started getting these strange feelings... Another sorcerer family directed me here saying that the people in the enclave might be able to teach me how to get control of and expand my skills."

I wasn't lying. I'd never really wanted to use the magic that turned shadowkind into slaves, but it didn't appear I had much choice. If I was going to use my sorcerer abilities to stop the fiends who'd been hunting me down for their malicious purposes, I'd need to be able to do a lot more than order around one little beast at a time, which was all I'd managed so far.

I simply wasn't going to mention that I had other goals I was hoping to achieve by coming here.

The man seemed to study me for a long moment—long enough that my skin started to itch. He raised his hand to his own face, motioning to his cheek. "You've been hurt."

My fingers twitched toward the fading bruise I knew lingered on my own cheek, where Crag had accidentally struck me with his rocky hand. There hadn't seemed to be any point in trying to conceal it when that deception would be easily uncovered too.

"A creature I wasn't strong enough to control," I said, which was kind of true.

The man hesitated again and then swiveled on his heel with a motion for me to follow him. "Come. Let's see where you're at."

I hurried after him, my sneakers thudding across the boards of the deck. As I approached the shadowy area, I spotted a set of double-doors set farther back from the protruding rooms we were walking between. A pine tree appeared to be growing right over the top of the doorway, its roots providing an extra frame.

As the man reached the doors, two more figures stirred—other members of the enclave who'd hung back while they'd observed me. They wore cloak-like jackets that fell to their knees with hoods that shadowed their faces. They flanked me as if to ensure I wouldn't run for it, as if they thought I might feel the need to make a hasty retreat. Uneasiness crept over my skin.

The man pushed one of the doors open, and I felt weirdly relieved to see bright light on the other side rather than some dank dungeon. These people lived here—even if they were isolated sorcerers, I shouldn't expect them to be skulking around in their own home like comic-book villains.

Ignoring my jittering nerves, I followed the man inside. This was what I'd come here for, after all.

I found myself in a long hallway with pale gray walls and light fixtures beaming at regular intervals down its length. Several doors were set along it —the man led me into the closest one on the left. The cloaked figures trailed after us inside.

We'd entered a small room with no windows and little furnishings—only a round, maroon rug that covered about half of the floor and a few metal boxes set along the far wall. As the door clicked shut behind me, I realized the boxes seemed familiar. They reminded me of the carrying cases Rollick had used to transport the shadowkind creatures he'd had me practice my powers on.

It seemed these served a similar purpose. The man wasted no time in walking over to one of the boxes and bending down to grasp the latch on the door.

"We'll want to know what we'd be starting with," he said. "Call this creature to you, as quickly as you can."

A sharper wobble radiated through my pulse, sending a tingling sensation all through my veins. I needed them to believe my story—I needed them to think it was worth spending time on helping me. I focused on the door of the box-like cage as the man swung it open.

Stark light flooded the inside, making the patch of shadow within it stand out starkly against the gleaming metal walls. My heart thumped faster. I imagined how the thing must feel, cooped up in that tight space, knowing people who wanted to manipulate it for their own ends were holding it captive. How it must long to be free again.

A twinge of sympathy formed in my gut. But I needed it to come to me. *Now.* Or I could end up just as screwed over.

And so many other shadowkind might suffer more.

The urgency of my resolve made the tingles of supernatural energy condense at the base of my throat. I opened my mouth, and the strange language I didn't understand spilled from my lips with an electric jolt. When I'd ordered my monstrous lovers away, the words had come out in English, but maybe I'd been able to use familiar words only because I'd known my targets so well. Every other time, my intention had translated into these foreign sounds.

At my command, the shadow leapt from the box, taking physical form as it darted toward me. It looked like a rat with spindly legs twice as long as they should be and several antenna-like whiskers poking from the top of its head. It dashed straight to my feet and then stopped there, quivering and looking up at me as if waiting for further instructions.

Someone made a soft sound that at first I took for consternation. When my gaze jerked up, one of the cloaked figures tugged back her hood as she stared at me. Her pointed features were framed by a cloud of salt-and-pepper hair. Her gaze was equally pointed, but her voice came out with a tone that was shocked rather than skeptical.

"What was your family's name?"

She had an accent too, but it sounded different from the man's. How many different countries had the sorcerers in this enclave come from?

"I don't know," I said. "I was adopted when I was really little—I just know that they died." It was kind of accurate—the heart that had brought my new powers with it had technically been adopted by me with its transplantation.

"You've never had any direct training, and you commanded the creature that quickly? How long did these other sorcerers guide you?"

I didn't know what the right answer would be, so I gave what was essentially the truth. "Not much. They offered me a few tips about how to focus and that sort of thing. I only found out about my powers about a month ago."

She blinked, her surprise echoing across her face. Then she schooled her expression into somberness as she swiveled toward the man who'd brought me in. She jerked her head toward the door.

"Wait here," she said to me, and all three of the enclave members stepped out of the room.

The shadowkind creature was still standing tensed on the floor in front of me. Taking pity on it, I let a little more of the wavery energy inside me bubble up from within and ordered it back to its box. At least it wouldn't have to worry that I was going to make it do something worse right now.

The sorcerers didn't return for several minutes. What was taking so long? Were they arguing about whether I should stay at all? Had I handled this scenario wrong?

Finally, the man stepped back inside alone. His mouth was pressed into a flat line as if he wasn't happy about what he was going to tell me. I braced myself for a dismissal.

"You can stay," he said brusquely. "As long as you follow our rules and don't interfere with activities that don't involve you. We'll have some tasks for you, and if you seem dedicated enough, you may be chosen to participate in the rites that could awaken more power in you."

Bingo. I raised my eyebrows. "Rites?"

He frowned at me. "If you're chosen, then you'll hear more. If you're unhappy with the terms, you can leave."

I couldn't shake the feeling that he was hoping I'd take that option. Instead, I forced myself to offer him a sunny smile. "No, not at all, just curious. Thank you so much for giving me this opportunity. I promise I'll do my best."

CHAPTER FOUR

Quinn

Vera looked over the notes I'd written across several pieces of lined paper which I'd set on the table in front of her. She raked a slim hand through her cloud of salt-and-pepper hair and nodded thoughtfully to herself.

"You certainly applied yourself to the task," she murmured.

I'd spent most of the last two days in the large room around us, which had a gloomy vibe that was more what I'd have imagined for an enclave of sorcerers off in the mountains. It was the enclave's library: the walls were lined with built-in shelves packed with books, journals, scrolls, and loose notes gathered into folders. If there was a set system of organization, I hadn't been able to decipher it.

It wasn't totally gloomy though, despite the relatively dim lighting beyond the lamps positioned on each of the several birchwood tables. A large fireplace lined with stones crackled at one end of the room, casting some extra warmth and an appealing whiff of pine smoke into the space. The floor in front of it was clear of furniture, holding only a thick fur rug that I'd sometimes seen a small group of sorcerers hunker down on to hold hushed discussions in front of the hearth.

The enclave did seem to use the library quite a bit, with many of the sorcerers coming and going while I'd been completing the tasks I'd been assigned. I hadn't been able to get a clear read on how many lived in this place, as there hadn't been any mass gatherings during my time here.

Vera, who'd appointed herself my examiner or mentor or whatever exactly she was, had told me everyone operated fairly independently—that I could grab food from the kitchen area when I was hungry without worrying about specific mealtimes and make use of the laundry facilities if I needed them whenever they were free. From the number of different figures I'd seen wandering through the vast network of rooms, I guessed there were a few dozen sorcerers in residence at the moment.

So far, Vera's assignments had felt a lot like schoolwork—in a way that'd given me a pang of homesickness for my architecture courses back home. The two summer classes I was increasingly falling behind on, in particular. But there wasn't anything I could do about that other than throw myself into the work here in the hopes that eventually I'd find something that would let me get my old life back.

Two days ago, right after I'd arrived, Vera had set me searching through the library's various volumes and documents to compile notes on the most established meditation strategies. When I'd finished that task yesterday, she'd gotten me gathering information on different types of identified shadowkind beings.

I'd actually learned a few things, but nothing I expected to help me conquer a duo of immense monsters with sorcerer powers of their own. Knowing the enclave had divided animal shifters into two distinct categories wasn't exactly earth-shattering information.

One benefit of the haphazard organizational system was that I'd encountered various items I wanted to come back to later. Like a journal written by a sorcerer who'd apparently specialized in enslaving particularly powerful shadowkind. And a book that sounded like it had strategies for dampening magical energies. But there were some questions I hadn't come across any answers to. Maybe now, while Vera was at least somewhat happy with my progress, would be an okay time to ask.

"It's fascinating," I said. "But I still find it hard to figure—how do we end up with the power to control these monsters at all? Why us and not everyone?"

Vera glanced up at me with a momentarily wary expression. "We put in the work—we made the sacrifices. Or those before us did. You don't understand because you had no one to teach you to honor those efforts."

I didn't think that was true, because none of the sorcerers I'd spoken to outside of the enclave, those who'd learned from their families, had seemed to have any clue where their powers had come from either. But arguing wasn't likely to get me very far.

"I want to understand—I'd be willing to make sacrifices too," I said.

She grunted and looked down at my notes again. "If you continue showing your dedication like this, perhaps you'll get there. We don't initiate newcomers without plenty of vetting."

I guessed that made sense, or they wouldn't have been able to keep this place or the powers they taught so secret. But if it was a year-long process, I really didn't have that kind of time.

I tamped down on my impatience, another question that had dogged me for as long as I'd known about my magic rising to the surface. "If there are ways of provoking the powers... are there also ways of removing them? No one could steal my potential from me, could they?"

It seemed wiser to frame it as something I was scared of rather than something I might hope for. Maybe my powers were the key to stopping the menace that might threaten everything I cared about, but they'd also made me a target in the first place. I couldn't help still wondering whether I might be able to get rid of them completely.

But Vera was already shaking her head with a wry smile. "Once it's in you, it's in you. No one can take your rightful inheritance away. Believe me, there've been a few I've thought should be shut down, but—" She shook her head again as if dismissing that thought. "That's why we're so careful about who we accept for the rites."

My heart sank even as I forced a sheepish smile in return. So much for that hope. If even the sorcerers here didn't believe there was a way, what were the chances I could find one elsewhere?

I'd heard about these "rites" multiple times since they'd first agreed to let me stay. I still didn't know anything more about them other than that they could apparently awaken sorcery in a person. But Vera and everyone else I'd overheard mention them had been incredibly tight-lipped on that subject.

Vera shuffled the papers into a neat bundle and handed them back to me. "You should hold on to these—you might want to look them over again to really absorb the information. The better you understand the creatures, the more adept you'll be at controlling them. But I think that's enough for today. You should get some dinner into you."

"I'll do that," I said, and then paused. There was one other subject I needed to broach with her, and I had no idea how she'd react. "Would it be a problem if I left the enclave for a little while tomorrow? I'm learning so much—I feel like I need to take a break so everything can get settled in my head before I stuff more in."

The wariness came back into Vera's eyes. "Where would you go?"

I made a casual wave toward the front of the building. "I figured I'd just take a little drive, maybe go back to the nearest village up the road and grab some lunch with a change of scenery. If that's not a problem. Obviously I wouldn't mention the enclave to anyone there. But if you have rules about everyone needing to stay in the enclave until they're finished their studies, I totally understand." I just had no idea how I was going to communicate with Rollick if that was the case.

To my relief, Vera's stance relaxed. She motioned for me to follow her out of the library. "It shouldn't be an issue. It's not as if you know significantly more now than you did before you came here. But if you're gone too long, we may not welcome you back, so don't disappear on us."

"Of course not," I said quickly. "I figured it'd just be a few hours."

Would their rules be different once they did let me in on their more guarded secrets? Obviously plenty of sorcerers did leave the enclave, or they wouldn't be living all over the world.

There was still way too much I didn't know.

As we walked down the hall toward the kitchen, we passed two men I'd seen before—an elderly sorcerer with a short, pointed white beard and a young man who I didn't think was much older than me, whose shaggy wheat-blond hair always seemed to be falling into his eyes. This time, the younger man was mumbling to himself, his eyes eerily vacant. His skin looked almost as pale as his hair. As we strode by, his body twitched, though he gave no other sign he'd noticed our presence.

"Who's *that*?" I whispered to Vera. "And what's going on with him? Is he okay?"

Vera's next smile was tighter. "That's one of our two current trainees. He's almost ready for his rites—it takes a lot out of a person. You'll need to be prepared for the same if you want to expand your connection to the shadows."

"Definitely," I said automatically, but I had to force myself not to glance back at the sickly-looking guy. Just what did the sorcerers put their new initiates through?

When I left the enclave building the next morning, I half expected someone to yell out at me to stop. But Vera must have passed on word about my plans, or else the sorcerers here really didn't care all that much about people coming and going. I guessed they had a certain amount of security simply in the fact that if I *had* tried to tell any regular person what was going on here, they'd think I was insane.

The drive back to the village where Rollick and I had spent our first two nights was a little faster than the trip to the enclave because now I knew where I was going. I reached the bakery he'd mentioned around eleven thirty. Not seeing him inside, I popped into the village's one corner store to buy a few snacks out of the unfamiliar options on display and then went back to the bakery to buy a slice of what the owner haltingly translated as "spinach pie" for me to eat for lunch.

I'd just sat down at one of the three small tables at the front of the bakery when Rollick ambled inside with a ding of the bell over the door. He asked the owner for a puffy pastry that was stuffed with a creamy filling and dropped into the chair opposite mine, looking no different from how he had the last time I'd seen him, three days ago.

We couldn't talk all that openly here. He glanced me up and down and seemed to make a similar assessment of my state as I had with him. "You've survived."

"It's been all right," I said. "But I haven't found out much yet. They know a lot, but they're very cagey. I'm keeping my eyes out and doing my best to get into their good graces. We'll see." I took a bite of the cheesy pie and almost groaned at the richness of the flavors. "How's your searching been going?"

The demon shrugged. "I'm chasing down some theories—and becoming increasingly convinced of what I thought I saw at that mountain camp by the lake."

I raised my eyebrows. "And are you ever going to tell *me* what your theories are? You think you know what kind of... things we're dealing with, don't you?"

Rollick gave me one of his sly grins that always turned his movie-star looks twice as striking. "I think you've got enough on your plate without me adding that to the heap." His gaze slid away from me, his expression turning unusually pensive. "If I'm right, there's no way that enclave will have anything useful to tell us about our specific foes. They're one of a kind or close to it."

My stomach twisted, diminishing my enjoyment of the lunch. I swallowed hard. "That would make them pretty hard to beat, wouldn't it?"

"Let me worry about that." Rollick flashed me another smile, and a different sort of twinge ran through my gut.

He was all I really had here—the only ally, the only being remotely on my side. Before, I'd had my three monstrous lovers to count on. Protecting them and taking this on without them meant it was just the demon and me in this mess together against forces I could barely comprehend.

Maybe some of my uneasiness showed on my face, because Rollick's smile softened a little. He tapped my hand, not drawing out the touch long enough that I'd have felt the need to flinch away, playful but with a gentleness I wouldn't have expected.

"Look at how far we've come already, Quinn," he said. "You ferret out those mortal secrets as quickly as you possibly can, and between the two of us, we'll be unstoppable."

He sounded confident enough to settle my nerves a little. I sucked in a breath and brandished my fork again. "One thing's for sure: I'm not giving up."

The demon beamed back at me. "And that's exactly what I like so much about you."

The warmth of his expression came with an underlying flicker of fear. Because I still couldn't say for sure that being "liked" by Rollick put me in any less danger than if he'd hated me.

CHAPTER FIVE

Quinn

Vera appeared to have decided to give me the rest of the day off. When I returned to the enclave in the early afternoon, neither she nor any of the other sorcerers rushed over to give me a new assignment. So I drifted into the library to conduct some studying in line with my personal interests.

I'd set the records I wanted to return to on a specific shelf so that I could find them again in the vast chaos of the library. It didn't look like anyone had disturbed them. Probably no one could tell they'd ever been anywhere else, unless there was some bizarre system of organization to this place that was beyond my comprehension.

I skimmed through the journal accounts of the sorcerer who'd made it his mission to attempt to enslave the most powerful shadowkind he could encounter, but found that it was full of a lot of self-aggrandizing with no real details about how he'd supposedly accomplished the feats. I kind of wondered if he'd even managed to pull off everything he claimed or if he just liked to pretend he had for an ego boost.

Some notes I'd set aside on tracking shadowkind were a little more useful, although mostly we'd been trying to avoid having our enemies track me rather than trying to track them. But you never knew when we might need to find them to enact a plan. Unfortunately most of the methods reported in the records hadn't worked. Dowsing, radio waves, and various other approaches the industrious sorcerers had experimented with hadn't shown any signs of being effective.

You must rely mainly on your sorcerer senses and the threads of commonality between you and the beasts, their finishing paragraphs instructed. Wonderful. Well, Crag was pretty good at picking up on the presence of other beings in the area and even identifying those he was already familiar with.

The thought passed through my mind in an instant and set off a fresh flare of loss. I closed my eyes for a second as I automatically choked up.

It was better that the gargoyle wasn't involved in anything to do with our powerful foes. That was the whole reason I'd sent him away. I just had to keep remembering that.

The last of my stash was the book on suppressing magical energies. As I flipped through it, a tingle of excitement rippled over my skin.

This I could really use. It was mainly focused on strategies for dampening or shielding against the effects of shadowkind magic, but they included the basics like using silver and iron to repel their powers, which had also worked to stop the beings from picking up on *my* powers. I was still wearing my custom vest for that exact reason.

Maybe some of the other tactics mentioned in the book would give me new options for deflecting shadowkind attention. It'd sure be nice to be able to take a shower without having to wash around the vest, or to have an alternative method of protection if I needed to go somewhere that required the kind of clothes I couldn't hide the vest under. No one here at the enclave had noticed my unique undergarment so far since I could hide it under baggy sweaters and sweatshirts. The temperature in the building was tolerable but hardly cozy.

I glanced around, confirmed no one else was in the library, and then surreptitiously tucked the small leatherbound volume into my messenger bag, which I'd carried with me for exactly this reason. Now I'd be able to examine the book at my leisure, maybe even show it to Rollick to get his input on the contents. There were so many books haphazardly stuffed into the shelves around me that it seemed unlikely anyone would notice one missing anytime soon.

I browsed through the library again, but I'd already done some pretty thorough circuits during my earlier assignments. Nibbling at my lower lip, I slunk out into the hall. My sneakers rasped faintly over the dark wooden floor.

No one had told me I couldn't go exploring. Vera had simply instructed me to stay out of any rooms that were locked. What else might there be around here that could tell me more than the human inhabitants were willing to?

I wandered through the halls, passing the laundry room and a couple of what looked like meeting rooms, and then another larger room with smudged chalk marks on the floor but no other sign of magical practice. The chill in the air thickened enough that I shivered. I had the impression that I was walking deeper into the hillside the building was constructed into.

Turning a corner, I found myself facing a door that appeared to lead into a wing of the enclave I'd never ventured into before. Another sorcerer was just unlocking it with a twist of a key. I halted, holding perfectly still, as she tugged the door open and slipped past it without noticing me. Then I darted forward as quickly as I could move without making a racket.

I grabbed the door just before it clicked shut. There. It wasn't currently locked. I wasn't breaking any rules.

Ha. I'd still better not get caught, no matter how well I was obeying the letter of the law.

I eased the door open slowly to peek past it. Another long hallway lay beyond. The woman I'd seen entering was just disappearing through a doorway up ahead. I darted into the hallway, afraid someone would come up behind me and notice my transgression, and let the door close behind me.

Where to go from here? I padded carefully over the floor, which I realized was stone here rather than wood. Another indication that I'd come right into the hillside. The walls were the same smooth, pale gray as the rest of the place, but I couldn't tell whether they were painted stone or the same material as the rest of the building.

It was definitely a feat of architecture. I wished I'd been in the right headspace to enjoy studying that aspect of the place.

I passed a couple of closed doors that I was too nervous to open in case someone was on the other side who'd accuse me of trespassing. Then a faint rattling sound reached my ears.

I followed the noise to a smaller side hallway that ended with a narrow doorway. This door was unlocked. Opening it, I stared into a room so brightly lit I had to blink several times before I could start making sense of its contents.

It was some kind of menagerie. Cages lined the walls, a few larger ones and many small ones stacked on top of each other, almost as haphazardly as the books in the library. Orderliness was obviously not something that went hand in hand with sorcery.

I could guess what I'd see inside the cages before I'd even squinted. Even more lights beamed from the tops of the cages, which were solid metal on all sides except the barred fronts. Those were held shut with latches and locks. Within the lights, blurs of shadows quivered and shuddered.

The enclave had its own shadowkind collection.

That wasn't surprising. Obviously most if not all of the sorcerers here were using their magic, which meant they'd all have at least one being enslaved. But Vera had indicated that most of those creatures were being put to work: guarding the enclave in various ways, hunting for food, luring fellow beings that the sorcerers wanted to trap closer to the building. These were simply being contained.

Maybe they hadn't been "harnessed" yet, if the sorcerers meant to at all. The assortment in front of me felt more like a set of collectables on display.

The thought made my stomach turn. I had no idea what creatures were trapped in these cages, but they were obviously miserable surrounded by all that toxic metal and pinned under the searing lights. Who knew if any of them had ever harmed another being? They might have been roaming around not much different from mortal animals before they'd been snatched up and shut away in here.

I walked closer to one of the larger cages. As I took in the details, my teeth set even more on edge.

The contraption, which came up to my shoulders in height, was obviously designed not just to hold the shadowy being inside it but also to hurt that creature if the sorcerers decided it was necessary. Maybe even to kill it.

Sharp blades that must have been silver, iron, or both poked from the walls on mechanisms that looked ready to propel them toward the creature hovering in the center of the space. A few crystals dangled from the top of the cage, the light beaming through them. Would they also move on command to concentrate the light even more painfully on the captive shadowkind?

My fingers itched to try to open the door and free it, even though I knew I couldn't break the padlock. I raised my hand, about to set it against the bars as if I could indicate to the prisoner that I sympathized with its plight, when the door squeaked open behind me.

I jerked back, my heart stuttering. God only knew what the sorcerers of the enclave would think if any of them saw me showing any kindness or concern to the beings they considered nothing but monsters.

I found myself staring at the pale, shaggy-haired guy I'd passed in the hall yesterday—the one Vera had told me was studying for his rites. He peered at me, looking briefly puzzled. "You're the new arrival, aren't you?" he asked with a mild British accent. "What are you doing in here?"

"I, um—" I groped for an easy explanation. If he was coming into this room, presumably the place was related to the rites in some way. "Just trying to get prepared," I finished with enough vagueness that it'd be hard for him to challenge me.

My answer must have made some kind of sense to him, because he hummed to himself. His gaze slid away from me as if he hadn't really wanted to be paying me all that much attention anyway.

He meandered farther into the room, focusing on the smaller cages along the back wall. "Have you picked one?" he asked.

Picked one? For what?

"Not yet," I hedged. "I figure it's a big decision. Better to take my time."

He nodded. "True. I've given it a lot of thought." He stroked the bars of one cage almost lovingly, with an avid gleam in his eyes that set my skin crawling. "I'm claiming this one, so take it off your list of possibilities."

"Oh, I hadn't even been considering that one," I assured him quickly, though I still wasn't sure what we were even talking about. The first shadowkind he'd enslave? That would seem to make the most sense. I was surprised that the sorcerers would simply hand one over rather than having him prove himself by capturing one from scratch with his new powers, but maybe the first "harnessing" was part of the rites.

"You'll be going through with it pretty soon, then?" I ventured.

An eerie smile curved the guy's lips. He stroked the cage again, gazing at the shadowy creature flickering within.

"Three more days," he said. "It's scheduled now. I can't wait."

Even as his tone sent another uneasy quiver through my nerves, I committed that number to memory.

"It's further off for me," I said, hoping I was keeping my tone appropriately casual. Like I was just shooting the breeze with a fellow initiate, not digging for info. "I'm not even sure where I'll be having my rite."

The guy's gaze flicked to me, and my pulse stuttered at the thought that there might be suspicion in his eyes. But he just chuckled in a slightly patronizing tone. "I think it's always done outside in the same spot. They lead us to the ceremony area. Wouldn't be fair to get an early look at it."

I made myself laugh in return. "Of course not. I can't help speculating, that's all. Lots to imagine. It'll be an intense experience, for sure."

He rubbed his hands together, his smile coming back. "I bet it's even more intense if you have a rite in the winter, when it'll actually be dark at night. But I wouldn't want to wait that long when I don't have to."

So the rites were held outside at night. This guy would be having his in just three days.

And I'd have to find some way of being there so I could find out exactly what it was he couldn't wait to experience.

CHAPTER SIX

Rollick

The trail I'd been following petered out along the outskirts of Berlin. The nature preserve I'd ended up in didn't hold much other than trees, grass, a murky stream, and a few low hills, but I was a lot surer of what I was looking for now and where I'd find it. Under the layer of vegetation and soil covering a slightly odd dip at the far edge of the park, I'd discovered a distinctive gouge in a buried stretch of rock.

I spent at least an hour swerving back and forth over the landscape in shadow form, extending all my senses toward the earth beneath me. There weren't any other markers of the being that'd spent a fair bit of time in this area decades ago. But it had hung around for at least long enough to dig into the local rocks.

I had to admit I didn't have any direct experience with the being I believed I was tracking, but from what I understood through hearsay, it either fed off stone or rubbed the stuff into its body to build strength. Not totally unusual among shadowkind—I'd watched Crag munch on chunks of quartz crystals before for similar reasons. But the slabs this thing dug out of the earth were nearly as big as Crag himself.

And somehow I suspected the beast's temperament wasn't anywhere near as cooperative as the gargoyle's.

I left the park behind and wandered through the suburbs that bordered the reserve. In the wilder terrain, I hadn't encountered any beings likely to be able to report their observations, but higher shadowkind tended to gravitate toward human habitations if they could get away with co-existing there. Out of all mortal beings, humans were the ones who provided by far the greatest variety of entertainment and indulgences, after all.

I'd reached a commercial strip with a few small shops, still far from the bustling core of the city, when I caught a whiff of not-entirely-mortal feline. Ah ha.

It only took a minute to trace the scent to its source. The shifter was curled up in the shadows of a garden shed, lounging there for the day like an actual cat might have.

The being's presence tensed at my approach. From the intricacies of his scent, I could tell he was decently established—at least a century under his belt. Of course, that didn't mean he'd spent all that time in this area, but in my vast experience, shifters were a territorial bunch. Once they settled in someplace they liked, they weren't inclined to leave unless they were forced to.

No doubt he could tell that I wasn't any kind of being he'd want to mess with just from whatever impressions of *me* he'd picked up already. I stayed in the shadows, propelling myself close enough that we were essentially face to face. If he'd tried to flee, I'd have pounced on him, but maybe he sensed that much. He stayed where he was, peering back at me, every nerve quivering through the atmosphere around us.

"I'd just like to have a quick chat," I said, flashing the shadowy equivalent of a smile. "I've got no beef with you. I only need information."

"Information about what?" the cat shifter asked in a voice with a hint of a lisp.

"How long have you been coming to this part of the mortal realm?"

The shifter let out a sound like a humph. "I saw the last king leave. Planes coming in. The big wall going up and down. I don't bother anyone. This is my little piece."

I held up my hands. "And I have no interest in taking it from you. I'm only hoping you can indulge my curiosity. There was a powerful being that came through here and maybe mucked around a bit probably toward the earlier parts of your time. Something ancient with ties to the earth. I doubt you'd have seen another one like it since, if you saw that one."

A shiver ran through the shadows from the cat shifter, and my spirits lifted. He knew what I was talking about.

"You don't want to mess with that one," he muttered, and I had the impression of him curling his tail around himself like a shield.

I didn't think I was going to have much choice, but there was no reason to share that observation with this stranger. I wouldn't have let him see me at all if my enemies didn't already know I was working against them. Quinn's little gambit had forced me into the center of the conflict, which meant there was no more point in trying to hide.

"I'd just like to know what he was doing here," I said. "Did he clash with any other beings in the area? Did he interact with the mortals at all?"

The shifter snorted. "He wanted to *crush* the mortals."

A chill prickled through me. I'd known the duo of ancient shadowkind was out to slaughter sorcerers for their power, but he made it sound like this one had wanted to destroy all humans. "What do you mean?"

"He started making the earth shake and crack. Buildings broke. A little bit here and there and then more. I think he was seeing what he could get away with. I didn't like it." The cat's tail twitched. "But the Highest must have found out he was getting too pushy. They sent some of their warriors, who drove him away. I don't know what they did with him, but he never came back here that I saw."

Wonderful. So we were dealing with a super-powerful being who'd added to his powers and also had at least used to be itching to wreak havoc throughout the mortal realm. Not that I'd assumed his other intentions were good, but they could definitely have been *better* than this.

I dipped my head. "Thank you. That's all I need to know. You can go back to your cat nap."

The shifter let out a wordless grumble, but I felt his attention on me as I slipped away. He didn't trust me to be any kinder than the fiend he'd just told me about.

As I drifted farther into the city, stewing in my thoughts, I let myself emerge into physical form in my human guise, keeping my usual veneers covering the pointed teeth I couldn't transform. The air had the usual chemical tang of city life, but it tasted fresher when I was breathing it into proper bodily lungs. The rhythm of my striding legs helped center my thoughts.

I'd seen signs of this one ancient shadowkind's presence in various spots across Europe and eastern Asia. This was the most recent spot, and the only one where I'd found a being who'd witnessed what he'd been up to. The other one, his partner, I hadn't found traces of in the same places, but then, I suspected theirs was a recent collaboration. The other's domain would be more difficult for me to explore and unlikely to contain many lingering traces.

A couple of tourists I passed stopped to raise their phones for a photo, and I glanced up to see what they found noteworthy. An immense tower jutted up in the near distance, slim with a spherical bulge partway up before tapering into an even thinner spire.

My sorcerer would have liked to see that, wouldn't she? It was along similar lines to her fanciful designs that she scrawled in her sketchbook. I found myself raising my own phone to snap a visual record myself.

I made it back to the little Norwegian village just a few minutes after noon. Quinn was already perched at one of the tables in the bakery, one foot tapping restlessly against a chair leg. Something had her more on edge than during our first rendezvous. Nervous energy radiated off every movement from the swipe of her pale hair back behind her ears to the pursing of her soft lips.

At least, I assumed they were soft from the look of them. She hadn't yet agreed to give me a chance to experience them for myself. Not for lack of interest, but out of the stubborn sense of loyalty she seemed to possess in spades. I still wasn't sure whether her defiance was ultimately going to turn out in my favor or against me.

But either way, it was impressive if sometimes irritating to watch.

The moment I stepped into the bakery, Quinn's spine jerked rigidly straight. Even now that we'd officially been working together for several days, she eyed me like I might pounce on her just as the cat shifter had been worried I would.

To be fair, I *had* pounced on her at least once in the past. But for good reason. And she'd kind of liked it, even if she didn't want to admit it.

I dropped into the seat across from her. She might have still been a little afraid of me, but she'd also generously bought me the same kind of pastry I'd picked up last time I was here. It had been pretty tasty. Such a mix of contradictions, this mortal woman.

Which was why I couldn't help speculating about how delicious she might be too. It really was too bad that we had to be stuck in a conflict that put her life, my livelihood, and who knew how much else on the line. Otherwise I could have focused on more enjoyable pursuits I'd eventually have persuaded her to join me in.

Well, plenty of time for that later.

"You managed to get away again," I observed. "They trust you that much."

Quinn shrugged. "I don't know how much it's trust. But I might get something really useful tonight." Her hands twined together on the table. She'd barely touched the slice of pie she'd bought. "One of the trainee sorcerers at the enclave is doing his 'rites' tonight. I'm planning on finding a way of watching and seeing what exactly it is they do to spark the magic in him."

I raised my eyebrows. "That will be a big step forward. Have you uncovered anything else that would bolster your own powers?"

She shook her head, her mouth twisting. "It's mostly been busy-work so far, making sure I'm dedicated to learning. They're being very secretive about the rites, so I'm guessing that's the key." She sighed and picked up her fork. "Have you gotten anywhere with your investigations yet?"

"I went out to Berlin yesterday," I said without thinking about it, and somehow both delighted in and regretted the glint of hopeful interest that lit in her eyes.

"It's one of my top ten cities I've wanted to visit," she said. "I mean, if I manage to fit in that kind of travel with the time I have..." Her hand dipped to the neckline of her shirt. Her sweater covered her entire chest, but I knew she was touching the spot where the top of her surgery scar was marked on the skin over her sternum. "Did you see the Upper West? We talked about it in one of my classes."

I felt abruptly ashamed that I didn't even know what she was talking about. “I took a picture of this one,” I said, showing her the photo on my phone.

“Oh, the Television Tower. That’s an amazing one too. Did you know it’s the tallest building in the whole country?”

I hadn’t actually given it that much thought. “And here I thought you’d be one of those women who say size doesn’t matter.”

Quinn wrinkled her nose at me, but the eager flush that’d crossed her face at the overall topic of conversation made up for it. “It’s an impressive feat of engineering. And I bet it’s breathtaking to see up close.”

“So you’re all about looks, then.”

She ignored my teasing tone. “It’s not just *looks*. It’s...” She paused, her bright blue eyes going momentarily distant as she searched for the right words. “There’s something special about being able to make people feel something, having an impact on them. That’s why so many people make art, right? To do it with a building—something that’s functional but also art in its own way—something that’s entwined in their lives and the city... Maybe it sounds silly, but I think that’s just about the most amazing thing possible.”

I was rarely lost for words, but in the first few moments after she stopped speaking, I had trouble deciding what to say in response. The passion in her words was obvious.

I hadn’t really been fair to her. I *had* assumed that her interest in architecture was mostly about making pretty structures and achieving acclaim. The way she phrased it... her reasons for her pursuits weren’t that different from my own reasons for setting up the hotels and other social venues I had over the years. Creating something that contributed to the larger community. Offering people something they might not be getting elsewhere.

Although in my case I was mainly concerned with inhuman sorts of “people.”

“I hope I’ll get to see what kind of functional art you offer up to the world someday,” I said, keeping my tone languid but meaning it all the same.

“Yeah, well...” She swiped her hand across her mouth, her expression tightening again. “I’m trying not to think about that right now. Until it’s more possible again.”

The gloom that passed over her face spoke of the other things she was trying to talk about. The beings she'd have preferred were sitting across from her right now. Her fingers curled toward her palm as if she were imagining wrapping them around someone's hand, and my jaw clenched.

I'd nudged her toward sending those three mutinous lackeys of mine away. She'd cared about them, and I'd used her caring to my advantage. But when I saw the pain from missing them rise up behind her eyes like it had just now, some small part of me wasn't completely convinced I'd made the right call.

They'd been a distraction to her, and her to them. They'd also brightened her up in a way I hadn't figured out how to replicate. Was she really better off for *anyone's* purposes with that loss weighing on her?

I shoved those doubts away. She was mine, and sooner or later she'd figure out she wasn't badly off like that. I could be patient. The rest didn't matter.

Or it shouldn't anyway.

Quinn seemed to shake herself out of her melancholy. She focused on me again, though the sadness still lingered at the corners of her mouth. "Were you just sightseeing, or did you find out anything useful off in Germany?"

"I determined that one of our sorcerer-killers isn't a fan of any human, magical or not," I said. "Which doesn't bode well for this villainous duo's ultimate plans. I suspect he ended up going across the ocean because his habits were becoming too well-known over here."

"And have you figured out *what* he is?"

I dragged in a breath. Why should I keep avoiding the subject now that I was sure? It wasn't as if she'd fully understand my trepidation over the fact anyway, from her mortal perspective.

"I'm now completely sure that it's a behemoth," I said. "Or rather, *the* behemoth, because as far as I know, the shadow realm has only ever spit out one of those."

Quinn studied me. "And that's bad, I take it."

I gave her a thin smile. "It's only one of the most powerful beings ever to exist, outside of the absolute Highest beings that never leave the shadows —and now for some reason it's got a vendetta that's put both of us right in its path."

CHAPTER SEVEN

Quinn

I'd worn every piece of clothing I'd brought with me, and still I was shivering as I crouched in the dimness just beyond the enclave's sprawling house. The chill of the high altitude had deepened with the night, even though the sun didn't quite go all the way down at this time of year. It was past eleven o'clock now, but a hazy golden glow still gleamed at the edges of the sky. It felt more like mid-evening than the middle of the night.

It wasn't enough sun to warm things up. My face was prickling in the cool air. I tugged the collar of my windbreaker up over my mouth and let my warm breath flow over my cheeks with the exhale. At least it was dark enough that I shouldn't be easy to spot, but not so dark that I had to worry about tripping over things I couldn't see.

I could have waited tucked into my bed, listening for the sound of footsteps in the hall outside. But I'd been worried that I might drift off and miss the sounds of the rite beginning if I was more comfortable, and it would have been harder to sneak through the building itself if many of the sorcerers were bustling around.

Staking out a spot in the nearby wilderness had seemed like the best strategy. I just hoped they hurried up with the whole ceremony thing. I'd rather not witness it as an ice cube.

A distant rumble made me perk up. To my surprise, it sounded as if it was coming from off in the distance rather than from the building to my right. I squinted through the trees. The gleam of headlights came into view, and moments later a van pulled into the parking area under the lowest deck. I heard the thump of the doors but couldn't see what was going on down there from my perch.

Had they brought something special for the rite that had to be organized at the last minute? What would that be? It'd sounded like the novice sorcerer had already picked out his first shadowkind slave. I had no idea what else might be involved in the process.

Maybe this meant they were almost ready to begin.

I adjusted my position cautiously, stretching my legs. My backpack shifted against my shoulders. I didn't have much in it now that all my clothes were on me, but I hadn't felt comfortable leaving my pills, phone, or first aid kit inside the enclave while I embarked on this mission.

If anything went wrong, I might need to make a hasty run for it. There'd be no chance to duck back into my bedroom and collect my things.

Finally, the soft creak of the building's double doors reached my ears. A rustling of footsteps followed. I peered through the dim light and watched a cluster of robed figures crossing the deck to the packed earth path in front of it—and then veering to the right, farther away from me.

I wasn't sure if their course was to my advantage or not. I wasn't going to have to scramble to get out of their way, but I'd need to hoof it to make sure I kept track of them rather than losing them in the semi-night.

Setting my feet carefully the way I'd learned in my not-always-legal urban explorations, I clambered farther up on the forested hillside and circled around the top of the building, picking out the moving figures when they came into view. They'd come around the building and now were heading upward like I had, along a path I couldn't make out from my current position.

Good. Less distance for me to close.

I slowed down, slinking from tree to tree, my ears pricked for their footsteps. No one spoke. I poked my head out over a narrow but obvious path between the trees just as the last of the cluster vanished around a bend farther up the hillside.

I followed the direction of the path through the trees alongside it so I still had some shelter. It was slow-going, both to make sure I stayed unnoticed and because of the steepness of the slope. Within minutes, I was sweating despite the chill in the air. Give me a set of skyscraper stairs over a mountainside any day.

A flare of firelight up ahead warned me to slow down even more. I crept onward, eyeing the dancing flame of the torch someone had mounted on a post. Creeping to the side where its glow shouldn't reach me, I knelt down a few feet from the edge of what I could now see was a clearing.

The cleared area was a rare section of the mountainside that was nearly level, about twenty feet across and roughly round. Nine torches blazed at even intervals around the border. They gave off a pungent smoke with an acrid scent that tickled my nose even though I was keeping my distance.

The cluster of robed figures had stopped in the middle of the clearing. It was hard to count them because they kept moving around and they were all wearing matching cloaks, but I decided there were ten. One of them eased back his hood, and I recognized the new initiate. His face was even paler than before but set in a mask of determination. He held his chin high.

The other figures had started murmuring some kind of chant. The initiate closed his eyes and swayed with the rhythm of their words. The eerie melody made the hairs on the back of my neck rise. I didn't understand the words any more than I did the sorcerous commands that directed my magic, but they resonated with power.

One of the sorcerers handed a couple of two-pronged metal blades to the guy. Then all the surrounding figures drew back to stand beneath the torches, still chanting. With the space around the guy cleared, I could now see that one of those shadowkind carrier boxes sat on the ground near his feet.

Well, that was fairly self-explanatory. But what was he going to do with those weird knives? He was just standing there on his own now, still swaying, his lips now moving in unison with the chant, though I got the impression he wasn't actually making any sound.

Abruptly, the chanting fell away. Somehow its absence felt twice as unsettling as the racket they'd been making before.

The wind warbled through the branches overhead. The initiate raised his hands, each clutched around one of the double-pronged blades, toward the violet sky overhead. A shudder ran through his slim body.

He dropped to his knees in front of the carrier box and unlatched it. Then he thrust both of his hands, still gripping the blades, through the large opening in one violent movement.

I didn't understand what was happening until he drew his arms back out and straightened up. A wiry-haired, hissing creature was writhing in his grasp, skewered between the two weapons that had dug into its flesh. Its shadowy blood was wisping up from those puncture points.

A jolt of horror socked me in the gut. What was he going to do with the little beast? He'd speared it like it was a cob of corn he was about to dig into.

I had no idea how accurate that comparison would prove to be until a few moments later. The guy held up the flailing, bleeding creature and called out into the night, "Now I become one with the creatures I will rule. I will take their essence into me and make it my own."

With the last words, he rammed the blades in twice as deep, twisting them with the same movement. The shadowkind creature screeched, but its voice faltered, its struggles weakening.

The initiate pulled it right to his face and closed his mouth over one of the wounds.

My stomach lurched, nearly propelling my meager dinner up my throat. *He* was making some kind of dinner of the creature, sucking in the smoke that poured off its body in audible gulps, inhaling more with each heave of breath. He sounded like some kind of beast himself, tearing into its food after weeks of starvation.

As I watched, he mashed the increasingly limp body right up against his face as if he could absorb even more of the smoky blood right through his skin.

I couldn't help it—I doubled over and gagged as quietly as I could manage. Thankfully the savage noises the initiate was releasing and the lingering squeaks of the dying creature drowned out what I couldn't muffle with my hand over my mouth.

As my thoughts spun and more nausea bubbled up through my chest, it occurred to me that this awful "rite" made a sick kind of sense. The villainous shadowkind duo was taking the power of sorcery into themselves by consuming the most vital organs of the practitioners. Based on what I was seeing now, those sorcerers—or their relatives, somewhere far down the line—had activated their sorcery at least in part by consuming the shadowkind they exerted control over.

The cycle had come full circle in the most gruesome possible way.

I was so focused on the initiate in his horrible act and suppressing my reaction to it that I didn't notice the other figures appearing at the edge of the clearing until the guy glanced over at them. Two more robed figures had stepped into view, with a few other people I couldn't clearly see gathered with them, shoulders slumped, one of them small enough that it must have been a child.

The creature the guy had killed had all but disintegrated into his hands. Dark veins crawled across his face beneath his skin as if the shadowy blood had infected him with a disease. He turned his head, and I saw his eyes had gone totally black, even the whites consumed with darkness.

He tossed the scraps that remained of the creature away and lunged toward the newcomers as if he were an animal himself.

Which maybe was the point. The sorcerers along the edge of the clearing took up their chant again, their voices rising louder, and the newer arrivals shoved one of the hunched figures into the clearing.

It was a woman, not much older than me, wearing nothing but a white nightgown that fell to her knees. She stared at the guy charging toward her and let out a shriek.

My body tensed, a cry of warning snagged in my throat. It was too late anyway. As she stumbled away on her bare feet, he tackled her.

His fingernails dug into her skin; he clamped his teeth around her throat. There was a crack as a bone broke, and then a sickening tearing sound. The woman's scream cut off in a wet gurgle.

The guy raised his head and shook it, spraying blood from the chunk of throat caught in his mouth. He spat it out and snarled a few words I didn't recognize, but some part of me, maybe the sorcerer energies pumping through my own veins, thrummed with a growing sense of recognition even as I held back the urge to vomit.

He has taken the beast into him, and now he is one with it. He is letting the monstrous energies move through him to gain the deepest possible understanding of the fiends he'll bind to his will. To control monsters, you must become a monster.

That was the gist of what the chant said, I was abruptly sure. The sorcerers were urging him on, cheering for him to let loose this savagery and fully absorb the energies he'd consumed.

Because this was all they believed the shadowkind were. Monsters, wild beasts, interested in nothing more than senseless killing. How could they spend so much time around them and not realize there was so much more to the beings they enslaved?

And what had the sorcerers' human victims done to deserve being dragged into these awful rites? Even now, they were propelling a girl who couldn't have been older than nine or ten out from the trees.

My body tensed, my pulse pounding so loud it nearly drowned out the chant. The guy who was now barely a man whirled on the girl, bloody teeth bared. She spun with a sob and dashed toward the nearest sorcerer, but the robed woman flung her away.

Oh, God. How could they? How could any kind of magic possibly be worth acting like this?

The initiate was already bearing down on her. And while the sorcerers around me might have been willing to watch this scene with nothing but approval, *I* couldn't just stand by.

As the guy leapt at the girl, a cry of protest I couldn't restrain burst from my throat. My legs threw me forward without consulting the rest of me, with a desperate urge to wrench that poor kid away from her terrible fate.

The chanting stopped. One of the sorcerers sprang at me and caught my arm, just as the initiate smashed the little girl's skull into the rocky ground with a crunch of her skull. A sob of my own snagged in my throat, and I found every face around the clearing had turned toward me.

CHAPTER EIGHT

Quinn

"What are you doing here?" the man who'd grabbed me demanded in a raspy voice, his face shadowed by the hood of his cloak.

"You can't let him—" I protested automatically, straining to run at the initiate as he continued bashing the little girl's body, even though I could tell she was beyond saving now.

Before I could get my entire sentence out, the man who'd grabbed me smacked his hand over my mouth to cut off my words and dragged me back toward the trees. I squirmed against his grasp, but he held me too tightly. The others took up their chanting again as if I'd never intervened.

Another figure appeared beside us. I didn't recognize her until I heard Vera's voice from beneath the hood, low and urgent. "That's the new one—the one I've been working with." She tugged her hood back enough that I could meet her eyes, hers cold and flinty. "How did you get out here? What do you think you're doing, Quinn?"

"Quietly!" the man ordered me in a harsh whisper as his hand loosened on my mouth. "You've already disturbed the rites enough."

As if I were anywhere close to being the most disturbing thing that'd happened out there in the clearing. A slightly hysterical laugh quavered up from my lungs through my constricted chest. I was afraid that if I let it out, I might puke again too.

"I heard you leaving, and I was curious about what was going on," I managed to murmur. "How can you— He's *killing* people."

But they already knew that. They'd brought those people to the enclave specifically for the guy to kill.

Where had his victims come from? How could the sorcerers possibly justify these murders to themselves?

They barely seemed to acknowledge how horrifying it was. "He's becoming one with the monsters," Vera said, confirming the impressions I'd gotten from their chant. "To be able to fully harness them, he must know them and their ways from the inside out. It's the *only* way to unlock the sorcerer power within. Your magic came from the same place, somewhere down your family line."

Not *my* family, I wanted to protest, but I didn't want to give away that much of my personal history—or the fact that I'd lied about the origins of my powers. More nausea flooded me. My heart was thudding so fast my body was trembling with the beat.

What were the sorcerers going to do with me now that I knew their secret? Now that they'd seen my reaction to it? Should I pretend I was accepting it after my initial shock to buy myself enough time to get away, or would they refuse to believe I'd changed my mind?

There was still another victim somewhere over amid the trees, waiting to be slaughtered. How could I stand back and let that happen?

All of those questions were rendered moot by the tramping of footsteps toward us and the rough clearing of a throat. A man I'd seen once or twice around the enclave was approaching us from lower down the slope, wearing a regular jacket and jeans instead of the ceremonial robes, his narrowed gaze fixed on me.

"I thought I might find her here when I saw her bedroom was empty," he said, shifting his focus to the sorcerers standing on either side of me. At his tone, the other man's grip on my arm tightened. "She's a spy."

My heart just about stopped. I opened my mouth, but no sound came out. I didn't know what he'd found out, what I needed to deny or explain.

"What are you talking about?" Vera demanded, her voice still hushed.

The new arrival lifted his chin toward me. "I followed her on her trip into the village like we discussed. She spoke with a man there, someone she was clearly familiar with. I stuck around after she left to see what he was up to. He was awfully shifty, but he couldn't completely evade me. I finally got close enough to tell it wasn't a man at all. It was one of *them*. She's working with the monsters."

Oh, shit. The bottom of my stomach dropped out. "I—what?" I stammered. I could still act like I hadn't realized, right? "The guy I talked to is just someone I met when I first got here. He seemed totally normal. He can't be one of those shadow things."

I couldn't tell whether I'd been convincing. Vera's lips pursed with a sour expression. She motioned to the man holding me, and he dragged me farther from the clearing, where the chanting and the sounds of a scuffle continued. Then she shook her head at me.

"It doesn't matter whether you knew or not. That *thing* will have known what it was doing. It was using you. Who knows what else it's up to?" Her gaze jerked to the man I'd had no idea had followed me to the village. "What did they talk about?"

"I couldn't get near enough to listen in," he said. "But they looked awfully chummy for two people who only just met."

I had the urge to protest the description of my relationship with Rollick as "chummy," but I didn't think that would do anything for my case. "We were just talking about our travels," I said hastily. "I didn't mention anything about the enclave, of course. This doesn't make any sense. He seemed like a totally normal—"

"We can't trust her," the newcomer snapped, cutting me off. "They've managed to infiltrate our ranks, whether because of her cluelessness or with her cooperation. Who knows how else the creatures have their claws in her? They might be maintaining a connection to her even now."

Vera's expression hardened even more, and my entire body went twice as cold as it'd been just from the chilly night air.

They were going to kill me. Maybe they'd even sacrifice me to their initiate alongside the other victims they'd tossed his way.

They saw me as being as much of an enemy as the shadowkind they despised, and eliminating me would be the only way to cut off the connection.

I reacted on instinct again, but this time it was all self-preservation. The techniques from my long-ago self-defense classes flashed through my mind, and I jerked my arm toward me with a twist of my elbow that broke the man's hold. Then I turned tail and ran as fast as my feet could take me.

I stumbled on the uneven terrain as I hurtled forward. The three sorcerers who'd been gathered around me sprang after me with restrained shouts and curses and the rustling of the underbrush. I swerved to head downhill, since that would give me more speed, but even as I careened onward, a sense of hopelessness closed around my heart.

The enclave lay downhill too—and it sounded like the man who'd spotted me with Rollick had already searched for me there. He'd have alerted the other sorcerers. They'd probably confiscated my car.

How the hell was I going to get back to any kind of safe place on foot? I wouldn't even be able to follow the roads without the sorcerers catching me. Assuming I could get far enough ahead of my current pursuers to even think about making the longer trek back to the nearest village.

I had my health essentials in my bag but no food and only a single bottle of water. As soon as the enclave's residents had the chance, they'd send some of their shadowkind slaves to hunt for me too.

I swung to the side to dodge a stump, and the chain around my neck shifted. A spark of hope lit in my chest.

I had the necklace Rollick had given me. I couldn't think of a time I'd have needed it more. The last thing I wanted was for him to have to sweep in and rescue me somehow, but if I could at least get away from this bunch and hide out someplace where he could pick me up—

Even as I thought that, one of my pursuers gained enough ground to snatch at my backpack. I lurched forward instinctively at the feel of the tug, wrenching free, but my pulse stuttered. Getting away even for a moment was seeming less doable by the second.

A metallic click carried from behind me. "Give me a clear line of sight," one of the men barked, and I realized what the sound had been: the safety being released on a gun. He was going to shoot me.

In desperation, I leapt sideways and landed on a particularly steep patch of hillside. I ended up skidding down on my ass, just as a gunshot boomed overhead. The second my feet hit firmer ground, I was darting away again, my hand leaping to the necklace.

Screw dignity. I needed to get out of here alive, and I had to admit I couldn't do it alone.

I dragged out the bird pendant, tugged on the wing, and twisted it the way Rollick had said. Then I dashed on, the metal charm thumping against my sternum.

Would he even get here in time? The man had suggested that Rollick had stuck around in the village for a while after I'd left, maybe because I'd told him about the rites tonight. He might have wanted to be nearby specifically for this reason. But he still had miles of territory to cover to reach me, and the regular shadowkind guards would be keeping watch along the edges of the sorcerers' domain.

But it could be that the demon had come as close as he could to the enclave's boundaries to wait. As I rushed on through the forest, one of my pursuers sucked in a startled breath. Then, between the thuds of my frantic feet, a distant shriek reached my ears.

I couldn't tell if it was angry or pained, but it sounded as though some creature off in the wilderness was not happy at all.

"Something's coming," Vera muttered to the men. They slowed as they took stock, and I pulled farther ahead, sliding down another steep portion of hillside. I fled to my right, through a denser stand of trees, and spotted a narrow crevice next to me in the rocky ground.

I didn't have time to think about it. I squeezed into the tight space that was barely a cave and pushed myself as far back into its darkness as I could get.

My legs were already wobbly from the exertion. I didn't know if I could outrun my pursuers for much longer, especially when one of them was taking literal shots at me, but maybe I could hide until help came.

Voices carried from the forest beyond, mumbled words in English and in the strange sorcery language I only vaguely understood. They were calling their "harnessed" shadowkind to them now. To fend off the intruder or to find me?

Maybe both.

I held perfectly still, keeping my breathing shallow. A thick mossy odor filled my nose. It was dark enough in the crevice that I didn't think anyone would be able to see me unless they leaned right into the opening, and then

I wouldn't be much more than a vague shape. I could hope that my pursuers wouldn't notice the crevice at all.

Another cry rang through the air, this one a little nearer than the first I thought. It definitely wasn't a victorious sound. My fingers curled into my palms as I waited.

Footsteps trod closer outside. The voices had fallen silent. There was some rustling as hands pushed through bushes in their search for me. I swallowed thickly, still afraid to move so much as an inch.

A few shouts went up somewhere farther away. From the enclave building or the clearing for the rites? I couldn't tell. My pursuers murmured something to each other too low for me to make out. I waited and waited as they rasped through the vegetation around the crevice, willing them away with each second that passed by.

Abruptly, the sounds of movement stopped. Then I heard one phrase that turned my blood to ice.

"Over there."

Shit. They'd spotted the opening to my hiding spot. I closed my hands into tight fists, planning to fight them off as well as I could if they came at me. Although they'd probably just shoot me where I crouched. Should I burst out and make another run for it?

Before I could decide, a shadow cast extra darkness across the entrance to the cave. A figure was bending down to peer inside—

And then that figure was shoved to the side by another, larger form I only saw as a blur. There was a bang of a gunshot and a strangled sound, followed by a crack of breaking bone. Then came a shout, a heavy thump, and the tearing of flesh. It made me think of the scene I'd just witnessed in the clearing, and my stomach heaved all over again.

A face appeared in the dim light beyond the crevice. Rollick gazed in at me, his human face flecked with what I had to assume was blood. His eyes shone darkly in the dusk.

"There you are," he said, somehow managing to make the remark sound jaunty despite the circumstances. "Come on out. I take it the rites didn't go all that wonderfully?"

A choked guffaw lodged in my throat. I pushed myself out of the crevice, scraping my shoulder against the rough stone surface, and found myself staring at the mangled bodies of two of the sorcerers who'd been pursuing me.

Vera must have left, possibly to warn the others of a potential attack or to summon more shadowkind to her side. The two men sprawled on the slanted earth, both of their necks sliced clean through, one with a gouge in his chest as if Rollick had punched straight through his ribs into his heart. Which maybe the demon had.

I drew in a breath and realized that I was shaking. But none of my horror was for the scene in front of me. Alongside my nausea came a surge of anger and defiance.

"They were killing people—a kid, even—for their awful rites," I said. "Then they tried to kill me. It's all—it's all some sick ceremony that isn't even *right*—"

I wasn't sure I was making much sense, but Rollick's gaze intensified. He grasped my arm, a brutal light flaring in his eyes. More shouts were carrying from across the forest in more than one direction.

"We can make them pay," the demon said, a hint of his monstrous nature coloring his voice in a husky note that promised vengeance. "I can tear more of them apart. You can call up the creatures they've been chaining to break free and turn on their masters. I know you could unleash all that fury on them if you give yourself over to the magic. Just say the word, and I'll be right there with you."

His words sent a shudder of yearning through me. Part of me did want to charge back to the clearing and rip the sorcerers to shreds for the horrible acts they'd carried out tonight and who knew how many times before.

But that kind of violence was exactly what had sickened me about them. I couldn't let my horror turn me into a person who was just as vicious.

"No," I said roughly. "Thank you, but— I think we should just get out of here. There's nothing else I can learn from them anyway."

Not even the sorcerers of the enclave seemed equipped to deal with shadowkind on the scale we were grappling with. And they were as monstrous as our other enemies.

"We'll deal with them," I added, my jaw clenching. "We won't let them keep doing this. But we're not going to slaughter them like the savages they think shadowkind are. Later, after we've handled the bigger problem, we'll come back."

Rollick considered me for just a few seconds and seemed to decide it wasn't worth a debate. He knelt down and shifted into his demonic form at the same time, his body expanding, his skin turning ruddy as his clothing vanished, his horns jutting up from over his angular features. As he held his hand out to me, his tufted tail lashed back and forth. "If you don't want the bloodshed, then we'd better run, or I'm not going to have much choice."

At his gesture, I stepped forward and let him heft me up so he could carry me piggyback-style. My arms wrapped around his neck, my knees bracing on either side of his expansive chest. His smoky scent flooded my lungs. As I secured my hold, he pushed off on his powerful legs, racing through the forest away from the enclave.

I closed my eyes against the rushing of the wind stirred by his swift pace. A lump clogged in the base of my throat.

The being I'd sworn never to trust had saved me. All I'd learned in the past week was that we were still on our own when it came to defeating the larger villains we were up against, with no more idea than before how to do that.

And the tremors of power rippling through my heart came from a source so horrifying I wished I could tear the borrowed organ right out of my chest.

CHAPTER NINE

Crag

A peculiar scent lingered along the shoreline in this part of the country the mortals called China. The notes of it had stuck in my memory after we'd barged into the mountain camp where our shadowkind enemies maintained a base of operations. It hadn't seemed like a smell that should be there, and it'd tugged at something deep in my memory.

I'd almost forgotten it in the chaos of the moment, but afterward—after Quinn had sent me away, when there wasn't much to think about other than mulling over the past couple of days and where I'd gone wrong—it'd risen back to the surface of my mind.

Quinn had ordered me to stay away. I couldn't have ignored that command if I'd tried—which I had. So I would help her whatever way I could. And the only way I could think of was by continuing to find out everything possible about the powerful beings that threatened her.

It'd taken me a long time to narrow down the smell. I hadn't been able to go back to the southwestern United States, at least not immediately after the mortal woman I cared for so much had cast me into the nearest rift. She must have still been nearby then. So I'd followed my instincts and shreds of memory across day after day until I'd ended up here.

No humans gathered on this lonely stretch of shoreline. It was a jumble of rocks and slimy seaweed that caught the froth of the hissing waves. Salt and all kinds of other ocean scents laced the air, but I could pick out that one specific odor clearly now.

What exactly was it? I allowed myself to emerge from the shadows, since there was no one around to see me here, and crouched down on the rocks. The smell wasn't coming from any of the bits of seaweed I raised to my nose, and it didn't seem specifically attached to the rocks, although I caught a slightly stronger whiff here and there. Hmm.

There was a flicker of bright green at the corner of my vision, and the next thing I knew, I was being bumped off my slightly precarious perch into the water. I spun as I fell, whipping out my wings, but I wasn't fast enough to stop myself from crashing into the shallows next to the shore.

I sprang back onto my feet in the waist-deep water, braced for a fight, and found myself staring back at Lance's grinning dragon face.

He shifted back into human-like form an instant later, nimbly leaping from one larger boulder to another with a rustle of his wild black curls. "Here you are. You wandered off far enough. It took us *days* to track you down."

Torrent wavered into being sitting on a rock beside him, his ever-present tentacles steadying his lean frame. He tipped his head to me, his rumpled dark red hair slanting across his pale forehead. "Sorry to take you by surprise. You know how the dragon is."

I did. But I found I didn't know what to say to either of them as I climbed out of the water, shaking it from my rocky limbs. I stayed in gargoyle form, both because it was more comfortable when I had the option and because I'd actually stand out less against the shoreline if anyone sailed at all within view of us. I'd look like one part of the scattered rocks.

"How did you find me?" I muttered. I wasn't sure I appreciated this interruption. I'd been in the middle of concentrating, and now my thoughts had scattered.

"I figured you'd be on the move," Torrent said in his typical coolly collected way. "You're trying to find something that'll help Quinn, aren't you? There aren't a whole lot of gargoyles roaming widely across the mortal realm. All we had to do was find one being who'd noticed you passing by and follow the trail from there."

I couldn't help scowling at him. We weren't exactly a squad anymore. He didn't have any official authority over me. "I was following a trail of my own. I don't know how useful it'll be."

"Oooh, the gargoyle is grouchy now," Lance declared, shooting a more human grin at me, his white teeth bright against his brown skin.

"I was in the middle of something," I informed him.

"What? We want to beat down the beasts who are after her too. We'll all tackle them together. And then we'll go back to Quinn and show her she doesn't need to worry about us. She doesn't get to tell us what to do. We protect *her*."

He said the last bit so firmly with a defiant jut of his chin that I might have chuckled if the sentiment hadn't jabbed right through my heart. The purposeful energy that'd buoyed me through the past several days deflated. My shoulders slumped despite my best efforts at keeping my inner turmoil in check.

Torrent, as usual, noticed everything. He leaned forward on his perch. "What's the matter? Have you come across anything that's made you more worried than we already were before?"

As if we hadn't been worried enough already. But that wasn't the reason for my reaction.

I debated telling him it was nothing, but I didn't think he'd believe it. And given that these two had hunted me down all across the mortal realm, I doubted he'd let the matter drop just because I tried to put him off.

"It was my fault," I said, low but even despite the pain that shuddered through my chest with the admission. "*I* pushed her away first. I made her feel like it was a problem for her to be around me. So she sent me even farther away—she sent all of us away. She thought *she* was the problem."

Torrent's sea-green eyes darkened with sympathy. "I think Quinn's concerns about us had to do with the way we *all* behaved after the battle in the sorcerers' valley." He looked down at his right hand, mangled to the point of barely being recognizable. Lance paused, following his gaze, and stiffened.

The dragon shifter had been the one who'd mangled that hand. He'd been in the grips of our enemies' stolen sorcery, so he hadn't *wanted* to attack us. But he had, and I'd seen before how guilty he felt about it.

And it was in trying to protect Quinn from him in his enraged state that I'd ended up hurting her. I'd smacked her across the face hard enough to make her cheek bleed. That had been an accident, no more purposeful than Lance's actions, but the thought of her bruised face still made me cringe inwardly.

"I was the one who made her feel unwelcome," I said, refusing to accept the out Torrent had offered me. I was the only one responsible for my own behavior. "Maybe she shouldn't *want* me back after the way I treated her. I damaged her body, and then I hurt her heart when I should have been there for her in every possible way."

Torrent's mouth twisted. "I don't think she would see it that way. But we don't need to harp on it right now. She can tell you herself when we're able to get back to her. Why don't you fill us in on why you've come out to the sea? This is more my domain than yours."

"I enjoy coastal terrain as well as higher elevations," I informed him, but I welcomed the chance to get back to actual work. Work that didn't require thinking about my past mistakes.

I turned back toward the water, giving myself a brief shake to remove the lingering droplets from my fall. "There's something here that was also in the mountain camp. Something that shouldn't have been there. I'm trying to figure out what it is."

Lance cocked his head. "What kind of thing?"

"That's what I'm trying to figure out. All I have is the scent..."

I prowled farther along the coastline, inhaling deeply. Lance and Torrent followed at a respectful distance, Torrent slipping into the shadows to travel more easily where his ruined legs wouldn't hold him back. My companions let me slip back into my zone of concentration.

That was better. I couldn't have explained the smell I was tracking anyway.

After several minutes of walking and pausing to lean closer to various spots on the ground, a sharper tendril of the odor reached my nose. I jerked around and spotted a scattering of bones in a notch between two of the rocks. As I bent to examine them, the scent grew even thicker, solidifying my certainty.

A jolt of memory passed through me—snatching a silvery body out of the water, digging my gargoyle teeth into its juicy flesh. A fish. It was a particular type of fish I'd found especially delicious and also enjoyable to catch.

Spinning, I caught a brief glimpse of a silvery body flashing amid the strands of seaweed farther from the shore. I'd only discovered them because I needed to do my hunting so far from human sight. They seemed to be particularly shy of people—I'd never noticed them when I'd lurked in mortal-made harbors.

But they were definitely an ocean fish. Why had I smelled them up in the mountains of Utah?

One of the shadowkind staying there must have brought them—for a snack or some other purpose? It would have had to be for one of the leaders, wouldn't it? I couldn't imagine them giving leave for their underlings—the ones supporting them of their free will and the ones they'd ensorcelled into helping them—to wander off to the ocean just to hunt down a particular delicacy to consume on their own.

Why hadn't the boss gone down to the ocean himself and simply had his meals there? Had it been difficult for him to make the trip? Had he enjoyed ordering his minions to do his bidding?

None of this made any particular sense to me. But I knew that this ocean was the same ocean as on the western side of the United States, the one by the beach of Rollick's hotel. It wouldn't have been *too* long an expedition from the mountain camp to reach the right waters if this sort of fish lived on both sides of the sea.

"One of the fiends from the camp was bringing fish from the ocean up to the lake," I said to my companions. "They couldn't have stayed alive there. I assume they were to eat. I don't know if the being that requested them *needs* them or not... but maybe we can assume it wouldn't go too far inland, if it prefers that meal so much?"

Torrent reappeared, picking up one of the bones I'd seen. "We have another piece of data to work with, anyway," he said. "Can you catch one of those fish for me now? Without killing it, if you can, since there's no need. I'd like to see exactly what it is so I'll recognize it in the future in living form as well as post-meal."

My renewed sense of purpose wrapped around me, lifting my spirits.

Just for that moment, I could believe that I might deserve the chance to earn back Quinn's trust after all. I was defending her in my own way, with every possible effort I could put toward keeping her safe, no matter how far from her I was.

"Give me a minute," I told Torrent, and launched myself over the ocean with a flap of my wings.

CHAPTER TEN

Quinn

For the past month, my life had kept getting more surreal, to the point that I was starting to expect that at any second I'd step through a doorway into an Escher painting. Like at the moment, I was somehow sitting on a smooth leather seat in the back of a fancy Cadillac, eating drive-through hamburgers for lunch with a millennia-old demon after fleeing for my life from a psychotic monster-enslaving cult.

It was hard to remember what it'd been like living a *normal* existence, without monsters or magic or death even more imminent than the possibility of a failing heart.

Rollick, through some supernatural ability he hadn't disclosed, managed to eat his entire hamburger and a carton of fries without getting a single drop of ketchup anywhere on his immaculate suit. I was still halfway through my burger because I was eating much more carefully, trying not to look like a slob, although I was starving. This was my first meal since he'd grabbed me from the forest near the enclave.

By the time we'd made it back to the car he'd stashed beyond their territory, I'd been so exhausted from the stress and the late night that he'd ordered me to sleep in the back while he drove us farther away. When I'd woken up to the morning sun beaming through the windows, he'd directed me to a motel room in whatever city we'd ended up in so I could shower and start to feel like a somewhat normal human being again. It wasn't until after we'd grabbed this quick meal and driven out to a secluded lane amid more hilly countryside that he'd allowed me to give my account of what I'd seen last night.

The hearty meatiness of the burger had fortified me, although my appetite was waning as I got to the most gruesome parts of the story. "They'd brought three people—I don't know where from. A woman around my age, a little girl, and I didn't see the third one because I couldn't help trying to intervene with the kid and they caught me then. The sorcerers sent them out into the clearing and the guy just tore into them like he was a rabid animal."

Rollick let out a soft huff, leaning against the door across from me in a casual pose that should have clashed with his formal clothing. "That's what they think shadowkind are—rabid animals. Monsters. It's not as if they're alone."

I grimaced and set aside the rest of my burger in its wrapper. "Most people don't even know you really *exist.* They're only going by stories and imagination. It's not their fault they don't know better. The sorcerers are interacting with actual shadowkind all the time. They should be able to see you're more than that."

"It wouldn't really be in their best interests to see anything worth respecting in us, though, would it?" The demon cocked an eyebrow. "That might put a damper on their enthusiasm for subjecting us to their whims."

I couldn't deny that he had a point. "It's still not right," I muttered, hugging myself. "Is it strange that those rites work at all? I thought you said that no shadowkind can manipulate other shadowkind. So how could something in them give humans that power?"

"I've heard of other ways a merging of human and shadowkind can create more than either was on its own," Rollick said. "That phoenix you met is an example. I'd guess that sorcerous power is generated by an interaction between the shadowkind qualities and whatever you mortals possess, transforming something inside you into an entirely new thing."

"A horrific thing. And then the shadowkind that kill those sorcerers are able to take that thing into themselves."

"So all available evidence suggests."

I sighed. "What do we do now?"

Rollick hummed to himself. "Well, I don't think we should stick around Norway now that they'll have their enslaved creatures on the hunt for us. I think I've found out all I can here about the beings we're up against. What matters more is what that villainous duo is getting up to right now."

"Back in the US. You think we should go home?"

He shrugged. "I think if we want to stop the menaces as soon as possible, we have to be where they are. And possibly the maniacal mortals here have given us some strategies for improving our chances of victory. You mentioned that the one who was mentoring you said that the rites could expand your powers just as they activate them for total novices, didn't you?"

At the recognition of where he might be going with that line of conversation, my spine stiffened. "She made it sound like that's the case. But what does it matter? I'm not going to murder and consume some innocent creature or run around attacking people just in case it gives a little more umph to my powers."

"I think we can assume that the attacking part isn't necessary," Rollick said with a chuckle. "Just their misinterpretation of what it takes to connect with the shadowkind experience on a visceral level. The absorbing of shadowkind essence might give your magic a boost that could tip the balance in the battles ahead, though."

I glowered at him, my stomach twisting. "I'm *not* killing some little beast the way they did. It was awful. And we don't even know for sure what effect it'll have on me. It didn't sound like the sorcerers usually did rites for people who already have the talent."

Rollick studied me with an intentness in his dark blue eyes that set me on guard. "To be clear, though, your main objection is to the slaughter of a random creature? If we happened to have some shadowkind essence on hand that you could drink in without any unwilling being suffering, you wouldn't object to giving it a go?"

"I—I don't know. I guess not." If it could make the difference between stopping more suffering, more murders, and whatever else our enemies had planned, then how could I say no? "But you don't have it bottled somewhere, do you? And if you're thinking you're going to wait until

Torrent and the others can come back, if they even decide to come when they can, and convince them to—"

"Oh, I don't have any interest in waiting that long." Rollick grinned. "Especially when we already have everything we need."

Before I could process what he'd meant by that, he was already moving —launching himself forward across the seat as if he'd been braced to pounce the whole time rather than lounging there all nonchalantly. I barely had a chance to flinch before he was grabbing me by the waist and yanking me under him.

My head bumped into the soft padding of the seat, my breath jolting out of me. Rollick loomed over me, trapping most of my body in place with his powerful legs. His clothes were rippling away as his massive demonic form emerged. The heat of him washed over me, almost smothering.

Panic sliced through my chest. I whipped up my arms in an effort I already knew would be futile, smacking against his muscular torso to try to dislodge him. "Don't—what are you doing—get off—"

Rollick's veneers had already wisped away to reveal the jagged demonic teeth underneath. Without paying my protests the slightest attention, he brought his arm to his mouth and gouged open his own wrist all the way to the bone. Then he slammed the wound down over my lips, cutting off my voice.

Smoky blood poured out of him into me so fast it was congealing in my throat before I'd even managed to shove at his arm. Rollick snatched my wrists with his other hand and pinned them to my chest. When I tried to shut my mouth against the flow of his shadowy essence, he pushed his limb even farther between my lips where I couldn't dislodge it. It was either suck down the smoky substance or suffocate.

I dragged a ragged breath through my nose and sputtered and gagged, but the billows of essence seeped down my throat into my lungs and stomach. It prickled through my nerves with an electric tingling everywhere it touched. The shadowkind blood didn't actually taste smoky, I realized as I struggled against Rollick's hold. It was cool and misty and laced with flavors that made me think of an autumn forest at night.

My muscles strained, and the demon gave me a tight smile, his ruddy demonic face gazing down at me with a flicker of fire in his darkened eyes. "There's a hell of a lot more essence in me than some little beastie. And the sooner your powers are up to snuff, the sooner we can deal with the real brutes we're up against. You don't have to let your morals stir up doubts this way. I made the decision for you. It'll be over faster if you relax and let it happen."

Maybe he was right, but my body still wanted to resist. Tension coiled all through my muscles. I tried to wrestle my arms away from his grasp ineffectually.

But even as I squirmed with defiance, a different sensation was sweeping through me. With each gulp of Rollick's essence, the prickles in my nerves were softening into something almost giddy.

I wanted to... I wanted to run and rove and feel how fast my limbs could move. I wanted to stretch my body, lunge and leap. There was so much—so much I could do. Gravity didn't hold me back. I was strong, powerful, impervious. Nothing could keep me down.

Was this how the initiate had felt in the clearing as he'd absorbed so much of that creature's hazy blood? And then the sorcerers' chants and all the preparation he'd done had made him turn those urges into something viciously murderous. Or maybe he'd been a brutal soul all along.

I didn't feel any inclination toward violence, only power and freedom. But I was restrained still—fixed in place by the weight over me. I inhaled, drawing even more of the smoky torrent into my lungs, and a weird tremor of sensation rippled through my senses.

I was aware, suddenly, of the rise and fall of Rollick's breaths. Of the fragility he noticed in my mortal body and how carefully he was holding his own much beefier form to avoid hurting me. Of a flicker of admiration at the fight I'd put up even as he was annoyed that I couldn't just accept what he'd done.

It was his essence I was drinking in, and more of who he was coursed into me alongside it. It woke up a hunger to have even more of him than that. To take in all of the hauntingly impressive body I'd seen on full display weeks ago, to merge with him in every possible way.

I'd been attracted to Rollick before. It wasn't a totally unfamiliar sensation. But my uncertainties about his motives and my knowledge of the screwed-up things he definitely had done had made it easy to ignore those impulses. Now, my mind seemed to have detached from my body. It was floating away, worries and longings dispersing in opposite directions, my physical presence taking its own initiative.

My hips arched up. My cunt bumped against the bulge of what I knew was not just one but two cocks, one over top of the other. A fresh wave of need rushed through me, sweeping away more of my distant protests.

No, I yelled at myself from wherever that part of me was floating now, but even more of me called out, *Yes!*

My muscles loosened beneath Rollick, and he relaxed his grip on me, his own breath quickening with a flare of desire I felt with the flow of his essence. My hand slipped free and reached to trail down the planes of his naked chest. My hips lifted toward him again, beckoning, practically begging.

The demon let out a growl. He dipped his head, his wrist still clamped over my mouth, and buried his face against the crook of my neck. His hot breath washed over my skin, and a needy whimper reverberated out of me. Every inch of me was on fire with him pressing so close. I wrapped my arm around his shoulder to tug him even nearer.

"You want this now, do you?" Rollick murmured in a dark, velvety voice that shivered through every cell. "A little taste, and you realized how much you were missing out on. That's my sweet sorcerer. Let me hear you say it, Quinn."

He eased his wrist away, and my lips parted as if seeking to gulp down even more of the smoky blood he'd poured into me. My thoughts were jumbled, the giddying hunger scattering every other concern. The only sound that came out of me was a moan.

I slid my hands down Rollick's body again, but his form had gone still over me. I rocked upward impatiently as he gazed down at me with an impenetrable expression. His essence was still gushing through the enclosed space of the car from the wound he'd given himself, but he barely seemed bothered by it. I had the vague sense that I should have been wondering how much he could afford to lose, but that worry drifted away.

He was so close and yet not close enough.

"Quinn," Rollick said, softer than before, "tell me what you want."

Why was he making this so hard? "I—I—" I managed to get out, but the craving seemed to choke me. "Please," I mumbled desperately, the burning need driving my hips toward him again.

He wanted it too. The hunger thrummed through him loudly enough that I could taste it even without the direct stream of his blood filling my lungs. But a hint of hesitation had risen up alongside it. Something cool and unyielding. I didn't like it.

"This isn't you," he muttered. "You're drunk on the stuff." His head bowed, and for a second I thought he might kiss me, but his mouth never quite reached mine. Then he pushed himself off me.

In the first moment when his body pulled away from mine, I cried out at the loss of contact. But as the cooler air slipped in between us, my gaze slid to the window, and the other desires that had gripped me first raced back into my mind. I scrambled up onto my hands and knees and peered through the window at the landscape that called me to run riot through it.

"I don't think letting you loose like this would be a good idea," Rollick said from behind me, his voice carefully even. When I glanced back at him, he was back in humanesque form, wrapping a bandage around his wrist to stem the flow of smoky blood while he healed. One of my hands lifted to scratch at the window, more wildness coursing through me.

Rollick shook his head. "I'm not losing you that way either." He rummaged around and found the blanket he'd given me to sleep with, wrapping it around me. The weight of it dampened my restlessness just a little.

"Just stay here until you come down from it," he said. "I'm going to find us the nearest airport. And then we'll see whether I've accomplished anything other than making a total mess out of things."

CHAPTER ELEVEN

Quinn

The dirt lane through the misty fields ended at a stand of trees. Rollick parked his new car there and got out without a word. I followed on the passenger side, taking a deep breath of the late summer warmth.

It was funny how the scenery in front of us could look so similar to the terrain on the other side of the Atlantic but feel so different at the same time. Although I wasn't sure I was all that much safer now that I was back in my home country.

"Are you sure this is a good idea?" I asked Rollick, resting my hand on the sun-heated glass of the window. "I mean, the big bad duo that wants to capture me—or their minions, anyway—must have been here just a few days ago."

Rollick shrugged in his typical languid way. "That's exactly why we should check out the scene of the crime. They might have left some useful trace of their presence behind. I doubt there'll be anyone all that important still lurking around." He shot me a grin that was a little more subdued than

I was used to, though that didn't stop his face from being as stunning as ever. "You've got me here to protect you, fair maiden."

All of his grins and smirks had been toned down ever since our encounter back in Norway two days ago when he'd forced his smoky blood down my throat—and I'd gone wild with it. Since I'd woken up from the essence-induced stupor, he hadn't referenced what'd happened, and all his other behavior toward me had remained unchanged. I'd kept my mouth shut about the whole thing because even thinking about talking about it made my cheeks flare so sharply I was afraid they'd literally ignite.

Like the time when I'd burst into tears in front of him, the demon seemed dedicated to pretending my momentary lapse in control had never happened. Which probably worked out in his favor at least as much as mine since it was his fault it'd happened in the first place.

"I think I'd like to be able to rely on myself too," I said, and jerked my chin toward the trunk. "You picked up all our stuff that you'd stashed away before we left, didn't you? The crossbow we got from the sorcerers in Arizona is still in there?"

Rollick arched his eyebrows, but he went around to open the trunk. "As you wish. You did seem to have gotten the hang of it when we stormed their camp. I doubt we'll encounter anywhere near as many beasties here."

"Better safe than sorry," I muttered.

He handed over the small weapon which was at least as much a gun as it was a crossbow and then stepped back so I could collect a handful of the slim silver-and-iron bolts that served as its arrows. Not much could stop a shadowkind creature in its tracks, but the combination of metals that were noxious to them did the trick well enough that even a powerful being like Rollick didn't want to handle objects that size.

I loaded three of the bolts into the crossbow and adjusted my grip, refamiliarizing myself with the weapon, which was about as long as my forearm. Its weight put a slight strain on my bicep, but I found it comforting all the same. "All right, let's go."

Rollick led the way along a foot path through the trees, and I was happy to let him go first. If we encountered any aggressive creatures, he was better equipped to fend them off than I was, crossbow or not.

At first the stretch of forest looked normal enough, but as we walked deeper, I spotted vicious gouges in the bark of the trunks up ahead. Near their roots, chunks of earth had been torn by what I had to imagine were thick claws. I braced myself for the sight we'd discover on the other side.

Word had gotten out through the shadowkind communities that another sorcerer family had been struck down while we'd been dealing with the enclave's sick rituals over in Norway. Rollick had heard about it within a few hours of our touching down back on American soil and decided it was as good a place as any to resume our stateside investigations.

I couldn't say I was super enthusiastic about the trip, but when the alternative was probably searching out random shadowkind for me to test my possibly enhanced sorcery on, I wasn't going to complain.

Because of sorcerers' frequent preference for setting up their homes far from civilization, no one in the human community had discovered the murders yet. We came out into a wide glade that showed no sign of police presence. More claw marks had churned up bits of grass and wildflowers. A long single-story house with patches of moss on its stone walls stood at the far end of the open space, the door closed but the windows shattered.

Even from this far away, a rancid smell reached my nose. A shiver ran down my spine.

Rollick glanced over at me. "I'd say you can wait out here, but I'd rather not leave you on your own for reasons already discussed."

"I'll be fine," I said, clenching my jaw against the queasiness already stirring inside me.

He scanned our surroundings as we walked over to the door, his gait casual but his eyes alert. Apparently he didn't see any reason for worry, because he didn't hesitate. At the door, he made a gesture with his hand, and there was a snapping sound from within. He'd used his demonic magic to break the lock.

"You couldn't have just willed it to slide open?" I asked him.

"Breaking is simpler. I don't think the owners are in a condition to be concerned about their security any longer."

He had a point there. We stepped inside, the smell thickening enough that I tugged my shirt up over my face so I could get a little relief by breathing through the fabric.

This family appeared to have been made up of five people. We found an elderly-looking couple first, slumped and bloody in the kitchen. Then a younger man and woman in the dining room, where it looked as if they'd tried to use the table as a barricade. When we came around the flipped-over slab of wood, a smaller body was sprawled right at its base—a toddler so mangled I couldn't even tell if it'd been a boy or a girl.

My stomach heaved at the sight. I jerked down my shirt just in time to vomit my lunch onto the floorboards. Acid seared the back of my mouth.

I'd been horrified by what the sorcerers in the enclave had been doing to activate their powers, but some of the shadowkind *were* exactly the sort of monsters those people believed them to be. I guessed that unlike the little boy they'd stolen before, the villainous duo had decided this child was too young to be of any possible use to them.

Rollick didn't comment on my reaction. His mouth set in an expression of distaste that I could tell was aimed at the carnage rather than me. He turned away from the bodies, cocked his head, and knelt in the corner to examine a different spot on the hardwood floor that looked exactly the same as the rest of the boards to my eyes.

I gulped a little water from the bottle in my bag to wash out the sour flavor in my mouth, careful not to swallow so much that I'd set off my stomach again. "What are you looking at?" I asked a little hoarsely.

Rollick touched the boards and sniffed his fingers. "Water damage."

"And that's important?"

"It contributes to the larger picture."

He didn't seem inclined to say more yet, and I wasn't in the mood to badger him. I left the dining room behind to see what I might find in the rest of the house, farther from the awful spectacle.

I'd only made it two steps down the hall when a shadowy blur flung itself at me from a doorway up ahead.

A yelp jolted from my throat, but thankfully my reflexes kicked in even as my nerves jumped with surprise. I jerked up the crossbow and squeezed the trigger in one swift movement, throwing myself backward at the same time.

The silver-and-iron bolt hit the creature that'd sprung at me as it shifted into physical form, catching it square in the chest. With a pained snarl, it crumpled on the floor, smoke wafting up from the wound. The sight reminded me of the enclave's rites and made my stomach lurch all over again.

A different, distant sensation rippled through me: a flicker of consternation and fear. It arrived in tandem with Rollick rushing into the hall.

That'd been happening here and there since he'd fed me his filmy essence, the stuff that shadowkind considered blood. Just as I'd sensed his lust and hesitation in the car, I sometimes caught a whiff of his other emotions, maybe only when they were particularly strong. Which wasn't very often, but it was still a bit unnerving having an internal tie to the demon.

I wasn't sure whether he was aware of that consequence of his force-feeding. It hadn't seemed like a good time to bring it up yet. Being aware of his true emotions could turn out to be a good if small advantage to have in my back pocket.

He was definitely concerned about my current well-being. He stalked over and toed the slumped creature with his loafer. It cringed and groaned.

"Good shot," he said evenly. "We're not getting anything useful out of a lesser beast like this." Then he raised his foot and slammed it down on the thing's head, crushing its skull.

I dragged in a breath and loaded another bolt into the crossbow, not wanting to reach into the creature's disintegrating body to retrieve the one I'd shot. "See," I said, summoning more bravado than I felt. "I can look after myself."

Rollick shot me a look somewhere between amused and annoyed. "Not against every being that's been here. But I think anything larger than this is long gone."

I held my crossbow at the ready as we searched the rest of the house, Rollick never letting me get out of his sight. My heart thumped at a faster pace, but I couldn't say I enjoyed the tension that'd built up inside me. My thrill-seeker side was getting exhausted by all the close calls I'd had in the past month. Even it wouldn't have minded a break to just chill for a little while.

The place didn't hold anything else all that useful, especially now that I'd gotten a much more in-depth glimpse of the inner workings of sorcery at the enclave. I didn't lower the crossbow until we made it back to the car, and then I brought it into the front seat with me, feeling a little better having it within reach.

"Are you going to tell me what picture you've been putting together?" I asked as Rollick started the engine. "Didn't you already figure out we're dealing with a behemoth?" I had no idea just how bad that was, but the name alone and remembering the way Rollick had talked about it sent a fresh chill through my veins.

Rollick paused for a moment, and I caught another quaver of emotion from him: a deep uneasiness that I didn't like at all. He wasn't half as confident about our chances as he'd been acting.

"I've become increasingly sure that the other half of this dynamic deadly duo is a creature of the sea," he said.

"Like Torrent?"

The demon snorted. "If he were like Torrent, we wouldn't have anything to worry about. Torrent isn't the type to go around wreaking havoc. No, considering the powers at play and the company he's keeping—and a few details that've been adding up… I think our behemoth has allied himself with a leviathan. Possibly the only leviathan, since like the behemoth I've only ever heard of one."

A deeper chill washed over me. I resisted the urge to hug myself, not wanting Rollick to see how unnerved I was. "And we're taking on these two one-of-a-kind monsters on our own."

Rollick's mouth twisted for a second, the only outward sign of his discomfort. "I have some ideas about that. Don't worry yourself about it for now. I won't be putting anything in motion until we reach our next destination anyway."

I tipped my head back against the seat and closed my eyes, but I was too keyed up to have any hope of dozing, even though last night's sleep hadn't been all that restful. The pangs of emotion I'd gotten from the demon, especially his concern when he'd heard me being attacked, tugged at my mind. Suddenly the weight of all the things we hadn't talked about pressed in on me too heavily for me to keep my mouth shut.

"We haven't talked about what happened the other day. In the car. When you—"

"I remember," Rollick cut in, but he sounded more resigned than irritated by me bringing up the subject. "I didn't think you wanted to talk about it."

"I'm not sure *want* is the right word." I hesitated, staring at the road ahead. "I didn't want to react the way I did then either. Your shadowkind blood seemed to bring out these urges, and I couldn't get control of myself." My cheeks started to burn, but the worse sensation was the guilt clogging my throat.

I hadn't discussed exclusivity with the three men I'd fallen for. They hadn't minded that they were sharing my attentions with each other. And maybe, after the way I'd sent them off, they didn't even consider themselves my... boyfriends, or whatever I should call them. But it would still have felt like cheating to get it on with any other person—or being.

Rollick kept his voice light but steady with none of his usual sly teasing. "I know. I'm not sorry about feeding you my essence, because it could make a difference in the long run, and your only objections had nothing to do with the situation I created. But I am sorry that my actions had effects we weren't prepared for. I had no intention of messing with your mind or your inhibitions."

How could he have known? It wasn't as if he'd gone around feeding his essence to mortals on a regular basis. He sounded like he meant the partial apology, which was as much of an apology as I could imagine him ever offering.

Of course he wasn't sorry about the other part. I wasn't even sure I was angry at him about the rest, since maybe it would be better that he'd juiced up my powers—if he actually had. I'd known that might be the right call, and I'd been having trouble making it, so he'd done it for me.

"You've always said I'd decide to hook up with you eventually," I said, taking on a similarly breezy tone. "You didn't take me up on it while you had the chance."

Rollick let out a huff. "I don't think you being addled out of your mind counts as a real chance—or a real decision." He glanced over at me. Even seeing him just from the corner of my eye, I could feel the intensity of his gaze. "When—if—we go there, it'll be because all of you is on board, not just a burst of hormones you're too drunk to control. I have no trouble finding fully willing sexual partners. Even as a monster, I find those much more satisfying."

"Ah." My cheeks heated more, and I didn't know what else to say. I couldn't help noticing that he'd revised his "when" to an "if" despite his previous insistence that I'd eventually jump his bones. "Well... that's good to know."

The demon chuckled, and the tension in the car subsided. His smile turned sly again. "Maybe what I have in store for you next will make up a little for my miscalculation."

I raised my eyebrows at him. "That sounds ominous."

"Just wait and see."

It didn't take all that long to figure out where we were going once we got onto a major freeway with regular signs. Rollick set a course toward Boston, and I sat up a little straighter as its downtown high rises came into view in the distance.

"Why Boston?" I asked, even as my pulse gave a giddy skip.

"You didn't get to come to Berlin with me, so I figured why not a different B city." Rollick tipped his head toward the cityscape. "From what I've seen, it's got one of the most interesting mixes of buildings in this country."

I doubted that was the only reason we were making the trip, but I wasn't going to complain. I could already pick out the Hancock amid the shorter buildings, its glossy sides reflecting the blue sky and tufts of clouds. And I'd love to see the stark modern design of the John F Kennedy Library up close after we'd talked about it in one of my college courses last year. I'd hoped to do a little road trip touring various cities around the country one summer, and Boston had been near the top of the list.

"Thank you," I said.

The demon shrugged. "You've been through a lot. You should get a chance to enjoy yourself a little along the way. Maybe your life's gotten off course, but that doesn't mean you're totally giving up what matters to you."

I supposed it mattered to *him* that I was relatively content so that I'd continue going along with his schemes. But I couldn't help saying, "It's not really the same, you know. It's not like all I wanted out of life was to look at cool buildings and admire them."

"Isn't that what those classes you've regretted missing are all about?"

"Yeah, but..." I gazed at the skyline we were approaching, and a knot formed in my chest. My voice dipped. "I wanted to make my own mark too. To add something to places like this. Like I told you before, great architecture isn't just about making something easy on the eyes. I wanted to create something that would keep inspiring people or at least making them feel something... after I'm gone. But I guess there isn't a whole lot of chance of that now."

Rollick frowned, an expression that sat oddly on his stunning face. Another waft of uneasiness tingled into me from him. "There's no reason to assume that."

I lifted my chin, stuffing down the pain that came with my growing sense of resignation. "I'm just trying to be realistic, seeing how things have gone so far. It was a long shot anyway, given my condition. I'm running out of time. But if I can save some people from *dying*, that matters a lot too. And I appreciate the chance to get to be inspired myself, even if I won't get to do a whole lot with that inspiration. So thank you."

The demon was silent for a long moment. Then he shot another grin at me. "Don't give up yet. That's not your style at all, is it? You still have your sketch pad. Consider me your professor for the week. I want to see two new designs by the time we're through here."

I rolled my eyes at him, though a flutter ran through my chest at the gesture. "Oh, first it's about me enjoying myself, and now you're assigning me homework?"

"Consider it my attempt at replicating the 'Quinn's real life' experience," Rollick said, and then sobered slightly. "It might not be such a long shot anyway, at least not any more than it already was. I've got my own plans while we're here."

Color me not at all surprised. "And what are those?"

He made a vague gesture with his hand. "There's a significant rift that leads to the shadow realm in one of the city parks. Big enough that one more being passing through shouldn't draw any attention. I'm going to go have a chat with the Highest."

My brow knit. "The Highest?" Something about the term sounded familiar—had he mentioned them before?

"The oldest and most powerful shadowkind," Rollick explained. "They're basically mountains in themselves, looming off in the deeper reaches of the realm. They themselves never venture mortal-side, but they've got a lot of lackeys at their beck and call, and they don't look kindly on any of us interfering with human society too aggressively. From what I heard, they've already cracked down on the behemoth once."

I perked up. "And you think they'd intervene again now?"

Rollick's mouth formed a tight smirk. "I believe our behemoth and leviathan have made more than enough trouble for the Highest to think it's worth stepping in. And if they send out the troops, all our trouble should soon be over."

CHAPTER TWELVE

Lance

We tumbled through the rift over a series of sprawling green hills that sent a crisp herbal smell into the air. I soared down through the shadows and twisted in a last-second flip to land in a patch of gloom at the edge of a boulder, enjoying the sensation of moving through the fresh mortal-realm air even in my invisible state.

I spun around to face Torrent and Crag as they descended the short drop from the rift after me. I had the vague sense that it was night in this area, but some sunlight still gleamed along the horizon.

"This is that Norway place?" I asked.

Torrent nodded, studying the landscape around us. "The country where Quinn thought the special group of sorcerers she heard about might be based. It's not that big a country. If we were able to come out here without her command pushing us back—"

I perked up with a burst of eager energy. "Her orders have worn off!"

Crag made one of his usual grim expressions. "Or she's left, so we're not so close to her that it's a problem. How long has it been since she planned to come here?"

Torrent hummed to himself. "I'm not sure. Let's find the nearest human habitation—there'll be some clue there."

I never paid much attention to the passing of days anyway, and it was particularly hard to keep track in the shadow realm, where there was no night and day, only that endless sort of twilight. It was good to be back. Good to think that maybe I could return to Quinn soon… even if the memory of her aiming that twisted power at me sent a shudder right down the center of my body.

But even as I tensed up inside, the ache of being without her pealed louder. I *needed* her, needed to be stroking her smooth skin and nuzzling her soft hair, needed to hear her gleeful laugh and the gentle voice she used when she was worried about me. I needed to make sure none of the beasties out there had gotten their claws into her in a much more vicious way than I ever would.

I needed to understand why she'd forced me to leave. How could she have turned that awful magic on me when she'd been so upset about how others had done the same thing? How could she think *I* needed protection, like Torrent said she must have believed?

I would get answers. I leapt after the others through the swaths of darkness, doing my best to ignore the jitters passing through my nerves.

There were other sorcerers around here somewhere. Powerful ones, maybe ones who taught new sorcerers how to bend our wills and enslave us. The thought set my fangs gnashing and my ghostly claws digging into the earth, and at the same time it made me want to whirl around and dash as far as I could get from any of them.

No. Torrent had found me, and we'd found Crag, and we would stick together. Once we'd just worked together, but now we were something more than that. We were tied to one another by our feelings for Quinn, but our association went beyond that aspect too.

I liked them. I trusted them. They'd helped me when no other being would have, and I'd helped them when I could as well.

I'd also hurt them. My gaze slid to the impressions of Torrent's tentacles moving through the dusk, knowing that one of the tips was mangled beyond repair by my fangs and fiery breath, and a fresh surge of horror welled up inside me.

I shoved it away and pushed onward as if I could run away from that memory too.

Quinn hadn't blamed me. Torrent and Crag hadn't either. But how could I not blame myself? It'd been me, too weak to fight off the sorcery that'd slammed into my brain. Me who hadn't been prepared enough to fend it off. My fangs and claws that'd slashed at both of them.

I would have killed *Quinn* if they hadn't stopped me. If—

I stiffened up just as I started to fling myself at a shrub we were passing with the urge to savage its brambles. To show I decided how I wielded my body now. I yanked myself away with gritted teeth, checking whether Torrent had noticed my lapse.

Going around destroying things and picking fights didn't help anything. I *knew* that, even if part of me still wanted to do it. My limbs itched with the uneasy restlessness.

"There's a cottage," Torrent said, veering to the right.

I trailed behind him and the gargoyle, burning off as much of the anxious energy as I could by taking unnecessary twists and turns to stretch my body. At one point I nearly crashed into a mortal animal that sensed me even through the shadows and hissed with a flash of pointed teeth. I snarled in return and was about to launch myself at it when the cuff of Crag's fist against my shoulder brought me back to the task at hand.

"Torrent's going in. Come on."

Chagrinned, I hustled after him to the wall of the cottage. It must have been night, because snores were carrying through the one window that was cracked ajar. Torrent had already vanished inside.

I circled the cottage, eyeing the weather-worn walls and the bed of flowers out front, but I'd only completed the circuit twice when Torrent emerged. He shook himself, flexing his tentacles. I could tell from his voice that he wasn't pleased.

"It's been more than a week. Plenty of time for her to have come and gone."

He paused, and I immediately filled in what he hadn't said with my mind. There'd been plenty of time for the sorcerers to have done something to Quinn that'd take her *out* of this world too.

"If she died, her magic would die too," I said, my lips drawing back with a growl. "When was the last time we felt it repel us?"

Crag drew his massive form taller as if to command our attention. "We can't make any assumptions from that. Hundreds of miles could be a fairly small distance compared to the entire mortal realm. It'd be easy for us not to have stumbled on that boundary."

"We need to be sure. We—"

"We will be sure," Torrent said in his firm but even way, so calm the growl faded in my throat. He rubbed his jaw thoughtfully. "If she came here and already saw the sorcerers or never found them at all and then left, she's most likely gone back to America, where she's most at ease. And where Rollick's most current resources are. That's where our enemies were making trouble. Once she finished with her investigations here, why wouldn't she return?"

That made sense. I spun around tightly enough that I could have snapped at my own tail with my jaws. "Then we go to America and see if we feel her magic pushing us away. Or should *we* track down these sorcerers first?"

Just asking the question made my skin bunch up beneath my scales. How many beings did that group have under their control? Would they try to grab our minds too? I wanted to snarl at myself for suggesting it, and to slash my frustration into the earth, and—

"We don't know where to start beyond getting to this country," Torrent said. "If Quinn didn't find them, then I doubt we could, and if she did, then she's already got it covered. I say we head to Jacksonville first and work from there."

He glanced at us as if checking for our approval rather than insisting on the course of action. Crag rumbled his agreement. I blinked at Torrent and then nodded too, although I'd have gone along with whatever he suggested.

Torrent always had good ideas. I'd have followed him to track down those sorcerers if he'd felt we needed to... but I couldn't promise what I might have done to them if they'd come within reach of my claws.

"Good. Let's go, then." Torrent turned back toward the rift we'd emerged through.

Thankfully, moving in our shadow forms didn't take up much energy. We traveled across the rolling landscape, leapt up to the rift, and then darted through the hazy plains of the shadow realm until Torrent found another rift he was satisfied with. When we sprang through that one, we found ourselves on a beach with salty ocean air wafting over us and the sun just setting beyond the buildings on the western horizon.

This was the city where we'd first watched Quinn. Where she'd clambered to the top of those tall buildings and looked so pleased as she gazed out over the city.

A pang hit me: the longing to have joined her properly for one of those expeditions, to have listened to her tell me what she loved about the view. And maybe to have offered some additional thrills near one of those precarious edges.

Then I registered that we had come out, and we were here, and nothing was deflecting us. But that didn't mean anything. She simply might not be here.

"If she's still with Rollick, they could have gone back to his favorite city," I pointed out, lashing my tail. It was hard to say whether I'd rather she was with Rollick for the protection he could provide or far from him after the ways he'd manipulated her in the past.

Torrent gestured to the rift. "We'll check there next. She said we had to stay 'hundreds' of miles away, so two hundred at a minimum. We'll keep moving from city to city until we've covered every two-hundred-mile span or encountered the barrier of the spell."

And if we never encountered it? I bit back the question as a renewed wave of restlessness swept through my body. How would we find her then? She could be anywhere. She might not even be alive. But Torrent and Crag knew that as well as I did. What was the point in saying it?

The ache of longing inside me spread through my chest with each rift we slipped through. The place called Los Angeles offered nothing of interest. We emerged into desert and forest and flat plains of golden grass, small towns and soaring cities.

My spirits had sunk when we approached what must have been the twelfth or so rift—and my senses jarred on the threshold.

My eyes widened. I whipped my head around to look at the others. "I can't go through. She must be close—close to wherever that rift leads to." And wherever that was, she was alive.

"I feel it too," Crag said gruffly.

A smile crossed Torrent's face briefly before he became stern again. "This one opens out to just north of New York City. She's in the northeast, anyway."

But we still had no idea exactly where. Or what she was doing there. Or if she was okay or simply hanging on to the barest thread of life after some major injury.

I pushed closer to the rift, unable to deny the impulse to tear my way through to her. The magic that'd clamped around my skull with Quinn's sorcery-laced voice clutched me harder, but I thought I felt a bit of a wobble through it that hadn't been there when I'd tried to double back to her before. I shoved myself even farther into the rift and caught just a glimpse of blue sky before my body forced me to recoil.

"It's getting weaker!" I rasped with uncontainable excitement. "The spell is wearing off." Hopefully that didn't mean there was something wrong with her. We'd expected the sorcery to dwindle over time on its own, after all.

Torrent's eyes glimmered with a trace of hope. "Then we'll stay nearby, figure out the exact boundaries we can't cross, and see what we can do to help her in the meantime. There are other rifts in this area." He paused. "Will you be okay, Lance? It might be... frustrating knowing she's there but not being able to reach her."

I understood why he was asking. The memory lingered in the back of my head of how I'd been careening around the shadow realm when he'd found me. Even now, my muscles were straining to fight the magic keeping me from Quinn with all I had.

But if I made a disturbance in the mortal realm, that could be bad for her and the three of us too. It could draw our enemies' interest. Or sorcerers' attention. Or who knew what else.

I closed my eyes and stretched my limbs one at a time, exerting my will over each of them in turn. The need to see Quinn, to hear the answers only she could give me, still jangled inside me, but I would control it. If I couldn't command *myself*, how would I ever stop sorcerers from enslaving me again?

"I'll be good," I said, and flashed a fanged grin at Torrent. "Let's get back to our woman."

CHAPTER THIRTEEN

Quinn

"What are you up to now?"

Rollick's voice came with a tone of amusement mixed with mild exasperation, but it was so startling I flinched and dropped my multitool on the floor of the hotel room. I snatched it up before twisting around to glower at him.

"You could start with a hello. Or knocking on the door instead of appearing in the middle of the room out of nowhere."

The demon propped himself against the wall, more mirth sparking in his dark blue eyes. "But where would the fun be in that? It's important that I keep you on your toes, or you might get complacent."

I snorted. "I don't think there's any chance of that happening." I motioned to the table I'd been sitting at, where I'd eaten a hasty breakfast about an hour ago while awaiting Rollick's return. "I noticed the table was pretty wobbly, so I figured I'd see if I could do anything about that. It looks like whoever assembled it tightened a couple of the screws too much and then couldn't tighten the others enough. I've balanced it out pretty well."

Rollick arched his eyebrows at me. "And that was the best way you could find to pass the time?"

"At least it's accomplishing something," I retorted, and straightened up for just long enough to flop onto the edge of the bed. "It's hard to just zone out and watch whatever's on TV with everything else going on, and you *still* haven't let me have my computer back or any internet access on my phone. And you did insist that I shouldn't leave the hotel room while you were gone." Not that I'd disagreed with that part.

"I'm simply protecting you from yourself," he reminded me with a grin.

And protecting my family and anyone else I might have been tempted to contact, which was the only reason I hadn't kept badgering him about my devices. What could I really have done online when I couldn't safely talk to my parents or professors?

The thought of how worried Mom and Dad must be getting after so long without even a brief text made my stomach knot up. I couldn't do anything about that, though, so I did my best to focus on the situation at hand. Our current plans might mean I *could* talk to them safely again before too long. "Did you manage to meet with the Highest like you wanted? Are they going to help stop the shadowkind we're up against?"

Rollick pushed off the wall, looking abruptly more serious. "It took some time, but I made my appeal, and eventually persuaded them of the severity of the concern." He let out a huff. "The Highest don't have the greatest sense of anything outside their own vast hollow in the shadow realm where everyone caters to their whims. But they really don't like the idea of anyone riling up the mortal realm enough that there's a chance their leisure might be disturbed."

I perked up. "They're sending someone, then? Their warriors or whatever?"

He nodded. "Through my connections, I've been able to locate another of the villainous duo's camps—the one it appears they've moved to for the most part since we crashed their party in Utah. I might have promised I'd help ensure the fiends they need to talk to are actually *there* when the warriors arrive tonight... although it'll be much easier to give that help if you're willing to flex those possibly enhanced sorcerer powers of yours."

A weird tingle passed beneath my skin, both uneasy and excited at once. I liked my powers even less after seeing how they must have been provoked by whichever of my heart donor's ancestors had undergone the rites generations ago. Still, it was hard not to enjoy the idea of taking down the monsters that'd spent so much of the past month hunting me down, either to kill me or enslave me themselves.

"I could do that," I said. "What exactly are you thinking we'd try?"

Rollick motioned for me to gather my things. "Once we get out there, if our behemoth and leviathan aren't already conveniently on hand, we'll hunt down a lackey or two of theirs and give them instructions. A panicked message to deliver to their overlords or something along that line."

I frowned as I grabbed my backpack. "Aren't their lackeys already controlled by *their* sorcery? Would I be able to override that?"

"I'm not sure," the demon admitted. "I haven't associated with sorcerers enough before you to find out the details of how their magic interacts. But we can try if necessary, and if it doesn't work, they do seem to have quite a few hangers-on who are in it of their own free will, just to suck up to a powerful leader."

"All right." I swung my bag over my shoulder. "What are we waiting for, then?"

By the end of the day, maybe this horrible situation would be over.

When Rollick indicated that we were getting close to the new camp, I started to understand how it might not have been all that hard for him to locate it once he'd seen their first base of operations. The Oregon mountain range we were driving up to after our flight across the country was a lot greener than the desert terrain in Utah, cloaked with trees lower down and other vegetation higher up, but the peaks were equally imposing. And we hadn't passed any human habitations in half an hour.

"They like the high elevations—because people are less likely to just wander through?" I said. "And they stay far away from any major hubs of human activity in general."

Rollick smiled thinly. "Those appear to be two out of the three key factors. The other is water. The leviathan must prefer the sea, and while he can't easily ensure he's close to that, he doesn't want to stay anywhere he can't get decently wet at all. There's a lake nestled up there just like at their other camp."

"You're sure they've been here recently?"

"Remember that I can hop across the country in a matter of minutes using the rifts," he said. "I've already been here to observe with my own eyes. There's definitely more shadowkind activity happening than I'd expect if the base were just on standby. And other than their detours for sorcerer-murdering, the head honchos have mostly been rounding up troops and hassling the local shadowkind along the west coast. They probably figure you're still around somewhere. Or that *I* am, and they'd like to murder me too."

He didn't sound all that concerned about the possibility, but I knew his nonchalance was at least partly an act. A few tremors of apprehension had passed from him into me during the drive out here.

He parked amid a stand of trees. "We'd better walk from here. It'll go a lot faster if you let me give you a ride like we did when we were fleeing the sorcerers' enclave."

He made the suggestion equally casually as if it was no big deal, but when I shrugged and said, "Okay," a flash of his surprise hit me. He was so good at keeping it cool that not a single hint of the emotion showed on his face.

I wasn't sure how much I trusted the demon now, but I believed that he wasn't going to take some kind of physical advantage of me while he had me in his grasp. If he'd wanted to do that, he'd had the perfect opportunity already. And I'd rather get this expedition over with as quickly as possible with a minimum of hiking.

As Rollick shifted into his demonic form, I secured my shoulder bag against my back, the crossbow tied to it with Velcro strips I'd constructed that should allow me to snap it off with a sharp jerk if I needed it quickly. The beads of my silver-and-iron vest slid between the two thin layers of fabric I wore around it, and I glanced over at Rollick, who'd hunched his massive frame down in a kneeling position.

"The metals I'm wearing won't bother you?" I asked.

He waved off my worry with a clawed hand. "With them covered up so they aren't directly touching me, it's just a minor irritation. I'd be much more irritated by having to match your much slower mortal pace going up the mountain."

He grinned to soften the criticism, and I made a face at him as I walked over. "We can't all be super-powerful demons with giant legs. Just be glad I'm taking you up on the piggyback ride."

Rollick chuckled. "Believe me, I am."

As much as I was trying to stay focused on the task at hand and not any other emotions that'd been stewing inside me, an ache spread through my chest with the heft of Rollick's hands fixing me in place where I could loop my arms over his shoulders and around his neck. Crag had carried me when we'd gone up the mountainside in Utah. Not like this, but cradled in his arms like an embrace... although an embrace he'd only given because he felt the alternatives were worse.

He'd hesitated to hold me close for any other reason in those last couple of days before I'd sent him and my other two shadowkind men away. His fear of hurting me accidentally had been too painful.

I swallowed the lump that'd risen in my throat and closed my eyes, but as Rollick loped through the trees at a swift pace, the thoughts kept filling my head anyway. What were my three shadowkind men doing now? Had my magical command really held firm for this long? Or had it worn off, but they'd decided I was right—that they were better off staying away from me? Especially when I'd proven that I was willing to use my sorcery against them.

With each day that passed without their return, it seemed more and more likely I was never going to see them again. It would have been nice if I could convince myself that possibility was for the best for all of us. The warriors sent by the Highest would deal with our enemies, I could go back to my regular life pretending I had no magic at all, and everything would be almost the same as it had been.

Almost, other than the fact that I'd know about the world beyond the one I'd been aware of before. I'd remember what it was like to be wrapped up in the affection and passion of three men totally unlike any human guy I'd ever met. I'd wanted to believe I could find some kind of balance between normalcy and my relationship with them... but now the choice was out of my hands.

Rollick's taut muscles flexed with smooth efficiency beneath me. His breaths stayed even despite his quick pace. It wasn't long before the trees dwindled and then disappeared completely, leaving a grassy landscape scattered with shrubs and rocks. He set me down carefully, peering around in the descending evening. "Now to find our prey. Stay close to me."

He shrank back into human-like form as he stalked forward, and I hustled along at his flank, pulling my crossbow into my hands. The slope we were on was still steep enough that I broke out in a sweat after several steps. The demon moved onward with unwavering focus. Then, without warning, he leapt forward and vanished into the shadows.

I froze in place, but I didn't have time to even start to panic. A moment later, he sprang into sight clutching a slim, pale-skinned being around the neck. The thing was vaguely humanoid, but with long sloth-like arms and a round face that intensified the animalistic impression. It stood only about three feet tall.

It'd gone limp in Rollick's grasp. He loosened his hold just enough that it would be able to speak. "Are you patrolling around here because your masters burned their orders into your brain, or because you think you'll get some kind of favors from them for your loyalty?"

"I don't know what you're talking about," the creature whimpered in a nasal voice. "I'm just looking out for myself like we all do."

Rollick snorted and clenched his fingers again, making the thing gag. He glanced toward me. "That sounds like a free mind to me. We won't need to strain your powers after all."

I squared my shoulders. My stomach was churning, but I'd come too far to back down now. "What should I have it tell the head honchos?"

The demon hummed to himself. "Let's stick with what's almost the truth—that the sorcerer Quinn has come to negotiate with them for her life. She'll be waiting by the lake. But she needs to talk to both of them before she'll come to any agreement."

I inhaled deeply and fixed my gaze on the sloth-like figure. Just thinking about using my powers sent the energy prickling through my limbs. A warbling sensation flooded my chest, more intense than I ever remembered it before. For a second, I lost my breath completely, and I hadn't even really started.

Oh, Rollick's essence had given my powers some kind of boost. I could already taste it in the electricity crackling up my throat onto my tongue.

I knew the creature in front of me even if I'd never encountered a being like it before. I could picture the conflicting desires tangled inside it—to roam wildly, to indulge its basic hungers, to ensure it allied itself with the right sorts of beings, to curry favor it might need later. It was wary of me now and frightened of Rollick but still confused. In the back of my mind, I could see how it would scurry across the terrain at my command.

The magic seared through my mouth and over my tongue. My lips parted, the language of sorcery spilling from my lips as I focused on the message I meant to convey.

You will go to the powerful shadowkind you serve. The two that give the final orders. You'll tell them that Quinn the sorcerer has come to their camp here to negotiate for her life. She's waiting by the lake. She will only speak with them if they both come. Go to them and deliver that message as quickly as you can.

Before, the casting of sorcery had left me drained. This time, as Rollick released the creature and it darted off exactly as I'd imagined, a fresh wave of energy surged through me. I was exhilarated rather than exhausted.

I could have commanded a hundred more beings like I had that one, I was suddenly sure.

Rollick was eyeing me. "Nicely done, sweet sorcerer."

I tamped down on my giddiness and met his gaze. "What happens if they get to the camp and find out I'm not there before the Highest's warriors get there?"

He offered a wry smile. "Not a problem. They're already here, waiting."

My head jerked around. "What? Where?"

"Closer to the camp, but they're aware we've arrived—and that we have no beef with them." He paused. "We could leave now and get you farther away where you'll be safer... or we could watch this villainous duo fall like they deserve."

The first option was probably the smart one, but the high of my casting and the thought of how much torment these monsters had put me through renewed my boldness. "I want to see them go down."

Rollick's smile widened. "Then come with me."

He led me along a winding path to a small outcropping of rock that looked down over a vast dip between a few different mountain peaks. Just as he'd said, there was a lake up here, at least a mile distant beyond my current perch, its waters turned black in the dimming light. We wouldn't be all that close to the battle.

"Will we definitely be able to see anything?" I couldn't help asking, hunkering down on the gritty stone. The wind whipped over us, chilly at this altitude. I reached to twine my hair into a hasty braid. "I mean, they might just fight in the shadows, right? And it's getting dark besides that."

Rollick sank down next to me with his legs sprawled out. "It's difficult to make as much of an impact as our shadowy selves. I expect the violence will be perfectly corporeal. And beings this powerful will bring out the special effects. You'll get your fill."

I glanced over at him, the angles of his striking face deepened by the falling dusk, and couldn't stop myself from thinking of the violence these fiends had dealt out toward him. Because of other choices I'd made.

"I'm sorry about your hotel," I said abruptly.

Rollick's gaze flicked to me. "What?"

I braced my hands against the cool rock, looking down at the rough surface. "It's my fault—that they realized you'd had me staying there. I set things up so there'd be a fight, and because of that you had to shut the hotel down."

The demon had obviously figured that out a long time ago. I didn't catch any hint of surprise over the revelation. He simply shrugged. "I'll go back when I can, or I'll set up a new one. It won't be the first time. I'm surprised you have any regrets—or is it only because your plan didn't work out the way you'd hoped?"

I grimaced. "I know the hotel was important to you. For good reasons —or reasons I understand, anyway. I don't hate you. I just—it was the only way I could see to get out of the situation. You'd already shown that you'd use every tactic you could to control me in your own way. I didn't know what else you might be capable of."

"Well, I'm glad I've risen above the level of outright hatred," Rollick said with a laugh. "And I don't suppose I can really blame you for thinking the worst of me when by your standards I had behaved pretty badly. But I don't think I've done too terrible a job of looking after you since then, have I?"

"No," I admitted. "You haven't."

The past several days when it'd just been the two of us had gone a lot less horribly than I'd been prepared for. Rollick had been a pretty decent traveling companion, and I'd been able to count on him when I'd needed someone to have my back. I still didn't really know how much he was doing this for his own selfish interests, but I was at least sure he didn't want to gain glory or security at my expense.

So no, I didn't hate him. I might even have liked him a little, right now as a companionable silence settled over us. It didn't really matter since after the night was over, I'd probably never see him again either, but at least I'd cleared the air.

Whatever came next, it had to be better than what'd come before… didn't it?

CHAPTER FOURTEEN

Rollick

From what my former employees had reported, Quinn was more used to clambering around on rooftops than mountainsides. That didn't stop her from looking perfectly comfortable perched on the ledge with a hundred-foot drop below its lip, her feet braced against the stone surface just a few steps away from a fatal fall.

There was a stillness to her that I hadn't often seen in mortals. I hadn't gotten much chance to notice or appreciate it while she'd technically been my prisoner back in L.A.—she'd been too restless in captivity, like any being would be when caged. But even then I'd gradually realized she wasn't a typical human in many other ways.

She really was lovely, poised there in the dwindling light with wisps of her pale hair floating free from the hurried braid she'd pulled the strands into. Not just in a way that called to my cock, but that made me think it really was a shame no one had tried to capture her form with paint or pencil to commit it to posterity.

Which then made me think of the dreams of her own that she'd talked about more than once now. The monuments she'd wanted to build for the rest of humankind to revel in after she was gone.

I knew that wish wasn't any kind of self-aggrandizement on her part. Most human buildings didn't come etched with the name of their architect. She didn't even care about being remembered for herself, only about leaving some kind of impact—and a positive one—on the world. A meaningful trace of her existence that would give people something more than they'd had before.

How many mortals would worry about something like that when they only had a handful of years left? She could have been making as many happy memories as possible with family and friends, squeezing all the joy and pleasure she could out of the small amount of time her illness had left her with—like most humans focused on even with their full lifespan—but this was what gave her the most pleasure: making a difference. Contributing something.

It wasn't as if I didn't understand. Probably it niggled at me precisely because of how well I *did* understand, despite our situations being so very different.

"What do you think they're even after?" she said, stirring me out of my thoughts. Her gaze was fixed in the direction of the camp.

"Our sorcerer-killing duo?" I paused, but I'd given that question a lot of thought over the past few weeks, and even now being fairly sure of what kind of beings we were dealing with, I had to admit I didn't have much clue about their end goal. "They want to be able to manipulate other shadowkind, obviously. And from what I heard during my travels through Europe, the behemoth has some animosity toward humans."

"So, what, they want to convince other shadowkind to make more trouble for us or something?" Quinn frowned. "Would they really need to go to all this trouble just for that goal?"

"No, probably not. And it'd be a stupid plan anyway, for exactly the reason they're about to pay for their actions now. As soon as they started messing with mortals in any significant way, their days were numbered. They only got away with it for this long because it's been sorcerers and I can't think of any of us who quite *mind* seeing them lose their lives."

The Highest themselves hadn't exactly reverberated with rage when I'd mentioned the duo's most popular current pastime. Their vast, dark shapes had simply glowered at me from within the depths of the cavernous space in which they passed their own time. But when I'd pointed out how careless the fiends and their followers were being in their kills, leaving the bodies for mortal law enforcement to find, clearly savaged in unusual ways, they'd stirred with a little more consternation.

It'd taken a fair bit more talking, emphasizing that the two ancient miscreants were taking on the powers we all hated for themselves and using them against our own kind, before one of them had said in her fathomless voice, "This cannot continue." Then it'd only been a matter of arranging the logistics.

Quinn rubbed her mouth, still gazing pensively at the darkening landscape ahead of us. "Yeah, I guess that's understandable."

It wasn't just stillness, I realized, watching her. There was an air of sadness to her that I hadn't quite recognized in the past. A sense of loss. Over what she'd already sacrificed or what she expected she'd have to next?

Maybe a little of both.

Her phone buzzed softly in her messenger bag. Her body moved with automatic swiftness, her arm reaching to unzip one of the pockets and retrieve her pill case, her other hand grabbing her water bottle. She popped her evening pills into her mouth and swallowed them with a single gulp of water as if it were nothing.

I knew what a lie that was. If it'd been nothing, she wouldn't have worried so much about the alarms and taking them at the exact same time. They were the only thing ensuring she kept whatever little time she did still have.

How could I say I understood her dreams and fears when I really didn't have any idea what it was like to see the end of your life approaching like headlights speeding toward you on a freeway? My own potential death rarely even crossed my mind.

My stomach twisted with an unfamiliar sense of discomfort. Before I could dwell on it, Quinn looked over at me. "Why would they want to mess things up for humans anyway? No matter what the sorcerers think, that's clearly not a standard attitude among shadowkind. Torrent and Lance and Crag didn't see mortals that way. *You* don't."

"I don't," I agreed. "But I don't think it's any great mystery. There are humans who go on killing sprees, aren't there? Animals that have a particularly aggressive streak. It happens in all species, so why not in shadowkind too? Most of us just want to continue our lives and make what we can out of them, and there are some who specifically want to make suffering for others."

"And unfortunately when you get a psychotic higher shadowkind or two, they can do a heck of a lot more damage than a serial killer or a rabid bear," Quinn muttered.

"Well, that's why the Highest exert some kind of rulership over the rest of us. So those of us who want to just live our lives can continue doing so in peace."

"Or even building something to help each other, like you have."

There was a wistfulness in Quinn's voice that twisted me up even more. But before I could put my finger on exactly why I was unsettled, a flare of light on one of the slopes below us caught my eyes.

"There," I murmured, touching her arm and pointing. Another glowing spurt and another burst into being along the inner mountainside to our right, close to the ridge. Not all that near the lake. My lips tightened into a caustic smirk. "Our enemies must have been poking around on the outskirts of the camp seeing what was up rather than heading right in. The Highest's warriors decided it was time to step in."

Quinn leaned forward, squinting at the distant slope. Enough light now dotted the landscape there for us to make out a wide ring of figures, large and humanoid but with wings and horns and other appendages that made it clear they were much more than any mortal. Several other figures stood in the middle of the ring, but I could tell most were cringing lackeys. Only two stood tall, one even blockier-looking than Crag and the other towering but sinewy. That was all I could make out from a distance.

"What are they doing?" Quinn whispered. "They're barely moving."

"The warriors will interrogate them first." I lifted my chin toward them, relief starting to spread through my chest. It was almost over. "They'll want to be sure they've got the right delinquents and to give them a chance to come back to the shadow realm and face their judgment willingly. Somehow I don't think these two are going to take that option."

And I was looking forward to watching the Highest's warriors crush them.

I'd hardly finished speaking when a few of the warriors leapt forward. Someone over there was bellowing loud enough that a hint of the sound reached my ears even across that huge distance, though I couldn't pick apart any words. They charged at their captives, swords and claws slashing.

The beings I'd taken for lackeys fell left and right with plumes of essence. Two of the warriors slammed the bulky being I assumed was the behemoth into the ground. A few more sprang at the leviathan.

I almost looked away, thinking the fight was basically over. But just before I did, another distant yell rippled through the broad valley between the mountains.

One of the warriors who'd pinned down the behemoth turned and stabbed his sword into the neck of his colleague next to him.

My gut lurched. I was on my feet before I'd realized I was going to move.

No. They couldn't—with just some sorcerer organs in their gullets—I'd *specifically* told the Highest to send the most powerful underlings they had working for them. How many actual sorcerers could have commanded a shadowkind that potent?

But somehow this duo had managed it, maybe working in tandem. The one warrior crumpled with the fatal injury, and the one possessed by sorcery hurtled toward those pinning the leviathan. The behemoth heaved himself upward at the same moment and charged into the fray too.

"What—what's happening?" Quinn asked, a waver running through her words. "You were sure whoever the Highest sent would be able to deal with—"

"I know what I said," I cut in roughly. My heart was thudding faster than I could ever remember. If these fiends could manage to cut down a whole squad of the Highest's top soldiers...

They were managing it. Even as denial clanged through me, the two beings who'd once been at the warriors' mercy were carving up their opponents with the help of one—no, now *two* dupes who'd fallen under their sorcerous spell. Other shadowy bodies were racing in from the camp to help them as they turned the tide. Another of the warriors fell, and another—

Quinn dashed to the edge of the ledge and crouched down there, sliding her legs over the lip. A different sort of panic jolted through me. I leapt after her. "What in the realms are you doing now?"

Her face had totally blanched, her eyes wide in the dimness. "I have to—they're not going to make it on their own. The warriors. But maybe if I can get to them—I can try to use *my* sorcery on the others, force them to stop..."

She was absolutely insane. She was also already easing her way over the edge, about to slide down the nearly sheer slope to the slightly more even ground farther down.

I lunged forward and caught her arms before she could get that far. Quinn squirmed against me with a hiss of protest. "I have to—there isn't much time—"

"There isn't *any* time," I snarled at her, somehow furious and anguished all at once. "It'd take you at least half an hour just to clamber your way over there. They'll have fallen ages before then. All that'll happen is those beasts will carve you open too—or worse."

"This was our only real chance—they'll be distracted—let me *go*. I have to try. I know I can't cast any magic at them from this far away, but if I got a little closer, maybe..."

Every particle of my being rejected that thought. I could already see them bashing open her fragile body, shattering the skull that held all those hopes and dreams.

She had such big aspirations, and she was willing to throw them away on a one-in-a-million chance. While I stood here with my millennia behind me, already knowing there was no point.

This woman deserved more than that. She deserved so much more than she'd gotten, so much more than I'd offered her since she'd come into my grasp. But I could do this one thing for her.

The resolve swept through me so abruptly and fully that it blanked every other thought from my mind. I released my demon form as I hauled Quinn up from the ledge, ignoring her protests and the smack of her limbs. Setting my hand on her forehead, I willed a rush of demonic magic into her mind to knock her into unconsciousness.

She went slack in my arms. I bit back my horror at the feel of her gone so limp and eased her over my shoulder. Then, casting one last glance at the carnage the victory I'd tried to orchestrate had turned into, I spun on my heel and stalked off to descend the mountain.

CHAPTER FIFTEEN

Quinn

I woke up with the sense of a cry lodged in my throat. When I opened my mouth, a sound more like a squawk tumbled out of it. I shoved myself upright on the leather seat, my pulse racing, getting my bearings.

I was sitting in the passenger seat of Rollick's car, wearing the same clothes I'd had on for our trip up the mountain in Oregon. My messenger bag lay at my feet. The driver's seat appeared to be empty. The car was parked on a city street, the buildings around me draped in the darkness of night.

Knuckles rapped against the window next to me. As I flinched, Rollick opened the door from the outside. He was holding my backpack, slightly unzipped. I made out the corner of my laptop through the gap.

I stared up at him, blinking against the glow of the streetlamp beyond him. The warm air that wafted over me smelled strangely familiar.

"What's going on?" I demanded, and memories rushed back to me. "You took me away! I could have—I was going to try—"

"It wouldn't have done any good," Rollick said, calmly but firmly. He motioned for me to get out of the car. "Come on now."

I eased gingerly out of the car onto the sidewalk and peered around me. Even in the darkness, my surroundings looked kind of familiar too. It was a residential street lined with two-story houses.

Wait. That one on the corner with the arched windows—I *knew* that place. It was just down the street from…

From my parents' house.

My gaze jerked to Rollick's face. I kept my voice low, thinking of the sleeping people in all the houses around us that we wouldn't want to wake up and notice us. "We're back in Jacksonville. What the hell are we doing here?"

The demon let out a huff of breath. "It shouldn't take too much explaining. If you're going to insist on it now, let's get more out of view."

He ushered me into the playground where I'd spent so many hours of my early childhood. As we walked past the swing set, I glanced around at the equipment with a sudden burn of tears behind my eyes.

What sick game was he playing at now? I'd thought we were past emotional manipulations.

I spun toward Rollick. "What the fuck are we doing here? What's *wrong* with you? I—"

He caught me by the shoulders, his expression so strangely intense that the words died in my throat. A smack of anguish hit me, like the turmoil of emotions I'd felt from him as we watched his plan fall apart… earlier this night? Last night? When the villainous duo of ancient monsters had overcome the warriors sent by the rulers of the shadow realm.

A chill of my own rippled through my limbs in the wake of the demon's anguish. Had something even worse happened since then?

I opened my mouth, but before I could say anything else, Rollick broke the momentary silence.

"I'm trying to fix this," he said raggedly. "I'm trying to put this one thing back the way it should have been."

I blinked at him, totally bewildered. "What are you talking about?"

"You—" He sucked in a breath, an almost frantic light dancing in his eyes in the darkness. "You weren't supposed to be a part of this. These aren't your powers. It wasn't your heart. You wanted to do so much with the little bit of time you have, and this conflict has stolen it from you. You belong *here*. You should get the chance to do as much as you can with your life, however long you can extend it."

My brain couldn't quite compute what he was saying. "You... want me to go back to my regular life? My parents—my classes—but the behemoth and the leviathan are still out there, aren't they?"

"It doesn't matter," Rollick insisted. "You can let me deal with them. I've already had thousands of years more than you're going to get. I should be the one taking that burden. I should have from the start, but I was too caught up—" He cut himself off with a growl. "I was selfish. I'm ashamed of that, but I'm trying to make it right. Let me do that."

I was still having trouble wrapping my head around this switch of attitude. "Won't they come after me? Isn't that why I've been on the run from the beginning anyway?"

He tipped his head toward my torso. "You've got your special vest now. You'll want to keep that on for the time being. I'm going to look into other options... I might be able to have some shirts constructed for you that simply have silver thread woven through them to enough effect that they'd effectively shield you, so it isn't quite so awkward." His mouth set in a grim smile. "And whatever I do next, I'll make sure the bastards are too distracted to even think about you."

"What the heck *are* you going to do?" I demanded. "I thought you said those warriors were the toughest shadowkind out there."

"They probably weren't the smartest. I have resources I haven't called on yet—a lot of them. I'll figure something out."

"This doesn't make any sense. *You* pulled me into this situation."

Rollick closed his eyes with a pained expression that echoed the emotions radiating off him. "I know. I realize I'm changing my tune. And maybe you still can't trust that I mean what I say." He fell silent for long enough that my nerves started to twitch. His fingers squeezed my shoulders gently. Then he met my eyes again.

"I didn't get into this business for myself, you know. At first, I was a lot like Torrent used to be, though lighter on the chemical indulgences. I enjoyed all humanity had to offer, and I could exude enough charm and authority to get pretty much whatever I wanted. But I was still getting my footing, and a demon who'd been around the block a few more times than me with similar inclinations took me under his wing."

I raised my eyebrows. "So, the two of you ran around partying like kings?"

"Something like that," Rollick said. "But as we roved around, I got to know other beings who couldn't enjoy themselves the same way. They had something about them that wouldn't allow them to move among mortals quite as easily... which is the situation most shadowkind are in, really. And it occurred to me that I could build the sort of place where the indulgences would freely come to them rather than them seeking out the fun they wanted and failing. Which did work out to my benefit as well."

"And your friend's," I suggested.

"My lover's," Rollick corrected without missing a beat. "For as long as he was that. He thought my venture was a waste of time. He stuck around for a little while and then he took off, and I haven't seen him since then. Which probably means some dire fate came for him, or our paths would have crossed by now."

For just a moment, he looked pensive, but I guessed that relationship was far enough in the past not to bother him all that much, because he focused his attention on me again.

"He wasn't totally wrong. I was too soft. I welcomed the beings who came to take advantage of my services and supported them as much as I could, and in return plenty of them took advantage of *me*. Mortals I should have protected died under my roof. So I stopped coddling anyone. I cultivated the persona I wear easily now—unpredictable and detached so my fellow shadowkind never feel totally sure of me or how I'll react, harsh enough that they fear crossing the line and so that when I am kind it's mercy rather than weakness. That's who I need to be."

He spoke so emphatically that my stomach knotted. "Why are you telling me all this?"

"Because I need you to understand. I didn't start out like this. I know how to care. I know how to stick out my neck for those in need. I've just... gotten out of the habit. But I decided to harden myself, so I can decide to allow a little softness when the moment is right. This matters. That vicious duo making their plans that can't be good for anyone—taking them down matters. And *you* matter."

Rollick lifted one of his hands to touch my cheek, and my heart stuttered. "If you see through what you want to do, you'll have accomplished more in the few years that might be all you have left than I've achieved in centuries. I'm not going to take that chance away from you any more than I already have. You deserve this life more than anyone. Let me give it back to you. *Take it.*"

I stared at him, his words sinking in. A strange heat had flooded my body at the touch of his fingers. I wanted to laugh and cry at the same time. But as much as my thoughts were spinning, it didn't take long before one clear fact surfaced in my mind.

"I can't."

Rollick bared his teeth. "What do you mean, you can't? I brought you back here. I'm giving you your things back. You have everything you need."

I reached up and set my hand over his, swallowing thickly. I *could* take his offer, couldn't I? I could walk back into my parents' house, resolve their worries, slip back into the life I'd left behind as if I'd never been torn away from it. Throw myself into achieving the goals that it'd wrenched at me to set aside.

Closing my eyes, I pictured myself slipping down the stairs from my bedroom in the morning, surprising my parents at breakfast, feeling the squeeze of their relieved hugs. Opening up my computer and digging into the latest assignments. Taking a moment to relax in the backyard with the sweet scents from Dad's garden wafting over me.

I let the image of that life settle over me... and my answer remained the same. The pang of homesickness that resonated through my chest couldn't change what I knew to be true.

"No, I don't have everything I need," I said quietly. "I need to know that people are going to be okay—not just the people I know, but people all around the world. I need to do everything I can to make sure those monsters don't hurt any more of them. Maybe some action I take will make the difference between other lives being lost or not. Maybe the whole world will go to hell if every person who could pitch in doesn't."

"After what we saw last night, I doubt even your boosted sorcerer powers could work on those menaces," Rollick said.

"That's not the only way I've pitched in. I haven't been completely useless."

"Of course you haven't. But, Quinn... it's not your responsibility."

I made a face at him. "It's not yours either. And I..." The truth of what I was going to say swelled in my chest. "I care about *you* getting through this mess okay too, all right? I would feel like a jerk to walk away and leave you to handle it on your own. This is my world more than it's yours. I know that it matters to you, and it matters to me too, so I can't back down any more than you will."

It was Rollick's turn to stare at me. His jaw worked. He exhaled in a rush. "You're really not going to change your mind, are you?"

The corner of my mouth quirked upward. "I think you already know how stubborn I can be."

"Yes, I'm very familiar with that particular quality of yours."

His hand swiveled so his fingers could twine with mine, his knuckles still resting against my cheek. His head bowed toward me. My heart skipped a beat with the sudden thought that he might be going to kiss me—and the awareness that I wasn't sure I'd want to stop him.

But then he stepped away, tugging at me through our joined hands. "All right, stubborn sorcerer. I can't *force* you to live a normal life, no matter how much I might want to. So we'd better figure out where we go from here."

CHAPTER SIXTEEN

Quinn

I bit into the Thai chicken wrap, taking a moment just to appreciate the crunch of the crisp lettuce, the tangy sauce filling my mouth, and the fresh breeze that brought a refreshing coolness over us in the glade where we'd stopped to eat our takeout lunches.

An elm tree offered a swath of shade over the sole bench that seemed to be left over from when this spot might have been a more happening park of some sort. At the moment, it didn't look like much more than a weedy field a short drive off the main road.

I chewed through a few mouthfuls, took a gulp of my water, and glanced over at Rollick, who appeared to be very pleased with the Caesar salad wrap he'd opted for. He licked a fleck of dressing off his thumb, and my gaze focused a little too long on the sculpted perfection of his mouth.

Jerking my eyes away, I brought my thoughts back to more important matters. Like what the hell I was going to do now that I'd doubled down on my commitment to this quest. It was still kind of hard to believe the demon next to me had offered me a free ticket out of this mess. But I'd been able to feel how much he meant everything he'd said.

He'd always been a strange mix of callous and considerate with me. I'd assumed the considerate parts were solely to advance his own agenda. Had that changed during the time we'd spent together, or had I always been a little too hard on him?

I guessed the answer to that question wasn't really important now, only how we moved forward.

"You said you don't think I could be powerful enough to use my sorcery on the head honchos," I said. "But you didn't think they'd be able to manipulate the warriors that the Highest sent either. We should test out my magic. Because if I *can* control the villainous duo, then all we have to do is find them and our problems are solved."

Rollick gave an amused hum. "Forgive me for not believing the solution could be that simple. But I agree that we should evaluate your newly enhanced powers. You seemed to work the magic faster than I remember from before when we sent off that lackey the other day."

I nodded. "It felt easier... like I was more sure of what to do, even though it's still instinctive. I had the feeling I could do a lot more than just that."

My companion grinned with his shiny veneers on full display. "You already had the benefit of a powerful lineage, and then you got a particularly strong demon's essence on top of it. I'm assuming most sorcerer families make do with lesser beings. That should give you some kind of leg up."

A surge of conviction gripped me. "Then maybe I *will* be able to work my magic on those two. I could try with you—you're at least almost as powerful as one of them, right?"

"I'd like to think we'd be on a similar playing field," Rollick said. "But it'd hardly be a fair test. You know me a lot better than you know them—at this point, you know more about what matters to me than just about anyone. It seems like having a personal understanding gives your powers a lot more punch. You might be able to turn me into your puppet, but it wouldn't prove anything about going up against those menaces."

I narrowed my eyes at him. "Are you just trying to get out of becoming a test subject? You didn't have any problem offering up *other* beings for that purpose."

He spread his hands, putting on an innocent expression. "Feel free to make me your slave if you can manage it. I'd be curious to see what you decide to do with me for as long as you can hold on to the control. But it's obvious that a deeper understanding makes it easier for you to command someone. How else could you have managed to keep my three mutinists away for so long otherwise? You hadn't gotten a power boost back then, and they were no slouches as far as shadowkind go."

He was right, but the reminder of how I'd sent the three men away—and the fact that they hadn't come back yet—put a damper on my enthusiasm. My throat constricted.

I forced down the last of my wrap, staring off across the field toward the sedan. "Maybe it has worn off. Maybe they just haven't wanted to come back in case I'd manipulate them again."

Rollick snorted. "I think it's more likely that they decided to start a rock-n-roll band and are currently touring New Zealand than what you just said. The only thing I can imagine that *could* keep those three from sticking close to you is magical compulsion."

He sounded so confident that I wanted to believe he was right, but the ache of loss didn't subside. I clenched my jaw. "I knew what I was doing. I knew it was kind of an awful thing to do to them. The most important thing is that they're safe."

"Quinn." Rollick let out a huff and turned toward me. He tucked his hand beneath my jaw, resting his fingers lightly on the underside of my chin to draw my gaze to his. "I saw how they were with you. I know you well enough by now to comprehend how you earned their devotion. There isn't anything in either realm that I can imagine keeping them away from you other than you yourself."

"You can't know for sure," I had to say.

"Well, if it isn't the case, then at least you have me for company, even if I'm not a very good substitute."

My eyebrows rose of their own accord. "Humbleness—not something I thought I'd ever see from you."

A sly smile curved Rollick's lips. "I have all sorts of dimensions you've yet to uncover."

A quiver that wasn't entirely unpleasant raced over my skin from where he was still touching my chin. The memory of the moment when I'd thought he might kiss me this morning flitted through my head, and my cheeks flushed with a mix of desire and shame.

I didn't want to be thinking like that. Why couldn't my brain get the memo?

I was tensing to pull back and wishing it didn't require as much effort as I was finding it did when three forms burst from the shadows amid the trees.

I startled and jerked around. Next to me, Rollick stiffened, but only until he'd recognized the figures facing us.

There was no more than an instant when Torrent, Lance, and Crag stood there a few feet from us, perfectly familiar other than the hint of uncertainty crossing all their expressions. I gaped at them, losing my breath. My lips parted, my heart leaping and stuttering at the same time, and then Lance was launching himself at me.

Angling his claws carefully away from my body as he always did, he caught me in his arms with no sign of concern about my vest, lifted me up, and spun me around with his face buried in my hair.

"We're back. The magic's gone. And you're okay." He paused and twisted around to press his hand over my mouth, gently but insistently. "No more magic-y words. You don't tell us what to do like that again. All right, baby girl?"

He stared me down, his violet eyes flaring beneath the tumble of his wild black curls. Tears welled up behind my own eyes.

He was here. They were all here, and it felt as if I could finally properly breathe again for the first time since they'd left. But at the same time, the terror that had gripped me before at the danger they'd already put themselves through and almost definitely would again wound around me. I couldn't move.

Lance nuzzled my temple and then resumed his hold on my gaze, his hand still fixed over my mouth to prevent any speech. "You have to say it. I'm not letting you go until you say you won't do that ever again. Promise us."

Even after everything, he trusted me to tell the truth—trusted that I wouldn't lie just to get free and then use my sorcery after all. As that fact sank in, my resistance melted. How could I deny that kind of devotion? How could I tell him that my worries for him mattered more than his dedication to me?

The tears behind my eyes overflowed. I grabbed him in a hug just as tight as the one he'd initially wrapped me up in and nodded emphatically.

Lance withdrew his hand, but only far enough to swipe at my tears as he drew back to look at me. His forehead furrowed. "Are you sad?"

"Not that you're back," I choked out. "That I made you leave at all. I didn't *want* to, I just—I didn't want to see you get hurt more than you already had been, because of me. It's my fault you're mixed up in this situation, and—"

Lance's growl cut me off. "Not your fault," he insisted. "None of the hurt had anything to do with you. You didn't ask for the beasties and whoever else to attack you. You didn't make them use their tricksy magic. *You* make me nothing but happy. Except when you forced me to go away. That's the only thing you ever did that hurt me."

I blinked hard, but the tears kept coming. "I'm sorry. I didn't know what else to do."

"You keep us with you, and you let us protect you from the vicious beings out there, and everything will be good."

I didn't think it was quite that simple, but then Lance pulled me into a kiss with all the eager passion he exuded so easily, and I couldn't bring myself to argue.

He was back. All three of the men I loved were back. Maybe the other two wouldn't forgive me quite as quickly, but they'd come, which had to mean they didn't hate me.

Lance drew out the kiss with a pleased thrum in the base of his throat and then eased back to stroke his knuckles down the side of my face. He cocked his head. "What were you talking about with Rollick when we got here? He was touching your face too."

Even though I'd been about to *stop* Rollick from touching me in that moment, guilt hitched in my chest. But the demon spoke up swiftly and smoothly before I had to figure out what to say.

"We were actually discussing the three of you—whether you would come back once our reluctant sorcerer's magic wore off. She wasn't sure. And she was quite despondent about it."

Lance beamed down at me, apparently more than satisfied with that answer, and I soaked up his brightness. Then I glanced past him to the two men who'd arrived with him.

Crag strode over, his stony jaw looking starker than ever against his bronze skin. He hesitated just before he reached me, and my gut clenched, but then he propelled himself the last short distance to tug me from the dragon shifter's arms. He enfolded me in his brawny embrace, holding me closer than he'd dared in the last day when we'd been together, and I let myself sink into his broad chest.

"*I'm* sorry, Softness," he muttered in his usual gruff tone. "I pushed you away first. I didn't mean to make you feel—I was so worried—but it was the same as you told me. It was the fault of those villains, not either of us. I won't let them tear us apart again."

My eyes started to burn again. "Good. You never need to protect me from *you*."

"As long as you remember that the sentiment goes both ways, Ms. Fix It," Torrent said, his tone as dry and even as ever.

I turned in Crag's arms, not forcing him to relinquish me when he seemed determined to keep hugging me, and met the tentacled man's sea-green gaze. He didn't rush in to embrace me, but then, my relationship with Torrent had always been a little more complicated. I couldn't tell whether he was being careful of my potentially awkward feelings or his own.

"How long did the spell last?" I asked. "How did you find me?"

"It only just wore off," Lance announced triumphantly. "We came straight to you the moment we could."

Torrent inclined his head. "We'd determined the general area you had to be in by keeping track of where your magic repelled us as that boundary shifted with your movements. And we spread out to get a sense of the larger reach of that magic, knowing you'd be in the middle of its circle. So we knew which direction to head in as soon as its effects dissipated. And once we were close to Rollick, Crag could pick up on his presence."

"Speaking of picking up on my presence..." Rollick brushed his hands together and motioned toward the car. "I think we've lingered in this spot for long enough, especially since our enemies now have even more reason to want to hunt me down than they did before. But I have a property not too far from here where we can regroup. As long as you weren't planning on ousting me from the group next. In the past, I think we've accomplished a lot more working together than going our separate ways."

A twinge shot through me at the thought of sending the demon off now, but Torrent gave him a small but amicable smile. "I think we can manage to cooperate for a little longer in the interests of keeping Quinn safe."

CHAPTER SEVENTEEN

Torrent

I peered through the tall window on the Mediterranean-style house into its inner courtyard, where Quinn had stretched out on a lounge chair by the pool. Her toned but slim torso was unencumbered by the layer of metal beads that had weighed it down for so much of the past month. It lifted a weight in my own chest seeing how relaxed she looked without that burden, but a twang of anxiety reverberated through my nerves at the same time.

"Are you sure the protections around this place are enough to ensure her powers aren't noticed?" I asked Rollick, who was sprawled on the modern sofa perpendicular to the window. "In that cabin in the swamp—"

"I'm well aware of what happened in the swamp," Rollick interrupted, "seeing as that incident was the start of my plans derailing. I hired some mortals to add to the silver and iron deposits around a few of my properties as soon as Quinn came to the hotel. I wasn't so naïve as to think I could count on remaining there as long as I'd have liked to."

I had felt the unnerving prickle of the metals' effects as we'd cruised up the winding drive to this sprawling estate in the Texas badlands. And we were far enough away from anyplace we'd clashed with our main opponents that it was unlikely they were searching for us too thoroughly anywhere nearby. But hearing Rollick confirm the property's security measures soothed the worst of my worries.

He'd been confident about his hotel, and no shadowkind had detected Quinn's presence there... until we'd purposefully tipped our enemies off to her location. Rollick wasn't the type to cut corners when it came to things he cared about.

And from the atmosphere I'd sensed between him and our mortal since our return, I was starting to suspect his caring had expanded in dimension. It didn't seem anything overt had actually *happened* between them, but it was clear he no longer viewed her as simply a tool.

I didn't know whether to see that change as more comforting or unsettling.

"Sit down," he added, tipping his head toward the chair across from him. "Rest those legs—there's no shame in it. She isn't going to vanish the second you take your eyes off her."

I grimaced at him, but I sat as he'd requested. We did have business to discuss. "You said there's something specific you think I can help with. What exactly is that?"

Rollick exhaled in a slow sigh that told me he wasn't happy about what he was about to say. "I believe one of the fiends we're dealing with is a—or *the*—leviathan."

Whatever I might have anticipated him saying, I hadn't expected that revelation. I stared at him for a beat in case this was some bizarre prelude to a joke, but he showed no sign of taking back the statement.

"What the fuck would a leviathan want with a bunch of human sorcery?" I asked. "Wouldn't he have better things to do?"

"Wouldn't it be nice if that were the case?" the demon muttered. "Who knows what goes through the mind of a being that ancient? Maybe he's simply gotten bored. It's not as if anyone's heard much about him or any being like him in ages, so he can't have been occupying himself all that thrillingly. But that's where you come in."

"With the thrills?"

Rollick chuckled. "Preferably not so much thrills, more with the hearing about him. The ocean is your domain. I want you to cruise around through the seven seas calling on whatever other watery shadowkind you come across and see whether anyone knows anything about what might have motivated our serpentine foe."

The request did make a certain amount of sense. All the same, I couldn't stop myself from saying, "So I just got back, and you're sending me off again on a mission of unknown length."

"You're allowed to say no," Rollick replied languidly, although the slight tensing of his fingers as he picked up his glass of expensive gin showed he wasn't quite so relaxed about it. "I think it's become very obvious that I no longer have much of any control over what you do or where you go. But it will be for her benefit." He glanced toward the window.

The sunlight was gleaming off Quinn's pale hair, but that wasn't what caught my attention most. It was the strange, almost wistful expression that crossed the demon's face. I found myself bold enough to say, "And *you* seem nearly as concerned about that now as about everything else that's at stake."

Rollick's penetrating gaze flicked to me. He smiled again, looking only amused rather than offended. "I don't think I need to tell you that she's a rather impressive example of her kind."

He hadn't even tried to deny his interest. I bit back the urge to shout out that she was mine, that he could make no claim on her—because what would the point be? If he'd been going to, he'd had every chance while the rest of us were gone. Maybe he *had*, and she'd rejected him. Although she hadn't exactly looked uncomfortable in that moment as we'd emerged from the shadows when he'd been sitting so close to her.

They'd spent a lot of time together just the two of them in the past several days. That was a recipe for either killing each other or developing some sort of closer rapport. And they definitely hadn't killed each other.

I willed my teeth not to grit and kept my voice even. "She is. You were the one who wanted her to tap into her sorcery to begin with. Now I can't help wondering if you encouraged her using it on us."

Rollick's smile tightened just slightly. "If I nudged her in that direction, it was only bolstering feelings she already had. I wasn't the one who put the idea in her head—she came up with it all on her own. And if it makes you feel any better, afterward I realized the emotional toll on her wasn't really worth the benefit of not having to argue with the three of you over our plans."

I folded my arms over my chest. "So you're not worried that we'll run off with her again?"

"You know what?" Rollick said with a wave of his hand. "Feel free to, if you can convince her. I tried to drop her off at her family's home, to hand her old life back to her, and she wouldn't take it." His attention slid back to the woman by the pool. "Much too stubborn for her own good. This shouldn't have been her battle to begin with."

The admission struck me momentarily speechless. He'd have let Quinn go? He'd already attempted to? After all the lengths he'd gone to in order to get his hands on her…

The prickles of apprehension and jealousy faded, and for a second I felt almost ashamed. It made sense that I'd been wary of his intentions. They hadn't always worked in her favor. But I'd misjudged just how much of an effect she'd had on him while we'd been gone.

"I think we'll just be lucky if she doesn't feel the need to send us away again so she can take on the entire battle herself," I said, more honestly than I wished I was being, and stood up. "I'll go scout out word about the leviathan. But we've only just gotten back. I need to talk with her first."

Rollick got to his feet too with a brisk gesture toward the courtyard. "Talk to her, do whatever you like with her. I've got my own business to attend to. It seems I need to raise an army." He made a face. "Just remember that the faster we get these menaces dealt with, the safer she'll be."

If we could deal with them, I thought but didn't say. I'd heard his account of what had happened with the Highest's warriors, and I wasn't sure I liked our odds.

But that didn't mean I was going to give up. I'd only just found real joy in this world; I wasn't going to let any monsters, no matter how ancient, steal it from me again.

And I'd better make sure the source of my joy knew it too.

As Rollick ambled off to see to his army-building, I opened the door to the courtyard and stepped out into the desert warmth. It would have been easier to simply leap through the shadows, but I forced myself to walk over with the support of my tentacles, ignoring the twinges of pain in my lower legs.

Quinn straightened up at my approach, setting aside the small, leatherbound book she'd started paging through. Concern flashed across her pretty face. I sank onto the chair next to her before she felt the need to express her worries about my physical limitations out loud and tipped my head toward the book on the side table. "Getting some reading in?"

She looked at it and wrinkled her nose. "I got that from the sorcerer enclave. It's a record of different strategies for warding off supernatural powers. I thought it might have something useful for keeping our enemies from sensing me, but so far nothing sounds as effective as my vest has been." She frowned. "I wish it had some method that would work to protect all of you from sorcery, but the approaches all seem to involve things that would be uncomfortable for shadowkind in general."

"A quick fix would be a bit much to ask for, I guess," I said. "But we'll get it figured out one way or another."

She glanced toward the room I'd come out of. "Is it time to get going again? Have you all been making plans without me?"

I offered a wry grin. "Not plans for you. I'm going to go information-seeking. Since I'm the most comfortable of us in the water, Rollick thinks —and I agree—that I'm the best one to learn more about the leviathan's intentions."

"You're leaving?" She couldn't quite smooth the disappointment from her voice, which made me feel both gratified and guilty. "For how long?"

"I'm not sure yet. But I didn't want to go without talking to you first. We haven't had much of a chance." After Lance and Crag had glommed all over her this morning, I hadn't known what to say. I didn't know how to crack open the walls around the churning emotions inside me without too much spilling out.

But maybe there wasn't such a thing as too much. This woman had told me she loved me. She'd sacrificed her own happiness and security to try to protect me. If I hadn't already known I didn't need to hide myself from her, that should have convinced me.

Even now, she was hanging her head. "If you're angry, I'd understand. It was a shitty thing to do, even if I was trying to look out for you. I—"

"Quinn," I broke in, scooting to the edge of the chair so I could lift my good hand to her cheek. "I'm not angry. I wish that you hadn't felt the need to do it, but I know it came from a place of caring. I just don't want you to ever feel like you should have gone farther or that you've made a mistake by letting us come back."

Her gaze slid to my other hand, the ruined one resting on my knee. It didn't ache as much as it used to. I could close the thumb and the remaining fingers in a sort of pincer grip, which seemed somehow appropriate. A little crab appendage to add to my overall sea-creature theme.

Quinn obviously couldn't see any humor in it. Her voice came out rough. "You've lost the most out of anyone. I hate that."

"I can't say it's my most favorite thing in the world either, but—" I tugged her face up so she'd meet my eyes. "I don't mind. You have to understand that. It's a tiny trade-off compared to everything I'm getting in return."

"How can you say that? You're about to go off nosing around after some uber-powerful, murderous monster, and—"

"I don't care." I cupped her jaw, willing her to understand how much I meant this. "The whole time, I'll be thinking about how I can come back to you. About what I've already had with you. And that makes it more than worth it. You told me that you love me, and I don't know what it would even mean for me to say it in return. But Quinn, you have no idea how empty my life was before. I used to fill it with drugs and parties, and then I filled it with carrying out jobs for Rollick, but none of that stopped me from feeling alone."

"You had Lance and Crag," she said, her voice dipping low.

"In a way. They were more colleagues than friends. I had to keep up an air of authority. I wasn't sure, if I let that waver, if they'd still respect me given my other weaknesses."

Quinn's eyes flashed. "There's nothing *weak* about you."

I smiled at her. "And you're the only person who could say that who I'd believe. Because you've seen every part of me, you recognize my difficulties, you've heard about who I've been, and you don't shy away from any of it."

"There's nothing to shy away from," she said with the stubbornness Rollick had commented on. He had been right about that.

"Not when I'm with you," I said. "You see me, and you embrace all of it—and when I'm with you, I know I can be the man you see. I still have a place in this world. I'm more than just an outcast. And I have more of a purpose than I ever did before. You gave me all of that. So losing part of a hand *really* isn't that big a deal. You're worth it. And I am too."

For a second, she looked as if she might cry. Then she leaned forward to wrap her arms around me and bury her face in my shoulder. I slung one of my tentacles around my waist to tug her closer, and she let out a ragged sigh.

"You are," she said. "You were before you met me too."

"Maybe so. But it didn't feel like there was anywhere near as much of a point before I met you."

She pulled back to look into my eyes again. "There is one part of you I haven't seen. You've never shown me your full shadowkind form. I'd like... I'd like to totally know you. If you don't mind."

Even with all the faith I had in her, doubt jabbed through my chest for an instant before I nodded. It seemed only fair. And maybe I wanted her to have that piece of me too before I had to leave again.

The pool gave off a faint oceanic tang, laced with salt rather than chlorine, which I was grateful for. It'd feel better on my skin. I stepped to the edge and dipped my feet in, not bothering to remove my clothes. They'd vanish as I transformed anyway.

With Quinn watching from her chair, I sank into the water. As it flowed over my head, I released the human guise I'd always worn with her even when I brought all of my tentacles out.

My body expanded, torso and head ballooning, tentacles widening and stretching. In a matter of seconds, I filled most of the pool. The cool water rushed over my pliant flesh with a welcoming sensation, but I turned my eyes toward the surface of the water with tension wound through my innards.

What if this had been a mistake—one step too far?

CHAPTER EIGHTEEN

Quinn

As Torrent's pale skin and auburn hair vanished amid a vast maroon body that expanded through the water, my breath caught in my throat. I got up, walking to the edge of the pool so I could see all of him properly.

I'd had a general sense of what he must look like in his most natural form from having seen his tentacles, but it hadn't really prepared me for the reality. The tentacles themselves had expanded to twice the length and width I was used to, and the body they attached to now was no more human than Lance's reptilian dragon form. Even *less* human, with twice as many limbs and no clear facial features other than the large eyes set low on either side of Torrent's immense, rounded head.

He was, in essence, a giant octopus. Large enough that he had to curve his tentacles to allow them to fit in the rectangular space, his head alone longer than I was tall. To accommodate him, the salty pool water sloshed over the lip of the walls onto the slate tiles.

Most people probably would have been terrified. But I'd spent most of my life pushing myself to my limits, turning the things that scared me into an adventure. As alien as Torrent's appearance was, there was also something sublime about it, like a vast mystery waiting to be unraveled. A secret I'd never quite get to the bottom of.

I'd taken my shoes off in the summer heat, and the water streaked over my feet, cooling my skin. After everything he'd said to me, an impulse gripped me to show him that I accepted him this way too, that our connection meant just as much to me as it did to him.

Normally I avoided pools like all stagnant water, but Rollick had specifically mentioned that he'd had this one replenished with clean water for our arrival, by whatever means the demon had at his disposal. Without hesitation, I pulled off my tee and shorts and darted around the corner of the pool to the steps in just my panties and bra. Unlike Torrent, I couldn't dry off my entire outfit with a quick trip into the shadows.

I waded down into the water until my feet reached the floor and the salt-laced liquid reached my chin. My hair floated out around my face like flaxen seaweed. I'd placed myself carefully in an open space between two of Torrent's tentacles. Now I reached out and rested my hand on one.

It might have been larger, but the soft yet firm skin felt the same as it always had. Torrent eased closer, the end of that tentacle wrapping loosely around my waist. As he moved into the shallower end of the pool, the top of his head protruded from the water. I stepped forward to meet him, my heart skipping a beat as I touched the spot at the base of his head between those two fathomless eyes.

He was even more awe-inspiring up close. "You're amazing," I told him, stroking the velvety slope of flesh. I had no idea how well he could hear me in his current state, but I had to say it anyway. "Totally amazing."

Another tentacle coiled around my calf, its tip trailing in a teasing line up my inner leg toward my thigh. I'd barely had time to consider whether the heat that abruptly flooded me was reasonable or deeply weird when Torrent surged toward me.

He shifted as he came, with a warble of the water. The next thing I knew his human body was pinning me to the side of the pool, his human head bowing over mine as droplets streamed from his drenched hair. Four of his tentacles held me in place with the kiss of their suckers. He clutched the side of my neck and slammed his mouth into mine.

The salt of the water lingered on his lips, and his human skin was slick when I wrapped my arms around his shoulders. I kissed him back hard, all of me aching for the ultimate closeness that I'd gone without for days.

His warped hand came to rest on my side. The other and the ends of his tentacles caressed my curves as he devoured my mouth. The hooks of my bra released, and the water washed over my breasts. Suckers plucked at one nipple while his palms and then his thumb swiveled over the other, sending jolts of pleasure through my chest.

My hips rose instinctively, my thighs splaying around his hips. He'd reappeared without bothering with clothes, and the head of his rigid erection slid against my sex through my panties so perfectly that I gasped into his mouth.

He pulled back just far enough to mutter words, his lips grazing mine with each movement. "I will always come back. There's no pain that could be greater than this joy. You are... everything."

His voice rasped, and then he was claiming my mouth again at the same moment as he wrenched at my panties. The fabric split, and his cock plunged into me.

He swallowed my pleased cry and rammed even deeper. I arched into him and groped at his shoulders, desperate to feel all of him, to solidify our connection in the most fundamental possible way.

It felt like it'd been forever since we'd come together like this. My body melted into his, bliss surging with every thrust, impossibly fast. I rocked with him, clung to him, gasped my eagerness into his ear.

The flood of pleasure stole my breath. A tentacle slid between us to pluck at my clit, and sparks of pure delight seared through my pussy. It only took a few moments of that monstrous, marvelous touch before I was shivering and shuddering my release against him.

Torrent groaned and bucked faster. I felt his own climax in the tremor that rippled through his muscles, pressed so tightly against mine.

As he caught my mouth again, our bodies sagging together against the side of the pool, a shadow fell over us.

"Hmm," Lance said in a teasing tone. "Getting up to so much fun already, and not inviting the rest of us. That's not very... what's the word humans use?"

"Sportsmanlike?" Crag suggested in a rumble from a little farther away.

I tipped my head back to peer up at them. Lance had crouched down at the edge of the pool over us—he reached to brush the tips of his claws over my hair. Crag loomed just a couple of steps behind him, his stance relaxed but his eyes smoldering.

I was still trembling with the force of my collision with Torrent, but more giddiness rushed through me at the desire in my other men's expressions. I lifted a hand toward Lance. "There's no reason you can't join in now."

He grinned wide and might have leapt into the water right then if Torrent hadn't cleared his throat. "Maybe we should take this to a more private venue. I actually found a little something in the guest bedroom that I'd like to try out with our woman if she's up for it... I just got a little caught up in the moment." He pressed a kiss to my temple as if in apology.

I laughed. "Feel free to get caught up whenever you're in the mood. But now I'm curious. What are we trying out?"

His pale eyes glinted with promise. "You'll see." He scooped me up in his arms with an extra boost from one tentacle and lifted me into the edge of the pool. "Can I count on the two of you to get her to the bedroom?"

Lance nuzzled my damp shoulder. "As fast as we can."

"I'll take care of that." Crag bent down to gather me in his arms the way I was used to.

I tucked my head against his brawny chest, weirdly turned on and yet also comforted by his embrace. "I'm getting your shirt all wet."

"It'll be gone soon!" Lance announced gleefully, and bounced ahead of us into the house.

Crag squeezed me a little tighter as he carried me after the dragon shifter. "You're as lovely like this as you are every other way, Softness." He paused, and a smile touched his usually somber lips. "And he isn't wrong."

Torrent vanished, trailing alongside us through the shadows where he could move more easily. Crag strode down the hall with its cream-colored walls and pale birch flooring and into the airy bedroom Rollick had assigned to me "in case you're in the mood to sleep before we leave again." I didn't suppose he'd be all that surprised by us making other uses of the king-sized bed.

Crag lowered me onto the fluffy duvet and climbed up next to me, lowering his head to seek out my mouth. As I kissed him, reveling in the tenderness he could offer even with his rocky jaw, Lance leapt up at my other side. The dragon shifter lapped his ridged tongue up the side of my neck and flicked the tips of his claws over my breast to send a rush of giddy quivers over my skin.

A bittersweet ache spread through my chest like melting wax. This was where I was meant to be. This was who I was meant to be with. I'd denied myself and these men what felt right to all of us for too long. But this interlude, right now, was even more of a homecoming than the moment when they'd appeared before me this morning.

Another presence knelt by my legs, and I knew Torrent had rejoined us. He trailed his fingers along my leg and let one of his tentacles nibble my toes with its suckers.

"Mine," Lance murmured with typical possessiveness. He eased down my body, swiping his claws back and forth with just enough pressure to leave me tingling, slicking his tongue along the same path. He teased them right over my clit and jerked them back when I couldn't stop my hips from bucking up to meet him.

"Needy girl." He nudged my knee to the side and bent his head between my legs as I gasped against Crag's mouth. "I'll take care of you good."

At the first swipe of his tongue over my pussy, I moaned. Crag swallowed the sound and lowered one of his massive hands to massage my breast. His calloused fingers worked over my nipple with a friction totally different from but just as thrilling as Lance's claws.

Torrent eased around to attend to my other breast with a tentacle. Watching over me, he reached to tug open the drawer on the bedside table. I was too occupied with my other lovers to see what he retrieved.

Lance plunged his tongue right inside me and then started pumping into me with his knuckles while he sucked on my clit. At my growl of need, he chuckled with a wash of hot breath over my sex. "I'll give you what you're craving, baby girl. I need it too."

He moved up my body in one smooth motion, his clothes disappearing somewhere along the way. As he nipped the edge of my jaw, he speared me with his cock, sliding all the way to the hilt in one go.

I arched to meet him, and he clutched my hip with the slightest prick of his claws. I pulled away from Crag to catch the dragon shifter's mouth.

As Lance's tongue delved between my lips, Crag crouched down to suckle the breast he'd been fondling. My men seemed determined to leave no part of me unattended.

My body thrummed with pleasure, every nerve alight. We'd only come together all three of us once before, and I'd forgotten just how exhilarating an experience it was. Lance's cock swelled inside me into its bulbous dragon form, stretching me and rubbing against the perfect spot inside with every stroke, and I started to tremble with delight. I bucked with his thrusts, matching his rhythm as well as I could, tipping my head to kiss Torrent and then meet Crag's mouth again.

Lance kept up his ferocious pace and trailed his claws down my side at the same time. The quiver of bliss they woke up twined with the pleasure swelling from my core. My head jerked back against the pillow, and I clenched around him as I came. Sparks danced behind my eyes.

The dragon shifter let out a strangled sound as he careened after me. He bowed over my body, panting and grinning with satisfaction. I ran my fingers down the side of his face, but I still had one more lover I hadn't fully reunited with yet.

As Lance withdrew, I pushed myself upright and turned toward Crag. He drew back far enough to take in my expression.

I nudged him into a sitting position. "Clothes off. Now."

He smiled with a hint of a flush beneath the bronze of his cheeks. "How do you want me, Softness? The man or the gargoyle?"

I let out an impatient sound. "I love both of them. Which feels better to you?"

He paused and then admitted, "I like it better when I know I'm not at all pretending."

"Then give me the gargoyle."

He blinked into the shadows and back again, a foot taller and nearly as much broader on his return. His wings arched from his back. The bed's frame creaked but held under the weight of his flexible stone body.

I clambered onto his lap and stroked my hands over the solid planes that felt rock-hard yet as warm as regular flesh. When I reached past his shoulders to trail my fingers along the tops of his wings, he made a sound somewhere between a growl and a purr of encouragement.

One part of him was *particularly* hard, stiffly erect in anticipation. I slid my cunt along it, licking my lips and closing my eyes as the friction brought a fresh surge of giddiness.

Torrent and Lance had warmed me up, but Crag's gargoyle cock was by far the biggest I'd ever taken. We'd managed it before, though.

He slipped one hand between us to prepare me, sliding between my folds carefully and then with more confidence. With each sweep of his fingers, he stretched me wider. A little moan escaped me. I swayed with the movements of his hand, kissing his rough-edged jaw, his cheek, his mouth again until he was groaning too.

"Now," I mumbled when I couldn't stand the wait any longer. "I need you now."

A rumble reverberated from deep in the gargoyle's chest. He withdrew his hand, and I positioned myself over him. I eased down a couple of inches, and then a couple more, a sigh escaping both of us in unison. I was so perfectly, incredibly full.

Another hand glided down my back to my ass. Torrent leaned in to kiss my shoulder. "This is the perfect position for my experiment." He glanced at Crag. "If you don't mind me collaborating."

Crag gave me a look that was both fond and hot enough to turn my blood scorching. "If it makes our woman even happier, I'm all for it."

I sank a little deeper, taking even more of Crag into me, and paused to absorb the heady sensation. Then I peeked at Torrent from the corner of my eyes. "What's this secret?"

His smile was sly. "Not really a secret. We've discussed it before. And Rollick seems to keep his guestrooms well-stocked." He held up a bottle of lube. His caressing hand dipped between my cheeks to my back entrance, and a jolt of unexpected pleasure raced through my body. "We could find out how you enjoy being taken from two directions at the same time. We'll go slowly with it—I'll use a tentacle so I have even more control."

The thought of one of those lithe appendages stimulating me there turned my breath ragged in an instant. "Okay. Yes. Please."

Lance chuckled. "So eager, baby girl. I want to watch this. And hear every sound you make."

I did make a lot of sounds as I slid up and down on Crag's cock while he palmed one breast and then the other and Torrent slicked gel-drenched fingers over my other entrance. When the tentacled man hooked one finger inside me, I whimpered. It turned out I *could* feel even more full, and that feeling was glorious.

He worked another finger inside me, careful but firm, pulsing in and out. "How are you liking that, Quinn?"

"Good," I mumbled before another moan escaped me. "So good."

His fingers vanished, but only for a second before one of his tentacles replaced them, nudging at my now pliant entrance. It slid into me and began to thrust in and out in an echo of my rhythm over Crag's cock.

I cried out at the rush of pleasure radiating all through my torso. Crag caught my cheek and yanked my mouth to his. We kissed wildly, and I bucked faster, and both men picked up their pace to match me. It was a whirlwind of blissful pressure and friction and then—

I came apart with a cry that must have rung through the whole house. My body sagged between the two men, quaking with the aftershock of my final orgasm. Crag roared at the same moment, spilling himself inside me as he caught me against his chest. He hugged me to him as if he never meant to release me from his hold.

Torrent propped himself against the headboard next to us, outright smirking now. "It seems like that was a successful experiment."

I laughed breathlessly. "Yes. Very."

Lance sprawled out at my other side, totally comfortable leaning against the gargoyle's bulk as he stroked my arm. "So lovely. So sweet. Our special mortal."

"So lucky, to have the three of you," I said with a wave of emotion.

Torrent leaned forward to tuck a few stray strands of my hair behind my ear. He studied my face with a sudden intensity. "Have you had any interest in getting even luckier?"

His voice came out soft with its usual evenness, but something about the words made my pulse jump. I raised my head to peer at him. "What do you mean?"

"I mean," he said, and hesitated as if grappling with the words, "I've gotten the impression you and Rollick have made your peace with each other over the past little while. Maybe even become somewhat fond of each other?"

Guilt tugged at my gut. "We haven't done anything," I said quickly. "I didn't *want* to do anything."

Torrent's gaze was knowing. "Because you thought you'd be betraying us, or because you honestly weren't interested?"

There was no judgment in his tone. Still, my shoulders slumped. I didn't want to lie to him—to all of them.

"He has a certain appeal. He always did. And now I trust him... more than I did before, anyway. I understand why he did what he did. But I have the three of you. I don't need anyone else. You're more than enough."

Lance hummed to himself, his violet eyes sparkling in his golden face. "But is there such a thing as being *too* happy? I think the more we can give our woman, the better."

I blinked at him. "*You'd* be okay with him being a part of this relationship? He used you too—all three of you."

Lance shrugged. "He did what he thought was the best thing without worrying too much about anyone else. That's what shadowkind do. None of us got hurt. And he did protect you. He's trying to protect you every way he can. That means he's all right now."

Crag nodded slowly, watching me with a thoughtful expression. "If you wanted him, Softness, I wouldn't resent you or him for it. He's tackling this problem alongside us, as one of us. I can't say we're somehow more deserving."

"It's not about *deserving*," I protested.

Torrent slung a gentle tentacle around my shoulders. "When it comes to whether we can accept it or not, it is. But I only brought it up because, after talking to him, I realized *you* might deserve what he can offer too. I think whatever he would bring to the table, it'd be honestly, not a game. But all that matters is whether you really do want it. I don't think any of us would object to getting to keep you all to ourselves either."

"I don't know," I said, my emotions whirling.

"Lots of time to decide," Lance said. "I don't think the tricksy boss is going anywhere."

Torrent nodded. "No. I didn't mean to put you on the spot. I just thought we should be clear that the option is there, if you wanted to go down that path. I wouldn't like to see you tearing yourself up because you wanted something you thought would upset us."

All at once, I choked up. Still braced over Crag, I pulled the tentacled man into a hug. "Thank you," I said.

I didn't know what I was going to do with the information he'd just presented, but at least it dissolved the guilt that'd lodged deep inside me. We could figure the rest out when we needed to.

For now, we had two of the most ancient shadowkind in existence to bring down, and we still didn't know for sure what their endgame even was.

CHAPTER NINETEEN

Quinn

Even though we'd only been here for a matter of hours and Torrent often stuck to the shadows wherever we were, the house felt quieter after he left. At least for the half hour or so before Rollick prowled into the kitchen where I was eating a pot of yogurt I'd found in the fridge.

"They have to be doing it on purpose," he was muttering. "Of all the fucking cities in the entire world..."

His angry tone made me immediately tense up, even as a flicker of heat raced through me at the memory of the conversation I'd just had with my lovers... about the potential of this man becoming my lover too. But any consideration along those lines went out the window when I took in his furrowed brow. There was obviously something more important going on.

Rollick didn't often let any emotions show through his cool confidence. He wasn't upset enough for me to have picked up on it through that weird one-way bond we now had, so maybe the situation wasn't that bad, but he was definitely irritated.

I set down my spoon, bracing myself. "What happened?"

Rollick swiped his hand over his face and composed it into a more typical nonchalant expression. "Oh, just that the bastards have decided to target the one city I particularly like around here. They're menacing mortals all over L.A."

A chill washed over me, deeper than the cool currents from the air conditioning system. "What? What are they doing to people?"

"Mostly just spooking them from the shadows, from what I'm hearing from my contacts back ho—back there. But a few humans have been outright attacked by their minions."

He'd almost called the city *home*, I thought. Did it bother him to think of any mortal place that fondly? Even if he wasn't willing to say it out loud, he clearly felt particularly protective of the place. And the thought of the kinds of shadowkind beasts I'd been attacked by threatening the entire city made my stomach knot, even though I'd only spent ten days there.

Lance leapt into being out of the patch of darkness by the doorway and clicked his claws against the counter near me. "They're hassling mortals openly? Isn't that against the rules?"

Rollick grimaced. "Slaughtering them openly is against the theoretical rules too, but that hasn't stopped this bunch. I don't understand their game plan, though. Terrorizing a city full of non-sorcerers hardly connects to their other activities."

I folded my arms over my chest, hugging myself. "Could they be looking for me there—or trying to provoke me into showing myself? They know I was staying in the city before."

"I think they'd be more likely to pick your hometown for that," Rollick pointed out. "It could be intended to rankle *me*, in which case, bravo, they're succeeding. But it's too random right now. It has to add up to a larger picture."

"Maybe they're just cuckoo," Lance suggested, making a spinning gesture next to his ear that he must have picked up from his mortal observations.

The demon sighed. "As much as I'd like to believe we're merely dealing with a couple of ancient beings gone ferally unhinged, they've handled themselves very efficiently so far. I don't think we can count on that."

Crag strode into the room then, back from the patrol-slash-hunt he'd gone off on after our interlude in the bedroom. He frowned at Rollick.

"Who's unhinged? What are the villains up to now? I didn't spot any concerning activity near the house."

"No one much comes near this part of the country," Rollick informed him. "That's why we're here. They're toying with the mortals in Los Angeles for purposes unknown."

"What are we going to do about it?" I asked, drawing my spine straighter. "I mean, we're not going to let them get away with it, right? If they're attacking people—innocent people, not just sorcerers now— Have you been able to get many of your contacts or whoever ready to push back against the behemoth and the leviathan in general?"

"I'm working on it." Rollick rubbed his jaw, his gaze going momentarily distant. "It'll take some doing, you know, considering I didn't develop my connections with the idea of building an army in mind. And most shadowkind aren't inclined to stick their necks out unless it's necessary to save their own hide. I'm having to start slow—planting the idea that their hides are actually at stake. I don't think they're ready to rush into battle just yet."

My spirits sank. "Then what can we do? What about Sorsha and the shadowkind she hangs out with? She said we should go to her if we need more help against our enemies. She's pretty powerful, isn't she?"

The demon gave me a baleful look. "How much do you know about the shadowkind who calls herself 'Sorsha' and her history?"

I paused, abruptly uncertain. Did Rollick know some reason to distrust her? I'd never gotten any bad vibes from her… but then, I wasn't all that experienced at judging shadowkind intentions.

"She's a phoenix, right?" I ventured. "She can conjure fire. I thought… she saved a whole bunch of people a while back. She said something like that when we first met her, and Torrent knew what she was talking about."

"Well, that's essentially true. From what I understand, she's some kind of hybrid: a nearly impossible mix of shadowkind and human origin that makes her powers particularly potent—and unstable. I've heard from beings who were there during the final showdown she was involved in, and they say she nearly burned down the entire continent before her friends managed to calm her down. The Highest believed she might destroy both this world and ours."

I blinked at him. "Oh. Um, she didn't mention that part."

Rollick smiled thinly. "I wouldn't either, if it were me. But I'd rather not count on allies whose main fighting skill is razing everything around them to the ground. Personally, I'd prefer if Los Angeles was at least mostly still standing when we're done dealing with these pricks."

I could see his point. But still… "Are you saying we're just going to hang out here and let them harass people until you can convince the other shadowkind you know to actually help, then?"

"No," he said. "I'm going back to L.A. to see if I can't decipher their motives. You should be safe enough here with—"

"No," I broke in, raising my chin. "You're not leaving me here to just sit around and relax either. The fiends are attacking humans—my people. I can help. You need to question the creatures carrying out the attacks—I can use my sorcery to compel them to answer, right? I don't mind wearing the vest, and no one should notice I've arrived in the city while I have it on."

Rollick fixed me with a steady, penetrating stare. I gazed right back at him. If he figured he could glower me into submission, he obviously didn't know me as well as he thought he did.

I didn't even have to make the stand alone. Lance bobbed his head and tucked his arm around me. "I want to tackle the beasties too. We'll keep Quinn safe wherever we are. Right, stony one?"

He glanced over at Crag, who hummed low in his chest. "Yes. We should all find out what we can. They're escalating the threat. We don't know how much time we have until they do something worse."

"There," I said to Rollick. "We're all agreed—well, except for you. Three to one. We can leave a note for Torrent for when he gets back to let him know where we've gone. Or maybe you have other ways of sending him a message."

Rollick exhaled with a sound of exasperation, and then, to my surprise, he grinned at me. "I shouldn't have expected anything less. Come along then, sweet sorcerer. We've got quite a trek ahead of us."

When Crag nudged me from the doze I'd fallen into in the back seat, the city ahead of us was nothing but gleaming lights amid the darkness of night. We'd flown into California on a small private jet that was apparently in Rollick's arsenal, but he hadn't wanted to land too close to L.A. itself in case our enemies were keeping a close eye on more blatant comings and goings.

I straightened up and rubbed my eyes. At my awakening, Lance blinked back into physical form in the passenger seat. He kicked out his legs, eyeing the oncoming buildings avidly. "Now we teach some beasties a lesson."

"We take a cautious approach," Rollick reminded him in a dry tone from behind the wheel. "We're not in a position to go head-to-head with the dastardly duo just yet."

"Do we have any idea where to start once we get into the city?" I asked.

"I'll touch base with my contacts when we're there."

That only took a few more minutes. Rollick pulled over to the side of the road and got out his phone. As he skimmed through his messages and placed a couple of calls, Crag tugged me closer to him with his arm around my shoulders. He seemed determined to show he wouldn't shy away from me anymore, and I couldn't say I minded. I leaned my head against his solid chest and let myself relax just for a moment.

It *was* only a moment, because then Rollick let out a sound of consternation. "They're really getting bold. Look at this."

He passed his phone back to me with no hesitation or warnings not to exploit the opportunity. I might have reveled in the trust he'd shown if my eyes hadn't widened at the sight of the news video he'd brought up on the screen. The headline said, *WILD DOG ATTACKS RAMPANT.*

"What the heck?" I muttered to myself, and hit play.

The reporter in the video feed talked in an urgent voice about the rash of brutal assaults across Los Angeles, which appeared to be the work of feral animals—they were assuming packs of stray dogs. One shot of a victim showed deep gouges across his face, neck, and chest. I winced at the sight.

"Six attacks already tonight," I said as the video finished, my gut churning. "What are the shadowkind thinking? What are they getting out of this?"

"I don't know," Rollick said. "They're really skirting the line of exposure. Some of those victims must know it wasn't dogs, but whatever they've reported, the human authorities will find it impossible to believe."

Lance growled. "The beasties should know better."

"Maybe they do," I pointed out. "They might be under a spell, not doing it because they want to." But we didn't know yet whether my sorcery might be able to break our enemies' hold on their enslaved minions. "If we could find the beings who are carrying out the attacks and question one of them—if any of them *can* talk—"

"Already one step ahead of you." Rollick started the engine. "Three of tonight's attacks and one of yesterday's two were in the same general neighborhood. It must be a favorite stalking ground for at least a couple of these creatures. And if they can't tell us anything, we'll see if they can lead us to someone better informed."

He drove into a part of the city much less posh and shiny than the neighborhood around his hotel. Low-rise brick and concrete apartment buildings stood amid a few smaller homes with scruffy lawns and the occasional corner store. Some of the streetlamps were broken, leaving the sidewalks cast in intermittent pools of light.

Not many people were out at this late hour. Most of the activity seemed to be centered around a few bars on the outskirts of the residential area, their windows still glowing and occasional shouts and barks of laughter carrying from within. Rollick parked down the street from them and motioned for us to get out.

I hefted the crossbow I'd left at my feet, fully loaded, and unzipped the pocket on my messenger bag where I was keeping a stash of extra bolts so I could grab them quickly if I needed to reload. Once I was out of the car, I held the weapon down by my thigh where it wasn't too obviously visible in the darkness.

"We'll patrol in the shadows," Rollick said. "Quinn, you amble around and keep a close eye on any pedestrians who could become targets."

"*She* could become a target," Lance pointed out.

The demon shot him an amused glance. "I think she's proven she can handle herself. At least for long enough to give one of us the chance to jump in there as need be."

His confidence in me didn't stop my nerves from jittering. I might be able to handle a shadowkind creature on the attack, but that didn't mean I enjoyed the thought of it.

Taking a deep breath, I set off down the street. The men vanished into the shadows, but I took comfort from knowing they were nearby. I walked past the bars, circled the block, and was just coming back into view when a man and a woman came out through one of the doorways.

I meandered along behind the couple for a short distance until they got into a car. No beasts showed themselves.

A guy who looked like he was probably homeless shuffled by. I trailed him for a few blocks without any interference. He hunkered down on a bench by a bus stop, and I watched from the other end of the street for several minutes until it seemed better to search for other potential targets. Who knew what criteria the creatures on the hunt were using?

After doubling back, a murmured voice reached my ears as I neared the bars. A woman strode my way from the direction I'd been heading, swaying a little on her feet, her phone pressed to her ear. I pulled back against the building I'd been passing, and she walked on by without showing any sign that she'd noticed me. I waited until she'd almost reached the next corner, then pushed myself forward to follow her.

She lowered her phone—and a clump of shadow burst from a nearby alley to hurtle toward her.

A yelp of warning broke from my throat. I dashed forward, raising my crossbow and registering that it was *two* creatures leaping at her, not just one. But I couldn't risk hitting her with one of the bolts.

I sprang to the side, bumping into a parked car, and fired at the smaller beast that'd landed on her shoulders as it solidified. It tumbled off with a squeal. The woman was shrieking and flailing out her limbs at the larger creature, which looked like a cross between a wolf and a sheepdog. It shoved at her from behind as if trying to knock her down.

I aimed at its head as it snapped its fangs, but it was moving too quickly for me to get in a good shot while avoiding its intended victim. My fired bolt hit it in the shoulder instead. It stumbled to the side, and the woman took off with a sob. She left her heels behind on the sidewalk, her bare feet pattering frantically across the concrete.

As I spun toward the wolf-thing, which was heaving itself back to its feet while smoke streamed from its shoulder wound, my three men materialized around it. Crag caught it by the shoulders, digging his thumb into the wound. "Shift," he demanded.

Before my eyes, the being shed its shaggy, course fur and canine shape, swinging upright into a man with rumpled hair and eerie yellow eyes. The wound from the bolt didn't disappear. He hissed through his teeth as Crag gripped him harder.

Rollick stepped over beside me to look the shadowkind in the face.

"Why are you hunting the mortals like this? Is it your idea, or did your masters force you?"

The wolf shifter simply growled at him. A quiver of my power raced through my nerves. I drew myself up as tall as I could and willed the energy from my heart to sizzle through my whole chest, into my lungs, and up my throat.

The words that spilled from my tongue weren't any I'd have recognized, but I understood the compulsion behind them. *Answer our questions.*

But the command seemed to smack against a barrier, the energy tremoring apart between us instead of taking hold in the being's mind. I'd never felt that sensation before.

"He must already have sorcery on him," I said. "It's blocking mine. But I might be able to break through."

I inhaled deeply to try again, and the man squirmed in Crag's grasp, panic flashing across his face where before he'd only looked defiant.

"My masters will it, so it is so," he snarled. "And they'll destroy all of you too."

Lance leapt in. "Be careful. The one I caught before—"

He was too late. The wolf-man jerked his head—and managed to smash it into the brick side of the building next to us so hard his skull caved in. Horror congealed in my stomach as his body crumpled.

That hadn't been an action I could imagine any creature, mortal or shadowkind, managing on its own. There must have been a suicide command implanted in the spell his masters had cast on him.

Rollick muttered a curse and motioned for Crag to release the body that was now gushing smoky blood. "Well, now we know for sure that some of the beings responsible aren't acting of their own accord. We'll have to restrain the next one more carefully. If we can find a next one." He glanced grimly down the street. "Back to the patrol."

CHAPTER TWENTY

Crag

After an entire night of stalking the city streets and failing to capture another being capable of speech, Quinn slept through most of the day. She only woke up in the apartment Rollick had brought us to when the sky beyond the narrow window was starting to darken with the next evening.

She came into the small living room with her messenger bag. I suspected it was nearly time for her next dose of pills. The sight of the surgery scar poking from the neckline of her top made something inside me clench up.

The new heart had saved her life when she was a child, but it might also have doomed her to a worse fate at the hands of these fiends we were facing off against.

Rollick had returned to the apartment just minutes ago and was pouring himself a sour-smelling drink in the kitchen area. Quinn flopped into the chair next to the window and glanced between me and him. "Any progress?"

"Lance is out having another prowl," Rollick said. "But we haven't turned up anything substantial. It's very clear the vicious duo are in the area, but I haven't managed to pin down where they're hiding out. If we knew where they were sending their minions from, that'd make catching those minions easier."

Quinn pinched the bridge of her nose. "There aren't any convenient mountain lakes nearby that they'd be using?"

Rollick guffawed. "Believe me, that was the first thing I considered. Maybe they realized after two invasions in a row that they'd become too predictable." He wrinkled his nose at his drink. "I often appreciate a challenge, but I wish these particular opponents weren't quite so on the ball."

Their comments about the mountain lakes stirred a memory in my head. After we'd gotten so focused on what was happening on this side of the ocean, I'd almost forgotten the evidence I'd come across when Torrent and Lance had found me in China.

"I noticed something at the first camp by the lake," I said, hesitating. Maybe it wouldn't be meaningful at all. But I should let the others decide how useful the information was. "There were traces of fish—a specific kind of fish I recognized after I did some more searching afterward. It's a fish from the ocean that must have been brought up into the mountains specially. I'm guessing one of the bosses—probably the leviathan, since he's the watery one—must like them a lot."

Rollick's eyes gleamed with an eager light that gratified me. "Good work! You should have mentioned that before. Do you know exactly what this fish is?"

I frowned. "I don't know what the humans call them. But I could tell from a picture. They're silver and about this big." I spread my hands in front of me. "They like waters near the coast where there aren't many people around. I first encountered them along the Asian side of this ocean, but I'm guessing they're on the American side too."

"It doesn't seem likely that the leviathan would be importing his fish from a distant continent," Quinn agreed, and knit her brow. "Unless they were taking them through a rift or something."

"Let's see what we can find." Rollick was already tapping on his phone. "Fairly small, silver, Pacific ocean, coastal... There we go." He held the device up with the screen facing me, a grid of photographs showing across its glossy surface. "Do any of these look right?"

I spotted the right one immediately, with a flash of memory of its tender flesh in my mouth. "It's that one," I said, pointing.

Rollick grinned. "*Very* good. That's just the sort of thing we need. I can send some people along the coast and other secluded areas within a reasonable distance from the city and see if they can't track down a trail of fish bones that'll point us in the right direction."

He brought the phone to his ear and breezed out of the room as he started talking to the person on the other end. A smile crossed my lips. My searching when I'd been forced to leave Quinn had been worthwhile after all. Maybe it would get us closer to ending the threat that loomed over her.

I looked at her where she was perched on the armchair. "Are you hungry? I brought back some food."

Quinn made a face. "Not really. Not yet. I'll eat later. I feel like my stomach is too full of worries to have room for anything else."

I couldn't quite picture that sensation, seeing as I never really felt hungry the same way mortals did, but it made a certain kind of sense. I didn't like seeing her plagued by those worries. Hoping to offer some kind of reassurance, I walked over to rest my hand on her shoulder—but just as I reached for her, a scream split the air from outside.

Quinn leapt to her feet, fear flashing across her face. "Someone else is being attacked. Shit. Where's my crossbow?"

She dashed into the bedroom and sprinted out a moment later clutching the weapon. I could have leapt right through the shadows outside the window, but I wasn't leaving her to rush down into the possible fray alone. I'd already pushed the door open. As she darted past me, I melded with the patches of gloom to follow her where no mortals would see my face with its clearly inhuman jaw.

The apartment was only the second floor of a building with a storefront below, the shop now closed for the night. Quinn raced down the single flight of stairs with thudding feet and burst out into the thickening dusk. Her head whipped around as she tried to locate the source of the scream. "Where did it come from?"

A yelp from around the corner gave us a clue. Quinn ran over, and I hurtled alongside her through the shadows.

Foot traffic was already diminishing in this part of the city, but there were still a decent number of people around. A small crowd had gathered around the mouth of an alley. Quinn rushed over to them, tucking her crossbow close to her body to avoid notice, and bobbed up on her toes to peer at the scene.

I slipped right through the clustered feet and halted. A young man's body was sprawled in the mouth of the alley, his eyes staring sightlessly, blood saturating his shirt from where his throat and chest had been torn open.

It wasn't like the sorcerer attacks. None of his organs had been taken, only mangled by vicious claws. I couldn't sense the creature that'd done it —it must have carved him up with a few brutal strokes and then fled.

Rollick came up beside me through the shadows. I sensed his grimace. "That's not promising. They're escalating from injuring to murdering. I'll tell my people on the hunt that they'd better move *fast*."

I shifted my attention back to Quinn. She'd eased back from the crowd, her mouth tight, her knuckles whitening where she was gripping the crossbow. My heart lurched for her, but I couldn't easily comfort her with all these mortal witnesses around.

Her gaze darted around the darkening street. Then she turned and marched swiftly back to the apartment.

I decided it was safe enough to emerge in the stairwell, since it didn't lead to anything other than Rollick's apartment. I leapt into physical being on the steps ahead of her, and Quinn kept moving forward, right into my arms.

I hugged her tightly as she let out a choked sound. She pressed her face against my chest. Her voice came out muffled.

"We weren't fast enough. He wouldn't have had any idea what the thing that attacked him even was. Why are they killing random people who never did anything to them?"

I didn't have any answers for her. My throat constricted. I held her close, abruptly aware again of the strength in my arms, the grip that could turn crushing if I let it.

I was like the thing that had killed that man. It would be so easy for me to hurt her—I'd done it before without intending to. How could I—

Closing my eyes, I shoved those thoughts away. They were what had wrenched us apart in the first place. I would never harm her like that. I'd protected her so many times. I had to focus on what I'd accomplished and not the rare mistakes.

Or I might lose her in a totally different way.

"I don't know," I said, trying to keep my voice from sounding too gruff. "They want to cause pain—they're more monstrous than most of us."

"I wish I knew how to stop them."

"We'll find a way. They can't get away with this forever." I let my determination color my tone. I wasn't going to *let* them get away with it, no matter what it took.

"They might hurt you too," she said.

They probably would. I didn't say that out loud. "Then I'll be hurt, and I'll recover, like I have many times before. You know I'm made of tough stuff."

But saying that didn't feel like enough. She'd spent the last few weeks running from catastrophe to catastrophe—and I'd contributed to those disasters. If I could just take her away from all the horrors for a little while, remind her of all the goodness that was still left, give her a glimpse of the peaceful future I wanted so badly to share with her...

An idea sparked in my head. I scooped her right off the steps and carried her upward.

"Where are we going?" Quinn mumbled.

"You've asked before what I love about being in the mortal realm. I'm going to show you one of the things around here that I love most."

She lifted her head. "What? Crag, don't you think we should—"

"I think right now you need to get away from all the awfulness we can't tackle yet," I interrupted. "I'm not taking no for an answer."

Quinn raised an eyebrow at me. "When did you get so bossy?"

I glanced down at her. "When I saw what happens when I let our problems tear us apart instead of bringing us together."

A hint of tears shimmered in her eyes. She leaned forward and wrapped her arms around my neck without any further protest. A faint prickle of discomfort spread through my skin at the sense of the metal vest beneath her shirt, but her embrace gave me more pleasure than that minor irritation could ever dislodge.

I'd noticed when we'd arrived at the apartment that there was a set of maintenance steps leading up to a small landing above the level of Rollick's apartment. After popping into the apartment so Quinn could leave the crossbow there, I busted the lock on the maintenance door open and stepped out into the warm night air at the edge of the roof.

Streetlamps still glowed below us and artificial light streaked the wisps of cloud and smog overhead, but it was dark enough that I didn't hesitate. I let loose my gargoyle form, my wings unfurling from my back, and pushed off toward the sky.

I didn't throw caution completely to the wind. I shot straight upward with swift flaps until I was sure no one would be able to make me out against the deep indigo of the sky. Only then did I turn and soar toward the spot I wanted to show the woman I—

The woman I loved.

The realization hit me so hard my wings stuttered in mid-flap. Quinn tensed in my arms with obvious concern, and I picked up my rhythm again even as my mind reeled.

She'd told me that she loved me when she'd said the same to the others, right before she sent us away. I hadn't really thought about the exact nature of my feelings toward her, because they had nothing to do with thinking, they simply were, as if they'd always been a part of me. But that was the word for it, wasn't it—this all-encompassing desire to see her safe and happy? Love.

And somehow she felt the same incredible emotion toward me.

I'd flown out over the ocean. I swiveled around and kept my wings sweeping up and down to bring us in a slow circle, adjusting Quinn's position in my grasp so she could take in the view with me.

"You asked me before where I like to fly, what sights I've enjoyed taking in," I said. "While I was working with Rollick mostly in this area of the world, I often came out here at night to enjoy the view. And do a little night fishing, but we'll skip that part while you're with me."

"Maybe another time," Quinn teased, but awe wound through her words. "It's beautiful. That's the highway?"

"Yes." A glowing golden line wove along the coast, undulating with the curves of the green-dotted hills. Starker lights glided along it as cars cruised by. The glow mingled with the moonlight to catch on the foam of the waves below, bringing out hints of lavender and turquoise against the blackness of the night.

It was amazing how humans had taken a landscape that was already striking by daylight and used their inventions to transform it into something eerily gorgeous after sunset.

"No matter what the fiends do, this view will be here," I said. "Mortals will survive and bring their light. And even if we can't do it perfectly, we are helping to protect that light. Together."

"Together," Quinn murmured, looping her arm around my bicep and squeezing. "Even if we get hurt."

"Even if we hurt each other accidentally." I kissed the back of her head. "I love you, Quinn."

She craned her neck to meet my eyes, a smile lighting her face so it shone as stunningly as the landscape before us. "I love you too. Thank you for this. I think I needed it. I—"

Her gaze slipped past me for a second, and her forehead furrowed. "What's that?"

I spun in the air just in time to see the starry sky before us ripple as if it were a pond someone had thrown a pebble into. My body tensed.

"That's a rift," I said. "And someone's messing with it."

CHAPTER TWENTY-ONE

Quinn

"And what makes you so sure this rift is important?" Rollick asked as he turned the wheel to follow the curve of the road.

I spoke up for the gargoyle. "Crag could sense that there was a lot of shadowkind activity near it—a bunch of them, and at least one particularly powerful one. It's got to be the sorcerer-killers, right?"

Not just sorcerer-killers now, I corrected myself silently. Human-killers in general. I restrained a shudder at the memory of the savaged man we'd seen on the street earlier this night.

"More tricks from the big beasts," Lance muttered in the back seat, clicking his claws together restlessly.

"We might be able to learn more about their plans," Crag says. "I could go ahead and—"

Rollick shook his head, peering down the road through the glow of the lights along the highway. "We all stay together until we find the spot. I want to get some idea what we're dealing with before we decide on a strategy."

I squinted at the sky, still black and dotted with stars. I couldn't make anything out, but then, I hadn't seen anything other than a brief, vague distortion when I'd first spotted the rift. It'd vanished before my gaze right afterward, even though Crag had still been able to identify it.

I guessed that made sense. If mortals had been able to see the rifts shadowkind used to travel between their world and ours, their existence wouldn't have been anywhere near as secret. But what were the villainous duo doing that had affected this one enough that I'd caught a glimpse of it?

Hopefully we'd be able to find that out.

Rollick must have been able to sense the rift in some way too, because he veered off onto a side road abruptly but with a clear sense of purpose. He drove up the slope of one of the hills along the coast, the road winding back and forth up the side with signs for a lookout point at the top. But halfway up, he pulled the car as far as he could onto the shoulder and parked. "We'll go the rest of the way on foot."

I gathered my bag and my crossbow, my pulse kicking up a notch. I had no idea what we were going to find out here—whether it might be even more horrifying than what we'd already discovered about these monsters.

The road here was cloaked in almost total darkness. I walked as briskly as I could along the shoulder while placing my feet carefully to avoid falling, thankful again for my past urban explorations tramping around in abandoned buildings and private skyscraper stairwells. Who could have predicted what handy preparation they'd be for this new phase of my life?

"Could it be they're just bringing more shadowkind minions through to the mortal realm?" I asked, keeping my voice low. "They were doing that over by Miami too, right?"

"We never saw any strange energy around the rift there like the one here tonight," Crag said.

Rollick nodded. "For something to be happening that would make the portal visible even to mortal eyes, they're up to more than standard immigration. I'm *very* curious to discover what that is."

We hustled the rest of the way in silence, Crag striding a little ahead to scan the vegetation for lurking beasts, Lance shifting into his dragon form to leap and weave between the shrubs with typical wild grace. Watching him brought a pang into my heart. I glanced at Rollick, who was still marching along beside me.

"Are you sure Lance should have come? If either of the leaders use their sorcery again..."

"I gave him strict orders to retreat immediately if he senses either of those ancients nearby," the demon said. "And I think, given his past experience with them, he'll actually follow my orders for once. We don't have many allies we can count on, sorcerer. We can't afford to coddle those who are willing to stand with us."

I narrowed my eyes at him. "*You* encouraged me to send them away for their protection. What happened to that perspective?"

He shrugged casually as if it didn't matter much to him, but a twinge of emotion carried into me that tasted like regret. "I didn't know how vast a threat we were up against. We've sorted out the situation now."

"So you're admitting you were wrong," I couldn't help needling.

He cast me a baleful look, his eyes gleaming in the darkness. "It does happen, though only on very rare occasions."

Ahead of us, Crag grunted. He was looking back toward the ocean. "There it is again."

We all spun around. I caught just the faintest waver in the sky beyond the top of the hill before its surface smoothed out again. My pulse stuttered.

Rollick frowned, apparently no surer than before what might have caused the phenomenon. "Our enemies do like to keep busy," he remarked. "Come on."

We left the road and scrambled the rest of the way up the hill more directly. At its peak, I hung back at the far end of the lookout's parking lot with Lance standing guard while the demon and the gargoyle approached the crest overlooking the sea. My fingers tightened around the handle of the crossbow.

After a minute, Rollick motioned us over. He pointed down toward a small peninsula protruding into the ocean, closer to the hill next to ours than to our own. Barely any of the light from the highway lamps reached it, but when I squinted, I made out a few thicker clots of darkness moving through the shadows there.

"That's right beneath the rift," he murmured. "There are a lot of beings around it, but they're mostly in the shadows, hard to pick out at this distance. I suspect if we got closer, we'd be able to sense at least one of the two head honchos in their midst."

"What are they *doing*?" I asked. It was all a vague, dark blur to me.

"I'm not sure. They—"

Lance interrupted with a startled hiss. I stiffened, my gaze flicking over the peninsula and the sky—and snagging on what looked like a wisp of smoke briefly obscuring a patch of stars, there and then swallowed into the brief wobbling of the rift's border.

"What was that?" I demanded. "What happened?"

"Carving up the beasties like they do the sorcerers," the dragon shifter muttered with a twitch of his head.

Rollick's forehead had furrowed. "It looks like they're making some kind of sacrifice out of lesser shadowkind. Killing them and sending their essence into the rift. I have no idea what they expect that act to accomplish, though."

A shiver ran over my skin. "So every time the rift has wavered like that, they've killed something?" I'd seen it three times already just in the short time I'd been within view. How many other creatures had they slaughtered in the hours it'd taken Crag and I to return to the others and then for us all to drive back here?

"Possibly. It could be they're up to other things as well. The being that killed the beast just now didn't even show itself." Rollick glanced at our companions. "You two see if you can get a closer look. Lance, stick to the north—Crag, go south. Don't let yourselves be spotted. They're busy for now, but once the sun rises, I expect they'll disperse."

It occurred to me then that if the behemoth and the leviathan could bring even the powerful warriors sent by the Highest beings under their sway, Crag wasn't necessarily any safer than Lance was. As they vanished into the darkness around us, my mouth went dry.

"What are *we* going to do?" I asked the demon.

"Stay here and keep an eye on the bigger picture." Rollick rubbed his jaw. "I don't like this at all."

I couldn't help thinking that his plan left me pretty useless, since I could barely see any of the picture with my human eyes. I shifted my weight from one foot to the other, restlessness itching at me—but what else could I do? I wouldn't be any more useful trying to scope things out closer to the gathering, and I'd be a lot more likely to get caught than the shadowkind men. I guessed the demon was keeping me in reserve until it seemed like a good idea to bring my powers into play.

We watched until the sky lightened just slightly to a deep blue, the first hints of dawn creeping over the eastern horizon behind us. Rollick stirred, maybe thinking it'd be time to get going soon.

"Stay here," he said. "I want to do a quick search closer by."

Without waiting for a response, he vanished into the night. I grimaced at what I imagined was his retreating back and then peered down the hillside again.

It couldn't have been more than a minute later when my gaze caught on a shape moving through the shadows far down the slope below me.

It was a humanoid form, bald and gangly, its pale skin showing against the darkened landscape as it raised the small animal it'd leapt out of the shadows to pounce on to its jagged teeth. My heart skipped a beat.

Could that be one of the duo's minions on patrol? It looked human-like enough to be able to speak. If I could use my sorcery on it, maybe we could find out what the hell was going on out here.

There was no sign of Rollick's return. I didn't know how long the creature would enjoy its meal before it slipped back into the shadows where I'd never find it. I wavered for only a few seconds, and then I readied my crossbow and hopped over the low crest of the hill.

The slope gave me the momentum for my strides to stretch wide. The creature's head jerked up at my approach, but its eyes only narrowed, probably seeing me as mortal prey just as much as the animal it was snacking on. I propelled myself faster, adrenaline thrumming through my limbs, and raised the crossbow.

Panic flashed across the thing's face. It dropped the furry body in its grasp, but before it could disappear, I fired a bolt into its knobby thigh.

Magic reverberated up my throat. "Stay where I can see you," I said, or at least something like that in the unfamiliar syllables of the sorcery language. My tongue sizzled with the energy my voice expelled. "No ducking into your shadow form."

The creature's body stiffened. My magic had taken hold. I hadn't felt any obstacle to the spell, so this must be a being that was helping the monsters of its own accord.

I was ten feet away and slowing when Rollick materialized, looming over the creature, which only came up to his waist in its hunched pose. He clamped a hand around the back of its neck as if to ensure it didn't go anywhere and then leveled a pointed look at me. "What in the realms do you think you're doing?"

"I saw it—I had to try," I said, drawing up short. "We can question it."

"You shouldn't go running at shadowkind creatures—especially ones probably allied with our enemies—on your own. What if it'd lunged at you before you could work your sorcery? What if you'd missed with your fancy weaponry?"

I glowered at him, my annoyance only slightly tempered by the concern that was wafting off him despite his snarky tone. "You brought me along. Do you trust me to handle myself or not? We need to know what they're doing here. If it's worth risking Lance and Crag to find out, then it's worth risking me too."

To my surprise, the demon looked momentarily chagrined. "Fine," he said. "Let's see what this lackey has to say for herself."

Apparently the thing was female. I wouldn't have been able to tell. I lowered the crossbow and fixed my attention on her. When I opened my mouth, more of that strange language coursed out of me like an electrical current, carrying my will that she should answer our questions truthfully. My skin tingled with the effort, as if it'd only exhilarated me rather than tiring me out.

Rollick's essence had definitely enhanced my abilities in ways I wasn't sure I'd totally discovered yet.

The creature twitched and bared its teeth at me, but it didn't—couldn't?—argue. I met Rollick's gaze again. "It should tell you whatever you want to know now."

He stepped to the side of the creature and jerked her around so she was facing him. "Are you working with the shadowkind who've been killing sorcerers and harassing humans in Los Angeles?"

She let out a little snarl, but she answered in a gravelly voice. "Yes."

The simplest, briefest possible answer. But the demon's lips curled with a smirk. No doubt he was perfectly fine with playing the game of how to squeeze the right information out of it. "And your masters are a behemoth and a leviathan, aren't they?"

The creature made a face at him. "Yes."

"Very good. Now, what are they doing over there with that rift?"

"Offering up dead shadowkind," she rasped, as brusquely as before.

Rollick tsked his tongue. "Yes, but *why*? What are they hoping to accomplish by doing that?"

Her jaw tightened, but she couldn't hold back the words. "The essence is making the rift bigger."

They wanted the portal between the realms to grow? I frowned at the sky and then at her.

Rollick appeared to be equally puzzled. "And why do they want it to be bigger?"

"I don't know," the creature growled. "We do what they say. They know what they're doing. Please stop. If they find out I've told you anything, they'll kill *me*."

The blood stains on her teeth made it hard for me to feel much mercy. So many other lives were at stake if we didn't find out all she knew.

"Why are you helping them?" I asked, stepping closer. "Why are you doing what they say?"

Her round, dark eyes fixed on me. "Why not? They're going to bring us out of the shadows. We can have everything—this world can be ours. Let me go!"

Her words sent a chill down my back. Bring them out of the shadows? The world would be theirs? What was that even supposed to mean? Nothing good—that much I could tell.

"And how exactly—" Rollick began, shifting his grip on her neck, and the creature must have felt the tiniest loosening of his grasp. She jerked from his hold and sprang straight at me, needle-sharp claws protruding from her fingers, bloody jaws yawning wide.

My chest shuddered with a flash of fear that was both mine and Rollick's. I stumbled backward, jerking my crossbow up—and the demon was already on her.

Rollick punched his fist straight into the creature's chest when she was only inches from me. She sagged with a few spastic twitches, hanging off his arm. He shook her off, looked down at his smoking, gore-smeared hand with an expression of distaste, and flickered in and out of the shadows just long enough to leave the mess behind.

He met my gaze. "We probably got everything useful we could out of her anyway."

He'd acted so fast, without thinking—and if he hadn't, I might be dead right now. I swallowed thickly, my pulse still hammering from the shock of the moment, grappling with the unexpected urge to hug him. "Thank you."

A strange emotion I couldn't identify wisped from him into me, warm but somehow melancholy at the same time. "Just because you want to take risks doesn't mean I'm going to let you succumb to them if I have any say in the matter." He glanced down at the smoking corpse. "It wasn't a bad gambit. We do know a little more than we did before."

"We do." I had no idea what to say next, but then it didn't matter, because a jaunty voice called down from the crest of the hill.

"What are you two playing around with down there?"

As we turned toward Lance, Crag appeared beside him. The expanding dawn shimmered in the sky behind them. At Rollick's gesture, I clambered up the slope beside him.

"We got to have a little fun of our own," Rollick said. "Now I think we'd better get out of here."

On the drive back to the city, Lance and Crag reported their observations, but they hadn't seen much more than we'd already observed, just closer up. "There were a couple dozen beings gathered around," Crag said. "And the one making the sacrifices was moving up and down to the rift through the darkness. I couldn't get close enough to get a strong feel for him, but he was powerful. He felt at home with the ocean."

"The sea serpent," Lance put in. "I could take him, dragon to dragon. If he didn't have his cheating magic."

"But he does, so you'll stay put," Rollick said dryly. "They're expanding the rift for some purpose, and it sounds like they want to establish more of a shadowkind presence in the mortal world. But they wouldn't need a *bigger* rift just for that. There are hundreds across this country already."

"Next time we'll have to catch a minion who knows a little more," I suggested, and he aimed a wry smile my way. But his uneasiness kept reaching me in flickers and flashes. He wasn't happy about what we'd learned at all.

We marched up to the apartment in the brightening morning light. As we strode in through the door, Torrent wavered into view in the middle of the living room, his expression grim.

My heart leapt with relief. "You're back!"

"I am," he said. "But I don't think any of you are going to like what I have to report."

CHAPTER TWENTY-TWO

Quinn

Before Torrent could get into his report, my morning alarm pealed from my phone. The shadowkind men fell silent while I popped my pills and grabbed a glass of water to chase them. Crag followed me into the kitchen and insisted on heaping a plate with slices of fruit and the premade sandwiches he'd obtained for me.

I hadn't eaten all night other than a couple of hasty snacks, so I guessed he had a point. But as soon as the plate was in my hands, I sat down on the linen sofa and focused on Torrent, who'd propped himself against the wall next to the window. "You found out something about the leviathan."

"Yes." His supporting tentacles flexed uneasily. "It took a lot of searching. I got the impression that a lot of the shadowkind who enjoy the mortal oceans have had some kind of encounter with him but were too nervous to admit to it."

Rollick sat down on the arm of the sofa. "And what did you learn from the ones who were willing to talk?"

Torrent's mouth twisted. "Apparently he's been hanging out in the area of the Bermuda Triangle quite a bit for more than a century. Wrecking boats and even managing to take down the occasional plane and hide them away to unnerve the mortals. But he hasn't stuck to that area all of the time. One merman speculated that he might have had something to do with a couple of tsunamis that've caused a lot of destruction on the other side of the globe."

Rollick's expression had darkened. "He's pushing the boundaries of what he can get away with without drawing too much attention to the supernatural source of the disasters. Sounds a lot like the approach I gather the behemoth was taking before they joined up."

As I forced down the last bite of the sandwich segment I'd been eating, my skin crept with apprehension. "And it's all directed against human beings. Is that their end goal? Is that how they figure shadowkind will have this world for themselves—they're going to kill *all* of us?"

Torrent blinked. "They're doing what now?"

I stewed in my horror as the other men filled him in on what we'd found out near the rift. Then Rollick turned to me. "That can't be it. They wouldn't get away with it."

"Even if they bring hordes of shadowkind through that enlarged rift to help them?"

"Even then. For one thing, they wouldn't need a *bigger* rift for that. They'd just need to call them through all over the world, and there are more than enough rifts to summon a massive army in minutes if they could convince enough to come over."

"You're not being very reassuring," I muttered.

The demon gave my shoulder a teasing prod. "Even the biggest army of shadowkind they could raise wouldn't be a match for humans eventually. There are already hunters scattered across the globe who know what our weaknesses are. If they saw that shadowkind were making themselves an open threat to humanity, they'd share that knowledge widely. Walmart would start carrying copies of that crossbow of yours. We might be powerful, but we do have a few very basic weaknesses. You could kill me right now with that contraption no matter how old I am or how much magic I have."

"They'd lose eventually," Crag put in. "It wouldn't be a good plan. It wouldn't make anyone happy for very long. But a lot of mortals and shadowkind would die if they decided to attempt it anyway."

"Then they're idiotic as well as tricksy," Lance declared. "Why would they want to get rid of mortals anyway? Humans are part of what makes this realm so much fun." He flopped down on the sofa next to me and tucked his arm around my waist.

I set my half-finished plate onto the side table and let myself lean into the dragon shifter a little. "These two don't seem to think so. Or maybe what's fun for them is seeing us suffer."

"I think they've been too strategic to simply be aiming for temporary chaos," Rollick said, frowning. "And it doesn't explain what they're doing with the rift. I don't think they *are* powerful enough to summon that large an army anyway. They only managed to take control of a couple of the Highest's warriors—they had to kill the others. They have enough of a force right now to put our small group in danger and menace a single city, but the entire world?"

"It does sound like there's a piece we're missing," Torrent agreed, his face gone even more somber.

Crag squared his shoulders. "Then we'll keep searching until we understand."

I scooted closer to Lance, tipping my head against the crook of his neck and letting his nuzzle of my hair comfort me as much as any gesture could. "Whatever it is, it's obviously going to be *bad* for humankind. And any shadowkind who don't want to see us tormented."

Rollick took on his usual confidently authoritative air. "I have contacts looking into all sorts of things around the city. Our opponents seem to mostly be active at night. We'll see what my people turn up in the meantime, and then we'll track down a minion who has a better idea of their masters' plans."

"What if none of the minions know?" I had to ask. "What if the two head honchos are keeping it to themselves?"

A gloom fell over the room. We all knew that wasn't just possible but actually fairly likely.

"Then we'll wait and see their next moves, and learn what we can from those," Torrent said evenly.

While more people would probably die in the meantime. There'd been at least a dozen more attacks across this city tonight. And more shadowkind would die too—the ones being sacrificed, and the ones who dared to go up against these monsters... which might end up including the men around me.

I closed my eyes, wishing I could sink right into Lance and never let him go. Wishing the catastrophe I'd gotten wrapped up in didn't seem to be growing with every passing day.

The dragon shifter pressed a gentle kiss to my temple and let his lips linger there, his claws stroking along the curve of my torso. "We're here with you, baby girl," he crooned. "We're not going anywhere."

He couldn't really promise that, though—not when we were up against enemies this powerful and brutal. But I wanted to believe it.

His head lowered, trailing kisses down the side of my face and nipping my earlobe. His claws skimmed my thigh with just enough force to send a giddy prickling sensation over my skin, and a wash of heat spread from where he'd touched to pool between my legs. Suddenly I wanted a whole lot more than just to believe him.

Lance picked up on the shift in my mood as quickly as he usually did. He dipped his mouth to my neck and tested the fangs he'd brought out against the tender flesh there, bringing a gasp to my throat. "Maybe our woman needs a more concrete reminder of just how much we're here with her."

Yes. If there wasn't any way we could fight these villains right now regardless, I wanted to lose myself in the pleasure my three lovers could conjure in my body. I wanted to hold them close enough to convince myself that they'd never slip from my grasp, no matter what we faced.

I cupped his jaw and tugged his mouth to mine. He threw himself into the kiss, letting his tongue shift from human-like to its ridged dragon form, and yanked me right onto his lap. The bulge of his already rigid cock pressed against my ass through my shorts.

As he caressed my breasts with a growl that seemed directed at the metal beads that made it difficult for him to properly fondle me, Crag sank down next to us. The gargoyle kissed my shoulder with absolute tenderness.

There was a soft rustling sound as Torrent used his tentacles to help him cross the room. He looped one of those tentacles around my bare calf and paused. I drew back from Lance's kiss to see he'd cast his gaze toward the fourth man in the room—the one who'd never been a part of an interlude like this with us before, other than watching unknown from a distance.

My gaze locked with Rollick's. Desire had flared in his eyes, echoed in the pulse of emotion that flowed from him into me. But his posture had stiffened where he was perched on the sofa arm.

So many memories rushed through me: the horror of discovering how he'd violated our privacy back at his hotel, the pained apology he'd offered after he'd saved me from what would have been a deathly fall. The way he'd rushed to my aid at the sorcerers' enclave, the moment in the park near my parents' house when he'd offered me my life back. He'd always intrigued me as much as he'd unnerved me, and I no longer saw *him* as a villain. He'd maybe even become kind of heroic in the past several days.

Of course, he was also a high-level demon used to commanding authority and getting his way. He'd wanted to claim me, but I had a feeling he'd intended that to be only for himself, shunting my other men aside.

Now... now I had no idea what he'd accept. What would win in the potential battle between his desire and his ego.

But I wouldn't get a chance to find out if he didn't realize I wanted him too—fully aware of what I was doing, not the slightest bit intoxicated.

He stood up with an expression of careful composure and gave us a wry bob of his head. "I'll leave you to it."

"Wait," I blurted out before he could disappear. As he paused, watching me with obvious uncertainty, I eased away from my other men. Not even Lance made a noise of protest as I walked over to the demon.

They'd accepted him. They believed he was with us in every way that counted, that he posed no threat to my body or my heart.

I stopped just a foot away from Rollick, starkly aware of the heat wafting off his body and the tangled emotions seeping into me with it. His hunger stirred more of my own.

"We're all together in this mess, aren't we?" I said quietly. "What if you were with us for the good parts as well? Can *you* handle that?"

More passion flared in Rollick's eyes. He glanced at the other men and then back at me. "What do you want from me, Quinn?" he asked, his voice so raw it sent a tremor right down the center of me.

My throat constricted. I stepped even closer, reaching to slip one hand around his neck. "I want you. But only if it doesn't have to be just you and no one else. Only if you can accept that I'm always going to want them too. And until I'm sure of that, they're going to come first."

A husky quality wound through his next words. "I suppose that's reasonable, if you're going to insist on laying down rules, sweet sorcerer."

He inclined his head, and I bobbed up on my toes to meet his kiss. More heat flooded me from the joining of our mouths, searing all through the rest of my body.

The demon did know how to kiss. His lips melded with mine at the perfect angle to set my nerves tingling alongside the surge of heat. I found myself pulling him closer as if I could absorb even more pleasure from the moment that way. He set his hands on my waist, his thumbs arching under my shirt to skim across the bare skin, an encouraging noise resonating from his throat. The quiver I caught of his own delight and something almost like contentment sparked more bliss inside me in turn.

We were really doing this, after weeks of teasing and resisting. But nothing about this moment felt like a mistake. The fire of his kiss burned away any final traces of doubt.

He wanted *me*. Not as a trophy or a tool or to prove a point, but because of the same hunger that was reverberating down to my core right now. He might have been claiming me with his kiss, but I'd claimed a part of him just as much. Somehow in the past several days, our hopes and desires had become intertwined far beyond the point of any scheming or strategy.

With a little growl, Lance came up behind me. He rested his hand on my hip beneath Rollick's fingers and nibbled the curve of my shoulder. "Mine," he murmured against my skin, as if reminding me that he'd been the one who'd started us on this path.

Rollick's grasp on my waist tightened momentarily as I pulled away from our kiss, but he relaxed enough to let me turn and yank the dragon shifter to me next. The demon's hands teased up under my vest and the thin cotton undershirt that kept it off my skin until they cupped my breasts through my bra. My breath caught, and I kissed Lance harder, swaying between the two of them.

Lance had been ready for more since the moment he'd pulled me onto his lap. He hooked his claws over the waist of my shorts and dragged them down my legs, catching my panties along the way. As he kissed me again, his tongue sweeping through my mouth, he tucked his hand between us and grazed the tips of his claws over my pussy. When they glided across my clit, I whimpered into his mouth.

The dragon shifter blinked away so swiftly I barely felt his disappearance other than a current of air before he was standing before me again—buck naked. He grasped my hand and tugged me down with him onto the thick rug, a sly grin stretching across his face. "Everyone can join in with this position. I want to see how you take all of us at once, baby girl. Are you ready for that?"

A thrill shot through me. I looked up, catching the other men's gazes. "Whenever you are."

Lance cocked his head toward Torrent. "I don't think we should unleash the gargoyle's equipment on places we still need to be careful with, hmm? Do you still have that slick stuff to make her really ready?"

Torrent wet his lips, the hunger in his eyes searing over me. "Just a second."

He wavered away too, and then returned seconds later with the tube from Rollick's guest bedroom clutched in his deformed hand. As the tentacled man knelt behind me, Rollick let out a low chuckle. "So glad you made such excellent use of my hospitality."

I reached one hand toward him and then the other toward Crag, beckoning them down around me on either side. Crag came at once and Rollick more warily, and then I was surrounded in a complete circle of heated desire.

All at once, I felt weirdly shy. I touched Lance's cheek and drew him into a kiss that started out chaste but turned passionate as our mouths lingered together. Torrent stroked his hand up and down my back, not reaching to any more sensitive areas yet. As one of his tentacles looped around my waist to press its suckered kisses against my belly, Crag followed Rollick's example and slipped his broad hand under my shirts to fondle one breast.

For a moment, Rollick just watched. Then I felt the press of his lips against my shoulder. "I look forward to times in the future when I'll hopefully get to see you in all your glory," he said, and eased his hand up my chest to work over my other breast in tandem with Crag.

The rush of pleasure through my body had me arching against the man I was perched on. My sex brushed against Lance's cock, and he let out an eager growl.

"Mine," he murmured again, rubbing his shaft over the wetness that'd collected between my folds and then sliding right up inside me.

I sighed as he filled me, that fantastic burn searing away any lingering doubts about whether we could make this group collision work. Grasping Crag's shirt, I pulled him into a kiss next, my lips shifting against his as I rocked with Lance's leisurely thrusts. "Clothes off," I ordered him.

Behind me, Torrent's hand dipped to my ass. As he delved lube-slick fingers between my cheeks, the tip of his embracing tentacle dropped to squeeze my clit. I gasped and found myself glancing at Rollick again.

So much passion lit his face now that flames seemed to dance in his eyes. "Fill her up," he murmured with a hint of command in his tone. "Let's see our mortal fully satisfied." He pinched my nipple between his thumb and forefinger, and I tipped my head back with a moan. Then I reached for him to claim another demonic kiss.

His mouth scorched mine as Torrent warmed up my back entrance. When the kiss broke, the tentacled man brushed his lips against the back of my neck and asked, "Are you ready for me?"

The pulsing of his fingers inside me already had me trembling for release. "Yes," I mumbled. "Please."

Lance tipped me forward against him to provide the other man with a better angle, and Torrent lined himself up. The feel of his solid cock sliding into me from behind was totally different from the flexible thrust of his tentacle, but even more giddying in its own way. A ragged moan spilled out of me as I found myself speared by two of my lovers, friction sending its heady bliss through my nerves from both sides.

Torrent matched Lance's relaxed pace as they warmed me up even more together. I kept just enough awareness beyond the surging sensations to motion for Crag to push more upright. The gargoyle had shed his clothes as I'd asked, and even in his human-like form, his cock jutted massively from between his thighs.

I knew I couldn't take it all into my mouth, but I was going to give it my best shot. I stroked my fingers over the silkily firm length and closed my lips around the head.

Crag groaned and swayed to meet my embrace. I sucked hard as my hand worked the rest of his shaft up and down, and his thick fingers tangled in my hair as if he needed to hold on to me through his own careening path toward release.

Lance leaned in to flick his tongue along my jaw. "Not quite all of us yet, baby girl. Can you handle four?"

Hell, yes, I could. With Lance and Torrent holding me balanced between them, I raised my other hand toward Rollick and curled my fingers into his shirt before trailing them down his chest. The demon edged closer, slipping his hand over mine and guiding it lower. When my palm came to rest on the bulge behind his slacks, a rough rumble emanated from his chest.

"Let's stick with one to start," he said in an equally rough voice. For just an instant, the impression of his body vanished. Then he was there again, no layers of fabric between us.

I teased my fingertips over the single taut shaft he sported in human-like form and then gripped it firmly. Rollick kept fondling my breast as I pumped him with a rhythm in time with the other men's movements.

"Let go," he murmured. "Give yourself over to the pleasure, and bring all of us with you."

As if on cue, Lance began to thrust faster, deeper. As Torrent matched his pace, the bliss sweeping through me tossed me even higher. I swirled my tongue around the head of Crag's cock, stroking both him and Rollick faster in turn. We'd all gathered together to form a tidal wave of delight that I couldn't have reined in now even if I'd wanted to.

Torrent seemed determined to make sure I came first. His sucker strummed at my clit as he bucked into me. I moaned onto Crag's shaft with a shudder of ecstasy. Then the pleasure building inside me exploded, crackling through me and whiting out my vision.

It blazed on and on as Torrent followed me with a choked sound and a squeeze of his arm around my torso. Crag grunted with the tightening of my lips, and the salty gush of his release spilled over my tongue. Lance chuckled breathlessly and pounded into me with even more force, and I shattered apart again right on the heels of my first orgasm.

My hand jerked faster around Rollick's cock. He wrapped his fingers around mine to clench them even harder and came with a muttered curse. Then the dragon shifter followed the rest of us, liquid heat spurting inside me.

Lance yanked my face away from Crag's and scraped his fangs over my neck. The pain added one final spark of bliss to my release before he healed it with a waft of fiery breath.

My head bowed forward, my body going slack. Rollick brushed my sweat-damp hair back from my temple and grinned fiercely. "That's our woman."

As the last quivers of ecstasy seeped out of me, resolve formed in my chest. I *was* theirs, in every possible way, as much as they were mine. And since I hadn't been able to protect them by pushing them away from me, I'd just have to hold them as close as I could—and put up every possible fight to defend the love I'd found with them.

CHAPTER TWENTY-THREE

Quinn

Somehow the darkened coastline looked eerier now that I knew what sorts of plots were being carried out under the cover of night. I rested my hands on my crossbow where it was lying across my lap in the back of the car and willed my pulse not to thunder quite so loudly.

"So, your spy said the leviathan sent some minions off on fishing duty?" I asked.

Rollick nodded from the seat ahead of me, where he was driving as usual. "Something like that. I warned the associates I've been able to call on not to get too close to any unusual activity, because we don't want to tip off the villainous duo that we've noticed. A small group of the minions were messing around on an isolated spot farther down the coast from the rift, pulling something out of the water."

"It would make sense that a being that powerful might send someone else off to catch his favorite food," Crag rumbled from beside me.

Lance huffed in the front passenger seat. "He and his buddy are too busy making their tricksy plans. We can let him starve."

Rollick gave him an amused look. "We're not going out there to put an end to the fishing. If he trusts these lackeys enough to handle his food, it's possible one or more of them has seen or heard things about his larger plans. We catch one, interrogate it, and if that one isn't useful, we move on to the next."

"I'd rather see the *both* of them starve," Lance muttered, propping his legs up on the dashboard.

"At least we shouldn't have to worry about anyone using sorcery on you during this mission," I said. "Since the bosses will be busy with other things." A small comfort.

Rollick veered onto a side road and parked out of view of the highway like he had when we'd observed the rift last night. As we got out of the car, Torrent materialized next to us, having ridden along in the shadows since there wasn't a whole lot of room for five in the car, especially when one of those was Crag. I didn't think the tentacled man minded the excuse not to hold his often painful physical form when he didn't need to.

He'd been listening to all of our conversation, of course. "Any thoughts on what being we should aim to capture first?" he asked. "Are there any that we have reason to believe might be closer to their masters than the others?"

Rollick made a face. "Unfortunately no. The head honchos themselves have managed to stay mostly out of public eye. I say we grab whoever's most easily available and work from there." He glanced at me. "You're staying here—with Lance, so you have a little backup. You'll be too noticeable tramping around over there, and we won't really need your skills until we've caught our first prisoner and need to convince them to talk."

I hadn't really thought that part through. It made sense for me to hang back when I couldn't merge with the shadows like the men, but I couldn't help grimacing at him. "So, I don't get to be anything other than a sorcerer for this mission, then."

Rollick's lips curved into a smirk that was unusually soft around the edges. "I think we all know you're much more than just a sorcerer—sweet, reluctant, or otherwise."

His smile sent a quiver of heat over my skin. I didn't totally know how to react to him after the intimacy we'd shared this morning. It was too fresh, and I wasn't even sure how *he* felt about it now that all was said and done. But this wasn't exactly the time to hash it out.

"Fine," I muttered, and brandished my crossbow. "But if any beings come sneaking around this way like last time, I'm taking them on."

Lance leaned close to nuzzle my hair with a much easier familiarity. "And I'll be here to help you."

Rollick took the two of us in with a twinge of emotion I couldn't quite decipher, though I thought I sensed a little jealousy in it. He didn't say anything, only stepped closer for just long enough to cup my jaw and press a quick kiss to my lips. My heart skipped a beat, and then he was stepping away, motioning to the other two men.

Crag shot me a concerned glance, and I waved him off. With the dragon shifter watching my back, I didn't think the gargoyle had anything to worry about. Torrent tipped his head to me, and then all three vanished into the darkness.

My human eyes couldn't make out much in the landscape around us, where a narrow road cut through a field with two more rolling hills on either side. We'd parked as far as possible from the sparse lampposts, and even the nearest of those cast small pools of light that barely extended beyond the shoulder of the road. Tonight was more overcast than yesterday, clouds blotting out the stars and all but the faintly glowing edge of the moon.

Lance shifted into dragon form to prowl around me and then sprang back up into his human-like body, flexing his arms. "Let's hope they catch a talkative beastie quickly," he murmured. "We should be part of the fun."

I nudged him with bemused fondness. "I wouldn't call this expedition *fun*."

He grinned at me. "Anything can be fun if you take the right approach. For example, while we're waiting, I could—"

He'd just started to trail his claws down my arm when he froze, his gaze darting away from me to search the darkness. I tensed automatically. "What?"

His tongue flicked over his lips. The lean muscles in his shoulders flexed. "There's something—"

In one massive surge, the darkness around us came alive. A wave of monstrous bodies hurtled down the slopes on either side of the road, rushing straight toward us.

A squeak of startled shock burst from my lips. As Lance snarled and leapt back into dragon form, I yanked my crossbow up.

My finger squeezed the trigger once, twice, three times, hitting targets because it was almost impossible not to with so many racing toward us all together. Those bodies crumpled, but the dozens of others dashed onward.

Lance whipped along their front lines, slashing through as many as he could reach with his claws and flares of roaring dragon fire. But the ring of protection he was forming around me contracted no matter how swiftly he flung himself onward.

I fumbled with the bolts in my messenger bag, snatching a few up and shoving them into the crossbow with all the speed I could summon. Even as I clicked them into place, my pulse thudded with a rapidly growing sense of futility. I wasn't sure I had enough bolts in my bag to take even half of these creatures down, whether I could load and fire fast enough or not.

We hadn't expected a horde to come down on us. How had they found us here? Why were so many lurking out here by what was supposed to be just a fishing spot?

Did the other men have any clue this was happening, or were they still investigating the supposed fishers on the coastline, totally unaware?

My instinct had been to stay quiet, but that thought jarred a panicked, wordless yell from my throat. I didn't know if we could get out of this if they didn't come back and join the fray on our side.

But I couldn't count on my other men hearing me or being close enough to help. I shot three more bolts into the oncoming horde and gasped for breath. I had to dodge to the side when one creature slashed at my thigh, its claws snagging on the fabric of my shorts in the instant before Lance pounced on it and tore its head off with his jaws. He hurtled onward, but more of the beasts were closing in.

I pushed my back against the side of the car for some minor sort of shelter. It'd be no good getting inside where the creatures could easily leap in after me through the shadows and I'd have no room to maneuver. Adrenaline thrummed through my body—and woke up the other sort of energy lodged in my heart.

I focused on the crackling sense of power with a jolt of hope. Willing it to sizzle up my throat and into my voice, I opened my mouth and shouted out a string of syllables in the language of sorcery.

The idea was to tell them to back off. To stand down and cower before us. But all through the onrushing crowd, I sensed the energy I cast out crashing into barriers like the one I'd felt on the being Rollick had snatched on the mountainside in Oregon.

Most of these creatures weren't here of their own free will. They had their masters' sorcery driving them onward.

I fired a few more bolts into the horde and let my voice ring out again, more forcefully than before. I had to break the hold on them. I had to shatter the sorcery that already gripped them. Even if I couldn't bend their wills with my own magic at the same time, they might not want to take up this battle if they had the choice anyway.

The power of my words rippled through the mass of creatures in a wave. I felt with tingling pricks across my skin as one hold and another snapped. But as even several of the beasts veered away and a spark of triumph lit inside me, one large creature lunged at me just after Lance had whipped by.

I hadn't been able to reload yet. I smacked the panther-like thing in the muzzle with the crossbow, but it was already shoving me to the ground. Its curved talons raked through my abdomen, slicing my shirt, the lower threads of my vest, and right into my flesh with a spike of agony.

I cried out with nothing in my voice but pain now. Lance ripped the thing off me and smacked its head right off its shoulders, but when I pressed my hand to my side, wetness pulsed against it. I was bleeding—gushing blood.

The dragon shifter kicked a few more fiends out of the way and dipped his head toward me. I jerked my hand out of the way just in time for him to send a blast of his fiery breath over my torso.

In his haste, Lance hadn't been able to work as carefully as usual. The heat stung badly enough to force another whimper from my lips. He must have sealed some of the wound, but I could still feel blood trickling over my skin and soaking into the rest of my shirt.

My entire abdomen blared with pain. I could hardly breathe.

Lance snarled in frustration, whirling to savage a few more creatures who'd leapt in at us. A lithe humanoid figure sprang onto the hood of the car, and he swung toward her with a threatening growl.

She held up her hands, the image of her doubling before my wavering vision. "I'm not going to hurt her. I want to help." She looked down at me. "Thank you for severing their spell. The beings that had me under their control want you destroyed by whatever means necessary. They see you as nothing but a threat now. Stay away from them if you want to live."

With that warning, she fled into the shadows. I clamped my hand to my side, too dizzy with agony to fully process her words, and groaned. Even if I wanted to follow her advice, I had the sinking suspicion it might be too late.

There was a shriek, and a tentacle lashed into view, slamming several creatures head over heels. A huge, stony body landed beside me with a heavy thump. Crag stared down at me, his eyes blazing with fury and horror.

"Get her out of here!" Rollick's voice rasped from somewhere nearby.

The gargoyle didn't hesitate. He swept me up in his bulging arms, his muscles flinching at my hiss of pain, and launched himself into the air. As the ground fell away, the dizziness swelled right through my brain, and my mind fell away into a blackness even deeper than the night.

CHAPTER TWENTY-FOUR

Quinn

Pain blazed all through my mid-section. I sucked in a breath, my eyelids fluttering, and winced at a sensation that felt like several shards of glass poking deeper into my belly.

Crag's rumble of a voice came from somewhere over me. "Quinn? Lie still—you need more time to recover." He raised his voice slightly to call to someone farther away. "She's waking up!"

The gargoyle's broad hand came to rest on my shoulder. As the shock of the pain ebbed, I became more aware of the other sensations outside my body: soft blades of grass covering a lumpy stretch of earth beneath me, hazy morning light seeping into my eyes, a rush of warm breeze carrying the scent of wildflowers and not a trace of salt.

I blinked, focusing my vision. I was lying on my side in a small clearing sheltered by looming trees. Pale clouds still covered most of the sky; the sun hadn't yet risen above the level of the treetops. Crag was crouched behind me. As I parted my lips, attempting to work sound from my parched mouth, my other three shadowkind men materialized around me.

"Bring her water bottle," Rollick ordered, coolly and briskly but with a waver of worry that passed from him into me. "She needs hydration after the blood she lost."

Torrent snatched the bottle from my bag and brought it to me with a tentacle. His expression was tight, his sea-green eyes stormy. "Don't move," he told me.

Lance leapt in to open the bottle and hold it to my lips. With Crag supporting my head, I raised it a little to sip the water. The liquid had warmed in the few hours since I'd refilled the container, but right then I wasn't feeling picky. It slid down my throat like some kind of elixir. My belly twinged, but the discomforts beyond my wound retreated.

"What happened?" I asked with a rasp. I couldn't feel any blood where my arm was leaning against my belly, although my shirt clung to me here and there with damp splotches. "Am I going to be okay?"

"We'll have to keep a close eye on you," Rollick said grimly. "But I think Lance managed to seal your wound all right once he didn't have those creatures swarming him. It'll take a while before the flesh all knits together properly—a lot of it will be scar tissue right now. I'll get you some painkillers when we're back in the city."

"Okay." Lance had patched me up enough times that I trusted his dragon fire to have seared away any chance of infection. I let my head droop back against the grass. "How did we end up getting attacked? What were all those creatures doing there to begin with?"

Torrent sank down next to me and stroked a careful hand over my hair. "It looks like they set a trap for us. Someone must have spotted Rollick's spies and reported that the site had been compromised. Instead of moving elsewhere, they prepared an ambush assuming we'd come investigate ourselves."

The thought of our enemies following our moves that closely made my pulse stutter. I shifted slightly, feeling the press of the silver and iron beads across my chest—but not as far down as the strands used to fall. "The one that got me broke my vest. If they track me down again—"

"It still seems to be offering enough protection to mostly disguise your sorcerer energy," Rollick cut in. "I can catch a little of it from here, but at the far side of the clearing, I couldn't pick it up at all. That should be enough protection until we can arrange something else. I've already had a few of my contacts working on putting together a few items with silver thread woven in like I talked about before. As soon as one is done, you can try it out instead."

I sighed and slowly rolled onto my back. This movement only set off the impression of a couple of shards of glass digging into me instead of a whole bunch like before.

I touched my belly tentatively and found the skin there was dry but rippled with the scar tissue Rollick had mentioned. Even the swipe of Lance's tongue with its special saliva hadn't been able to smooth this spot out completely.

Oh, well. I wasn't any stranger to scars.

"So, what now?" I asked the group around me. "What else can we do to find out what they're doing—to stop them?"

Lance let out a little growl. "You need to rest and get better. No more fighting. If they'd hurt you any more..." His face darkened with a haunted expression that looked totally wrong there. My dragon shifter was meant to be smiling and laughing.

"They know for sure that we're in the area now," Crag said. "We should leave, go somewhere they won't think to look for Quinn."

"No," I protested. "We can't—that'll give them even more time to prepare whatever it is they're working toward. And we know they're out to hurt people however they can. If we back down now, we might not get another chance."

Torrent's mouth twisted. "I don't know how much of a chance we have even now."

"That being you snapped out of their sorcery, she said they're out to kill you now, not just capture you," Lance reminded me, slinging a possessive arm over my legs.

The memory of her words left me cold, but I couldn't let that shake my resolve. "It doesn't matter. I'll be in danger no matter where we go and what we do. I'll be in *more* danger if these monsters gather more power than they already have. We have to... Maybe we should stop trying to figure out what they're doing and why, and just go straight to shutting them down."

Rollick let out a dark chuckle. "If accomplishing that was as easy as saying it, we'd already have done it."

"There has to be a way..." My mind drifted through the events of the past few weeks. "I'm a sorcerer. Sorcerers have ways of controlling shadowkind. That's *why* they want me dead, isn't it? They don't think there's any chance they could really use me now, but they're afraid I might be able to control them. They can't control me themselves, right? The sorcery they've absorbed only works on other shadowkind."

"We can't count on you being able to overpower them," Torrent said.

"No, but... what if we used more sorcerer strategies in general? They have all kinds of ways of manipulating shadowkind. They kill them to bring out their own powers. They know how to weaken them and threaten them..."

The image swam up from my memory of the cages where the enclave had held the creatures for the rites—and who knew what other purposes. Made out of silver and iron, yes, but also with those blades ready to spear right into the beings if need be.

"We could set a trap for *them*," I said slowly. But how the hell would we get one of those immense beings into any kind of cage? Even making a cage big enough seemed like a monumental task—and neither my men nor Rollick's other shadowkind allies could construct anything made out of the toxic metals.

But mortals—mortals could handle silver and iron without any trouble. I glanced at Rollick. "You have contacts who are human—the ones who're working on my new protective gear. The ones who set up the protections around your properties and inside the hotel. If we gave them a design, they could build whatever you asked, couldn't they?"

Rollick raised an eyebrow. "I suppose I could pull together the manpower and resources to construct just about anything, given enough time. What are you scheming now?"

All at once, my fingers were itching for a pencil and sketch pad. An image of the trap I wanted to design was unfolding in my mind, a larger and more concealed version of the vicious cages from the enclave.

"I think I could make plans for a structure we could use to... to kill the behemoth and the leviathan," I said. "I might need someone with more advanced engineering knowledge to adjust the mechanical parts, but I'm almost sure it should be doable. We could take a similar approach to something I saw the sorcerers in the enclave using."

Lance shuddered. "Nothing they do is good."

His response sent an ache through my chest that had nothing to do with my injury. I reached out to squeeze his forearm. "I know. They're horrible to the shadowkind. But now we're dealing with shadowkind who are horrible too. The sorcerers have spent their entire existence honing their ability to control beings like that—and destroy them if they feel they need to. We're running out of time. We have to make use of every advantage we can."

"She's right," Crag rumbled. "Whatever it takes. They've done too much damage already."

Torrent nodded. "I'm on board. Our usual tactics haven't gotten us far enough."

Lance grimaced but then dipped down to kiss my hip. "I don't want them or their beasties getting any more claws into our woman. If we need to act like sorcerers to do that, then fine."

Rollick folded his arms over his chest with a contemplative air. "I think we're forgetting one thing. We can make a trap, sure. But how are we going to get these menaces to stroll on into it?"

"They came to the camp in Oregon when we compelled one of their lackeys to say I'd show up," I said.

"Yes, but they're not likely to fall for the same trick twice. And I'd already used similar tactics to redirect their attention before, so I think using *you* as bait in any way is all tapped out."

I stared up at the drifting clouds, considering the situation. When the idea came to me, my stomach twisted, but I couldn't think of anything better to suggest.

"What if we don't present me as willing bait? What if we make them think I'm an even bigger threat than they already believe, and they've got to hunt me down and ensure I'm destroyed if they want to go through with their plan?"

Lance's growl revealed exactly what he thought of that plan. Crag let out a similar ragged huff. "I'd rather you weren't in their sights at all, Softness."

"But I am anyway," I pointed out. "We might as well use that fact. We can make our trap in a building, and let word get out that I'm gathering an army of my own there. Subtly, so they think we're trying to hide the information from them. I can... I can enslave at least a few shadowkind, make sure other minions of theirs are nearby to witness it. I can break the duo's sorcery. They won't like that."

"I don't know if that will be enough," Rollick said with obvious reluctance. I got the sense he didn't particularly care for this strategy either.

I bit my lip. "What if we also—we could reach out to whatever sorcerer families you're aware of that they haven't already attacked. Send a message asking them to come ally with me. Make sure at least one of those messages gets intercepted, so our enemies know we're gathering those sorts of forces too."

"Bring the actual sorcerers in?" Lance said with a hiss of breath through his teeth. "They'll try to capture *us*."

"We won't let them. And they probably won't even come. It'll look like a trap to them. We just want to make the big bosses worried that they might come. And if they do show up... then that'll just be extra bait."

My gut knotted just for a second at the thought of luring fellow humans into my scenario. Only for a second, because then I thought of all the ways these humans had manipulated shadowkind over the years.

Did it make *me* a monster that I was willing to risk sacrificing them to take down an even greater evil?

A few weeks ago, I'd have shied away from that thought. Now, it settled inside me next to my resolve, not a blessing or a curse, just the way things were.

I'd do whatever it took to protect the people who deserved it—and there were a heck of a lot more of them than there were innocent sorcerers.

"What if the fiends send a bunch of beasties in again and don't come themselves?" Lance asked. "Like they did at Rollick's hotel."

I'd already pondered that point. "Rollick has made buildings where most shadowkind can't get past the silver-and-iron barriers without a special access point, right? In the hotel, he'd let them in to try to prove his innocence. We could set up this entire building like that—and obviously we wouldn't let the less powerful beings in. It'd make the story that I'm gathering my forces to take down the big baddies more plausible too. We'd make the protections strong enough to ward off all but particularly powerful shadowkind. If they wanted to get at me, they'd *have* to come themselves."

Crag frowned. "That'll make it hard for all of us to protect you in there."

"If the trap works the way it's supposed to, I won't need anyone protecting me. As soon as they come into the building, we can activate it, and it'll kill them all on its own."

Talking so casually about slaughtering another living being—even mostly immortal beings like the shadowkind—sent another jab of nausea through me. But then I thought of the man we'd found dead in the alley, of the toddler slaughtered in that sorcerer house near Boston, of the being last night who'd thanked me for freeing her from them.

These two monsters were threatening all of us. Something had to be done about them. And if we were in the best position to do it, then it was up to us not to let the rest of the world down.

"It sounds like you have your mind made up," Rollick said in a ghost of his usual breezy tone. "And you figure you're going to set all this up while recovering from a near-fatal disembowelling?"

I glowered at him. "Get me back to your apartment, bring me a sketchpad and my laptop—you can keep the wifi password to yourself, I don't need the internet—and I'll have a blueprint worked out within twenty-four hours." I paused. "And then most of the rest will be up to the four of you."

"Until you have to go into the trap to lure them after you," Lance said discontentedly.

I set my jaw. "Yes. Until then."

CHAPTER TWENTY-FIVE

Lance

It was a strange kind of tricksy, pretending to be sneaky while actually trying to catch other beings' attention. I slunk through the shadows as if I intended to avoid getting noticed, weaving to the side here and there, glancing at the houses and sprawling lawns all around me regularly. But I'd purposefully never gotten too far ahead of the being that'd been tracking me since shortly after I'd left Los Angeles. I could sense it at the very edge of my awareness, just distant enough that it was believable I might have missed it.

It needed to think I was on a special secret mission. That my woman, my friends, and I didn't want it knowing what I was up to. Because if it realized our whole plan was for it to overhear the message I was going to deliver, it would know this was part of a trap.

Rollick had shown me the sorcerers' house on a map, although my memory of the paper landscape didn't seem to have much in common with the paved terrain I was crossing over. I knew what direction I had to go in, though. And with each mile I crossed, the apprehension prickling over my skin dug deeper.

I didn't want to be anywhere near the mortals who warped shadowkind minds. I didn't want to tell them anything, even if it wasn't really for their benefit.

But I wanted the brutes who'd been threatening Quinn and so much else in this world gone even more. So I kept going, keeping up my ruse of caution.

Thankfully, I didn't have to get too close to the actual sorcerers. Like most, they had their own minions lurking around in a wide radius around their home, watching for threats. This family was less isolated than others we'd dealt with, living in a quiet stretch of widely-spaced homes that Quinn had called a "suburb." Rollick said they were hiding in plain sight, which didn't make a whole lot of sense to me. How was it hiding if people could see you?

In any case, they had creatures staked out in the shadows well before I could catch so much as a glimpse of their actual house. I could tell the one under a mailbox was a fierce but lesser being, unable to convey my message for me. I veered away from her until I came across the next sentry, this one a young-feeling nymph in the shade of a vast tree.

I paused several feet away from it and postured a bit both to get its attention and to give my follower time to catch up. The nymph shivered when it noticed me, but it slunk a little closer to the edge of the tree's shadow.

"Go away," it told me. "No shadowkind should come this way."

"You're here," I couldn't help pointing out. "I have a message to give to some people who live nearby."

"I'm not supposed to let anyone pass," the nymph insisted, but I could taste the tension in the air with its movements. It was struggling against the hold of their magic, the power propelling the words from its mouth, and failing to free itself. If I pushed the issue, its orders might compel it to try to fight me—a battle it wouldn't win. Or maybe it'd just run to warn its masters.

My skin itched even more at the thought. This being should be roaming around as freely as I could now, but instead the sorcerers had forced it into their service. Did it get any enjoyment at all out of its life? A memory flickered up of how it'd felt when that kind of power had locked around my mind, caging me from the inside out, and I held back a shudder.

And here I was using its state for my own benefit.

For good reasons, I reminded myself, and forced out the words. "I think the people I need to give the message to might be the ones you work with. You protect some sorcerers, don't you?"

The nymph gave me a narrow look. "I won't speak of that."

"Fine. You can speak to them about what I'm going to tell you. There's a new sorcerer in Los Angeles, one who's gathering enough power to challenge two very powerful shadowkind beings who've been killing other sorcerers and bending our kind to their will. She's building up her strength to enslave them herself, but that'll take a lot of her power, so she's hoping to get help from other sorcerers to deal with their minions."

"Why should anyone help *your* sorcerer?" the nymph muttered.

"Because otherwise these beings will probably kill all the sorcerers out there. Quinn is going to stop them. It'll just be faster with your masters' help. Tell them, and let them decide. They can find her in the building where she's preparing for the battle and stockpiling her resources."

I rattled off the address I'd memorized, slow and clear the way Torrent had reminded me to. It was very important that not just the being in front of me but the lackey who'd trailed me this far heard exactly where Quinn would be—exactly where we wanted those massive beasts to come looking for her.

Not yet. It wasn't quite ready yet. But Rollick's people were already hard at work following the design Quinn had worked out. He thought it would only take a few more days. It wouldn't be until it was ready that she'd walk in there, and by then we hoped that our enemies would be watching, waiting for the chance to strike.

But we'd be the ones who'd strike out at them.

My claws flexed at the thought, bolstering my determination despite my discomfort seeing this enslaved being. I dipped my head to him, hoping he understood that I wished for his freedom too. "Please let them know. Whether they come or not is up to them."

Then I hurried back the way I'd come, still acting like I wanted to dart away before anyone else realized what I was up to.

The images of the nymph's shiver and the tension wound through its presence dogged me as I rushed through the streets and across the countryside beyond as fast as I could. On the highway, I leapt into the shadows on a passing bus and sped off before my follower would have any hope of tracing me back to the apartment where Quinn was currently staying. I didn't need him watching me any longer.

When I made it back to the apartment, still slinking through the patches of darkness throughout the building, I passed Crag in the stairwell. He nodded to me without emerging from his own shadowy state. He was standing guard while Rollick oversaw the construction of the trap and Torrent reached out to a couple of other sorcerer families.

I found Quinn in the living room, curled up on the sofa, frowning at the blueprints on her computer. I dropped onto the cushion next to her and lifted her feet onto my lap where I could stroke my claws over them. "Is there something wrong?"

"No." She sighed and set the device aside. "I'm just triple-checking that I've thought of everything. The engineer Rollick talked to made some tweaks. I think it's really going to work. As long as we can get the big bads in there to begin with."

She pushed herself a little more upright with just a hint of a wince. My claws curled toward my palms, away from her skin, even though I knew I hadn't provoked that response.

I wanted to find the being that'd dug his own claws into her and eviscerate him all over again. Shred him into itty bitty pieces. The sight of the blood gushing from her side in the dimness of the night flashed through my mind, and my fangs sprang from my gums of their own accord.

She was much better now, able to walk around the apartment on her own and only showing a little pain now and then, partly with the help of the pills Rollick had gotten for her. But I knew how close she'd come to dying. I knew she would have died if the others hadn't leapt into the fray as soon as they did. I hadn't been able to protect her from that onslaught all on my own.

It wasn't my fault. No being could have fended off a whole army alone. But thinking about it still chilled all the fire that normally coursed through my body.

How long would it take before she could move around as swiftly and gracefully as before her injury? Would the scar on her side ever completely heal? Last night I'd given it another several swipes with my tongue, bathing it in dragon saliva, but the skin had remained a bumpy peach shade against the rest of her pale abdomen.

There was one other thing I could offer her that might at least improve her spirits. "I delivered the message I was supposed to—and one of the sorcerer-killers' minions was definitely spying on me. *They'll* get the message too."

"Oh, good," Quinn said, and then studied me more carefully. I smiled at her, but my insides still felt wobbly after the mission I'd just carried out.

Our woman didn't miss very much. She knew us so well.

Her brow knit. "I'm sorry. I'm sure it wasn't easy for you going that close to where you know sorcerers are living—or talking with a being they've captured."

I shrugged. "It needed to be done, so I did it. Now it's over." But her sympathy struck a chord in me, bringing out a peal of longing. I leaned closer and eased all of her onto my lap. Tucking her close against my chest, I buried my face in her soft hair and drank in her fresh, tangy-sweet scent.

Quinn slipped her arm around me and hugged me in return. "I'm sorry that I put you through that kind of magic again too. I know I said it before, but I want you to know how much I mean it. I was just so worried about you—but it was a mistake. A horrible mistake."

"I know you were trying to stop me from being hurt, not to hurt me," I told her, but a tremor ran through my body even as I spoke. Having *her* strange energy rippling through me, stealing my will and compelling my limbs, had been its own kind of horror. I wished I didn't have to connect that experience to her, but there was no getting away from the fact that she was the one who'd caused it.

"It'll never happen again," she said, so firmly her voice reverberated into me from where her face was tipped against my shoulder. "I promise you I'll never use my power on you for any reason. And when this is over, when that monstrous duo is dealt with, I won't use it again on anyone at all."

I wouldn't have asked her to go that far, to completely shun the power she'd found in herself, but the words sent a rush of relief through me. I hugged her tighter. "I know you wouldn't do bad things with it."

"It's a bad power," she said. "It comes out of hurting beings that don't deserve it. I'm going to try to force whatever other sorcerers have survived the battle to stop too. No one deserves to go through what you did."

And this was why I could still hold her now despite what she'd done, still take comfort in the feel of her against me, still want more than anything to absorb every smile and laugh she could offer. Her love for *me* rang through her voice and into me, right down to my bones. I meant that much to her, when I'd never meant much of anything to anyone before.

So I needed to do whatever I could to preserve the most special being who'd ever entered my life.

I glanced toward the kitchen and scooped Quinn up. I couldn't carry her quite as deftly as the gargoyle managed to with his vast arms, but it wasn't much strain bringing her over to the stools by the kitchen island. As I set her down on one, she raised her eyebrows at me. "What are you up to?"

I grinned at her, more freely this time. "You need to keep your strength up, baby girl, and I'm going to make sure you do. It's just about lunch time, isn't it? Let me know what you'd like me to slice and dice or charbroil, and I'll make it happen."

And I wouldn't let myself think about what might happen if this plan went wrong and none of us could save her after all.

CHAPTER TWENTY-SIX

Quinn

I adjusted the leather belt around my waist, making sure it didn't dig into the still slightly tender spot above my hip where my wound had mostly healed. I wanted to balance the pouches that held my crossbow ammo on either side so they didn't throw off my equilibrium if I needed to move quickly.

Never had I been more grateful for the reflexes I'd honed wandering around abandoned and supposedly inaccessible urban terrain for the past several years.

And hurray for shadowkind healing powers too. I doubted I'd have been feeling anywhere near as limber as I did with regular human medical treatment rather than Lance's supernatural breath and tongue. Other than when I got the occasional twinges of pain, I could mostly forget I'd been sliced wide open a week ago.

I took a stroll around the apartment's bedroom, getting comfortable with the belt on. In just a few hours, I was supposed to make my debut at the old factory-building-turned-monster-trap that Rollick's people had just put the finishing touches on.

We didn't know if the villainous duo would turn up right away. It could be a while before they came hunting me. But my men had noticed other beings spying on the area from the shadows. Rollick had been careful to ensure they'd get no glimpse of what was going on inside the building, but they knew we were up to something big there. The two sorcerer-killers would hear the moment I was seen entering.

Hopefully I wouldn't need to shoot them or any other beings anyway. Hopefully I'd be able to dash out via the trap's human escape route before I was in any significant danger. But I intended to go in prepared for worst case scenarios, and my men definitely hadn't been arguing about that. Although they'd have preferred if I hadn't needed to be there at all.

It'd been hard enough staying hidden and recovering when I knew the duo's minions were still out there attacking more humans across the city every night, when they were conducting more sacrifices at the rift for who knew what awful purpose. But getting spotted and cut down before the plan was ready might have doomed so many more people.

My men had been intervening and preventing the attacks as much as they could, both to reduce the carnage and to put the pressure on our enemies. The behemoth and the leviathan needed to believe that me and my "army" of shadowkind posed a real threat to their plans.

I undid the belt bucket and set it on the armchair in the corner, thinking I might lie down for a bit to settle my nerves before it was time to go. But before I'd made it to the bed, a jolt of intense emotion that wasn't mine socked me in the chest.

It was a sharp, ragged burst of anger. My head jerked toward the door, knowing that if I was picking up on Rollick's inner state, especially this intensely, he had to be nearby. I hadn't realized he'd gotten back to the apartment, but shadowkind didn't typically make a whole lot of noise with their comings and goings.

Had our plan been ruined somehow? Had something happened to one of the other men? I pushed past the door and hurried into the living room.

"What's going on?" I demanded the moment I spotted Rollick standing by the sofa, his back to me. "What's wrong?"

Rollick turned slowly, revealing his phone clutched in his hand. His grip was loosening, but his knuckles were pale as if he'd been gripping it tightly a second ago. He'd composed his expression into casual bemusement, his eyebrows arching with a quizzical look. "What makes you so sure that something's wrong?"

"I—I just had a feeling." I tipped my head toward his phone. "Did you get some bad news? Is everyone okay?"

"The three mutinists you're so enamored with are just fine," Rollick said, still studying me. "And 'just having a feeling' doesn't explain why you burst into the room like the place was on fire. You're not the type to jump at, well, shadows. *Something* set you off. I think you'd better tell me what."

I swallowed thickly. If I'd realized that revealing my concern would take us down this path, I would have reined myself in, pretended to only notice something might be bothering the demon after I'd greeted him.

But then, maybe he deserved to know. A flicker of guilt rippled through my gut at the thought of how long I'd been hiding our connection from him. Of course, he'd forced it on me in the first place. But I understood why. And I no longer saw him as someone I'd need a secret advantage against.

We were on the same side in every possible way now.

I couldn't help folding my arms over my chest in a defensive stance as if to ward off any criticism. "I—When you fed me your essence, I started sensing how you were feeling. It faded afterward, but with any strong emotions, if you're nearby, I still get a taste of them. And just now you were feeling very angry about something."

Rollick blinked at me. He kept his expression nonchalant, but he couldn't obscure the tremor of uneasiness my revelation had stirred up. It wasn't surprising he'd react like that—I'd known him for long enough to realize how much he prized his ability to hold his cards close. It couldn't sit well with him that I had a direct inside line to his deepest feelings.

"Well," he said. "I thought the sharing of energies might encourage some sort of bond of trust, but I'll admit that wasn't exactly what I had in mind. I guess I should be glad that you haven't picked up on anything that's sent you running for the hills all over again."

He didn't even ask why I hadn't told him right away. Maybe that was as obvious as his own preference for discretion. I wet my lips and dared to press the point. "So what were you angry about? What's the matter?"

For a few seconds, I thought he might not answer. Then he sighed and glanced at his phone before stuffing it into his pocket. "The bastards know that I'm still helping you. They're clearly peeved about that fact. I just got word that they've completely destroyed the Sunshine Sin Hotel."

His hotel here in LA—the one where I'd stayed for ten days while we started to figure out where we stood with one another. The business he'd set up to help shadowkind enjoy the mortal realm while protecting the mortals they mingled with, the current addition to his millennia-long legacy.

My stomach twisted. Even when I hadn't trusted Rollick at all, I'd been able to see how much the hotel meant to him. "Destroyed as in…?"

He kept a flippant tone. I didn't know whether he was trying to convince himself or me—or possibly both of us—that he didn't really care. "As in reduced to rubble. It was a little damaged after the fight there, but nothing I couldn't have patched up within a few days. Now I'd have to rebuild it from the ground up."

My heart sank. "I'm sorry. That was a low blow."

"They haven't been the most sportsmanlike of opponents in general. I'm not even really surprised." Rollick gave a dismissive wave of his hand. "The news disturbed me on first hearing it, but I've rebuilt hundreds of times over. I'll take this as a sign that it was time to set down new roots."

"You don't have to pretend to be okay with it," I said.

"I'm not pretending. When you've been alive for thousands of years, it takes a lot to really get under your skin." He stepped closer, still studying my face. "I'm more interested in the fact that you noticed that a very powerful demon in your presence was enraged, and your first instinct was to come running *toward* me."

I rolled my eyes at him. "I knew you wouldn't hurt *me*."

The words spilled out into the air, and it was only as I heard myself saying them that I registered just how momentous they were.

Rollick's eyes sparked with a rush of pure delight. "Is that so?" he purred, stalking closer, his mouth curving into a sly grin. "Not a single shred of fear left for the mighty demon?"

I gazed back at him with my chin high as he paused just inches away from me, standing nearly a foot taller than my average height. But there was nothing menacing about his loom. The force of his nearness sent a heady tingle all through my veins.

I held myself back from reaching for him to pull him the last short distance to me. "Nope," I said. "I've seen who you are. I know why you do what you do. I know you'd sooner take on the kind of fiends who could challenge the strongest warriors from the shadow realm alone than put me in harm's way, if you have the choice. What's there to be afraid of?"

Rollick let out a low chuckle. He brushed his fingertips over my cheeks with the faintest scrape of the claws he'd let loose. "You make me sound so tamed. I do have a reputation to uphold."

The corner of my own lips quirked upward as my whole body thrummed with anticipation. "I'm not saying you're not a monster. Only that I know you'll be one for me, not to me." Just as I would be for the ones I cared about.

I paused, desire coursing deeper inside me. I could have this now—I could have *him*. And depending on what happened tonight, I might never get another chance.

I wet my lips and added, "Maybe unless I ask nicely?"

The new light that glinted in the demon's eyes was all heat. He bowed his head toward mine. "And what are you asking for right now, sweet sorcerer?"

There seemed to be no possible answer other than the words that bubbled up my throat. "Show me what it's like to be taken by a demon."

A soft growl escaped Rollick's throat, and then he was surging forward, his form shifting as he did. He caught me up in arms already bulging with more muscle as his dress shirt fell away, lifting me both with his grasp and the spurt of height that shot him at least another foot taller. His dark eyes glittered at me like embers amid the sharp angles of his ruddy, monstrous face.

He strode into the bedroom so fast the door hinges squealed at the shove and set me down in the middle of the bed. Then he braced himself over me in all his demonic glory, his lips pulling back in a smile that showed off his pointed teeth.

I couldn't resist the sight of his horns, sprouting in their graceful curves from his temples. As he opened his mouth to speak, I reached up to trace one hand along the smoothly spiraled surface, and Rollick's breath caught around whatever he'd been going to say. Instead, he leaned in and captured my mouth with a searing kiss.

He had a smoky taste I hadn't been able to savor quite so intently when he'd joined me with my other men before. I'd been too focused on his outward reactions then. Now, I drank in the flavor of him with every movement of my lips, wanting to get as high on him as I had when he'd fed me his essence. Except this time, I'd have thrown myself into that wild delirium willingly.

I might die a few hours from now or be injured beyond even Lance's ability to repair. I'd found something strange but wonderful with all of my monstrous men, and I hadn't really gotten to appreciate everything the demon could offer yet. If there was one thing I'd believed in since I'd needed my transplant, it was squeezing every bit of joy out of life that I could while I had the chance.

Rollick deepened the kiss with a flick of his tongue around mine. He dipped his body closer so the heat of his massive demon body wrapped around me, but I could tell he was being careful not to press too firmly in case he aggravated my mostly-healed wound. A weird thread of tenderness wove through my hunger. The emotion flooding me from him was all eager desire.

"And what can you sense from me now, my sorcerer?" he murmured as he kissed the edge of my jaw and then my neck.

I shivered with my own eagerness. My voice came out husky. "I sense that you want me just as much as I want you."

He made a rough sound in his throat even as he smiled against my skin, and teased the sharp tips of his teeth down to the crook of my shoulder, drawing giddying lines across my skin. At my whimper, he nibbled my shoulder a little more forcefully while his hands slid my shirt—and the silver-threaded undershirt he'd had made for me, as promised—partway up my ribcage.

He licked my collarbone and gave my shirt a momentary glower. "I'm looking forward to a time when I can spread you naked and enjoy all of you like the delicacy you are. For now, I'll just have to work with the territory I have access to."

Easing to one side, Rollick lifted my arm and pressed a kiss to my palm. He nibbled his way over the heel of my hand, across my wrist, and down the inside of my arm, until the movement of his lips against the sensitive skin had me quivering. When he reached the short sleeve of my shirt, he reached for my other hand.

By the time he'd worshipped both of my arms, my panties were drenched and I was swallowing whimpers. Then in one swift movement, he dropped to the skin he'd cleared on my belly.

The demon kissed and licked and sucked at every inch of my lower abdomen, grazing me with his teeth here and there, trailing his claws up and down my sides. When a gasp burst from my throat, he smirked up at me.

"I've barely even gotten started on the good parts."

Having seen his reaction the first time I'd touched one of his horns, I curled my fingers around both of them now. As I stroked them up and down from the base to the tips and back again, Rollick gave a little shudder with a waft of his own giddy enjoyment.

He yanked my shorts and panties down and dappled kisses across my hips, leaning into my caresses here and there. Then, with a faint noise of consternation, he pulled lower, tugging my clothes completely off.

This time, he started at my feet. He kissed the soles and my ankles, charted every curve of my calves and thighs with his short claws, nipped the undersides of my knees, and breathed close enough to the apex of my thighs that I moaned in frustration.

"Have I not quite satisfied you yet?" he teased.

"Rollick," I growled, grasping his horns again.

He hummed with a mix of amusement and pleasure and lowered his head between my legs.

The first swipe of his tongue over my cunt had me shuddering. He knew exactly the right pressure and pace to have my clit pulsing in a matter of seconds, my pussy gushing with arousal to the point that it would have been embarrassing if he hadn't lapped up the reaction to his attentions so enthusiastically.

Retracting his claws, he slid a finger between my folds to swirl inside me in a slow circle, stretching my inner walls. When I rocked into his touch, he chuckled before sucking on my clit again. Bliss swelled all through my core.

"I need to get you ready for all of me," he said. "If you want to be taken by the demon, you're going to need to be ready for both of my dicks."

The moan that spilled out of me at the next swivel of his tongue was nothing but approval. He spread the slickness seeping from my slit down to my other opening and then tucked a finger into that entrance as well.

More pleasure quivered through me. With a strangled sound, I pushed into his touch.

"So impatient, lovely mortal. But you're right—I don't want to hurt you. I want you to get nothing out of this encounter but the highest of pleasures. So we'll do this right."

He pumped his fingers in and out of me, rotating them in expanding circles as he did. His lips closed around my clit, and then he brushed the edges of his teeth over it, and all at once I careened over my peak. Bliss rushed through my body in a wave. I rocked with it, letting out a sob that was nothing but joyful.

"Hmm. A very good start." Rollick crawled up over me again, tucking my legs around his hips. I trailed my hands down his sculpted chest to the two cocks jutting down below, one right above the other.

The first twitched at my grip. I slid my fingers up and down it a few times experimentally, and the demon let out a muted snarl. But he didn't stop me from reaching lower and stroking the other one too. That one had already beaded with a thick precum that glided over both his shafts under my exploring fingers with a consistency not much different from the lube Torrent had confiscated. He was obviously built for penetrating multiple holes at once.

The discovery sent a quiver of delight through me. I spread my legs wider and teased my hands back up Rollick's body to grasp his shoulders. "I need you."

The words set off a flare of contentment in the demon that I didn't have time to consider too closely, because the next moment, he was sliding into me, both dicks in their separate openings simultaneously.

At the heady rush of being penetrated both ways in tandem, my head tipped back into the pillow with a cry. As Rollick pushed deeper, the blissful burn spread all through my body. My breath broke into panting.

Even in the haze of pleasure, I couldn't help remembering how the demon had promised he'd have me like this—willingly—one day, back when I'd recoiled from the thought. My hand tightened around his shoulder, the other rising to caress one of his horns again. "Is this... how you thought it would happen?"

Rollick plunged the rest of the way into me with a groan. He held there, claiming a kiss and then bowing his head next to mine.

"No," he said quietly. "This is much better. This is something I didn't know I could even aim for."

Then he began to move again, thrusting in and out with quickly increasing speed. His renewed claws curled against my side, my hip, and my thigh in time with his rhythm. His tail swooped around his own hips so the tufted tip could trace its own delightful trails across my skin.

"Oh, God," I mumbled. My second orgasm was building so swiftly I couldn't do anything but clutch onto Rollick. He thrust into me deeper, angling himself so the base of his upper cock brushed my clit. His shafts pounded in and out of me, filling me with bliss again and again, sending me spiraling higher and higher until everything around me was a searing mist of pleasure—

And then ecstasy crackled through me twice as hard, my pussy clamping around one of his cocks, my body arching. Rollick slipped his hand under my back to press me to him and stole one last kiss with a groan as he came with me. His release sent a fresh flood of delight through me that had me shuddering and gasping all over again.

He lowered his head so his forehead rested against mine, his breath only slightly broken. A glow of satisfaction radiated from him into me. I slung my arms around his neck in a loose embrace that was the best I could offer in my current bonelessly sated state.

"Well," I said, "I really hope I don't die tonight, because I'd like to do that again sometime."

I'd meant to make Rollick laugh, but he tensed, his happiness vanishing with a surge of fiery protectiveness. "If they get to you, it'll only be over *my* dead body."

I gazed up at him, somehow still startled by the proclamation—and horrified by the thought of him losing his life over me, no matter how willing he might be to give it.

"Let's hope it doesn't come to that, then."

His lips curled into a tight but affectionate smile. "Yes, let's."

As if we'd have a whole lot of choice in the matter.

CHAPTER TWENTY-SEVEN

Rollick

Quinn didn't show an inclination to leave the bed, and we didn't need to head out of the apartment for a couple more hours anyway. So I lay there next to her, absorbing the sensation of her body unwinding in my arms.

After those couple of hours, she'd have to tense up again to meet the threat we'd called down on us. But for now, she deserved all the peace I could offer her.

It was a strange thought—that I might be bringing *peace*. The momentary contentment that had settled over me was equally unfamiliar. I provoked passion and pleasure, excitement as well as horror when I needed to, but quieter emotions weren't generally my domain.

How much could she sense of my inner state right now? She'd said it was only strong emotions that she picked up on, but I had no idea where the threshold might be.

She had a direct line to my soul, whatever I had of one. It'd be a trial trying to hide anything from her from now on. But even though I'd recoiled from the idea of her reading my inner state when she'd first told me, my instinctive discomfort had faded.

I didn't want to hide anything else from her. After everything she'd been through—everything I'd had a hand in putting her through—the least she deserved from me was honesty. I couldn't promise the truth would always or even usually be pleasant, but I could give it to her.

The connection I hadn't known I'd forged might even have worked in my favor. Would she have trusted me as much as she appeared to now without it? Would she have believed that my attempt to give her life back was genuine and not a ploy?

Somehow she had come to me, on her terms rather than mine, and I couldn't have said I'd have preferred it any other way.

I didn't like how small she felt next to my demonic body—how breakable. I stroked my fingers down her side, skimming the edge of scar tissue where the dragon shifter had done his best to heal her. My dignity insisted that I keep my tone wry rather than revealing the full extent of my concern. "I hope you didn't strain anything during that workout."

Quinn laughed and snuggled closer to me, which I liked far too much for my dignity to have any hope at all. "I have no complaints."

"Good. Because I have a reputation to keep up there too."

She tipped her head to look up at me, her sky-blue eyes thoughtful but not worried. "You have gotten around quite a bit, haven't you? You've kind of mentioned it a lot. Is that—are you going to be hooking up with other people too? I mean, when there's much of a chance once we've dealt with all the problems we're facing right now. I obviously can't complain about it when I'm with three other men, but... it would be good to know."

So she could decide how invested or not to get in me? I had no doubt that my three former employees had completely devoted themselves to her. Picturing them with her, even after having joined in that group love-fest once, set off a brief flare of jealousy in my chest.

But I couldn't have her all to myself. She'd made that abundantly clear... and when I thought with my head instead of my dicks and my monstrous impulses, which was part of what had kept me alive this long, I couldn't see it as a bad thing. Possessing her for myself but in the faded, melancholy state she'd fallen into with their absence wouldn't be any kind of victory.

A different instinct gripped me: to be noncommittal, to leave a touch of uncertainty to keep her on her toes. But I didn't really want her on her toes either. I wanted her sure. If I was going to share her with three other beings, I didn't want any chance of her thinking I was the spare she could cast aside.

"I've had millennia to experiment and spread my talents around," I informed her. "A little monogamy might be a nice change of pace." I paused, grappling with how to express the rest of it without rubbing her mortality too much in her face. "I don't know how long I'll get to enjoy your company, so I intend to savor as much of it as possible as long as you'll bestow it on me."

My formal phrasing brought out another light laugh, but her expression had softened. No doubt she was aware enough of her uncertain lifespan without any reminders to fill in the blanks.

I'd already lived more than a hundred times longer than she might survive in this world. What could I possibly lose by focusing on her for such a short part of *my* life when that was all I'd get of her?

The thought of losing her made me want to bare my teeth with a snarl. But the greatest threat to her survival might not even be the menaces we'd go up against soon but that borrowed heart beating in her chest. I couldn't fight it into doing right by her.

If there was some way I could ensure she got as full a life as any mortal should, I'd see it happen.

A glint of mischief lit in Quinn's eyes. She cocked her head. "I suppose we're all one happy family now. You mentioned that you've been involved with men before. Have you ever thought about propositioning my other three?"

I should have seen that question coming. I chuckled and tucked one claw under her chin. "None of them is really my type. And I doubt any of them would want to be diverted from you anyway. But you don't need to worry. Somehow I doubt that I'll ever get bored while I'm with you."

Quinn huffed. "I never thought I'd say this, but I wouldn't mind a little less excitement following me around. Or at least if it was of the less deadly variety."

"We'll see if we can't set you on that path tonight."

I kissed her, hard and long enough to draw one of those lovely, eager sounds from her throat, but my heart wasn't totally in it. The conversation had stirred up too much apprehension about the job ahead of us. When I released her, I sat up, contracting my demon body into my typical human form.

"I should call in the others so we can hash out the final details. We don't want to leave any possibility unconsidered."

"Of course." Quinn pushed herself upright with a stretch and scrambled out of bed. As she pulled her clothes back on, I stalked into the living room with my phone in my hand.

Torrent had agreed to check for messages from me regularly, and while he might have played the traitor before, he was generally good to his word. He answered my beckons right away, and within half an hour had rounded up the gargoyle and the dragon shifter and returned with them to the apartment.

We gathered in the living room, Quinn with her crossbow already in hand and the custom belt I'd commissioned slung around her waist. She didn't look small or breakable now. No mortal would have stood a chance against the resolve she possessed. If the contraption she'd designed worked as intended, no shadowkind would either.

"Have you seen any new activity monitoring the streets around the building?" I asked the others.

"The minions are still watching it," Lance said with a click of his claws. "Waiting for us to put on our show." He grinned. "I think we're going to like it a lot more than they will, though."

"I haven't sensed either of the bosses nearby," Crag put in. "I think they must be keeping their distance until they hear more from their followers."

Torrent nodded. "After the moves we've already made against them, it's unsurprising that they're being cautious. But they've also seen how far we'll go to interfere with their plans. I can't imagine that they're *not* concerned about what else Quinn might have up her sleeve."

"They wouldn't have their lackeys watching the building so closely otherwise." I rubbed my chin, contemplating the best opening strategy, but Quinn spoke first.

"Has there been any sign of the sorcerers we reached out to?" she asked quietly. "Have any of them turned up looking for me?"

The three exchanged a look I could instantly read. But they appeared to be as dedicated to honesty as I'd newly become, at least when it involved our shared lover.

"A woman who we believe was from one of those families was found dead in an attack near the city limits a couple of nights ago," Torrent said, his tone as even as usual but with a gentle note to it. "If we'd known she was on her way, we'd have done our best to guard her..."

Quinn's face tightened. Then she let out a sigh. "I guess she was in almost as much danger staying where she was. Only one of them was willing to risk coming out here to help? This plan might have been easier to pull off if they'd work with us on this one thing."

I grimaced. "It's possible that the enclave in Norway has spread out a warning about you through the wider community. A not very accurate one, of course, but sorcerers aren't much for socializing outside their trusted allies anyway."

Quinn squared her shoulders. "That's fine. We weren't counting on them helping. Is there anything else we need to go over before I make my grand entrance?"

I glanced at the other men. "I think it's best if the three of you stay outside the building. The amount of silver and iron in that place will weaken even you quickly. We need you at your best. My suggestion would be that Lance and Torrent monitor opposite sides of the place and take down any minions these fiends send into the building—as many as you can. If we can avoid anyone getting in other than the main duo, that would be best."

I turned to the gargoyle. "Crag, since you're the most able to identify other beings at a distance, you could patrol a little farther abroad to sense when the villains are approaching and give the rest of us a warning." My lips slanted into a crooked smile. "That's how I'd handle it, at least. I'm well aware that none of you are obliged to follow my orders at this point."

Lance let out a little hiss, clearly unsettled by having to protect our woman from a distance rather than right beside her, but he didn't argue. Torrent inclined his head. "That all sounds reasonable to me. And you'll be Quinn's last line of defense against whatever does breach the walls?"

"Yes. I've been inside the building multiple times. I won't *enjoy* it, but it shouldn't hamper my abilities too much." I cast my gaze toward Quinn. "Assuming you're fine with all of that too."

She nodded immediately. "I don't think we should weaken ourselves any more than we absolutely have to. But—the secret exit has the chime we talked about built into it, right? Everyone else will know when I've left so they can meet me there?"

"I've tested it myself," I assured her. The last thing I'd want was for her to dart out into the street and fall prey to a horde of other minions right outside.

"I'll have returned to the building by then," Crag said. "I'll stay close to the back door so that I can grab you as soon as you're out."

"Perfect." I clapped my hands. "I think we're all set. Why don't the three of you get into position, and I'll escort Quinn over once you've had time to prepare yourselves?"

Torrent and then Crag and then Lance each stepped toward Quinn to offer her a tight embrace and a kiss. More jealousy flickered in my chest, but it passed in a moment as I saw how she beamed back at them, bolstered by their affection.

The dragon shifter held her for the longest, as if he thought if he kept hugging her he might just not have to stop. He finally dragged himself away, started to turn to follow the others, and jerked back toward her with a flash of determination crossing his golden face.

"Wait," he said. "Before we go out there, I think there's something Quinn should do first."

CHAPTER TWENTY-EIGHT

Quinn

Lance looked so resolute, his violet eyes both bright and hard, that my stomach flipped over. His words reverberated through my head. *There's something Quinn should do first.*

"What?" I asked. "Anything you need, just ask." It was bad enough having to watch them go out there ready to do battle on my behalf where I'd have no way of helping them or even knowing what they were going through. If I could make their fight easier, I'd do it in an instant. But the dragon shifter didn't look exactly *happy* about whatever he was going to say.

A little twitch ran through his stance, making me even more sure that he was uneasy about his suggestion. But he flicked his tongue over his lips and put on a smile that was only a little forced.

"We know the big baddies are supposed to be coming to get you. We know how much sorcery they have that they could use on us. When their beasties are compelled by them, it's harder for you to hook them with your own magic. So… I think you should give us some kind of command. With sorcery. That'll go against anything they might want us to do."

I stared at him, losing my breath in shock. "You *want* me to use my sorcery on you?"

He held my gaze, still tense but not backing down. "It wouldn't be to control us. You could tell us to do something we'd have been doing anyway. It'd just be like a shield to stop their magic from getting in. Or at least make it harder."

Torrent sucked in a breath. "Lance does have a point. It wouldn't be perfect protection against them affecting us, but it could buy us enough time to get out of the way or take other precautions before their magic took hold."

Crag glanced at the others and then at me, his expression somber but unworried. "That makes sense to me."

Sure, it made sense the way the dragon shifter had put it. But nausea had coiled in my gut at the thought of aiming any of my power at these men again. Even if it was technically for their own good, what if the gambit misfired? What if I gave them an order that they'd end up needing to go against to protect themselves—or me?

"I don't know," I said slowly. "It seems pretty risky. I'm still getting the hang of how the magic works at all. We don't know exactly what you'll encounter out there or what tactics you might need to use. I don't want to force you into a situation where you can't defend yourself because of what *I* told you."

Rollick set his hand on my shoulder, tentative despite the intimacy we'd shared just an hour ago. "I'm sure we could come up with wording that allowed a lot of flexibility while still being a command in essence. If you want to be extra careful, you could skip me. I'll be inside the building with you beyond their reach anyway, but if something goes wrong, I'd be able to act quickly enough."

Even with that compromise, my stomach kept roiling. But a lot of that was my own guilt over using my power on these men against their will before. They were asking me now—they could use my protection. How could I say no?

I dragged in a breath. "All right. But we have to be *really* careful about what exactly I order you to do. Let's not rush this."

We spent the next half hour hashing out various wordings, debating some and discarding others immediately, tweaking the ones that seemed like the best bet, until I was finally satisfied. I'd been doing most of the vetoing, but my men hadn't shown any impatience. If anything, Lance still looked like he kind of wished he'd never suggested this strategy in the first place.

Still, he stepped in front of me first, his jaw tight. "You should put all the power you can into it. Each of us, one at a time. That'll give us the most possible defense."

He was probably right. I readied myself, reaching toward the now-familiar sizzle of energy rippling through my chest. It didn't take much coaxing to expand it and urge it up my throat. I fixed all my attention on Lance and the precise phrase we'd chosen.

Several syllables in the sorcery language tumbled out first as I focused on my intent, but with the men I was so close to, I was able to channel the energy into English words as well, just like in my earlier orders. "While I'm inside the building where we've laid our trap, you will prevent shadowkind beings from entering that building using tactics based on your best judgment, and refuse any orders given to you by the behemoth or the leviathan."

The command was open-ended enough that only a twinge of worry remained in my chest. I repeated it with Torrent and then turned to Crag, who needed a slightly different version with his separate duties. "You will keep watch for the behemoth and the leviathan approaching the building where we've laid our trap as long as you feel it's wise to do so, and you will refuse any orders given to you by those two beings."

"There," Rollick said, brushing his hands together. "That's settled. If it comes to sorcery against sorcery, I know who I'd place my bets on. Now get going without any more dawdling, the three of you."

Each of my men offered me one last swift embrace and then faded into the shadows. I paced the room, knowing they were racing across the city toward the factory while we waited. It wouldn't do us any good if I arrived before they were ready and faced an attack before we had all the pieces in place.

It felt like I'd been waiting forever when Rollick said, "That's enough time. Come on—let's get the car."

Nothing stirred in the underground garage as we walked to his sedan. I sank into the passenger seat with my crossbow on my lap and the ammo pouches on my belt clinking faintly. Dread wound all through my body.

"What if it doesn't work? What if we haven't done enough?" I really didn't know how much else we *could* have done, but that didn't guarantee success.

"Then we'll lick our wounds and come back stronger," Rollick said with his usual confident air. I didn't sense any deep concern or fear from him, so maybe he really was that sure of us. As he started the engine, he glanced over at me. "You've come a long way, and you already had one of the strongest wills I've ever encountered when I first met you. You're going to get through this."

His words from our bedroom interlude rose up like a ghost. If I didn't get through it, it'd only be because he'd fallen too.

Oh God, please let it not come to that.

The demon had carefully planned our route ahead of time. We wanted to be sure the villainous duo's spies saw me arriving, but we knew they most likely had orders to try to slaughter me before I could make it to the building when they did. He'd picked a car with tinted windows so I couldn't be identified from outside, and he parked right outside the door.

There, Rollick flicked through the shadows to emerge next to me the instant I stepped out of the car. In the few seconds it took for him to usher me across the sidewalk to the factory door like a bodyguard, I ran my fingers through my hair to toss it so it caught the late-afternoon sunlight to make sure my arrival was marked in the brief time I was visible.

My other men had noticed multiple minions keeping watch over the front door. They'd clearly spotted me as I'd hoped—and sprung into action even faster than expected. Just as I pushed open the door, a barrage of shadowy forms blinked into being in mid-pounce.

Rollick shoved me into the front hall and whipped around with a growl. Bodies thumped and whimpers of pain sounded behind me. As I spun toward the doorway, he slammed the door shut, only a few wisps of smoky essence wavering through the air before dissipating. He swiped his hands together. "Those beasties won't be making it past the barriers. The few that survived can go off to notify their masters now."

I exhaled shakily. So far so good.

Rollick locked the door for good measure, and we hurried past the factory's old office rooms to the big space farther back where we'd constructed our trap.

The room had once been forty feet long by thirty feet across with a ceiling some fifteen feet high. It'd shrunk quite a bit since Rollick's workers had built the additions called for in my designs.

Stark white lights blazed over us from various small but bright fixtures on the lowered ceiling, ensuring that any beings that made it this far inside wouldn't have shadows to hide in. The floor was the same scuffed linoleum it'd been before, marks showing where tables and conveyer belts had once been set up, but smooth gray walls surrounded us. You could barely make out the outlines of the slots that would pop out when the blades hidden behind them and the ceiling shot forward.

When the trap went off, any shadowkind within this space would find itself speared by a barrage of mechanized blades, each of them constructed out of melded silver and iron. Rollick had confirmed that they would do enough damage for even the most powerful being to quickly bleed out, if not die on impact.

Now we just needed to get at least one of our foes, ideally both, in here.

The place had the lingering new construction smell of sawdust and mechanical grease. It tickled my nose as I walked all the way to the back of the trap room with Rollick still trailing behind me.

Under more searing lights, there was a little booth built into the new walls there with a window where I could watch over the space like a foreman might have decades ago when the factory was still in regular use. A control panel with a large, red button was mounted right beside the door where I could smack it easily the second I needed to.

At the other end of the booth, a narrow passage led to the factory's original back door. The door was locked with a deadbolt and reinforced with so much silver and iron even Rollick wouldn't be able to exit that way unless I opened it for him.

I sank into the office chair set up in the booth and rested my crossbow on my lap. Rollick scanned our surroundings with a satisfied air. "Everything appears to be in order. Now it's time for the great camp-out. Aren't you lucky you have me for company to stop you from getting bored?"

He shot me a smirk, but I knew he was only teasing. I stretched out my legs. "I don't think we should get *too* distracted. Let's hope the creeps don't leave us waiting too long." If need be, there was a sleeping bag and some non-perishable food stashed in the booth's built-in cupboard, but I'd rather not have to resort to using them. Especially for multiple nights.

But who knew how cautious the villainous duo would be?

It'd only been about twenty minutes when the ping of Rollick's phone had me jerking upright with a jolt of adrenaline. He glanced at the screen, and his smile flattened. "More minions incoming. The poor bastards. Well, any of them who wanted to be in this fight of their own accord will get what they deserve."

The men outside were supposed to be dealing with the lackeys, and any lesser creatures wouldn't be able to make their way into the building to begin with. But we had no idea how many higher shadowkind would come. I stood up, rechecking the bolts in my crossbow, and moved to the main room where the lights were brightest. My heart thumped erratically in my chest, and suddenly I regretted my wish for the battle to come to us sooner rather than later.

The duo had obviously sent more powerful minions to try to drag me out of my protected space than my other men could handle all at once. But not many of even the higher shadowkind could handle the protections easily, even if they managed to slip inside through the shadows we couldn't totally eliminate beyond the main room. The first being that wavered into sight by the wall lurched at me with a clumsiness that showed how the metals embedded in the building had drained its strength.

A startled squeak broke from my throat, but I whipped up my crossbow and squeezed the trigger before its knobby fingers closed around me. The bolt hit the thing square in the throat. It flinched backward, and I shot it again in the middle of the forehead. That was enough for it to crumple, gushing essence.

There was a thump behind me at the same moment. I jerked around to see Rollick punching the head right off another two-legged being that'd leapt at my back. He crushed its ribs under his heel for good measure and then stalked over to pummel the other creature's skull into the floor.

"Can't risk them getting up again," he said, his voice cool but taut.

He'd barely finished speaking when two more beings materialized, leaping from the slots on the walls on either side of us. We each spun toward one, backs to each other in an instinctive protective pose.

The harpy-like woman who charged at me looked steadier on her feet than the first beings to make it through—a little stronger, a little less affected by the building's protections. But I was ready now, my nerves humming with determination and adrenaline, my reflexes honed. I shot her in the head and kicked her away from me as she stumbled.

As I yanked more bolts from the pouch at my hip to reload, Rollick gave the being he'd faced one last slash and sprang past me to ensure the harpy was gone from this world. He glanced over his shoulder at me, a gleam lighting in his eyes. "Not so hard. But it's a good thing you kept me with you to have your back."

The corner of my mouth twitched upward. Sometimes it was fun to take his ego down a peg, but not when I agreed with him so much. "Yeah, it is."

He smiled back at me, and for that moment, everything seemed okay.

Three more beings came at us, streaks of shadowy bodies racing across the floor and rising into physical form for their final lunge, and we tackled them with the same efficient teamwork. The swift pounding of my pulse steadied me rather than unnerving me now.

When we had a lull, I grabbed a drink of water from the bottle in the booth and then returned to wander carefully through the main space. I was on high alert now, my gaze twitching toward the slightest sound or movement, my finger hooked around the trigger. Rollick left his phone on the floor by the wall and prowled around the edge of the room in his demon form, his hooves rapping against the linoleum and his tail lashing.

My flow of adrenaline had ebbed when five monstrous forms rushed at us from different ends of the room.

I whirled around, shooting at one being and then another. In motion, it was hard for me to aim as well. I caught one in the shoulder, another in the side of the chest, the third in the gut. They staggered, one slumping to its knees, but the other two kept hurtling toward me.

Rollick's phone started to ping. He couldn't do anything about that or my oncoming attackers while he tore through one and then another of the beings at his end of the room.

I fumbled for more bolts while sorcerous energy crackled through me. Words I didn't know burst from my throat and smacked into the barrier of existing magic in the beings' heads. My power didn't quite crack it on the first try—and I didn't have time for a second before they were on me.

The one that looked like a skinny, patchy polar bear swung a massive paw at me, and I managed to dodge. I scrambled away, shoving one and another bolt into the crossbow. The third being I'd shot was heaving back onto its feet. Were they slowing down a little with the continued exposure to the silver and iron?

When I opened my mouth to attempt another sorcerous shout, the bear-ish one flung itself at me. I shot it in the underside of its jaw just as its claws raked across my arm. It collapsed on top of me, which might actually have worked in my favor, since it shielded me from its companions.

As I squirmed out from under it, the sounds of ripping flesh reached my ears. Rollick was carving his way through the rest of them, having an easier time of it with those I'd already wounded. I looked at the smoking remains scattered across the floor, shuddered, and clapped my hand to the talon marks on my upper arm.

Rollick was at my side in an instant. He couldn't seal the wounds with his breath like Lance, but he'd come otherwise prepared. He snapped back into human form for long enough to pull a roll of gauze from his pocket and wrap it tightly around my arm.

"Can you still handle the bow all right?" he asked.

"Yes," I said, the pain a distant throbbing compared to the renewed roar of tension and anticipation filling my head. "What was the text you got?"

Rollick swore and dashed to the device. He flicked through to the messages. "At least one of the head honchos on the move this way. Crag felt he'd better pull in to the entrance now."

"Okay." One was enough. Even taking down one half of the duo would diminish their power significantly. Then tackling the other wouldn't be so bad.

The thought had barely crossed my mind when the floor shook beneath my feet. There was a creaking sound followed by a drawn-out screech as if the building itself were being wrenched apart.

My pulse stuttered. My gaze shot to Rollick, who stepped closer to me, looming into his demon form again. He flexed his clawed fingers.

I felt it. The immense, ponderous presence that'd intruded on the sorcerer village in Utah and ravaged their bodies. Every nerve in my body twanged with alarm. But before I'd even seen it, a low groan of a voice reverberated across the walls.

It spoke in words I knew and yet didn't—and Rollick clapped one hand to his head. He reeled, his face contorting as if he were in pain.

"What's the matter?" I blurted out, but then understanding hit me like a smack of frigid water.

The being that'd come was using its sorcery on him, and the magic was starting to work.

If Rollick couldn't fight it off, I was as good as dead.

CHAPTER TWENTY-NINE

Quinn

My voice tore up my throat as I backed away from Rollick, my hand clutched unwillingly around my crossbow. "Listen to me, not him. You belong to *me*." At least, that's what I thought I was saying in the eerie syllables that spilled from my mouth with a rush of power.

But it didn't matter. The villain's magic was already fighting its way into the demon's brain, and my own power bounced off him like it had their minions.

Rollick clamped his other hand to his ruddy temple, his claws digging into his own skin to set off tiny plumes of smoky essence.

"No," he snarled under his breath. "You're not having me. *No*."

I hurled another command with my sorcery at him, but it didn't connect. At the same time, the thing at the front of the building gave another bellow that seemed to rock the demon on his feet. It must have been driving its influence in even farther.

Rollick's body swayed on his cloven hooves. A tremor ran through his body. He squeezed his eyes shut, his jaw flexing, the turmoil inside him as he struggled wafting from him into me.

I stood rigid, my crossbow half raised, my hand moving automatically to reload it again, although I found it hard to imagine shooting *him*.

This couldn't come to that, right? He was a millennia-old demon. Even if our opponent was a little more ancient, a little more powerful, sorcery wasn't its natural talent, only something it'd borrowed.

But then, you could say the exact same thing about me.

Rollick swung his head toward me. His penetrating eyes smoldered with rage... and what I knew was a flicker of fear. The most assured being I'd ever known wasn't totally sure he could fight this off.

"Go back to the booth," he rasped at me. "Get ready to do what you have to do once he's here. You shouldn't be near me like this. I—"

Another roared phrase echoed through the room, and Rollick snapped his mouth shut. I backed up toward the short hall with the booth, but my stomach twisted with queasiness.

Did he expect me to set off the trap with him still in the room? Why hadn't I cast my own sorcery on him ahead of time?

I would have if we'd known early enough that this fiend was on its way, but we'd been too caught up in the fighting—and I'd been too afraid of my powers to insist on that protection up front.

And my refusal to fully accept what I was and what I could do might mean the death of one of the men I'd come to care for in ways I'd once doubted were even possible.

I stopped by the entrance to the hallway, ready to bolt for the booth if Rollick turned on me, willing more of my sorcerer energy to swell up inside me with a surge of the newfound exhilaration it could bring. I'd broken the villainous duo's hold on other shadowkind—but this monster was pummeling Rollick with his influence right in front of me, far fresher than anything I'd shattered before.

It wasn't coming into the trap either, I realized. My sense of it still quivered over my skin with an unsettling tingle, but it hadn't pushed closer since I'd first felt it shoving into the building. The floor had stopped trembling, the walls stopped groaning.

It must suspect that I had something else up my sleeve. It was hoping to use my companion to finish me off where its own minions had failed.

Maybe I was focusing on the wrong monster here. The thing that was assaulting Rollick with its magic didn't have any sorcery on it for me to break. I didn't know it the way I did my men, but I'd compelled less powerful higher shadowkind.

I had to try.

I dragged in a breath and shouted toward the entrance of the building as forcefully as I could. The sorcerous words hurtled up my throat with a crackle of electricity. I focused all my attention on the vast, ominous presence at the front of the building.

Do as I say. Come toward me. Leave my companions alone.

For just a second, I thought I had it. I had the impression of my influence catching on the massive being like the tug of a fishing line when a fish has just taken the bait. But however much I'd hooked it, the next second, it slipped free, shaking off my energy.

My shoulders slumped, my chest heaving as I recovered from the effort I'd put into that spell. I'd thrown enough of myself into that command and the ones I'd aimed at Rollick that even the exhilaration of my enhanced magic was dwindling into exhaustion.

Rollick spun and staggered toward the side wall. He smacked his head into it, his horns digging into the drywall, as if he thought he could propel the fiend's influence out of his skull through physical force.

It didn't seem to be working. He shook himself with a furious growl, and the flare of emotion that hit me was laced with hopelessness.

My sense of his inner state was fading. The sorcery was dulling his resistance and the emotions that came with it. How much longer did we have before he succumbed completely?

I'd given everything I had to my attempt to control the monster that still hadn't entered the trap room. If even that hadn't worked—

My gaze stalled on the trickles of smoke trickling from the scratches Rollick had carved into his face. A memory hit me of being pinned beneath him in the back of his car, that cloudy essence coursing down my throat—and waking up all kinds of unearthly energies in me.

There was more smoke pouring up all throughout the room from the bodies of the minions we'd killed. Minions the creature that threatened us had compelled and forced to carry out his orders.

They were the closest things to a connection to the beast itself that I could get.

A wave of horror washed over me at the thought that'd just unfurled in my head, but I shoved it away as I dashed across the floor toward the nearest fallen creature—the torso of the polar-bear-ish thing.

It didn't matter if the idea sickened me. It didn't matter if this act took me farther down a path I'd never wanted to be on in the first place. My men were willing to be total monsters for me, so I shouldn't shy away from any bit of monstrousness if it meant saving one of them—maybe all of them. Maybe the whole city around me as well, and who knew what else.

When I looked at it that way, it was a minor sacrifice. I wouldn't be around all that long to regret whatever the act did to me anyway.

I threw myself to my knees beside the smoking torso and dropped my head to its ragged ends. Opening my mouth wide, just an inch from the disintegrating flesh, I inhaled the deepest breath of the stuff that I could.

The essence flowed into my lungs and sizzled through the rest of my body, waking up the chaotic sensations I'd felt with Rollick's. But they were familiar now, less stupefying now that I recognized them.

I was in control. I was *deciding* to take this step. I was a sorcerer, and I'd take in all the power I could.

I gulped mouthful after mouthful of the acrid essence as quickly as I could. A thump and a dwindling snarl from behind me told me that Rollick was still fighting, but continuing to weaken with every passing moment. I drank in another waft and another, every nerve lighting up with the wildness of the shadowkind—and then I yanked myself upright.

Electricity seemed to sizzle over every inch of me. I wouldn't have been surprised to catch a glimpse in a mirror and see my body lit up with a vicious glow.

"Go to the back door," I yelled at Rollick, hoping he had enough will left to manage that much even without my magical compulsion, hoping he'd listen if he did. I sucked in one more lungful of the essence and focused on all the energy zinging through my veins.

I was powerful. I was invincible. I was a monster, and nothing could stop me.

Then I flung the full force of my renewed power at the monster lurking beyond the room.

The words tore my vocal cords as they burst out of me, leaving my throat raw. *Do as I say. Come toward me and show yourself. Leave my friends alone.* I battered the presence in front of me with every shred of strength I had in me.

My legs wobbled, but with a burst of joy, I felt the hook snag deep. The fiend moved, finally. My awareness of its immensity expanded as it trudged toward me, its steps thundering over the floor.

"Keep coming!" I shouted at it, every particle of my body quivering. "All the way in."

The doorway at the far end of the room shuddered and split—but we'd been prepared that these massive beings might not fit. The beast that shouldered into the room past the chunks of wood that fell around it was nearly as tall as the ceiling and half as wide as the entire space.

It looked like a cross between a hippo and an ox—if ten times more immense than either of those animals would have been. Its rounded snout opened to reveal a gaping maw of crooked teeth. Curved horns protruded forward at an aggressive angle from its forehead. Each of its hooves on its thick legs, solid rather than cloven like Rollick's, was wide enough around to stamp me flat.

Bristly hair sprung from all across the thick, wrinkled hide that covered its broad body. A smell like the darkest, deepest cavern wafted off of it, sending a chill through me.

This must be the behemoth.

He was still coming, step after heavy step. I whirled around and saw Rollick stumbling by the back hallway, still clutching his head and shaking it. Throwing caution to the wind, I ran at him and shoved him forward.

"Go, go, *go!*" I screamed, and more of my amped up magic seared through my voice with the command. I didn't manage to break the behemoth's hold on him, but I felt it crack. With a ragged breath, Rollick lurched on down the hall.

He stopped by the door, waiting for me. I glanced back at the beast heaving himself into the room, my pulse racing.

I could only be sure of our victory if it made it all the way inside so the trap would fully spear it. Come on.

The behemoth pawed the linoleum, and a spark of fear jittered through me. Was he throwing off my influence?

"Get in here," I screeched at him, not caring what I sounded like as long as the sorcery reverberated through my voice. My body outright shook with the energy jittering out of me. "Come all the way in *now.*"

My fingernails dug into my palms, but the behemoth pushed farther forward. I spotted the flick of his tail behind its haunches as its rear end finally passed the larger entrance he'd smashed into the far wall.

He was in. We could do this.

My triumph was muted by the panic still blaring through me. Every part of me was aware that the thing just ten feet away from me was powerful enough to squash me like a flea.

I ducked into the booth and slammed my hand on the red button. Then I bolted for the back door.

Gears squealed. A vicious light flared in Rollick's eyes, and he swung one clawed hand toward me. Moving only on instinct, I threw myself forward, ducking down at the same time, and rammed my side into his legs to propel him into the door.

We hadn't bothered to lock it, since no being should have been able to touch it anyway. As it popped open with the force of the impact, we both tumbled onto the sidewalk outside. Crag grabbed my shoulders an instant later, but my gaze was glued to the scene at the other end of the short hall.

The silver and iron blades slammed forward simultaneously. They lanced into the behemoth's body from all sides, slicing into his abdomen, his neck, his skull. A groan loud enough to shake the pavement in the alleyway where I stood resonated from his throat. A vast cloud of smoke exploded from his form. He twisted once, twice...

And then he sagged between the weapons that'd skewered him, the presence I'd felt snuffing out like a forest fire doused by a downpour.

CHAPTER THIRTY

Quinn

A gasp caught in the back of my mouth. Then a laugh of relief jolted out of me.

The beast was down—one of them anyway. I didn't know what the continuing effects of my gamble might be, but I had no regrets about making it right now. Even if I felt so drained I needed to lean into Crag's grip to keep myself upright.

Rollick shook himself with a ragged exhale and contracted into his human-like form. Of course—out here in the relative open, who knew what mortals might see him? He stepped over beside Crag to grasp my arm as he stared past me at the immense smoking corpse. Tendrils of his own essence seeped from the smaller scratches he'd carved into his face, but they were already shrinking.

"Nice work, reluctant sorcerer," he said with a bit of a rasp in his voice that provoked a flutter of concern. The behemoth's influence over him had ended with the beast's death, but he didn't sound totally recovered yet mentally either. The hint of emotion I caught from him was full of turmoil.

Lance appeared beside us. "The beasties are going haywire. Most of them are running away—or around in circles like they don't know where to go." He chuckled.

"They were probably all under the behemoth's sway," Rollick said. "Since he was the one who came. I'd imagine that he bolstered his control over them before sending them at Quinn to make it harder for her to shake his hold." His smile down at me might have been a bit tight, but I felt the warmth in it all the same.

"Halfway there," I said, smiling back at him. "Should we go to the apartment? I'm sure you'd say we deserve to celebrate." My gaze flicked back to the sagging beast. "Or do we have to do something about the corpse?"

The demon shook his head. "I can keep any unwanted intruders off the property until the essence totally dissipates. I definitely think this warrants breaking out the—"

He froze, his gaze darting to a spot in the near distance. I tried to follow it, but I couldn't see anything there except the dusk-shadowed side of a nearby building.

Rollick swore under his breath. He motioned to Crag. "Get her out of here."

My pulse skittered. "Why? What's happening?"

Crag didn't wait around for the demon to answer. He hauled me up toward the sky despite the dim evening light still wavering over us. But from that height, I got my answer.

A serpentine form as tall as the factory wavered into being as it smashed through the outer wall. Bricks crumbled and beams toppled. The monstrous, finned snake I knew had to be the leviathan reared back and plunged its head into the depths of the building, heedless of the shrieks that rang out from nearby bystanders who couldn't miss that terrifying form.

"What is it *doing*?" I cried out as Crag hefted me higher.

"Whatever it's doing, we don't want you anywhere near it," the gargoyle growled.

He was right. I couldn't summon more than a faint crackle of magical energy at the base of my throat. I'd hurled everything I had at the other half of the villainous duo just minutes ago.

It shouldn't have mattered. I'd already known we still had the second ancient monster to tackle. But as the roof collapsed around the huge serpent, I abruptly understood.

The leviathan had lowered his head right to the behemoth's body—and was tearing it apart. Swallowing down every shred of its smoking corpse.

My heart plummeted, my blood turning to ice. He'd been waiting nearby, not helping his partner while I got control over the behemoth, while the beast had died, and then he'd leapt in to reap his own benefits.

He didn't care that his ally was dead. Maybe he'd always wanted to rule whatever world he meant to create on his own.

And now he was absorbing every bit of sorcery the other monster had possessed, the sorcery that I'd already struggled to deflect, to make himself twice as strong.

I blinked hard as Crag whirled me away, but I couldn't stop the rush of hopelessness from flooding me.

Oh, fuck. There was nothing to celebrate now.

We were so, so screwed.

HAILED BY FIENDS

THE HEART OF A MONSTER #4

CHAPTER ONE

Quinn

The reporter on the TV screen looked like a fish dragged out of the water, her eyes bulging and her mouth opening and closing breathlessly as she tried to explain what had happened on the outskirts of L.A. just a couple of hours ago. Shaky footage that looked like it was from a cellphone showed a distant view of a massive dark shape moving over a large building I recognized far too well.

"Reports are coming in of a huge form that smashed into an old factory building, causing most of the roof to collapse. Some witnesses to the event saw smoke billowing into the air, though no signs of fire have been observed. The form itself appears to have been long and cylindrical, leading some to describe it as a 'giant snake.' Presumably it was a large machine, but it has since been removed with no traces remaining other than the ruined building."

There mustn't have been much video captured, because the footage quickly switched to the wreckage around the factory. Next to me on the sofa, Lance snorted. "A machine," the dragon shifter said with rough amusement, shaking his head so his dark brown curls jostled wildly. "Mortals don't have very good eyes."

I made a face. "It's hard for us to accept that something we assume couldn't possibly exist is actually real. I had trouble to begin with, but having the three of you right in front of me made it pretty much impossible to deny the facts."

It was still difficult to believe that this was the life I was living right now. I had a man who sprouted tentacles from his sides and could turn into a massive octopus-like creature sitting at my other side. A gargoyle still in his hulking, rocky form with wings flexing over his shoulders leaned against the back of the sofa behind me. The demon who owned this apartment stood near the sofa's arm, at the moment looking more like a movie star who'd walked straight off a theater screen than any kind of monster.

And the incident the reporter was attempting to describe had been caused by a being even more immense and monstrous than any of the men around me: an ancient sea serpent the shadowkind called a leviathan.

He and his partner in crime, an earth-shaking behemoth, had been terrorizing this city and sorcerers around the world for months. I'd thought we'd struck a victory against them with the trap we'd put together, which had killed the behemoth. But his co-conspirator had been lurking in wait, springing out at the first opportunity to feast on the behemoth's essence.

Which meant instead of two very powerful, ancient, murderous monsters, we were quite possibly dealing with one very *very* powerful fiend. I sucked my lower lip under my teeth to worry at it.

I didn't know if I could tackle the leviathan if it'd taken in the behemoth's powers as well as what it'd already possessed. I'd only been able to draw the behemoth into our trap using my sorcery—sorcery enhanced further by drawing in the essence of one of its fallen minions—and I'd barely been strong enough. I wasn't sure I could make myself twice as powerful to match the leviathan's new strength, if its macabre meal had worked the way it must have hoped.

I glanced at Rollick, the former leader of this group of shadowkind, who still had more authority and resources than the rest of us. "He appeared so blatantly," I said. "It was only evening—lots of mortals saw him, even if they don't totally believe what they saw. That's against the most basic shadowkind rules, isn't it? Will the Highest shadowkind send more of their warriors to try to deal with him?"

Would it matter even if they did? The last time the oldest and most feared of all the shadowkind had sent their underlings to the mortal realm from the shadowy world where they lived, the villainous duo had managed to capture two of the warriors' minds and slaughter the rest.

I suspected Rollick was remembering that incident too. The demon rubbed his sculpted jaw, his dark blue eyes pensive. "They may hear about this situation. It depends on how much fear and magical control the leviathan has been able to exert over the other shadowkind in the area. But even if they hear about it, I'm not entirely sure what they'd *do.*"

Crag straightened up behind me, his muscles flexing across his brawny gargoyle body. "They have to do *something*. Showing his shadowkind form like this—openly destroying mortal buildings—it's even worse than having his lackeys attacking humans from the shadows. Even harder for them to explain away."

Beside me, Torrent's forehead had furrowed under the fall of his scruffy dark red hair. "Did he need to make that much of a spectacle of it? He could have slipped inside through the shadows and kept out of view while he devoured his 'friend.' It's almost as if he *wanted* to be seen."

I shivered, liking that idea even less than what I'd already been thinking. "Maybe with all the silver and iron, he needed to smash his way in to get good access."

"No point in overthinking the problem," Rollick said in a typically languid voice, but when footage of the battered factory building appeared on the TV screen, his body stiffened in a way that brought my gaze jerking to him.

He seemed to recover within seconds, lifting the remote to switch off the TV, but a chilly flicker of uneasiness had passed from him into me in that moment. Ever since he'd force-fed me a bunch of his essence, I'd been able to pick up on his stronger emotions. Something had unnerved him deeply.

The demon caught my eye with a warning look that seemed to say, *Don't bring it up in front of the others*. I shut my mouth against the question I'd wanted to ask, my teeth gritting. But I guessed I couldn't blame him for not wanting to advertise his unexpected vulnerability to the entire crew. He'd only just found out about it himself earlier today.

How could so much have happened in just one day? I pressed my hand to my forehead, where a faint ache pulsed. My limbs still felt heavy, the crackling sorcerer energy that'd become familiar now simmered down to a soft sizzle in my chest.

I'd expended a lot of power getting the behemoth under my control. I'd have insisted on racing back to the scene and trying to harness the leviathan too, but I'd been able to tell in the moment that there was no way I could command even a lesser shadowkind beast, let alone one of the most intimidating monsters out there.

I'd recovered a little in the past couple of hours, but I didn't think I'd be back at full potency for a day or two. And probably only with some sleep, not that I felt much in the mood to rest my head while my nerves were still jangling with a sense of impending disaster.

Lance stirred restlessly on the sofa cushions, his bright green eyes flashing. "He's a problem for sure. Giving dragons a bad name. I'd carve him into little pieces if I could get my hands on him." He made a jabbing gesture in the air with the three-inch-long, viciously sharp talons that protruded from his fingertips even in human-like form.

I found myself checking him for any signs of deeper anguish. I'd used my sorcery on him, Torrent, and Crag before we'd gone to launch our trap, to try to block any chance that our enemies would manipulate their minds. Casting magic on any of them had made me nervous, but I'd been particularly concerned about Lance. He'd gone through a lot of trauma at the hands of crueler sorcerers in the past. I hated reminding him of those times, even when my power might help him.

I touched his arm, giving his bicep a light squeeze. "Are you okay after the sorcery I worked on you? It didn't rattle you at all?"

Lance shot me a smile that was somehow sharp and sweet at the same time and slung his arm around my shoulders, careful as always to angle his claws away from my skin. He nuzzled my hair with the open affection he offered up so easily. "You were my shield while I was yours. There's nothing to be rattled by."

A warm glow lit in my chest at his phrasing. If it could always be like that, I wouldn't have minded using my magic. But it was hard not to cringe away from it when I knew how the sorcerers before me had awakened that power in themselves—the horrible rites where they tore apart shadowkind and human lives alike.

I'd shied away from doing everything I could with my supernatural talent, and we'd almost paid the price. I hadn't given Rollick any commands, and when the behemoth had come up on us faster than we'd been prepared for, the ancient being had cast enough power at the demon to leave him reeling in a struggle for control. He'd nearly attacked me in the last few seconds before the monster had met his end.

I couldn't balk again. I had to do whatever it took to protect the men around me and all the other beings, mortal and shadowkind, the leviathan threatened.

Even if we still weren't totally sure what the beast's endgame was.

"We can't just wait around and see what the leviathan's next moves are," I said, sitting up straighter with a rush of determination. "We know he wants to hurt people—we know he's got worse things up his sleeve, and now he'll have an easier time carrying his plans out with the extra power he's consumed. Where would we be able to find out more about what he's up to?"

My men looked grim, but none of them argued with me. "He's been sacrificing shadowkind at that rift down the coast," Torrent said. "He might be back to that as soon as tonight. It seemed like the two bosses wanted to handle that process themselves."

"He might have other beings seeking out those fish he likes," Crag added. "If we can find them without it becoming a trap." His last few words turned into a growl, and he gripped my shoulder protectively with his firm hand.

"That's a couple of starting places," I said, trying to lift my spirits and hopefully theirs at the same time. "And Rollick has his people keeping an eye on things. We could—"

A sudden jolt of pain shot through my body, so abrupt and unexpected that I doubled over in response. A gasp tumbled from my lips.

My men gathered around me in an instant, Crag's grip on my shoulder tightening, Lance and Torrent scooting closer, Rollick striding over from across the room.

"Is it your wound from the attack?" Lance asked, worry and anger twining together in his voice. "If I didn't heal it well enough—"

"I—I don't think it's that," I mumbled, breathing raggedly. The pain ebbed but also seemed to spread, radiating down my back and unfurling into stiff fingers that squeezed at my chest. I couldn't seem to pull enough air into my lungs.

I pushed my hands back through my hair, riding out the sensations. A tendril of nausea wound through my stomach as the pressure higher up finally started to ease off. I inhaled and exhaled as steadily as I could, waiting as the pain continued to dwindle.

Even when I straightened up again, an impression of tightness lingered, wound through my ribs. I felt as if I'd just run a mile, even though I hadn't left the sofa.

Rollick peered at me intently. Concern wafted off of him. "What's the matter? What are you feeling?"

"I don't know. Just cramping up or something." I dragged in another breath, and the realization smacked into me like someone had thrown a bucket of water over my head.

I knew the warning signs. I'd been watching for them carefully my entire life. Lately I'd just gotten so distracted by the external threats to my life that'd become so vivid in the past few weeks that I hadn't focused that much on the other risks.

The chill that tickled through my limbs had nothing to do with any physical ailment. I swallowed hard and wet my now-dry lips.

"I think—I think my heart might be starting to fail."

CHAPTER TWO

Quinn

At my statement, Lance spun all the way toward me with a snarl as if he thought he could intimidate my transplanted organ into behaving itself. He stared at my chest and then at my face, his eyes wild. "What can we do? We need to fix it!"

Crag had come right around the sofa, his wings unfurling. "She would need a hospital, wouldn't she? I can get her to one quickly."

One of Torrent's tentacles curled around my wrist protectively as he glanced around the room. "Where's your medicine? Did you miss a dose?"

"She didn't," Rollick said before I could answer, with a firm certainty that sent a more welcome twinge through my chest. I knew immediately from the way he said it that he'd been keeping track, monitoring to make sure I was as safe as possible. As much as the demon liked to pretend he didn't care all that much about anything, he hid an awful lot of compassion.

He crouched down next to the looming gargoyle so his face was level with mine and held my gaze, all serious intensity. "You know your specific condition better than any of us could, Quinn. What do you need?"

The flurry of concern and affection around me had me choking up. It took a second before I could speak.

"I don't think we can really do anything right now. My medical team is back in Jacksonville."

"Then we go back to Florida," Lance broke in before I could go on, leaping to his feet.

I shook my head. "I need to be here, dealing with the leviathan. We might *all* be dead if he goes through with whatever he's planning, no matter what happens with my heart."

I tested my body, shifting my arms, and found the pain had almost completely dissipated other than a faint pressure in my chest that I only noticed when I focused on it. Maybe it was all nerves now.

"It was just a brief spell," I said. "Usually these things don't happen in an instant. That's just an initial warning sign. I probably have months before my heart is weak enough to give out completely." As long as nothing sped along the process.

Torrent was frowning, his whole body tensed. "I thought you should have at least a few more years before that happened."

I offered a tight smile. "So did I. I don't know—maybe using the sorcerer magic that came with this heart is putting a strain on it that's worn it out faster. Maybe it wasn't the strongest heart to begin with. The estimate they give you is just an average. Some people get more... and some people get less. And I could be wrong. Maybe it was just the stress getting to me and my heart's fine."

My men didn't look convinced, and to be fair, I wasn't really either. Rollick stood again, folding his arms over his chest. "There are medications to help sustain the transplant in a situation like this, aren't there? I can bring in a doctor. We'll do what we can without drawing attention to you. If you went back to your team in Jacksonville, there's a possibility the leviathan has minions keeping an eye on the hospitals there."

I hadn't even thought about that. I nodded, hating how weak I felt, worn out by the brief but intense burst of symptoms.

I had the impression that Rollick meant to summon up a doctor from someplace or other right away, but before he could so much as reach for his phone, Crag stiffened. The gargoyle jerked around, his gaze skimming the room as his muscles flexed.

The other men braced themselves too, knowing Crag was the most sensitive to the presence of other shadowkind out of all of them. I pushed myself to my feet, relieved to find that my legs only wobbled a little, and grabbed my trusty crossbow off the coffee table. I kept it loaded with the three silver-and-iron bolts it could hold at all times, just in case.

"Please don't hurt me," a squeaky little voice said from the vicinity of the window. A small form moved in the shadows beneath the ledge. "I wanted—I wanted to say thank you."

My men formed a barricade in front of me, even though the creature that'd arrived hardly seemed like much of a threat. One of them could probably have stomped on it without breaking a sweat.

"Show yourself," Rollick said in a voice that was both smooth and ominous.

A miniature human form eased into the glow of the overhead lights, only tall enough to reach my knee, with spiky blue hair poking up over her pinched face and iridescent bug-like wings fluttering at her back. She cringed looking up at the much larger shadowkind, but she held her ground.

"Pixie," Crag muttered. "What are you doing here?"

She quivered before she spoke. "The behemoth had my mind. I saw you all leaving after the sorcerer killed him and freed us. So I followed you. I—I'm so grateful that you stopped him from using us any more, but I'm so scared—the being he was working with—the leviathan..." Her words seemed to dry up as her whole body shook.

"So you came here looking for protection?" Torrent said dryly.

"Not just that," the pixie insisted with a sharper squeak to the words. She sought out my gaze where I was peeking from between the men. "I'll help any way I can. Whatever you're going to do next. Whatever you need. I know you're not like the usual sorcerers." Her gaze flicked over my companions. "You obviously know that too. And there are others—lots of the beings who broke free from the behemoth's sorcery would help too. They're waiting nearby. I said I'd talk to you first."

They'd realized that a whole horde of them invading the apartment at once probably wouldn't have gotten them the result they were looking for, no doubt. I took a step forward, but Lance caught my arm.

"We don't know if she's being honest or tricksy," he said. "That little friend of Torrent's turned on us before."

Goldie the leprechaun. Torrent grimaced at the memory, but Lance did have a point. Rollick cocked his head, with another tic of his muscles that I only noticed because I was standing so close. What was up with him?

"You could be under the leviathan's compulsion right now," he said to the pixie.

She held up her hands. "No, I swear, everything I said was true. Please—if you don't want my help, I'll leave. It's enough just to say thank you. But I don't like what they've been doing. It feels wrong. And I don't know what it'll take to stop the leviathan now."

"Do you know anything about their plans?" I asked. "What they were trying to do?"

She shook her head with a miserable expression. "They didn't tell us very much. But they were killing other shadowkind by a rift near here. They were making some attack the mortals when they didn't want to. And now, bursting into that building in front of the whole city... I have a very bad feeling."

As did we. I hesitated, and then the most obvious solution came to me. "I can use my sorcery on her—to confirm that she isn't under anyone else's sway and make sure she's answering us honestly."

Lance spun to face me. "You can't work more magic. It could make your heart worse."

I squared my shoulders. "It's the one way I can contribute. It's the whole reason I'm in this mess to begin with. We probably won't get *out* of this mess if I back down. Anyway, it shouldn't take much just to ask a few questions." I yanked my attention back to the pixie. "If you're okay with it."

I didn't want to use my powers on an ally without their permission—that was one line I hoped I'd never feel the need to cross again.

The pixie raised her chin without hesitation. "I have nothing to hide."

I couldn't help admiring her spirit despite her small stature and the four deadly, not particularly friendly beings she was facing off against. My men watched me warily as I stepped to the front of the group.

"If you feel at all out of sorts," Rollick started.

I glanced back at him. "I know. I like defying death, not running headlong into it."

The demon gave me a crooked smile. "From what I've seen, you're not always clear on the difference. But go ahead."

I glowered at him half-heartedly and then focused on the pixie. The energy inside me had faded with my earlier efforts, but enough of a tingling remained in my chest that I should be able to pull off a little sorcery.

I willed the magic up into the back of my mouth. The words in the odd language sorcery almost always seemed to come out in spilled over my tongue. *You will answer my questions truthfully.*

The energy leapt out of me and sank into the pixie without any sign of other sorcery blocking my command. "She isn't under anyone else's control," I announced quickly, keeping my gaze on her. That fact didn't guarantee that she was trustworthy. "Why are you here? Tell me the truth, like I instructed you."

The pixie's voice came out fierce. "I want to stop the leviathan from enslaving me and other beings like me the way the behemoth did. You brought down the behemoth, so you seem like the best person to turn to. And I at least wanted to say thank you for breaking me from that spell."

"Do you intend any harm at all toward me or these beings?" I asked, gesturing to the men around me.

She shook her head. "I only want to help. I don't want to see anyone else get hurt."

I couldn't sense any reason to doubt her in her words or her body language. I glanced around at my men. "Is that enough to convince you?"

"Well, she isn't some kind of traitor, anyway," Torrent said, still looking skeptical. I guessed it was kind of hard to figure just how much help the pixie would actually be.

She didn't appear to be affected by his tone. She jerked straighter as if standing at attention and beamed at me. "Thank you for giving me a chance! Can I bring the others who'd like to offer their gratitude and support too?"

Rollick hummed to himself, the sound casual but the ripple of emotion I caught from him unsettled. "We should probably test all of them to be sure of their intentions. I'm not sure our lovely sorcerer is quite up to that at the moment. How many beings are we talking about?"

The pixie bobbed eagerly on her feet. "Oh, at least a hundred when I left them to come to you. More might have gathered since then. A lot of them are lesser creatures who probably don't totally understand what's going on, but they want to put an end to all this trouble too. I think there were a couple dozen higher beings like me or, well, bigger." She let out a little giggle.

I blinked, having trouble wrapping my head around what she'd just said. Rollick had been working on building his connections up into some kind of shadowkind army, but he hadn't made a whole lot of progress from what I'd gathered. Shadowkind didn't tend to band together for larger causes—they liked to look out for themselves.

Now we had a couple dozen higher beings and over a hundred shadowkind altogether ready to push back against the leviathan's attacks? A shiver of exhilaration ran through me that lifted me above the melancholy of my uncertain health.

Maybe we really could do this. Defeating the leviathan, enhanced powers or not, no longer felt like quite such a huge hurdle to conquer.

Rollick's expression had turned unusually grim, though. He narrowed his eyes at the pixie. "And how close is this swarm that's waiting for you? They followed you most of the way to the apartment?"

She nodded. "I told them to stay a little ways off—they don't know exactly where you are. I understand you're being cautious."

"Not cautious enough." Rollick snapped his fingers at the rest of us. "Grab your things. We're going to regroup elsewhere. A flood of shadowkind in the neighborhood will almost definitely have caught the attention of other beings we *don't* want finding us. The leviathan's minions have been spread out all over this city."

My pulse stuttered. I whirled to grab my shoulder bag and backpack, keeping my crossbow close by as I stuffed the smaller bag into the larger and swung the pack over my shoulders.

Rollick had turned to the pixie. "Tell the bunch waiting for you to head to the grotto near the southeast rift and wait there for further instructions. You can come with us for now, but not the rest of them—not until we've had a chance—"

The rest of the orders he would have given were cut off by the crash of heavy bodies through the two windows, the glass panes shattering. Several more forms sprang from the shadows beneath the door. I yelped and snatched up my crossbow as the first of the new arrivals lunged at me.

It was too late. Our enemies had already found us.

CHAPTER THREE

Crag

It was obvious from the first instant that the beings who'd charged into the room had just one goal in mind: tearing Quinn apart. My body immediately sprang into action with the only acceptable response: tear *them* apart first.

Already in my gargoyle form, I didn't even need to shift. With a roar, I sprang at the nearest beings. I smashed one's skull with my rocky fist, its brains exploding into a smoky pulp, and pummeled another's head right off its neck. Hazy essence gushed through the air from their crumpling bodies.

More shadowkind were flooding into the apartment from what seemed like every direction, many of them animalistic lesser beings interspersed with a few higher beings who made their lunges at Quinn more strategically. Hisses and snarls rang through the air.

Lance whipped around the sofa in his dragon body, incinerating a beast with a gush of scorching breath here, ripping another into fleshy shreds there. Expanded into his demon shape, Rollick gouged out a vampire's throat with his bare, clawed hand and drove his other fist straight through another attacker's chest.

Torrent had brought out every tentacle he could while staying upright. The sinewy appendages lashed around us, knocking creatures off their feet, crushing their bones with vicious slaps. He swiped his limbs through the air more frantically as the barrage of shadowkind kept growing in their onward charge, his jaw clenching beneath the hollow of his scarred cheek.

And in the middle of it all, Quinn's breath rasped as she fired off shot after shot with her crossbow, fumbling for the bolts she'd stashed in her bag in between. I whipped my head around to take a glimpse at her, and my chest wrenched at the paleness of her face, the sweat that'd beaded on her forehead.

How much was this fight taking out of her when she'd already started to feel ill? These brutes were putting even more strain on her heart while it was struggling. What if it failed completely because of this onslaught of fiends?

Anguish and rage seared through my body in tandem. Every being that was threatening the woman I loved should pay in the most painful way possible.

A deeper roar reverberated up my throat. I flung my fists even faster, leaping from place to place, carving a gap with battered flesh and plumes of essence in the incoming flood.

Part of me wanted to hurtle right out into the street and track down the shadowkind who'd led our enemies to us. Smash and pummel the leviathan until even that gigantic menace lay bashed and bleeding. But I couldn't leave Quinn behind. There were too many vicious maws and sharp talons snatching at her right here.

And more and more kept coming. I had no idea how many the leviathan might have already had under his sway and how many were new recruits, but it seemed as if every shadowkind in Los Angeles must be racing into the apartment with murder on its mind. The air was thick with smoke that pricked at my eyes and blurred my vision. My companions were little more than blurs of motion rippling through the clouds.

A reptilian beast wriggled close enough to Quinn to snap at her arm, and I slammed my heel down on its spine with a fleshy crunch. My teeth set on edge. There were even more swarming us every moment.

Rollick hadn't given any instruction, but I didn't need his commands to know what I needed to do. I flung my arms around Quinn, yanking her off her feet into my embrace, and bellowed out to the others, "I'm getting her out of here!"

Quinn froze in my arms, tensed from the battle but obviously not wanting to make it harder for me to carry her. She was always so starkly aware of how her protections against our foes might hurt me, but the silver and iron threads woven into the undershirt Rollick had gotten made for her only sent a faint pinching of discomfort through my skin, not even as bothersome as the beaded vest she'd used before.

It hadn't stopped these monsters from finding her, though. We had to get her so much farther away from here and the ancient being that wanted her dead.

As I barreled toward the nearest window, Quinn clutched her crossbow to her stomach and hunched her head under my chin. I threw myself through the already broken pane and whipped out my wings to propel us up into the sky. The warm night air rushed over us, sweeping the acrid essence from my lungs.

Unfortunately, the leviathan's minions had gotten wise to our usual tactics. Several winged beings leapt into the air to soar after us. They must have been waiting outside in case we attempted an escape.

I wasn't going to let those beasts bring me low this time. Before, that thicker metal vest had weakened me in ways the new undershirt didn't, and I'd gotten more used to fighting while carrying her. I bared my teeth. These creatures were going to regret ever tangling with a gargoyle.

With vast flaps of my wings, I careened straight upward into the darkening sky. There was no point in heading toward our precautionary meeting spot outside the city until I'd dealt with these fiends, or one of them might follow us and then tell the others to bring another attack down on us.

My thoughts narrowed down to the movements of my body, the feel of Quinn nestled safely against me, and the strikes I'd have to make to end each of the lives closing in on us.

Somehow, my fierce mortal had managed to maneuver her crossbow around to take aim. The moment I swung toward our pursuers, she shot three of them in quick succession. The first bolt slammed into a harpy's shoulder, making her spasm but not falter more than that. The other two projectiles caught beasts in the forehead and the neck. As they plummeted with blood steaming from their wounds, I tightened my grip around my woman.

The fact that she was so capable, so determined to fight for herself, only made me more furious at the creatures that wanted to wrench her from this world. I bellowed a battle cry that resonated up from my chest and heaved toward them.

While I held Quinn with one arm, I could do damage with my other fist, but my best weapons in the air were my legs. I kicked and clawed, whirling this way and that with rakes of my broad feet. I grabbed the harpy's hair and rammed her head into my knee hard enough to split her skull open. The talons on my toes tore open a hawk shifter's gut. My body twisted, jerked, and jabbed with all rage-driven might behind it, lending me strength and speed.

By the time the last body fell, my shoulder was aching where I'd taken a swift but shallow slash and my breath was coming hard, but we were alone. I pushed off a forceful current of air and soared toward the spot Rollick had picked out where we should meet if anything went wrong in the city.

Quinn shivered against me. I glanced down at her with a pang of concern. "Are you all right? Did any of them manage to hurt you?"

Had *I* inadvertently hurt her while I fended off our attackers?

Before guilt could dig in too deeply, she shook her head. "I'm just... I'm tired of all this fighting. Of always having to be on the run. And seeing so many creatures dying."

She nestled her head under my chin, and a different sort of guilt rose up through my chest, more an ache than a jab.

I'd dealt out a lot of the death she'd witnessed today. I'd pummeled dozens of creatures without any thought but of her safety, as savagely as I could manage. I didn't think she'd have told me I'd done anything wrong, but I didn't like that I'd contributed to the violence that had disturbed her.

"We'll do whatever we can to make sure they don't follow us again," I said gruffly, even though I had no idea how we'd accomplish that. Our enemies kept tracking us down nearly everywhere we went, and the leviathan would be even more desperate to get rid of Quinn now that she'd managed to destroy his partner. Now that she'd shown that she *could* tackle a being that powerful.

She was in more danger now than ever before. Both from the

weakening organ inside her and our most unshakable enemy in the outer world.

That knowledge had me sweeping my wings faster. We careened over the suburbs and onward until the lights of buildings and roads below came few and far between. The chemical tang that laced the city air gave way to fresher natural scents.

"How can you tell where the right spot is from up here when it's so dark?" Quinn asked, craning her neck to peer at the ground, which was drenched in black.

"I feel it rather than see it," I said. "The patterns of earth and stone all have their own resonance. I made note of the sensations when Rollick showed us the place."

My stomach itched with the urge to gulp down some quartz to bolster my gargoyle strength and awareness. I hadn't had the chance to munch on many minerals since I'd started down this chaotic path with the woman in my arms weeks ago.

I could manage without it. But maybe Rollick would be able to obtain some for me quickly without much hassle if I asked.

I picked up on the vibe I'd been watching for and swerved to the left. A few minutes later, we descended through the air with a rush of wind to land on a rocky hill where several boulders would have hidden us from view even if the sun had been out.

Quinn shifted so she could stand, and I released her carefully, studying her in the thin moonlight for any sign that her heart was affecting her badly again. Her legs held her firmly enough, and her face might have been a bit pale, but her eyes scanned our surroundings with total alertness. Remembering how she'd hunched over earlier this evening, the pain that had marked her lovely face, made my gut twist up.

"I guess it could take a while for the others to get here," she said. "They'd have left as soon as we did, right?"

"That would make sense," I said. "There'd be no point in them lingering once you're not there to protect. If they can catch a ride on a vehicle, it will carry them close pretty quickly."

She nodded and rubbed her mouth. "I hope the pixie was okay. After she tried so hard to offer us her help... She looked terrified when the other beings burst in. I think she hid under the TV, but I didn't see what happened to her."

With a jolt of chagrin, I realized I hadn't even remembered the pixie had been in the room. I couldn't recall seeing her after the moment when the attackers had swarmed us, I'd been so focused on destroying them.

Nothing had mattered to me except Quinn. Quinn, and pulverizing anything and anyone that might threaten her.

"I—I'm not sure," I admitted. "I don't imagine the beasts would have bothered her. And she was swift enough finding us—she should have been able to slip away."

Quinn frowned. "I hope so."

I didn't know how to answer this soft side of her. It'd always been her softness that'd both called to me and left me uncertain, so different from my own nature.

I would batter, maim, and kill to keep her safe. But even if I managed to avoid ever hurting her by accident again, how could she *not* see me as the same sort of being as the creatures who'd meant to do the same to her?

And how long would her love last, the more she saw of my brutality?

That question dug into me as sharply as Lance's claws could have, but it came with a resigned sort of resolve. This was what I could contribute. Defending her with all my strength was what I did best. And with everything that'd happened, the next few days might call on me to become even more brutal than ever before.

If Quinn ended up seeing me as nothing more than a monster after all, that was how it had to be. I wasn't letting any of those fiends touch one hair on her head if I could help it.

CHAPTER FOUR

Quinn

I skimmed my fingers over the smooth plaster walls as we descended the concrete steps into what I could only describe as an underground bunker. Cool air closed in around us despite the summer heat above. Ahead of me, Rollick flicked a light switch at the bottom of the stairs, and a room that looked like an immaculately Ikea-furnished studio apartment flashed into sight.

"Wow," I said, taking it in. "You put a lot of work into this setup. You were expecting the apocalypse to come sometime soon?"

The demon shot me an amused glower. "It's brand new. I commissioned it and a few others around the country after it became clear what level of threat we were facing. But it's not for *my* protection. With the amount of silver and iron embedded in the earth around this room, I'd rather be outside it in the safety of the shadows if worse came to worst. This is all for you."

I blinked, studying the elegantly functional space again with a lump rising in my throat. I'd thought a lot of harsh things about Rollick over the past month, and early on he'd deserved some of them. But he'd been more devoted to my well-being than I'd had any idea about for longer than I'd imagined.

"Oh," I said, groping for the right words. "You managed to get this built that quickly."

He shrugged. "I pulled together your massive sorcerer-inspired trap in just a few days, didn't I? It's amazing how speedily things can come together when you simply ignore red tape and pay your workers enough."

I could believe that. I ventured a little farther into the space, my sneakers whispering over the thin but soft rug. There was a kitchenette at one end, a small birch dining table and a linen sofa, a TV mounted on the wall, and a big boxy shape that I guessed was a Murphy bed, ready to drop down when it was time to sleep but kept upright for the time being to maximize the floor space.

The only thing the room was missing was windows. I could feel that I was underground in the lack of natural light, and a faint sense of claustrophobia itched at me as if I could feel the earth all around us pressing in.

"The leviathan and his minions won't stand a chance of finding Quinn here!" Lance declared happily, but I noticed he gave a tiny shiver as he bounded around the room, peering at all its contents. The metals toxic to shadowkind would affect him and my other men even more than they irritated Rollick, who was the oldest and strongest of the four.

I glanced at the demon. "Just how much silver and iron *are* there around this spot? You had plenty at your house in Texas, and it didn't seem to bother the rest of you there."

"I pulled out all the stops," Rollick said. "And those layers are concentrated much closer to the living space here. But we should all be able to tolerate it for as long as necessary, and we can take turns ducking out for a break before it wears on any of us too much. You can remove your threaded shirt while you're down here without any worry at all that your presence will be detected. I figured a safe house should be as comfortable for its primary occupant as possible."

A safe house. As he said the words, it sank in that this wasn't just a temporary resting place. "You're expecting me to stay here for a while."

"The leviathan does seem very eager to get you out of the way," Torrent put in from where he'd appeared at my other side. "If you stay down here, we can be sure you're safe."

Rollick nodded. "If your heart is acting up, we don't know how that might affect the energy it's giving off. The threads in that shirt might end up not being enough to ward off notice if you're walking around in the open."

A surge of defiance cut through my exhaustion. "No. I can't just hide away for who knows how long while that monster does whatever it's planning to do to the rest of the world. I might be the only person who has any hope of stopping it before things get so much worse."

Crag frowned. "Quinn—no one could ask you to take all that on by yourself."

"I'm not by myself," I insisted. "I have all of you, and whatever other beings we can rally. We defeated the behemoth, and we'll figure out what to do about the leviathan." I rubbed my temple, the momentary spurt of energy fading under my exhaustion. It had to be well past midnight by now, and it'd been a very long day.

Lance veered back around to catch me in his arms. He nuzzled my jaw. "You need to rest now, baby girl. You'll make yourself sicker if you push yourself too hard, right?"

Torrent nodded. "You've been through a lot in the past twenty-four hours. Once you've gotten caught up on sleep, you'll be in a better position to make decisions."

I made a face at him. "I don't think any amount of sleep is going to make me think it's a good idea for me to bury my head in the sand while the world goes to hell."

He gazed back at me, his sea-green eyes as steady as ever. "Then you'll be in a better position to make plans about how we'll stop it from going to hell. You're wiped right now."

"As owner of this humble abode, I whole-heartedly agree with what my mutinous former employees have said." Rollick strode over to the bed and hit the control to bring it swinging down from the wall. "I'll only entertain further arguments about your next exploits *after* you've recovered."

Lance eased off his embrace, but only so he could tug me toward the bed, which was already made up with ivory sheets and a thin blanket. "I'll keep you company. And not in the distracting way. So you know for sure there's no way anything could hurt you here."

I swallowed thickly and let him guide me over to the bed. They weren't *wrong*. I wasn't going to do anyone any good if I collapsed before I got around to figuring out my next brilliant plan.

"Fine," I muttered, and crawled onto the bed. Lance tucked the covers over me and snuggled in next to me, perfectly chaste as he'd promised. Rollick flicked the light off again. As I leaned my head against the dragon shifter's warm shoulder, breathing in his smoky scent, his warmth did ease my jangling nerves.

I closed my eyes, and despite the chaos of the day, it wasn't long at all before I drifted off.

When I woke up, finding my head muggy but my body somewhat refreshed, I was alone. As I squinted in the darkness around me, the lights flickered on and Lance appeared at the other end of the room by the stairs that led to the main door. I had the impression he'd just returned from a jaunt outside.

"You're awake," he said eagerly. "How do you feel?"

"Not too bad." I sat up. "Where did you go? Where's everyone else?"

He tipped his head toward the door at the top of the stairs. "That little pixie woman who came to the apartment managed to follow us here. We were all having a chat with her."

I pushed off the covers and shoved myself off the bed. "I want to talk to her too. Has she brought along any of the other shadowkind she said wanted to pitch in?"

Lance shook his head. "She's very sorry about causing any trouble in the city, so she was careful. But she says she can find them again." He paused. "I don't think Rollick will like you coming out of here until we agree on a plan, but I can tell the others that you're up and they can come down."

I glanced down at myself, abruptly aware of the clothes clinging to me with a day's accumulated sweat and other grime. I'd been so wiped last night that I hadn't even taken off my threaded undershirt despite Rollick's assurance that I could. "Give me five minutes to wash up a bit."

The bunker had a tiny bathroom with a sink, toilet, and shower stall all crammed next to each other. My phone alarm went off in the middle of the world's hastiest shower, and I hopped out to take my morning pills. My schedule had changed so much with the different time zones I'd traveled between that I had no idea how I'd have managed without the automated reminder.

Within five minutes, I managed to pull on a reasonably fresh change of clothes from my backpack. I'd just grabbed a granola bar from the box I found in one of the kitchenette's cupboards when four shadowkind figures appeared in the living room area.

Crag wasn't with them—I assumed he'd stayed aboveground to patrol the way he liked to. The other three of my men surrounded the little pixie, who looked even tinier with their tall, well-muscled bodies looming over her.

"She's very persistent," Rollick remarked.

"I think that's a good thing." I swiped my damp hair back from my face and sat down on the floor so I was almost eye to eye with the little winged woman. "I have a feeling we're going to need all the help we can get. I'm glad you made it through the fight all right."

She ducked her head. "I went to warn the others and made it back in time to see the gargoyle and you flying off. I was able to follow—but I made sure no one noticed me. It was my mistake, letting the others gather so close by before. I'm sorry."

"Anyone could have made that mistake. You don't know what we've already been through with the leviathan's people."

I sighed and leaned back on my hands, glancing up at my men as well. Torrent and Lance had sunk onto the sofa while Rollick propped himself on its arm. The demon took one look at my expression and chuckled softly. "You're still determined to throw yourself right back into the fray, aren't you, stubborn sorcerer?"

I let out a huff. "I don't think that should be a big surprise. The question is how."

I inhaled and exhaled slowly, gathering my thoughts, and the men waited to see what I would say. My thoughts gradually came together. "We still need to find out what the leviathan is up to. And the more of his supporters we can peel away from his ranks, the better. I think targeting his minions, especially the ones he's forced into serving him, is our best bet. If we can figure out where to find them without getting swarmed again, anyway. Do we know for sure that he's still active at the rift?"

Rollick inclined his head. "I took a little trip to check while you were sleeping. He's sacrificing away, tossing up lesser beings like they're nothing more than shark chum. If that doesn't make the ones watching eager to find a new master, I don't know what would." He shot me a narrow grin, but I caught one of those odd twitches of his jaw and a flicker of emotion that sent a jolt through me that was too swift for me to focus on it.

"You wouldn't want to go at him there," Torrent said before I could worry too much about the demon. "There are too many minions milling around, and he'll be reinforcing his sway over them regularly. We need to pick off stragglers."

I turned to the pixie. "He and the behemoth were working pretty closely together before. You might have some idea where the leviathan would have sent beings like you in smaller groups where it'd be easier for us to deal with them."

Her eyes brightened. "Yes! I can think of a couple of places near Los Angeles that might work. The rift could be a good start, actually. There would be a lot gathered right around it, but they always sent out a few here and there to make sure no mortals came near, even during the day, between the nighttime sacrifices."

I smiled. "Perfect. Then we can start there."

Lance let out a faint hissing sound. "We're going right back to the place where they attacked you so many times? I don't like it."

"I'm not exactly excited about it either," I told him. "But holding off on tackling the problem isn't going to make anything better. The leviathan is out there already, probably terrorizing the city and who knows how much else of the world even more than before."

Rollick pushed to his feet. "You're going to need to put your protective gear back on, then. And we're giving the areas he's claimed a *very* wide berth this time." He checked his phone. "And I have a medical professional I'm going to insist you speak to before we go anywhere else."

I glared at him, but he simply gazed back at me without any sign of budging. I could tell from the expressions on Torrent's and Lance's faces that they'd side with the demon on this particular subject no matter what I said.

Grumbling wordlessly, I stood up. "All right. If that'll make you feel better."

The visit with the doctor Rollick had picked out went both more smoothly and more awkwardly than I'd anticipated. She checked me over quickly and efficiently, listening to my heart and my breathing and running a handful of tests. But there were hesitations between her questions and moments where she knit her brow that reminded me that she had no idea of my patient history beyond what we could fill her in on. This wasn't an ideal scenario for giving a diagnosis or treatment.

In the end, she wrote out a prescription that Rollick grabbed and then told me to take it easy for a little while. I managed not to laugh out loud at those instructions. We also hadn't been able to explain to her how the supernatural powers I'd been wielding might have been speeding along my borrowed heart's demise. She did look concerned, though, which left me with a knot in my stomach.

The transplanted organ was definitely starting to falter. And I had no idea how the trials ahead of us might rush me toward my end even faster.

Our next stop was the beach quite a stretch up the coast from L.A. My men had wanted to scope out the area near the leviathan's chosen rift from a distance first. As I stepped onto the rocky shoreline where we'd come down to the ocean, my gaze was immediately drawn to the swath of dark clouds that smothered the sky from just a little south of us to as far as the eye could see across the water. Even where we stood under hazy afternoon sunlight, the waves were frothing wildly as they smacked the shore.

"It looks like a storm's settling in," I said.

Torrent dipped a tentacle into the water, and his expression turned grim. "The water's being churned up. I did hear that the leviathan has summoned tidal waves in other parts of the world in the past several years. He might be attempting the same thing here."

My heart sank. When I looked at Rollick, he was eyeing his phone again, scrolling through something on the screen. The tensing of his mouth unnerved me even more.

"There's been quite a barrage of weather hitting L.A. and the nearby coastal regions since early this morning," he said. "I was hoping from the early reports that it was a natural stormfront, but from what I'm seeing now, the way they're intensifying… I'm sure that menace is behind it. There's already been flooding along the beaches."

A shiver ran through me. "We might not even be able to get close enough to look for his minions. And what about all those people—the mortal ones?"

"The city is starting to evacuate everyone in the neighborhoods closest to the sea," Rollick told me.

Crag scowled at the roaring waves as if he could frighten them into chilling out. "We should get Quinn away from here."

I set my hands on my hips. "Forget about that. We only just got here."

Torrent turned to face the rest of us. "I'll take a closer look, see exactly what's going on. The ocean is my domain. I'll have the best chance of determining how he's working his powers on it and whether there's a way to interrupt the effect. It shouldn't take very long."

I hadn't thought I could get any more worried than I already was, but it turned out I was wrong. My lungs constricted. But I couldn't tell Torrent not to go when I was insisting on taking my own risks, could I?

"Be careful," I said instead.

He held my gaze for a moment with a small smile. "I told you I'll always come back to you, and I plan on keeping that promise."

Then he leapt into the waves.

CHAPTER FIVE

Quinn

The pixie—whose name, I'd finally learned, was Paisley—stamped her foot as she looked around the shallow grassy dip a few minutes' walk from the coast where she'd hoped to find some of her former fellow lackeys.

"They must have moved on from here," she said in her squeaky voice. "I don't know where else they'd have gone."

"The leviathan might have moved all his operations since the behemoth's death," Crag rumbled. "He knows we've been looking into his activities and trying to interfere."

"Wonderful." I hugged myself, my tee and the protective undershirt beneath it clinging to my skin with a growing dampness. It wasn't exactly cool, considering we were in the midst of a southern California summer, but the storm clouds condensed around L.A. had been creeping ever closer. The gray haze overhead had been spitting on us for at least a half hour now.

Lance shook himself as if he didn't appreciate the moisture either. "His minions have to be around somewhere."

I glanced back toward the sea—and toward the gloom hanging over the distant city. "We could go closer to their main base of operations. We'd probably run into someone eventually."

Crag frowned. "We don't know how many we might run into all at once or who else might see us. I don't like it."

"You don't like me being here at all," I reminded him. "You think we're going to get pummeled by a tidal wave at any moment."

He glowered at me, but he couldn't manage to put much annoyance behind it. "We might. Rollick said the flooding was getting worse all around the city."

The demon had gone off to meet with some contacts and sort out business he hadn't gone into a lot of detail about, but that I gathered had something to do with arranging the army we were supposed to be building. Paisley had also told him where to find the freed beings who'd wanted to pitch in. I expected to be spending a lot of time tonight casting minor sorcery on one after another to confirm their loyalty the way I had with the pixie.

"Well, we're not getting anything done here," I said, holding in a huff of my own frustration. I was a powerful enough sorcerer to have compelled a behemoth to his death, and here I was wandering around mostly trying to avoid running into our enemies. How was that helping anything?

But I knew that getting caught—and maybe killed—wouldn't be particularly helpful either.

We trudged back to the shoreline not far from where Torrent had left us a couple of hours ago. I wasn't sure how long his investigations would take. He'd been gone for a few days the last time he'd slipped into the ocean to find out more about the leviathan, but then he'd traveled all around the world. I'd gotten the impression he was planning to stay local this time.

What if *he* was caught? I couldn't imagine the leviathan would go easy on him if the monster realized he'd gotten his hands on one of my closest companions.

I clambered along the rocky shoreline restlessly. The waves splashed higher than before, drenching my sneakers, and I grimaced with a prickle of apprehension. The giant serpent was definitely stirring up the salty waters in ways that could be awfully destructive.

Lance let out a little shout of triumph and vanished from view. I hustled over to find him in a small dip where a stretch of sand had gathered within a circle of taller rocks that framed it from three sides, a few trees looming even higher around the edges. Their branches rattled with the rising wind, but between them and the arched boulders, they held off most of the rain.

Lance was stalking around on the sheltered sand. He gave a disgruntled sound. "I thought this looked like a good place for beasties to want to hide. No one down here, though."

Crag was studying the spot with a pensive expression. He rubbed his rocky jaw. "Maybe it would be a good place for Quinn to hide—as long as you keep an eye on the water and make sure it's not surging too high. I could fly farther down the coast and see if I can find a minion to pick off from the rest. It'd be better for me to bring one back here to question than for Quinn to get closer to the leviathan's territory."

It said something about how concerned he was about what the ancient shadowkind might do to me that he'd rather leave me with just Lance for protection than bring me with him on his quest. I sighed and hopped down into the natural alcove. "Fine. But search quickly, and if you don't find anything, come back. Otherwise I'm going to do more searching on my own."

Paisley fluttered her wings. "I can fly with you," she offered to Crag. "Cover more ground. I mean, I'll need to come to you to do the rest if I spot any of them, since I can't carry much of anyone off myself, but it could mean we find them faster."

Crag paused, eyeing the tiny woman, and seemed to decide that she'd be more use scanning the terrain than protecting me from whatever threats might arise. "Fine," he said gruffly. "Let's go."

As they vanished into the shadows, I walked across the sand, testing the grains under my feet, until I reached the driest section where the overhead rocks formed what was almost a cave. I sank onto the ground, finding that the pale grains were at least pleasantly soft, and Lance dropped down next to me. He tucked his hand around mine. The gesture came so easily now that I barely noticed the claws that could have sliced open my skin in an instant if he hadn't maneuvered them so deftly.

"It's good for you to have a little time to relax," he told me in his breezy way. "You've been on your feet for a long time now. Did you bring some food? Maybe you should eat something. I could try to hunt if you don't."

A crooked smile crossed my face at the barrage of concerned suggestions. I reached into my trusty messenger bag and pulled out the apple I'd packed. "Not a bad idea, but no hunting necessary. And I'm fine. I had that bad spell with my heart yesterday, but I don't feel so different from usual today. It was probably just the strain of tackling the behemoth and—"

Before I could finish my sentence, my hand tremored. As if my body was determined to prove my words wrong, my pulse started to race, a chill washing over me that had nothing to do with the damp air. The clenching sensation that'd gripped me before tightened around my chest, making my breath hitch as I struggled to catch it.

Lance leapt to kneel in front of me, his eyes blazing with urgency. "You're sick again. What do you need? Did you take the medicine Rollick got with that paper from the doctor?"

I managed to nod, my fingers digging into the sand as I fought for control over my body. My voice came out ragged. "Yeah. But it'll—probably take a while for that—stuff to kick in." If it did at all. If the reasons my heart was acting up had anything to do with normal transplant issues and not the supernatural energies that'd been passing through it.

Lance stroked my arm from shoulder to elbow, obviously uncertain about what else to do. But I didn't think there was anything he *could* do for me right now. I breathed as deeply and evenly as I could, focusing completely on the rhythm of the air moving in and out of me, and I wasn't sure how much time passed before I felt like myself again. I inhaled shakily and raised my head, barely aware of having lowered it.

The dragon shifter peered at me with concern shimmering in his violet eyes. I'd rarely seen him look so serious. "It was bad again. Two times in two days, when it never happened before since I've been around you. Should we go look for Crag and tell him we need to go? Or I could find a way back to Rollick's safe house on my own, I think."

I wasn't sure how likely that was. We'd driven here, and Lance didn't know how to handle a car. I could drive, but I doubted Rollick would appreciate us taking off with his ride anyway. If he'd even left it where we'd parked instead of using it himself on his business, which I didn't know.

And besides...

"It's okay," I said, grasping Lance's forearm. "It's over now. I'm probably going to have to deal with moments like that every now and then for the time being, and that's okay. They're not really doing any damage."

They just meant that my heart was starting to wear out to the point that it was giving off warning signals.

Lance's brow knit. "Maybe you *should* stay in the bunker. Away from everything. Then you can get better. We'll fight the leviathan, the four of us and the other beings who want to. Shadowkind to shadowkind is more fair anyway."

I wished fairness was a factor that mattered. A lump rose in my throat. I scooted closer to the dragon shifter, my forehead coming to rest against his.

"I won't get better," I told him, more steadily than I'd expected—but then, these facts weren't news to me. I'd just never before had to explain them to someone I cared about who didn't already know. "No matter how much I rest or what medications I take, a transplanted heart was never going to last me my entire life. If I'd been really lucky, I might have gotten twice as long as I have so far. But it was a strange heart, and obviously I'm not so lucky." I paused. "Well, I wouldn't even say that. I don't regret that the strangeness of the situation let me meet you."

Lance growled low in his throat, a pained sound. "You made us go away, and you promised you wouldn't do that again. *You* aren't allowed to leave us either. I want you to stay right here with me. That's where you belong."

I leaned into him more, an ache spreading through my gut. "It is. And I don't want to go. But I've known since I first had the operation that this was going to happen someday. To some extent I'm lucky I even made it past the first year. I've been prepared for this moment my whole life since I had the transplant. That's why I tried to make every day count. To experience as much as I could while I could. So holing up underground and doing nothing really isn't my thing."

"I don't want to see you hurting," Lance said, and looked down at his claws, curling them away from me as if suddenly scared that *he* might hurt me, the way Crag had once feared.

A spark of inspiration lit in my head. The idea wouldn't fix everything, but maybe it would help him accept the way things were and make the most of them like I hoped to. It was exploring excitement that'd brought us together in the first place, after all.

I slid my hand down to his palm and unfurled his fingers. Then I raised his hand to my face to trace the tips of his claws over my cheek. Even now, with the dreary weather around us and my body still a little shaken from the brief glitch of my heart, their delicate touch woke up a quiver of delight that ran straight to my core.

"I *still* want to enjoy every moment as much as I can," I said. "In all the ways that you can help me enjoy it. The thrills you give me won't hurt me at all—I promise. They'll just make the time I have sweeter. Will you remind me of how good we can feel together?"

Lance made a rough sound. Then he was sliding his fingers from my cheek into my hair, his other hand rising to trace across my neck. His mouth collided with mine.

As his tongue flicked between my parted lips, its dragon ridges forming across it the way he knew I liked, I couldn't think of any place I'd rather be, no matter how much longer this heart kept beating.

CHAPTER SIX

Torrent

I caught the siren just outside the underwater rift that lay out in the depths of the Pacific. She'd been traveling through the shadows that swirled around the ocean currents, but that suited me just fine. I could only talk to her in our shadow forms, since my physical shadowkind form couldn't produce speech and my human form would have drowned down here.

I shot out my shadowy tentacles and snagged them around her essence, holding her tight when she tried to squirm away.

"I'm not going to hurt you," I said in the strange voiceless way we spoke through the shadows. "I just want to talk for a minute."

The siren shuddered, still trying to work her presence free. But I had twice as many limbs as she did, even if a few of them were no longer whole.

"I have nothing to say to you," she spat at me.

I picked up more panic than anger in her ephemeral voice. Had she been compelled toward her destination? I'd sensed her leaving a small group of water-dwelling beings that'd clustered around the much vaster impression that I knew belonged to the leviathan.

"I want to know where you're planning on going after you pass through that rift," I said. "Are you simply going back to our home, or were you supposed to continue on to some other part of the mortal realm through another portal?"

"Why should I tell you?"

"Because I don't think you really want to be doing whatever that menace sent you to do. And maybe if you tell me, I can make sure you won't have to."

She snorted, but there was desperation to the sound. That convinced me even more that she was under the leviathan's magical compulsion. I'd have to tread carefully with her—past minions we'd interrogated had ended their existences rather than allowing us to continue to question them.

But I had no means to really force her to answer. Quinn was leagues distant, and I wasn't sure I could drag this being all the way to her unnoticed. We'd be in even deeper shit if I led more of our enemies back to the woman who was determined to save us all.

Possibly that lack of direct threat stopped the siren from attempting to harm herself. She thrashed in my grasp again to no avail. Then she went still for a moment. I felt more than saw her attention on me, studying me.

I didn't know what she saw, but she seemed to decide it was worthwhile to offer up a small tidbit—probably the most she could without violating the commands on her. Whether it was an attempt to bargain for her freedom or in the genuine hopes that I could help, I couldn't tell.

"There are many oceans in this world," she said. "And mortals live alongside all of them. Pressure is more effective from more than one side."

Uneasiness rippled through my amorphous body. She was heading to the Atlantic ocean then, I guessed—to carry out some destruction on the opposite coastline of this country? Many sirens could conjure sea squalls, a talent the more vicious among them used to put their sailor prey in a vulnerable position or punish those who eluded them.

She was the only being who'd headed toward this rift, but others had moved off from the apparent meeting in different directions. How many spots was the leviathan directing his minions to? How much destruction did he intend to carry out?

And what was the point of all this anyway?

I doubted the siren I held prisoner could have told me any of that even if she'd wanted to. I paused and said, in recognition of the covert way she'd replied to my first question, "It's a shame when a disaster causes many of those mortals to die all at once."

"Yes," she said grimly, "it is. But sometimes it can't be helped."

"I wonder what possible reasons an ancient being might have for wanting that to happen. Hypothetically speaking."

She sighed. "So do I."

She didn't know his plans any more than the other minions we'd captured did. Did *any* of the lackeys he'd drawn into his scheme have a clue, or were we kidding ourselves that we had a chance of undermining him this way?

Well, I knew more than I had before. And at least I could take a little comfort in the awareness that one siren could cause a lot less watery turmoil than the leviathan already was on this coast.

But it would be better if she didn't go at all. I relaxed my grip slightly. "Can you delay? If you can manage a detour, I know someone who could—"

Apparently not, or at least she didn't trust me to have her well-being in mind. She twisted sharply and slapped hard against the newly damaged tip of one tentacle that still ached now and then even when it wasn't being attacked. Agony speared through my limb, and the siren's shadowy presence managed to wriggle free.

I lunged after her, but she'd already caught a current that sent her careening right through the rift.

I hesitated outside the portal to the shadow realm for a moment, debating giving further chase. But what was I going to do if I caught her? Kill her to prevent her from carrying out orders she didn't want to follow anyway? Or rather, if I found her in the shadow realm, try to batter her essence into such a state that she couldn't follow through with her mission, since shadowkind couldn't die in our natural environment?

No. I didn't want to torment a being who'd had no choice in the matter, and it hadn't seemed as if she was a critical piece of the plan. The leviathan had hundreds of lackeys now. It was a waste to spend much time focusing on just one.

I turned away from the rift and moved on through the sea, letting myself solidify into physical form to make full use of my body and enjoy the caress of the water over my skin. I tasted every movement and flavor in the currents with my suckers, watchful for any other minions who'd headed this way. But I wasn't sure there was much else to learn.

Before the siren, I'd caught a kelpie who'd known even less than she had and followed a school of shark-like lesser beings who'd disappeared into that same portal. They'd been too animalistic to offer any answers, so I hadn't bothered trying to question them. The leviathan was definitely rallying his watery minions to a much greater extent than I'd encountered when I'd first gone searching for information on his activities several days ago.

Maybe there *wasn't* anything else to learn. It'd been hours now. I should check in with the others, let them know what I'd discovered and see if any of them had big ideas about what to do about it or how it might fit into the leviathan's larger intentions. Or if they'd encountered something more informative in their own search.

The span of ocean near the L.A. coast, where the water closer to the surface was churning and heaving, had nearly emptied of mortal creatures. The disturbance and maybe the leviathan's presence in general had driven most of them off. They might not have been able to tell what kind of threat he posed, but they had their own instincts. They knew danger when they saw it.

As I swam onward, a twang of discomfort reverberated through my gut. I'd roamed all over the mortal world, partying and indulging in every possible vice, when my physical body had been undamaged, but I'd spent a lot of time enjoying the seas in my monstrous form as well. Even after my beating, after I'd started working for Rollick, I'd come out to these waters regularly to claim this one small bit of enjoyment I still could.

But I'd never sensed anything was amiss in the expanse I'd soaked in so often. The leviathan had been traveling all around the globe, stirring up catastrophes, and I hadn't caught wind of the wrongness that was growing in the part of this world where I most naturally fit in.

Before, I'd been too caught up in my selfish pleasures to care. And after, I'd still mostly dwelled on what mattered to *me*—avoiding any more blows to my ego, impressing the boss I'd dedicated myself to so I had some sense of achievement and purpose. That had been selfish in its own ways too.

Would the leviathan and the behemoth have managed to get so far in their plans if I'd cared more about the world I'd derived so much enjoyment from? If I'd been inclined to do something about any strangeness I noticed rather than dismissing it as irrelevant?

Would I even be sticking my neck out now, doing everything I could to stop whatever new catastrophe the fiend was planning, if Quinn's life and safety weren't at stake? That was a kind of selfishness too. I wanted her to survive because I wanted her in my life, with all the joy she'd woken up in me.

The uncomfortable thoughts followed me all the way up the coast. Finally, I tasted the shifting traces of minerals and organic matter that told me I was nearing the spot where I'd left the rest of the group behind. Hopefully they hadn't needed to depart in a hurry because of some new threat, but I could make it to our agreed-upon backup meeting spot if they had. It'd just make for a longer journey.

As I came closer to the shore, I noticed another creature that wasn't quite mortal slinking through the shallows. Was it a shifter of some kind in its mortal-like animal form or a lesser being? The vibe it gave off made me think it was more purposeful than a thoughtless creature would be.

I eased closer, following its movements, and lashed out in an attempt to snatch at it. But the fishy body dipped and dodged before darting through my grasp with its slippery scales. I whirled to chase after it only to find it lunging at me, transformed into something now human shaped and sized but with fins jutting from its forearms.

Fear flashed through me. I had to stop this thing before it stopped *me*. It might have already spotted the others—it might mean to report their location to its master. No normal being would have gone on the attack with me like that when I still had a huge advantage of size.

I snatched at his limbs, and he sank spindly teeth into one of my tentacles. With a grunt, I shook him off. Seeming to decide he'd made a miscalculation, he leapt away from me, back into fish form.

But I couldn't let him leave either.

If I could capture him—if I could bring him to Quinn—I might have brought back real answers after all.

I hurtled after him with swishes of my tentacles. I could move faster than his small body, no matter how he veered one way and another in an attempt to lose me. I closed in on him, my tentacles braced to lash out—

Some instinct or a thread of sorcery in the fish shifter's brain must have told him there was no escape. Instead of racing onward, he jerked downward without warning—and speared his skull on a sharp spire of bone protruding from a half-crumbled skeleton on the sea floor.

I stared at his sagging body for a minute as his smoky essence flowed into the water, my chest tight. Then I returned to the shore empty-handed.

At least, if he had been a spy, he wouldn't be reporting to anyone now. Small comforts.

I passed from the water into the thin shadows that draped the shoreline beneath the clouded sky, knowing I'd move faster that way once I was on dry land. All the same, my heart felt heavier than usual as I flitted across the terrain, feeling for impressions of any of my companions nearby.

I heard Quinn first—a gasp that echoed through me with a jolt of desire. I knew that sound so well. As I veered toward the spot it'd come from, the dragon shifter's eager growl reached my ears next. I glided around a stretch of larger rocks toward a hollow shadowed by looming boulders and a few trees, and spotted the two of them entwined on a sheltered patch of sand.

I'd thought I was beyond jealousy when it came to Quinn and the beings I trusted my life with. But seeing Lance swipe his tongue along her jaw as he traced his claws over the bared skin around her waist woke up an emotion that wrenched at me.

In the back of my mind, I could hear him announcing his love for her in that brashly confident way he had. Completely certain of the depth of his emotions and what label he could put on them.

She'd said it back to him before... and she'd said it to me too. But I hadn't been able to answer her with a similar declaration of my own. What did love mean to a shadowkind? How could I say that what I felt matched the devotion she'd shown me, as much as I adored her?

So maybe I didn't really deserve her the way the others did. After all, what had I done to prove my worth as a partner beyond offering the same indulgences I'd once treasured?

But how could I change who I'd been for centuries in a way that would transform me into someone who'd truly earned my spot by her side?

CHAPTER SEVEN

Quinn

Lance paused in his death-defying caress of my torso with a cock of his head. "Torrent's come back."

Now that we'd started on this course, every nerve in my body was quivering with the need for him to continue toward its blissful end. But that didn't mean I *only* wanted him. I teased my fingers into his chaotic curls. "Is that a problem?"

The dragon shifter flashed a grin at me, baring the fangs he'd already grazed along my neck with glee. "Not at all. The more thrills for you, the better, right?"

I beamed back at him. "Definitely." But even as the generosity of his love lit a warm glow inside me, a sharper pang hit me underneath.

This interlude wasn't just about thrills, as much as I enjoyed those. Depending on what I had to do to stop the leviathan, I didn't know for sure whether we'd ever have another moment like this again. This might be the last time I'd get to soak in my men's carnal affections and offer my own devotion so intensely and concretely in return.

I didn't know how much of an impact losing me might really make on their vast lives, but if I was going to have to leave them, I wanted it to be with them knowing how fully I embraced and appreciated every part of them.

As he resumed his stroking of my stomach, Lance glanced over his shoulder. "Don't just stand around watching from the shadows. Bring those tentacles over here."

Torrent wavered into view just a few steps away at the base of one of the looming boulders. I couldn't read his tense expression, but his eyes looked stormy with the emotion behind them.

For a second, I forgot the moment I'd wanted to create here, the little bubble of happiness I'd known would only be temporary anyway. I rested my hand against Lance's knuckles to stop his caress. "Did you find out anything in your search?"

Torrent shook his head. "Nothing clear enough that we could do anything about it immediately. You can carry on." He paused. "I wasn't sure that you'd want me to join in."

Lance snorted. "I can give our woman my claws and fangs and tongue, but you can make her feel even better on top of that. We might as well put all we have to good use." His mouth stretched into an even broader grin.

In case the other man had any doubts about whether I agreed with that sentiment, I held out my hand to Torrent to beckon him over. "I wasn't accomplishing much wandering around here," I said, as if I needed to explain why I wasn't saving the world this instant. "It seemed like... a worthwhile way to pass the time. While we can."

I'd only meant to refer to the fact that we'd been pretty busy with tackling and then fleeing from our enemies in the past couple of days, but I suspected from the tightening of Torrent's jaw that he understood the other implications as well.

I didn't want him thinking about the limited time *I* might have in general. "Come here," I added softly, and something about my tone convinced him.

He sank down onto the sand next to me, leaving me encompassed in heat between him and Lance. As the dragon shifter nuzzled my jaw and pressed another kiss to my neck, I turned my head toward Torrent. His gaze held mine as my breath hitched and my eyelids fluttered with the sliding of Lance's claws farther down my body to the apex of my thighs.

Torrent raised his hand to trace his fingers over my cheek, but he didn't lean in for the kiss I was anticipating. "Always trying to find a way to make everything better, Ms. Fix It," he said lightly, though his expression was still pensive.

My lips twitched with a smile. "I'm not trying to fix anything right now. Just to make the most of what I have. Which I think is an awful lot."

His throat worked. Then he finally kissed me, his mouth capturing mine at the same moment as he trailed one of his tentacles across my chest. Even through the fabric of my tee and undershirt, my nipples stiffened at the brush of the suckers over them. The tingles of pleasure brought an eager murmur up my throat.

I gripped his shoulder and kept my other hand tangled in Lance's hair. The tips of the dragon shifter's claws grazed my cunt through my shorts, and I only partly swallowed the moan that followed.

He swiped his tongue over my throat as Torrent kissed me harder. When the exploring tentacle slipped right under my clothes, trailing bliss up my torso, Lance tugged my face around to claim my mouth for himself again.

Torrent swept my hair back from my shoulder and pressed kisses to the crook of my neck as his lithe limb worked over both of my breasts in tandem. He didn't give any sign that the contact with the threaded undershirt bothered him, and I didn't want to offend him by implying any physical weakness.

He knew what he could give, what he was comfortable with. I wanted my men to trust that I knew what I could handle, and I should respect them just as much.

I reached for Torrent's shirt and unbuttoned it blindly so my hand could roam over his leanly sculpted chest. Every ripple and dip of a scar was a testament to how far he'd come to be here with me now. He hesitated at first and then pushed even closer to me, welcoming my touch. When I stroked my fingertips over the dappling of suckers on the back of his upper arms, a hungry noise resonated through his breath over my skin.

Lance let out a grunt that sounded like a mix of amusement and impatience and vanished from my grasp for a split-second. I wasn't at all surprised to see him reappear fully naked, his well-muscled, golden-brown body on full display with his erection jutting impressively from between his thighs, ready for action.

He'd thrilled me in so many ways with that dragon tongue of his that I wanted to return the favor. I leaned in, bringing my mouth to his golden-brown skin. His warm, smoky scent filled my lungs as I kissed my way down the planes of his chest and abdomen, all the way to his groin.

When I reached his cock, I didn't hesitate to swirl my tongue around its thick head. As it twitched under my attentions, Lance groaned.

"So good, baby girl," he murmured, teasing his claws around my thigh and across my lower back. He stroked back and forth as I took him deeper into my mouth, pressing just hard enough to send the prickling of pain that came laced with delight through my flesh. Then he tugged at the waist of my shorts as well as he could without severing the fabric. "A little help getting these off?"

The second comment was directed at Torrent. A moment later, another tentacle flicked across my belly to undo the fly and yank the shorts down. As I helped squirm out of them, sucking Lance hard enough to provoke a growl as I did, Torrent kept squeezing my nipples with his suckers. His second tentacle delved right between my thighs to glide over my pussy.

A tingle raced through my clit. I moaned around Lance's shaft, and the dragon shifter grazed his claws across my scalp. His hips pumped instinctively, seeking even more stimulation.

When I tucked my hand lower to fondle his balls, his breath turned ragged. But with my next slick of my tongue around his cock, lapping up his musky flavor, he gripped my hair and tugged my head up.

"I don't want to finish there," he said in a rough voice. "Too many other parts of you I'd like to be inside."

At the raise of my eyebrows, he didn't elaborate, only pulled me into a kiss. I clung on to him, my body undulating as pleasure radiated through it from Torrent's attentions, pouring all the emotion I could into the meeting of our mouths.

But it didn't feel like enough. When I drew back, I caught Lance's violet gaze. My pulse stuttered for no reason other than the joy of having had this man in my life. "I love you."

Lance gave another growl and slammed his mouth back into mine, kissing me so hard my head spun. "I love you too, Quinn," he murmured against my lips. "So much. You are *mine*."

Not only his, though. I kissed him back just as passionately, but when he released me, I shifted onto my side to let Torrent wrap me even more fully in the embrace of his tentacles. The pluck of a sucker against my clit had me gasping, but it couldn't distract me from my sense of purpose.

I brought my mouth to his and kissed him as eagerly as I had Lance, reveling in the wild, salty flavor that laced his lips. Then I cupped his jaw with my head bowed close. "I love you."

Torrent let out a rough sound, the storminess coming back into his eyes. "I will always come back. You're the brightest thing in my life. But I don't know if—"

"I know," I said quickly, without any disappointment. Torrent had made it clear before that love wasn't a concept he knew what to do with. I wasn't looking for him to pretend a feeling that didn't come naturally to him. The affection he did offer me was more than enough in return. "I just want you to remember. Always. I'd be right here with you forever if I had the choice."

His mouth twisted, but then it crashed into mine again. His tentacles picked up their rhythm, strumming at every sensitive spot on my body faster. Pleasure swept through me, but I didn't want to reach my release like this either.

I groped at Torrent's pants, and he flickered away and back again like Lance had, leaving behind everything but the boots that covered the damaged ends of his legs. I pushed him over onto his back. As I straddled him, he adjusted his tentacles around me, still stroking my breasts but easing up to uncover my cunt.

Lance knelt at my flank and licked his tongue along my shoulder blade. "I like this position. I'd like to feel you the way only Torrent has gotten to before." He grazed a knuckle over my back entrance.

Ah, so that's what he'd meant about other places, plural. I couldn't help pushing back into his touch at the quiver of bliss it sent through my nerves. "Yes, please," I mumbled.

Torrent let out a dry chuckle that was cut off by a groan when I rubbed my pussy against his rigid cock. "Make sure you get her good and ready first," he instructed his friend.

I sensed Lance's grin in his intake of breath. As I sank down, taking Torrent inside me, the dragon shifter peppered kisses down my spine—and kept going.

At the first swipe of his tongue over my other entrance, I both whimpered at the shockingly heady sensation and started to tense. It felt even more intimate than anything we'd done before. But Lance showed no sign of hesitation or reluctance, lapping at me there and coating me with his slick dragon saliva until my uncertainty unwound.

Torrent stroked my clit with his tentacle and gave my nipples a tighter squeeze. A jolt of giddiness shot through me. I took that as my cue to start moving over him, rocking up and down, taking his cock deeper with every iteration.

The tentacled man lifted his hips to meet me, and the dragon shifter matched our pace unwaveringly. As Torrent thrust forcefully enough to hit the perfect spot inside me, a whole chorus of sounds tumbled from my mouth. Lance worked me over with his tongue for a few seconds longer and then lined himself up behind me. The head of his cock—the slimmer humanesque version—nudged against my opening.

"All good, baby girl?"

"The best," I said in a ragged voice.

As wild as Lance could be, he was nothing but careful when he knew one wrong move could hurt me. He slid in slowly, letting each pump of my hips against Torrent's guide him another inch. And with every one of those blissful inches, the pressure inside radiated farther through me, making me tingle all the way to my toes.

Lance wrapped an arm around my waist and hummed happily against the back of my neck. "Different and yet just as wonderful."

I started to giggle and lost the sound to a moan as he and Torrent both thrust deeper at the same time. After that, I wasn't aware of much at all other than the ecstatic sensations unfurling through my body and the grunts and groans of my lovers' pleasure alongside mine. We moved together as if we'd always been meant for this, even though a few months ago I'd had no idea beings like these two men even existed.

"Fuck, Quinn," Torrent muttered raggedly. "You are amazing."

I could only whimper in response. I bucked harder, faster, chasing the release we were all hurtling toward. Torrent pushed himself upright with his good hand to close his mouth around the tip of my breast. Lance dragged the tips of his claws down my sides, Torrent nipped my nipple in time with a flick of my clit, and I tipped over the edge, feeling as if I were both soaring upward and careening from a great height at the same time.

My body shuddered, and Lance growled. He slammed into me with the most force he'd yet dared and let out a choked sound as he came with me.

Torrent thrust up into me with his tentacles gripping me tight, and I cried out again with one last wave of bliss as he flooded me with his heat.

Lance didn't pull back as he softened inside me. He nuzzled my back and hugged me close. "Still strong, our baby girl. We won't let anything take her."

I glanced down and met Torrent's gaze. I had the feeling he understood better than the dragon shifter did how little say they'd have when it came to certain problems threatening my life, but he didn't correct the other man. Instead, he pushed his torso even farther up so he could form the other side of our joint embrace more fully.

I nestled between their bodies for several minutes until the thump of heavy feet sounded just beyond the trees, as if a large form had landed on the ground.

"Crag!" Lance said cheerfully, leaping up and flickering into his clothes as easily as breathing.

My cheeks flared with the awareness that I couldn't make myself presentable quite that quickly. Thankfully fixing my shirt was a simple matter of tugging the hem farther down. Torrent snatched up my shorts with a tentacle and passed them to me. I'd managed to squirm into them and was just buttoning them up when the gargoyle appeared at the seaward end of the sheltered hollow.

Paisley fluttered after him, but she wasn't Crag's only companion. He had a rotund figure about half his substantial height in his grasp, his massive hands clutched around the being's stout neck. It squirmed in his fingers, its eyes bulging, but obviously couldn't flee.

If Crag had taken notice of what we'd recently been up to and had any feelings about it, he didn't show them. He nodded to me with a grim smile. "I caught one."

"So you did." I let out a halting laugh, jarred by the sudden switch in mood. I had to gather my powers quickly and focus on the important tasks at hand.

But reconnecting with Lance and Torrent had been important in its own way. As I sucked in a breath, I found the passionate interlude had refreshed my spirits. It wasn't that hard to concentrate.

I focused on the plump human-like being the gargoyle held and willed a surge of sorcerer energy up from my chest. The words spilled off my tongue with a crackle, compelling him to answer our questions.

My energy smacked against a barrier inside him like it had with other beings in the past. No surprise—he was under the leviathan's sway. I squared my shoulders and braced for a much bigger punch of power. I had to shatter the magic that already bound him… and then, if he was still unwilling to cooperate, use more sorcery to force him to.

"Quinn?" Crag said with obvious concern, but I shook my head. It wasn't any good preserving my strength if the world fell apart around me in the meantime.

I repeated the order in the sorcerer language, flinging the words at the being and my sense of the magic inside his head with all my might. My pulse hiccupped—but the barrier cracked. With a flash of triumph, I hurled the command at him once more.

The leviathan's sorcery disintegrated completely. The stout little man blinked and gulped a breath through his constricted throat.

"Put him down," I told Crag. "But don't let him leave yet." I drew myself even straighter, this minor victory steadying me on my feet.

We were finally getting somewhere. Maybe I'd end up getting a chance to fix this mess after all.

After Crag lowered him to the ground, the being rasped a few more breaths. He shook himself and peered up at me. "You broke me out. I can do what I want again."

"You can," I said. "But I'd appreciate it if you tell us what you know about your former master's plans first."

The round face fell. "I—I'm not sure of much. He just ordered me here and there, back and forth." He made a wiggling gesture with his thick fingers. "But…" His equally round eyes brightened. "I did hear just this morning—he was sending a bunch of watery shadowkind off into the ocean. He wanted them to gather in a few different places in the sea around this country."

A chill tickled down my back. "And what were they supposed to do then?"

"I only got the gist of it. But I think… they're supposed to summon the big waves."

"Big waves?" Lance repeated. "How big?"

The little man grimaced. "Big enough to wash away all the mortals near the shores, all around this country. 'Drown them all,' he said."

CHAPTER EIGHT

Quinn

Drown them all. The portly shadowkind man's words were still ringing in my ears when Rollick returned to our shoreline location not long afterward. He took in our combined gloom and cocked his head with his usual authoritative air. "All right, what's gone wrong now?"

"We managed to catch one of the leviathan's minions that knew a little about his plans," I said. "And Torrent talked to a siren near a rift in the ocean whose story lined up with it. The leviathan is sending a bunch of water-based beings through the oceans all around the country to hurl tidal waves at as many places as they can."

I rubbed my arms against the growing chill, which wasn't all internal. The clouds overhead had thickened even more, their spitting turning into a full if light rain.

Rollick frowned at the sky and motioned us toward his car to get out of the weather. "I'm not sure how much he could accomplish by attempting that. *He* can create a real tsunami, but a siren isn't going to have much impact. It takes at least a few of them just to upend a boat."

"A big boat," Torrent put in, walking stiffly in his physical form with his tentacles for balance so that he could continue the conversation where I could hear. "And we don't know how many beings the leviathan has under his sway at this point—or helping him willingly. How are things in L.A.?"

"The flooding is getting worse," Rollick admitted. "But that's more due to a bunch of small waves rather than one particularly big one. I'd imagine he's in the process of building one at least for that spot. But he can only tackle one place at a time himself."

My heart skipped a beat. "They'll need to evacuate even more people. A tidal wave can cover a lot of ground. If it comes on too quickly..."

Rollick nodded as he opened the passenger-side door for me. "They're already moving a lot of the residents to temporary shelters farther inland. I'm not sure about this approach our foe is taking. He could have stealthily built up a wave with less obvious preamble. It's as if he wants us to be aware of the threat."

"Maybe he likes knowing we can't do much about it," Crag rumbled somberly.

Rollick's forehead furrowed. "I can't help thinking there's more to it than that. But I haven't been able to put my finger on it yet. I took a look at his pet rift that he's been expanding, and while it's noticeably bigger and giving off more energy than I usually see, I can't tell why he and the behemoth were so obsessed with it either."

"I don't trust anything that big snake is doing," Lance muttered. He leaned past the open car door to steal a kiss from me before hopping into the back seat. Paisley fluttered after him, and Torrent and Crag disappeared into the shadows. There wasn't much more for them to report anyway.

As Rollick started the engine, I hugged my messenger bag to my chest. "If the leviathan is sending shadowkind to the Atlantic side too, and we know he has it in for me... He'll probably have them targeting Jacksonville before anywhere else, won't he?"

My parents didn't live super close to the ocean, but I didn't know how far any of the waves the leviathan's minions summoned might reach. Or whether Mom and Dad would be at home if one hit and not taking a stroll on the beach. Or what other problems our enemies might cause out there.

The villainous duo hadn't figured out who my family was, as far as we knew. But they'd been aware I'd been staying in Jacksonville. It wouldn't be hard for the leviathan to guess that there'd be people I cared about in the city. If he targeted the entire area, no one was safe.

My stomach knotted. I didn't want *anyone* dying because of the monster's campaign against me. But my parents had already been through so much both because of my childhood illness and now my long, unexplained absence. How could I leave them unprepared when the threat might be coming right to their doorstep and it wouldn't take more than a quick call to warn them?

The demon could obviously guess at my concerns. As heavier droplets started to drum on the windshield, he shot me a tight smile. "I whisked your parents away to safety once before. I'm sure I can manage to do it again if it seems necessary. We'll keep a close eye on the reports from all North American coastal areas."

"Why is he specifically after *this* country?" Lance asked from behind us, clicking his claws restlessly. "The worst sorcerers are over on the other side of the ocean."

He had to mean the enclave where experienced sorcerers led novices through the vicious rites that granted them the power to "harness" shadowkind. I couldn't disagree with his assessment of them, having witnessed those rites and the sorcerers' attitudes about the shadowkind they enslaved firsthand. Oh, and also after having those sorcerers almost murder me. That gesture hadn't made me feel all that friendly toward the bunch of them either.

"I don't know," I said, glancing at Rollick. "It sounded like the leviathan and the behemoth were going around in Europe and Asia plenty before, although maybe that was before they joined forces. You said there doesn't seem to be anything special about that rift other than the way they've expanded it. They could have done that to any rift anywhere, right?"

"As far as I know." Rollick rubbed his jaw. "It could simply be that they joined up and decided to go on their sorcerer-murdering rampage, and they found it easier to track down the families here in the 'new world.' Many of the sorcerer lines on the other side of the globe are more established and practiced at hiding themselves."

"And the storms?"

He shrugged. "I'm already unconvinced that he'll be able to wreak all that much havoc with his lackeys even on one country. If he tried to take on the entire world all at once, he'd be spreading his forces even thinner. He probably wants a certain amount of concentrated impact. The real question is, toward what end?"

I thought back to the minions we'd managed to capture before. There'd been one who'd been helping the duo of its own free will. "That one creature did say something about taking the mortal world for themselves. But a few tidal waves and some storms... I mean, they'd cause a lot of destruction along the coasts, and that's horrible, but it wouldn't really turn the tide for an all-out invasion. You didn't think they had any hope of managing that no matter what they did."

To my relief, Rollick responded with the exact same confidence as before. "An attempted takeover would be bloody and catastrophic on both sides, but there's a reason it's never been attempted before. There are far too many mortals, and you have an abundance of the substances that can easily weaken or even kill us. I truly hope he's not so delusional that he's going to attempt that kind of invasion anyway."

"It'd be a strange way of launching it," I said, knitting my brow as I gazed out the window into the falling rain. "Where are we going now?"

"I thought we'd take a little detour over to—"

Rollick's remark was cut off by a strangely fleshy thump from behind me. A thump that sounded like it'd come from *inside* the car.

I spun around just as Lance lunged at Paisley. The pixie was flinging herself at the window next to her headfirst, her skull smacking against it for a second time. She pounded at it with a few swings of her fists as well before the dragon shifter caught her in his grasp and clamped her arms to her sides, holding her well away from him to dodge her now-flailing legs.

"What are you doing?" he demanded, looking bewildered.

"Have to go," Paisley muttered through clenched teeth. "Have to get to him. He needs us."

My eyes widened. "I broke the behemoth's hold on her. The leviathan shouldn't have any control—unless the sorcery can hide and activate later—"

Before I could finish that thought, Lance twitched. He snarled and whipped his head around as if trying to shake something out of it. Next to me, Rollick shuddered. The wheel jerked in his hands with a screech of the tires.

I jolted against my seatbelt, my breath knocked from my lungs.

Swearing, the demon swerved all the way onto the shoulder and slammed on the brakes. His hand fumbled as he reached to shut the engine off. A cold smack of terror passed from him into me, like nothing I'd ever felt from Rollick before.

"Quinn," he grated out, sounding as strained as Paisley had. "You need to drive. East. As fast as you can. There's a"—he cut himself off with another shudder, smacking one hand to his temple—"a turn off onto another highway up ahead. Take that and keep going."

I shoved open my door and stumbled out into the rain, my heart thudding. "What's happening?"

Lance was twisting and squirming in the back seat, groaning with frustration. "He's trying to take us. The slippery magic is tickling around in my head. I can't get it out."

The pixie had darted from his grasp. I yelped as she shot past me, her wings fluttering so fast they were a blur. In an instant, she'd vanished into the shadows along the darkened road.

Rollick heaved himself out of the car and around the hood to the passenger side, unsteady on his feet. The sight of him so off-balance sent a flare of panic through me. I dashed around to take the steering wheel like he'd said.

"Our serpentine 'friend' is sending out a general call," the demon managed to growl as he threw himself into the seat I'd just vacated. "I wouldn't have thought—for him to reach this far with this much power—but he did absorb so much from his partner." He let out a hiss through his teeth.

I started the engine, but my mind was spinning. "If it's his sorcery, I could try to cast my own to block it."

"No. We don't have time for that. We don't know if you're strong enough, and if you don't manage all of us—I can feel Torrent and Crag grappling with it too—it isn't hitting us as forcefully as it would have up close. Even Lance is holding off the leviathan's influence for now. You just need to get us farther away before the bastard ramps it up even more."

I didn't need to be told twice. I hit the gas and tore down the road as fast as I felt I could control the car on the increasingly slick road. My pulse pounded louder than the raindrops drumming on the roof. Lance was still thrashing in the back seat, the leather tearing as he dug in his claws. Rollick had bowed his head over with his hands clutched around it, breathing in halting gasps I could tell he was fighting to even out. More fear wafted from him into me.

How far were we from the leviathan right now? L.A. was at least fifty miles away. And the leviathan had managed to extend its influence all the way out here.

How many other shadowkind, not quite as powerful as my own or closer by, had already fallen completely under his sway like Paisley had?

I couldn't answer any of those questions. All I could do was take the exit Rollick had mentioned and speed farther away from the coast and the city that was the leviathan's current haunt. Thankfully with the stormy weather, there was even less traffic than when we'd driven out here. The gas tank was still three quarters full.

We'll be okay, I told myself over and over. *We'll be okay.*

As we roared along the highway to the east, the rain dwindled. The drumming became a patter and then faded away completely. Afternoon sunlight streaked out across the landscape up ahead where the clouds thinned.

Rollick gradually straightened up. His stance was tense, but even so, he couldn't hold in the tremor that ran through his body. He glowered through the windshield for a few minutes before he let himself speak again.

"Just when I thought that fiend couldn't become any more of a menace."

He glanced toward the back and sighed, I assumed at whatever wreck Lance had made of his seats. The dragon shifter had quieted down, but I still heard the occasional grunt and rustle as he fought off the lingering effects. It was several more minutes before his bright voice, unusually mournful, carried to us. "I'm sorry."

"It's all right," Rollick said in a resigned tone. "Blame the beast that caused it. You did a good job fending off his commands."

"I think... I think there was still a little of Quinn's sorcery in me from taking on the behemoth. I reminded myself of her orders, even though they didn't totally make sense anymore. That helped."

At least my magic had done a little good. I swallowed thickly. "Can I assume Torrent and Crag are all right?"

Rollick nodded. "Still with us in the shadows, taking a much-needed rest after dealing with that crap." He shifted his gaze back to the horizon ahead. "It seems we won't be doing much more investigating around L.A.

for the foreseeable future. But I don't think that's where we'd want to be heading right now anyway."

I glanced at him. "What do you mean?"

His mouth twisted. "If the leviathan is powerful enough to send out his sorcery that far, he'll have enslaved hundreds more beings than he had under his sway before. Maybe enough of an army that he *will* be able to send tidal waves all along both coasts. We'd better get your parents out before he has time to see that plan through to its brutal conclusion."

CHAPTER NINE

Quinn

I couldn't sit still in the back of the limo parked on the tarmac. Rollick had insisted on going to collect my parents on his own, since he could travel through the rifts to reach Jacksonville in a matter of minutes, faster than even the private jet he'd be taking Mom and Dad on to return to the area near his bunker. But I could only imagine how confused and terrified they'd be once some stranger had forced them to leave their home, no matter what he said to them.

Crag had commandeered the seat next to me, peering out the car windows watchfully and rubbing my shoulders with his solid hand when I shifted in my seat for the hundredth time. Lance had gotten restless himself and gone out to prowl along the edges of the airfield, even though we were well away from L.A. and anywhere the leviathan was likely to send his minions searching for us now.

Torrent's voice carried from the front passenger seat, speaking into a cellphone in his usual low, even tone but getting a bit louder here and there as he added emphasis to his message. "Yes, I know the data you're seeing might not show any reason for concern yet, but our experimental systems have been accurate in the past. I'm only asking that you keep a closer eye on the situation than usual. I thought it was important to convey a warning, given how serious the potential consequences are."

When he hung up, I leaned forward in the expansive back area of the limo. "Are they listening to you?"

Torrent glanced back with a grimace. "So far, all of the monitoring stations I've spoken to have been skeptical, but at least we're putting the possibility into their heads. They'll be primed to notice any concerning changes in the weather patterns or tidal behavior."

I blew out my breath in a huff, but that outcome might be the best I could have hoped for. We couldn't whisk *everyone* across the entire coastline away from the threat of a tidal wave, but there was more chance of saving lives if the people watching for problems had advance warning and could spot the signs of trouble sooner.

A distant rumble reached my ears. A jet appeared against the stark blue of the sky. As it soared toward us, dipping lower, I tensed in my seat.

It was right on time. I guessed Rollick hadn't had that much trouble getting my parents on board. I wasn't sure if that boded well for the methods he'd needed to resort to or not. I had a flash of an image of him working some demonic magic on them to knock them out, slinging them over his monstrous shoulders, and hauling them back to the plane like that.

Well, he couldn't have gone quite that far. I was at least sure that he wouldn't have walked around downtown Jacksonville in full demon form.

I still didn't know how I was going to explain any of this situation to them: my absence, my new companions, why they were in danger. The truth sounded totally insane, but there were no alternate explanations that sounded more normal. My general plan was to start out as vague as I could get away with and only get into details where Mom and Dad pushed for them.

They trusted me. They knew I'd never gotten into any significant trouble or made up wild stories before. But who knew how far that trust would get me, especially after I'd vanished on them for weeks on end?

The roar expanded until it filled my ears. Crag lowered his hand to wrap his fingers around mine. "Do you want us to stay with you for this or would you rather they didn't see us?"

I looked at him, nearly human but huge and with that jaw of literal stone, and at Torrent, with his tentacles braced on either side of his waist. Torrent could probably have sat reasonably comfortably without his extra appendages out for a short time, since he didn't need to put any significant weight on his lower legs in his current position, but I didn't like asking him to.

Anyway, even if they'd been totally human, I couldn't imagine my parents being super comfortable with even more strange men taking part in the conversation beyond the one who'd essentially kidnapped them.

"I think it'll be better if I talk to them on my own first," I said. "But I might need backup at some point... if I need to prove the supernatural side of the story to them. So, I guess stick around in the shadows and follow along with the conversation, if you don't mind? If I need you, I'll make that clear."

"That's no problem," Torrent said without hesitation, shooting me a tight smile that seemed to say, *Good luck*. Crag nodded. As the private jet touched down on the runway with a faint bump of its wheels, both men slipped away into the patches of darkness within the limo. I knew Lance would rejoin us shortly too, heading our way from the moment he noticed the plane's arrival.

Not for the first time, I wished I could still sense them in the shadows the way they could track each other's presence. Even with all this supernatural power of my own, I was still nearly as unaware as any other human being.

The plane slowed to a stop only about twenty feet from where the limo was parked. The door swung open with a soft hiss, lowering into a short flight of stairs. Rollick appeared first, the sunlight gleaming off his tawny hair. He drew himself a little taller and beckoned behind him, and two other figures stepped hesitantly into view.

My chest constricted at the sight of my parents. It'd been more than a month since I'd last set eyes on them. Which wasn't *that* long in the grand scheme of things—I'd gone longer without visiting them in person while I was at college, although we'd usually video chatted once a week then. But so much had happened in the past several weeks that it might as well have been years.

And they had no idea about any of what I'd experienced yet.

The confusion was clear on both of their faces as they followed Rollick down the stairs and across the pavement to the car. I wavered for a second and then gave in to the impulse to push open the door and meet them outside. Let them see me sooner rather than later.

The moment I stepped out, Mom's eyes widened. "Quinn!" She rushed forward to meet me and flung her arms around me, hugging me against her compact frame.

Dad hurried after her on his longer legs, his pale hair unusually rumpled as if Rollick had pulled them out of bed for the trip. The second Mom had released me, he hugged me next, with a tight squeeze that had a bit of a tremor to it.

"We've been so worried," he said roughly. "Where have you *been*?"

"We tried texting and calling," Mom put in. "I don't like to interfere with your life on campus, but after a while with no response, I checked in with the college and found out you hadn't participated in any of your classes since last month. After that we filed a missing persons report, but they won't do much for adults. No one had seen you."

She sounded so relieved and frantic at the same time that my heart ached. I gripped her arm and Dad's and guided them toward the back of the limo. "I'm so sorry. There's been so much going on—I know Rollick will have told you a little about it—and I was afraid if I got in touch with you, I might send the wrong kind of attention your way. Put you in danger. Unfortunately, now you're in danger anyway. But we're going to get you someplace safe, and I'll explain everything as well as I can."

Mom balked a little at the car, peering over at Rollick, who'd stopped by the driver's side door with a mild expression. She turned back to me, lowering her voice to a murmur. "I don't understand. He said you've been helping against some group that wants to attack the country? Who even *is* he? How did you meet him? He isn't forcing you into some kind of cult situation or... or I don't even know what, is he?"

I swallowed hard and nudged them toward the car. "No. And that's a pretty good basic explanation. I want us to get going, but I'll try to give you the whole story while we're in the car."

My parents both hesitated for a few seconds longer, but then they climbed into the back of the limo with me following. They sat on the seat facing backwards, and I took the one across from them where I'd been sitting before. As Rollick started the engine and the car rolled forward, I could tell they were taking in the luxurious trappings of the vehicle with even more bewilderment.

"Rollick has a lot of resources," I said. "He set up this safe house for you too." I didn't have to mention it'd originally been for me. "But—let me start at the beginning."

It wasn't that simple, of course. At a halting pace, I laid out how I'd first been attacked back home in the park near their house, the way the group of men I was now with had come to my rescue, the discovery that my heart gave me unexpected powers, and a summarized version of the enemies we'd realized we were up against. With each additional piece of the tale, my parents' expressions shifted from confused to utterly bewildered.

"I know it sounds crazy," I said for what might have been the tenth time as I wrapped up the truncated version of events. "I'd think it was crazy too. But I've been living in this craziness for weeks now. I know the shadowkind are real. I know how much destruction the really monstrous ones can cause. Maybe you've even seen reports of the strange stuff that's been going on in L.A."

Mom and Dad exchanged a glance. "They said there've been attacks by wild animals," Mom said. "Not *monsters*."

"That's the best way they can explain it. No one would believe anything else, right?"

Dad was frowning. "You've always had a good head on your shoulders, Quinn. You have to be able to see that none of this fits with what you know about the real world."

"Yeah," I said with a humorless chuckle. "That's because there's too much of the real world that we weren't aware of. I... Let's wait until we get to the safe house, and then I can really show you." Somehow I didn't think they'd handle an encounter with my shadowkind men in the confines of the car all that well. Better not to freak them out too much while Rollick needed to concentrate on driving.

Mom leaned forward to grasp my hand. "Whatever's going on, we'll get through it together. I'm just glad you're here with us again."

I smiled back at her and was about to say something intended to be reassuring when a hitch in my chest stole my breath. The increasingly familiar pressure clamped around my heart, tight enough that my head momentarily spun.

I fought to keep my expression blank, but Dad's eyes flickered with concern. "Are you all right, kiddo?"

"Yeah," I lied, speaking slowly so that I could get out the words without my voice turning ragged. I pushed my posture a little straighter despite the urge to hunch in on myself, unable to stop my jaw from clenching briefly at the pain. A deeper discomfort wound around my gut.

I wasn't going to let them know that my heart was giving out on me on top of everything else going on. They didn't need worries about my shortened lifespan hanging over their heads when there was a much more pressing problem threatening all of us. If I still could spare them one little bit of anguish, I was going to do everything in my power to do so.

Mom's brow had knit. I forced my smile back into place, willing it to stay relaxed, taking careful breaths through my nose. The worst of the pressure eased off, but a prickling sensation remained, spreading farther through my chest and across my back and shoulders.

I was lucky all three of my other men hadn't sprung out of the shadows to make sure I was okay. They'd no doubt been able to tell my heart had acted up again. But it wasn't as if they could have done anything to help regardless.

"I'm really glad to see you again too," I went on, easier now that the vise in my chest had released. "It was really hard not being able to talk to you, knowing you'd be worried. I was just even more scared that the monsters that want to hurt me would realize they could use you to get to me. I didn't want to totally upend your lives the way we're having to now."

"Don't you worry about us," Mom said firmly. "Whatever you need, we'll figure out how to make it work. That's our job, sweetheart, not yours."

Sudden tears pricked at the back of my eyes. They had no idea how much I'd worked at keeping our family time happy and worry-free all through the past several years. How much responsibility I'd felt not to drag them down any more than my childhood illness already had.

When we reached the bunker, my parents climbed out of the car and peered around across the desolate desert. I led them over to the door in the small shack-like structure that was the only part of the building above ground. When Rollick unlocked the door, they halted, looking down at the stairs that would take them under the earth.

"This is all a little much," Dad said. "What exactly is going to happen to us here?"

"Nothing," I promised. "It's just a little apartment, basically, with everything you could need to stay comfortable. We've set it up with a TV and a computer so you can follow the news, and Rollick made sure there's a cell signal if you're near the top of the stairs so I'll be able to call you and touch base while we're... trying to deal with the rest of the problem. Hopefully you won't need to stay for too long. There's no way any of the creatures after us should be able to find you down here."

Honestly, the setup was a bit overkill since the silver and iron protections around the place were mainly there to prevent shadowkind from sensing my sorcery magic. Mom and Dad didn't have any of that. But the protections would also repel any shadowkind that ventured near here, and being under the ground would keep my parents completely out of view. I couldn't complain about them being *too* safe.

But I could see from the tightening of their faces that this was one step too far without further evidence. Sucking in a breath, I glanced at Rollick. He raised his eyebrows in question.

No. I didn't think a massive naked demon would be the best example of the shadowkind to present them with first.

"Lance," I said, knowing all three of the other men would be nearby. "Could you come out so my parents can see that shadowkind beings like you are actually real?"

Lance wavered into view a few feet away from us without hesitation, in his human-like form but with his hands held up, clawed fingers splayed to show them off. He gave my parents his usual jaunty, crooked grin. "Quinn is working very hard to protect you. And because you're important to her, we are too."

My mom blinked, taking in his talons, and Dad gripped her shoulder. Before they could make some excuse about makeup or prosthetics, I tipped my head toward Lance. "Show them your dragon form."

He bobbed his head and stretched forward, shifting effortlessly with a rippling of his jewel-toned scales over his now-reptilian body. He twined around on the dry earth and flashed a fanged grin at my parents.

Mom let out a little shriek and clapped her hand over her mouth. Dad was simply gaping. I walked over to Lance and rested my hand on his smoothly scaled neck, giving him a gentle stroke with my fingers. He turned his head to nuzzle my hip.

"I—I don't understand," Mom mumbled.

"I know," I said. "It's crazy. But it's also real. Wait until you meet the other friends I've made."

Both of my parents stared at me, momentarily lost for words. But I could see the change in their eyes as disbelief gave way to horrified acceptance.

CHAPTER TEN

Rollick

I let Quinn sit in silence for a good while after we'd gotten into the car before I glanced over at her. "I'd say that could have gone at least twice as badly as it did. Consider it a win."

She exhaled in a rush as if she'd been holding most of her breath for the past hour. "I know. I still don't like it. I don't like that I can't stay with them while they're wrapping their heads around all this. It's so much to lay on them at once."

In the back, Lance slid down to prop his feet against the back of my seat. "We take down the leviathan and his beasties, and then your parents won't have to worry about it anymore anyway."

Next to him, Crag let out a wordless rumble. "We don't know how long that might take. But they'll be safe until then, even if they're still confused."

"Yeah." Quinn rubbed her face. "I just hope they stay there. I'll have to call them regularly to make sure they know I'm okay and everything's on track... as much as we have a track at the moment."

"They'd have trouble getting very far," I said. "Torrent's taking the limo back to where it belongs, and this car was the only other vehicle I had nearby. They seem like practical enough people not to attempt a hike across the desert when they have perfectly comfortable accommodations where they are—and their daughter's assurances."

My remark didn't appear to put Quinn at ease. She folded her arms over her chest, gazing broodingly out the window. "Do we even know for sure that any of Paisley's friends will be waiting for us? They might have gotten caught up in the wave of sorcery the leviathan sent out, just like she did."

"I expect we'll have a few new allies, and those will be the most eager ones of the bunch too. I told them to meet us at a spot near the New Mexico-Arizona border, which would have put them well out of range if they set off fairly quickly. Her mistake was glomming on to us so early."

I said the last bit flippantly, but even as I spoke, an icy jolt shot through my nerves. For just a second, my thoughts scattered as if they were dandelion fluff in a sharp gust of breeze.

My hands tightened on the steering wheel as I clamped down on the abrupt reaction. I trained all my attention on the road ahead and the steady, even breaths I was sucking into my lungs.

Quinn's head twitched toward me. No doubt she'd gotten a flash of the strange panic that'd come over me, through the blasted emotional connection I hadn't meant to forge. I hadn't minded it so much when it'd allowed her to trust my loyalty to her, but I wasn't pleased at all with her sensing my moments of weakness. Which had been happening far more often than I liked in the past few days.

I kept my expression relaxed and let out a light chuckle to follow up the remark, emphasizing how absolutely fine I was. From the corner of my eye, I saw Quinn's mouth tighten, but she didn't badger me about what she'd sensed. I was managing to convince her it wasn't a big enough deal to impinge on my dignity in front of the other beings in the car. Maybe she was being kind enough to wait until I was comfortable discussing it with her, as long as I wasn't at the point of driving us off the road.

If I *never* had to discuss what was plaguing me, I'd be satisfied. It should go away on its own, as randomly as the unwanted bursts of emotion had begun.

All right, their arrival hadn't been entirely random, but I'd prefer not to think about that fact either. The less I thought about it, the less likely I'd provoke another discomforting response.

I was a millennia-old demon with more power than the majority of beings in either realm possessed. I could handle this small problem on my own while we tackled the much larger one ahead of us together.

It was the physiological responses of the woman sitting beside me—the woman who'd come to matter more to me than just about anything in either realm—that I should be more concerned about. Especially when we pulled up at the wooden hut that was all that marked the meeting spot I'd picked and I sensed not just a few but dozens of beings lurking in the shadows around us.

"We'll want to go through the same test we did with the pixie on all of them," I said reluctantly as I parked the car. "Confirming that they're all free from any enemy's sway and joining us with the right intentions. But expend as little energy as you can get away with on each of them. And if you start to feel tired, I expect you to give yourself a break."

Quinn gave me a quizzical look. "I don't see why that should be a problem." She pushed open her door, stepped out onto the dry earth, and froze as the multitude of beings of various shapes and sizes rippled into physical form around us. Her breath caught with a hint of a gasp. "Oh."

"We do have an army!" Lance declared eagerly, springing out of the car and then leaping onto the roof of it in dragon form. I couldn't tell whether he thought he was offering them a warmer greeting by meeting them in his shadowkind appearance or attempting to intimidate anyone who might not give our mortal woman the respect she was due.

But our reluctant sorcerer knew how to handle herself just fine by now, initial hesitation aside. Her shoulders had already squared as she gazed out over the crowd of what I could now see was several dozen beings—and at least half of them higher, capable of more than just animalistic fighting. Twice as many as I'd spoken to yesterday. Many of the lesser shadowkind had wandered off since the pixie had first approached us, but the arrival of more thoughtful beings more than made up for their absence. They must have gathered more numbers like a snowball picking up new layers of frost as they'd moved across the country.

The leviathan's gambit might even have worked a little in our favor, despite what we'd lost to him. Any being that'd sensed what he was attempting to accomplish but managed to escape the sweep of his sorcery would be that much more motivated to make sure he never got the claws of his unnatural magic into their heads. More motivated than the various contacts I'd established over the centuries, most of whom still preferred to protect their own necks while they hadn't seen the full impact of the threat.

But then, how could I blame them when I'd taken the same tactic myself for so long? Too long.

"All right," Quinn said, moving to the hood of the car and propping herself against it. "Can you all get into some kind of line so we can be a bit organized about this? I just need to make sure none of you are under any compulsion from the shadowkind that wants to, y'know, kill me. I'm sure you can understand why I'd be cautious."

I'd already told the original bunch I'd talked to what would be required. They shuffled forward without argument, though they appeared to have some trouble with the whole idea of assembling in a line.

As Quinn got started, aiming a few sorcerous words at the first being to approach her to check for existing magic gripping its mind and then to question its intentions, Lance sprang back off the car. He and Crag prowled around the crowd like monstrous sheepdogs surveying their flock.

I stayed next to the car, within easy reach of Quinn should I need to yank her away from a troublesome being, though they seemed peaceful enough so far. Standing in one spot also made it easier to ride out the faint tremors of chill that rippled through me here and there as the odd syllables spilled from her tongue.

They reminded me too much of the commands the behemoth had hurled at me when he'd tried to force me into becoming his slave. The memory of that time was the deepest, darkest chill in the back of my mind.

I'd fought him off enough that I hadn't hurt Quinn or interfered with the trap we'd managed to set off. He hadn't gotten the best of me.

But he *almost* had. There'd been that moment, right before the trap had closed its metal jaws on him, that something had fractured in my self-control. There'd been nothing ringing in my head except his orders. I'd been about to attack Quinn.

Maybe I'd have wrestled control back and stopped myself, but I'd never know that for sure. And now I'd spend the rest of my ancient life living with that uncertainty.

As well as the uncertainty of whether another time, if a foe like that tried me again, I might lose myself altogether.

But that possibility didn't matter right now. Right now I held the most authority out of any being around us, and I wasn't going to let them forget that.

I stretched into my full shadowkind form, letting my hooves paw at the dusty earth and smiling to show off my jagged teeth. Any shadowkind who'd had the slightest inkling of turning on my woman had better think twice.

Quinn moved through each of the beings in just a minute or two, but I noticed when that time started to stretch a little longer. Once she'd spoken to maybe half of the crowd, finding them all honest about wanting to stand up to the leviathan, she exhaled so raggedly I was about to enforce a break. But then she got up herself and took a brief walk around to stretch her legs, drink some water, and eat a pear that Lance insisted on dicing up for her, show off that he was.

Even so, I wanted to tell her to give it a rest. That we would bring the beings we'd confirmed were trustworthy back with us and let the others linger here for another day or two until she'd recovered. But I could already imagine how well the suggestion would go down. I settled for eyeing her closely for any signs of deeper discomfort.

By the time she'd checked the last of the shadowkind who'd come to our aid, the sun had touched the horizon. Quinn sagged back against the hood with a sigh of relief.

"All good," she said. "Where do we go from here?"

I glanced to the east. "I was thinking we'd gather our forces and decide on our next steps in my badlands house—the one you visited briefly before. It's well out of the way of any ocean and also well-protected. Any beings in this bunch who can't handle the metal installations can stay outside them, and you'll go out to them when you need to make arrangements."

Quinn cocked her head but seemed to decide my strategy was solid enough. "Fine. Let's get going then."

I turned to the crowd around us. "There are plenty of shadows on and around the car. Hitch a ride if you like and can find room. The gargoyle will stay back with those who can't and show you the way. Stick to the gloom—we don't want to be spotted by any of that beast's minions who might have wandered this way."

A murmur mixed with grunts of agreement spread through the mass of beings. I didn't know how much of an army they'd prove to be, but at this point, I wasn't going to be choosey. At least every shadowkind with us was one that the leviathan hadn't bent to his will.

As we got into the car, I settled back into the driver's seat and started the engine. Quinn pulled out her phone, equipped with the SIM card I'd newly restored to her. I thought she might be going to place a call to her parents even though we'd only left them behind hours ago, but instead she flicked at the screen. I didn't know what she was up to until a few minutes later when she sucked in a horrified breath.

My gaze flicked from the road we were cruising down to her. "What?"

"A big wave hit Jacksonville just forty minutes ago. Half of the city is flooded. A bunch of people who were near the beach drowned or were killed by wreckage in the currents." Her voice wobbled.

"It's a good thing we got your parents out of there, then," I said. "The rest... We did our best to warn them. There are probably fewer casualties than there would have been otherwise."

"Yeah. It's just scary thinking of how close a call it was. If we'd waited even another day..." She ducked her head. "And I'd bet the leviathan told his minions to start with Jacksonville because of me. If I wasn't involved in this—"

"Hey," I said, sharply only so I could cut through her self-recriminations. "He'd have had them hit *somewhere* no matter what. He's the one responsible for the deaths, not you. You're doing everything you can to stop him."

"I know. I know." She closed her eyes for a minute and appeared to gird herself. Then she started scrolling through the news reports again. I kept most of my attention on the road, but I noticed when her frown deepened.

"It isn't just that one wave," she said. "There was another near Seattle. And people have finally figured out there's a huge one building off the coast of L.A. But it's not just waves either. There are strange cloud patterns in the skies where all the storms are happening. People are saying they're seeing faces there, glowing eyes, that sort of thing." She glanced at me. "I thought shadowkind like to keep a low profile. This is even more over-the-top than the attacks on the streets in L.A."

"They generally do lay low." A frown of my own crossed my face. What was the leviathan up to? "It's sounding more and more like our enemy wants to make his influence known. I guess he isn't scared of the Highest stepping in now that he's already faced off with some of their warriors and won. Maybe he's even rubbing his disobedience in their face for some sadistic reason."

Lance let out a short growl from the back seat. "Maybe he wants to scare all the other shadowkind who see it hoping they'll obey *him*."

"That's also possible," I said, but my stomach had knotted with uncertainty. None of those reasons quite added up with what I knew about my kind.

But if the leviathan was going for something beyond the obvious, what *was* he hoping to achieve?

And how the hell was our little makeshift army going to stop him?

CHAPTER ELEVEN

Quinn

It seemed like every time I glanced at the news feeds, the situation on the coasts had gotten worse. I woke up in the guest bedroom in Rollick's Texas badlands house and immediately grabbed my phone to find reports of more storm activity and a couple more tidal waves that'd crashed along the coastal regions. By the time I ventured out into the common areas, showered and theoretically refreshed for the day, my stomach was a mess of knots.

Lance was already in the kitchen, crisping bacon and frying eggs with his fiery breath. He motioned for me to sit at the gleaming central island and nudged the plate toward me before swiftly slicing an orange into crescents with his claws. I guessed he'd sensed as soon as I'd woken up and decided to be ready for me. I wasn't going to complain.

"Thank you," I said, and he beamed at me.

"You have to keep your strength up, baby girl. I'm always going to take care of you."

I couldn't bear to tell him that bacon wasn't exactly the best option for heart health. I doubted a little grease really mattered at this point when so many other things were putting much more strain on my transplanted organ.

As I dug in, my other three men wavered into sight around the island. Crag grabbed a bottle of water from the fridge and set it in front of me as if he was afraid I'd forget to hydrate. Torrent leaned against the counter with a pensive expression.

"We had a few more beings turn up overnight," he told me. "Wanderers who noticed the increased activity here and wanted to find out what's going on. They've opted to stay. You'll need to test them."

Rollick gave a tight grin. "For the moment, we have a few of our confirmed allies keeping watch over them to make sure they don't get up to anything nefarious. And the most competent beings standing watch at a farther distance to make sure no one else meanders close enough to see what's happening here without being vetted."

My gut clenched even more with that new worry. "Do you think the leviathan's minions will realize we've come out here—or what we're doing?"

"I expect we're reasonably safe," the demon said. "He's focusing his attention on the coasts, which are his natural habitat anyway, and he has no idea what our current plans might be or where we might have gone to. It's unlikely he has enough minions to spare to closely investigate every corner of the country. But the patrols will guard against any of those minions happening to stumble on our little army on the off chance that they do head this way."

"There aren't many beings hanging around out here at all," Lance put in. "Not much to do. Very boring. No people, no buildings, and everything is so flat."

Rollick shot him a light-hearted glower. "The boring-ness is what makes it safe. You always seem to find plenty of ways to entertain yourself no matter where you are."

"The storms are getting more volatile," I said. "I read that there's a major hurricane brewing in the Atlantic now, bigger than they usually see at this time of year. Will that be shadowkind-generated too?"

Torrent nodded. "There are definitely beings that can affect the weather that way, and I'm sure the leviathan has the reach to bring them under his sway."

"The humans have been evacuating many of the coastal areas—all across the country, not just in L.A. now," Crag said in an obvious attempt at reassurance. "They'll get to where it's safe for them too."

"If they can." I rubbed my mouth, forcing myself to finish chewing even though I couldn't take much pleasure from the food. Rollick might have had a general idea of the logistics after how thoroughly he'd involved himself in urban life, but I doubted the other shadowkind had any concept of how difficult it was to move entire cities' worth of people and keep them fed and sheltered.

Maybe it was the stress of that added concern or maybe it was just random, but a moment later, my chest contracted with a now-familiar vise. I braced my hands against the island, closing my eyes as I breathed through the painful sensation. My pulse skipped and raced, and a chill washed through me, deeper than the air-conditioned coolness.

A hand came to rest on my shoulder, rubbing it gently. I focused on that contact rather than the pressure in my chest. Lance let out a rough noise of frustration, but there really wasn't anything else any of them could do—as they had to be recognizing by now as much as I had.

When the pressure released, a sheen of sweat had formed on my brow. I wiped it away and stared down at my plate, a faint queasiness in my stomach making it hard to imagine eating more.

"We can put your food in the fridge for later," Torrent suggested, his even voice unusually soft.

"Yeah, that might be a good idea." I dragged in a breath and glanced toward the windows that looked out onto the house's yard and the desert terrain beyond it, where all of our new "army" was hiding in the shadows. "First I'm going to check in with my parents, and after that I'll confirm that the newcomers are above board, and then I think we should get on with figuring out who in this 'army' can actually do anything to fend off the leviathan."

I went back into the bedroom to make the call in private, my chest constricting in a different way at the sound of Mom's voice. She still sounded shaken but resigned. I didn't sense any sign of rebellion in her tone.

"It's good to hear from you," she said. "Are you all right? What we're seeing on the news is pretty frightening."

"I know," I said. "But I'm far away from it right now, and I'm making sure we're totally prepared before we try to fix things." As much as we could be prepared anyway.

"I feel so selfish staying here out of the way when so many other people are suffering."

A lump rose in my throat. I could have said the same thing. People were dying out there, losing their homes, struggling to survive, and I was living in relative comfort, even though I was one of the few people who had any chance of tackling the threat. I hated that we'd had to run away, as necessary as I knew that move had been.

"You're helping by giving me one less thing to worry about," I told her. "Knowing you two are okay makes it easier for me to concentrate on finding ways to stop this disaster that won't put *me* in too much danger."

I talked with her a little longer and then with Dad. After, I walked out of the room with my emotions in a muddle, pulling on my protective vest so I could go beyond the house's yard without fear of detection. Out under the searing sun, I pushed my worries to the back of my mind and went through the motions of making sure the new arrivals to our shadowkind gang weren't operating under enemy influence. Then I sat down on a bench in the shade of the pair of scrawny trees at the edge of the yard.

My men had followed me out to oversee the proceedings. "Let's find out exactly what we're working with," I said to Rollick.

Torrent leaned his forearms against the back of the bench, one resting next to my shoulder companionably. "The most important factor in tackling the leviathan is going to be making sure no one we send into battle will get caught up in his sorcery."

Lance clicked his tongue. "Quinn's magic shielded us from the behemoth. He didn't get into my head at all."

"Yeah, but the behemoth was only half as powerful as the leviathan is now," I pointed out. "And my sorcery has a stronger effect on you four because I know you so well. I don't know the beings that've joined us since then at all."

"And there are too many of them," Crag put in firmly. "Quinn would wear herself out if she tried to cast a powerful command that'd last long enough on all of us." He loomed over me with a concerned frown, not mentioning the possible consequences beyond simply making me tired.

I swallowed thickly, and Rollick let out a faint huff. "I doubt we'd want to send all the beasties right into the fray regardless. If we can pick out a few key allies, Quinn's magic would at least give them some protection. We can't decide how to proceed until we're aware of the possibilities."

He stepped forward into the sunlight, snapping his fingers. "All right, all of you who want to help stop the leviathan from carrying out whatever other horribleness he has planned, our sorcerer wants to speak with you. Let's start with the higher beings. Show yourselves a few at a time, and let us know any supernatural abilities or other skills you can bring to the table."

I raised my voice to carry across the desolate terrain. "If any of you have some kind of power that allows you to ward off other beings' supernatural abilities, that would be particularly useful. Or anyone who can manipulate water and weather, since that's what the leviathan is mostly using against us right now."

A slim woman with bluish skin materialized out of the shadow by a patch of desert grass. She approached me with her head bowed low. "I don't know about warding off, but I'm a sea nymph," she said. "All of my powers have to do with water."

My spirits rose a little. This was a decent start. "Do you think you'd be able to push back against the tidal waves that are being summoned—maybe even break them apart before they reach the shore?" We could send her to the east coast or farther north on the west where she'd only be contending with the leviathan's allies, not him and his sorcery directly.

"I could try. The way they're stirring up the oceans, throwing the water around—it isn't right. It'll be hurting the other shadowkind who like to live in the water too."

Lance had perked up. "Maybe you have some friends who could help? That way you could push back more."

She offered a shy smile. "I'll reach out to whoever I can find. I don't know how many others like me would want to get involved. I know what it's like to be caught up by that awful magic... I don't want it to happen again. But when they haven't had their minds taken over, they don't realize what's at stake."

"Whatever you can do would be great," I assured her. "Let's see who else is here to help, and then we'll decide the best place for you to go."

A gangly man with shaggy yellow hair had appeared while I'd been talking to the sea nymph. As she stepped aside, he gave me a jaunty bow and brandished a gleaming flute. "I don't know about deflecting powers, but I have a sort of sorcery of my own that I can use on mortals. I managed to get away from the leviathan before his magic totally caught me, so maybe my own powers have given me a little resistance."

"Maybe" and "a little" didn't give me a whole lot of hope, but it was better than nothing.

I smiled back at him. "That's good to know. Is that your only supernatural ability?"

"I can work minor glamours, but I'm not sure how much use they'd be."

Neither was I, but I forced my smile to hold. "You never know. Thank you." I glanced around the terrain. No other beings had emerged yet. My temporary good spirits started to fade. "Is there no one else here who has abilities related to persuasion or water?"

When no other shadowkind showed themselves, I sat up a little straighter, willing myself to hold steady. "That's all right. I'd still like to know what the rest of you can do. Let's hear from all of you."

But if the ones I'd already spoken to were the best of the bunch... I wasn't sure we had a hope in hell of defeating the fiend we were up against.

CHAPTER TWELVE

Quinn

"All right," I said, staring down at the puppy-sized frog, which peered up at me with its round eyes. "I'm guessing that you prefer a watery home. Anything else you can show me?"

The lesser shadowkind simply croaked. I couldn't tell whether it'd understood my question or not, but then, most of the lesser beings hadn't. From what I could tell, they'd joined up with us more for their own protection than to help with ours.

I dipped my head to it in acknowledgment. "That's fine. Glad to have you with us."

As it bounded back into the shadows, I stood up and stretched. I hadn't been doing much other than talking for the past few hours, but exhaustion rolled over me as if I'd barely slept last night.

That was another symptom of a failing heart—getting tired faster. I gritted my teeth against that knowledge and headed into the house, moving slowly but steadily.

Though I'd stayed in the shade outside, stepping into the air-conditioned cool was a welcome relief. As I let out a little sigh, watching my men emerge from the shadows around me, Lance slipped his arm around my waist and nuzzled the side of my head.

"What do you think of our army?" he asked.

I made a face. "Honestly? It's not much of an army. If the sea nymph can convince some of her fellow nymphs and whatever other beings to help counteract the magic that's driving the tidal waves, that'll be great, but it won't do anything to stop the leviathan himself. None of them seem to have much hope of deflecting his sorcery."

Crag had headed into the kitchen, where he was now leaning into the fridge to grab one of the pre-made meals they'd stocked the place with for me. He was clearly determined to make sure I never went thirsty or hungry. "It's unfortunate that they can't all wear shirts like yours. Or some kind of hat to shield their minds? I don't know how it would work."

"It might not do any good even if they could tolerate the silver and iron," Torrent pointed out, dropping into one of the chairs at the kitchen table with his tentacles arcing on either side. "Those metals can deflect the kinds of persuasive magic shadowkind use on humans. There's no reason to assume they'd protect against human-based magic, even if it's being wielded by a shadowkind."

"That's true." I sat down across from him and rubbed my brow. "The only beings who'd be able to stand up to the leviathan without getting caught up in his sway are other humans like me. And the only humans like me who could do anything at all to affect *him* are other sorcerers. And apparently they're all just as selfish as the average shadowkind, since pretty much none of them responded to our request for help."

And the one sorcerer who had turned up had been promptly slaughtered. I had no illusions about the vulnerability of our human bodies, even those that weren't harboring borrowed hearts.

Lance hissed through his teeth. "That bunch off in their enclave tormenting beasties to make new sorcerers—but they can't be bothered to come when there's a shadowkind who actually deserves to be messed with."

"Well, to be fair, I haven't asked *them*."

Rollick propped himself against the kitchen island. "I think we'd better keep it that way," he said dryly. "If they found out where you are after you disrupted their rites—and brought a demon into their midst who murdered a few of their people—I suspect we'd have two sets of enemies to contend with rather than new allies."

"Yeah." So it still came down to me. I dragged in a breath. "If I could just control him enough to make sure he didn't enslave any other beings, maybe the rest of you could restrain him. Or if I could force him to admit what he's really planning, we could focus our defenses better." I paused. "There really isn't any way to completely stop him other than killing him like we did with the behemoth, though, is there? I mean, after everything he's done, there's obviously no reasoning with him or convincing him to give up his plans."

"I think that's a fair assumption," Rollick said. "So fair that I've already had my human contractors building another trap on the outskirts of L.A., since we had solid blueprints on hand for what that should look like. What we really need is a way to get our serpentine adversary in there, and then it'll be game over."

"I don't think we're going to trick him," Torrent pointed out. "Even the behemoth only came all the way into the first trap when Quinn compelled him."

I nodded, biting my lip. "But it took everything I had to manage that."

"And it hurt your heart," Lance said with a frown.

I didn't think that really mattered in the long run. If I died stopping the leviathan, that'd be a hell of a lot better than living another few months while watching it wreak havoc across my world. But I knew the dragon shifter wouldn't like hearing me say that out loud.

Crag set a ham and cheese wrap in front of me, and I picked it up gingerly. I was still wiped from the morning's activities, and suddenly all I wanted was a few moments away from the horrible problem looming over us.

"Thank you," I said to the gargoyle, and stood up. "I'm just going to check whether my parents have left me any messages and take a look at the latest news. Then we can talk some more, see if we can figure anything else out."

As I walked to my bedroom, the men's voices continued to murmur behind me. Their conversation fell away after the door shut in my wake.

I actually had my phone on me, so I knew I hadn't gotten any alerts, but I double-checked for new texts or voicemail anyway. Then I found I couldn't quite bear to look into what other disasters might be going on around the country that I couldn't do anything about yet. I sank down on the edge of the bed, grappling with my uneasiness.

And then a sharp jab of panic lanced straight through my chest.

I jumped up instinctively, my pulse racing before I recognized that it wasn't a more potent effect of my failing heart. It was a flash of emotion, and not mine—it must have come from Rollick.

I'd been catching flickers of what felt like uneasiness and even fear from him over the past few days, but none quite as intense as this. With all my nerves jangling, I rushed back to the kitchen.

The men were still poised around the room, Torrent in mid-sentence, his voice fading when I came charging in. Rollick had kept his spot by the island, his stance typically languid, but as I came through the doorway, my gaze shot to his hand gripping the edge of the counter. His knuckles had turned pure white.

His eyes darted to me, and I caught a whirl of tumultuous emotion there in the instant before he managed to will it away.

"What's going on?" I demanded. I knew he didn't want me bringing it up, but he'd refused to say anything to me all the other times that rush of emotion had come over him, even though he must have realized I'd been picking up on what he was feeling. And something about the conversation with the other men must have provoked it, so if he wouldn't give me answers, they would.

We were all in this together now. He shouldn't be hiding something important enough to make him react like that.

Rollick offered me one of his movie-star smiles, as if that was going to distract me. "I don't know what you're talking about. We were simply having a conversation."

I folded my arms over my chest. "You do so know what I'm talking about. Something upset you—a lot. Something's *been* upsetting you ever since we faced off with the behemoth. If we're going to fight his partner, I think we need to know what's going on with all of us. If something's come up that makes the situation worse, we have to deal with it together."

Lance cocked his head. "What made you think something's wrong with Rollick? He didn't do anything."

I opened my mouth and closed it again. Not only had Rollick and I never discussed the emotional connection that'd formed between us with the other men, we hadn't told them about the incident that'd caused it. I'd been so relieved to have the three of them back, and I'd already been avoiding thinking about the way Rollick had forced his essence on me—

and the way my body had responded to him in that moment. They'd been aware that my sorcerer powers had been developing in general. It hadn't seemed important.

But maybe I shouldn't have been hiding any of it.

Rollick stared me down for a moment, but it didn't take him long to figure out that he wasn't going to intimidate me into backing off. He sighed and rolled his shoulders. "Fine. The rest of you have heard about the rites we discovered at the enclave. It seemed obvious that a similar process could enhance our reluctant sorcerer's abilities too. So I took it upon myself to insist that she consume a significant amount of my essence."

Crag's brow furrowed. "'Insist'?"

The demon waved off his implied objection. "She wasn't totally on board, but she was mainly hesitating out of fear of harming someone, and I didn't mind making the offering. We've hashed it all out since then. In any case, along with heightening her magic, it also seems to have left her unusually sensitive to my emotional state. Unfortunately, I haven't figured out how to turn off that connection." He grimaced.

"It's a good thing, considering you like to hold everything that's going on with you so close to the chest," I muttered. "So, what *is* going on with you right now?"

He hesitated in a very un-Rollick-like way, another tendril of anxiety reaching me, although this one didn't have the same urgent flavor. Whatever it was, he didn't like the idea of how we might respond.

"She's right," Torrent said quietly. "We need to know exactly where we stand—with each other and with our enemies. It's not as if the rest of us haven't had plenty of problems of our own to work through."

Rollick let out a disgruntled sound, but the reminder that his companions weren't likely to get particularly judgmental appeared to spur on his confession.

"It wasn't at all pleasant when the behemoth tried to wrap his magic around my mind," he said in a voice that might have been breezy if not for the thread of tension woven through it. "I've spent thousands of years never bowing to anyone else's will unless I chose to for my own reasons, and the sensation of nearly being taken over has left me... unsettled. And in random moments, I get flashes of memories from that time that unsettle me even more all over again. That's all there is to it. No new villains to worry about or additional problems to heap on our plates."

A pang ran through my heart. It sounded like a problem to me. My fingers curled into my palms against the urge to reach out to him, not knowing if he'd appreciate a comforting touch or find it embarrassing.

"That makes sense," I said. "Is the effect getting worse? This time just now... it *felt* worse than before."

He shrugged as if his answer didn't really matter. "I'm keeping it under control. My emotional state doesn't affect anyone but me. I assure you that if you need anything from me, this minor issue won't get in the way."

As if I only cared about his mental stability when it affected my plans. "I don't like that it's happening to you at all—because I don't want you to be going through any kind of emotional pain. If it isn't getting better over time—"

"Then I'll just have to keep coping," Rollick cut in, sharper than before. He paused with a wince and continued in a gentler voice. "You don't need to worry about me, Quinn. I've survived far too much already for this little setback to bring me all that low. And we definitely have much *bigger* problems to contend with."

Lance let out a wordless grunt, glancing from me to Rollick and then to the other guys. "We do have lots of problems—but maybe this is also a way that we can solve them."

CHAPTER THIRTEEN

Lance

Quinn blinked at me, confusion clouding her pretty blue eyes. "What do you mean? How could Rollick's panic attacks fix anything?"

"Not that," I said quickly, with a flick of my gaze toward the demon. He had stood by her side when the rest of us couldn't—he had kept her safe. I didn't want him to think I'd want him to suffer, even if it would have helped us. "I meant taking in his essence and getting that connection to him. You could do the same thing with all of us."

Quinn's lips parted, but it took her a moment before she seemed to be able to speak. "You—you know that would make my sorcery stronger. You don't like that part of me."

It was true that remembering the magic she'd cast on me to force me to leave her side sent a jolt of horror through me. My stomach turned at the thought of how much more easily she'd be able to work a spell like that even now, with the extra benefit of Rollick's essence. If she took a long drink of mine, she might be able to control me with a single brief word, with no effort at all.

But she wouldn't. She was my Quinn and I was her dragon, and she'd promised never to use her magic on any of us again unless we asked her to for our own benefit. She'd told me she was never going to use it on *anyone* again after we'd defeated the leviathan. She was as horrified by what other sorcerers did as any shadowkind was.

"I like that it could be what stops this unhinged leviathan from enslaving any more beings himself," I said. "Or hurting more mortals. That's a good enough reason. And—if you could sense how we're feeling, then you'd worry less about us, right? You'd know that if you're not noticing anything bad, then we must be okay."

Something in her face softened. "And if I did realize that you were in danger, I'd know to come help."

Well, that hadn't been exactly what I was aiming for. I'd rather Quinn stayed as far away as possible from wherever the danger was and let us deal with it when we could. But we couldn't always, and it was hard to tell her she shouldn't be allowed to help us when we were so determined to help her.

If I expected her to keep her promise not to force us out of harm's way, then I shouldn't try to force *her* to keep away from the danger we all faced either.

I let out a light huff. "Yes. But hopefully less of that. The most important thing is that we're all pretty strong, so if we give you some of our strength, the three of us might be enough to put you on the same level as the leviathan. Rollick's contribution made you powerful enough to control the behemoth."

Quinn's mouth twisted. "Not on its own. I—when I was trying to get the behemoth to come into the trap, it didn't work at first. I had to take in some essence from one of the higher shadowkind minions that'd attacked us before I managed it."

I shrugged. "Still. That was one and there are three of us. It could work. Maybe you could take a little more of Rollick's too."

The demon chuckled. "I'm not sure I want to give her even more of an open invitation inside my mind, as eager as you seem to be." He paused, and his voice turned more serious when he looked at Quinn again. "But I would offer more regardless if it could mean we can end this catastrophe for good."

"You're welcome to my essence, as much as I can spare," Torrent said.

"It won't only boost your sorcery to tackle the leviathan. It'd also give you an even closer connection to us so that your commands can shield us from him better."

I clicked my claws happily. "Yes, that's good too." Torrent always thought of all the aspects of a plan. And if he didn't see any problems with my suggestion, it couldn't be a bad idea, could it?

Crag let out a rumbling sound. "You can take whatever you need from me, Softness. But will it tire your heart to absorb more power?"

Guilt flashed through me. I hadn't considered that possibility. But Quinn was already shaking her head.

"I didn't feel any effects like that when I consumed Rollick's essence," she said. "The symptoms only started after I exhausted myself controlling the behemoth. I don't think the process itself should affect me. Who knows what'll happen when we confront the leviathan... but I've got to try. Having more energy might mean it's less of a strain."

Crag dipped his head in a nod. "Then I think you should do it. I know you'll use the power well."

Quinn glanced at each of us in turn, her eyes wide and a little shiny, like they'd collected a few tears. She did cry sometimes when she was pleased as well as when she was sad. I hoped this was one of the happy times.

"I don't really like the idea," she said. "I don't like the thought of doing to you what other sorcerers have done to so many other shadowkind selfishly. But... in this case, it wouldn't be selfish. And you're giving me permission rather than having it stolen from you. So I guess it'd be silly to refuse. I don't want more people dying because I have hang-ups about the power in me."

"You've never tried to hurt anyone," I reminded her. "You're always protecting all the people and beings you can. I wouldn't say we should do this if I didn't know it'd be okay."

She beamed at me, and a warm glow lit up in my chest as I grinned back. It was such a miraculous sensation, this emotion of love. And when she was connected to me the way she was to Rollick, she'd be able to feel just how strong my devotion to her was.

Maybe I liked that more than any other part of this plan.

Quinn raised her chin. "If we're going to do it, I suppose we'd better get on with it right away. Rollick, you said you've already constructed another trap. All we need is a way to propel the leviathan into it. Let's see if we can't accomplish that and put an end to his reign of terror before he takes it any further."

"All right." I stepped forward, my heart suddenly thumping faster. "I'll go first, since I made the suggestion. Does it matter what form we're in? Where should we do it?"

"I carried out the process in my demon body, but that made it easier for me to inflict the necessary wound," Rollick said. "Your claws should do the trick just fine either way. It might be more reassuring for Quinn to look into that pretty face of yours while she's still feeling conflicted about the situation."

I snorted at him. "I'm a very pretty dragon too."

Quinn's mouth twitched with another smile. "Yes, you are. I think I'd be fine either way. How would you feel more comfortable? You're the one who'll be bleeding."

Of course she would think of my well-being first. I weighed the options and decided, "Like this. I want to hold you while we're doing it. We can sit on the sofa."

I headed into the living room, and the others followed. As I sank down onto the sofa's soft cushions, Quinn hesitated.

"When I took in Rollick's essence, I kind of lost my mind in the moment. Went a little wild, feeling all-powerful and like I should be roaming around, stretching what I was capable of." She arched her eyebrows slightly at me. "Knowing how energetic you typically are, I might get even more that way when it's your essence. Just so you're prepared. If I can't control the reactions, you'll want to hang on to me, make sure I don't go running off."

She was putting a lot of trust in me too, then. I motioned her over and collected her onto my lap. "I won't let you go, baby girl."

Quinn tipped her head against my shoulder, molding herself against me as if she belonged nowhere else, and even more affection swelled in my chest. I adjusted her position against me so my arms could wrap all the way around her, flexed my claws, and slashed through my forearm deep enough to open a vicious gouge.

Quinn flinched in my embrace, but she tilted her head so I could easily bring the smoking wound to her mouth. The pain that radiated through my arm was diluted by the thrill of knowing that soon we'd be merged in new ways I'd never imagined could be possible.

My essence streamed from the cut in rhythmic billows with the thudding of my heart. Quinn had opened her mouth wide, inhaling steadily, but plenty of the stuff wafted up from the edges of her mouth and dissipated into the air around us. I kept my own breath steady. If I started to feel unwell, I'd have to stop and seal the wound, but I didn't want that to happen any sooner than it needed to.

The lingering tension in Quinn's body gradually released. Her muscles relaxed against me, her posture slackening as she absorbed more and more of my essence. She barely moved. At first, I thought she'd been mistaken about the likely effects.

Then the first tremor ran through her limbs. Her legs shifted against my lap, starting to squirm. I couldn't hold them in place with one arm around her waist and the other pressed to her mouth, but Torrent stepped closer, resting a tentacle over her shins to keep them still. Crag and Rollick eased nearer as well, ready to step in if I needed more assistance.

We were all in this together even now.

That recognition might have pleased me if Quinn's muscles hadn't flexed in my grasp at the same moment. The restlessness seemed to be rippling through her entire body.

One of her hands clutched my shirt, her fingers tightening and easing in an erratic pattern. A disgruntled murmur emanated from her throat. Her eyes darted from side to side, barely focusing on me. I couldn't tell if she was all that aware of anything in the room anymore.

Should I stop now? I could keep going—I should give her as much as I could, shouldn't I? But as I watched her quiver and jerk against my and Torrent's hold, a sudden chill washed away the warmth that'd filled me earlier.

This wasn't my Quinn in my arms right now, not really. A wildness had gripped her—the wildness of her expanding sorcery. I was giving her even more power to enslave shadowkind to her will, and it was muddling her head, making her fight me. She didn't remember the intentions she'd come to me with.

What if I'd gone too far by making this suggestion? Was I betraying my own kind, all the beings like me, by giving her the power to perform even more sorcery?

I might not know until we'd seen this war through to its end.

CHAPTER FOURTEEN

Quinn

I woke in a daze, blinking and finding myself staring up at the white ceiling in the guest bedroom. In that first second, my body felt weirdly numb, giving me the impression that I was floating over the bed rather than lying on it. Then my awareness sharpened, and I felt the silky texture of the sheets wrapped around me. A waft of cool air brushed my cheek.

"She's awake!" Lance bounced right onto the bed but slowed down his movements as he reached for me. He gazed down at me with obvious concern and stroked his knuckles over my temple, brushing the hair away from my face. "How are you feeling, Quinn?"

I cleared my throat before speaking. "All right. A little disoriented. Did everything go okay? I remember getting kind of stir-crazy—trying to run off—it's a good thing you held on to me. But the rest is blurry." I had distinct impressions of drinking in Lance's essence but not whether the other men had managed to contribute theirs as well.

Torrent's voice spoke up from near the foot of the bed. "After a little while, you seemed to realize you weren't going anywhere and resigned yourself to the process, just testing us a little here and there. We offered as much essence as we safely could—even Rollick again. Do you notice any change in your powers?"

I focused my attention on the ripples of energy that often passed through my chest. I had a sense of my sorcery whirling around my heart, but it was vague. "I didn't really feel the difference the first time I took in Rollick's until I actually tried to use my magic. I'm sure it's done *something*."

"You should try it on us," Lance declared. "Come up with a command that'll protect us from the leviathan's magic. We're about to go off and do battle with him anyway, right? As soon as you're up to it."

He spoke easily and without any outward sign of concern about me using my sorcery on him, but a twinge of anxiety quivered into me that I could tell was his. It had a Lance-like flavor somehow, which was a relief, because it would have been a huge muddle if I'd been getting hit by emotions constantly with no idea how to tell who might need my help.

I pushed myself upright and knit my brow at him. "I don't need to start giving commands. Not yet, anyway. We've got to get back to California first."

Rollick appeared in the bedroom doorway. "We do, but we don't know how far the leviathan is extending his reach now or how often he's putting out a call with his power. I think it'd be better if we're protected as much as we can be before we venture anywhere near his chosen domain. You can top up our protections when we're closer, of course."

He didn't sound at all bothered by the thought of me using my sorcery on him, despite the distress he'd talked about experiencing leftover from the behemoth's attempt at enslaving him, and I didn't catch any flicker of emotion that undermined his tone. I guessed he didn't associate my magic with the power that monster had used on him. Small comforts.

Crag loomed next to the demon. "You wanted to go right away to confront him, didn't you, Softness? Are you well enough to?"

I sat up and stretched my arms. "I'm totally fine. Just must have needed some rest after the whole essence-consuming thing. But we need everything else to be ready too."

I gave Rollick a questioning look, and he offered a slightly crooked smile. "The trap is ready whenever we are. If you want to flex those extra-enhanced powers of yours and see if we can hook a sea serpent, I say we go give it our best shot."

"I guess we'd need to find him first," I said.

Torrent nodded. "I don't think that'll be much trouble. He's mostly sticking to the ocean now and sending his minions to do his inland work. I might be able to draw him farther up the coast toward the trap so you don't have to go quite as far into his territory. We'll have a better idea once we get there."

"Okay." I dragged in a breath, ignoring the knotting of my stomach. I *had* wanted to get this confrontation over with. And I should make sure my powers were noticeably revved up before we took that step. Maybe I'd maxed out my potential with Rollick earlier and my other men's essence wouldn't have done anything other than forge those tenuous emotional connections. "What command should I give you that won't get in the way of anything you might need to do?"

"You had good phrasing last time," Crag rumbled. "It didn't cause any problems. You could stick to just the part about refusing orders from the leviathan for now, since we don't know exactly what we'll be doing out there yet."

"Yeah." Relief trickled through me at that thought. Protecting them really could be that simple.

I just had to hope my sorcery would be strong enough to fend off the leviathan's magic as well.

I turned to Lance, reaching to grasp his hand. "Do you want to go first again?"

No more tremors of anxiety reached me. He simply beamed. "Absolutely."

I fixated on the power I knew I held inside me, willing it to activate at my call. When I opened my mouth, it burst up my throat more like a bolt of lightning than a sizzle of electricity. The words flew out in its wake. "You will refuse any orders the leviathan gives you."

The command rushed out of me, leaving my skin tingling. Lance blinked and grinned. "That went in faster than before, and deeper I think. I can feel the magic wriggling around in my mind. But it's a good order. That's okay." He cocked his head at me. "Did it feel more powerful to you?"

A giggle bubbled my throat. Now that I'd stirred up the sorcerous energy inside me, it was jittering all through my veins. "Oh, yeah. You know, we might just be able to do this."

Torrent's lips curved in one of his rare smiles. "I like the sound of that. Then the rest of us had better receive our orders."

It was hard to maintain my optimism for the entire, long drive out to the L.A. area. Even with Rollick handling the car tirelessly and using some demonic power to ensure we didn't get caught speeding, night had fallen by the time he slowed at the edge of the terrain he considered reasonably safe.

He pulled off onto a smaller road and parked just beyond a desolate-looking gas station. Rain drummed against the roof, and wind warbled overhead. He glanced toward the back seat. "I think we'd better split up here. If any of you have concerns about your part in this scheme, you'd better mention them now."

Lance shifted impatiently. "I just want to see that big snake fall down."

"Well, you might not get to *see* it, but if all goes well, you can come watch the aftermath. One big bonfire of essence." Rollick chuckled darkly.

Torrent slipped a tentacle around my wrist to give it a quick squeeze. "You're stronger than him in the ways that matter most."

Then he and Lance vanished into the shadows.

The rest of us waited in the thickening darkness for half an hour, letting the two of them get a head start on us. The plan we'd come up with during the drive was that the dragon shifter and the tentacled man would create multiple disturbances across the city—making it look as if my supposed army was launching an attack. If it worked as intended, the leviathan would send a bunch of his minions to go deal with the threat but not bother going himself, which was his usual MO. That would leave much fewer lackeys hanging around guarding *him*.

We'd never come right to him or his partner before, not like this. I didn't think he'd be expecting it. The only question was whether I could pull off my part of the plan once we were close enough for me to cast my sorcery at him.

When Crag nudged me, I obliged his concerns by eating the rest of the drive-through meal we'd picked up for dinner. My stomach was still tight, but he wasn't wrong that I could use all the energy I could get. Whether it worked or not, the attempt was going to take a lot out of me.

I popped my pills at the right time, trying not to think about whether they were really making a difference at this point. At the ping of Rollick's phone, he started the engine. That was our signal that the other men's gambit was underway.

We didn't know exactly where the leviathan was. All Rollick's shadowkind contacts in southwest California had been swept up in the fiend's waves of magical influence. So we were going to go down as close as we could get to the most central beach and work from there. Knowing the leviathan's preferred habitat, Rollick had possessed the presence of mind to arrange for the second trap to be constructed not far from the coastline, in an old warehouse on the outskirts of the city.

The roads were eerily vacant even once we reached the suburbs. The streetlamps glowed off the rain-slick asphalt, and the only sound was the pounding of the rain and the distant thunder. The west-most end of the city had been totally vacated, flooded by the earlier smaller waves that we knew were just a precursor to the immense one the leviathan was building.

I wasn't totally sure how Rollick determined when we'd better leave the car ourselves. He parked outside a bar that was closed far earlier than I'd imagine it would have been under normal circumstances. "Out into the deluge we go."

I pulled on the ankle-length rain slicker he'd gotten for me, tugging the broad hood as far forward as I could so that it would shield my face. This wasn't going to be a fun excursion. But Crag's head had already lifted, his gaze focusing on something in the distance beyond his actual sight.

"He's close," he said. "Just a little farther north, out in the ocean shallows. I can fly out there in just a minute."

In just a minute, I'd be facing our ultimate foe. I swallowed thickly. "All right. Let's do this."

Rollick grasped my shoulder. "I'll be right there with the two of you. In this darkness, I can travel almost anywhere." He glanced at Crag. "If Quinn's sorcery isn't working and that serpentine monster comes at you, get her out of there as quickly as you possibly can. You know where we'll regroup."

Crag dipped his head in a brisk nod. He wrapped his arms around me, and I adjusted my position against his chest in the way I'd learned was more comfortable for both of us. The vinyl layer of the rain slicker gave him another barrier of protection from the silver and iron threads woven into my undershirt, but they were thin enough that they didn't bother him as much as my old vest had even without that. He showed no sign of irritation as we lifted off together into the downpour.

The cool rain spilled over the brim of my hood and streaked across my rain slicker as well as Crag's granite-like gargoyle skin. My hands were immediately drenched. I kept my feet tucked under the hem of the slicker so my sneakers didn't end up sopping too. The drops battered us in waves with each sweep of Crag's wings, lifting us higher.

At least the weather hid us from view—and stopped many people from coming out where they might have been able to see us in the first place. And as Crag soared closer to the churning sea, the buildings beneath us looked totally abandoned, no lights gleaming in the windows. The only glow was from the streetlamps that hadn't been toppled by the earlier waves.

I fixed my gaze on the frothing water beyond the coast. Somewhere amid those currents, our greatest enemy was lurking. He must have been deep beneath the surface or hidden in the gloom for now, because I couldn't make out the monstrous serpentine form I'd watched devour his partner just days ago. He was too massive to hide his physical form very easily.

Crag's sensitivity to shadowkind presences guided him. He flew farther north along the coast, gripping me firmly. It would have been difficult for him to speak in the storm, but for the most part, my sense of *him* was steady and calm. Only a few brief, faint quivers of apprehension filtered through the connection we'd formed.

Finally, he stopped and swung around in mid-air. He ducked his head so his mouth came close to my ear.

"He's down there," he rumbled through my hood. "I took us a little past him. You see where that red car is halfway in the water? He's almost directly across from there, maybe a hundred feet out."

"Okay." Now I just needed to call the leviathan toward us—and keep calling him all the way to Rollick's trap farther north. No big deal. Ha.

I closed my eyes and trained all my attention on the whirling energy inside me, tuning out the damp and the chill and the battering of the rain. Just with that internal gesture, the magic spurted and sizzled, crackling through every nerve. I felt like a live wire, ready to zap anything I touched. My pulse thumped faster as I opened my eyes and my mouth.

As always when I aimed my sorcery at any beings other than the men I knew so well, the words that seared from my mouth came in a language I couldn't understand myself. But I knew the intent I was putting into the shout, the command I was hurling at the invisible being below.

Show yourself and follow me. Now.

My skin quivered and my tongue tingled as the energy rushed out of me. It rang through my body so intensely that my vision briefly whited out. I reached toward the monster in the crashing sea with every ounce of strength I had in me, as if the foreign syllables were talons I could dig into its flesh and yank it forward with.

Something twanged deep in my chest. Exhilaration flared through my veins in the wake of the sorcery. I'd snagged the beast; my magic had caught hold.

Crag grunted with a mix of uneasiness and approval as a sinewy blueish green form materialized below us, a few shades darker than the wild waters that swept over and around it. The creature raised its head, its smoldering orange eyes large and fierce enough that I could make them out even across the distance between us. But it pushed forward through the water, heading our way.

"Good," Crag murmured, propelling us backward with flaps of his wings. "Very good. You're doing amazing, Quinn."

I hugged his arm and braced myself before flinging the command at the leviathan again for good measure. My heart stuttered with the blast of energy that surged through me as the words left my mouth, but the massive serpent slid forward a little faster than before.

It was working. I'd really made it happen. I was controlling this immense fiend.

I couldn't tell whether it was exhaustion from the energy expended or giddiness at my victory that'd left my head spinning. Maybe some of both. My mouth had gone dry. I clung to Crag even tighter, doing my best to ignore the increasingly erratic thump of my heart and the prickles of pain that were starting to dig into my rib cage.

I had to concentrate on the leviathan. I had to reel him in all the way to the trap, or this whole effort would be for nothing.

He was still coming, weaving through the waves, more of his seemingly endless snake-like body revealed as I drew him into shallower waters. I wasn't sure exactly how much farther it was to the trap; I wasn't sure how far we'd already come. My sense of time had fallen away along with everything else other than the hitches of my pulse and the magic shivering between me and my prey.

The ache in my chest spread down my back and out through my arms. Crag nuzzled my head through the hood. "Halfway there, Softness. We've got him."

The reassuring words had only just left his mouth when the leviathan reared up. Seawater streamed off its dark scales. It shook its upper body from side to side like a dog drying its fur and then smacked itself down on the road right at the edge of the coast.

I flinched automatically at the impact, the thud of it carrying all the way to my ears. And then the jitter of energy inside me fizzled. I knew in an instant, with a gaping horror that stretched wide through my chest, that I'd lost my hold.

A cry burst from my lips. I grappled with the magic twined through my heart, willing as much of it as I could still summon up to my tongue, and hollered out another command so forcefully it turned my throat raw.

My pulse lurched. The constricting sensation squeezed harder, pushing the air from my lungs. I gasped and choked on a sob as the answering jolt of a successful command didn't come.

My efforts hadn't been enough, and I didn't know what else to do. My limbs felt like jelly; my heart was on fire. My head was spinning so fast that the leviathan seemed to double and triple before my eyes as he surged farther out of the surf.

He threw himself upright and shrank at the same time, his body shifting into a mostly man-like form that stood at least seven feet tall. His wet, tangled hair hung halfway down his back, and his eyes glared up at us. A sheen of smaller scales dappled his bare torso and arms.

"You tried and lost, sorcerer and traitors," he bellowed at us. "Now you'll just have to sit back and watch. I'll bring the depths of the shadow realm down on this place and make it ours even if I have to summon them myself."

Then he whipped around and dove into the water. His body never resurfaced that I saw; he'd probably melded into the shadows there as he made his way back to his former haven.

I couldn't pay much attention anyway. My lungs were heaving and my breaths rasping as I gasped to fill my chest. I couldn't tell if I was suffocating or having a heart attack—maybe both.

"Quinn," Crag muttered in a mournful voice with a flash of fear that rushed from him into me. He whipped around. "Relax now. You can't do any more. Just—just breathe, and I'll take you someplace safe."

As he soared onward and I grappled for control over my body, one clear thought penetrated the growing haze in my head.

There *was* nowhere safe. Not in the entire world. And from what the leviathan had said, even if I didn't know exactly what he'd meant, soon our home would be even more dangerous for all of us.

CHAPTER FIFTEEN

Quinn

By the time we made it to the meeting spot and the new car Rollick had arranged to have waiting for us there, breathing was no longer a fight. The vise in my chest had eased off enough that I wasn't afraid I was going to die right this moment. But an ache still gripped my sternum, prickling more sharply when I moved. If I turned my head too quickly, it started spinning again.

Crag yanked open the back door and set me down on the seat with the gentleness he could offer in contrast with his hardened body. Rollick immediately emerged into physical form next to him.

"Do you need water?" the gargoyle was already asking, flicking on the overhead light. "More of your medicines? Should we get you to a hospital?"

I shook my head—slowly so that I didn't set off the dizziness. My voice came out with a rasp but not too wobbly. "No. There isn't much they'd be able to do anyway. I think if I just rest a little, I'll recover like I did before. It's already getting better."

"Get her that water," Rollick instructed, and Crag leapt to the front of the car to grab the bottle. With shaky fingers, I peeled off my rain slicker and tossed it on the floor. Here beyond the reach of the storms, the air held only a hint of dampness.

As I tipped back on the seat, letting out a relieved sigh as soon as I was lying on the firm cushions, the demon leaned through the doorway. He peered down at me, his concern for me rolling through our collection to mingle with the jolts of fear I was picking up from Crag.

"I almost did it," I muttered. "I got him halfway there. I wasn't strong enough." A sense of hopelessness swept over me that was far more uncomfortable than the physical pains.

Rollick's mouth twisted. "You're plenty strong. The leviathan is a menace beyond anything any of us has ever had to deal with. Including the Highest, I suspect, or they'd have..."

He trailed off with a furrowing of his brow, his gaze veering away from me. The emotion that wafted from him next was a mix of shock and horror that set my own nerves jangling.

"What?" I gasped out, moving to push myself upright again.

Rollick jerked out his hand to nudge me back down. "All you need to focus on right now is recovering that strength of yours. We can talk about everything else once you're back to your regular self. I want you contributing to the full extent of your abilities." He managed a tight smirk.

I grumbled inarticulately at him, but he'd dampened his emotional response down to a faint, dull current of uneasiness that reassured me a tad. It didn't seem like whatever had upset him was an immediate emergency, anyway.

Crag got into the back seat at the opposite end so he could help me drink some water without my having to get up. I leaned my head against his now human-like thigh, still pretty damned solid but a little less rocky than his gargoyle legs would have been, and he stroked my hair with careful fingers. *His* worry for me had barely ebbed.

Rollick must have called Torrent to let him know that no further distractions were needed. Several minutes after an engine rumbled by on some distant road, the tentacled man and Lance appeared by our car, presumably having hitched a secretive ride with that other lone traveler.

By that point, the pressure in my chest had eased off enough that it didn't hurt at all when I sat up. My muscles still felt jellified, but I figured that was regular exhaustion more so than any kind of symptom. It was pretty late, and I had pushed myself hard.

Could I expend that kind of magic even once more without pushing my heart past its limits? I really wasn't sure. What I'd experienced tonight had been at least twice as bad as any of the fits I'd experienced before. I was speeding my borrowed organ toward its end faster than any medical guidelines could account for, that was for sure.

"Quinn!" Lance exclaimed, and sprang past Rollick to dive into the back, yanking me into his arms. I nestled in his embrace with the contentment of knowing he'd survived creating his "diversions" without any significant problems.

I glanced past the dragon shifter to Torrent, who didn't look any worse for wear than he normally did either. "The minions didn't give you too much trouble?"

He shook his head, though his expression was even grimmer than usual. "We knew what we were doing. They weren't difficult to dodge when that was always the plan." He glanced to the west. "You weren't able to compel the leviathan?"

"I did," I said, with a twinge of shame as I remembered my failure. "I got him to follow us part of the way to the trap. But it wasn't enough. He managed to throw off my sorcery before we made it there. And he sounded like he was sure that now that he'd figured out how to, I'd never be able to conquer him again."

Crag frowned. "He said other things too. About summoning the shadow realm *here*. That doesn't make any sense."

Rollick sighed. "Actually, I think it does. If I'm right about what he was hinting at, it's the first bit of information we've gotten that ties all his actions together into a coherent picture."

I lifted my head from Lance's shoulder. "What do you mean? You understood what he was talking about?"

"The pieces only clicked together after I'd had a little time to think about it." Rollick folded his arms over his chest, unable to keep up his usual nonchalant expression. In the darkness beyond the interior of the car, his blue eyes glinted sharply. "He said he was going to bring 'the depths' of the shadow realm here—that he'd summon 'them.' He's been expanding that one rift. And he's been carrying on for the past several days as if he doesn't care whether the chaos he's causing here gets noticed."

Torrent sucked in a breath, the chill of his surprise reaching me. "You don't *really* think—how could that even be possible?"

"What?" I demanded, looking from one of them to the other. "The rest of us would like to be completely filled in, please."

Rollick glanced away for a moment before meeting my eyes. "I've told you before about who the Highest are—that they're the most ancient and powerful shadowkind in existence, and to some extent they monitor what happens here in the mortal realm through their underlings to make sure no one gets out of hand. They live in the deepest parts of the shadow realm. The trouble the leviathan has been stirring up is exactly the sort of thing I'd expect to draw their notice."

"But they couldn't stop him before," I said. "He and the behemoth overpowered the warriors they sent."

"They may have sent more since then. Or after that initial defeat, they may be waiting to see how far he'll go and if he'll betray any clear weaknesses before making another attempt. But I believe the fiend wants *them* to come. The Highest themselves, entering the mortal realm."

Lance let out a startled sound. "They don't go anywhere! They stay in their cavern and let beings come to them."

"But maybe the leviathan thought that if he disrupted the mortal world enough and subdued their underlings, they'd have to venture out," Crag put in, his expression still gloomy.

Torrent nodded. "It hasn't worked. I'm not sure how easily the Highest even *could* come through a rift at their size and how strongly they're tied to our home." He glanced at Rollick. "But you figure that's why the leviathan has continued expanding the rift. It's not to allow *more* beings to come through. It's to ensure that it's large enough for the largest of us all to fit."

"Yes. And believe me, I'd love to be proven wrong." Rollick sighed. "But it makes an unnerving amount of sense when you have that piece of the puzzle. Even the sorcerer-killing—why the leviathan has amassed so much of that human-based magic."

A chill of my own washed over me. "He's going to summon these Highest beings right out into the mortal realm? *Can* he do that?" Could he really have gotten that powerful?

"I don't know," Rollick admitted. "I'd imagine it'd take a tremendous amount of sorcery—possibly more than anyone could gather. But he seems to think he has a chance."

I shivered. "And from the way he talked about it, he figures that bringing the Highest here will make the mortal realm belong to shadowkind. Would it really change things that much?"

"It might," Torrent said quietly. "They might bring a lot of the shadow realm's energies through with them, whether they want to or not. And their very existence contains so much power that there's no way of knowing what impact their presence will have on this world. I can't imagine it'll be good."

Lance drew a breath through his teeth with a hiss. "The leviathan thinks it'll change the mortal world to be better for shadowkind. That's what he was telling his minions—that we'd own this world when he's done. I don't *want* to own it. I like it the way it is."

"Me too," I said, my heart thumping faster. "What can we do? I tried using my own sorcery on him. There's not much chance we'd be able to come up with another trick to get him into our trap, is there?"

We all sat in silence for a minute, pondering. "Well," Rollick said slowly, "I believe if he's hoping to summon the Highest, he'd need to put every shred of sorcery he has to that task. So he'll have to let the magic he's cast on all his minions fade rather than continuing to hold them bound to him. And while he's actually doing the summoning, it's unlikely he'd be able to enslave anyone else without risking his whole scheme falling apart."

A flicker of hope lit in my chest. "Then we'd have a chance once he actually makes a move. The shadowkind who've come to help us—they'd be able to intervene without getting swept over to his side. And I wouldn't have to worry about protecting the four of you quite as much, maybe. Then I'd have a little more of my own magic—maybe enough to overwhelm him after all."

Rollick rubbed his chin. "We can't be sure of that. And I doubt that our current motley crew of beings would have much hope of making an impact on him. But we can gather more, call on every shadowkind we can find in the mortal realm who'll have seen what's at stake. The damage he's causing is becoming increasingly obvious." He paused. "We should also make another appeal to the Highest. Let them know our suspicions. If they could send more of their underlings to join us, that'd give us even more of a fighting chance."

Crag bared his teeth with a brutal smile. "If Quinn can't compel him to the trap, we'd get together and drag him there."

Lance chuckled. "Yes. I'd like to see him squirming."

"Or even better," Rollick said, "we could bring the trap to him. If we know where he'll be, there by the rift, maybe my mortal contractors can work out a somewhat portable version. All we need is to fling a lot of iron and silver into him. He'll have to be in physical form to use his sorcery, since it requires a voice. I'll get them at the ready, since we can't put anything in place near the rift ahead of time or he'll notice and destroy it."

A spark of hope lit inside me. "All right. We do have a chance then." Even if it was a small one. I tipped my head toward Rollick. "Will you go appeal to the Highest again?"

He grimaced. "I'm not sure that would be the most ideal option. They might not be very pleased with me if they feel I didn't sufficiently prepare them for what their warriors would face."

"And you're needed here to continue appealing to your own contacts, as much as you can convince them to take part in the battle," Torrent said. He raised his chin with a resigned but determined expression. "I'll go. I'll be the least useful here. Any beings we could reach out to as potential allies who are strong enough to be much help will look down on my weaknesses—they won't see me as someone worth banding together with. The rest of you can focus on building our army and our weapons, and I can go to the Highest. They might not respect me, but they don't much of anyone. I don't need their respect to deliver a warning."

A pang shot through me at the thought of Torrent going off on his own again. "Are you sure?" I asked. "You've taken on so many of the jobs like that." And, selfishly, I didn't like how little I'd gotten to see him in the past several days.

He offered me a small but warm smile. "I've got to take the jobs I'm best equipped for. I'll speak to the Highest as quickly as I can manage and then come straight back."

Rollick clapped his hands together. "It's settled then—the start of a new strategy, anyway. Let's get back to the house, ensure Quinn gets a proper rest, and begin some real recruiting."

CHAPTER SIXTEEN

Crag

As I soared over the depths of the Atlantic, I couldn't help thinking that this was really Torrent's domain. I might have spent many hours coasting on wafts of wind over ocean waves, hunting for marine life and enjoying the scenery along various coastlines, but he was most at home in the actual water. I'd rarely dipped in other than a brief dive to snatch a particularly tasty looking fish.

But he had his own task to see through, and I couldn't say I'd have done a good job of making a verbal appeal to the Highest. I'd probably have ended up offending them with whatever blunt comments slipped out. There was no reason I *couldn't* travel through the darkness beneath the waves nearly as easily as he could. The currents barely tugged at our shadowy bodies.

It turned out, though, that I didn't have to plunge in just yet. In the distance, I spotted a few sleek heads poking from the water. Their short gray fur gleamed wetly under the early morning sun. They looked every bit the seals they were pretending to be, but real seals wouldn't have swum out this far. I could tell from that and my growing sense of their presence as I approached that these were shadowkind. Selkies.

I slowed as I came up on them, starkly aware of how my gargoyle bulk might unnerve them. "Hello," I called out, wishing my voice wasn't quite so rumbly. "I was hoping—"

Two of the four dropped beneath the waves with barely a ripple, vanishing from view. The other two bobbed farther away from me at the surface, their faces transforming into human-like ones: a man and a woman.

The man flashed animalistic teeth. "What do you want?" he hollered.

The two of them were clearly tensed, ready to swim away at any second. I stopped where I was, still twenty feet distant, hovering with swift flaps of my wings. "I'm not with the one who's been stirring up the seas," I said quickly, figuring it was important to make that point first. "I assume you've seen some of his minions riling up the waves near the coasts."

The frowns that crossed both the selkies' faces confirmed it without either of them speaking. "This could be some trick," the woman spat at me.

They seemed awfully hostile despite the leviathan's watery schemes not reaching this far out. How had it even affected them?

"Why would I want to trick you?" I asked, honestly puzzled. "The leviathan is making the beings under him do what he wants with sorcery, but he's the only shadowkind who's grabbed that kind of power. Many of us are working out a way to stand up to him and end the destruction, but I don't see how I could force you to do anything you don't want to do."

The words might have come out a bit gruffer than I'd have preferred in my confusion, but to my relief, I thought the selkies relaxed a little rather than becoming even more defensive. The man pushed a little higher amid the lapping waves, raising his chin. "What are you doing here then? Why are you talking to us?"

I would have thought that was pretty self-explanatory after what I'd just said, but apparently not. And this was why it was a good thing Torrent was doing the talking with the Highest, not me.

I cleared my throat. "Those of us who want to stop the leviathan are trying to gather as large a group as possible. He's so strong that it'll take a lot of us to overpower him. Beings comfortable at sea like yourselves would be particularly useful to the cause, since you can work against him in his natural habitat."

The woman let out a disgruntled-sounding huff. "Why should we? We don't even know you or this group you're gathering. You could be just as bad as him."

I could picture Quinn rolling her eyes at the statement. I restrained myself to a brief grimace. "I think that would be awfully difficult, considering that he's made himself the biggest menace I've ever seen in the centuries I've been in existence. You *have* seen what he's forced his slaves to do, haven't you? The way they're churning up the ocean along the coast, the waves they're hurling at the mortal cities. It's even worse on the Pacific side. And what he plans to do next..."

I trailed off, abruptly uncertain of whether I should mention what Rollick had deduced about the leviathan's ultimate plans. I didn't know how much I could trust *these* beings. What if they ended up reporting back to the villain somehow? It was better if he didn't know we'd figured out his end game.

The woman's eyes narrowed. "What's that?"

"Nothing that would be good for any of us who enjoy the mortal realm," I settled on as my answer. "He wants to turn this place as dark and dreary as our original home. I don't want that, and I doubt you do either. But if not enough of us are willing to take a stand, that's what we'll get."

The two selkies glanced at each other. The man's expression tightened. He looked at me with narrowed eyes. "We're not built to fight like you are. I doubt there's much we can do. One of our own was already badly injured in the recent storms."

My heart sank. So *that* was why they'd reacted so fiercely. "I'm sorry to hear that. If there's anything I can do..."

Both of them gave me a skeptical look. Then the woman said brusquely, "There's a particular kind of seaweed that's helpful for sealing our sort of wounds—for holding in the essence. I don't suppose you know anything about it?"

Her statement tugged out a memory from ages ago, when I'd chatted with an elderly merman while we shared the meat of a shark that I'd caught while it was in the middle of attacking him. He'd gathered some ocean plant to wrap around the wound on his arm.

"Reddish with broad leaves?" I asked, bringing up the faded image in my mind.

They couldn't keep their surprise from their faces. The man nodded. "That's the one. It's usually closer to the shore, but with all the churning of the waters, we haven't been able to get close. We've been searching for strands that were torn up and drifted farther out, but there hasn't been much. If you want us to help you, maybe you should help us first."

His caustic tone suggested that he expected me to disagree, but my spirits lifted at the opportunity to take concrete action. "I'll see what I can do. Where will you be if I find some?"

The woman waved toward the east. "There's a small island several miles that way. We're using it as a temporary camp."

Without another word, they both slipped under the water, transforming into their seal bodies as they did. I had the sense of a dismissal —that they assumed this was the last time we'd ever speak.

My jaw clenched. I could battle storms just as well as I could fight any creature.

I flew in the opposite direction, keeping low to the water, scanning as far into the depths as I could for a telltale hint of red. As I got closer to the coast, still well out of view of any mortals who might have dared to brave the storm on land, the waves grew choppier, forcing me to lift higher overhead. Rain first pattered against my hardened skin and then pelted me.

I swerved to the side and followed the angle of the shoreline, sweeping a little farther east again to avoid the worst of the storm. The leviathan must have enslaved a lot of seafaring beings to his cause for them to be stirring up this much turmoil on the opposite side of the country for him. My teeth gritted with frustration.

Just as I started to think I'd have to give up the search, that I'd wasted too much time on it already, my gaze snagged on a flash of a ruddy leaf tossed by one of the waves. I dove without hesitation, my hands shooting out to snatch at my target.

It was a lot more than just one leaf. A huge clump of the weed had been uprooted from its coastal grounds and floated out here. I bundled enough in my arms to have wrapped around an entire human body and, with a small smile of triumph I couldn't suppress, soared out of the storm toward the selkie's island.

Trickles of salty water streamed down from the mass of seaweed to patter against the ocean, and its pungent herbal scent filled my nose, but it wasn't difficult to carry. I had lots of practice flying around with Quinn in my arms by now, and I had to worry a lot less about the seaweed's well-being.

It was a matter of minutes before the little island came into view up ahead. The place was barely more than a cluster of boulders poking out of the water with some sparse bushes sprouting from the bits of dirt that'd managed to catch in the cervices between the rocks.

Several seals were gathered on the stones, most of them forming an attentive circle around one of their number, who was lying limply in the most sheltered area of the island. As I drew closer, I made out trickles of essence gusting from the prone body. However that one had been caught up in the storm's violence, the wounds hadn't fully healed yet. No wonder the others were worried.

One of the seals noticed me and barked an alarm. All the others' heads swiveled my way. I couldn't easily wave while holding the seaweed, but two shifted into human forms that I recognized. They leaned toward the others, their mouths moving hastily with words I couldn't make out.

As I swooped down toward them, a few scooted to the edges of the island, their teeth bared. But a couple of the seals and the two I'd spoken to before stayed with their injured companion, braced protectively around the slumped body.

I landed on a bare rock. "This is the weed you wanted, isn't it?"

The woman took in my cargo, and her eyes widened. "You found so much!" Her head whipped toward her partner. "We must wrap her up quickly. She's lost so much essence already."

They both darted forward, their stances still wary. I shoved the clump toward them so they didn't have to get too close to me. Then I watched from my rocky perch, feeling more fully gargoyle-like than I had in decades, as they bandaged up the injured seal. I'd have offered to help, but my thick fingers wouldn't be able to handle her wounds with as much care as their slimmer ones.

They layered the slick leaves over the wounds, and the trickling essence faded away. The unconscious seal let out a shuddery breath. The woman who'd bandaged her sat back on her heels and swiped her hand across her forehead, looking weary but relieved. I understood the kind of anguish she was going through better than I would have even a month ago.

"She means a lot to you," I observed in as subdued a tone as I could manage.

Her gaze flicked to me. "All of my pod-mates do. We stick together—we look out for one another, both here and in the shadows."

Her voice came out taut, as if she thought I'd been criticizing her. I did my best to form a sympathetic smile. "I'm glad I was able to help stabilize her then. It looks as if the seaweed helped. I hope she has an easy recovery from now on."

"We'll see," the man said, frowning. "She hasn't woken since she took those blows in the storm. There was so much wreckage floating in the waves."

I glanced around. "I passed a rift a few leagues from here. If you wanted to bring her back to the shadow realm so she might recover faster, I'd be happy to carry her—and I could probably manage one or two others—to get her there right away."

The woman blinked at me. "Why would you offer that?"

I knit my brow. "For the same reason I found the seaweed. I'd rather she isn't suffering if she doesn't need to be. And the same for all of you, worrying about her. It's... it's good to find some of our kind looking out for each other, supporting each other, after everything I've seen recently."

I meant the statement totally honestly, without any ulterior motives. It seemed unlikely that they'd volunteer to dive back into any kind of battle regardless of what I did now. But maybe because of my honesty, something softened in the woman's face.

"Yes," she said. "It is good. And maybe we shouldn't only think of our pod. Maybe *for* our pod, we should do more. How is it you think we can help stop the one causing these storms?"

A jolt of startled joy shot through me. I paused, grappling for the right words to show how much I appreciated her response, and it occurred to me that it hadn't been my strength that'd convinced her. It hadn't been my ability to take the storm either.

It'd been the kindness I'd offered, even though kindness wasn't a trait I'd ever thought of as my own.

Possibly I was more than just a monster after all.

CHAPTER SEVENTEEN

Quinn

Of all the places to ride out the intensifying symptoms of a failing heart, Rollick's badlands house was probably one of the best. I had innumerable softly cushioned surfaces to stretch out on when my chest clenched up. There was a salt-water pool to take a refreshing dip in while I shook off the effects of the latest attack. And all the food and drinks I could possibly want were on hand, regularly replenished by Crag and fried or sliced up by Lance as need be.

Most other places I could have ended up would definitely have been *worse*. But I couldn't say I was enjoying my stay all that much regardless.

None of the spasms in my chest had hit me as hard as the pain right after I'd compelled the leviathan, but they were coming frequently enough that my men had insisted I stay here while they did their recruiting—and from a practical standpoint, I couldn't really argue. It wasn't as if the average shadowkind being was going to respond better to overtures from a human sorcerer than from one of their own kind anyway.

So I was doing my best to recover more fully and to not go stir-crazy from boredom. When I felt steady enough, I went out into the yard and chatted with the newer beings who'd come to join us, getting a feel for their strength and skills. When I didn't, I paged through my sketchpad, looking at the designs I'd set on paper with pencil and fighting the constricting of my throat.

I wasn't going to see any of those plans to fruition. My chances of seeing my career through to any kind of real accomplishment had always been uncertain, and now it was pretty much impossible. I suspected I'd be lucky to have as much as another month or two before my borrowed heart crapped out on me completely, and that was if I didn't put any more significant strain on it. I wasn't on any waiting lists; my medical team didn't even know I might need a replacement. Even if I had been, the chances of getting the right match at the right time were always iffy.

That was the way it was. I'd resigned myself to my probable limited lifespan before, and I could deal with it now—as long as I knew I'd stopped the threat to everyone else's lives before I went.

Today, there hadn't been a whole lot that I could accomplish toward that goal. I'd talked with several new shadowkind arrivals in the morning, and no other beings had turned up since then. Walking around had left me feeling faint enough that eating a proper lunch had been a bit of a struggle.

I'd dug my trusty multi-tool out of my bag in the hopes it might give me a sense of purpose, but as far as I could tell, Rollick kept his property in such good repair that there was nothing for me to fix even a little. And anyway, when I thought about it, making some tiny tweak to a fixture or piece of furniture seemed so pointless now compared to the vast problems looming over me.

Finally, I went out onto the inner patio around the pool in the hopes that soaking up some sun—after a careful layer of sunscreen, as if I really needed to worry about minor precautions like that at this point—would rejuvenate me, and ended up drifting off in a brief nap.

I woke up feeling annoyed with myself for dozing when there was so much to do, even if *I* couldn't really do any of it at the moment, and headed inside to see if there'd been any news I'd missed. I was just coming through the patio door when a pressure like a massive hand digging its fingers into my ribs squeezed around my chest.

My breath hitched. I stumbled and caught my balance on the back of one of the living room chairs. A chill washed through me from head to toe.

"Quinn!" Crag appeared by my side out of the shadows, sliding his arm around my shoulders.

I opened my mouth to tell him I'd be okay, but all that came out was a choked gasp. Making a rough sound of dismay, the gargoyle swept me up in his arms and carried me into my bedroom.

Inside, he set me gently on the bedcovers and then seemed at a loss for what else to do. I gritted my teeth against the pain that was gripping me and jerked my hand toward him in a vague beckoning gesture.

Crag eased onto the bed next to me as gingerly as a man that large could manage. He tucked me against his massive form, brushing his fingers over my hair and humming in what I could tell he intended to be a soothing sound. "I've got you, Softness. You'll get through this. I know how strong you are, even if you shouldn't have to be strong enough to endure this pain."

I managed a ragged chuckle and nestled myself closer against him. The warmth of his body radiating over me and the tenderness of his attentions melted the worst of my discomfort. I breathed in and out as steadily as I could, and gradually the tightness released me. My heart thudded on, if with a beat that was a little erratic.

"Thank you," I said. "I'm all right now. No big deal."

Crag grunted. "Of course it's a big deal. I don't like to see you hurting." He pulled away from me just as tentatively as he'd gathered me against him, and I felt his nervousness about hurting me *himself* through the connection between us. "Is there anything else you need? Would you like help getting back to the living room—or wherever you want to go now?"

I rested my hand against his chest, where the planes of muscle were covered in human-like skin that now felt not quite as familiar as his rocky gargoyle form. Now that my body was no longer fighting itself, a different sort of heat was tickling through my veins.

Lance had needed a particular kind of assurance that my health problems hadn't made me totally fragile. And Crag had always been the most worried about how his monstrousness might damage me.

And I had even less time than I'd had before to make the most of the life I'd gotten. The love I'd discovered in that life.

"I think I'd like to stay right here," I said, looking up at him through my eyelashes. "As long as you're here too."

Desire flared in the gargoyle's eyes even as I caught another tremor of uncertainty from him. "Are you sure that's a good—" he started to ask in a tone that showed his reluctance at balking, and I answered him the fastest and most effective way I could: by slipping my hand around his head and pulling him into a kiss.

As our mouths melded together with the delicious friction of Crag's rocky lower lip against mine, he let out a groan that reverberated through his chest. More desire licked at me like flames through our emotional connection. He sank down again to slide closer to me, but the hand he rested on my waist still felt too careful.

I ran my fingers over the sheen of black hair on his scalp, curling them to tease my fingernails over the bronze skin in an imitation of claws. An eager quiver passed through Crag, and he kissed me harder. The bulge behind the fabric of his shorts was already stiffening.

A rush of wildness caught me up. I wanted him. I wanted every part of him. He needed to know that.

I tore my mouth from his and met his eyes, my cheeks flushed from the passion we'd already kindled between us. "When you've been with other shadowkind, it wasn't just with your gargoyle size. You brought the gargoyle fierceness too."

A whole lot of other parts of Crag stiffened at those words. He frowned. "They could handle it. They—"

"They didn't have delicate human bodies, I know." I cupped his cheek. "But I'm not that delicate either. I've taken Lance's claws and Torrent's tentacles. I don't want to be just pampered, as nice as that can be. I want to be ravished too."

Crag's tongue flicked over his lips in a way that sent sparks right down the center of me to my cunt. "I don't need to let out that side. You shouldn't have to witness any more of my brutality than you've been forced to before."

I stroked my thumb over his prominent cheekbone. "I love your tender side *and* your brutal side, Crag. I appreciate your hardness as much as you enjoy my softness. And what I'd really like right now is for you to rip the clothes right off me and take me like you can't stand to wait another second without us fucking."

A guttural sound emanated from Crag's throat. His eyes flared with a hotter light as his body expanded into his full gargoyle form: skin turning rock hard, horns jutting above the sharper angles of his face, wings extending from his back.

With a growl, he flipped me onto my back and loomed over me. The claws that had sprouted from his fingers were much shorter than Lance's but no less deadly. He raked them down the front of me with a swipe of his hand, shredding open my tee and shorts without doing more than grazing the skin.

That prickling, not quite painful touch woke up even more desires in me. I trembled with giddiness, a gasp tumbling from my lips. As Crag shoved the tatters of my clothes aside, I raised my arms to pull him closer, rising up to seek out his mouth. He needed to see just how into this I was now that he'd accepted my demand.

He let his lips crash into mine with a force that left my head spinning with a heady pleasure that was echoed through our connection. His forceful hands swept aside the last fragments of my panties and the cups of my bisected bra. He gripped one breast, massaging it firmly and pinching the nipple between his thumb and forefinger with a jolt of bliss. I whimpered eagerly against his mouth.

Crag raised his hand to scrape the tips of his claws over my breast the way he'd have seen Lance do a dozen times. I pressed my lips against his while holding the rest of me still so that he didn't sever anything important with his thrillingly dangerous touch. Then he reached farther down, trailing his claws over my sternum and belly until he reached the mound between my legs.

When he cupped my pussy, I arched to meet him, my lips parting to let him devour me even more fully at the same time. With a heated rumble, Crag swept his long gargoyle tongue into my mouth and flicked his claws up over my slit to my clit. I moaned, shuddering against him with nothing but enthusiasm for all he was offering.

His mouth wrenched from mine as he teased his fingers over my sex at an aggressive pace. My head tipped back into the pillow, my breath breaking into pants. Crag let out another growl as he gazed down at me.

"I want to make you mine in every possible way. I want to plunge into you so hard it knocks every other thought from your mind. I want to feel you shaking with delight."

An impatient noise formed between my ragged breaths. "Then what's taking you so long?"

He snarled and heaved my hips up to meet him with one hand. I knew how large he was, but I was used to him now—and the savagery of his foreplay had left me drenched and ready. I hefted my ass a little higher to show just how on board I was, and the next thing I knew he was thrusting his entire thick shaft into my pussy.

The giddily searing friction had me gasping for more. I shook in his arms like he'd asked for, clutching him and pressing closer. With a flurry of noises that were half growl, half groan, Crag pounded into me. I bucked to meet every thrust with all the hunger scorching through my veins.

"So soft," he muttered, "but so strong. I love you, Quinn. Always. Always."

"Always," I gasped in agreement, and lost my voice completely with the next plunge of his cock. I was seeing stars, pleasure blazing through me like a flashfire, burning away everything but this moment. Me and one of the monstrous men I loved so much.

His claws dug into my thigh with a flash of pain that I knew meant I'd need a quick swipe of Lance's tongue later, but in the moment it brought nothing but a deeper shock of bliss. I cried out, a tremor wracking my body as the building ecstasy exploded in a final, epic firework. But even in the haze of my pleasure, I kept rocking my hips to meet Crag, wanting more, wanting him to come with me.

"Want to feel you come," I muttered, and Crag slammed into me with a roar that shook the walls. His cum flooded me, perfectly hot and thick, his cock pulsing with the effort he'd expended.

He eased me down on the bed and held himself over me on his hands and knees, his chest heaving, his fiery gaze seeking out mine. I beamed up at him, a little delirious in the afterglow, and only then did he relax. A smile crossed his lips that was broader and brighter than anything I'd seen from the usually solemn gargoyle before.

"I satisfied you well," he said with a hint of pride in both his voice and the emotions traveling between us.

I couldn't restrain a giggle. "Very well. But then, you always do. My stony gargoyle."

He leaned in to nuzzle the side of my face with a gentleness that was the total opposite of the beast he'd brought out on my request. "My soft-but-strong mortal. The leviathan is a fool if he thinks he can beat you."

My smile faltered just slightly. I sure hoped my lover was right about that.

CHAPTER EIGHTEEN

Quinn

"So your idea is that you could distract him?" I said to the pair of impish demons who'd just carried out a demonstration in how they could belch puffs of smoke. "Obscure his vision with the clouds so he can't tell what else we're doing?"

One of them nodded eagerly. The other emitted another burp, which honestly barely contained enough smoke to obscure *my* sight, let alone a giant sea serpent's. But I wasn't going to say that to their faces when they were trying so hard to be helpful.

Instead, I jotted it down on the notepad where I'd been keeping track of our allies and their abilities and shot them a grateful smile. "Thank you. I'm sure that'll come in handy when we confront the leviathan."

From an indistinct noise behind me, I thought Lance might have muffled a skeptical snort. He came up behind me and kissed the back of my head. "I'll find more useful beings to bring back," he murmured. "If I keep searching, there've got to be more who won't turn their backs on the rest of us."

"You've been doing your best," I reassured him, knowing it was true.

He, Crag, and Rollick had only been back at the desert house for an hour or two at a time in between ushering new recruits here. For the first little while, they'd insisted that one of them had to be present at all times to watch over me, but now that we had enough loyal beings prowling around the house that they really could be considered an army, I'd persuaded them that all of them working toward stopping the leviathan was better for my well-being than acting as additional bodyguards.

That didn't mean I didn't miss them while they were gone, though.

I gazed out over the desolate landscape where I knew hundreds more shadowkind lurked in the patches of gloom at the bases of the straggly vegetation, around stones and boulders, and everywhere dips and cracks had formed in the dry earth. They were keeping out of sight when they weren't talking to me, but enough of them surrounded me that my sorcerer energy vibrated in my chest with the sense of their presence.

Unfortunately, the majority of them were lesser creatures or not particularly powerful higher beings who couldn't contribute much more to a battle than nipping at the leviathan's heels... or blowing puffs of smoke at him.

A burly, man-shaped being with small tusks jutting from beneath his square jaw appeared in front of me. He flexed his bulky arms and swung his fists a few times through the air. "Maybe I can help pummel him unconscious. I might not be able to do it alone, but if enough of us go at him..."

"We'd have to make sure he falls where the new moving trap can hit him," Lance pointed out. "Hard to move him anywhere once he's out."

I sucked my lower lip under my teeth. "That or just weaken him rather than knocking him out completely. Getting him out of sorts, dizzy and disoriented, would make it harder for him to fight back. And maybe easier for me to use my sorcery on him if I need to." I tipped my head to the man, who I thought Rollick had told me was a troll when he'd escorted him in earlier. "How hard can you hit?"

He grinned. "When the behemoth had my mind, they only saw half of what I was capable of. I was fighting them the whole time inside, dragging against their commands. Watch this."

He marched over to a narrow boulder that stood beyond the edge of the yard's protections, cracked his knuckles, and slammed his fist into the rock. A crack opened up from the top about halfway down the middle of it.

Lance let out an approving whistle. "A leviathan skull is probably stronger than that," he couldn't help saying, though. "Also, it'll be moving, not standing still for you to punch."

I swatted him. "It's a start. Don't become a pessimist now." But something the troll had said was niggling at me. I studied him as he walked back over to us. "You said that you didn't use as much strength when the behemoth ordered you to do things. He couldn't make you put in your full effort?"

The troll grunted. "It *felt* like a full effort by the time it happened. Just pushing back against the influence meant I used up some of my strength on that. Like punching through water rather than air—the drag holds it back."

I wasn't sure I totally followed his explanation, but it sparked a flicker of excitement in me. "Do you think... if you were ordered to do something you *wanted* to do... that the magic might add more to your effort instead of taking away from it? If it was propelling you forward instead of you fighting against it?"

The troll's eyebrows rose. "I don't know. I didn't like anything he wanted me to do... mostly because *he* wanted me to do it and didn't care how I felt about it." He paused, seeming momentarily wary of me. "I guess we could try and see what happens."

I swallowed thickly, knowing what an expression of trust it was that he'd even offered. "Are you sure? I know that having any kind of sorcery worked on you would probably bring up bad associations."

He shrugged, lifting his chin as if in defiance of his own worries. "We've got to find out what's possible. I'd rather have you in my head than the beast that's tearing up the coastlines."

I couldn't argue with his logic, and I didn't want to. Jittery anticipation was already tickling through my nerves—jittery because I was afraid I might be wrong and my hopes would be dashed all over again. But he had a point. We needed to know if my suggested strategy would work, and as soon as possible.

We had no idea how soon the leviathan might be able to carry out the final stages of his plan and actually drag the Highest beings through the rift he was preparing.

"All right." I stood up. "I'm not going to exert full control on you or anything like that. I'll just command you to punch that boulder again, and as soon as you have, the magic should wear off. Nothing permanent."

The troll nodded, his eyes gleaming. He looked like he was starting to get excited about the possibilities too. Lance hummed thoughtfully, watching us both with a growing smile. I had the impression that an awful lot of the eyes in the shadows were fixed on the unfolding scenario.

I dragged in a breath and drew on the magic twined through my heart. It took no effort at all to throw just a flash of it at the being in front of me. *Punch that boulder as hard as you can*, I thought as the odd syllables spilled from my lips.

The troll's muscles twitched, and for an instant I was scared he was going to react to the sorcery with panic or anger after all. Then his grin came back. He strode across the dusty earth without hesitation, heaved back his arm, and flung his fist at the boulder like he had before.

Except it wasn't exactly like before. This time his knuckles slammed into the stone surface with so much force the rock split right apart. It tumbled over in jagged chunks, nothing left but a stump no higher than the troll's knees.

He let out a triumphant laugh and spun to face me. "I could feel it! The magic, flowing through me, and I moved with it instead of straining against it. And it was like it was *my* magic, making me more powerful. How else can you use that power?"

Hope was expanding through my chest, light and fluttery. "I don't know," I admitted. "But it seems like it should help with just about anything we want to do."

The impish demons might be able to produce more smoke. Lance might be able to lunge faster, Torrent wrench harder with his tentacles. The magic that most sorcerers used to constrain the shadowkind might also be capable of boosting their supernatural abilities, transforming them into even stronger versions of themselves. The irony of it provoked a giddy chuckle of my own.

I might have continued the experiment, called for more volunteers to see what other ways we could make this new discovery work for us, when a few beings wavered into sight about a half a mile from the house, one of them letting out a shout of warning.

"Hey! We've got a sneaky one here. What should we do with him?"

Three of the figures I recognized as beings who'd volunteered for the security patrols: a svelte guy I believed was some kind of large cat shifter, a skinny harpy woman with slate-gray feathered wings and taloned feet, and the beefiest member of the selkie clan Crag had sent our way. It was the selkie who'd hollered. I didn't understand what he was hollering about until he tugged a much smaller figure in his grasp into better view.

The petite man whose neck he was clutching didn't stand much higher than the selkie's waist. But it was the reddish-gold curls and his forest-green suit that made him instantly identifiable.

I stiffened where I stood at the same moment as Lance hissed through his teeth. "The leprechaun," he snarled.

The small, spritely man who went by the name Goldie had been a friend of Torrent's. *Had*, because not long after I'd first met him, he'd sold us out to the villainous duo's minions. I'd never expected to see him again, and I couldn't say I particularly wanted to.

But he must have come out here looking for us for a reason.

"Are you sure he's alone?" I called across the scrubby field. "And no weapons or anything dangerous on him?"

"Just him," the harpy confirmed. "I flew around to scan the area and make sure of it before we brought him over. He says he has an important message, but he wouldn't give it to anyone except you or the kraken and his friends."

I gritted my teeth but waved them over. "Keep him at a distance, but I'll talk to him. I'd rather not have to scream the whole conversation. All three of you, stay on guard around him."

Lance shifted into dragon form to encircle me with his scaled body like a living shield. I rested my hand on his shoulder, feeling the distrust and protectiveness radiating off him as our patrollers led their prisoner closer.

"He's been in with the leviathan and his lackeys," I said in an attempt at reassuring him. "He might know something useful. He did *use* to be Torrent's friend."

Lance's growl told me exactly how little that fact warmed him to the new arrival. I didn't disagree with him. But I could admit that Goldie hadn't seemed totally *happy* about the whole betrayal business. He'd been risking us killing him where he stood by coming out here. His reasons had to be important. We'd just be careful about the conversation.

I held up my hand when the group was about twenty feet away. Crossing my arms over my chest, I stared Goldie down. His face looked ruddier than I remembered under that heap of curls, and now that he was closer, I could see that his suit had gotten scuffed and torn. The best smile he managed was tight and pained-looking.

"Thank you for giving me a chance to speak," he said, looking right back at me without flinching. "It's been a long time, with a lot happening in between, and I know we left things on a very bad note the last time you saw me."

"The last time I saw you, you were arranging for me to be kidnapped and eaten," I replied. "I think 'a very bad note' might be understating the situation a little."

His smile pulled into a grimace. "Yes. Well. I'm free of those degenerates now. I wish they'd never gotten a hold on me. I don't like what I've seen of them since at all. You seem to be doing *something* to make their lives harder, so I figured if there was anyone to tell what I know, it'd be you."

"And what do you know?"

Goldie rubbed his mouth, wincing when the selkie tightened his grip on his neck. "The big serpent doesn't think he's got enough power to pull off his plan yet," he said with a cough. "He's figured out that there's a bunch of top sorcerers living in Norway. He might be headed out there already to look for them. I don't want to think about how it'll tip the scales if they're really out there and he finds them."

The blood turned cold in my veins. *I* knew for sure there was an enclave of powerful sorcerers in Norway—and that they wouldn't have a hope in hell of defending themselves against a creature as ancient as the leviathan. It was possible he wouldn't find them, but Rollick had managed to locate their home with very little information to go by, so I didn't think we could count on the monster failing.

I'd hated what I'd seen there. Those sorcerers were monsters too. But having the leviathan chow down on them and absorb their magic was just about the most horrible outcome I could imagine.

He might not be quite strong enough to summon the Highest yet, but after that grand feast?

I tensed against the nausea rising through my abdomen. "Why should we believe you?" I asked, and then remembered I didn't even need to get into those kinds of questions. I could confirm the truth of his statement in a matter of seconds.

Squaring my shoulders, I gathered my own magic and opened my mouth. *Tell me why you're really here.*

My voice pealed across the terrain in those strange sounds of the sorcerous language. The energy smacked into Goldie's head without any resistance—he wasn't under the leviathan's control.

The leprechaun shivered, and his mouth popped open. "I'm afraid of what'll happen to this world if the leviathan gets what he wants. I was hoping the warning might help you stop him. And that maybe I'll be a little less likely to get killed if I'm on your side instead of his."

The selfish admission at the end fit what I knew of his character. And I didn't think he could have lied while my magic was compelling him. But that didn't mean what he believed he knew was the truth.

"How did you find this out?" I asked him in my regular voice.

Goldie spread his hands. "After our last encounter, those brutes hauled me off to the leviathan, but I managed to keep a very low profile among his minions. And he didn't have much use for me. He forgot I was there, and his magic wore off eventually. He also didn't notice me around when one of his other slaves gave the report about the Norway sorcerers. I saw how interested he was. It's not like it's a secret what he's done with other sorcerers and why."

No, I supposed it wasn't. That didn't sound like a staged conversation. I bit my lip.

Even if it wasn't guaranteed to be true, I needed to warn the enclave. If they got out of there in time, holed up in some other country where the leviathan didn't know to look for them, maybe he'd never find them.

But how in the world was I going to send that warning—across the ocean, to people who'd enslave or slaughter any shadowkind that crossed their paths?

CHAPTER NINETEEN

Torrent

Lingering in one place in the shadow realm had a similar effect to soaking in the depths of the ocean, getting lulled by the rhythms of the currents. It was a lot less enjoyable without the more varied textures of the water and the endless tastes and sights that would pass by, but the sensation of time passing without my being able to track it was familiar.

Had it been hours since one of the beings standing sentinel at the entrance to the Highest's vast hollow had told me to wait there and that they would speak to me when they were ready? Days? I hoped by all the water in the oceans that it hadn't been weeks.

My only small comfort was that the leviathan clearly hadn't gone through with his final plans yet if the Highest were still there in their home, immense presences that I could sense with an uneasy quiver through my essence even from a distance.

I'd told the lackey that this was an urgent problem that directly affected the Highest. Had she not bothered to pass on that part of the message? Did they not care? I adjusted my position in the shadowy currents restlessly, my tentacles twisting and twining.

I'd never spoken to the beings that were so old they were practically part of the realm itself before. I had no idea how they typically handled appeals from unexpected visitors. Rollick hadn't suggested it was likely to take very long, though.

A more prickly thought rose up in the back of my mind that maybe it *hadn't* taken them anywhere near this long with him. The lackey would have been able to evaluate me and report what kind of being had come calling. I was decently established, but not as ancient as the demon—and he had all his limbs in full working order. My physical disabilities had certainly worked against me before.

It wasn't difficult to imagine that the most potent beings in existence might assume a being like me couldn't possibly have anything all that important to say.

I drifted a little to the left and then to the right, pushing those self-recriminating thoughts away. I was what I was. I'd probably still been the best choice to make this trip out of the four of us. The realms only knew what Lance would have gotten up to if we'd sent him here and he'd been left to contend with this seemingly endless boredom. Or how gruff the gargoyle would have become by the time the Highest welcomed him in.

I'd be ready, whenever they got around to giving me the time of day. Or night, as the case might be. Neither really existed in this world.

How could that monstrous serpent really think it'd be better if the mortal realm was *more* like this one? All his years wandering the seas must have pickled his brain.

More time passed without any ability to measure it. Then a different being, one I hadn't noticed before, glided over to me. He bobbed his head with its elephantine ears to me and gestured for me to follow him without saying so much as a word.

I moved through the gloom after him. My awareness of the gargantuan beings ahead of me expanded as I approached the deeper, thicker depths of their shadowy home. I couldn't tell how many of them there were, other than there were definitely at least a few. I got the impression that their attention had fixed on me, so weighty it dragged me down like an undertow.

"What business have you come here with, kraken?" one of the beings demanded in a voice that echoed right through my bones. I had to tense my limbs to avoid wincing. "What is so important?"

So they had heard that I'd insisted I needed to see them quickly. Apparently they hadn't believed my claim.

I drew myself up into as authoritative but respectful a pose as I could manage. "Thank you for seeing me. I've come because of incredibly severe troubles in the mortal realm. As you may already be aware, a leviathan has been openly slaughtering mortals, taking in human sorcery and using it to enslave his fellow beings, and—"

A different, equally impactful voice let out a huff. "We are aware. Our loyal servants are monitoring the situation."

Then why the fuck hadn't they done more about it already? I bit back the bitter question and forced a brisk nod. "Good. But what you might not know, because a few of us only found out about it right before I came here, and only because we've managed to observe a lot of evidence and talk to the leviathan himself briefly—"

"Get on with it," another Highest said with a warbling growl that made every nerve in my body vibrate like a struck funny bone. My most recent deformity, the mangled end of my tentacle that Lance's teeth and breath had damaged beyond repair, started to throb.

It took all my effort to hold an ingratiating if thin smile on my face. "His ultimate plan seems to be that he'll compel *you* into the mortal realm using the sorcery he's stolen. He believes he has or can accumulate enough to force you through a rift against your will—and that your arrival in that realm will permanently alter it to be more to his liking. There's no telling how much destruction he might cause if he manages it."

One of the Highest let out a sound that might have been a rumbly laugh. Another sneered in a harsh voice, "You think another being could command *us*? That is what you've come here to jabber about?"

I swallowed, willing my voice to stay steady in the face of their disdain. "I have no idea if he's really capable of it. But I thought—we all thought—that you should be warned so you're prepared in case he attempts it. And maybe you'd want to take some action against him, to ensure that there's no chance you would ever come under threat."

The next sound that emanated from the gathered Highest was more of a hiss, with a definite angry edge to it. "It sounds as if *you're* threatening us.

Trying to force us to deal with this being the way you'd prefer by telling us how we'll be harmed if we don't."

Shock hit me in a chilly smack. "What? No. Of course not. I'm not making any demands. I'm just passing on the information to—"

"Information about how frightened we should be," another bellowed. "We will not stand for this kind of insult. You bring these threats to our faces and try to bend us to your will yourself, and you think we won't realize?"

"That's not at all what I intended," I said in what was more of a babble now. My body instinctively pulled backward, away from them. "I promise you I—"

"And now he tries to run. Don't let him! Show him what happens to anyone foolish enough to attack we who own the shadow realm."

"No!" The protest burst from my mouth unbidden. I whirled around, panic overcoming rational thought, my mind whirling with no idea whether I'd be better off running or attempting to prove my peaceful intentions by holding my ground.

I didn't get a chance to decide. Bodies hurtled at me from multiple directions. Claws raked into me—horns gouged me—hooves battered me.

In our shadow forms, the pain didn't radiate through solid nerves the way it would have in the mortal realm. But their presences tore at mine all the same. Agony spread all through my essence as the Highest's guards shifted in turn without letting up their assault. Their ephemeral forms had enough friction against mine to choke and smack and pierce. My being frayed, life gushing out of me in billows in all directions.

Shadowkind couldn't die in the shadow realm, but we could come awfully close.

I hurled myself away from the onslaught with every fragment of will I had left in me. Again and again, nothing in my mind but the searing pain and the need to get away. Onward, onward, dragging myself inch by broken inch...

I wasn't even sure when the beating ended. By the time I realized no new blows were reaching me, my awareness of myself was so scattered and wrenching that they might as well have still been tearing me apart. With a guttural groan I couldn't hold in, I forced myself to crawl farther.

Just a little more. Just a little more. In case they decided they hadn't done enough. Get away. Get away.

Then I couldn't move any farther. The agony simply short-circuited my brain. I curled in on myself, pulling together all of my essence that I could still hold on to, and held there as the particles of my being started to ever-so-slowly knit themselves back together.

More aches jabbed and sizzled through me. I had the sense of gritting teeth I didn't currently have. But even through the pain, I willed myself to come back together, to heal, as quickly as I could, even if the speed amped up my anguish.

I had to get back to the others. I had to let them know that the Highest didn't believe us—that they'd scoffed at the idea of the leviathan as a threat—that they knew what he was doing and were looking the other way in their pompous over-confidence.

I had to get back to Quinn. I didn't even know how she was doing right now, whether her heart was failing faster, whether the leviathan had managed to launch another attack against her.

If I couldn't make it back in time to stand by her side at least a little longer, to hear her bright voice and revel in her touch, to bask in her determination and affection, I'd rip *myself* apart. There was no pain I could imagine that would be worse than that.

The truth hit me then like a glowing beacon shining fiercely through a storm: I loved her. I did, with every shred of my being. The fact of it felt so true and obvious that I could have smacked myself for not acknowledging it sooner, for shying away from the words as if they were somehow dangerous rather than a statement of devotion. As if she'd be disappointed in me if I somehow didn't make good enough on them.

She wouldn't, and that was part of the reason I loved her. Quinn had embraced all of me—man, kraken, injuries, past, and all. The statement wouldn't be a promise or a guarantee. It'd only be three words that she deserved to hear back after how freely she'd offered them to me and how deeply I felt them resonating through me now.

I had to get back to her and let her hear them. Let her understand that *I* understood just how much she meant to me. I wouldn't let those hulking assholes with their even more inflated egos stop me from reaching her in time.

With that resolve coiling around me, I braced myself and pulled my essence together even faster than before, ignoring the torment of the sensation.

CHAPTER TWENTY

Quinn

I gnawed on the lid of my pen and stared down at the piece of paper I'd only managed to add a couple of sentences to in the past hour. Writing my message to the enclave by hand had seemed like the best option. A printed note would come across as much more detached. But deciding on the actual words had been even more of a struggle than I'd anticipated.

I wanted to warn them. I didn't want the leviathan to eat them for dinner. That said, there were a pretty large number of other uncomfortable fates I couldn't say I'd have minded them meeting. What I'd seen during my time there had shown me those humans were more monstrous than most of the beings they called monsters. I was more concerned about stopping the leviathan from getting a power boost than saving the enclave from destruction.

It was kind of hard to figure out how to convey my concern in a way that'd sound like I meant it—and not grudgingly.

Rollick appeared at my bedroom doorway with a glass of lemonade in hand. He set it on the night table next to me and glanced down at the paper

I had braced on the cover of my sketchpad on my knee. "Not going so well?"

I made a face. "I don't think 'Please don't let a huge sea serpent eat you, but if you wouldn't mind falling off a cliff during your escape, I'd appreciate it' is going to go over the way we'd want."

The demon chuckled. "That's a sentiment I fully agree with, though. Do you want me to handle the letter? I've conducted an awful lot of negotiations in my time. I know how to keep my less helpful feelings under wraps."

"No." I scowled at the paper. "I should do this. I was the one who lived with them for a little while. Who knows if they have some way of telling that a shadowkind wrote it, and then they won't pay attention at all. I'll figure it out."

"Have it your way, sweet sorcerer." He rumpled my hair teasingly and left me to it.

I scowled at the lemonade too, but gulping some of the sweet-and-sour liquid did revive my spirits a little. I squared my shoulders and forced myself to keep going.

To the members of the sorcerer enclave,

I'm sure you're aware of the murders of sorcerers that've been happening around the world, most recently across the United States. You might also have noticed the news about storms and tidal waves that've been battering the coasts here.

All of that destruction has been caused mainly by one vicious, ancient monster who's set on further ruining our world. I've heard from a source I trust that he's discovered that there's a group of powerful sorcerers living in Norway and he intends to hunt you down. I have no idea how likely it is that he'll find you, but for everyone's safety, I thought you should know so you can relocate before he even has the chance.

We're doing whatever we can here to stop him and make sure he can't hurt anyone else. If you hear that the storms have ended, you'll know it's safe.

"And then I'll be heading over there to stop all the crap *you're* doing too," I muttered to myself. I hesitated, and then simply signed the letter as "A concerned ally," as much as the "ally" part made me wince. Then I added my phone number for good measure with a note that they could call me if they wanted to ask questions to confirm my story. The more opportunity I could give them to believe what I was saying, the better.

And hopefully they'd never realize that their "ally" was the same woman who'd crashed their rites and called a demon straight into their midst a few weeks ago.

I folded the letter and tucked it into the small protective case Rollick had given me for that purpose. We were going to have to send the letter to the enclave in the hands of a shadowkind, because one of them could travel to Norway nearly instantly, way faster than me going by plane and car. And anyway, if I'd shown up at the enclave's borders again, they'd probably shoot me on sight. They'd already tried to shoot me before, and that was before I'd called on Rollick for help and he'd killed at least two of the sorcerers while rescuing me.

But sending the letter with a shadowkind meant the messenger might face a similarly hostile greeting. It was a dangerous mission, and we didn't want to risk the message being burned up or shredded in whatever defenses the enclave raised against a supposed intruder. A protective case had seemed like an important precaution.

When I'd decided to take this course of action, I'd asked the beings hanging out around the house for a particularly speedy volunteer. A few had offered their services, and when I stepped out into the yard, the hawk shifter I'd chosen shimmered into human-like physical form. He bobbed his head to me in a distinctly bird-like motion, his sharp eyes fixing on the case. "It's ready to go?"

"Yes," I said. "I know Rollick's already gone over the directions to the enclave with you. Remember, don't linger there. Just drop the message off at the edge of the boundary, set off the flare, and get away from that place as fast as you can."

He gave another bob. "I'll have no interest in sticking around. Shouldn't take any more than an hour. Happy to be able to pitch in."

He took the case from my hands and vanished back into the shadows faster than I could blink.

I dragged in a breath and resigned myself to a tense, uncertain wait.

It didn't take even a fraction as long as I'd anticipated.

In less than an hour, as promised, the hawk shifter reappeared at the house. His hair was slightly singed, and a scrape marked his jaw, but he'd made it back in one piece.

"They had a lot of beings lurking along the borders," he reported when I hurried out to meet him. "I couldn't even get all the way to the edge of their territory. But I flew the letter as close as I could, dropped it, and shifted for long enough to yell at them to bring it to their masters. Hopefully someone listened."

"Thank you," I said emphatically, meaning it. "That's the most I'd have asked from you. If it doesn't work, it's their fault, not yours."

But it'd be the whole world paying for it, not just the enclave.

I paced through the house, wanting to be focusing on figuring out battle strategies but too wound up and distracted to make much progress. I was just simmering down and getting my focus back when my phone rang.

My pulse stuttered. No one had that number who'd be calling in any situation that wasn't important. I yanked it out of my pocket, took in the unknown number on the screen, and hit the answer button. "Hello?"

"Who is this?" said the caustic male voice on the other end without any preamble.

My throat closed up. I inhaled deeply, groping for my inner calm. The man who'd spoken didn't need to introduce himself for me to be sure he was one of the enclave's sorcerers.

"That's doesn't matter," I said. "What matters is that I know about the enclave and about the monsters who come out of the shadows, and I know that everything I wrote in my letter to you is true. What you do about it is up to you, but I hope you protect yourselves."

There was a rustling sound and the murmur of breaths, and I realized he wasn't the only one following this call. "It sounds like her," someone else muttered in a firm female voice I thought I recognized as belonging to Vera, the sorcerer who'd mentored me during my brief time at the enclave. I hadn't known for sure that she was even still alive.

She'd been with the bunch who'd caught me at the rites and then tried to hunt me down before Rollick had rushed in to retrieve me.

"Quinn?" she demanded now. "That is you, isn't it? I can't think of who else would have known where to send a message like that—or be friendly enough with the fiends to have one deliver it for you."

I wasn't sure there was any point in denying it, but her tone didn't make me particularly inclined to confirm her suspicions either. "Like I said, it doesn't matter. If you need any more information about what's happening here in the States or the monster that's searching for you—"

"As if we'd listen to anything you'd say after what you already put us through," she interrupted. "This is probably some new conspiracy with those murderous beasts to get us away from our protections. We're fine where we are. You can't scare us into fleeing."

My spirits sank. "You've never dealt with any being like this one before. It's thousands of years ancient, and it's already consumed the power of dozens of sorcerers, maybe hundreds."

"It can't turn that sorcery on us. We'll fend the thing off if it makes it here. We aren't leaving our home. And if we ever find out where *you* are, you'd better believe you'll pay for the havoc you already caused."

The line went dead with a swift thump as if she'd slammed the phone down. I lowered my own from my ear with a heavy heart, my stomach knotting.

Was there some other way I could have delivered the message that they'd have received better? Was the leviathan going to get his potentially world-ending meal *because* I'd betrayed the enclave already?

Of course, if I'd never gone out there to investigate them, I'd never have known where to send the message to begin with. And witnessing their sick practices had taught me how to increase my own powers to use them for good. So I couldn't say it would have worked out better the other way.

I'd done the most I was capable of. Now I just had to hope that clearer heads would prevail over there. If they didn't leave right away, hopefully they'd at least ramp up their security even more. Maybe if one of their enslaved shadowkind sensed the leviathan approaching soon enough, they'd be able to make a run for it and get away before he reached them after all.

Those hesitant hopes didn't do much to dislodge the lump of uneasiness that'd expanded in my gut. I went back to my laptop, going over the chart I'd created of our main allies and their abilities. I'd been working out possible strategies for keeping the leviathan's minions busy while Rollick's human associates put the weapons that would make up his portable "trap" in place.

If we'd had the enclave's sorcerers on our side for this one thing, between me and them, we probably could have compelled the leviathan straight into the trap and ended all of this. But they wouldn't even leave the enclave to save their lives. There was obviously no way in hell they'd cross the ocean to purposefully face this creature beside me.

I was still ruminating on the problem when a shout went up outside. Panic jolted through my body. I was up and running to the door, snatching up my crossbow as I went, before I'd even had time to think about what the problem might be.

When I reached the yard, I still couldn't tell at first. Several of the shadowkind had emerged into physical form, crouched in a ring around something I couldn't see. Thin wafts of smoke rose up from their midst.

As I hurried over, a few glanced over their shoulders at me. The nearest eased to the side so I could join their circle.

"The injuries are already sealing," one of them said. "We'll do what we can to help him recover."

Those last words reverberated through my head as I found myself gazing down at Torrent: his eyes squeezed shut, his body halfway between its human- and octopus-like forms, twisted in agony. The smoke I'd seen was the essence seeping from multiple breaks in his flesh, drifting away into the open air.

CHAPTER TWENTY-ONE

Quinn

The fae woman leaned over Torrent's crumpled form on the bed. The flowers attached to stems that seemed to grow right out of her scalp swayed with her silvery hair. She pressed a hand to his side just above where one of his tentacles was twisted around his human-like torso and murmured. I caught a faint ripple of energy in the air.

His wounds had finished sealing as a bunch of the shadowkind outside had carried him into the bedroom. No more smoky essence dissipated into the air around us. But he was still unconscious, his limbs tensed at awkward angles as if braced against some internal pain.

At the fae woman's attentions, at least some of the stiffness in his expression had faded. She moved her hands to his shoulders and murmured again, and the final furrow smoothed out of his brow. Her lips pursed as she looked down at him.

"He should have stayed in the shadow realm longer to properly heal. But I've done what I can for the internal damage. The rest will have to knit together on its own over time."

I swallowed thickly. "How much time?"

She shook her head with a rustling of the flowers. "I don't know for sure. But he should wake up."

That didn't sound like a promise.

I tucked my legs up onto the bed where I'd perched next to Torrent's feet, hesitant to even touch him in his potentially fragile state. A couple of the beings who'd been gathered around him when I'd found them outside eased closer.

"He must have come through the rift that's about twenty miles from here," the hunched goblin said. "That's the closest one. I don't know how he managed to make it as far as he did from there on his own. We found him on our patrol about halfway here already, crawling along through the shadows but barely able to talk."

The fanged man next to him nodded. "He conked right out when we went to help him. We had to carry him back. Someone really wasn't happy with him, wherever he ended up." His gaze slid to Torrent with a sympathetic grimace.

"Thank you," I said. "For bringing him back so quickly. It sounds like... it sounds like he'll probably be okay." I was afraid to say anything more certain like that, as if I might jinx his recovery.

They dipped their heads and wavered away, leaving me alone with Torrent. None of my other men had returned from their most recent expeditions yet. I had no idea what else I could do.

Gingerly, I sank down on my side facing Torrent. I'd never seen my tentacled man really sleeping before. Shadowkind didn't technically *need* to sleep as part of their regular routine, and he'd tended to slip away into the shadows when he wanted to take a break.

His scarred chest rose and fell with slow but now steady breaths. His mouth twitched and then stilled. I wanted to reach out to him, but I had no idea how much internal damage might be healing beneath his skin.

Taking in the bruises and scars that mottled his body and remembering the battered state I'd found him in sent a wild rush of emotion searing through my chest. I could make sure that didn't happen again. I could send him away from all of this, from every being that might hurt him, like I had before. How the hell could I be so selfish to keep the men I loved in this fight?

Especially when at the end of it, there'd only be more heartbreak even if we won. Because I was becoming more and more certain that I wasn't going to make it past the final battle with my heart still beating.

I closed my eyes against the wave of anguish, hot tears welling up at the corners. As much as the ache inside wrenched at me, I knew I couldn't give in to it. I *had* taken that approach once before—and I'd seen how much pushing my men away had hurt them too.

There was no getting out of this scenario without some pain along the way—for any of us. But the sweet parts of life, the thrills and the beauty, had made the hard parts worth it for me. I knew all of my monstrous men would have said the same.

We were as connected as any beings, human or shadowkind, could become. And that meant we'd stand together through whatever happened next.

The body next to me stirred. As my eyes popped open, one of Torrent's tentacles flexed. It slid across the sheets to loop around my waist, looking instinctive in its movements.

His jaw flexed. His brow knit, and he blinked. His gaze fixed on me blearily and then with increasing focus. A whiff of confusion and then another of relief passed from him into me.

"Quinn," he said in a ragged voice.

With a leap of my heart, I sat up. "Can I get you anything? There was a fae who helped heal you—if you think you need more of her powers—"

"Quinn," he repeated, a little steadier, and tightened his grip on my waist. "I want you here. That's what I came back for. Don't go running off on some new mission, Ms. Fix It."

The old nickname brought a lump to my throat. I lay back down, letting Torrent tug me closer. When I rested my hand on his chest, his eyelids lowered to half-mast with an expression contented enough to absolve my guilt about not insisting on doing more.

"What happened?" I asked quietly. "Who did this to you? Was it the leviathan's minions—did they catch you on the way to the Highest—"

Torrent's dark laugh interrupted my question. "It *was* the Highest. Or their underlings, anyway. They took my warning as a threat, an attempt at manipulating them, and they were deeply displeased."

An icy jolt lanced through my chest. "You told them what was happening, and they attacked *you* for it? What the hell is wrong with them?"

"A very good question." He sighed and rolled toward me with a wince at the movement. "They've been holed up in the deepest parts of the shadow realm for so long I wouldn't be surprised if their minds are as muddled as the leviathan's seems to be. Which is all the more reason it'd be a very bad thing if they were dragged into the mortal realm. They didn't think it was possible."

"Which means they're arrogant and over-confident as well as being vicious jerks," I muttered.

A soft smile touched Torrent's lips. He raised his hand to my face and stroked his fingers over my cheek. "So angry on my behalf."

"Of course I am. They practically *killed* you. The beings who found you said you should have stayed in the shadow realm longer to heal. Did something else happen that we need to be ready for?"

He shook his head slightly against the pillow. "No. That was just— I didn't know what was going on here. I was worried—" He cut himself off, holding my gaze so intently that my pulse stuttered.

A warm wash of emotion carried with his next words. "I love you. I want to be here with you for as much time as I possibly can. If that means it takes a little longer for my wounds to heal, I don't mind."

He'd never said those three words before. He'd specifically told me he wasn't sure he'd ever be able to. I hadn't minded, but hearing them fall from his lips so emphatically set off a swell of answering emotion in my chest.

I scooted even closer to him and wrapped one arm around him, hugging him as tightly as I dared. "I love you too. So much. I'm sorry— You went through so much and they didn't even listen—"

"It wasn't your idea for me to go," Torrent said gently. He kissed my forehead. "It was the right thing to do. We had to try. Now we try something else. I'm sure you and the others can bring me up to speed on where we're at now."

I thought of everything that we'd learned since he'd left, and my stomach started to ache. I was going to need to tell him about all of it, but first I raised my head so I could meet his mouth for a lingering kiss. The quiver of joy that passed from him into me through our connection confirmed just how worth it this moment was to him.

Afterward, I sucked in a breath to gird myself. "There's been a lot. And the humans we've had to reach out to are being just as stubborn as the Highest. This is what you've missed..."

When Torrent drifted back into the sleep-like state that seemed to be helping him recover, I eased off the bed and went back to the bedroom where I'd been sleeping. The words he'd said and the devotion he'd offered me were still humming through my body. There were so many things wrong with the world, but that brief conversation had made everything feel a little more right.

I'd spent so much of my life trying to protect everyone around me from the impact of the problems I was facing. Going it alone. Keeping them at a distance or shoving them completely away. Suddenly I couldn't help wondering if I'd actually accomplished anything close to what I'd hoped to that way.

I couldn't do anything about the friends I'd pulled back from or never let in to begin with, but there were two other people I loved who I hadn't been fully honest with in a long time. I might not see them again before I died. Maybe they deserved my honesty more than my attempt at protecting them.

With my pillow propped against the headboard, I sat back and dialed Mom's number. Beyond the guestroom window, evening was falling, pink and orange streaking across the clouds with the setting sun.

We'd survived another day. That counted for something.

Mom picked up on the second ring. "Quinn? How are you, sweetheart?"

So eager to get an update on my well-being before anything else. The affection and concern in her tone decided me.

"Right now, okay," I said. "Are you two hanging in there all right still?"

"As well as can be expected, I suppose. I don't like staying here rather than being out there helping stop what's happening... but I can admit I have no idea how I would help."

"Staying safe helps," I reminded her. "It means I can focus more on fixing all this."

"I know. But I wish it didn't come down to you. I still don't understand how any of this could be true."

"Yeah, it doesn't make a whole lot of sense to me either. But it is what it is." I paused and raised my chin in defiance of my own hesitation. "Is Dad up? Could you put the phone on speaker so you can both hear me? There's —there's something else I'd like to talk to you about."

"Of course." Mom couldn't disguise the tremor of worry in her voice as she clicked the phone over.

"Hey, kiddo," Dad said from somewhere slightly more distant.

"Hi, Dad. It's good to hear your voice." But beating around the bush would only leave them to wonder anxiously longer. Better to rip off the bandaid.

I closed my eyes. "I didn't tell you everything the last time I saw you. I didn't want to make you worry even more. But I feel like you should know. I'm not sure if it'd have happened anyway or if it's because of all the supernatural stuff that I'm wrapped up in now, but I'm getting symptoms like my heart is starting to fail."

"Oh, sweetheart." Something about Mom's voice wrapped around me like an invisible hug. "How long has that been happening? You know there are medications that are supposed to moderate—"

"I know," I cut in, unable to listen to her offer up false hope. "One of my friends was able to arrange for me to get some. And it's only been for a couple of weeks. But it seems to be getting worse quickly even so, which is why I think the supernatural stuff is probably a factor. I'm okay. I always knew it could start to go at any time. I knew I wasn't going to live to eighty or something. I just—I didn't want to keep that from you. I wanted you to be able to prepare, and to tell you that you really did everything you could for me. You were exactly what I needed as parents."

"Quinn." Dad sounded choked up. He paused before continuing hoarsely. "You've been everything we ever wanted in a daughter. Isn't there some way that these... creatures, whatever they are... I mean, some of them have something like magic...?"

I let out a rough chuckle. "This seems to be beyond anything they're capable of fixing. Believe me, they'd be doing it if they could. But I'm happy. I've been happy. I still had a lot of great things in the life I did get. And there's nothing I'd rather be doing with the rest of it than making sure as many people as possible get more life too."

"You've always been so strong," Mom said. "I know you haven't liked to talk all that much about anything you're worried about. I'm glad that you told us. You have to know how much we love you. Our thoughts are going to be with you the entire time. And if you can come back here and see us again, I hope you will."

Her voice wavered, but she didn't let herself beg to see me, even though I had the feeling she wanted to. My eyes teared up all over again. "I definitely will. I don't know if it'll be possible, but if I can, I'll be there."

A nostalgic note crept into Dad's tone. "I still remember the time when you were fourteen and you insisted on going on that new rollercoaster at Busch Gardens, and you were laughing the whole time while your mother and I hung on for dear life."

A bittersweet smile crossed my face. "That was a fun trip. We had a lot of good times."

"We did," Mom said softly.

We reminisced back and forth for a while longer, until my heart felt full and my gut heavy. When I hung up, I slumped back into the pillows—and a tall form wavered into being just inside the doorway.

Rollick had returned. He studied me with his incisive gaze. "I didn't want to interrupt your call. It sounded important. You told your parents about your health?"

I nodded. "It seemed like the right thing to do. Now the fact that I haven't isn't hanging over me." Then I pushed myself straighter, my melancholy falling away under a sharper wave of apprehension. "What's happened? Has something changed?"

He held up his phone with a twist of his mouth. "Unfortunately, yes. There's breaking news out of Norway."

CHAPTER TWENTY-TWO

Quinn

I sat on the sofa with my computer poised on my lap, staring at the article on the screen. My stomach felt as if it'd plummeted right out of my body, through the floor, and possibly all the way down to the center of the earth.

Massacre in Isolated Commune, the headline read. The rest of the report went on to describe how the bloody bodies of nearly thirty men and women had been found in a tiny community in the wilderness of northern Norway just a few hours ago.

"Each of the bodies was brutally mutilated," Rollick read aloud. "I think we can guess what those mutilations involved."

"All their vital organs torn out as if by some kind of wild beast," I muttered, and let my head drop back against the sofa. "I tried to warn them."

Crag came up behind me to rest his hand on my shoulder. He'd made it back to the house shortly after Rollick had arrived with the bad news. "They might not have had time to escape anyway. We only found out about the threat this morning. The leviathan must have already been over there searching for them."

Of course he had been. As soon as he'd realized he had such a simple opportunity to expand his powers, he'd have wanted to jump on it before there was any chance of it slipping through his fingers… or talons, or whatever exactly leviathans had.

I rubbed my forehead. "I didn't like the enclave. The things they did were sick. But now the result of their psycho behavior is helping an even bigger psycho. How the hell are we going to stop him now?"

"We don't know if this will be enough to allow him to carry out his ultimate plan," Rollick said, though his tone wasn't all that confident. "Even taking in the behemoth's essence wasn't enough."

"But this is so many more sorcerers' powers, and they were strong sorcerers too." I groaned. "We don't have much time. We have to figure out some kind of plan to counteract his, or we might not be able to do anything at all before he's hauling the Highest through that rift."

Rollick got up, tucking his phone into his pocket. "I have human associates watching that area from a distance. As soon as there's any change in activity there, we'll know."

"We don't know what we'll do when that happens. We've got all these shadowkind here, but most of them won't be able to do much against the leviathan, especially now that he's got even more sorcery to wield. We can't get close until he's focusing it on compelling the Highest, and then it'll be almost too late. Are your weapons using the materials from the trap even ready?"

The demon gave a curt nod. "Everything's prepared. They're almost like a larger version of your crossbow." He aimed a tight smirk at the weapon lying on the coffee table between us.

"But we still have to figure out how to get them in place without the leviathan or his minions destroying them first."

Crag squeezed my shoulder. "We've got a lot of allies on our side now to push them back, and you have your own magic that can strengthen the rest of us. He won't be prepared for that. Maybe we should give you more of our essence. If—"

I shook my head to cut him off. I didn't want to say it, but there wasn't any avoiding the truth. My hand rose to press against my clavicle. "At this point, I don't think a lack of magic is holding me back. It's whether my body—my heart—can handle having that much magic moving through it. It doesn't do any good making yourselves weaker if I can't even use all the power you've given me."

Rollick let out a rough sound and started to pace. "We won't give up. There are a lot of us willing to stand against the leviathan, even if the Highest are too arrogant or cowardly to."

His words echoed through my head. *A lot of us willing to stand against him.* There was someone like that who we hadn't called on yet, wasn't there?

I sat up straighter, fumbling for my phone. "We have to ask Sorsha for help. She and her friends—you said they're really powerful, didn't you? It seemed like they'd want to stop this from happening."

Rollick frowned. "We talked about this before. She's unstable. I don't know the men she runs with at all. And a phoenix isn't going to be much help against a being of water anyway."

I glowered at him. "If her fire won't be much use, then there isn't any chance of her burning the world down either, is there? She'd be able to do *something*, even if it's just helping keep the other shadowkind organized. And—you told me that she's some kind of hybrid, right? Part human? Maybe she can handle silver and iron. Maybe the leviathan can't compel her any more than he can me. That would count for a lot."

Rollick and I stared each other down. Crag seemed to decide it was wisest to stay out of the argument and let us duke it out on our own. The demon's mouth twitched, and then he sighed, dropping his gaze. "I don't even remember why I was so adamantly against her involvement. Fine. Call her. You're right—we need all the help we can get, and quickly."

"I'd imagine the whole 'nearly destroyed the world' thing was a pretty legit reason before we got to the point where the world was probably going to end anyway," I said, to be fair. "Also, you have issues with letting anyone in on your plans or even giving away that you *have* plans. That probably had something to do with it too."

Rollick went back to glowering at me. Wielding my phone, I marched into my room where I could figure out what to say to the phoenix without my monstrous men distracting me. I'd only talked to her briefly a couple of times in the past.

Once I was in the solitude of the bedroom, apprehension settled over me. I had trouble letting people in on *my* plans too, even if that hesitation came from a different place than Rollick's.

I was asking Sorsha and her friends to risk their lives to help us. My men wanted to stand with me because of their feelings for me—and because they'd seen the destruction the leviathan was causing. The allies we'd gathered so far had come of their own accord. To reach out to someone who'd already helped me more than once and ask her to stick her neck out again...

I grimaced at my phone—or really at myself. My stomach was all knotted up over something Sorsha had specifically told me to do. I'd met her because she was investigating the sorcerer killings. I knew that she'd want to hear what we'd discovered and have the chance to contribute, didn't I?

And we did need the help.

I just didn't like the feeling that it was my responsibility if something happened to her. But she was just as much a being with her own free will as Torrent and the rest of my men were.

My jaw clenching, I hit the call button and raised the phone to my ear.

It took longer for the phoenix to pick up than it had with my mom. I guessed Sorsha probably had more on her plate than the average human in general, and definitely more than my parents did in their little underground bunker. But just when I was starting to think I'd end up going to voice mail, there was a click and a voice that sounded a bit breathless, as if she'd been running. "Hello?"

"Hey, um, Sorsha, it's Quinn—"

"Oh!" she said, her voice brightening and steadying at the same time. "Sorry. I really need to remember to label my Contacts better. What's going on? Got another kid you want to shoot my way? That's not actually an invitation. We do have plenty."

Her irreverent tone set me at ease before I'd realized I was relaxing. A small smile even crossed my lips. "No kids this time. But—this is a much bigger ask."

"Please tell me you know what asshole shadowkind are behind the mess we're seeing with all these storms, because I'd really like to kick their asses."

A relieved laugh spilled out of me. It suddenly seemed absurd that I'd hesitated to reach out to her. "That is actually why I'm calling. It's not so much a they but a he. A leviathan. Well, there was a behemoth involved too, but we dealt with him... sort of. It's a long story. Anyway, the leviathan is basically trying to destroy the mortal world as we know it, and we're having some trouble making sure that doesn't happen, so any ass-kicking you want to bring to the table would be totally appreciated."

"You've got it. We've already been on the go trying to figure out what the hell is going on. Where exactly are you? We'll have the Everymobile out there as fast as its supernaturally enhanced engine can take us... Maybe faster if we decide to risk a rift. That's always a gamble."

"Whatever you think is best," I said. "Here, let me get—this isn't actually my house—the demon who owns it will be able to give you clearer directions."

"A demon house, hmm. Keeping even more interesting company than before these days."

I couldn't tell whether Sorsha was just amused or being suggestive, but my cheeks flared anyway. "That's a long story too. I'll tell you when I see you—when we're not busy with the whole saving the world thing. Just a sec."

I hustled back out into the living room. Rollick gave me a look that suggested he knew exactly what I was there for—which, considering the keenness of shadowkind hearing, he quite possibly did. I handed the phone over. "Be nice and tell our very helpful friends how to find your super-secret house."

He huffed, but he said his hello with his usual charming drawl, so I figured it was safe to leave him to it.

I found myself heading into the guest room where Torrent was recovering rather than to my own bedroom. The tentacled man was still out cold since our earlier conversation, but the deep, rhythmic murmur of his breaths reassured me. I lay down on the bed next to him and imagined telling him that soon we were going to be bringing a phoenix and... whatever the rest of Sorsha's friends were into the fray. I thought he'd understand better than anyone else how hard making that ask had been for me.

For now, I closed my eyes and let myself revel in my victory over my self-doubts for a minute. Maybe Sorsha and her companions would be a big enough force to turn the tide. If Rollick hadn't been such a stick-in-the-mud about getting them involved before, I'd have thought to reach out sooner.

We were getting so close to having a real army. If the leviathan just allowed us another few days to finish preparing—

The attack came on me so suddenly I didn't even have time to catch my breath before the clenching sensation squeezed all possibility of breathing out of my lungs.

My lips parted with a silent cry of pain. My shoulders went rigid as I braced against the pressure, trying to think about anything other than the vise clamped around my chest.

But it wasn't just the pressure that I had to endure. A hot flash rippled through me, followed by a chill as if someone had doused me with icy water. A shiver ran through my limbs. Sweat had broken out on my forehead. The thud of my heart rang loud in my ears, sounding too slow and then too fast, thundering erratically like a train about to rattle right off the tracks.

It was impossible to say how long it took before the symptoms eased off again. Finally, I became aware of my hands balled in the fabric of the sheet beneath me, my breath coming again—now with a faint rasp. An ache lingered around my ribcage after the worst of the effects had subsided.

I dragged in a deeper breath and blinked hard, staring up at the ceiling. I was relieved that my fit hadn't woken Torrent from the healing rest he needed, but I was also feeling so very alone.

A few more days. Maybe we had that. And then we'd need to face the leviathan, and I was going to have to put every bit of power I had into winning that fight for my parents, all the beings who'd put their faith in me, and everyone else in this world.

And then, I was now surer than ever, my heart would give out completely.

But that was just how it was. At least going this way I didn't leave millions of others to go down with me.

CHAPTER TWENTY-THREE

Rollick

These days, the house that'd once been a sanctuary to me rarely offered much peace or solitude. The heaps of shadowkind who'd joined our crusade stuck to the yard and the areas beyond the ring of protections depending on their tolerance for silver and iron, but I was always aware of them nearby. And more often than not, if I was here, at least one of my mutinous former employees was too.

But I couldn't say their presence was necessarily a bad thing, because at least having other beings around kept me a little distracted. Kept my mind from veering in directions I'd rather it didn't go but couldn't seem to prevent.

Five in the morning was about as quiet as the place got. I wandered into the kitchen, having just finished a call with a few old associates overseas, wheedling them to the limits my pride allowed to join this fight and gritting my teeth as they balked. They saw the current disaster as a distant problem, nothing for them to stick their necks out over.

When I'd told them what we believed the leviathan intended to do next, they'd laughed. But they hadn't seen him in action.

None of us had seen him in action since he'd devoured the entire enclave's worth of sorcerers. That much more magic now hummed through his veins—

My pulse lurched, and I found myself clutching the edge of the island as if it were the only thing holding me upright. My thoughts had scattered, my heart hammering at my chest so hard I half expected to feel a rib crack.

I closed my eyes, clenched my jaw even tighter, and breathed evenly in and out until the rush of panic receded.

So ridiculous. The being that'd bound me was gone, dead. The other fiend that could wield as much power was hundreds of miles distant. I wasn't even *thinking* anything when the fear took over. It was pure, random emotion.

I didn't let emotion dictate my life, especially not irrational fears. Why the hell didn't this after-effect wear off already?

What if it never did?

The discomfort that came with that consideration brought a milder chill but one that lingered longer. I tried to walk away from it, ambling back to the living room where the solar lights still glowed dimly around the pool, and soft footsteps reached my ears.

"Hey," Quinn murmured, coming up beside me. "Is everything okay?" She winced as soon as the words came out of her mouth. "I mean, no more horrible than things were a few hours ago."

"I know what you meant. There's been no news." I also knew exactly why she was asking—that damned connection I'd inadvertently forged. Every time the panic hit me, she felt it too. "I hope I didn't wake you."

She shook her head, peering past me over the rectangle of dark water rippling with a breeze. "I woke up a while ago and haven't been able to get back to sleep. I figured maybe taking a break from trying would help."

"You need your rest," I couldn't help telling her. Her face definitely looked paler than it had when I'd first met her, with a sallow tone creeping into her normally peachy skin that I didn't like at all. And she moved a little slower these days, as if her usual briskly determined pace would have worn her out too quickly.

"I'm fine," she said emphatically, fixing me with a sharp look. In that moment, I was more annoyed than ever that the connection between us didn't flow both ways.

How was she really coping? She could be as stubborn as I was. I wasn't totally sure how much she'd admit to struggling, especially with all the responsibility that'd been piled on her shoulders.

"Well, so am I," I retorted.

She narrowed her eyes at me. "The flashbacks have gotten stronger. They're hitting me harder through you, which means they've got to be hitting you harder too."

"And I keep living through them just like you keep living with your heart."

Quinn frowned. "They might get even worse when we go out to confront the leviathan, though. I don't know if I can protect you enough."

The fact that *she* was worried about protecting *me* when I was the all-powerful demon around here rankled me. I slipped my hand around her head to turn her to me and tucked her against my human-like frame. "I've survived just fine being near one enhanced sorcerer. I'll manage the shadowkind one out there too."

Quinn's body went still, not tensed but as if she were trying to listen hard to something she couldn't quite make out. She glanced up at me, close enough now that her breath brushed across my neck in a ghostly sensation. "You said it was having the behemoth work his sorcery on you that set this off. The idea of losing control again is what makes you panic."

"Something like that." I didn't really want to talk about it at all.

Thankfully, my lovely mortal seemed to have decided she'd had enough talking too. She curled her fingers into my shirt and tugged me with her, and I followed willingly. The spark that had lit in her eyes promised something interesting to come, whether I ended up liking it or not.

When she led me through the doorway to her bedroom and kicked the door shut behind us, I decided that chances were good that I'd approve. As she drew me over to the bed, I raised my eyebrows at her. "If you're in need of some carnal satisfaction, you only needed to say so."

Quinn hummed low in her throat, a sound that sent a heady shiver straight to my cock. But the heat in her gaze was as much determination as it was desire. "I think we can do a little more than that in here," she said, and hopped onto the bed, pulling me with her.

When I clambered after her, she shifted to the side and pushed me onto my back. I sank down without complaint, watching her curiously. She obviously had something specific in mind, and I saw no need to rush her.

Quinn gazed down at me, wetting her lips. She straddled my waist, her ass settling against my groin with enough pressure to bring a groan to my lips even with at least three layers of fabric between us. Her hands splayed against my chest.

"Maybe being commanded doesn't have to be a painful thing," she said. "Maybe it'd help your mind stop freaking out about it if you got to experience a more enjoyable enchantment."

A quiver of anxiety wound through my growing sense of anticipation, but I resisted giving it much attention. I'd seen how distraught Quinn got over even the thought of hurting any of us. I didn't fear her intentions at all.

"What did you have in mind?" I asked, keeping my voice languid.

She leaned forward, her hair falling like a golden veil on either side of her face, until her nose nearly touched mine. Then she spoke at a volume barely above a breath. "Touch me."

Magic resonated through the words and wound through my mind. My body stiffened against it instinctively—but there wasn't anything brutal about this sorcery. It was tentative enough that I could have thrown off the order if I'd wanted to.

I didn't, though, did I? I could play along with her little game and see where it led us. If I wasn't strong enough for that, then the leviathan might as well kill me now.

I unclenched my muscles and let my hands rise as they'd itched to do at her words. My fingers stroked up her back and twined in her silky hair. I pulled her the last few inches down so our lips could meld together the way I'd been hungering for since she'd mounted me.

A soft noise worked from Quinn's throat. She kissed me back just as eagerly. I tilted her head to the side with a twist of her hair so I could delve my tongue into that hot mouth, and earned my first whimper in return.

It wasn't bad. No, it was absolute fucking paradise going along with her vague instruction. After a few minutes, the tendril of magic that'd gripped my thoughts gradually eased away, barely enough to direct my will, and I felt a sudden, strange thrill at the idea of continuing on this course.

I tipped Quinn's head even farther and pressed my mouth against her neck. A swipe of my tongue and the scrape of my teeth drew another gasp from her. Then I eased back just enough to speak, my lips grazing her smooth skin. "What does my sweet sorcerer want from me next?"

A tentative smile crossed her face, as if she'd been waiting for the confirmation that I was on board—and still wasn't totally sure she could accept it. She gave her next order in the same whisper with its faint whiff of compulsion. "Uncover me."

I sure as shit didn't object to that request. Even less anxiety twanged through me as I reached for the hem of the tank top she'd been sleeping in and peeled it off her. She'd used broad enough wording that I didn't feel overly controlled. It was like the gentlest sort of bondage, restraints I could have slipped in an instant but that gave a little jolt of excitement having them in place.

Somehow I doubted the sorcerers who'd developed and spread this magic had ever intended it to be used like this—and knowing that only made the moment more delightful.

Quinn wasn't wearing a bra under her shirt. I cupped my hands around her breasts and tweaked the peaks before pushing up on my elbows so I could suck one into my mouth. The feel of her nipple stiffening beneath my tongue made me growl. I hadn't been able to do this the first time we'd come together on our own—she'd had to wear that damned protective undershirt the whole time.

Quinn's hands traveled down my chest, making quick work of my button-up shirt and sliding across the planes of muscle beneath. It felt as if she were drawing flames across my skin with her touch, but only the most blissful kind.

Her command still tingled through me. I knew that I hadn't completely uncovered her yet. I could have fought the pull, but why would I want to when it aligned so well with my own interests?

As I suckled her breast, teasing the nipple with my teeth until she started to pant, I glided one hand down her body to her pajama shorts. As soon as I grasped the waist, her hips lifted to allow me better access. I dragged the shorts off her as quickly as I could manage, and then I couldn't stop myself from tucking my fingers between her legs.

She was so wet already, her pussy slick with arousal, that I groaned against her breast. As I stroked her from clit to slit, a matching moan spilled from her lips. She rocked against my hand, and another command tumbled out of her. "Let me see the demon."

I knew what she meant, even if I could have satisfied the tug of the magic by simply blinking in and out of my shadowkind form for a brief glimpse. She was after a more extended experience.

With a growl, I flipped her over on the bed, letting my demon form stretch my body at the same time. The cool air washed over my abruptly bare back while the front of me seared with the heat we'd already generated between us. My second cock jutted below the first, equally hard already.

I claimed Quinn's mouth again, letting my sharp demonic teeth nick her lower lip. She whimpered encouragingly, squirming beneath me until our bodies were almost perfectly aligned. My upper cock brushed against her mound, and she swayed up to meet that contact. The need to fill her burned through me—but the tension of waiting for her orders had become increasingly delicious.

"What should your demon do for you now, my lovely mortal?" I murmured.

Quinn made a needy noise and ran her fingers along the curves of my horns, sending a tremor of pleasure down them and through my scalp. "Take me—however you'd most like to."

Somehow I hadn't even been aware of my deepest urges until her sorcery unlocked the answer inside my skull. All at once, I was picturing her on all fours, crying out in ecstasy as I slammed into her from behind. A rumble carried from my chest, and without thinking I was already flipping her over and yanking her ass against my groin.

Quinn gasped, but there was nothing fearful in the sound. I knew without any supernatural bond necessary just how much she trusted me. That thought caught at the base of my throat, stalling me in my tracks as I bowed my head to her shoulder blades. My hand delved between her legs again to tease even more pleasure out of her. But this bodily unification wasn't all I was craving.

"You are mine," I muttered against her back, and kissed the faint bumps of her spine. "*Mine*."

"And you're my demon," she said, so happily I couldn't suppress the affection that swelled from my heart. I hugged her tighter against me, and in that moment, the most important thing was her knowing how much this "taking" meant to me.

"I love you. My sweet sorcerer. My defiant mortal. Everything you are."

She'd helped me find the parts of myself I'd buried so far within me that I'd started to forget they existed. The only other partner I'd ever said those words to had shunned that side of me, the side that could be generous, that cared about making the whole world better. But Quinn didn't reject the selfish, vicious side of me either. She accepted them all together, everything that *I* was.

And that was why I wouldn't let anything defeat her, not that leviathan, not her treacherous heart.

Quinn shivered beneath me, but the emotion that thickened her voice told me her reaction was all joy. "I love you too. My wicked fiend. My reluctant hero."

I chuckled at that second label and finally gave in to the other longing twined through my body. My fingers traveled up the crease of her ass to her other opening, smearing my own growing arousal with them.

My lover pressed into my fingers as I stretched her, her breaths fragmenting even more. It was the sweetest torture waiting until the give of her inner muscles convinced me I wouldn't cause her any pain—at least not any that would do more than heighten the pleasure that came with it.

With my first thrust into her, filling both her openings at once, she buried her face in the pillow with a strangled moan. I spread her legs farther apart so I could plunge even deeper into her slick channels and braced myself on one arm so I could fondle her breasts at the same time. With each smack of our bodies colliding, she rocked back into me, the gasps and moans escaping her in a chorus electrifying me.

The craving for release was already building in my balls. I rolled her nipple and then trailed my hand down to circle her clit with a careful claw, matching the movements with the pounding of my cocks.

Quinn broke, her body shuddering and clenching, the cry I'd imagined bursting from her in a peal even more beautiful than what my mind had conjured. The passion of her welcome unraveled what remained of my self-control. I thrust into her faster, harder, and felt a second release ripple through her as I tumbled over the edge myself with simultaneous surges of cum inside her.

"Fuck," Quinn mumbled as she sagged onto her side beneath me.

I grinned down at her. "Yes, that's the word for what we just did."

She swatted me with an amused wrinkling of her nose at the joke. Then a hint of somberness touched her expression. "Was that okay? The way I brought my magic into it—"

I eased myself down next to her and pulled her against me. "I enjoyed it quite a bit. And I don't think I'll ever be able to think about sorcery quite the same way again, so thank you for that."

She smothered a guffaw. "Just don't get any ideas about romancing the leviathan."

"Believe me, there's no chance of that," I said dryly, but as the words left my lips, a flicker of hope darted through me.

The mention of the ancient beast and his magic hadn't set off even the slightest flicker of panic this time. I couldn't say for sure that this creative interlude had completely cured my lingering fears… but maybe my precious lover's touch had been the salve that'd healed the worse of them.

If only I could heal her troubles just as quickly.

CHAPTER TWENTY-FOUR

Quinn

"These ones can move the earth," Lance said proudly, pointing to two beings he'd identified as ogres, who looked just as rocky as Crag's gargoyle form but were much more... lumpy about it. They squatted on the dry earth in the desert outside the house with their heads cocked curiously atop their stocky bodies. But at least they were here.

"That could be useful," I said. "For pushing the leviathan around or holding him in place if he's near the shore. Or even if he's not. There's earth under the ocean too."

Both of them nodded in jerky motions. "Yes, yes," the one on the right said. "We'll do our best. Mostly we crack things, but we can also make them collide."

And my magic should amplify whatever effects they could normally accomplish. I gave them a weary but grateful smile. "Thank you for coming."

As they waddled off, I turned to Lance, who was beaming. "They were a good find. I'm starting to feel like we might actually have a proper army here." If we could get them all working together in unison without having their powers collide with each other. It wasn't as if we could easily practice our strategies without any leviathan around and on terrain pretty much the opposite of the coastline.

The dragon shifter grinned even wider. "I think so too." Then his good humor dimmed. "Crag said the biggest wave hit Rollick's city."

I grimaced with a lurch of my stomach, remembering the images I'd seen from the news websites this morning. "Yeah. The leviathan finally threw that tidal wave he'd been building at L.A. Thankfully they'd already gotten a lot of people evacuated, but there were still some deaths, and it destroyed a bunch of property. The storms are still battering the whole area... It's a mess." I couldn't help feeling guilty that I'd been able to escape to someplace so comfortable and, well, dry.

"We should go challenge him right now," Lance said, rolling his shoulders as a fierce light sparked in his violet eyes.

"And that'll just add to *his* army," Rollick said dryly, coming up behind us. "I'd rather not make a contribution to his cause. You know we need to wait until he's focusing his sorcery elsewhere before we have a real chance."

Lance grunted with annoyance, but he didn't have any more solution to that problem than the rest of us did. I swallowed thickly, folding my arms over my chest just shy of hugging myself. "I guess now that we know he's accumulated all the sorcery he's likely to, we should get ourselves closer to California again so it's less of a trek when we need to reach him. Do you have any houses that—"

Before I could finish my question, a clanging like a warning at a train crossing split the air. I spun around to see a familiar RV in the distance, roaring along the narrow road that led to the house and kicking up dust under its wheels. A figure I could barely make out appeared on the top of the vehicle, heedless of its speed, and brought his arms down on something protruding from the roof a few times. Whatever he'd smashed, the clanging sound cut out.

Rollick sighed, but my lips twitched with a smile. Sorsha's vehicle might be unusual, but she and her companions were the last definite allies we'd been waiting on. It'd be better to start moving toward California with them already with us.

As the RV approached, my other two men emerged from the house, Crag striding over from the doorway and Torrent only wavering into physical form when he could stand with us. The tentacled man had all four of his supporting tentacles out, his posture still a bit unsteady.

I moved to him, grasping his arm. "Are you sure you shouldn't keep resting?"

Torrent slipped his arm right around me, the damaged hand on that side resting against my waist, and pressed a gentle kiss to my temple. "I get the sense that final plans are being made. You're not leaving the cripple out of them."

I narrowed my eyes at his self-derogatory wording, but he'd said it lightly enough that I wasn't too worried about his emotional state. All the same, I had to say, "Don't beat yourself up. The jerks back in the shadow realm already had that job more than covered."

A startled laugh tumbled out of Torrent, and he tightened his sideways hug for just a second with a ripple of affection through our connection. "As I'm well aware."

I had the sense that all of the shadowkind gathered around the house were watching the vehicle's arrival, even though most of them remained in the patches of gloom beyond my sight. It was hard not to find the RV kind of momentous with its various streamers and spinning accessories. I'd gathered that most if not all of those were the result of previous trips through rifts, which would explain why Sorsha might not have been super keen to travel by that route again.

The so-called Everymobile jerked to a halt just shy of the garage that held Rollick's multiple cars. The door chimed as it opened, and Sorsha strode out with the unflappable energy I was starting to expect from her, her appropriately fiery red hair swinging in its wavy ponytail. The four shadowkind men who I suspected were more than just friends of hers followed more cautiously. They flanked her with a mildly protective air that seemed a little absurd if Rollick was right that this woman had enough power in her to destroy both realms all on her own.

They were certainly a varied assortment of beings. One loomed as tall and brawny as Crag, his pale blond hair contrasting with his burnished brown skin. He'd had wings at least once before, but darkly feathered ones, so he definitely wasn't a gargoyle. At the moment his only obvious monstrous feature was the crystal-like surface of his knuckles. I didn't think it'd be fun to get punched by that guy.

An equally tall but much slimmer guy rested his hand on Sorsha's shoulder, his golden curls as sunny as his smile. A forked tongue darted briefly from between his lips. I had no idea what kind of being he was either.

The dark-haired guy, who had his leanly muscled frame clothed in a posh button-up and slacks combo like he was about to head to a fancy nightclub, eyed us all with a faintly amused expression that didn't seem to fit the situation. Sorsha had mentioned he was an incubus. Two short horns poked from his chocolate-brown locks.

And then there was the well-built, tawny-haired man who didn't show any shadowkind features at all, though I knew he had to have one somewhere. His mouth was tight as if he was holding back a growl, and I had a flash of a memory to seeing him transform into that human-like shape from that of a monstrous, glowing dog. A hellhound, one of my guys had said.

Seeing them all in front of us, feeling how much more powerful they were than the vast majority of the beings who'd already joined our "army," I couldn't help finding it twice as ridiculous that we'd only just called on them for help. Rollick and that stupid shadowkind hesitation to ever depend on each other.

The demon himself stepped forward with an air that was all polished charm and a wariness I could sense underneath it. "Welcome to my humble home. Although we've just been talking about leaving it."

Sorsha nodded with a swish of her ponytail and a flex of her toned shoulders. "I heard about the tsunami that hit L.A. overnight. The leviathan's still out there, you figure?"

"That's where his favorite rift is, so that's where he'll be."

She glanced around, and I could tell she was aware of the beings lurking around us too. "Quite the motley crew you've assembled. We were talking on the drive down about how we could best pitch in. Feel free to make suggestions, since you've all dealt with this prick firsthand and we haven't. Ruse is probably best on crowd control." She motioned to the incubus. "He can make sure all mortals steer clear of the battle grounds, if there are any around."

I hadn't even thought about random mortals getting caught up in the clash. "That would definitely be useful."

Sorsha patted the slim guy's hand on her shoulder. "Snap can use his 'tasting' skill to see if he can pick up any useful impressions that would tell us more about the leviathan's plan of action, what steps he'll take next, so we can anticipate his movements. And also figure out if there are any deadly surprises he's arranged. Unfortunately the whole devouring souls skill seems to mainly work on mortals, not other shadowkind."

Rollick raised his eyebrows. "It sounds as though he'll be quite helpful all the same," he said, while I re-evaluated the cheerful-looking guy.

Sorsha jabbed her thumb toward the big dude. "Thorn can give the leviathan a shove if you need him on the move and generally distract him with a good pummeling. His wings allow him a lot of maneuverability."

Crag let out a grunt and dipped his head to the other hulk. "We'll coordinate our attacks, then."

Thorn nodded in return, his expression even more solemn than the gargoyle's. "It will be an honor to fight alongside such courageous beings."

I decided not to ask what century he'd come from. The sentiment was appreciated.

Sorsha gestured between herself and the hellhound shifter last. "Omen and I should be able to have some impact with our fire, even against an enemy who's all about the water. We can boil the area he's hanging out in. Flambé any minions that come at the rest of you."

"As long as you don't flambé the rest of us too," Torrent said evenly.

The phoenix flashed him a smile. "Don't worry, I've got much better control over my powers now that I've had more than a couple of weeks to figure out what the hell I even am." She paused. "None of us have gone up against anything quite as ancient and powerful as this leviathan before. But we'll do all we can. Between everyone here, we should be able to kick his butt."

I realized with a jolt that I hadn't told her one important part of our plan. "We've actually found that we can, er, rev up the powers everyone already has. Well, I can, anyway. Using my sorcery. If I order shadowkind to do something they already want to do, it seems to amplify their strength."

Sorsha's eyebrows shot up. "Fascinating. And very handy."

Omen snorted. "Maybe with beings like *this*," he said, tilting his head toward the shadowy crowd around the yard, his voice slightly disdainful. "I doubt it'd do much for us."

I wavered, not sure that arguing with him was the best idea, but Sorsha clearly had no such qualms. She spun toward him with a sly grin. "There's an easy way to find out, isn't there? I think you've just volunteered yourself as a test subject. After all, you're the most ancient being here, except maybe our demonic host. If it works on you, it should work on anyone."

The man glowered at her, his tawny hair ruffling even though I didn't feel any breeze. "I'm not sure I can burn things even more to a crisp than I'm already capable of."

"Ah, but maybe you can burn them even faster!"

"Er, I don't actually have to use my powers on any of you," I said quickly. "It's totally fine if you'd rather not."

"No, no, our Disaster wants a demonstration, she'll get a demonstration." There was a weird fondness to the words despite Omen's grouchy expression. "Let's work with water, since that's what we'll be dealing with out there. Someone want to bring out a couple of glasses?"

Lance bounded into the house and returned moments later with two large tumblers brimming with tap water. Omen rolled his shoulders and then hunched over into his hellhound form—which was even more massive and unnerving than I'd remembered. He did look like a hound—one whose shoulders came up to the top of my head and whose charcoal gray fur was streaked through with magma-like currents of fire. Lance let out a whistle of approval.

Omen lashed a paw at the first cup, I supposed to establish a baseline. Even as the glass smashed into the hard terrain, the water was sizzling away into steam. Not a dribble touched the dirt. It was pretty impressive.

He looked at me impatiently with eyes that glowed just as searingly as the streaks in his fur. My pulse skipped a beat, but I tamped down my nerves and focused my sorcerous energy on him. A short string of syllables burst out of me. *Destroy the other glass.*

Omen lunged at the second cup. He smacked at it just like the first—but this time the vessel didn't shatter. It hissed alongside the water.

We all stared down at the blob of melted glass that now lay on the dirt. A giddy quiver raced through my chest.

I'd helped make that happen. Maybe we really did have a chance against the monster who meant to upend both our worlds.

Ruse started to laugh. Sorsha clapped her hands with a chuckle of her own as Omen returned to his human form. He ran his hand over his ruffled hair and gave me a warier glance. "All right. There's something to it. I mean, I *could* have melted the first one too if I'd been trying to. But I did the second without even trying."

"Yes, yes, you're very great and powerful," Sorsha teased. "Now that we've gotten the testing out of the way, how about—"

Rollick's ringtone interrupted her. The demon frowned and snatched his phone out of his pocket. "What?" he said smoothly, and then his expression tensed. "*What?* When did this start? Yes, yes. Just keep me updated."

He hung up, his jaw clenched, and glanced around at the rest of us. "We have to get going, *now*. The leviathan's gathering an even bigger mass of beings around the rift and has started slaughtering them faster than before. It looks like he's making his final bid to bring the Highest through—and he's not going to wait around for us to arrive before he makes that call."

CHAPTER TWENTY-FIVE

Lance

Watching Quinn disappear past the door of the phoenix's huge vehicle wrenched at me more than anything had since the time our sorcerer had sent us away from her with her magic. My limbs twitched, and I almost threw myself after her, but Torrent caught me with a tentacle around my wrist.

I halted instantly, knowing that he was still weak from the beating he'd gotten in the shadow realm—not wanting to hurt him worse.

"This is the best way to get her there with enough time for her to make a difference," he reminded me. "She can't travel through the rifts, and that vehicle is enhanced to go faster than any of Rollick's cars can."

I grimaced at the RV as the engine roared to life. It tore down the dusty road so fast it wavered against the desert landscape. "I know. But I don't like her being away from us. We won't know what's happening to her. And we hardly know those shadowkind with her."

"We know they fought enemies the Highest refused to tackle before," Rollick put in, though he didn't look much happier than I felt. "I may have concerns about their specific methods, but I don't think we have to worry that they'd suddenly take the leviathan's side." He motioned to us. "Come on. Let's lead this army of ours to the battlefield. We'll get there well ahead of our woman, which means we can make sure her arrival is as safe as possible."

I didn't think there was any way that approaching the rift the leviathan wanted to bring the Highest through could be *safe* for Quinn, but Rollick couldn't have picked an argument more likely to motivate me. I whirled around and dove into the shadows. Winding through the patches of gloom scattered across the sun-drenched terrain, I snapped my teeth at and nudged my dragon shoulders against the ephemeral bodies I brushed past.

"Let's go, let's go. It's time to stop that watery fiend from ruining this entire realm. If you're with us, come along!"

Now that the fight was actually in front of us, something real they'd have to face in the very near future, I tasted a ripple of hesitation spreading through the crowd. A growl reverberated out of me. "If we don't stop him right away, there won't be *any* stopping him! He'll turn us all into slaves, cage our minds. All the wonderful mortal things will be gone. But there are a lot of us, and only one of him. And our sorcerer is going to help us stand up to him. We can do this."

Many beings were already moving toward my three companions, who merged with the shadows as well. Rollick led the charge, continuing to beckon everyone as he headed toward the nearest rift that we could use to take a shortcut across the country. Crag and Torrent fell back near me, herding the more reluctant beings along with the crowd like shepherds.

"We could use all of your help," Crag boomed through the sporadic shadows. "But if you aren't willing to fight, we won't force you to come. *He's* the one who treats beings that way. We need everyone who's with us to be committed to stopping him. There's no shame in being scared."

I suspected the gargoyle thought there was plenty of shame in it, especially when it came to his own emotions. But his words seemed to rouse the slower beings, as if prodding them to action. They didn't want to be seen hanging back, cringing in fear, while their companions raced off to risk their lives defending everyone else. A hint of a smile touched my lips.

We ran on, darting through the narrow shadows in the cracked earth and leaping across stretches of sunlight when we needed to. The mass of beings condensed until we were all surging forward together like one creature.

I felt the vibration of the rift up ahead. Rollick was still leading us, a powerful presence at the front of the pack. He hurtled all the way to the patch of earth just below the rift, which hung several feet above the ground, invisible to mortal eyes.

"Keep following me," he hollered when the whole crowd was close enough to hear him. "I'll find the route that'll take us to California—but not so close that we should be within range of the leviathan's sorcery. If you lose track of the rest of us, try to get yourselves to a spot northeast of Los Angeles and look for us nearby."

He spun around and sprang up into the rift. We leapt after him in a flood, rushing through into the dull but familiar gloom of the shadow realm, tracing his presence as he hustled past other rift openings, ignoring the beings who stopped to stare at the mass of us charging by. There was no time left to do any more recruiting—and anyway, beings who liked to hang out on this side of the boundary between the realms probably didn't care that much about what happened on the mortal side anyway.

When Rollick paused at a rift up ahead, my spirits lifted. The force of his nod carried through the gloom. He waited a moment for the beings around us to register the spot he'd marked, and then he jumped through it with the forerunners of our army right at his heels.

We burst out into much less pleasant conditions than we'd had back at his house. Storm clouds smothered the sky and spat fat raindrops down on us. Thunder rumbled in the distance. When I pulled myself out of the shadows into physical form, the grass squished beneath my feet. I wrinkled my nose, swiping my wet hair back from my forehead.

The demon clapped his hands together, somehow looking perfectly composed even with rain dripping off his own hair and soaking into his suit. "We've still got a trek ahead of us, but we need to be wary from here forward. My friends and I will take the lead. We've gotten the sorcerer's commands to deflect the worst of the leviathan's magic. The rest of you should keep at least half a mile of distance from us. If we sense that he's trying to send out more manipulative magic, we'll signal all of you, and you'll need to back away as quickly as you can. Through another rift if need be. But we're hoping that he's focused on conserving his energy for now."

So that he could use all his sorcery to compel the Highest into this world. My fangs itched in my gums at the thought. Those hulking brutes in the depths of the shadows had bashed around Torrent for nothing other than trying to warn them. I didn't want them in *this* world for any reason, even if they'd been coming of their own accord.

I hurried over to join Rollick alongside Crag and Torrent. We melded back into the darkness, which there was a lot more of here, to begin the final stage of our journey.

I scanned the damp, dreary landscape, finding that none of it looked particularly familiar. "What about the weapons you had the humans making? To throw the metal blades at the leviathan. Will we be able to use those?"

"We should," Rollick said. "But we have to be even more careful with the timing when it comes to them." He sighed, an uneasy sound that he'd been careful not to make when the rest of our allies were closer by. "I don't think it's even the leviathan we need to worry about the most for now—at least, not what he'll do from here on. It's what he's already done. I'm sure he'll have gathered all the minions he could call on to guard the site of his grand display."

A quiver ran through me. All those beings he'd enslaved, many—probably most—of whom hadn't wanted this fight any more than we did. But we couldn't let them stop us from stopping him. They'd suffer even more if he went through with his plan.

"Do your mortal workers know we're coming?" Torrent asked.

"Yes. They've been building the contraptions in the warehouse that was originally meant to be the trap, so they aren't far from where we need them to end up. But I'm not calling them to cart the things into position until I'm sure we have a clear route for them. If they're attacked and cut down... none of us will be able to haul those things around."

"Quinn could," Crag pointed out. "And maybe the phoenix as well."

Rollick hummed to himself. "True, but I expect them to be busy with other equally urgent concerns. And I gather these things are heavy. I'm not sure they'd be able to move them *out* of the vehicles very quickly, just the two of them. Let's try not to get my mortal assistants slaughtered is all I'm saying."

I let out a huff. "I can agree with that."

I peered through the haze of rain. I'd expected it to pelt us harder as we approached the coastline, but if anything, it was tapering off a little. I shook my body even though the drops did no more than tickle through my essence while I was in the shadows. "The rain's letting up."

"The leviathan must have brought in the elemental spirits he had amplifying the chaos to join him by the rift instead," Torrent said grimly. "He thinks their energy, like his, would be better spent on making sure he can carry out his plan."

I decided to look on the bright side. "At least it'll be easier to see!"

Rollick chuckled. "Yes, that is a minor benefit."

I kept my senses on the alert for any hint of sorcerer energy. Quinn had given the four of us quick but careful commands before she'd climbed into the RV—to resist the leviathan and refuse his commands. That magic was already humming through my head, ready to deflect any attempts the fiend made to conquer our thoughts. But it was looking increasingly certain that he meant to aim whatever magic he had left in just one direction.

What if he still couldn't summon the Highest at all? Would he go looking for more sorcerers to devour?

I guessed it didn't matter. Whether he could have accomplished his goal today or not, we meant to destroy him before any of us had to find out.

The landscape became more uneven, rising into the low rolling hills I remembered around the coast where we'd seen the leviathan and the behemoth working on their rift. How many beings was he eviscerating in his final attempt to open it as wide as possible? How wide would it *need* to become?

I had no idea what the Highest's physical forms might look like, or how big they might be. I wasn't sure they'd ever taken on a true physical shape before. I'd never even gotten near them in their shadowkind form, but I'd passed close enough to the deep place where they lived to know their presence stretched far and felt uncomfortably heavy.

Rollick slowed and then stopped. The rain had eased off to a mere drizzle, but the clouds overhead still shut out all but a faint glow of sunlight. He pointed to a road that wound between the hill we stood at the base of and the one farther north. "Quinn and the phoenix's people should come along this route. Keep a close watch for any patrolling minions."

I stretched my long body, tension twined through my limbs. "Should we start harassing the leviathan now? We don't know how soon he might be ready to call on the Highest."

"If we send our allies in now, they won't have the benefit of Quinn's sorcery strengthening them," Crag pointed out.

"We'll wait as long as we can," Rollick said definitively. "Better to hit them as hard as possible all at once than to get into an extended battle that'll wear us down. You wait here and rally the troops as much as you can. Destroy any of the leviathan's lackeys that come near. And flag down the RV when you see it. I'm going to venture a little closer to see how much progress he appears to have made."

"On your own?" Torrent asked quietly.

Rollick raised a haughty eyebrow. "I've never needed a babysitter. I'm the one with the easy task." Then he raced off into the shadows stretched across the hill.

As we'd talked, the beings who'd followed us this far had amassed a short distance away, waiting for a signal one way or another. Rollick hadn't told them what to do if we stopped moving. Crag and Torrent motioned for them to join us.

Voices carried from the restless crowd. "What now?"

"Is he already calling the Highest through?"

"Should we attack?"

"Rollick has gone ahead to get a read on the situation," Torrent told them all. "We'll wait here for the sorcerer and our other allies who were traveling by road. Quinn will be able to enhance your powers so you're even better equipped to take on our enemies."

I was surprised by the uneasy murmur that spread through the swarm of beings. They'd seen what Quinn's help could accomplish, how it could make us stronger instead of restraining us. Why would they hesitate?

The answer came to me without needing to think. Because it was sorcery. It was the stuff meant to twist our wills and overcome our minds. *I'd* balked the first time Quinn had been going to use her magic on me as a shield, and I'd been the one to suggest the idea.

But since then, I'd fed her my own essence to increase her powers. And while I'd wondered if I was betraying my kind at the time, I found that I didn't have a single doubt left in me.

Quinn was good. What we were doing here was good. Somehow we'd worked together to transform something evil into something amazing.

I'd helped make that transformation happen—by thinking of the possibilities, by trusting Quinn enough to let her try.

Not that long ago, I'd have said the best thing a being could do to a sorcerer was cut them down. But changing their magic into something that fueled our own powers rather than binding them was even better.

I could show every being here how true that was. I could lead them just like Rollick had led them here.

I scrambled partway up the hill and turned to face them again. "She'll be here soon. And as soon as she is, I'm going to be the first to accept her magic. It's going to make me faster and stronger and the flames in my breath burn hotter. She isn't just *a* sorcerer. She's *our* sorcerer. She's more ours than that beast of a sea serpent ever will be."

Not everyone in the crowd had been hesitant. A chorus of approving shouts rose up—the beings who'd been freed when Quinn had killed the behemoth, the ones who'd already experienced how her magic could protect and empower them. I even spotted Goldie, who'd hung back with obvious discomfort among the others after his arrival at the house, pumping a fist in the air.

With that rush of whoops, more voices rose with increasing eagerness. "All hail our sorcerer!"

A grin stretched across my face, but my heart sank a little as I looked down the road. There was no sign of the RV yet.

Our sorcerer might be beloved, but she still needed to make it to us in time.

CHAPTER TWENTY-SIX

Quinn

The Everymobile didn't feel as if it was moving faster than a regular car. The engine's thrum sounded strangely soft within the steel walls, and the floor only swayed a little with bumps and turns of the road. But when I eased back the curtain to peek out through one of the windows, the blur of the passing landscape made my mind whirl and my stomach flip over.

As I yanked the curtain shut, Sorsha came up beside me. "I find it's best not to look out there when we've got the special boost going," she said with a wry smile. "Unless you enjoy car sickness."

"Ah, that would be a no." I flopped down in the C-shaped seat around the RV's table and willed my queasiness down. "How much longer do you think it's going to take to get to the coast?"

"We're pulling out every possible trick we can. I don't know how long we can keep this speed up for, but if the Everymobile holds together, we're on track to arrive in the area your demon friend indicated in a little more than an hour."

My mouth pulled into a grimace that wasn't only because of my lingering nausea. "It'd be a lot easier if I could travel through rifts."

Or if my shadowkind allies had left me behind in Texas, I thought but didn't say. But maybe I didn't need to express that doubt out loud for my current companions to pick up on it. Ruse appeared in the short hall between the living-dining-kitchen area and the driver's cab where Omen was at the wheel. The incubus cocked his head at me.

"We all have our flaws. Our phoenix still isn't great at navigating the shadow realm herself."

"The fact that the rulers of that realm spent most of my life trying to *kill* me doesn't exactly bolster my motivation," Sorsha muttered.

Ruse shot her an amused glance before turning to me again. "It's good that you'll be out there with the rest of us. And not just because of the benefits you can obviously offer to us shadowkind going into battle. You've given those beings a heroic leader to focus on. Shadowkind aren't great at working together. I think we need a focal point even more than mortals do."

"Yeah." And I knew that the increased strength I could offer our allies with my sorcery might make the difference between stopping the leviathan and not. It was just that with every passing minute we were on the road while I knew the others had to be gathered and waiting for us, my gut clenched tighter.

Sorsha dropped into the seat kitty-corner from me. "We can do this. It doesn't matter how powerful that asshole is—there's just one of him and tons of us. The fight will determine how many lives continue or end in the process of stopping him, and I don't think there's any way every being with us will make it through alive, but we *will* stop him. I promise you that."

Her confidence eased my nerves just a little. I nodded. "Good." There wasn't any point in mentioning that I was pretty sure *my* life was forfeit no matter what else happened.

Maybe that was the other reason for the heaviness in my gut. Sorsha and her guys were perfectly fine company, but I wished I was spending my last hours with the men I loved. I didn't know how much I'd even get to see them or talk to them once we leapt into the fray. The brief embraces we'd exchanged before I'd hurried onto the RV might be our last. My emotional connection to them only seemed to work when they were nearby—I couldn't sense anything at all from them now.

A lump rose in my throat. It didn't matter. I couldn't let it matter. I'd gotten a lot out of our short time together. If all this craziness hadn't happened, I'd never have gotten to have them in my life at all. I couldn't lament the events that had brought us together, as horrible as those events might be.

The alarm on my phone went off. I startled, almost having forgotten that constant reminder of my mortality. Sorsha didn't comment as I popped my pills, including the new one from Rollick's doctor that didn't appear to be doing a whole lot to stave off my heart's impending failure.

Okay, that might not be fair. For all I knew, I'd already be dead without the new medication.

But Sorsha and her friends were aware of my transplant. They knew it was the reason for my powers. I set my hand against my chest, feeling the shudder of energy rippling from behind my sternum all through my limbs and up across my scalp like a static charge. It was hard to imagine that it was completely contained in that one organ now.

"I don't know if my magic will work on you," I said to Sorsha. "Because you're part human. The things that work against shadowkind don't normally affect you, right?"

"They don't," she agreed. "And shadowkind powers that work against humans often do affect me if I'm not taking steps to protect myself. But in this case, that works in our favor, because the leviathan isn't out to brainwash mortals. We'll see how he likes a boiling bath."

Her smile turned sharp. I guessed a phoenix with enough power to burn down two realms didn't need any sorcery to amp up her strength.

Snap slipped into view, peering at me curiously. "Do you want anything to eat? We didn't have time to pick up much before we left, but we always have fresh fruit."

Sorsha grinned. "Because this one is a fructose addict."

I raised my eyebrows at the golden-curled man because the question sounded so like one I'd been getting repeatedly from my own men. "Is this typical hospitality or did someone tell you to keep me fed?"

He dipped his head, abashed. "The rocky one said I should make sure you keep up your own strength."

Well, that was totally on brand for Crag. And he wasn't even wrong. My stomach gurgled right then as if to join their conspiracy.

"I probably *should* eat something," I said in resignation. "Thank you."

I picked from the broad assortment of fruits Snap brought out and also accepted a yogurt cup he exclaimed over when he found it in the fridge, still a few days shy of its best before date. By the time I'd eaten as much as I could handle in my anxious state, I got the sense that the motions around us, dampened as they were, had started to slow. I perked up, glancing toward the front of the RV. "Are we getting close?"

"Almost there," the hellhound shifter called back in his curt voice. "Don't get too excited yet. I still need to figure out—oh, wait, there they are. Of course."

There was a faint lurch as the RV veered to the side. I gripped the edge of the seat cushion. It seemed like only seconds before we were jerking to a halt. My pulse stuttered, and I propelled myself toward the door automatically.

Sorsha stepped ahead of me with the athletic swiftness she could bring out in an instant that transformed her into something a little more than human. She poked her head out the door, peered around, and then bounded out with a motion for the rest of us to follow her.

When I stepped onto the shoulder of the road to find all four of my men waiting for us, a deeper relief than I'd ever felt before swept through me. Quivers of the same happiness reached me from each of them. I couldn't stop the smile that was stretching across my face, even though it probably looked manic, even though we were about to enter a battle to the death.

We'd made it this far. We were in it together.

"The leviathan is at the rift," Rollick said without preamble, grabbing my hand to give it a quick squeeze of welcome. "Carving up dozens of beings by the hour. The rift has grown noticeably just since we've arrived. But he hasn't cast any more sorcery since then, and his minions are clustered pretty tightly around him."

I dragged in a breath. "That's all what we were hoping for. So we follow Plan A. Divert the minions, make sure the path is clear for our souped-up crossbows to get in place, and harass the leviathan enough that he can't summon the Highest while keeping him in about the same place for when the weapons are ready."

I raised my voice, ignoring my tremor of nerves at the thought of the responsibility I was taking on by acting as the leader of this group. Ruse had said the shadowkind might need a figurehead to look to even more than mortals did, and humans liked their figureheads a lot.

I could be that for this group. I was going to need to speak to all of them anyway.

"Come to me in the order we discussed yesterday," I said to the crowd I had to imagine waiting in the shadows beyond my mortal vision. "As soon as I've given you your command, get started with your part of the plan. We have to move quickly. We don't know how close the leviathan is to taking his final steps."

Lance sprang in front of me as the last words passed from my lips, shifting into dragon form as he did. *That* wasn't totally according to plan. We'd discussed starting with Rollick and Omen, since they were the most ancient of the shadowkind on our side. But Lance would have come soon after, and something about his haste and the way he dipped his gleaming reptilian head to me told me that he was making some kind of point, something he felt was important.

My sorcerer energy crackled at the base of my throat. I urged it into my words. "When you attack the leviathan or his allies, let them feel your speed and strength and the heat of your dragon fire."

Lance flashed a dragonish grin at me and leapt away. He showed no sign of discomfort, but my stomach twisted anyway. We'd agreed on the "When" part of the command to allow room to maneuver if, for example, it wasn't a great idea for any particular being to be attacking at some specific moment. If I'd just told them outright to attack, I wasn't sure if they'd be able to do anything else. But I still didn't totally understand how the magic worked. I didn't want to inadvertently cause more of the lives around me to be lost.

We'd been as careful as we could, and it was too late to re-think the plan. Rollick stepped forward next, stretching into his full demonic form. He held my gaze with total trust in his darkened eyes, and the anxiety inside me loosened a little. Another sizzling sentence traveled over my tongue. "When you're attacking the leviathan or his allies, let them feel all the demonic force you can aim at them."

He inclined his horned head, and then he was vanishing into the shadows. Omen was already stepping forward to take his place. I squared my shoulders, willing more magic into my mouth to give a similar order.

I drew up more and more energy, giving command after command with sparks of electricity dancing through my nerves. The beings were soon flickering in and out of view in front of me so swiftly I barely had time to think between each jolt of sorcery. But I'd prepared well. On sight, I knew which of our allies was meant for which part of the plan and what powers I was supposed to enhance in them.

Even as my voice grew hoarse, a sense of exhilaration spread through me that came from more than just my magic. There *were* a lot of us. We were powerful in ways most of the leviathan's lackeys couldn't be when he was ordering them to fight a battle they didn't want to be in. We had our weapons; we had a human-shadowkind hybrid on our side.

Maybe we really could win this.

Suddenly there were no more beings to cast my sorcery on standing in front of me. My head was spinning, exhaustion and excitement mingling. Sorsha grasped my shoulders from behind with gentle fingers. "Let's get you in position now."

I lifted my arms slightly so she could lower her hands to grip my waist. Then, with a strength that was shocking even after everything I'd already witnessed from her, she lifted me with her into the air. Wafts of heat washed over me from the blazing wings that flapped at the edges of my vision.

I'd seen them before, but only very briefly and before I'd known anything else about her. They'd almost seemed to be a trick of the light. There was no denying their existence now.

"You really are a phoenix," I said inanely.

Sorsha laughed. "So they tell me."

We flew over a few low hills. The sounds of the battle reached me before I could see it, penetrating the warbling woosh of Sorsha's flaming wings. Grunts, snarls, and cries of pain carried through the air. I willed my body to stay as relaxed as possible, knowing that tensing up would make me more difficult cargo.

Sorsha landed on the crest of a hill right over the coastline—the hill where Rollick's human accomplices were meant to set up the oversized crossbows—and I stared down over the mix of grass and rocky terrain below leading to the frothing ocean waters. In the dwindling daylight, smoky essence gushed from hundreds of forms, some of them still moving, others lying crumpled. I couldn't tell how many were from our side and how many the leviathan's.

The leviathan himself had been forced into physical form. The giant sea serpent, as tall as a low-rise apartment building, thrashed and roared as smaller shadowkind lashed out at him from multiple sides. They were doing exactly what we'd planned, keeping him too occupied to carry out his own plan but not letting him stray from this spot.

As we touched down, a ring of guards wavered into being around me. Sorsha wiped her hands together with an air of a job well-done and gave me a jaunty salute. "Off to see about boiling a snake," she said, and launched herself back into the air.

I had the urge to sit down on the grass now that I wasn't needed for at least a little while, but I had the sense that position would be undignified. Figureheads could stand on their own two feet, right? Even if those feet were attached to increasingly wobbly legs. Even if both a fever and a chill seemed to be trickling through that figurehead's veins.

But maybe I wouldn't have to extend myself any farther. Even though the minions must have spotted our arrival—the blazing wings were a pretty clear giveaway—none even made it far enough up the hill to challenge my ring of guards. Flickers of emotion reached me from my men, but they were all determination and fury, no fear or pain so far.

I couldn't see any fighting near the road that was the key to our plan. And as I looked along it, headlights gleamed in the distance through the dusk.

The trucks transporting our weaponry. They were on their way—they'd be here in a matter of minutes.

A smile that was outright joyful crossed my lips. We were so close. Somehow, everything had worked out the way we'd imagined it. Now all we had to do was—

A surge of thicker darkness barreled toward the approaching trucks so abruptly I barely had time to yelp in warning before the vehicle in the lead swayed on its wheels with the impact—and tipped onto its side with a thunderous crash. The other trucks screeched to a halt. Bodies whipped back and forth across the road: a mass of attackers we hadn't been prepared for racing into the fray and my allies charging to meet them.

Another shadowy surge hurtled toward the leviathan—but not to assault him. The minions who'd either been told to hang back in reserve or who'd only just arrived flung themselves at the beings who'd been harassing their master.

I caught the flash of Lance's scales as he snapped and slashed at them with a flare of hotter rage. Sorsha soared around the turbulent ocean shadows, sending a being here and there up in bursts of flame—but she had to be careful not to light up our own people, who didn't look particularly different from the leviathan's slaves. My knees locked as I watched the struggle in horror, torn between the urge to tell my guards to race down there to help and the fear of what might happen to me without their protection.

Before I could decide on the best course of action, the leviathan shook off the majority of his attackers and reared up even higher toward the spot where the rift must be. Either he'd already been ready to take the final step, or he figured he might not get another chance.

His monstrous voice tore through the night, a feral bellow that reverberated right into my bones. Syllables somehow foreign and familiar at the same time shook every cell in my body. He roared his sorcerous command again, its meaning smacking me in the face with the force of it.

Come to me. Come to the other realm.

Then he plunged his enormous snake-like head right into the rift.

CHAPTER TWENTY-SEVEN

Quinn

The top of the hillside trembled beneath my feet. I gaped at the leviathan's immense serpentine form, looking deceptively headless with the wavering darkness I knew was the rift around its neck.

I couldn't hear its bellowed commands anymore, but somehow my nerves still vibrated with them, as if he were putting so much energy into them that the air leaving his lungs was setting off tremors through the atmosphere. It wasn't hard to imagine that his call might be felt all across the shadow realm. All the way to its intended targets in the deepest depths.

My skin turned to ice for reasons that had nothing to do with my physical health.

We had to stop him. We had to turn the tide back in our favor before we had even bigger monsters to grapple with.

If we could kill him—if we could take our shots while he was totally immersed in his scheme—that would solve everything. Any sorcery he'd cast would die with him. This could all be over.

But the battle was still raging around the vehicles that'd been carrying our weapons. With the lead truck toppled and shadowkind rampaging all around the road, there was no way for them to reach this hill where they'd have a clear trajectory. No way for Rollick's people inside to try to shoot the leviathan even from where they'd stalled without being savaged.

As I watched the skirmishes going on all across the terrain below the hill, bracing myself without any idea what action I'd need to take, it became increasingly, nauseatingly clear that we weren't winning quickly. We might not be winning at all. Beings whirled around each other, more essence plumed into the air, but the leviathan's horde of minions had managed to surround and divide us. It was too vast for my allies to overcome in a few decisive strikes, no matter how much my magic had ramped up their abilities.

My magic.

The answer came to me like a punch square in the chest, unmistakable and painful. There were two ways the leviathan's minions could be stopped: through killing, which wasn't working out at the moment, and through shattering the hold on them with someone else's sorcery.

And the only sorcerer anywhere nearby was me.

For a second, my legs locked and my breath caught in my lungs. There were *so* many of them—thousands, swarming all across the landscape around me. Undoubtedly there were more in the shadows where I couldn't see them. How the hell could I reach all of them?

I didn't need to snap every single one of them out of their magical compulsions, I reminded myself. Just enough of them that the beings on my side could get the upper hand. If I didn't try, if I didn't do it fast, I'd never get the chance at all.

I closed my eyes, still seeing the carnage below playing out in the back of my mind, and yanked all the fizzing electric energy inside me into my voice.

The magic blazed through me, its searing crackle drowning out everything beyond my body. A yell so loud it scraped my throat raw burst from my mouth. Words I didn't recognize blared from my lips through the dusk. But I knew exactly what I was saying. *Don't fight for the leviathan. Shake off his control. Go free.*

Here and there, all across the battlefield, the breaking of the leviathan's spell reverberated into me with little pops like cans shot by a BB gun. They rattled through my awareness so swiftly I couldn't count them, but there had to be dozens.

It was working. The leviathan mustn't have shored up his hold on his minions in a while as he'd stockpiled his energy for his larger goal. I was shattering his magic with my own.

My heart lurched with the power resounding through my body. My chest clenched up. But I shouted again and again, hurling the energy in me as far as I could, even as my legs gave and I sank to my knees.

My head was spinning. I coughed and bent forward, my fingers digging into the grass. There was no exhilaration in my sorcery now. My entire torso was on fire. A shiver passed through me as I struggled to catch my breath.

A loud, creaky thump jolted through my awareness with enough force that I managed to raise my head. My eyes widened.

The area along the road was clear again other than the scattered, smoking bodies of fallen shadowkind. A bunch of the beings who were still moving had just heaved the first truck back onto its wheels.

Its windshield was spiderwebbed with cracks, but either the driver had survived the crash without much injury or one of the other human workers had hurried forward to take his place. The engine sputtered and settled into a low rumble. Then the truck pulled forward with a slight hitch. The others growled to life behind it.

They were coming again. I'd managed to free enough of the leviathan's minions to turn the tide like I'd hoped.

I swiveled my head, staring blearily across the darkened landscape while the turmoil inside my body radiated through every cell. The fighting had mostly moved to the rocky terrain right along the coast, near where the leviathan's eerily immense form was still poised with his head immersed in the rift. Flares of fire glinted here and there as Sorsha, Omen, Lance, and whatever other beings could bring flames to bear let loose their heat.

Had we really done it? I couldn't quite summon much sense of triumph through my dizziness, but my lips managed to form a small smile.

I sat back on my butt. I could tell that my legs still wouldn't hold me up, if they ever would again. The throbbing in my chest hadn't let up at all —my breaths were strained, as if I were trying to suck in air through the tiniest crack in my throat. But none of that mattered if we saw this moment through to the end.

The trucks roared onto the hill behind me. Shouts rang through the spaces between them as the workers hustled to drag out their cargo. I turned my head to see them setting up the half a dozen bulky contraptions, which looked like something half cannon, half crossbow, along the crest of the hill on either side of me.

One of Rollick's people paused, looking at me, but I waved him off with a feeble gesture. "We've got to shoot that monster," I croaked, tilting toward the leviathan. "As soon as you can, as much ammo as you can."

He nodded and dashed back to the truck. I wondered vaguely what story Rollick had given these people to explain the crazy task he'd assigned them with now. They clearly understood the urgency. I guessed after everything they must have seen tonight—and in L.A. for several days before—their acceptance wasn't totally surprising.

They loaded the weapons with blades like sharpened shards of a vast metal frisbee. Like the blades that had been loaded in the walls of the factory where we'd killed the behemoth. Maybe they'd even repurposed the exact same ones, just altered a little so they'd fly through the air properly when launched.

Those killing edges had brought down the behemoth. These ones *had* to work on the leviathan too.

If they didn't, we were simply doomed.

The last blade had just clanged into place when one of the workers let out a yell that sounded more like a warning than a call to action. I jerked my attention in the direction he was staring.

The leviathan was moving again. His serpentine body shook off the beings that'd gone back to harassing him, and his head was pulling free from the rift.

Panic shot through me. Did that mean he was finished? That the Highest were on their way?

I gritted my teeth against a fresh wallop of pain and forced more words from my throat. "Shoot him! Now! Keep reloading until you've hit him with everything."

Before I'd even finished speaking, the workers were springing into action. All across the line of weapons, Rollick's people yanked the firing levers.

The blades released with a series of twangs. They whirled through the air, catching the faint beams of moonlight that penetrated the thinning clouds, and slammed into the leviathan's body one after the other, each a little higher than the last.

The monster's body flinched harder with each impact. He pulled his head completely free of the rift to let out an earth-shaking snarl full of pain and fury. The clouds of essence that poured up from the wounds were so thick I could see them even against the dusk.

The beings around him fell back except for Sorsha with her flaming wings. She whipped herself toward the blades, kicking them deeper into the leviathan's flesh. The metals in our projectiles would prevent most of the other shadowkind from getting close enough to attack. But now that we were launching them, the blades were enough.

Rollick's people scrambled to reload the weapons. They fired again, marking a path up the serpent's undulating body almost all the way to its jaw.

The leviathan twisted and shuddered, dodging a couple of the blades, including one that would have struck it in the skull. We could only hit it from the one side, and I didn't know how deeply the metals were digging in even with Sorsha's assistance.

But it was faltering. With the next barrage, it only avoided one. Its body sagged, slowly crumpling over toward the sea. Smoke gushed upward from its huge carcass like it was the burning wreckage of a vast ship.

The men at the weapons stepped back. They still had a few blades left, but they couldn't aim properly while the monster was slumped over in the water instead of stretched upright. It didn't seem to matter anyway. The leviathan was barely even thrashing now, just twitching here and there without finding the strength to get up. Those wounds couldn't heal while the metal was embedded in him.

We'd done it.

I almost gave in to the relief of that thought and slumped over myself. The soft grass called out to me. But as I tipped forward, leaning my weight onto my arms, a quaver of energy surged across the hillside, dissonant enough to set my teeth on edge and make every hair on my body stand on end.

I yanked my gaze upward. A gasp snagged in my throat.

Something was coming through the rift. Something huge and bulbous, like the head of a whale with an eye that must have been larger than my entire body. That eye blazed blood red, rolling beneath its heavy lid.

It was *wrong*. That was the only way I could describe it. Shivers wracked my body just looking at it. The air around it vibrated; an off-key pealing sound split the air.

The ocean hollowed out beneath the leviathan's still spasming body. The water twisted and churned. Rocks along the shoreline cracked open or outright disintegrated, pebbles blasting across the ground. My skin felt as if it were about to crawl right off my body.

That—that thing had to be one of the Highest. The leviathan had called them through after all… and he wasn't gone yet. He wasn't totally dead, which meant his magic was holding on, and the immense being whose very presence was unraveling the fabric of my world was pushing even farther out.

I thought I saw lips pulled into a grimace on that gigantic head. The blazing eye kept flicking this way and that. Along with the bone-deep wrongness, my strongest impression was that it didn't want to be here at all—but it couldn't pull itself back.

Would it be able to retreat now that it'd started passing through even *if* the leviathan finally died, or would the momentum be too much? How much damage was it going to do even before we could answer that question?

The grass beneath my fingers was crinkling, suddenly parched dry. A cloud overhead burst apart with a boom of thunder and a shower of lightning bolts. The beast in the rift groaned, and a crack opened up right through the shoreline into the ocean floor.

Terror and pain screamed together all through my body. I could barely feel my limbs. But my eyes fell on the leviathan's smoking body, and one tiny thought penetrated my stupor like a needle threading the last inspiration I might ever get through my mind.

The leviathan had the power to call that horrifying thing through… and his power was now up for the taking.

I shoved myself down the side of the hill. My limbs flailed like they were made of jelly; every choked breath burned in my chest. I dug my fingers into the grass and heaved out with my knees, propelling myself forward with every bit of strength I had in me.

Dark wings flapped overhead. Crag grasped my shoulders. "Where are you going, Softness?" he asked in a low, pained rumble that I barely heard through the rising thrum of wrongness.

"Get me to the leviathan," I rasped out. "Please."

I didn't think he wanted to follow that order, and I hadn't put any sorcery into it, but the gargoyle granted my final request. With a growl, he lifted me into the air and carried me over the shattering rocks to the monster's crumpled body.

I flung myself out of Crag's arms down on the nearest wound. As I opened my mouth, the fiend's essence rushed up my throat, nearly suffocating me. Stiffening my body, I gulped and gulped, no matter how the noxious smoke seared at my insides, no matter how tightly the vise around my heart clamped.

The leviathan's essence prickled through every nerve in my body. My pulse stuttered and faltered. It was too much, like I was trying to drink down the entire ocean, more than any one body was meant to hold.

But I needed it. I needed to hang on just long enough to—to—

There was no room left in my head even for thoughts now. Just drink, drink, drink.

When I couldn't stand to suck in one more puff of essence, I flipped over onto my back and stared up at the rift. My mind was whirling like the whipped-up clouds overhead. The huge, unnatural presence above me felt as if it were about to tumble down onto me and squash me flat.

I opened my mouth and let out the sorcery I'd swallowed, all of it, on top of the talent I'd already possessed, pleading to whatever other powers might exist to let it be enough.

"*Go home!*" I screamed in the language of the magic. "*Go back through the rift. Get away from here!*"

Agony cut through the center of my chest. My heart seemed to split in two. My vision hazed with growing blotches of black. But I felt my magic smash the leviathan's last lingering spell with a cracking sensation that rebounded into my body.

The Highest being groaned again, but there might have been relief in it this time. As my pulse dwindled to nothing and the pain spread through every inch of my frame, it jerked back into the rift. The last thing I saw before my vision blanked completely was its bulbous head slipping out of sight.

The catastrophe was done... and so was I. I had the sense of a tear tricking down my cheek, but a strange contentment swept over me before my awareness blinked out.

CHAPTER TWENTY-EIGHT

Quinn

Something was beeping. In kind of an annoying way too. If there was an afterlife, surely I'd earned a spot someplace that didn't come with irritatingly repetitive noises?

And if there wasn't an afterlife, why the hell was I hearing anything at all?

My eyelids fluttered. My body twitched on the firm padding it was lying on, and a thin fabric surface shifted with it. An ache woke up in my chest, but weirdly distant and fuzzy, as if the parts of my body were scattered around me instead of all attached in one piece.

I registered groggily that I'd felt this way before. The bright lights, planes of white around me—

A deeper sense of recognition jolted my eyes all the way open. I blinked, staring at the hospital room I'd somehow ended up in. The ache sharpened and eased, intensifying and retreating with every thump of my heart.

Of my heart?

As I stared down at myself, at the hospital gown cloaking me, a nurse hustled into the room. "You look like you're doing well," she said in a soothing voice. "Everything's on track. Your immune system has responded well so far. It's a long process fully adjusting, but of course you're an old hat at this—you know how it goes."

She flashed me a smile, but I was too distracted by taking in the fresh stitches marking my chest to return it. Fresh stitches sealing a fresh incision, right over the area where my last surgery scar had been.

How could— It didn't make sense. Was I dreaming? I blinked hard as if that might wake me up if I was, but all that happened was my head spun a little before my thoughts settled down again.

The nurse said something else that I missed completely. Then she bustled out of the room. The second the door clicked shut behind her, four monstrous men wavered into being out of the shadows, surrounding the bed.

I gaped at all of them, but I had enough of my wits to quickly check them over for any new damage. I thought Crag had a few more scars marking his face and arms than he'd sported before, and Lance had a new one cutting across the golden skin at the crook of his shoulder, but otherwise they weren't noticeably worse for the battle we'd somehow all survived. They smiled down at me in their own ways.

"What—" I croaked, and swallowed hard. "How—"

Rollick chuckled softly and brushed his fingertips over my hair as if he were afraid to touch me too firmly right now. "I have enough resources at my disposal to get giant crossbow-cannons manufactured with a few days' notice. Did you really think I couldn't find you a new heart?"

"But I—" My gaze shot directly to him, focusing on his face. "Where did it come from?"

He held up his hands. "I took a perfectly legitimate route. I wouldn't go against your sense of morality, even if it doesn't totally align with my own. I simply saw to it that you were bumped to the front of the list."

A strange emotion swelled inside me, so bittersweet it brought tears to my eyes. "That's cheating," I mumbled. "I stole someone else's spot, and—"

"Stop right there," Torrent said in his best no-nonsense tone, folding his arms over his chest. "If things had been the way they were supposed to be, you'd have had months if not years of warning to work your way up the list in priority. There's nothing *fair* about anything you've been through in the past couple of months."

"And I bet none of the other people on that list just defended the entire world from destruction," Lance pointed out with a broader grin.

Crag let out a rumble of agreement. "You can't save billions of lives and tell us we're not allowed to save yours," he informed me gruffly.

I sank back into the hospital bed. Maybe they kind of had a point. Maybe I didn't need to feel guilty. Maybe... maybe I actually deserved a second chance at this whole transplanted heart thing, without a legacy of toxic magic attached to it.

I glanced at Rollick again. "I hope you made sure this one doesn't come with a supernatural bonus."

He outright laughed. "No more sorcery for you. Such a shame when for a few minutes there, I'd imagine you were by far the most powerful sorcerer the universe has ever known."

I made a face and closed my eyes. "Not a title I had any interest in claiming."

Rollick hummed to himself. "There are a couple of people here I think you might want to see. Your parents are in the waiting room. I can have the doctor let them in if you're ready for other visitors."

My spirits leapt, and my eyes popped open again. "They're out of the bunker? Of course they're out of the bunker. Everything really is okay?"

Lance beamed at me. "No more storms, no more waves. No more tricksy ancient beings enslaving the rest of us."

Torrent's smile turned crooked. "The Highest were so offended by the assault on their autonomy that they collapsed that particular rift completely. So, as far as I know, there isn't even a portal left that's large enough to fit them if someone decided to give it another shot."

"Good," I said, a renewed wave of relief washing through me. I paused, studying each of them in turn. The familiar faces that didn't look at all monstrous to me now stirred up a pang of affection not even the aches of the transplant could overwhelm. "What happens after this?"

Rollick shrugged. "We assumed you'd go back to your regular life, your college courses and the rest. Unless you had some other plans."

"No. That's good. I just mean—what about you? What about *us*?"

I didn't need their protection anymore. They didn't need the special powers that had emanated from my chest. Neither of those facts made a difference to me, but these men didn't think or feel like regular humans did. I couldn't take anything for granted.

But Crag was leaning down to press a gentle kiss to my temple. "We'll be with you as long and as much as you want us there, Softness."

"Nowhere I'd rather be, baby girl," Lance declared.

Even Torrent's expression brightened. "If we can make it work when we're being chased by murderous fiends, I think we can handle a peaceful regular life just fine."

"Unless you've had your fill of us," Rollick said in a teasing tone.

"No," I said with total determination. "Not at all." Not ever, I suspected. And now... now I might have decades more with them.

I didn't want to have to totally hide that fact. I paused. "I would like to see my parents. But... I'd like you all to be here while I talk to them too. Where they can see you. They should know that you're sticking around."

The demon nodded. He vanished for a moment, and my stomach twisted at the thought of how Mom and Dad might react. They'd been stunned and horrified by the realization that monsters existed at all. How were they going to accept four of those monsters as a permanent presence in my life?

Well, they'd just... have to, one way or another. I wasn't hiding who I was or what mattered from them again. It wasn't my job to act as a human shield, to protect people from *myself*. If I deserved anything, it was to set that one worry aside after all the protecting I'd already accomplished.

Rollick reappeared in the same spot as before. The other men flickered out of view when the doctor opened the door to motion my parents in. As soon as Mom and Dad were inside and the door had closed, they solidified into physical form again.

Mom let out a soft yelp that she smothered with a hand to her lips. Dad flinched. But then they relaxed, presumably recognizing the men as the companions I'd introduced them to back at the bunker. Their gazes jerked back to me, and they hustled over.

"Sweetheart, I'm so glad you're okay," Mom said in a voice taut with emotion, leaning over to hug me gingerly. "The doctors say all your results look fantastic so far."

"You've always been a fighter, kiddo," Dad said, sounding pretty choked up himself, and squeezed my hand.

"I've still got a lot left to do," I said. Fatigue rolled over me, reminding me that no matter how long I'd been lying in this bed, my body had just been through more than one kind of marathon. My eyelids drifted down, but I held on to alertness long enough to add, "There won't be any more monsters around. Not like the ones that were hurting people. But these guys—they're staying with me. We're going to keep looking out for each other."

My parents lifted their gazes to the monstrous men. I couldn't say they looked overjoyed at the thought. Mom's attention lingered on Lance's claws and Torrent's supporting tentacles, and Dad's brow knit as he considered Crag's stony jaw. But Mom simply rubbed my shoulder.

Dad tightened his grip on my hand reassuringly. "They've done a good job of that so far."

Mom inclined her head. "And it's good to know you have someone else to turn to when you need it. You should have someone other than us. No matter what kind of people—or... whatever—they are." She shot my men a smile to show she didn't mean her comment as an insult.

Rollick gave them one of his charming grins. "We're people enough in all the ways that count. And Quinn definitely has us."

"Good." Mom sounded like she meant it.

The relief I'd felt before sank right through to my bones. My eyes drifted all the way shut. Rollick teased his fingers over my hair again, and I started to drift off, content with the certainty that everyone in the room was perfectly happy to see me get my rest.

It was really over. I really *could* rest, for the first time in weeks. No more sorcerer heart. No more magic pulsing through my veins. No more murderous, psychotic fiends out to kill me.

I was a one-hundred-percent-normal human being again. But that didn't mean I wasn't changed. I knew about so many amazing things out there in our world that most mortals had never imagined could be true. And *that* magic would stay with me no matter how short or long the rest of my life might be.

CHAPTER TWENTY-NINE

Five years later

Quinn

I got out of the car on the opposite side of the street from the building and hesitated before turning to face it. I'd come out to see the construction while it was in progress several times, of course, but not since all the outer walls, one of the final steps, had been put in place. Now it was finally going to look whole. Real.

I swiveled on the sidewalk quickly, wanting to take it in all at once. Gazing up at the looming skyscraper, my breath caught in my throat.

It was somehow even more than I'd imagined when I'd first started sketching the building out years ago, not long after I'd returned to my classes. More than any of the concept drawings or blueprints or even my visits during the earlier stages of construction had prepared me for.

I'd never told anyone this, but in my mind, from the very beginning, I'd thought of it as *The Monster*. To everyone I worked with, that name would have called up negative associations. But in the building before me, I saw everything the concept had come to mean to me.

It was broad as well as tall, huge and imposing and a little twisted with ripples breaking through the upward jut of the otherwise straight edges. But the outer walls with their reflective panes were tilted at just the right angle to reflect the southern sunlight without bouncing it into a passerby's eyes. The massive structure *glowed*, like something magical that'd sprung up on this city block.

It was my ode to the types of monstrousness and magic I'd learned to appreciate. And somehow it was standing here in front of me, the first major solo design I'd ever had accepted and constructed. I'd accomplished that dream.

How many more were still ahead of me?

As a smile crossed my lips to match the swell of awe and joy inside me, a figure drew to a stop on the sidewalk a few feet away. I glanced over to see a girl who looked to be in her early teens, a wave of hair so pale it was nearly translucent curving against her cheek as she gazed up at my building from beneath the shade of her sweatshirt's hood. Her bright brown eyes had widened. Her sinewy frame was weirdly tensed, as if she were grappling between stepping closer to the structure and yanking herself away from it.

"Wow," she said in a soft voice, her fingers tightening around the strap of her backpack. And then she shivered in a way that instantly set me on the alert.

"Are you all right?" I asked. She'd sounded appreciative when she'd spoken, so I couldn't tell whether the shiver had been provoked by the building or something else—maybe whatever had made her so tense in general.

Her eyes darted to me with a flicker of anxiety. "Yes," she blurted out. "Sorry. I just—I've got something to do."

She spun on her heel and hustled off before I could say anything else.

I watched her go, my smile dwindling. But then a gaggle of tourists halted farther down the street to exclaim over the building, and the rush of happiness came back. I glanced the way the girl had gone, but she didn't reappear.

I hadn't spent all that much time here in San Francisco. Maybe it was weird for strangers to talk to each other here, and that was why she'd hurried off. In any case, there wasn't much I could do about it.

A tickle of someone else's joy seeped into my chest. My smile returned, and I crossed the street to walk around the side of the building.

Even though my sorcerer powers had vanished when I'd lost the heart that'd granted me them in the first place, a thread of my connection to my monstrous men had remained, possibly from the traces of their essence that must have wound into my other vital organs. I could only sense the faintest hints of their strongest emotions, but sometimes that was enough to recognize their presence.

I was just coming up on the maintenance door partway down the side alley, which *should* have been locked, when it swung open to reveal Rollick's handsome face and his usual sly smirk. "Are you going to come in and check out your opus from the inside or what? The rest of your entourage is getting impatient."

I laughed and slipped inside, finding myself in a shadowy hall where the three other men who couldn't simply stroll down the street without being stared or even screamed at were waiting.

Lance tugged me to him with a pleased hum. "Is it everything you wanted it to be?"

"It's perfect," I said, returning his embrace.

"Wait until you see the view." The dragon shifter shot Crag a pointed look, and the gargoyle held out his hand to me. I stepped toward him and let him scoop me up into his arms.

"I'm doing well enough that I could manage the stairs, even this many," I had to inform him, though I didn't exactly mind being cradled by his stony strength. After the usual precarious first year, my doctors had gradually eased off monitoring my new heart. It thumped away in my chest now as if it'd always been a part of me. And hopefully, given that it hadn't come with any supernatural strings attached, it'd keep pumping for many years more.

Crag let out a gruff sound. "This is much faster. The elevators aren't running yet. No power."

"And we're not letting you play around with the electricity, Ms. Fix-It," Torrent teased in his dryly even voice from behind us.

"Fine." I patted Crag's well-muscled shoulder. "You can be my winged elevator."

He gave a rumble of a chuckle and stepped to the edge of the elevator shaft. I spotted the car down below on one of the basement levels, leaving the space above us totally empty other than the cables. With a push of his clawed feet and a flap of his wings, the gargoyle leapt up into the air.

My other men disappeared into the darkness, but I knew they were traveling with us. Crag couldn't move quite as fast as he normally might have when he was working with such a narrow space, but we soared past a few floors with every sweep of his wings. The exhilaration rushed through me, leaving me grinning.

At the top floor, Crag set me down by a ladder to a maintenance hatch that reminded me with a hitch of my pulse of my last urban exploring adventure before my life had become full of monsters. I clambered up the rungs without hesitation, shoved the hatch wide, and pulled myself up onto the rooftop of the first ever building I could take full credit for designing.

The sprawl of the city spread out before us, glinting with lights of different colors as evening started to creep over the streets. We were high enough up that I couldn't hear the thrum of the traffic passing by below. When I turned, I could make out the glinting ocean waters beyond the buildings along the coast.

"Who needs walls when you can be up here," I said with a laugh, and inhaled deeply with a gust of wind that tossed my hair back over my shoulders.

Rollick, who'd emerged from the shadows alongside the others to join me, arched his eyebrows. "Rethinking our current living arrangements, sweet mortal?"

I thought of the apartment back in Jacksonville we all shared now—as much as my shadowkind men needed a physical living space. Rollick had insisted on contributing enough funds that I could afford a corner penthouse, which had almost as amazing a view as this, the ocean in one direction and the city streets along the beach in the other.

Since none of the men needed to sleep, we could manage with a two-bedroom, the second bedroom set up in case they wanted to relax with a little privacy. Or entertain themselves while keeping out of my hair when I was working from home. Mostly, though, we'd fallen into a rhythm of living alongside each other that had quickly felt completely natural.

I could have had the place to myself whenever I wanted—I knew all I had to do was ask—but there was something comforting about knowing that just about anytime I called out, at least one of them would be in hearing distance.

"I'm always happy coming home to Jacksonville," I told the demon with a playful swat. "Which means you're also not convincing me to move to Miami anytime soon."

He grabbed my hand and pressed a kiss to my knuckles. "Then it's a good thing there are handy rifts I can jump through between the two, isn't it?"

My other three men had been content to putter around Jacksonville and the area nearby with occasional daytrips abroad, enjoying their favorite aspects of the mortal realm without straying for long from my side. Torrent had started anonymously donating small sculptures he made out of found natural objects to a local gallery that'd been excited by them, but that was the grandest of their ambitions.

Rollick, on the other hand, hadn't waited much time before getting started on rebuilding his legacy as he'd always said he would. His new hotel stood on the most popular stretch of Miami Beach, flocked to by human and shadowkind guests alike.

From what he'd said, the shadowkind needed a refuge like that even more now. The Highest hadn't stirred from the depths of the shadow realm again, and no other monsters had rampaged across the mortal realm since the leviathan's death, but the near-catastrophe had left a lot of the mortal-side beings shaken. Humankind seemed to have brushed off the craziness of those few weeks with our usual dogged resistance to anything beyond our understanding, but the shadowkind wanted to know they had like-minded companions they could turn to if anyone tried to steal their freedom or the land they considered a home again.

Lance let out a soft growl at the sight of Rollick's affectionate gesture and grabbed my other hand. He leaned his head close to mine and nipped my earlobe before murmuring, "I heard there's something humans like to do to make a place really their own. 'Christening' it, I think they call it?"

My cheeks flushed. "And you figured we'd do that up here, huh?"

An unusually mischievous glint had lit up in Torrent's sea-green eyes. He extended one of his tentacles to tease around my calf. "What better spot to celebrate our daredevil lover's great achievement?"

A thrill shivered through me, affection and excitement twined together. The men I loved knew me so well, both what was important to me and what got me off. And I couldn't say the proposal didn't have a significant appeal.

I nudged Lance with my elbow. "What are we waiting for, then?"

He let out an eager little snarl and pounced, snatching me up and flipping us over with his usual acrobatic grace. The next thing I knew, I was sprawled on top of his lean frame while he stretched out on a flat section of roof, and he was pulling my mouth down to his.

The sudden movement had left my pulse racing, and the flick of Lance's tongue between my lips only keyed me up more. I kissed him back hard, reveling in the wonder of the moment—that I'd accomplished this much, that I had these men with me. That I was here, alive and well, at all.

Seconds later, the rest of my men had gathered close around me and Lance. Crag lowered his head to kiss the side of my neck. Rollick slid his hand up under my shirt, tracing the line of my spine with a giddying caress. Torrent stroked my thigh with his hand while his tentacles glided over my legs where my skirt left them bare.

When one tentacle rose to the apex of my legs, squeezing my clit with a deft sucker, I whimpered against Lance's mouth. He took the opportunity to adjust the angle of our heads and kiss me even more deeply, as if he were trying to devour me whole. Then he released my mouth to nibble along the line of my jaw, pushing me up over him high enough that he could grab the bottom of my shirt.

He yanked the thin cotton garment over my head, and then Rollick claimed my mouth for himself. The demon's kiss was as searing as ever, with no hesitation about participating in this joint effort now that we had years of collaboration behind us. He trailed his hand back down my spine and snapped open my bra in the same movement.

As the straps slid down my arms, Lance dipped his head to catch the peak of one breast between his lips. Crag closed his rocky hand over the other, the warm but rough texture of his palm brushing over the nipple to perfect effect. I rocked helplessly against Torrent's pulsing tentacle, already feeling way too close to the edge. But then, these men could always take me there so quickly.

Lance tapped the tips of his claws against my side and, when I gasped, scraped them delicately over the skin. At my shiver, he sucked harder on my breast. Torrent picked the exact same moment to tuck the tip of his tentacle right inside my panties, the suckers plucking directly at my flesh, and I came with a rush of bliss that propelled a cry from my throat.

Rollick drank the sound down, and then Crag was tugging my head toward him, his strength tempered by the gentleness he always offered me. "We'll take you even higher than that, Softness," he said gruffly, and melded his mouth with mine.

Torrent was busy sliding the panties right off me. He nudged my hips a little higher and turned toward Lance, with a grin I could hear in his voice. "I can think of other places our woman would appreciate those claws."

I quivered with anticipation as Lance lowered his hand. He grazed the vicious talons ever so carefully over my folds and clit. Needing to hold so perfectly still only amplified the thrill of the sensation. I gasped, aching for more.

Torrent didn't leave me hanging. The second Lance withdrew his claws, the other man plunged his tentacle into me with just enough force to send my thoughts spinning with the surge of delight. I moaned and clutched at Lance beneath me, then pressed my lips harder against Crag's.

Rollick flicked his own shorter claws over my untended breast, adding to the symphony of pleasure that was swelling through me all over again. My mouth tore from Crag's with a guttural groan, and Lance beamed up at me.

"What do you want now, baby girl?"

"You," I mumbled. "Inside me. Give me the dragon cock."

He chuckled. "I'll never deny you that."

He was so good at his vanishing act now that my body barely shifted from where it'd been braced above him before he'd returned to physical form, now sans clothes. His monstrous cock with its thicker head rubbed against my clit, and Torrent withdrew his tentacle to make room. The wind licked over my back, chilling me for just an instant before Torrent leaned close enough for his warmth to envelop me. "Will you take me too, Quinn?"

Lance thrust up into me at the same moment, so my first answer was nothing more than a gasp. "Please," I said, breathless and shaking.

My gargoyle and my demon were still kneeling on either side of me, now fully naked in their monstrous forms. I gazed down at Rollick's two cocks and lowered my head to take the upper one into my mouth. It slid past my lips as Torrent prepared my back entrance with strokes of his tentacle, and the heady sensation of being triply filled careened through my nerves.

When I tested my teeth against Rollick's shaft, he hissed a breath and clutched my hair. I sucked him down as far as I could, swirled my tongue around him as I eased back, and released him only to draw his second cock into my mouth. He swore at the pursing of my lips around his rigid length.

I might have teased him more if Torrent's cock hadn't filled me then, gliding into my ass to match Lance's rhythm from beneath. Instead, my groan reverberated over Rollick's cock.

I brought my mouth back to his upper shaft and gripped the lower one with my hand, knowing from experience how to best ensure he unraveled. Crag kissed my shoulder and resumed his fondling of my breasts, not one to be left out. I pumped the demon's pair of dicks with the same blissful force my other two men were applying to me, bringing tongue, lips, teeth, and fingers to bear.

"I'm never going to get tired of seeing that hot mortal mouth around my cocks," Rollick rasped. His head tipped back, and he stiffened for just a second with a twitch of both shafts before he came, his smoky, salty release spilling down my chin and over my hand.

Before I could wipe my mouth, he leaned in and lapped his own cum off of me. I shuddered at the unexpectedly hot gesture, adding to the fire of passion searing through me with every rock of my lovers' bodies beneath and behind me. Then I turned to my gargoyle, wanting to bring him with us too.

Crag showed no qualms about kissing me while the taste of his fellow shadowkind must have lingered in my mouth. When I reached for his stunning gargoyle cock, he groaned. His hips pumped into my grasp instinctively.

I couldn't fit my mouth around more than the head of his shaft, but that was enough to make him shudder with delight. Then everything blurred into one string of motion, my body swaying between all of my men, the bliss blazing through me higher and hotter. And here we were up on top of a towering building, one that I'd helped bring to life, a dizzying distance from the regular world below.

The thought of that height and a fresh gust of wind over me somehow spurred my pleasure on even more. I whimpered around Crag's cock and pumped him faster, and just as he jerked with the first spurt of his release, Lance and Torrent hit the most sensitive spots inside me in perfect unison.

I came again, shivering and clenching around them, my mind blanking with the flare of total ecstasy. Torrent's breath broke and Lance let out a choked snarl beneath me as they followed me over the edge.

For a few minutes after that, I wasn't aware of much other than the bliss still racing through my nerves and the heat of my lovers' bodies around me. As I came back to myself, I found I was lying on my back, propped up between the four men to keep my skin off the surface of the roof, gazing up at the seemingly endless indigo of the evening sky. I grinned up at it, flooded with hope.

"This is just the beginning," I declared—to the sky, to my men, to the world stretching out all around me. "There's so much more I want to do, and there's no power in existence that can hold me back."

Lance hummed happily. "Especially not while you have us by your side. And we're not going anywhere."

Torrent tucked a tentacle around my waist, adding to the joint embrace. "I can't wait to see what you'll pull off next."

I closed my eyes, drifting on pure joy. "Neither can I."

DESIGNING A LEGACY
A HEART OF A MONSTER BONUS EPILOGUE

Quinn

Lights glowed throughout the vast atrium. All around me, men in tuxedos and women in evening gowns clustered together, chattering and laughing. Champagne flowed, and crystal goblets clinked.

Momentarily alone at the edge of the crowd, I sipped my own drink. The bubbly tang tickled down my throat. I was only going to allow myself one glass, but if this wasn't a time to let loose a little, what was?

I'd experienced a lot of magic in my life, but nothing quite compared to the thrill of seeing a building I'd imagined and worked out on paper made real around me.

Possibly the most magical part of the current thrill was wandering over to the sweeping windows along one wall and glimpsing the Eiffel Tower in the distance. The condominium and shopping complex hosting tonight's opening gala was my first completed international project—but I'd recently gotten calls from developers in London, Vienna, and Berlin inquiring about my availability.

It was hard to believe it'd only been eleven years since I saw the first of my designs constructed into an actual building. Even in my wildest teenaged dreams, I'd never imagined this kind of success.

But then, at that time I hadn't known I'd live long enough to have a chance to establish myself so well.

Of course, if there was a "unique perspective" and "sense of otherworldly grandeur" to my designs as the architecture magazines often said, it was mainly because of the other sorts of magic that'd swept into my life sixteen years ago.

The most concrete manifestations of that otherworldly presence had contrived to attend the gala with me—as best as each of them could. As I turned back to face the circulating gala-goers, Rollick ambled up to me with Crag close behind him.

As usual, Rollick didn't need to make any significant adjustments to blend into this upscale crowd. He looked as stunningly movie-star handsome as ever—maybe even more so in his perfectly fitted tux—with a gleaming smile that only me and my other lovers knew was composed of veneers hiding his sharp shadowkind teeth.

Crag had a trickier challenge with his stony jaw, but we'd discovered a gambit that worked well enough these days. He wore a medical face mask covering him from nose to chin, and if I heard anyone commenting on it, I told them he was being extra cautious because of his fragile health. That was enough to stop most gossip in its tracks.

Never mind that the gargoyle's constitution was as sturdy as everything else about his bulky body. He wanted to be able to celebrate my milestones with me, and I was simply happy to have him here.

Crag set one broad hand on my shoulder with an affectionate squeeze and scanned the atrium with typical protective wariness. His voice rumbled through the mask. "Everyone appears to be having a good time."

Rollick grinned. "What's not to enjoy?" He teased his fingers down my other arm in a subtle caress that nonetheless sent sparks over my skin. "I've heard many compliments about your work. I think they might be even more awed than usual."

I'd like to believe that was true and not just him showing bias in my favor. "It was the most ambitious project I've taken on so far. I'm glad it came together this well."

How much more could I still accomplish? The new heart Rollick had arranged for me what felt like a lifetime ago had held up well over the past decade and a half. Knowing him, he was keeping a constant eye on the lists of newly available donor organs in case this one gave out without warning.

With every design I created, I was doing my best to be worthy of all of my second chances.

Crag peered up at the immense, vaulted ceiling. "I could soar in here." He paused with a quick cough. "I mean, if people could fly."

I knocked my elbow teasingly against his. "I'd love to see that. You never know... I might be able to come up with an excuse to take a totally private stroll around the building before the tenants move in. As long as I get to come along for part of that flight."

An eager gleam lit in the gargoyle's eyes. "I'm always happy to have you with me, Softness."

Rollick gave a hum and pitched his voice in an undertone. "It looks as if you're being called on again, sweet mortal."

I glanced over to see one of the managers from the development company beckoning me over. With a quick squeeze of the demon's hand, I parted from my men to join the necessary hobnobbing.

You never knew who might become a client somewhere down the road. And as exhausted as these big events left me, it was always exhilarating talking about my work.

The investors the manager wanted me to meet were the best kind—they asked about some of the design decisions I'd made with obviously educated eyes for detail and exclaimed over my answers as if my explanations were brilliant.

One of the women motioned to a particularly fanciful area sectioned off at the far end of the atrium. "I hear the indoor playground was your inspiration too, even though it isn't exactly in the architecture realm."

I nodded. "I actually designed a lot of the equipment, with some help from a couple of engineers who are more experienced in that area. I wanted everything about the space to fit the airy, uplifting atmosphere I was aiming for."

The man beside her chuckled. "I'm sure the shoppers will appreciate it. As a few of our fellow guests already are."

The invitations had mentioned that free child-minding would be provided at the gala for those who wanted to bring along their kids. Not many families had taken us up on the offer, but several children ranging from preschoolers to upper elementary school age were roaming around the play structure under two attendants' watchful gazes.

As my conversation partners drifted off to join other conversations, I found myself meandering over to the glinting white wall that surrounded the play area like a line of crystals jutting from the ground. All of the equipment was similar shades of translucent pastel, turning the childish figures romping amid it into shimmery blurs when they passed behind.

A faint tapping alongside slightly unsteady footsteps told me another of my men had found his way to me. I looked over as Torrent reached the wall a short distance away.

The kraken shifter had taken inspiration from Crag's masks to come up with a medical accommodation of his own. He didn't need his tentacles for balance if he used a couple of forearm crutches to steady him.

I knew he didn't love the occasional stares the metal posts drew, but he'd hate missing the chance to witness my victories in the flesh even more.

"Not tired out yet?" he asked, his familiar dry tone tinged with warmth.

I shook my head. "With the time it takes to finalize a project, I only get to revel in the work I do once every year or two. I can survive the whole night." My gaze dropped to his legs, to the dressy leather boots hiding his broken feet. "Are you doing all right? You know that if walking around gets painful, I wouldn't expect—"

"I know," he broke in, with the softly crooked smile that never failed to set off a glow of affection inside me. "But I only get to revel with you once every year or two. There's nothing here for you to worry about, Miss Fix-It."

He cocked his head and gave a light laugh. "Lance says the caterer did an excellent job. Crag snuck some hors d'oeuvres into the bathroom so he could sample them."

When I concentrated, I got a faint impression of the dragon shifter in the shadows along the play area wall. To his dismay, Lance was the only one of us for whom we hadn't yet figured out a solution to let him blend in among regular human beings. There was no easy explanation for or way to disguise three-inch claws protruding from a guy's fingertips. But he always came along in his own way and participated as much as he could.

I aimed a smile at the shadows where he was lurking. "I think I heard there'll be ice cream served later. I'll smuggle some into the ladies' room for you."

A shadowy caress grazed my calf in appreciation. I could almost feel the provocative prick of those claws.

A shriek from the play area brought me jerking around, but before I'd even set eyes on the girl who'd let it out, I could tell from the tone that it was laughter, not distress. She giggled as she chased an older boy who looked like he was probably her brother under the slide and up into the castle-like structure.

The pure glee on their faces sent a pang through me that was both happiness at seeing how much they were enjoying my creation and a twinge of sadness. The latter must have shown on my face just as Rollick and Crag rejoined us.

The demon shifted his gaze from me to the playing children and back again. His voice came out in the gentle tone I'd only ever heard him use with me. "Wishing you had one of those small beings for yourself?"

A laugh caught in my throat, because I hadn't been wishing it consciously—but maybe some tiny part of me kind of had underneath. "We've talked about this before. I wouldn't want to risk the strain a pregnancy would put on my heart."

Torrent eased closer so his arm brushed against mine. "You know we aren't against adoption. It isn't as if any of us could easily contribute the typical way as it is."

Because shadowkind couldn't reproduce—at least, not except through some highly secret ritual none of us knew the details of. But that didn't matter anyway. I'd pondered this question more than I'd ever shared with my men, because I knew they'd insist on supporting whatever mattered most to me.

And only I could decide what mattered most.

"I don't think I have the energy to run around after a kid anyway," I said. "Not while getting everything else I want to accomplish done."

Crag dipped his head toward me. "You have the four of us to help. If it's something you really wanted—"

I held up my hand to stop him. "I know that. I really do. I've thought about it a lot, lots of times, and I always come to the same answer."

I paused, watching another girl careen down the slide with a giddy gasp, and that tiny part of me clenched up. "It's just a little sad that I never got to make the choice without having to take my shaky health into account, like most people can."

With a little shrug, I glanced around at my men. "It really is okay, though. I've gotten to have tons of other things most people never do—like the four of you. And my buildings are my kids." I motioned to the atrium around us, taking in the beaming lights with a rush of pride that was almost maternal.

Rollick was still studying me with a slyly pensive sort of expression that I knew meant I wasn't exactly off the hook.

"I suppose they are," he said. "But maybe your work can be even more. Will you have time to take a little trip with us back home before you're whisked off to create even more architectural magic?"

I arched an eyebrow. "I always take at least a week off to consider my options between projects. What did you have in mind?"

His smile grew. "I'll explain when we're there."

The demon kept his secret until we were stepping off his jet onto a private airfield. My sneakers rasped against dry, ruddy earth. Most of the nearby terrain was the same, with patches of coarse grass along the edges of the runway. Towering plateaus of similarly reddish stone rose in the distance, but my eyes were quickly drawn to the sprawling adobe building about a mile away.

As Rollick ushered us into the waiting car, the pieces clicked together in my head. "We're in New Mexico, aren't we? Are we going to the school you set up for the shadowkind a couple of years ago?"

Lance slid into the seat next to me and slung his arm around my shoulders with a click of his claws. "Our woman is very clever."

Rollick watched the embrace without the slightest hint of jealousy. "One of the many reasons we love her."

Somehow even after all these years, it still made me tingle when any of them used the L-word. Maybe because I knew how rare that kind of devotion was among the shadowkind.

I smiled back at him, nudging my foot against his. "It wasn't that hard to make an educated guess."

I'd never been out to Rollick's school before. All I knew was that he intended it to serve a similar purpose to his nightclubs, only on a more beginner level: offering a space for "monsters" who were having trouble fitting into the human world, allowing them to appreciate the mortal realm without causing any terror or destruction. The goal of the curriculum was to teach the students how to integrate well enough that they could more freely enjoy everything else my world had to offer once they were finished.

"But what are we doing here?" I asked. "I mean, I'm curious about how it's been going, but why did you specifically want me to come now?"

The demon waved his hand toward the building we were swiftly approaching. "I'll show you around, and then we'll get down to the real business."

His driver parked the car in a large garage off to the side of the main building, where several other vehicles—mostly less fancy than the one Rollick had called for—filled the spots. As I stepped out, Crag and Torrent materialized out of the shadows which had been more comfortable for them for the drive.

Crag flexed his arms and expanded into his full gargoyle form, his bat-like wings extending from his back, his skin turned limestone gray. There weren't many places where he felt comfortable showing his true self, for understandable reasons. I rested my hand on his rocky but warm forearm and tipped my head against his bulging bicep to show my approval.

Torrent's full kraken self wouldn't enjoy the desert climate, but he kept two tentacles extended to take some of the weight off his legs. As we walked inside, he set his uninjured hand against the small of my back. "Some of the students are a little... rough around the edges. They're here mainly because they don't know how to act around humans. You might need to forgive some odd behavior."

Crag grunted. "And if it's anything unforgivable, we'll put a stop to it fast. No one's bothering our woman."

Rollick let out a low chuckle. "I doubt any of them will act out very much in my presence. I have maintained my demonic reputation."

The main school building was simple in design, but as we strolled through the halls, I found plenty to admire about it. Scattered windows and skylights let in plenty of sun to glow off the cream-colored walls. It was structured like some of Rollick's homes that I'd visited—Mediterranean style with a broad square of rooms around an open inner courtyard. Except this structure was several times bigger than any of those houses.

The delicate perfume of desert flowers drifted in from the courtyard through sliding screen doors. I paused at one pane to take in the bright bursts of color.

Near the garden, a couple dozen figures were lounging around in the courtyard at picnic tables and on the grassy span of lawn. Some could easily pass for human, but I caught sight of spiraling horns jutting from the sides of one head, feathery wings protruding from another back, a bushy tail whipping from side to side as the owner stalked across the patio stones.

The woman with the bushy tail snapped at one of the totally human-looking figures, who bared his teeth to reveal a set of fangs. The woman raised her hand, but before she could show any further aggression, another being emerged from the shadows, shoving his burly arm between them.

"That's one of our staff," Rollick said with obvious satisfaction. "There are always several around keeping a careful eye on the residents, whether you can see them or not. We try to cut off any trouble before it becomes much of a problem."

He showed me the airy gym where a bunch of students were caught up in an intense basketball game, the cozy library where a few others were curled up in the armchairs pawing through books, and the vast kitchen where various helpers were preparing lunch alongside a couple of instructors talking about typical mortal cuisine.

Everywhere we stopped, some of the students stared at me—one's eyes taking on a pinkish glow, another's narrowing warily. Rollick stayed close with a possessive air. Maybe he was right about his reputation, because none of the strangers spoke or made any move at me despite Torrent's concerns.

The demon led us upstairs to a long hall with doors along each side. "These are the dorms. I thought I might have been excessive when I first approved the plans, but we're close to overflowing."

Somewhat literally. Several of the inhabitants had chosen to sprawl out in the hallway amid crumpled clothing, abandoned plates... and a few claw-like gouges carved into the floor.

Lance noticed those too and clicked his tongue. "The new beasties haven't been behaving themselves. They didn't even make an interesting decoration."

Rollick sighed. "It takes time for quite a few of them to adjust to the expectations of a cooperative living situation. And not everyone is completely happy to be here at all."

I shot him a puzzled glance. "Why would they come to the school if they don't want to learn?"

I saw a hint of his demonic self in his tight grin. "In some ways, this place has become a reform school as well as a voluntary learning center. No one is *forced* to participate, but if we catch higher shadowkind causing harm in the mortal world, they're given the option of rehabilitating here rather than immediately being banished back to the shadow realm. That doesn't mean everyone who chooses to stay rejoices the opportunity."

One of the students must have had keen ears, because he responded from his cross-legged pose at the other end of the hall. "But they all know better than to cross *you*, sir. It'd be more peaceful if you were here all the time."

"Hmm, but then how would you learn how to manage yourselves without a babysitter?" Rollick retorted in good humor. The guy shrugged and laughed.

We tramped after the demon back downstairs and stopped outside the courtyard again.

Rollick turned to me. "When I first set up this facility, I didn't realize just how much demand—and need—there'd be for the education we're offering. Word has only had a little over a year to spread, and we're already at capacity. I'd rather not have to resort to sticking students in patches of shadow rather than proper human-style accommodations. That would go against the whole principle of the place."

My spirits lifted at the thought of all those beings gathering here. "That's tough, but it's great that so many shadowkind want to integrate properly." When I'd first been introduced to the shadowkind world sixteen years ago, I'd certainly had my fill of the type who preferred disdain and destruction.

"It is." Rollick considered our surroundings. "I originally planned to simply build a cluster of matching structures. But after our conversation the other night... How would you like to design a school for shadowkind, Quinn?"

"Oh." That was all I could say before I lost my breath with a leap of my heart. "I've never worked on an educational building before."

But I could already picture it, expanding across the desert in my mind's eye. My pulse thumped faster in anticipation.

"I'd see that you're more than adequately compensated, of course," Rollick continued. "And offer all the guidance I can—and naturally you can speak with the staff and residents about their requirements and preferences. That should offer plenty of inspiration. I know you can come up with something both suitable and far more impressive than anything I could dream up."

He paused, taking in my probably dreamy expression, and his voice softened. "It wouldn't be something you could include on your resume... but you said your buildings are your children. I'd like you to be the mother of this strange little facility I've founded."

All at once I was grinning at him, my chest flooded with affection. The idea felt so right I didn't even need to think about it. "Yes. Of course. I'd love to."

I had other proposals, but I trusted that there would be more. None of them, no matter where in the world they took me, could be quite as meaningful as this project.

Lance clapped his hands, rattling his claws. "You'll make something perfect, baby girl. There can't be any other architect who knows the tricksy beasties like you do."

"They aren't *all* beasts," Crag put in, unmistakably fond as he watched the inexperienced shadowkind in the courtyard mingle.

How much had it meant to *him* to be able to help guide fellow shadowkind so they wouldn't see themselves as hopeless monsters like he'd once assumed he was?

Torrent's voice turned wry. "But knowledge of our kind and our various peculiarities should definitely help."

He turned his head at movement down the hall. Several beings were spilling out of a room at the other end. The kraken shifter straightened up with a curl of his fingers around my elbow. "There's someone here you already know, if you want to get started surveying the staff for ideas."

I craned my neck. "Is Sorsha giving some lessons?"

Rollick took my other arm to guide me down the hall. "She and her associates do stop by from time to time to share their wisdom, but I don't believe they're on the campus at the moment. We have a more permanent member of staff you should recognize, though."

We reached the doorway to what I saw was laid out a lot like a regular classroom, though with long tables rather than individual desks. A young man stood by the whiteboard at the front of the class, wiping off whatever he'd written for the benefit of his pupils.

At the sound of our feet, he glanced over with a swipe of his wavy black hair away from his eyes. I was struck by a jarring sense of recognition. "Jonah?"

The guy blinked at me and then broke into a grin. "Quinn? What are you doing here?" His gaze slid to Rollick, and his expression became a tad abashed. "Did the headmaster think I needed some more tutoring before I keep going with my work?"

The demon huffed softly at the title I guessed he hadn't claimed. "Quinn is going to be making the building designs for our expanded school."

Jonah snapped his fingers. "That's right! You're an architect as well as a former sorcerer, aren't you?"

My answering smile felt a little shy. Jonah's life had been entangled with mine since he was just a toddling kid—when I'd accidentally led an army of hostile shadowkind to the settlement where his sorcerer family was living, seen him kidnapped by those shadowkind, and insisted on rescuing him.

He'd grown up under the watch of Sorsha and her men, but they'd arranged periodic visits while he was growing up so that I could give him whatever guidance I could offer when it came to his burgeoning sorcerer powers.

The last time I'd seen him was several years ago, when he was thirteen. He had to be twenty now. All the lingering childhood softness had left his face, turning his chiseled features striking, and he'd grown into his tall, broad-shouldered frame with muscles that showed through his thin collared shirt.

I couldn't help seeing him as a kid still, but I'd bet he'd turned quite a few heads of the shadowkind who were inclined that way.

"I am," I said, coming into the room to lean against one of the tables. "And you've taken up teaching?"

He shrugged, a trace of a blush coloring his cheeks. "I've got a little wisdom I can pass on since I've sort of straddled the two worlds—human and shadowkind. It keeps me busy between... the times I've got to do my other job here."

Something about his hesitation tugged at my gut. I was about to ask what that other job was when Rollick cleared his throat. "I'm going to check in on the other staff. See if you can think of any suggestions for Quinn to keep in mind while she's putting together her initial plans."

"We'll be back," Crag assured me before following the demon, as if I'd have any doubts about that.

With a thoughtful expression, Jonah turned back to the whiteboard. He rubbed off the last few words and then tapped the brush against his hand. "I'd guess Rollick will have already covered the basics. We definitely need more dorms. It might be good to have at least two separate areas for them—so we can keep the residents who are here under sanctions separate from the willing students if their supernatural powers are causing problems."

My men hadn't mentioned any concerns along that line. I frowned. "Does that happen a lot?"

"I mean, for maybe half of the type who are dragged here rather than showing up out of interest, the reason is that they can't control their powers well enough around regular humans to avoid notice or outright harming them. They're not likely to hurt fellow shadowkind that much, but it can still be disruptive."

I pulled out my phone to start making notes. "I'll keep that in mind. What else do you think would be useful? I can't promise I'll be able to fit in everything, but feel free to make a dream list and I'll see what I can incorporate."

Jonah rubbed his mouth. "Let's see... The dorm rooms can be pretty small but the common areas, classrooms, that sort of thing—should be as large as possible. Room to maneuver. Wide halls. Some of the shadowkind can be pretty protective of their personal space. The enclosed outdoor area is great, so if you can work in more of that, wonderful... It might actually be nice to have a few separate buildings too. For some buffer if there are conflicts."

I tapped all those ideas into my notes app. "Anything else?"

He paused. "I'm not sure how much this would be on the architect side vs. the construction crew... but some kind of containment building for when we first bring in disruptive shadowkind could be helpful. Build to be secure both supernaturally and physically. For when we're figuring out whether they'll even be staying here, and they may be looking to escape judgment altogether."

I looked up from my phone. "It's sounding like you've had a lot of trouble with the involuntary students."

Jonah ducked his head with a sheepish chuckle. "I don't mean to make it sound as if we don't have them under control. I think about it a lot because that's my main purpose here."

"What do you mean?"

He made a vague gesture with his hand. "My sorcerer skills... When there's a being disturbing a human community, I can get them under control. Call them away and keep them subdued until the rest of the team has a chance to restrain them."

Rollick had been sending him out to do *that* kind of work? Or whoever ran things at the school all the times the demon couldn't be here?

My stomach sank. Most sorcerers saw shadowkind as lesser beings and monsters, creatures who deserved to be bent to their will. But I knew firsthand that if you'd gotten to know some as equals, come to care about them, it could feel sickening to inflict your power on them.

"That must be hard," I said quietly.

Jonah gave another shrug, but it didn't look quite as casual as the first. "It's the way I can be most useful. I *want* to help. Can't see going out into the 'real' world and finding some job surrounded by people who have no idea that shifters and fae and the rest exist."

His gaze jerked to me with a sudden widening of his eyes. "Not that I think there's anything wrong with getting that kind of job if there's something you really want to pursue."

I held up my hands. "No offense taken. I just—when I had my sorcerer powers, I had to do things that didn't sit right with me. Even when you're working for the greater good, it can feel pretty crappy. You don't *have* to do anything just because the people who run the school ask, you know."

Jonah nodded emphatically. "I never felt pressured. I'm just still figuring out how I fit in." He glanced toward the doorway. "Everyone knows. All the shadowkind. I've never used sorcery on anyone who *wasn't* acting out, but... there's still a vibe. I haven't been here that long, though. Once they see that I'm only doing what's necessary, I'm sure it'll be fine."

He sounded as if he was putting more confidence into his voice than he actually felt, but I wasn't going to tear down his hopes. I stepped closer and gave his arm a quick squeeze. "I'll give you my current number. You can call me if you think of anything else that would make for a better school design—and if you want to talk to someone who's been there when it comes to the uncomfortable parts of sorcery."

A smile flashed across his face. "Thanks, Quinn. You've always looked out for me. My savior."

I choked on a sputter of a laugh at that label and shook my head. "I was making up for the shitty situation I caused by coming to see your parents. If I hadn't visited them..."

Jonah's mouth twisted. "You didn't know the dangerous shadowkind would follow you there. You were trying to figure out what you were and what to do about it. *I* know what that feels like too. I'm glad you were there. The monsters might have found us anyway, and then there'd have been no one to even know I'd been taken."

I inhaled with a hitch of my lungs and found that my chest felt lighter than it had a moment ago, though I hadn't realized I was tense. I swallowed thickly, shedding a little of the guilt I was still holding on to. "That's true. I'm glad I was there to get you out. And to teach you however much I've been able to."

I might not ever be a mother in the traditional sense, but I'd passed on some kind of guidance about living one's life. Looking at Jonah, listening to him talk, I thought I'd done a decent job of it.

Lance poked his head into the room with a jostle of his wild curls. "You've taught all of us a thing or two or ten. My Quinn is a very good instructor." He sauntered over and stroked his claws carefully through my hair, thankfully not mentioning the more intimate subjects we'd explored together.

In the dragon shifter's presence, I relaxed even more. "You didn't need that much help."

"There were times and places where I wasn't sure how to act properly. You led the way." He cocked his head. "Maybe you should come to the school not just to design but to do a little teaching also. Torrent and Crag and I visit every couple of months. The things you could tell would have to be just as useful as anything we say."

A wider grin crossed Jonah's face. "He's right. You absolutely should."

I wasn't sure what I'd offer to a bunch of shadowkind who wanted to meld into the human world, but my spirits lifted all the same. "I'll think about it. If it'd make a difference."

"You always do," Lance insisted, and tugged me toward the doorway. "There are some other people Rollick thinks you should talk to."

I waved my farewell to Jonah and set off on a rambling route that took me to the kitchen staff, then a cheerful succubus who specialized in tutoring on intimate relations, and then a tattooed shadowblood man who ran various physical conditioning programs. By the time I'd finished talking to him, the rest of my men had rejoined me.

Rollick led me around the back of the building to a section I hadn't entered before. "There are a few more staff members you should speak with when they're on the campus—and a few who'll insist on weighing in even though their input will be somewhat questionable." He winked at me. "But I think you've made a good start. We can relax in my private room here. This trip shouldn't be all work."

My fingers were already itching for my sketchpad. "It isn't only work for me. I want to get some of the aspects I'm picturing down on paper before I lose the inspiration... Can someone grab my messenger bag from our luggage in the car?"

Crag vanished into the shadows without a word and reappeared in the office-slash-lounge room we entered a minute later, holding out the requested bag. I dug my sketchpad and a good pencil out of it and hunkered down on the floor with a blank page open on my lap.

The gargoyle settled behind me as if to provide a surface to lean against if I needed it. Torrent sank down at my side, a tentacle curving over my knee, and Rollick sat on the other while Lance sprawled out by my feet. Just like that, I was surrounded in monstrous warmth.

I glanced around at them. "This can't be all that interesting for you. You don't have to just sit here while I brainstorm."

Torrent leaned in to brush his lips against my cheek. "There's nothing quite like seeing you when you're caught up in a vision. I think we're all happy to bask in that glow."

When he spoke in that low voice, I felt like I really was glowing. I tipped my head toward his and let my pencil fly across the page.

As the shapes formed and expanded, the warmth spread through every particle of my body. I'd designed so many buildings with the shadowkind as my inspiration, and now I was designing one specifically for them, to give them a place that catered to them in my world.

What better legacy would I leave for the two realms I'd once been caught between?

Lance started to massage one of my feet with his knuckles, and Rollick slipped his arm right around my waist. Crag leaned forward to watch the lines spreading across my first page and then the next. And even though I'd never entered this room before today, I couldn't have been more at home.

Looking down at the images my pencil was conjuring on the paper, I had a sudden glimpse of those buildings rising from the ruddy earth I'd first seen when I emerged from the jet. Of figures both human and monstrous passing by the windows and strolling through the yards, smiling with just as much contentment as I had wrapped around me right now.

The memory of the gala in Paris passed through my mind and then other opening parties before. I thought of all the people living in the buildings I'd pulled into being from my imagination, all the shoppers and office workers who'd spent time in them too.

I wasn't leaving my mark just on the physical structures I designed, was I? Decades ago, a fluke chance had left me with a heart that had entangled me with the men around me, whose touch made me feel whole. And with every building I brought into existence, I touched so many more beings, human and now shadowkind as well.

No matter what else the future brought, those people would always be a part of me—and I would be part of them. Long after my final heart gave out.

A sense of peace deeper than I'd ever experienced before welled up in my chest. I set down the sketchpad.

"Pleased with your progress?" Rollick asked in a purr of a voice, his lips brushing my temple.

I tugged him and the others closer around me, sinking into their joint embrace. "It's going to be nothing short of wonderful."

ABOUT THE AUTHOR

Eva Chase lives in Canada with her family. She loves stories both swoony and supernatural, and strong women and the men who appreciate them. Along with the Heart of a Monster series, she is the author of the Rites of Possession series, the Shadowblood Souls series, the Gang of Ghouls series, the Bound to the Fae series, the Flirting with Monsters series, the Cursed Studies trilogy, the Royals of Villain Academy series, the Moriarty's Men series, the Looking Glass Curse trilogy, the Their Dark Valkyrie series, the Witch's Consorts series, the Dragon Shifter's Mates series, the Demons of Fame series, and the Legends Reborn trilogy.

Connect with Eva online:
www.evachase.com
eva@evachase.com

www.ingramcontent.com/pod-product-compliance
Lightning Source LLC
Chambersburg PA
CBHW020345310726
48979CB00015B/2509/J